About the Authors

USA Today bestselling author **Lynn Raye Harris** burst onto the scene when she won a writing contest held by Mills & Boon. The prize was an editor for a year – but only six months later, Lynn sold her first novel. A former finalist for the Romance Writers of America's Golden Heart Award, Lynn lives in Alabama with her handsome husband and two crazy cats. Her stories have been called "exceptional and emotional," "intense," and "sizzling." You can visit her at www.lynnrayeharris.com.

Caitlin Crews discovered her first romance novel at the age of twelve. It involved swashbuckling pirates, grand adventures, a heroine with rustling skirts and a mind of her own, and a seriously mouth-watering and masterful hero. Caitlin has made her home in places as far-flung as York, England and Atlanta, Georgia. She currently lives in California, with her animator/comic book artist husband and their menagerie of ridiculous animals.

Maisey Yates knew she wanted to be a writer even before she knew what it was she wanted to write. It wasn't until she was pregnant with her second child that she found her very first Mills & Boon book in a local thrift store – by the time she'd reached the happily ever after, she had fallen in love. Maisey lives with her supportive, handsome, wonderful, diaper-changing husband and three small children, across the street from her parents and the home she grew up in, in the wilds of southern Oregon.

Scandals
COLLECTION

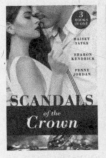

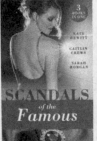

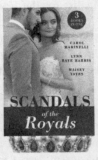

June 2018

July 2018

August 2018

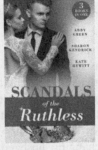

September 2018

October 2018

November 2018

Scandals of the Rich

LYNN RAYE HARRIS

CAITLIN CREWS

MAISEY YATES

MILLS & BOON

Published in Great Britain 2018
by Mills & Boon, an imprint of HarperCollins*Publishers*
1 London Bridge Street, London, SE1 9GF

Scandals of the Rich © 2018 Harlequin Books S.A.

A Façade to Shatter © 2013 Harlequin Books S.A
Special thanks and acknowledgement are given to Lynn Raye Harris for her contribution to *Sicily's Corretti Dynasty* series

A Scandal in the Headlines © 2013 Harlequin Books S.A
Special thanks and acknowledgement are given to Caitlin Crews for her contribution to *Sicily's Corretti Dynasty* series

A Hunger for the Forbidden © 2013 Harlequin Books S.A
Special thanks and acknowledgement are given to Maisey Yates for her contribution to *Sicily's Corretti Dynasty* series

ISBN: 978-0-263-26725-9

11-2018

MIX
Paper from
responsible sources
FSC® C007454

This book is produced from independently certified FSC™ paper to ensure responsible forest management.

For more information visit: www.harpercollins.co.uk/green

Printed and bound in Spain
by CPI, Barcelona

A FAÇADE
TO SHATTER

LYNN RAYE HARRIS

For all those who serve in the armed forces, thank you for your service.

CHAPTER ONE

ZACH SCOTT DIDN'T do parties. Not anymore.

Once, he'd been the life of the party. But everything had changed a little over a year ago. Zach shoved his hands into his tuxedo trouser pockets and frowned. He'd thought coming to Sicily with a friend, in order to attend a wedding, would be an easy thing to do. There'd been no wedding, it had turned out, but the reception was taking place anyway. And he stood on the edge of the ballroom, wondering where Taylor Carmichael had got to. Wondering if he could slip away and text his regrets to her.

His head was pounding after a rough night. He'd been dreaming again. Dreaming of guns and explosions and planes plummeting from the sky.

There was nothing like a fight for survival to rearrange a man's priorities. Since his plane had been shot down in enemy territory, the kinds of things he'd once done—fundraisers, public appearances, speeches, political dinners—were now a kind of torture he'd prefer to live without.

Except it was more impossible to get out of those things now than ever before. Not only was he Zachariah James Scott IV, son of an eminent United States senator and heir to a pharmaceuticals fortune, he was also a returning military hero.

Zach's frown deepened.

Since his rescue—in which every single marine sent to extract him had perished—he'd been in demand as a sort of all-American poster boy. The media couldn't get enough of him, and he knew a big part of that was his father's continual use of his story in his public appearances.

Zachariah J. Scott III wasn't about to let the story die. Not when it could do him a world of political good.

His son had done his duty when he could have chosen an easier path. *His* son had chosen to serve his country instead of himself. It was true that Zach could have sat on the Scott Pharmaceuticals board and moved mountains of money instead of flying jets into a war zone. But the jets were a part of him.

Or had been a part of him until the crash had left him with crushing, unpredictable headaches that made it too dangerous to fly.

Yes, everyone loved that he'd bravely gone to war and survived.

Except he didn't feel brave, and he damn sure didn't feel like he'd done anything extraordinary. He didn't want the attention, didn't deserve the accolades. He'd failed pretty spectacularly, in his opinion.

But he couldn't make them stop. So he stood stiffly and smiled for the cameras like a dutiful military man should, and he felt dead inside. And the deader he felt, the more interested the media seemed to get.

It wasn't all bad, though. He'd taken over the stewardship of the Scott Foundation, his family's charitable arm, and he worked tirelessly to promote military veterans' causes. They often came back with so little, and with their lives shattered. The government tried to take care of them, but it was a huge job—and sometimes they fell through the cracks.

It was Zach's goal to save as many of them as he could. He owed it to them, by God.

He made a visual sweep of the room. At least the media attention wasn't directed at him right now. The Sicilian media was far more interested in the fact the bride had jilted the groom at the altar. Zach was of no interest whatsoever to this crowd. That, at least, was a bonus.

It wasn't often he could move anonymously through a gathering like this one.

Still, he was on edge, as if he were being followed. He prowled the edges of the crowd in the darkened ballroom, his headache barely under control as he searched for Taylor. She wasn't answering his texts, and he was growing concerned. She'd been so worried about this trip, about her return to acting, and about the director's opinion of her.

But Taylor was tough, and he knew she would have gone into the press event with her head held high. She wanted this film badly, wanted the money and respectability for the veterans' clinic back in Washington, D.C., where she'd spent so much time working to help others. He thought of the soldiers, sailors, airmen and marines—most suffering the debilitating effects of posttraumatic stress—the clinic helped, thought of the constant need for funding, and knew that Taylor would have entered that room determined to succeed.

What he didn't know was how it had turned out.

He stepped into a quiet corner—if there was such a thing—and reached into his breast pocket for his phone. A small medal hanging from a ribbon came out with it, and he blinked as he realized what it was. The Distinguished Flying Cross he'd been awarded after returning from the high Afghan desert. Taylor must have put it in there when she'd picked up the tux from the cleaners for him. He fingered the starburst, squeezed it in his palm before putting it back into his pocket.

He hadn't wanted the medal, but he hadn't had a choice. There were other medals, too, which his father never failed to mention in his speeches, but Zach just wanted to forget them all.

Taylor insisted he had to realize he deserved them. She meant well, damn her, but she drove him crazier than any sister ever could have.

He dialed Taylor's number impatiently. No answer. Frustration hammered into him. He wanted to know she was all right, and he wanted to escape this room. The crowd was swelling—never let it be said that Sicilians let a chance to party go to waste—and the noise level was growing louder.

He was in no mood.

He turned toward the exit just as the DJ blared the first track and the crowd cheered. The lights went completely out and strobe lights flashed. Zach's heart began to thud painfully. Against his will, he shrank into the wall, breathing hard.

It's just a party, just a party. But the flashes didn't stop, people started to shout, and he couldn't fight the panic dragging him down any longer.

No, no, no...

Suddenly he was back in the trench, in the pitch of night, the bursts of gunfire and explosives all around him, the thrumming of their bass boom ricocheting into his breastbone, making his body ache with the pressure. He closed his eyes, swallowed hard, his throat full of sand and dust and grit.

Violence and frustration bloomed inside his gut. He wanted to fight, wanted to surge upright and grab a gun, wanted to help the marines hold off the enemy. But they'd drugged him, because he'd broken his leg, and he couldn't move.

He lay helpless, his eyes squeezed tight—and then he felt a soft hand on his arm. The hand moved along his upper arm, ghosted over his cheek. The touch of skin on skin broke his paralysis.

He reacted with the instincts of a warrior, grabbing the hand and twisting it until the owner cried out. The cry was soft, feminine, not at all that of a terrorist bent on destroying him. Vaguely, he realized the body pressed against his was not rough. It was clad in something satiny that slid against the fabric of his own clothing.

He forced his eyes open after long moments. The lights still flashed, and his heart still pumped adrenaline into his body. He blinked and shook his head. Was he not in the desert? Was he not the last one alive in the trench?

The sounds began to separate themselves until he could pick out music, laughter and loud conversation. He focused on the elegant paneled wall in front of him—and realized he held a woman against it, her hand high up behind her back. He could hear her panting softly.

"Please," she said, her voice calmer than he expected it to be. "I don't think I am who you think I am."

Who he thought she was? Zach blinked. Who did he think she was?

A terrorist. Someone bent on killing him.

But she wasn't, was she? He was in Sicily, at the infamous Corretti wedding, and this woman was a guest. Her blue-green eyes were set in a pretty face. Dark hair was piled on top of her head, and her breasts strained against the fabric of her gown, threatening to pop free at any moment. He hadn't spun her around, but instead held her against the wall with his body practically wrapped around hers.

One hand held hers behind her back, nearly between her shoulder blades, while the other gripped her jaw and forced her head back against the paneling. Her soft curves melded against him, filling all the hard angles of his body in ways he hadn't experienced in a very long time.

He'd had no room for softness in his life since returning from the war. He'd viewed it as something of a regret, but a necessary one. Now, he found that he was starving for the contact. His body began to stir, the telltale thrum of blood in his groin taking him by surprise.

Zach let the woman go as if she'd burned him and took a hasty step backward. What the hell was wrong with him? This was why he didn't like public appearances anymore—what if he lost his mind the way he just had? What would the media say then?

Son of a bitch.

"Forgive me," he said tightly.

"Are you all right?" she asked.

It was such a normal question, in response to an abnormal situation, and yet he couldn't formulate an answer. He simply wanted to escape. For once, instead of standing stoically and enduring whatever was flung at him, he wanted out.

There was no one here to stop him, no reporters or cameras, no duty pressing him to remain where he was and endure.

He turned blindly, seeking an exit. Somehow, he found a door and burst through it, into the cool and quiet hallway. Behind him, he heard movement. He didn't know why he turned, but he did.

She was there, watching him. Her hair was dark red and her dress a shocking shade of pink that looked as if it was about to split across her generous breasts.

"Are you all right?" she asked again.

"Fine," he replied in crisp Italian. "I apologize. You startled me."

She came forward then, hesitantly, her hands clasped together in front of her. She was lovely, he decided, in spite of the horrible dress. Her shape was imprinted on his mind, her curves still burning into his body. His hands itched to explore her, but he kept them clenched into fists at his sides. He used to take whatever women offered him, as often as they offered it, but that man had ceased to exist in the months after he'd returned from the war.

At first, he'd indulged in sex because he'd thought it would help him forget. It hadn't. It had only sharpened the contrast between life and death, only made him feel worse instead of better.

Now, denying himself was a matter of routine. Not to mention safer for all involved. His dreams were too unpredictable to sleep with a woman at his side.

Worse, they seemed to be sliding into his waking life if what had just happened was any indication.

The woman was still looking at him. Blue-green eyes fringed in dark lashes blinked up at him as a line formed on her forehead. "You really don't look well."

He glanced down at her hands, at the way she rubbed the thumb of one hand into her wrist. He'd hurt her, and it sickened him. What kind of man had he become? He was coming unglued inside, and no one could help him.

"I'm fine," he clipped out. "I'm sorry I hurt you."

Her eyes dropped. "You didn't really. You just surprised me."

"You're lying," he said, and her head snapped up, her eyes searching his. Something in those eyes called to him, but he shut it off and backed away.

"You don't know that," she replied, her chin lifting. "You don't know me."

He almost believed her. But her lip trembled, ruining her brave façade, and Zach loathed himself. "You should go," he said. "Walk away. It's safer."

She blinked. "Safer? Are you so dangerous, then?"

He swallowed. "Perhaps."

Her gaze was steady. Penetrating. "I'm not afraid," she

said softly. "And I don't think you're dangerous to anyone but yourself."

Her words hit him like a punch to the gut. No one had ever said that to him before. The truth of it was sharper than any blade.

More frightening.

Anger and despair flowed over him in waves. He wanted to be normal again, wanted to be what he'd once been. But he couldn't seem to dig out of the morass, and he hated himself for it. He simply didn't know what normal was anymore.

"I'm sorry," he said again, because there was nothing else he could say. And then he turned and strode away.

Lia Corretti sucked in a disappointed breath as she watched the tall, dark American striding down the hall away from her. Something fell from his hand and bounced on the plush carpet. Lia hurried forward, calling to him.

He did not turn back. She stooped to pick up the small object on the floor. It was some kind of military medal suspended from a red, white and blue ribbon. She clutched it in her hand and looked down the long corridor at his retreating back. He walked so precisely, so stiffly, with the bearing of a soldier.

Of course he did.

She looked at the medal again. He'd dropped it on purpose. She did not doubt that. She'd seen his fingers open, seen the shiny object tumble to the floor, but he hadn't stopped to retrieve it.

Why?

Her wrist still smarted where he'd twisted it behind her back. She didn't think he'd been aware of what he'd been doing. He'd seemed…distant, as if he were somewhere else. It's what had made her go to him, what had made her touch him and ask if he was all right. He'd been plastered against that wall, his eyes squeezed tight shut, and she'd thought he'd been ill.

Lia closed her fingers around the medal. It was warm from his skin, and her heart skipped. She could still see the raw look on his face when he'd realized what he was doing to her.

She knew that look. It was one of self-loathing, one of relief and one of confusion all rolled into one. She knew it because she'd lived with those feelings her entire life.

In that moment, she'd felt a kinship with him. It was so strange. After a lifetime of isolation, one moment of looking into a stranger's eyes had made her feel less alone than she'd ever felt before.

She turned to go back into the ballroom, though she'd rather be anywhere else, and caught a glimpse of her reflection in one of the full-length mirrors lining the corridor. Revulsion shuddered through her.

No wonder he'd wanted to get away.

She was a whale. A giant pink whale bursting at the seams. She'd been so excited when she'd been asked to be a bridesmaid. She'd finally thought she might be accepted by the sleek, beautiful Corretti family, but instead she'd been forced into a blazing pink dress at least two sizes too small for her bust. Carmela Corretti had laughed when she'd walked out of the fitting room, but she'd promised to have the dress fixed.

She hadn't, of course.

Lia's grandmother was the only one who'd seemed to sympathize. When Lia put the dress on today, despair and humiliation rolling through her in giant waves, her grandmother had hugged her tight and told her she was beautiful.

Tears pricked Lia's eyes. Teresa Corretti was the only one in the family who had ever been kind to her. Her grandfather hadn't been unkind, precisely, but he'd always frightened her. She still couldn't believe he was gone. He'd loomed so large in her life that she'd started to think him immortal. He'd been intense, driven, the kind of man no one crossed. But now he was dead, and the family wasn't any closer than they'd ever been. Not only that, but Lia wasn't certain that her cousin Alessandro wasn't to be more feared as the new head of the family.

Lia screwed up her courage and reentered the ballroom. A glance at her watch told her she'd put in enough time to call it an evening. She was going to find her grandmother and tell her she was leaving. No one would care that she was gone anyway.

The music pumped and thumped as it had before, and the crowd surged. But then another sound lifted over the din. It took Lia a minute to realize it was Carmela, shrieking drunkenly.

Lia despised her late uncle's wife, but thankfully she hardly ever had to be around the woman. She didn't care what Carmela's problem was tonight. She just wanted to go back to her room and get out of this awful dress. She'd curl up with a book or something inane on television and try to forget the humiliations of the day.

But, before she could find her grandmother, the music suddenly died and the crowd parted as if Moses himself were standing there.

Everyone turned to look at Lia. She shrank instinctively under the scrutiny, her heart pounding. Was this yet another ploy of Carmela's to embarrass her? Did she really have to endure another scene? What had she ever done to the woman?

But it wasn't Carmela who caught her attention. It was Rosa. Carmela's daughter stood there, her face pale, her eyes fixed on her mother's face.

"That's right," Carmela said gleefully, her voice rising over the sudden silence of the gathered crowd, "Benito Corretti is your father, not Carlo! That one is your sister," she

spat, pointing a red-tipped finger at Lia as if she were a particularly loathsome bug. "Be thankful you did not turn out
like her. She's useless—fat and mousy and weak!"

Rosa looked stricken. Lia's heart stuttered in her chest.
She had a sister? She wasn't close with her three half-brothers. She wasn't close with anyone. But a sister?

She'd never had anyone, not really. She'd often longed
for a sister, someone she might get to know in a way she
couldn't get to know brothers. Her three half-brothers had
one another. Plus they were men. A sister, however—that
felt different somehow.

A surge of hope flooded her then. Perhaps she wasn't really alone in this family, after all. She had a sister.

A sister who was every bit as lost at this moment as Lia
had been her entire life. She could see it on Rosa's face, and
she wanted to help. It was the one thing she had to offer that
she knew was valuable. But suddenly, Rosa was storming
away from Carmela, coming across the room straight for Lia.
She reached out instinctively to comfort her when she came
near. But Rosa didn't stop. The look she gave Lia could have
frozen lava. Lia's heart cracked as Rosa shoved her hands
away with a growled, "Don't!"

A throb of pain ricocheted through her chest where her
heart had been. Rejection was nothing new to her, but the
freshness of it in the face of her hope was almost too much.
She stood there for long moments after Rosa had gone, aware
of the eyes upon her.

Aware of the pity.

Soon, before she could think of a single pithy remark,
the crowd turned away, their attention waning. Self-loathing
flooded her. No wonder Rosa hadn't wanted her comfort. She
was so pitiful. So naive.

How many times had she let her heart open? How many

times had she had the door slammed in her face? When was she going to learn to guard herself better?

Shame and anger coiled together inside her belly. Why couldn't she be decisive? Brave? Why did she care how they treated her?

Why couldn't she just tell them all to go to hell the way her mother would have done?

Grace Hart had been beautiful, perfect, a gorgeous movie star who'd been swept off her feet by Benito Corretti. She'd had no problem handling the Correttis, until she'd accidentally driven her car off a cliff and left Benito a lonely widower with a baby. Soon after that, Benito had sent Lia to live with Salvatore and Teresa.

She knew why he'd done it. Because she wasn't beautiful and perfect like her mother. Because she was shy and awkward and lacking in the most basic graces. She'd grown up on the periphery, watching her cousins and half-siblings from a distance. Wanting her father's love but getting only cool silence.

No, she wasn't beautiful and perfect, and she wasn't decisive. She hated crowds, and she hated pretending she fit in when everyone knew she didn't. She was a failure.

She wanted to go home, back to her small cottage at Salvatore and Teresa's country estate, back to her books and her garden. She loved getting her fingers in the dirt, loved creating something beautiful from nothing more than soil and water and seeds. It gave her hope somehow that she wasn't as inconsequential as she always felt.

Useless. Fat and mousy and weak.

Lia turned and fled through the same door Rosa had stormed out of. This was it. The final straw in her long, tortured life as a Corretti. She was finished pretending to fit in.

She meant to go to her room, but instead she marched out

through the courtyard and found herself standing in front of the swimming pool.

There was no one in it tonight. The hotel had been over-run with wedding guests, and they were all at the reception. The air was hot, and the blue water was so clear, the pool lit from below with soft lights. For a moment Lia thought of jumping in with her dress on. It would ruin the stupid thing, but she hardly cared.

She stood there for a long time, hot feelings swelling within her. She wanted to be decisive. Brave. She wanted to make her own decisions, and she didn't want to let anyone make her feel inferior or unneeded ever again.

She took a step closer to the edge of the pool, staring down into the depths of the water. It would ruin her dress, her shoes, her hair.

So what?

For the first time in a long time, she was going to do what she wanted. She was going to step into the pool and ruin her dress, and she damn well didn't care. She was going to wash away the pain of the day and emerge clean. A new, determined Lia.

Before she could change her mind, she kicked off her shoes and stepped over the edge, letting the water take her down. It closed over her head so peacefully, shutting out all the sounds from above. Shutting out the pain and anger, the humiliation of this day.

She didn't fight it, didn't kick or struggle. She was a strong swimmer, and she wasn't afraid. She just let the water take her down to the bottom, where everything was still. She'd only sit here a moment, and then she'd kick to the top again.

Above her, she heard some kind of noise. And then the water rippled as someone leaped into the pool with her. It annoyed her. She wasn't finished being quiet and still.

Guests from the reception, no doubt. Drunk and looking for a good time.

Lia started to kick upward again, her solace interrupted now. She would get out of the pool and drag her sodden body back to her room. But her dress was heavier than she'd thought, twisting around her legs and pulling her back down again.

She kicked harder, but got nowhere. And then she realized with a sinking feeling that the suction of the drain had trapped part of her skirt. Panic bloomed inside her as she kicked harder.

Stupid, stupid, stupid.

She couldn't cry for help, couldn't do anything but try to rip herself out of the pink mess.

The dress didn't want to come off. Her lungs ached. Any minute and they would burst.

She kicked harder—but she was caught by her own folly.

No, by Carmela's folly, she thought numbly. Carmela's folly of a dress. Wouldn't everyone laugh when they discovered her bloated body in the pool tomorrow?

Poor, pitiful, stupid Lia. She'd been decisive, all right. She'd made a decision that was going to kill her. She wondered if her mother had thought the same thing in those seconds when her car had hung suspended over the cliffs before plunging onto the rocks below....

CHAPTER TWO

LIA WOKE SLOWLY. She coughed, her throat and chest aching as she did so. She remembered being in the pool, remembered her dress getting caught. She pushed herself up on an elbow. She was in a darkened room. She sat upright, and the sheet slid down her body. How had she gotten out of the pool? And why was she naked? She didn't remember going back to her room, didn't remember anything but that last moment where she'd thought of the Correttis finding her pink-clad body trapped at the bottom of the pool.

She pushed the sheet back, intending to get out of the bed, but a movement in the darkness arrested her.

"I wouldn't do that if I were you," a deep male voice said.

Lia grabbed the sheet and yanked it back up. How long had he been standing there?

"Who are you? And why are you in my room?"

His laugh was dry. "I'm Zach. And you're in my room, sugar."

Sugar. "You're American," she said, her heart thumping steadily. The same American as earlier?

"I'm sorry," he said.

"For what?"

"You sound disappointed."

She shook her head, stopping when her brain couldn't quite keep up. She felt light-headed, as if she'd been drinking, when she hadn't had more than a single glass of champagne all evening.

"How did I get here?"

"I carried you."

"Impossible," she scoffed. She was tall and awkward and fat. He couldn't have done it without a cart and a team of horses to pull her.

"Clearly not," he told her. "Because you're here."

"But why?" The last thing she remembered was water and darkness.

Wait, that wasn't right. There'd also been light, a hard surface under her back and the scalding taste of chlorine in her throat.

"Because you begged me not to call anyone when I pulled you out of the pool."

She vaguely recalled it. She remembered that she'd been worried about anyone seeing her, about them laughing and pointing. About Carmela standing there, slim arms folded, evil face twisted in a smirk, nodding and laughing...fat and mousy and weak.

"It was the only thing you said. Repeatedly," he added, and Lia wanted to hide.

She put a hand to her head. Her hair was still damp, though not soaked. And she was naked. Utterly, completely naked. Her face flamed.

He sat beside her on the bed, holding out a glass of water. "Here, take this," he said, his voice gentle.

She looked up, met his gaze—and her heart skipped several beats in a row. It was the same man. He had dark eyes, a hard jaw and the beginnings of a scruff where he hadn't shaved in hours. His hair was cropped short, almost military style, and his lips were just about the sexiest thing she'd ever seen in her life.

She took the water and drank deeply, choking when she'd

had too much. He grabbed the glass and set it aside, no doubt ready to pound her on the back if she needed it. She held a hand up, stopping him before he could do so.

"I'm fine," she squeaked out. "Thank you."

He sat back and watched her carefully. "Are you certain?"

She looked at him again—and realized his expression was full of pity. Pity! It was almost more than she could bear to have one more person look at her like that tonight.

"Yes."

"You were lucky tonight," he said, his voice hardening. "Next time, there might not be anyone to pull you out."

She knew he was trying to say something important, but she was too weary to figure out what it was. And then his meaning hit her.

"I wasn't trying to kill myself," she protested. "It was an accident."

He raised an eyebrow. "I saw you step into the water. You just decided to go swimming while fully dressed?"

She dropped her gaze from his. "Something like that." What would he know of it if she told him the real reason? He was beautiful, perfect. She'd thought they had something in common earlier tonight, but she'd been wrong.

Of course.

She usually was. It disappointed her more than she could say. And made her feel lonelier than ever. This man, whatever his flaws, had nothing in common with her. How could he?

"What's your name?" he asked, his voice turning soft.

"Lia. And I hated my dress, if you must know. That's why I jumped in the pool."

His bark of laughter surprised her. "Then why did you buy it in the first place?"

"I didn't. It was a bridesmaid dress, and it was hideous."

"Pink is not your color, I'm sorry to say." His voice was too warm to take offense. "Definitely not." She was slightly confused, given his reaction to her earlier, and more than a little curious about him. It occurred to her she should be apprehensive to be alone with a strange man, in his room, while she was naked beneath his sheets.

But she wasn't. Paradoxically, he made her feel safe. As if he would stand between her and the world if she asked him to. It wasn't true, of course, but it was a nice feeling for the moment.

"I'm afraid I couldn't save the dress," he said. "It tore in the drain, and the rest rather disintegrated once I tried to remove it."

She felt heat creeping into her cheeks again. "You removed everything, I see."

"Yes, sorry, but I didn't want you soaking my sheets. Or getting sick from lying around in cold, clammy clothing."

What did she say to that? *Did you like what you saw? Thank you? I hope you weren't terribly inconvenienced?*

Lia cleared her throat and hoped she didn't look as embarrassed as she felt. "Did you find your medal?"

It was the most benign thing she could think of. She'd tucked it into her cleavage when she'd returned to the ballroom. She would regret it if it were lost. Something about it had seemed important to her, even if he'd cast it aside so easily.

"I did."

"Why did you drop it?" It seemed a harmless topic. Far safer than the subject of her body, no doubt.

"I have my reasons," he said coolly.

Lia waited, but he didn't say anything else. "If you intend to throw it away again, I'll keep it." She didn't know where that had come from, but she meant it. It seemed wrong to throw something like that away.

"It's yours if you want it," he said after a taut moment in

which she thought she saw regret and anger scud across his handsome face.

She sensed there were currents swirling beneath the surface that she just didn't understand. But she wanted to. "What did you get it for?"

He shoved a hand through his hair. She watched the muscles bunch in his forearm, swallowed. He'd been in a tuxedo the last time she'd seen him, but now he wore a dark T-shirt that clung to the well-defined muscles of his chest and arms, and a pair of faded jeans. His feet, she noted, were bare.

So sexy.

"Flying," he said.

"Flying? You are a pilot?"

"I was."

"What happened?" His face clouded, and she realized she'd gone too far. She wanted to know why he'd reacted the way he had in the ballroom, but she could tell she'd crossed a line with her question. Whatever it was caused him pain, and it was not her right to know anything more than she already did.

"Never mind. Don't answer that," she told him before he could speak.

He shrugged, as if it were nothing. She sensed it was everything. "It's no secret. I went to war. I got shot down. My flying days are over."

He said it with such finality, such bittersweet grace, that it made her ache for him. "I'm sorry."

"Why?" His dark eyes gleamed as he watched her.

"Because you seem sad about it," she said truthfully. And haunted, if his reaction in the ballroom earlier was any indication. What could happen to make a man react that way? She didn't understand it, but she imagined he'd been through something terrible. And that made her hurt for him.

He sighed. "I wish I could still fly, yes. But we don't always get to do what we want, do we?"

Lia shook her head. "Definitely not."

He leaned forward until she could smell him—warm spice, a hint of chlorine. "What's your story, Lia?"

She licked her lips. "Story?"

"Why are you here? What do you regret?"

She didn't want to tell him she was a Corretti. Not yet. If he were here at the wedding, he was someone's guest. She just didn't know whose guest he was. And she didn't want to know. Somehow, it would spoil everything.

"I was a bridesmaid," she said, shrugging.

"And what do you regret?" His dark eyes were intent on hers, and she felt as if her blood had turned to hot syrup in her veins.

"I regret that I agreed to wear that dress," she said, trying to lighten the mood.

He laughed in response, and answering warmth rolled through her. "You'll never have to wear it again, I assure you."

"Then I owe you an even bigger debt of gratitude than I thought."

His gaze dropped, lingered on her mouth. Her breath shortened as if he'd caressed her lips with a finger instead of with his eyes. She found herself wishing he would kiss her more than she'd ever wished for anything.

He sat there for a long minute, his body leaning toward hers even as she leaned toward him. Her heart thrummed as the distance between them closed inch by tiny inch.

Suddenly, he swore and shot up from the bed. A light switched on, and she realized he'd gone to the desk nearby. The light was low, but it still made her blink against the sudden intrusion into her retinas.

"You don't owe me anything." His voice was rough, and it scraped over her nerve endings. Made her shiver.

She blinked up at him. He stood there with his hands shoved in his pockets, watching her. A lock of hair fell across her face, and she pushed it back, tucking it behind her ear.

Zach's gaze sharpened. He watched her with such an intense expression on his face. But she couldn't decide what he was feeling. Desire? Irritation? Disdain?

Dio, she was naive. She hated it. She imagined Rosa would have known what to do with this man. Lia wished she could talk to her sister, ask her advice—but how silly was that? Rosa was as estranged from her as she'd ever been. This new connection between them meant nothing to Rosa.

Lia's hair fell across her face again and she combed her fingers through it, wincing at how tangled it was. She would need a lot of conditioner to get this mess sorted.

She looked up at Zach, and her heart stopped beating. His expression was stark, focused—and she realized that the sheet had slipped down to reveal the curve of a breast. Her first instinct was to yank the fabric up again.

But she didn't.

She couldn't.

The air seemed to grow thicker between them. He didn't move or speak. Neither did she. It was as if time sat still, waiting for them.

"Are you staying in the hotel?" Zach asked abruptly, and the bubble of yearning pulsing between them seemed to pop.

Lia closed her eyes and tried to slow her reckless heart. "I am," she told him.

What did she know of desire, other than what she'd read in romance novels? Her experience of men was limited to a few awkward dates to please her grandmother. She'd been kissed—groped on one memorable occasion—but that was the sum total of her sexual experience. Whatever had been going on here, she was certain she had it wrong. Zach did not want her.

Which he proved in the next few seconds. He turned away and pulled open a drawer. Then he threw something at her.

"Get dressed. I'll take you back to your room."

Embarrassment warred with anger as her fingers curled into the fabric of a white T-shirt. "This will hardly do the job," she said, turning to self-deprecation when what she really wanted to do was run back to her room and hide beneath the covers. *Fat and mousy and weak.*

"Put it on and I'll get a robe from the closet."

Lia snorted in spite of herself. "The walk of shame without the shame. How droll."

He moved closer, his gaze sharpening again, and her heart pounded. "And is that what you want, Lia? Shame?"

Between the horrendous dress she'd had to wear while people stared and pointed, to the very public brush-off she'd had from Rosa, she'd had enough shame today to last her for a while.

Lia shrugged lightly, though inside she felt anything but light. She was wound tight, ready to scream, but she wouldn't. Not until she was back in her room and could bury her face in the pillow first.

"A figure of speech," she said. "Now turn around if you want me to put this on."

He hesitated for a long moment. But then he did as she said, and she dropped the sheet and tugged the shirt into place. It was bigger than she'd thought, but she still had her doubts it would cover her bottom when she stood. She scooted to the edge of the bed and put her legs over the side.

She stood gingerly. Her head swam a little, but she was mostly fine. The shirt barely covered her bottom, but it managed.

"I'll take that robe now," she said imperiously.

Zach walked over to the closet and pulled out a white, fluffy Corretti Hotel robe. Then he turned and brought it back to her, his gaze unreadable as he handed it over. He did a good job of keeping his eyes locked on hers—

But then they dropped, skimming over her breasts—which tingled in response, the nipples tightening beneath his gaze— then farther down to the tops of her naked thighs, before snapping back to her face. His eyes glittered darkly, and a sharp feeling knifed into her.

If she were a brave woman, a more experienced woman, she'd close the distance between them and put her arms around his neck.

But she wasn't, and she didn't. She was just a silly virgin standing here in a man's T-shirt and wishing he would take her in his arms and kiss her.

Lia shrugged into the robe and tied it tight around her waist. "Thank you for your help, but there's no need for you to come with me. I can find my own way back to my room."

"I insist," he said, taking her elbow in a light but firm grip.

She pulled away. "And I'd rather you didn't."

"It's nonnegotiable, sugar."

Something snapped inside her then. Lia lifted her chin. She was so very tired of people telling her what to do. Of not being taken seriously or respected in any way. She was tired enough of it that she was done putting up with it.

This day, as they say, had been the last straw.

Lia plopped down on the edge of the bed and performed her first overt act of defiance as she crossed one leg over the other and said, "I suppose I'm staying here, then."

Zach fought the urge to grind his teeth. It was everything he could do not to push her back on the bed and untie that robe. His body was painfully hard. Lia tossed her hair again—that hot, tangled mess that was somehow sexier than any polished style could have been—and Zach suppressed the groan that wanted to climb up his throat.

Nothing about this woman was typical. She wasn't afraid of him, she didn't seem to want to impress him and she'd jumped into a pool fully clothed because she hated her dress. And now she sat there glaring at him because he was trying to be a gentleman—for once in his life—and make sure she got back to her room safely.

She crossed her arms beneath her breasts and he fought the urge to go to her, to tunnel his fingers into the thick mass of her auburn hair and lift her mouth to his.

That was what she needed, damn it—a hot, thorough, commanding kiss.

Hell, she needed more than that, but he wasn't going to do any of it. No matter that she seemed to want him to.

And why not?

Tonight, he was a man who'd dragged a drowning woman from a pool, a man who hadn't had sex in so long he'd nearly forgotten what it was like. He wasn't a senator's son or an all-American hero. He wasn't a broken and battered war vet. He was just a man who was interested in a woman for the first time in a long time.

More than interested. His body had been hard from the moment he'd stripped her out of that sodden pink dress, her creamy golden skin and dusky pink nipples firing his blood. He'd tried not to look, tried to view the task with ruthless efficiency, but her body was so lush and beautiful that it would take a man made of stone not to react.

Holy hell.

She stared at him defiantly, her chin lifting, and he had an overwhelming urge to master her. To push her back on the bed, peel open that robe and take what he wanted. Would she be as hot as those smoldering eyes seemed to say she would? Would she burn him to a crisp if he dared to give in to this urgent need?

"If you stay, you might get more than you bargained for," he growled. Because he was primed, on edge, ready to explode. It had been so long since he'd felt desire that to feel it now was a huge adrenaline rush.

Like flying.

"I've already had more than I bargained for today," she said hotly, color flooding her cheeks. "I've had to parade around in front of everyone in a hideous dress that made me look even fatter than I am. I've had to endure the whispers and stares, the laughter, the humiliation."

Zach blinked. Fat? No way. But of course she would think so. Women always did, unless they happened to be about five-six and weighed one hundred pounds. This one was taller than that, about five eight or so, and stacked with curves. She wasn't willowy. And she damn sure wasn't fat.

She choked out a laugh. "I also found out I have a sister—of course, she wants nothing to do with me—and on top of all of that, I finally did something daring and jumped in the pool fully clothed, only to nearly drown."

She sucked in a sharp breath, and he knew she was hovering on the edge of tears. "And then I wake up here, with you, completely naked—"

He thought she was going to cry, but she got to her feet suddenly, her eyes blazing, her chin thrusting in the air, though he could see that it still trembled. Her hands were fists at her sides.

"Even then, the only reaction I arouse in you is pity. I'm naked in front of a man and all he thinks about is the quickest way to get rid of me—so you will excuse me if I fail to cower before this latest pronouncement!"

Zach could only stare at her, mesmerized. He'd have sworn she was going to cry, sworn she would blubber and fall apart—but she hadn't. She was staring at him now, two high red spots on her cheeks, her dark auburn hair tumbling over her shoulders, her eyes flashing fire. The robe had slipped open a bit, exposing the inside of a creamy thigh.

Lust flooded him until he had to react or explode. He meant to turn away, meant to put distance between them. Hell, he meant to walk out of the room and not come back—

But instead, he closed the distance between them, gripped her shoulders as he bent toward her.

"Pity is the last thing I feel for you, Lia," he grated, still determined in some part of his brain to push her away before it was too late.

But then he tugged her closer, until she pressed against him, until she'd have to be stupid not to know what he was thinking about right now.

She gasped, and a skein of hot need uncoiled within him.

"Does this feel like pity?" he growled, his hands sliding down to grip her hips and pull her fully into him.

Her eyes grew large in her lovely face, liquid. For the barest of moments, he thought she seemed too innocent, too sweet. But then she reached up and put a palm to his cheek. Her thumb ghosted over his lips. He couldn't suppress a shudder of longing.

"No," she said, her voice barely more than a whisper. "It doesn't."

He thought there was a note of wonder in her voice, but he ignored it and pressed on, sliding a hand around to cup her round bottom. She wasn't fat, the stupid woman. She was curvaceous, with generously proportioned boobs and hips that other women could only envy.

"Is this what you want, Lia?" he asked, dipping his head, sliding his lips along her cheek in surrender to the hot feelings pounding through him.

Her only answer was a soft gasp. Desire scorched into

him, hammered in his veins. He'd wanted her to go back to her room, wanted to remove the temptation when he had no idea what might happen if he had sex with her, but now that she was in his arms, sending her away had suddenly become impossible.

Her arms went around his neck, and he shuddered. She should be frightened of him after what had happened in the ballroom, but she showed no fear whatsoever. Then again, he had been the one to pull her from the water. Perhaps that redeemed him somewhat in her eyes.

"Why aren't you afraid of me?" he asked against the soft skin of her throat.

"I'm only afraid you'll stop," she said, and he squeezed her to him in reaction as emotions overwhelmed him.

He wanted to tell her not to trust him, wanted to tell her to run far and fast, that he could give her nothing more than a night of passion. He wanted to, but he couldn't find the voice right now. Not when what he so desperately wanted to do was slide his tongue into her mouth and see if she tasted as sweet as she looked.

Zach drew back just enough to see her face. Her eyes were closed, dark lashes fanning her cheekbones, and her pink lips parted on a sigh. She arched her body into his and heat streaked through him. It had been so long. Too long...

He shouldn't do this. He really shouldn't. He didn't know this woman at all.

But it felt like he did. Like he'd known her for ages.

With a groan, Zach fell headlong into temptation.

CHAPTER THREE

As ZACH'S MOUTH came down on hers, Lia's first thought was to freeze. Her second was to melt into his kiss. She'd been kissed before, but nothing like this. Nothing with this kind of heat or raw passion. He wanted her. He *really* wanted her. This was not a dream, or a fever, or an illusion. This was a man—a hot, mysterious, dangerous man—and he wanted her, Lia Corretti.

His tongue slid against hers, and she shivered with longing. She didn't really know what she was doing—but she knew how it was supposed to feel, how she was supposed to react.

And she had no problem reacting. Lia arched into him, met his tongue eagerly, if somewhat inexpertly. She just hoped he didn't realize it.

The kiss was hot, thrilling, stomach-churning in a good way. Her body ached with the sudden need to feel more than this. To feel everything.

She knew she shouldn't be doing this with him. Wanting this. But she did.

Oh, how she did.

To hell with what she was supposed to do. To hell with feeling unwanted and unloved and unattractive. What was she waiting for? *Who* was she waiting for?

Zach made her feel beautiful, desirable. She wanted to keep feeling that way.

When Zach loosened the robe, her heartbeat spiked. But she didn't stop him. She had no intention of stopping him. When would she ever get another chance to feel this way? Eligible men weren't exactly thick on the ground in her grandparents' village.

And even if they were, they'd have been unlikely to risk Salvatore Corretti's wrath by sleeping with his granddaughter out of wedlock.

Zach's warm hand slid along her bare thigh, up beneath the T-shirt he'd loaned her. His touch felt like silk and heat and she only wanted more. She shifted against him, felt the evidence of his arousal. He was hard, thick, and her body reacted with a surge of moisture between her thighs.

A sliver of fear wormed its way through her happiness. Was she really going to do this? Was she really going to have sex for the first time with an American whose last name she didn't even know? Was she going to keep pretending like she knew what she was doing even though she didn't?

Yes.

Yes, most definitely. Today was a new day for Lia Corretti. She was finally going to be brave and decisive and in control of her own destiny. No one would force her to wear an ugly pink dress—or call her fat, mousy and weak—in front of hundreds of people ever again.

The robe fell from her shoulders and then Zach swept her up into his arms. She gasped at his strength as he put a knee on the bed and laid her back on the mattress. And then she froze as he came down on top of her, his jeans-clad body so much bigger than hers.

He must have felt her hesitation because he lifted his head, his dark eyes searching hers. "If you don't want this, Lia—"

She put her fingers over his mouth to stop him from uttering another word. "I do," she said. And then she told a lie. "But it's been a long time and I—I..."

The words died on her lips. Surely he would see right through her, see to the heart of her deception. She had no experience at all, and he would be angry when he figured that out. And then he would send her away.

He pulled her hand from his mouth and pressed a kiss to her palm. "It's been a long time for me, as well." She must have looked doubtful, because he laughed softly. "Cross my heart, Lia. It's the truth."

She lifted a trembling hand to trace her fingers over his firm, sensuous lips. She barely knew him, and yet she felt as if she'd known him forever. But what if she disappointed him somehow? What if this was nothing like she'd read in novels?

"But you are so beautiful," she said.

He laughed, and she realized she'd spoken aloud. Heat flooded her. Oh, how simple she was sometimes!

"And so are you," he said, dipping his head to drop kisses along the column of her throat.

"You don't have to say that." She gasped as his tongue swirled in the hollow at the base of her throat. "I'm already in your bed."

"I never say things I don't mean." He lifted his head, his mouth curling in a wicked grin. "Besides, you're forgetting that I've already seen everything. And I approve, Lia. I definitely approve."

She didn't get a chance to reply because his hands spanned her hips and pushed the T-shirt upward, over her breasts, baring her to his sight.

"Still perfect," he said, and then he took one of her nipples in his mouth, his tongue swirling around the hard little point while she worked so hard not to scream.

She'd had no idea it would feel like this. No idea that a

man's mouth on her breast could send such sweet, aching pleasure shooting into her core. Her sex throbbed with heat and want, and her hands clutched his head, held him to her when she feared he would leave.

He did not. He only moved his attentions to her other breast, and Lia thought she would die from the sensations streaking through her. How had she missed out on this for so many years? How had she missed so much living?

Zach's tongue traced the underside of her breast, and then he was moving down, kissing a hot trail over her stomach. She was torn between anticipation and embarrassment that he could see the soft jiggle of her flesh. Why hadn't she insisted on turning out the light?

But then his tongue slid along the seam of her sex and she forgot everything but him. Lia cried out, unable to help herself. Never had she imagined how good this could feel, how perfect.

He circled her clitoris with his tongue, growing ever closer, until he finally touched her right where all those nerves concentrated. Lia stopped breathing. Her body clenched tighter and tighter as he focused his attention on that single spot. She wanted to reach the peak so badly, and she never wanted it to end, either.

She tried to hold out, tried to make it last, but Zach was far too skilled at making her body sing for him. Lia exploded in a shower of molten sparks, his name on her lips.

She turned her head into the pillow, embarrassed, gasping, trying to gather the shards of herself back together again. What had he done to her? How had he made her lose control so quickly, so thoroughly?

She felt Zach move and she turned to look at him. He stood beside the bed, tugging off his clothes. He looked fierce, and her heart thrummed at the intensity on his face.

She had no idea what she should be doing, but she didn't think she could go wrong by trying to help him remove his clothes. She sat up and started unbuckling his belt while he ripped his shirt over his head.

"Just a minute," he said, turning and disappearing into the adjoining bathroom for a second. When he returned, he was holding a condom package that bore the Corretti Hotel logo. She nearly laughed. Leave it to Matteo to think of everything in his hotels.

Zach's jeans disappeared, and Lia's breath caught at the sheer beauty of his body. He was hard, muscular—but he was also scarred. There was a long red scar that ran along his thigh, and a smaller round scar near his rib cage. Emotion welled inside her as she realized what it was: a bullet wound. She wanted to ask him what had happened, but he knelt between her thighs and rolled on the condom—and all thoughts of bullet wounds fled from her head as her breath shortened at the knowledge of what came next.

He bent and took her mouth with his, stoking the fire inside her instantaneously. When he stretched out over the top of her, she could think of nothing but how perfect this felt, how amazing to be naked beneath a man, his body stretched over hers, dominating hers in all the right ways.

Lia wrapped her legs around his waist, arched her body into him, her hands sliding down his back until she could grip his buttocks. It was natural, instinctual, and she gloried in the sound of approval he made in his throat.

She wanted to explore him, wanted to remember this night forever. But the fire between them was too urgent to go slowly. Lia gasped as she felt the head of his penis at her entrance. She knew this would hurt. What she didn't know was how badly.

Zach reached between them and stroked her. "Are you ready, Lia?" he whispered. "Or have you changed your mind? Last chance to say so."

Lia loved that he would ask. Now, like this, with his body poised to enter hers, he stopped to ask if she still wanted him. Part of her wanted him to stop. Part of her was terrified.

Brave. She nibbled his earlobe between her teeth, felt a ribbon of satisfaction wind through her at the soft growl he emitted. She was brave.

There was no other answer she could give except yes. Her body was on fire, humming from the way he touched her, the way he made her ache for more.

"Please," she said, the only word she could manage. It came out sounding like a sob. Zach stilled for the briefest second—and then he was sliding forward, his body entering hers.

She tensed when there was a slight resistance, but it didn't last. Zach's eyes clouded as he looked down at her, as if he were thinking, but then she shifted her hips, and he groaned softly. He was fully inside her now, his length stretching her in ways she'd never experienced before.

It was the most astonishing feeling. She arched her hips upward, gasping as sensation streaked through her.

"Lia, you make me forget—" She didn't know what else he planned to say because he took her mouth then, kissing her hard, urgently, his tongue sliding against hers so hotly.

They lay like that for a long moment, kissing deeply, their bodies connected and still.

Then he began to move, slowly at first, and then faster as she took everything he had to give and asked for more. The air between them shimmered with heat, with power.

Everything about making love was foreign to her—and yet it wasn't. She felt as if she'd always known how it would be, as if she'd only been waiting for him to take her on this sensual journey.

As they moved together, as their bodies lifted and separated and came together again, she could feel something just out of reach, something wonderful and shattering and necessary. She strained toward it, needing it, trying to catch it—

And then, with a gasp of wonder, she did.

"Yes," he told her, his breath hot in her ear as he threaded his fingers through hers and held her hands over her head, "like that. Just like that, Lia."

Lia sobbed as she flew out over the abyss. And then her breath caught hard in her chest before it burst from her again in a long, loud cry, her senses splintering on the rocks below. Zach captured her mouth, swallowed her cries as she moaned and gasped again and again.

Soon, he followed her over the edge, gripping her hips and lifting her to him as he found his own release. He gave her cries back to her then, and she drank them in greedily, until the only thing that remained was the sound of their breathing.

Zach moved first, lifting himself up and rolling away from her. Lia lay stunned at the intensity of the experience. Like a slow drip from a faucet, uncertainty began to erode the surface of her languor.

What happened now? Did she thank him for the good time, put on the robe and leave? Or did she roll over and run her fingers over the smooth muscle of his abdomen?

She knew what she wanted to do. She wanted to touch him again. Explore him when her body was calm and still.

But she was paralyzed with indecision. And then Zach decided for her. He didn't say anything as he got up and walked into the bathroom. Lia's heart performed a slow dive into her belly. They'd had sex, and he was finished.

She scrambled up and grabbed the robe, slipping it on

and swinging her legs over the side of the bed before he returned. Before she'd gone three steps, he walked out again.

Both of them crashed to a halt, staring at each other.

He was, she thought with a pang, beyond gorgeous. Beautifully, unconsciously naked. Tall and dark, packed with muscle that flexed and popped with his every movement. He looked like something she'd dreamed up instead of a flesh-and-blood man she'd really just had sex with.

Dio, she'd just had sex....

"Zach—"

"Lia—"

They spoke at the same time, their voices clashing. Lia dropped her gaze to the floor.

"Are you hungry?" Zach asked, and she looked up to see him watching her, a half smile on his handsome face. She couldn't keep her eyes from roaming his perfect body, no matter how she tried to focus solely on his face.

"Not that kind of hungry," he added with a laugh. "Though I'm definitely game for another round later."

Another round. Oh, my... Her insides thrummed with electricity at the thought.

"I haven't eaten since breakfast," she managed, her pulse thumping at the idea of doing it all again. And again.

Zach walked over to the desk and picked up the menu there. "Any suggestions?" he asked.

She had to struggle to concentrate. She knew what was on the menu without looking, but she could hardly think of food when Zach stood naked before her.

"Some antipasti, a little pasta alla Norma, some wine. It is all good," she finally managed, knowing that her brother would serve nothing but the best in his hotel.

"And dessert," Zach said, grinning. "Let's not forget dessert." He picked up the phone and ordered in flawless Italian—adding cannoli and fresh strawberries to the list—while Lia went into the bathroom to freshen up.

Her reflection surprised her. She'd thought she would look different—and, indeed, she did in a way. She looked like the cat that'd gotten into the cream. Yes, it was a terrible cliché, but it was truly the best way to describe that look of supreme satisfaction. Her skin glowed and her eyes were bright. Her lips were shockingly rosy and plump.

From kissing Zach. Her stomach flipped hard, and she wondered if she'd be able to eat a bite when he sat there with her, looking so tempting and yummy.

Lia forced herself to focus. She used the comb on the vanity to smooth her wild tangle of hair—as much as possible anyway—and wiped away the mascara that had smudged beneath her eyes. Then, heart pounding, she returned to Zach's suite. He'd pulled on his jeans and sat in a chair by the window, staring at the screen of his smart phone. When he realized she was there, he put the phone on the table.

His gaze was sharp, hot, and her skin began to prickle.

"Your Italian is perfect," she said, casting about for something innocuous to say. Something that would give these butterflies in her belly a chance to settle again. "Where did you learn it?"

"My grandfather was from Sicily," he said. "And I learned it from my mother. She refused to teach me the Sicilian dialect her father spoke, but she did teach me Italian."

Her gaze slid over him again. Now that she knew he had Sicilian blood in him, she could see it. He had the hot, dark eyes of a Sicilian. "Then you have been to Sicily before, yes?"

He inclined his head. "But not for many years."

She went and perched on the edge of the sofa, facing him. His gaze slid over her, warmed her in ways she hadn't known were possible before tonight. "You are friends with the bride's family or the groom's?"

He laughed. "Neither. I came with a friend." He picked up the phone again and frowned as he glanced at the screen. "I can't seem to find her, though."

Her. Lia swallowed as her stomach turned inside out. Of course a man who looked like this one was not alone. But where was his girlfriend, and why hadn't she come searching for him? If it were Lia, she wouldn't let him out of her sight.

But now she needed to do just that. Lia stood. "I should go," she said. "It's late, and you must be tired…."

Words failed her. She turned away, blindly, fighting a sudden rush of ridiculous tears. But then he was there, a hand wrapping around her arm, pulling her back against him so that she could feel the hot press of his body through the robe.

"Forgive me."

"There's nothing to forgive," she said stiffly.

His mouth was on her hair, her temple. "I'm not here with another woman, Lia. Not like that. Taylor is a friend, and she's here to work."

"Taylor Carmichael?" Lia knew of only one Taylor who would be in Sicily to work right now, and that was the gorgeous former child star. She'd heard her grandmother talking about Santo's film, and the troubled woman who was slated to star in it.

She heard Zach sigh. And then he turned her in his arms, put his hands on either side of her face and held her so he could look into her eyes. "Yes, Taylor Carmichael. Yes, she's beautiful and desirable—but not to me. We've only ever been friends. She's the sister I never had."

Lia bit her lip. It was almost impossible to believe that two such gorgeous creatures weren't sleeping together. "I think you need glasses, Zach."

He laughed. "Hardly. I know when I have a beautiful woman in my arms."

Lia flushed with pleasure. She'd never felt beautiful.

Until tonight. Oh, she still worried that she was too fat and too awkward, but she could hardly deny the evidence of his desire for her. She was quite a good dreamer, but she had definitely not dreamed what had happened in his bed only minutes ago.

What she hoped would happen again.

She closed her eyes. One time with him, and she was already becoming a woman of questionable morals.

He tipped her chin up with a long finger and pressed his lips to hers. Desire, so recently sated, still managed to lift a head and send a finger of need sliding down the pathways of her nervous system.

She stepped closer, her lips parting beneath his…and the kiss slid over the edge of polite and into the realm of hot and amazing. He was in the process of shoving the robe off her shoulders when there was a knock on the door.

He took a step back, breaking the kiss, and tugged the robe into place with a sigh of regret. "Food first," he said with a wicked smile. "And then we play."

Lia could only shudder in response.

They spent the night entangled together, their bodies craving the pleasure they found in each other. Lia learned more about sex, about her own body, than she'd dreamed possible.

They showered together in the morning, and then spent the day walking around Palermo, ducking into churches and restaurants, stopping in ancient alleys to kiss and touch, drinking espresso and eating pasta.

It was a perfect day, followed by another perfect evening. They were strangers, and not strangers. It was as if they'd known each other forever. Zach's smile made her heart throb painfully whenever he turned it on her. His laugh had the power to make her ache with raw hunger.

They talked, in Italian and in English, about endless

things. She confessed that she was a Corretti. Zach didn't seem to care, other than a brief lifting of the eyebrows as he connected her to the hotel owners.

She discovered that Zach lived in Washington, D.C., and that he'd met Taylor Carmichael at a clinic for military veterans. She didn't ask about his scars because he'd grown tight-lipped when he'd told her that much.

They returned to the hotel, to his room, and spent the entire night wrapped in each other once more. He left the balcony doors open so that a breeze from the sea blew in. Church bells chimed the hour, every hour, but sanctuary was in this room, this bed.

And yet it was ending. They both knew it. Lia had to return to her grandparents' estate, and Zach was going back to the States. He'd heard from Taylor, finally, and she'd told him everything was fine, though she was somehow now engaged to Lia's brother Luca. Zach didn't seem too happy about that, but he'd accepted it after they'd talked a bit longer.

He did not, Lia noticed, tell Taylor about her.

Yet she kept hoping for more, for some sign this meant more to him than simply sex. It had to. She couldn't be the only one affected by this thing between them. Could she?

But when she awoke early the next morning, Zach was gone. She hadn't heard a thing. His suitcase was gone, everything in the bathroom, everything that indicated he'd once been here.

All that remained was a single rose in a vase and a hastily scribbled note propped beside it. She snatched it up and opened it. The military medal fell out and hit the floor with a plink.

Lia's pulse throbbed as she read the note.

Be well, Lia.

Her heart crumpled beneath the weight of those words. Words that meant well, but ultimately meant nothing. She retrieved the medal, and then sank onto the bed and lifted his pillow to her face. It still smelled like him and she breathed it in, seeking calm.

Zach was gone, and she was alone once more. Like always.

CHAPTER FOUR

THE EVENING WAS hot and muggy, and Zach stood off to one side of the crowd gathered at the country club. He took a sip from his water glass, cleverly disguised as a mixed drink by the addition of a lime slice and a cocktail stirrer, and then set it on a passing tray.

He never drank at functions like this. It was something he'd learned growing up. Always keep your head and always be prepared for any eventuality. His father hadn't made a career in politics out of being imprudent, and Zach had learned the lesson well.

These days, however, he was less concerned with the good impression than he was with the opportunity to escape. Once he'd done his duty—made the speech, shook the hands, accepted the honor, cut the ribbon, got the promised funding for the Scott Foundation's causes—he was gone.

Tonight, he'd had to give a speech. And right now, his father was holding court with a group of people he no doubt hoped would become campaign donors. His mother was circulating with the skill of a career politician's wife, smiling and making polite small talk.

There were reporters in the room—there were always reporters—but the cameras were thankfully stowed at the moment. They'd come out during his speech, of course, and he'd had to work hard to concentrate on the crowd and not the flashes. A matron came over and started to talk to him. He nodded politely, spoke when necessary and kept his eye on the exit. The second he could excuse himself, he was gone. He'd already been here too long, and he was beginning to feel as if the walls were closing in.

He scanned the crowd out of habit, his gaze landing on a woman who made him think of Sicily. She was standing near the door, her head bowed so he couldn't see her face. The crowd moved, closing off his view of her. His pulse started to thrum, but of course, she wasn't Lia Corretti. Lia was in Sicily, no doubt making love to some other lucky bastard. A current of heat slid through him as he remembered her lush body arrayed before him.

If he'd been a different man, he'd have stayed in Sicily and kept her in his bed until they'd grown tired of each other. It's what the old Zach would have done.

But the man he was now couldn't take that chance. He'd spent two nights with her and she'd made him feel almost normal again. Yet it was a lie, and he'd known it.

He didn't know Lia at all, really, but he knew she deserved better than that. Better than him.

"Zach?"

His head whipped around, his gaze clashing with the woman's who'd moved through the crowd unseen and now stood before him. Shock coursed through him. It was as if he'd blinked and found himself whisked back to a different party. Almost against his will, his body responded to the stimulus of seeing her again. He wasn't so inexperienced as to allow an unwanted erection, but a tingle of excitement buzzed in his veins nevertheless.

Lia Corretti gazed up at him, her blue-green eyes filled with some emotion he couldn't place. Her dark red hair was twisted on her head, a few strands falling free to dangle over one shoulder. She was wearing a black dress with high heels and a simple pair of diamond earrings.

She wasn't dripping in jewels like so many of the women in this room, yet she looked as if she belonged. The woman who'd been talking to him had thankfully melted away, her attention caught by someone else.

"Hello, Lia," he said, covering his shock with a blandness that belied the turmoil raging inside him. He spoke as if it hadn't been a month, as if they'd never spent two blissful nights together. As if he didn't care that she was standing before him when what he really wanted to ask her was what the hell she was doing here.

But he was afraid he knew. It wouldn't be the first time a woman he'd slept with had gotten the wrong idea. He was a Scott, and Scotts were accustomed to dealing with fortune hunters. She hadn't seemed to be that type of woman, but clearly he'd been wrong.

He noticed that her golden skin somehow managed to look pale in the ballroom lights. Tight. There were lines around her lips, her eyes. She looked as if she'd been sick. And then she closed her eyes, her skin growing even paler. Instinctively, Zach reached for her arm.

He didn't count on the electricity sizzling through him at that single touch, or at the way she jerked in response.

"I'm sorry," she said in English, her accent sliding over the words. "I shouldn't have come here. I should have found another way."

"Why are you here?" he demanded, his voice more abrupt than he'd intended it to be.

She looked up at him, her eyes wide and earnest. Innocent. Why did he think of innocence when he thought of Lia? They'd had a one-night—correction, two-night—stand, but he couldn't shake the idea that the woman he'd made love to had somehow been innocent before he'd corrupted her.

"I—I need to tell you something."

"You could have called," he said coolly.

She shook her head. "Even if you had given me your number…" She seemed to stiffen, her chin coming up defiantly. "It is not the kind of thing one can say over the phone."

Zach took her by the elbow, firmly but gently, and steered her toward the nearest exit. She didn't resist. They emerged from the crowded ballroom onto a terrace that overlooked the golf course. It was dark, but the putting green was lit and there were still players practicing their swings.

He let her go and moved out of her orbit, his entire body tight with anger and restlessness. "And what do you wish to say to me, Lia?"

He sounded cold and in control. Inhuman. It was precisely what he needed to be in order to deal with her. He'd let himself feel softer emotions when he'd been with her before, and look where that had gotten him. If he'd been more direct, she wouldn't be here now. She would know that her chances of anything besides sex from him were nonexistent.

He would not make that mistake again.

Lia blinked. Her tongue darted out over her lower lip, and a bolt of sensation shot through him at that singular movement. His body wanted to react, but he refused to let it. She was a woman like any other, he reminded himself. If sex was what he wanted, he had only to walk back in that ballroom and select a partner.

Her gaze flicked to the door. "Perhaps we should go somewhere more private."

"No. Tell me what you came to say, and then go back to your hotel."

She seemed taken aback at the intensity of his tone. She ran a hand down her dress nervously, and then lifted it to tuck one of the dangling locks of hair behind her ear. "You've changed," she said.

He shook his head. "I'd think, rather, that you do not know me." He spread his hands wide. "This is who I am, Lia. What I am."

She looked hurt, and he felt an uncharacteristic pinch in his heart. But he knew how to handle this. He knew the words to say because he'd said a variation of them countless times before.

"Palermo was fun. But there can be nothing more between us. I'm sorry you came all this way."

He'd expected her to crumple beneath the weight of his words. She didn't. For a long moment, she only stared at him. And then she drew herself up, her eyes flashing. It was not the response he expected, and it surprised him. Intrigued him, too, if he were willing to admit it.

"There can be more," she said firmly. "There *must* be more."

Zach cursed himself. Why, of all the possible women in the world, had he chosen this one to break his long sexual fast with? He'd known there was something innocent about her, something naive. He should have sent her back to her room. Unfortunately, his brain had short-circuited the instant all the blood that should have powered it started flowing south.

"I'm sorry if you got the wrong idea, sugar," he began.

She didn't let him finish. Her brows drew down angrily as she closed the distance between them and poked him hard in the chest with a manicured finger. He was too stunned to react. "The wrong idea?" she demanded.

She swore in Italian, curses that somehow sounded so pretty but were actually quite rude if translated. Zach was bemused in spite of himself.

"There were consequences to those two days," she flashed. "For both of us, *bello.*"

Ice shot down his spine, sobering him right up again.

"What are you talking about?" he snapped.

Her lips tightened. And then she said the words that sliced through him like a sword thrust to the heart.

"I'm pregnant, Zach. With *your* baby."

Lia watched the play of emotions over his face. There was disbelief, of course. Anger. Denial.

She understood all those feelings. She'd experienced each one in the past few days, many times over. But she'd also experienced joy and happiness. And fear. She couldn't forget the fear.

"That's impossible," he said tightly. His handsome face was hard and cold, his eyes like chips of dark, burning ice as they bored into her.

Lia wanted to sit down. She was beginning to regret coming here tonight. She'd only just arrived in Washington today, and she'd hardly rested. She was suffering from the effects of too much air travel, too much stress and too many crazy hormones zinging through her system.

This was not at all how she'd pictured this happening. She hadn't thought beyond seeing him, hadn't thought he would force her to tell him her news standing in the darkness and watching men tap golf balls toward a little hole in the ground.

She also hadn't expected him to be so hostile. So cold.

Lia swallowed against the fear clogging her throat. She had to be brave. She'd already endured so much just to get to this point. There was no going back now.

"Apparently not," she said, imbuing her voice with iron. "Because I am most assuredly pregnant."

"How do you know it's mine?"

His voice was a whip in the darkness, his words piercing her. "Because there has been no one else," she shot back, fury and hurt roiling like a storm-tossed sea in her belly.

"We spent two nights together, Lia. And we used condoms." His eyes were hard, furious.

"There was once," she said, her skin warming. "Once when you, um, when we——"

She couldn't finish the thought. But he knew. He looked stunned. And then he closed his eyes, and she knew he remembered.

"Christ."

There'd been one time when they'd been sleeping and he'd grown hard against her as they slowly wakened. He'd slipped inside her, stroked into her lazily a few times, and then withdrew and put on a condom. It had been so random, so instinctive, that neither of them thought about it afterward.

"Exactly," she said softly, exhaustion creeping into her limbs. Why hadn't she just stayed at the hotel and slept? Her plan had always been to see him privately, but when she'd seen the announcement in the paper about his speech tonight, she'd become focused on getting here and telling him the news. On sharing this burden with someone who could help her.

But that wasn't the only reason.

For an entire month, she'd missed him. Missed his warm skin, the scent of soap and man, the way he skimmed his fingers over her body, the silky glide of his lips against hers.

The erotic pulse of his body inside hers, taking her to heights she'd never before experienced.

Lia shivered, though it was not cold. A drop of sweat trickled between her breasts. She felt...moist. And she definitely needed to sit down.

Zach stood ramrod straight on the terrace before her. "You may be pregnant, but that doesn't make the baby mine," he said. She swallowed down the nausea that had been her constant companion—it was lessening thanks to medication the doctor had prescribed—and tried to bring him into focus. "We were together two nights. How do I know you didn't have another lover?"

Lia's heart ached. She'd known he might not take the news well—what man would when a spontaneous encounter with a stranger turned life-altering in such a huge way?—but she hadn't expected him to accuse her of having another lover. Of basically coming all this way to lie to him.

"I need to get out of this heat," she choked out, turning blindly. She couldn't stand here and defend herself when she just wanted to sit down somewhere cool. When her heart hurt and her stomach churned and she wanted to cry.

She'd only taken a few steps toward the door when she felt as if the bottom was dropping out from under her. Lia shot a hand out and braced herself on the railing near the door as nausea threatened to overwhelm her. She turned to lean against it, grateful for the solid barrier holding her up.

"What's wrong?"

She looked up to find Zach standing over her, his stern face showing concern where moments ago it had only been anger.

Lia put a shaky hand to her forehead. "I'm hormonal, Zach. And you aren't helping matters."

He blew out a breath. And then his hand wrapped around her elbow as he pulled her to his side. "Come on."

He led her away from the door and then in through another door farther down. It led into a dark bar with tables and chairs and only a few patrons. Zach steered her to a table in the corner, far from anyone, and sat her down.

"Wait here."

She was too tired to argue so she did as he ordered, propping her head against one palm as she fought her queasy stomach.

He returned with a glass and a bottle of San Pellegrino, opening it and pouring it for her. She took a grateful sip, let the cold bubbly water slide down her throat and extinguish the fire in her belly.

Zach sank into the chair across from her. His arms were folded over what she remembered was an impressive chest when it was bare. His stare was not in the least bit friendly as he watched her. She thought of the military medal she'd tucked into her purse and pictured him in a flight suit, standing tall and proud beside a sleek fighter jet.

"Better?" he asked shortly.

She nodded. "Somewhat, yes."

"Good." His eyes narrowed. "Why should I believe this baby is mine, Lia?"

Her heart thudded. There was no reason she could actually give him. *Because I was a virgin. Because you are the only man I've ever been with.* "A paternity test should clear it up," she said coolly, though inside she was anything but cool. "I will submit the first moment it is safe to do so."

He turned his head and stared off into space. His profile was sharp, handsome. His hair was still cut in that military style, short and cropped close. On him, it was perfect. Not for the first time, she wondered what he'd seen in her. No doubt he was wondering the same thing.

"You seem to have it all thought out," he said evenly. Coldly.

Lia clutched the glass in her hands. "Not really. All I know is we created a baby together. And our baby deserves to have both parents in his or her life."

It was the one thought that had sustained her on the long trip from Sicily. The one thing she'd had to cling to when everything else was falling apart.

Zach would want his child. She'd told herself that over and over.

But she didn't really know if it was true.

What if he was exactly like her father and just didn't care about the life he'd helped to create? Despair rose up inside her soul. How could this be the same man she'd lain in bed with? That man had been warm, mysterious, considerate. He wouldn't abandon a helpless baby.

But this man...

She shivered. This one was cold and hard and mean.

He looked at her evenly. Across the room, a few people sat at tables or lounged at the bar. One woman leaned in toward the man across from her and said something that made him laugh. How Lia envied that woman. She was with a man who wanted her, a man who was happy she was there.

"I don't know what you expect, Lia, but I'm not the father type. Or the husband type." His voice was low and icy, his emotions so carefully controlled she had no idea if he felt anything at all.

"You don't have a choice about being a father," she said, her throat aching.

His dark eyes glittered. And then he smiled. A cruel smile. "There is always a choice. This is the twenty-first century, not the dark ages. You don't have to have this child. You don't have to keep this child."

His words seared into her. Lia shot to her feet and clutched her tiny purse to her like a shield. Her hands were trembling. Her body was trembling.

"I want this baby, Zach. I intend to give my child the best life possible. With or without you," she added, her throat tightening over the words. Though she didn't know how she was going to do that. She had nothing. The money she had from her mother wasn't in her control. She didn't even know how much there was; her grandfather had always managed it. Now, she supposed, Alessandro was managing it.

She didn't really know Alessandro, but he was her grandfather's handpicked successor. And if he was anything like Salvatore had been, then he was not a man you demanded anything from.

When she walked out of here, she had nothing more than

she'd walked in with. The bit of cash she'd saved from her allowance and the credit card on her grandmother's account. She kept hoping her grandmother wouldn't notice the charges, though she had no idea how much longer that could last. She'd fled while her grandmother was out of town, but Teresa would return any day and find Lia gone.

Then what? The family would shut down her ability to spend a dime other than her cash. Then someone would come for her. Lia shuddered.

Her heart thundered while Zach stared her down. *Please*, she silently begged. *Please don't reject us. Please don't send us back there.*

His eyes did not change. There was no warmth, no sympathy. No feeling at all. She'd been too hasty with that ultimatum. Too stupid.

"Without me," he said, his voice low and measured.

She considered him for a long moment, her eyes pricking with tears, her breath whooshing in and out of her chest as she fought to maintain control. He was a bastard. A horrible, rotten bastard.

What had happened to the man who'd been frightened and alone in that ballroom back in Palermo? The man who'd been vulnerable, and who'd dropped his military medal because he must believe, on some level, that he didn't deserve it?

She'd come here with such hope for the future. She'd come here expecting to find the man who had charmed her and made her feel special.

But this man was not the same man. She despised him in that moment. Despised herself for being so weak and needy that she'd had sex with a stranger—not once, but many times over two days. It was as if she'd wanted to challenge fate, as if she'd been laughing and daring life to knock her in the teeth one more time.

Well, it certainly had, hadn't it? She'd let herself feel

something for a man she didn't know, let herself believe there was more to it than simple biology. Not love, certainly not, but…something. Some feeling that was somehow more than she should have felt for a man she'd only just met.

She was so naive.

The pain sliced into her heart. "I spoke with Taylor Carmichael after you left Sicily. She thinks you are a good man," Lia told him. Something flickered in his gaze, yet he said nothing. "But I think she doesn't really know you the way she thinks she does."

She turned and headed for the exit, though the door was a blur through her tears. One of the patrons in the bar looked up as she passed. He grinned at her, an eyebrow lifting, but she kept walking, her entire world crumbling apart. She hoped Zach would stop her. Prayed he would.

Prayed that she was wrong and he was just very surprised and not reacting well.

But she reached the door and tugged it open, and still he wasn't behind her. Lia stepped into the corridor and hurried down it, her heels sinking into the plush carpet. And then she was outside, nodding to the doorman's query if she would like a taxi. Here, the world moved as it had before. Nothing had changed. Inside her soul, however, everything was different.

She was pregnant. She was alone.

She wished she had someone to talk to—a friend, a sister, anyone who would listen—but that was wishful thinking. She'd never had anyone to talk to.

A taxi glided up the rounded drive and the doorman opened it with a flourish. Lia handed him a few dollars and then slid inside and turned her head away from the elegant building as the taxi drove away. She refused to look back. That part of her life was over.

CHAPTER FIVE

LIA DIDN'T SLEEP well. She'd returned to her hotel, ordered room service—soup and crackers—and then taken a hot bath and climbed into bed with the television remote. She'd fallen asleep almost instantly, but then she'd awakened when it was still dark out. She lay there and stared at the ceiling.

Her entire life was crashing around her ears, and there was nothing she could do about it. Zach had rejected her. She had no choice but to return to Sicily. No choice but to tell her grandmother everything that had happened. She could only pray that Alessandro was a better man than her grandfather had been, and that he wouldn't force her to marry someone she didn't love simply for the sake of protecting the family reputation

She didn't hold out much hope, actually.

She put her hand over her still-flat belly. What was she going to do? Where was she going to go? If she tried to keep running, the Correttis would find her. She couldn't melt away and become anonymous. She couldn't find a job and raise her child alone. She had no idea how to begin. She had no skills, no advanced education. She'd never worked a day in her life.

But she would. She would, damn it, if that's what it took. She wasn't half-bad with plants. Maybe she could get a job in a nursery, or in someone's garden. She could prune plants, coax forth blooms, mulch and pot and plan seasonal beds.

It wasn't much, but it was something.

Tears filled her eyes and she dashed them away angrily. Eventually, she fell asleep again. When she woke this time, it was full daylight. She got up and dressed. She thought about ordering room service again, but she needed to be careful with her expenses. She would go and find a diner somewhere, a place she could eat cheaply.

And then she would figure out what to do.

Lia swept her long hair into a ponytail and grabbed her purse. She was just about to open the door when someone knocked on it. The housekeeper, no doubt. She pulled open the door.

Except it wasn't the housekeeper.

Lia's heart dipped into her toes at the sight of Zach on the threshold. But then it rose hotly as anger beat a pulse through her veins. He'd been so cruel to her last night.

"What do you want?" she asked, holding the door tight with one hand. Ready to slam it on him.

"To talk to you."

He was so handsome he made her ache. And that only made her madder. Was she really such a pushover for a pretty face? Was that how she'd found herself in this predicament? The first man to ever pay any real attention to her had the body of a god and the face of an angel—was it any wonder she'd fallen beneath his spell?

This time she would be strong. She gripped the door hard, her knuckles whitening. "I understood you the first time. What more can you have to say?"

He blew out a breath, focused on the wall of windows behind her head. "I called Taylor."

Her heart throbbed with a new emotion. Jealousy. "And this concerns me how?"

"You know how, Lia. Let me in so we can talk."

She wanted to say no, wanted to slam the door in his

face—but she couldn't do it. Wordlessly, she pulled the door open. Then she turned her back on him and went over to the couch to sit and wait. He came inside and stood a few feet away, his hands shoved into his jeans pockets.

"You went to see Taylor," he said. "To find out where I lived."

She lifted her chin. "I knew you lived in Washington, D.C. You told me so."

"Yes, but it's a big city. And you needed an address."

She toyed with the edge of her sleeve. "I'd have found you. You did tell me about your father, if you recall."

But it would have been much harder, which was why she'd gone to see Taylor. And how embarrassing that had been. She'd had to explain to a complete stranger that she needed to find Zach because she had something to tell him.

Taylor hadn't accepted that excuse. She'd demanded to know more. Lia hadn't blamed her, since she was Zach's friend, but it was still a humiliating experience. Taylor hadn't actually believed her—until she'd produced the medal. Lia still wasn't certain that Taylor believed everything, but she'd relented at that point because she'd believed enough.

"You've gone to a lot of trouble," he said.

Lia swallowed. What could she say? *I had no choice? My family will be furious? I'm afraid?*

"A baby needs two parents," she said. "And a man should know if he's going to be a father."

"And just what did you expect me to do about it, sugar?"

Irritation zipped through her like a lash. *Sugar* wasn't an endearment, spoken like this; it was a way of keeping her at a distance. Of objectifying her. "You know my name. I'd prefer you use it."

His eyes flashed. "Lia, then. Answer the question."

She folded her arms and looked toward the windows. She could see the white dome of the Capitol building sitting on the hill. Why had she chosen this hotel? It was far too expensive. If her grandmother cut off her credit cards, she'd be doing dishes in the hotel kitchen for the next ten years just to pay for one night.

"I thought you would want to know."

"You could have called."

She swung back to look at him. "Are you serious? Would you want this kind of news over the phone?"

He didn't answer. Instead, he pulled something from his rear pocket and tapped it on his palm. "How much money do you want, Lia?"

Her heart turned to stone in her chest as she realized he was holding a checkbook. And though she needed money—desperately—it hurt that he thought all he needed to do was buy her off.

And it hurt that he didn't want this child growing inside her. That he could so easily shove aside that connection and have nothing to do with a person who was one half of him.

My God, she'd really chosen well, hadn't she?

"You think I came here for money?" It would solve her most immediate problem, but it wouldn't really solve anything. She'd still be single and pregnant, and her family would still be furious—and the Correttis had a long arm.

"Didn't you?"

Lia stood. She had to fold her arms over her middle to hide their trembling. "Get out," she said, fighting the wave of hysteria bubbling up inside her.

He took a step toward her and then stopped. The checkbook disappeared in his jeans again. He looked dark and broody and so full of secrets he frightened her. And yet a part of her wanted, desperately, to slide into his arms and experience that same exhilaration she had back in Sicily.

"You expect marriage," he said, almost to himself. "That's why you came."

It seemed so silly when spoken aloud like that, but she couldn't deny the truth of it. She had thought she would race to D.C., tell Zach she was pregnant and he would be so happy he'd want to take care of her and the baby forever.

Lia closed her eyes. What was wrong with her? Why was she always looking for acceptance and affection where there was none? Why did she think she needed a man, any man, in her life anyway?

"This is your baby in here," she said, spreading her hand over her abdomen. "How can you not want it?"

He raked a hand through his hair and turned away from her. Once more, she was studying his beautiful, angry profile.

"Assuming what you say is true, I'm not good father material." He said it quietly, with conviction, and her heart twisted in her chest.

Still, she couldn't allow sympathy for the pain in his voice to deflect her from the other part of what he'd said. "If you don't believe me, why are you here? Do you usually offer to pay women to get them to go away?"

He turned back to her, his expression cool. "I've encountered this situation before, yes. It has never been true, by the way." He spread his hands wide. "But my family name encourages the deception."

Lia stiffened. "I really don't care who your family is," she said tightly. "I did not come here for them."

"Then what do you want, Lia?"

She swallowed. She'd thought—naively, of course—there had been something between them in Palermo. Something more than just simple animal attraction. She'd thought he might be glad to see her. God, she was such a fool.

The only thing she had was the truth.

"My family will be very angry when they find out," she said softly. "And Alessandro will likely marry me off to one of his business associates to prevent a scandal." She dropped her gaze and smoothed her hand over her belly again. "I suppose I could deal with that if it were only me. But I'm afraid for my baby. A Sicilian man won't appreciate a wife who is pregnant with another man's child."

She could feel his gaze on her and she lifted her head, met the tortured darkness of his eyes. And the heat. It surprised her to find heat there, but it was indisputable. The heat of anger, no doubt.

"You know this to be true," she said. "You are part Sicilian yourself."

"A small part, but yes, I know what you mean."

She could have breathed a sigh of relief—except she didn't think he'd changed his mind about anything. "Then you will not want your child raised by another man. A man who will not love him or her, and who will resent the baby's presence in his household."

Zach was still. "You should have chosen better," he said.

She blinked. It was not at all the response she'd anticipated. "I beg your pardon?"

"That night. You should have chosen to leave instead of stay."

She'd bared her fears to him and this was what he had to say. Anger spiked in her belly. "It takes two, Zach. You were there, too."

He took a step toward her, stopped. His hands flexed at his sides. "Yes, and I tried to send you away, if you will recall. Considering how we first met, you should have run far and fast."

Her skin was hot—with shame, with anger, with self-recrimination. "It's not all my fault. Perhaps you should have tried harder."

As if anything would have induced her to leave after the way he'd looked at her: as if he wanted to devour her. It had been such a novel experience that she'd only wanted more.

"I should have," he said. "But I was weak."

"This baby is yours," she said, a thread of desperation weaving through her. If he walked out now, if he sent her back to Sicily, what would become of her and the baby? She couldn't face her cousin's wrath. Her grandmother would do what she could, but even Teresa Corretti would do what the head of the family dictated in the end. And he would dictate that she not have a child out of wedlock. Or he would throw her out and cut her off without a cent.

For a moment, she contemplated that option. It would be…heavenly, in a way. She would be free of the Correttis, free of the pain and anger that went along with being the outsider in her family.

Except she knew it wouldn't happen that way. Salvatore Corretti had ruled his family with an iron fist. And no wayward granddaughter would have ever brought shame on the family name in such a way. A Corretti grandson could father illegitimate children all day long, and he would not have cared. Let one of his granddaughters get pregnant, with no man in sight, and he most certainly would have come unglued.

Alessandro was a Corretti male and would be no different. He'd learned at their grandfather's knee how to run this family and she could not take the risk he was somehow more enlightened. He'd never been enlightened enough to pay attention to her in all these years, which told her a lot about how he already felt about her. Add in the humiliation of his aborted wedding, and she was certain he was in no mood to be sympathetic.

"How can you be sure, Lia?"

She had to give herself a mental shake to retrieve the thread of the conversation. He wanted to know how she could be sure the baby was his, as if she was the kind of woman who had a different sexual partner every night.

"Because I am. Because I've been with no one else."

He swore softly.

Her cheeks heated. Hot emotion whipped through her. She was tired of feeling guilty, tired of feeling as if she was the one who'd done something wrong. She felt snappish.

"This isn't ideal for me, either, you know. I didn't ask to get pregnant, especially not my first time ever having sex—"

She broke off as she realized what she'd said. His face grew thunderous. He closed the distance between them, stopped just short of grabbing her. His hands were clenched into fists at his sides. "What did you say?"

Lia's heart pounded. Adrenaline roared through her veins. She felt light-headed. "Nothing," she whispered as his eyes darkened. "It was nothing."

"You told me that night it had been a long time...." His voice was diamond-edged.

"I thought if I told you the truth, you'd send me away."

He swallowed, hard. "I would have. I should have anyway." His gaze dropped, his dark lashes dipping to cover his beautiful eyes. "I thought something was...different with you. But it had been so long since I'd been with anyone that I dismissed my intuition. You didn't act like a virgin, but you felt like one when I..."

He swore again, his eyes meeting hers once more. "I'd have done things differently if I'd known. Been more gentle. You should have told me."

Lia couldn't stop herself from lifting a hand and sliding it along the bare skin of his arm. It was the first time she'd touched him, really touched him, in a month. And the electric sizzle ricocheting through her body told her just how little had changed for her.

"I should have. I know it. But everything was so surreal, and I was afraid it would end. You were the first person to make me feel wanted in a very long time. I liked that feeling."

He moved away from her, went over and sank down on a chair. Then he sat forward and put his head in his hands. Lia didn't say anything. She didn't move, though her heart throbbed at the sight of him looking so overwhelmed.

"This is not what I expected to happen at this point in my life," he said to the floor.

"I don't think either of us did," she replied, swallowing. "And though I could make it all go away with a visit to a doctor, as you intimated earlier, I can't do that. It's not who I am or what I want."

He lifted his head. "No, I know that." He blew out a breath, swore. And then he stood again, his presence nearly overwhelming her as his eyes flashed fire. "The press will have a field day with this."

Lia bit the inside of her lip. In all the drama, she'd never considered the press. It was true the paparazzi flocked around her family like piranha. But she'd never been their target, probably because she was so humdrum and uninteresting in her family of brilliant swans.

But this baby was a game changer, especially considering who Zach was. His family was even more famous than hers. American royalty, if there was such a thing. A family with incredible wealth and power. She'd read all about the Scotts on her way across the Atlantic.

And she'd read about their heroic son, a man who'd returned from the war after a dramatic plane crash behind enemy lines. Her gaze drifted to where she'd set her purse. Inside, in a little zippered pocket, she still had Zach's medal. A medal he hadn't cared about.

She thought of him flat against the ballroom wall in the Corretti Hotel, his eyes tightly closed as he fought against something, and knew there was more to the story than had been reported.

"We're the only ones who know," she said. "And I have no plans to inform them. I think the secret is safe for now."

His gaze was steady, cool, and she realized he didn't entirely trust her. It stung.

"There are always leaks." He shoved a hand through his hair. "There's only one way to deal with this. One way to keep everything from exploding into an even bigger problem than it already is."

Her heart thundered in her chest. And it hurt, too. Hurt because he'd called her—and their baby—a problem.

"Congratulations, Lia," he said, his voice chilling her. "You've won the jackpot, after all. You're about to become a Scott."

"This is not how I wanted this to happen," she said on a throat-aching whisper. Tears pressed the backs of her eyes. She couldn't let them fall.

"You came here," he said, his voice hard. "What did you expect? Did you think I would be happy?"

She dropped her gaze. A single tear spilled free and she dashed it away, determined not to cry in front of him. Not to be weak.

"I had hoped you might be, yes." She lifted her chin and sucked back her tears. "Clearly, I was mistaken."

"We'll marry," he said. "Because we must. But it's an arrangement, do you understand? We'll do it for as long as necessary to protect our families, and then we'll end it when the time comes."

Anger started to burn in her, scouring her insides. He was no better than her father had been. He didn't care about his child any more than Benito Corretti had cared about her. He was making a deal, nothing more. It made her sick. And furious.

"Fine," she said tightly. "I accept. But if we are having an arrangement, as you so nicely put it, then I want it understood that this arrangement is in name only."

She didn't know what made her say that, but once she said it she knew it was right. Because this situation was so out of her power that she needed something she could control. Something she could have a say about.

He stared at her for a long moment. And then his sexy lips curled up in a smile, surprising her after he'd been so hard and cold. "I can't guarantee that, sugar. But we'll try it your way to start. Just know that when you do surrender to me, I won't be saying no."

Lia pulled herself erect and looked at him with all the haughtiness she could muster. Which wasn't much, she was sure. But damn if he hadn't infuriated her. "There will be no surrender, Zach. Not ever again."

"We'll see," he said with all the arrogant surety of a man who was accustomed to getting his way. And then he headed toward the door. "I'll let you know when the arrangements are made."

"How long will this take?" she asked as he opened the door.

He turned back to her. "Eager, Lia?"

She sucked in a breath. No, she was just worried about her ability to stay in this hotel. And about her family sending someone to fetch her if they figured out where she was. "No, but I have no idea how long these things take in America. I can't stay in this hotel for weeks, Zach."

His eyes slipped over her. "No, you can't. The media will descend soon enough. You'll move in with me. I'll send someone for you later."

He closed the door before she could say another word. She

stood there for a long time, uncertain whether she'd found salvation by coming to D.C.

Or whether she'd damned herself instead.

CHAPTER SIX

ZACH LIVED IN a sprawling house in Virginia. It was gated, with manicured green lawns and a view of the Potomac River. Here, the Potomac was still close to the source and was wilder and freer than it had been in Washington. It tumbled over huge boulders, rushing and gurgling toward the city where it would become wide, placid and subject to Chesapeake tides.

Lia stood in a room that overlooked the backyard and the cliffs of the Potomac. Glass doors opened onto a wide stone balcony that ran the length of the house. Immediately outside was a small seating area, with a chair and a table. Perfect for reading.

The gardens weren't overly ornate, but there were a lot of gorgeous flowering plants in manicured beds. Roses bloomed in profusion along two stone walls, red and pink and white. Fat flowering hydrangeas, blue and pink, sat in the shade beneath tall trees, and a host of bright annuals bloomed in beds that ran down toward the river.

Lia's fingers itched. She wanted to lose herself in the garden, to go dig into the dirt and forget all about Zach Scott and the Correttis for a while.

But that was impossible right now.

She hadn't seen Zach since she'd arrived. A chauffeur had come to get her at the hotel earlier, after a terse call from

Zach informing her to be ready. Once she'd arrived, a uniformed maid had showed her to this room and offered to put her things away. Lia only had one suitcase and a carry-on, so she didn't really have much with her. She'd declined and hung everything herself.

Now she felt like she was in stasis. Just waiting for something to happen. The garden called to her, but she resisted. What would Zach think if he came looking for her and she was on her knees in the dirt?

As the minutes dragged by, she resolved to go out on the balcony and run her fingers through the potted geraniums and lavender, just for something to do, but a knock at her door stopped her. "Yes?" she called.

The door opened and Zach stood there, tall, handsome and brooding as ever. Lia folded her arms over her chest and waited.

"If you've no objection, I've brought a doctor who is going to take a blood sample."

"Why?"

Zach came into the room, his hands shoved into the pockets of his faded jeans. *Dio*, he was sexy. Lia shook herself and tried not to think about him that way. She failed, naturally. Her heart thumped and pumped and her bones loosened in the shell of her skin.

"There is a paternity test that will isolate the baby's DNA from your blood. Just to be certain, you realize."

Lia lifted her chin. "I have nothing to hide."

It hurt, of course, that he didn't believe her. But if a test would erase all doubt, she was for it. Not only that, but she also looked forward to the apology he would have to make when the test proved he was this baby's father.

"I'll bring her up, then."

"Yes, do."

He left and then returned a few minutes later with a smiling woman who took Lia's blood and asked her questions about how she was feeling. Once it was over, and the woman was gone, Lia was left with Zach.

"I have an important dinner to attend tonight," he told her. "You will accompany me."

Lia swallowed. She wasn't accustomed to large gatherings. Aside from the wedding-that-wasn't, and a few family things that happened once a year, she spent most of her time alone or with her grandmother.

"I don't have anything to wear," she said. She didn't even know what kind of dinner it was, but if it was anything like that gathering she'd crashed last night, she knew she didn't have anything appropriate. She'd put on the nicest thing she had for that event.

Zach didn't look perturbed. "There is time. I'll send you to my mother's personal shopper."

"That is not necessary," she said, though in truth she wouldn't begin to know where to start in this city.

"I think it is, Lia. It'll go much faster if you simply let her help you pick out what you need. For tonight, you'll need formal wear. But select a range of clothing appropriate for various events."

"And do you attend many events?" she asked, her heartbeat spiking at the thought of being out among so many people so frequently.

Plants she understood. People not so much.

His eyes were flat. "I am a Scott. And a returning war hero. My presence is in demand quite often, I'm afraid."

She didn't miss the way his voice slid over the words *war hero*. It was like they were oily, evil words for some reason. As if he hated them.

"You don't sound as if you enjoy it."

One corner of his mouth lifted. "No, I don't. Not anymore."

She wanted to ask what had changed, but she didn't. "Then why do it?"

"Because I am a Scott. Because people depend on me. And if you are going to be a Scott, too, then you'd better get used to doing things because you have to instead of want to."

Lia nibbled the inside of her lip. She was no good at the social thing. She had no practice at it. But, for tonight, she would have to try and be something she wasn't. She would have to navigate the social waters without falling flat on her metaphorical face.

"I'm no good at this, Zach," she told him truthfully. "I don't have any experience."

Not to mention she was awkward and grew tongue-tied around too many people. She'd always been so self-conscious, so worried about whether or not others liked her.

Because she'd never felt very wanted and she didn't know how to fix it.

"Then you'll learn," he said. "Because you have no choice."

Zach slipped into his tuxedo jacket and tugged the cuffs of his shirt until they were straight beneath the jacket arms. Tonight was another event, another speech, where he would be speaking to some of Washington's elite about the need for funding for veterans' causes. Everyone tended to think, because the military worked for the government, that returning vets' care was assured. It was to a point. Where that point ended was where Zach stepped in.

But tonight was different in a way he had not expected. For the first time since he'd returned from the war, he was taking a woman with him. A woman who was his date.

His fiancée, for God's sake. An unsettled feeling swirled in his gut at the notion, but it was too late to back out now.

He'd had the call from the doctor. They'd rushed the results—because he'd paid them a great deal of money to do so—and he knew the truth.

Lia Corretti was pregnant with his child.

He wasn't quite sure how that made him feel. He was still stunned at his reaction to her earlier today, in her hotel room, when he'd suddenly decided that marrying her was the thing to do. It had been a preemptive strike, because though he'd fully intended to get an answer to the child's paternity before proceeding, he'd also known on a gut level that she was telling him the truth.

She'd been a virgin. He'd realized something was different about her that night in Palermo, but she'd distracted him before he'd puzzled out precisely what it was. Not that being a virgin made someone truthful, but he imagined it was highly unlikely she'd turned around and taken a new lover so quickly.

His gut had known what his head hadn't wanted to admit. And now he had a fiancée. A fiancée he didn't quite know how to fit into this life of his. She hadn't wanted to accompany him tonight, but he'd insisted she would anyway.

He'd been angry and resentful toward her all day. But now he felt a twinge of guilt over his reaction. Still, he'd told her the truth. She would learn to deal with her responsibilities as his wife because she had no choice.

They had appearances to maintain and commitments to keep. If he was going to have a wife, then she was going to be at his side. It's the way it worked in his world. The way it had always worked.

He went downstairs and into his office, where he opened the wall safe and extracted a box. He'd told Lia to shop for clothing, but he'd not thought of jewelry. He had no idea what she would wear tonight, but he knew what would look good with her coloring. He opened the box and slid a finger over the art deco rubies and diamonds. These had belonged to his grandmother. She'd left them to him on her death and he'd put them away, certain it would be years before he found a woman to give them to.

He flipped the box closed after a long moment and held it tight. His life was changing in ways he hadn't expected. Ways he wasn't quite sure how to cope with. He resented the changes, but he would deal with them the way he dealt with everything else in his life these days.

By hiding his feelings beneath a mountain of duty and honor.

She was learning, or trying to. Lia stood beside Zach at a posh gathering being held in the National Gallery of Art. It was past closing time, and the museum was only open for this exclusive party.

She'd chosen a gown in a rich cream color, and swept her dark hair off her shoulders and pinned it up. She'd applied her makeup carefully, slid into her heels—not too high because she was already self-conscious about her height—and wrapped a shawl around her shoulders. Her jewelry had consisted of her simple diamonds, until she'd arrived downstairs and found Zach waiting for her in the foyer of the big house.

His gaze had flicked over her appreciatively, and she'd felt warmth spread through her limbs. She liked the way he looked at her. And she wasn't happy about that. After the way he'd behaved since she'd arrived, she didn't want to like anything about him. She kept telling herself that the man she'd spent two days with was gone—except she couldn't quite convince herself when he looked at her the way he had earlier.

"Wear these," he'd said, flipping open a box that held a

ruby-and-diamond necklace and matching earrings. It was ornate, but somehow simple, too. An impressive feat for an expensive necklace.

"I shouldn't," she said. "I'm too clumsy—"

"Nonsense." His tone had been firm. "You're a beautiful woman, Lia. And you are about to be my wife."

He'd taken the necklace from the box and clasped it on her once he'd removed her small pendant. Then he placed her necklace carefully in the box he'd taken the larger necklace from. She was grateful for that, considering it was the only jewelry she had that had belonged to her mother. It might be small and unimpressive, but Zach didn't treat it that way, and that touched her even though she did not want it to. He held out his hand for her earrings, which she handed over, and then she put the diamonds and rubies on.

When she was finished, he gave a satisfactory smile. "Excellent. You look lovely."

They'd climbed into the Mercedes, and the chauffeur—Raoul—had driven them here, where Zach had been greeted like the political royalty he was. Now, they were sipping cocktails and waiting for the dinner to begin.

She didn't miss that women slanted their gazes toward her. Some were appraising while others were downright hostile. Zach kept her at his side. Periodically, he would drape an arm around her, or slide his hand into the small of her back to guide her through the crowd. His touches made her jumpy yet she found herself craving them.

Soon they were seated at a large round table toward the front of the gathering. Lia wasn't intimidated by the array of cutlery and plates before her. She might not be any good at the socializing part of this, but she'd been brought up by Teresa Corretti, the most elegant woman in all of Sicily. Lia knew which fork to use, and which bread plate was hers.

She also knew how to sit through a multicourse meal and how to pace herself so that she wasn't too full before the last course arrived.

But tonight she was finding it hard to concentrate on her food. She was still tired from the trip, and the stress of everything was starting to overwhelm her. She'd left Sicily on impulse, and now she was here with Zach, and he wasn't the man she'd thought he was.

He was an automaton, an aristocrat, a man who did what he had to do because he cared about things like social standing and reputation. While it wasn't a foreign concept to her, coming from the Corretti family, it wasn't what she'd thought she was fleeing toward when leaving Sicily.

She could hardly reconcile the man he was here—dressed in a bespoke tuxedo and sporting an expensive watch—with the stiff military man who'd thrown a medal at her feet. The two did not seem to go together, and it confused her.

"You aren't eating."

His breath ghosted over her ear and a shiver of something slid down her backbone. She turned her head, discovered that he was frowning down at her, his dark eyes intense.

"I'm tired," she said. "My schedule is all messed up. In a couple of hours, I would be waking up and having breakfast, were I still home."

"You need to eat something. For your health."

She knew what he meant. And why he didn't say it. "I've eaten the soup and some of the bread."

"Beef is good for you. There's iron in there."

"I've had a bite of it."

"Eat more, Lia."

"I can't eat just because you order me to," she snapped quietly.

Zach glanced at someone across the table and smiled.

Then he lifted his hand and slid it along her jaw, turning her head as he did so. To anyone else, the gesture looked loving and attentive. But she knew what it really was. He was attempting to keep her in line.

His eyes held hers. She couldn't look away. His mouth was only inches away, and she found herself wanting to stretch toward him, wanting to tilt her face up and press her lips to his.

His gaze dropped to her mouth, and one corner of his beautiful, sensual lips lifted. "Yes, precisely," he murmured. She felt her face flood with heat. "And I am not ordering you to eat, Lia. I'm concerned about your health."

She dropped her gaze from his. "*Grazie.* But I will not let my health suffer, I assure you."

"Excellent," he said. "Because you are mine now, and I take care of what is mine."

A shiver slid through her. And a flash of anger. "Are you certain about that? What if the test results aren't what you want them to be?"

His eyes sparkled with humor that she sensed was at her expense. "I've already had the result. And it is precisely what you said it was."

Lia wanted to jerk herself out of his grip, but she knew this was not the place to show a bit of temper. "You could not have told me this earlier?"

He shrugged. "Why? You already knew the answer."

"Perhaps I would like an apology. You did suggest I was lying, as well as exceedingly promiscuous."

"My mistake."

"You consider that an apology?"

"I do. You must realize, sugar, that you aren't the first to try and trap me this way. You're just the first to succeed."

Lia shoved her chair back, uncaring how it looked to the other guests at their table. The murmur of conversation ceased and all eyes were on her. She swallowed and stood, hoping the trembling didn't show.

"If you will excuse me, ladies and gentlemen," she said. "I believe I must freshen up."

Then she turned and marched away without waiting for a response. She was certain the fashionable ladies were appalled with her. The gentlemen probably shrugged it off as foreign eccentricity. Nevertheless, she didn't quite care what they thought. She wasn't about to sit there and let Zach talk to her like that.

She found the ladies' room and went inside to perch on one of the settees and calm down. She refreshed her lipstick in the mirror and smoothed a few stray hairs into place. As she gazed at her reflection, it hit her how unusual her reaction just now had been. She'd sat through enough humiliating Corretti functions in her life to know how to be invisible for the duration.

She also knew how to be a lady whenever any attention happened to turn on her, and she knew that marching away in a huff was not a part of the training her grandmother had instilled in her. Teresa Corretti would be disappointed at that display of temper just now.

Lia curled her hands into fists on her lap and took a deep breath. Damn Zach, he had a way of getting beneath her skin and irritating her so much that she simply reacted without thinking. It wasn't like her to draw attention to herself, or to argue, but she couldn't help it with him.

Still, she should not have let him get to her like that. But he'd suggested she'd purposely set out to trap him into marriage, and it made her furious. What kind of God's gift to women did he think he was anyway? It was ludicrous. And she planned to tell him so just as soon as they were alone and she could give him a proper piece of her mind.

Lia stood and smoothed her dress. She studied herself in the mirror and was pleased with what she saw. Oh, she was still too plump—and too tall—but she cleaned up quite nicely when she was able to wear designer dresses someone had picked out specifically for her shape and coloring.

When she left the ladies' room, Zach was standing across from the door, leaning against the wall in a sexy slouch that made her heart kick up. He really was spectacular. Tall, broad and intensely handsome. The kind of man that, yes, would have women falling all over him.

"You've been gone awhile," he said.

Lia tilted her chin up. "Yes. I needed to get my temper under control."

Zach laughed. She didn't like the way the sound slid beneath her skin. Curled around her heart. Warmed her from the inside out.

"I wasn't aware you had a temper, Lia."

"Of course I do. And you know just how to aggravate it." She'd never really realized precisely how furious another person could make her until she'd met Zach. He had an ability to make her feel things she'd never quite felt before—and to say things she would have never said to another person. Usually, she hid her emotions down deep.

Except with him. With him, she couldn't help but say what she was feeling.

It was that or burst.

She crossed the hall and stood right in front of him, nearly toe to toe. She was tall in her heels, five-eleven, but she still had to tilt her head back to look up at him. "You might think you are some sort of priceless gift to womankind, Zach Scott, but I'll have you know that I would much prefer to be back home and for none of this to have happened."

It wasn't quite true, but she wasn't going to tell him that.

She wasn't sorry for the two nights they'd spent together. She wasn't even sorry about her baby. She was sorry for the way it had happened, and for the man it had happened with. Why couldn't she have chosen a good Sicilian man for her night of rebellion? A single, sexy Sicilian who had no hangups about women and their motives.

Even as she thought it, she knew she didn't really want that, either.

"For your information," she continued, "I did not set out to 'trap' you. That is the most arrogant, conceited, unbelievable thing you have said yet. No one forced you to do what you did in Palermo. No one forced you to take that risk."

His expression was dark. "No, you're right about that. No one forced me. It was a mistake, and I was stupid enough to make it." His eyes slid over her, came to rest on her face again. "Everything about those two days was a mistake."

Lia tried not to let that hurt her, but she didn't quite succeed. It stung her in places she'd thought she'd locked away long ago. "Well, now that we have that out of the way, I think it must be time for the dessert course."

She turned her back on him and started down the hall, back toward the dinner. Tears pricked her eyes. Angry tears, she told herself.

Zach's hand on her elbow brought her up short. She whirled around and jerked out of his grip.

He was a dark, brooding presence. "Look, I didn't mean that the way it sounded." He shoved a hand through his hair, blew out a breath.

Lia glared at him steadily. "I did not trap you, Zach. I'd like you to admit that."

His expression remained dark. "Fine. You didn't trap me."

"And what about not believing I was telling the truth? Are you going to admit you were wrong about that, too?"

His eyes gleamed. "No."

She stiffened. "Of all the rude, arrogant—"

"What reason did I have to believe you?" he said heatedly. "We're strangers, Lia, regardless of what happened in Palermo."

She swallowed against the knot of anger and pain clogging her throat. But she knew what he said was true. Would she have believed a story like hers if she were Zach? Considering his previous experience of women, perhaps not.

"I will concede that point," she said coolly, though her heart beat hot at the admission. "But I don't like it."

He reached for her hand, slipped it into his. Her entire body went on red alert just from that simple touch. She wanted more of him, more of what they'd had in Palermo. And yet she knew that was the last thing she should want. The very last. They had an arrangement in name only, to protect their families, until such time as they could go their separate ways and not cause a scandal.

She had to remember he didn't truly want this child. Or her.

She tried to pull her hand away, but he held it tight.

"Darling, we're returning to the event," he chided her. "We have to look happy together if they are to believe our whirlwind romance."

"I'm not very good at pretending," she said stiffly.

He tugged her closer. "Then I will have to give you a reason to smile," he said, slipping his hand around to the small of her back and pressing her against him. He pulled the hand he'd trapped up to his chest, pressed her palm against the smooth fabric of his tuxedo.

"There is nothing you can do to make me smile, Zach," she said, though her heart beat harder and faster as the look in his eyes changed. Heat flared in their dark depths and her body responded by softening, melting. She held herself rigid, unwilling to give in to the feelings swirling inside her. Feelings that wanted her to tilt her head back and offer her lips up for him to claim. "I want you to let me go."

His eyes were hooded as they dropped to her mouth, and a shot of adrenaline pulsed into her veins.

"I will," he murmured. "But not quite yet."

CHAPTER SEVEN

ZACH WAS ON the edge of control. Not in a way that made him sweat as helpless panic rose in his throat and threatened to squeeze the life from him. But he had a need to dominate. A need to take this infuriating woman to his bed and not let her out of it for several hours.

Not until she sighed her pleasure into his ear. Not until she gasped out his name the way she had in Palermo. Sweet, innocent Lia. He wanted to taste her again. Wanted to know if she was as sweet as he remembered. As intoxicating.

She stood very still in his grasp. He didn't hold her tight. She could have broken free with a single tug. Oh, not when he'd first gripped her hand. Definitely not then. At that moment, he'd been intending to saunter back into the gathering with his woman at his side, looking happy and enraptured for the world to see.

He knew how this game was played. He could have a fast romance and marriage, but first he had to be seen with Lia. And they needed to appear as if they couldn't keep their hands off each other. So far, they'd looked as if they might prefer to touch anyone else rather than each other.

He had to change that perception, especially since there were at least three reporters circulating at this party tonight. Tomorrow, on the society pages of the local papers, they'd

mention his date. By tomorrow evening, they'd know everything about Lia Corretti.

And what he wanted them to know was that she was mad
for him.

Except she didn't look so much mad for him as mad at him
at the moment. Furious, with her snapping blue-green eyes
and dark auburn hair that caught the light like a flame. Her
lips parted slightly as he stared at them. Her breathing grew
shallow, her creamy breasts rising and falling more rapidly.

He could see the pulse thrumming in her neck. A very
male sort of satisfaction slid through him. Lia was not immune, no matter how she bristled and glared.

Zach reached up and ran his thumb over the pulse at her
throat. She gasped, but she didn't pull away.

"We were good together," he purred. "We could be again."

Her eyes were wide as she gazed up at him. "This is an
arrangement, Zach," she said, her voice hardly more than a
whisper. "An arrangement that does not include sex."

He was beginning to regret that he'd used that word with
her. She was intent on keeping it strictly business since he'd
told her this was a temporary solution to protect their families from the media.

He'd fully intended it to be temporary when he'd said it.
It had seemed the perfect solution. He didn't know the first
thing about being a father, wasn't sure he could even do it.
If he married Lia, gave their child a name and a legacy, they
could go their separate ways in a few months and everything
would be fine.

Except, strangely, since the moment the doctor had given
him the test results earlier, he'd felt a sense of duty that
warred with those thoughts.

And more than duty. When Lia had come downstairs tonight, he'd felt the same shot of lust he'd experienced in his

room in Palermo. The same hard knot of desire had coiled inside his gut and refused to let go.

He bent toward her, breathed in her scent. "What is your perfume, Lia?" he asked, his breath against her ear. A shudder rolled through her. He could feel it in his fingertips where they pressed into her back and throat.

"It's my own," she said, her voice husky. "I went to a perfumer in the village. She made it for me."

Zach breathed again. "Vanilla. A hint of lavender. Perhaps even a shot of lemon. For tartness," he finished.

"I—I don't know," she said quickly. "I didn't ask."

Zach couldn't stop himself from what he did next. He touched his tongue to her throat, glided to the sweet spot beneath her ear. The sound that came out of her made him hard.

Her hands were on his lapels, clutching him. "Zach, stop…"

"Do you really want me to?" he said against her sweet flesh.

She shuddered again, and he reacted with animal instinct, pushing her into an alcove where they were hidden from prying eyes. Unless someone was standing right in front of the opening, they would not be visible from down the corridor.

It was appalling behavior for a public event, but right now Zach was operating on a pure shot of desire.

"I definitely taste lemon," he said, tilting her chin up and back until her eyes were on his. "You are so beautiful, Lia. So hot."

"You are trying to seduce me," she said, closing her eyes. "You would say anything to further your purpose."

His hand slid around her back, up her rib cage. He shaped her breast, his thumb caressing her nipple beneath the fabric. He was gratified when it pebbled beneath his touch.

"Why do you say such things? Why don't you want to believe the truth? If you weren't hot, I wouldn't be unable to control myself with you. Don't you remember how it felt? How we burned together?"

"I remember it every day," she said, still not looking at him. "I carry a reminder."

He let his hand fall to her belly, pressed gently against her there. She uttered a little protest, but he didn't take his hand away. He knew it bothered her that her belly wasn't hard and lean. No, she was soft and pliable, womanly. Her body was curvy, not angular and hard from exercise. He liked it just the way it was.

"Maybe we should alter the arrangement," he said, his tongue suddenly feeling thick in his mouth. As if he didn't know the right thing to say. As if he were so new at this game of seducing a woman that the outcome could be in doubt.

She turned her head toward him, as if she was going to speak, and he knew the answer wouldn't be what he wanted to hear from the way she stiffened at his words.

But he wasn't going to give her a chance to say a thing. He brought his mouth down on hers, trapping her body between him and the wall. His heart was thundering in his chest, the way it did when he'd gotten that adrenaline rush after he'd aimed his jet straight up and climbed the sky like it was a mountain. Once he'd stopped climbing and starting racing toward earth again, only to pull up before it was too late, the g-forces holding him tight to his seat, he'd gotten another huge rush that made him laugh out loud at the sheer joy of flight.

Kissing Lia was similar to that feeling. Her lips were soft beneath his, though he sensed she didn't want them to be. Her hands curled into fists on his lapels—but she didn't push him away. He ghosted a thumb over her nipple and she gasped, letting his tongue inside her mouth.

Another shot of unfiltered desire ricocheted into his groin, making him painfully hard. He'd not been with a woman since he'd been with her. And before that, he'd not been with a woman in months. Lia had been the one to break the drought—and, strangely, he still desired her the way a man desired cool water after a hot trek in the desert.

Zach slid his tongue along hers, coaxed her into responding. She made a little noise in her throat—desire, frustration, he didn't know which—but she stroked him in return. He tightened his grip on her, pulled her in closer to his body.

And then he assaulted her mouth more precisely, more urgently, taking everything she had to give him and demanding yet more. Her arms went around his neck, and then her body was arching into his, her hips pressing ever closer to that hardness at the core of him.

He cupped her ass with both hands, pulled her tightly to him, so tightly there could be no doubt what he wanted from her. He flexed his hips, pressing his hardness into her, finding that precise spot that made her gasp and moan.

He could make her come this way. He *would* make her come this way. He needed to hear her pleasure, needed to be the one to make her feel it.

Dimly, the click of heels against tile registered in his brain. The sound was coming closer, closer. With a frustrated groan, Zach broke away from the sweet taste of Lia. She looked up at him, blinking dazedly, her eyes slightly unfocused and distant, her lips moist and shiny. By degrees, her features changed, set, hardened into a cool mask.

"I'm sorry," he said right before the heels clicked to a stop in front of the alcove. Except he didn't know what he was sorry for.

"Mr. Scott?"

Zach closed his eyes for a brief moment. Then he turned to greet the socialite who stood there. "Yes, Mrs. Cunningham?"

Elizabeth Cunningham's gaze darted past him to Lia,

then back again. He didn't miss the tightening of Elizabeth's mouth, or the disapproving gleam in her eye. It pissed him off. Royally. Elizabeth Cunningham was thirty years younger than her husband, and much too judgmental for one who'd reached the pinnacle of society by marrying into it.

Zach reached for Lia's hand, pulled her to his side. Claimed her. He thought she might move away from him, but she didn't. She seemed to grasp the importance of appearances, after all.

"It's time for your speech," the other woman said, her gaze settling on his face once more.

Zach made a show of looking at his watch. "Ah, yes, so it is. I lose track of time when I'm with my lovely fiancée, I'm afraid."

Elizabeth's eyes widened. They darted to Lia. To Lia's credit, she didn't flinch or give away by look or gesture that she was anything other than what he'd said she was.

"Come, darling," he told her, tucking her hand into his arm and leading her back toward the gathered crowd. Another speech, another event to tick off his social calendar.

Afterward, he would take Lia home…and then he'd finish what he'd started here tonight.

Lia was shell-shocked. She sat through the rest of the evening in a daze. Her mouth still tingled where Zach had kissed her. Her body throbbed with tension and need. She'd been so furious with him, so convinced she would never, ever be susceptible to his charms again.

She'd been wrong. Woefully, pitifully wrong.

She was still the same lonely girl she'd always been, the same girl looking for acceptance and affection. She despised herself for that weakness, despised Zach for taking advantage of it. She took a sip of her water and let her gaze slide over the crowd before turning back to Zach.

He stood at a podium close to their table, talking about his father, about the war, about the night he was shot down over enemy territory. He said the words, but she wasn't convinced he felt any of them.

He was detached. Cold. The crowd was not. They sat rapt. And Lia couldn't help herself. She was rapt with them. She learned about how his plane took a hit and he'd had to bail out. How he'd broken his leg in the landing, and how he'd had to drag himself to shelter before the enemy found him.

Then she listened to him talk about the six marines who'd been sent in to extract him after several days. They had all died trying to save him. He was the only survivor. It sent a chill down her spine and raised the hairs on the back of her neck.

He'd suffered much, she thought. So much that she couldn't even begin to understand. She wanted to go to him, wanted to wrap her arms around him and lower his head to her shoulder. And then she just wanted to hold him tight and listen to him breathe.

Toward the end of his speech, a photographer started to take photos. His flash snapped again and again. Zach seemed to stiffen slightly, but he kept talking, kept the crowd in the grip of his oratory. The photographer moved in closer. No one seemed to think anything of it, but Lia remembered that night in Palermo and her palms started to sweat.

Zach gripped the sides of the podium, his knuckles white. The flash went off again and again and she didn't miss the way he flinched in reaction. It was so subtle as to seem a natural tic, but something told Lia it was not. Then he seemed to stumble over his thoughts, repeating something he'd just said. Panic rose up in Lia's chest, gripped her by the throat.

She couldn't watch him lose his way like he had in Palermo. She couldn't let him suffer that kind of public meltdown. She didn't know that he would, but she couldn't get past the memory of the way she'd met him, plastered against that wall with his eyes tight shut and the flashing and booming of lights and bass all around.

She didn't have to look at this crowd any longer to know it would be disastrous if he did.

Right now, everyone seemed to be paying attention to Zach. She didn't quite know what to do, or how to deflect their attention—and then she did. She coughed. Loudly. After a moment, Zach's gaze slid in her direction. She kept coughing, and then she reached for the water, took a swallow as if she were having trouble. Zach's attention was firmly on her now. He darted his eyes over the crowd, but they inevitably came back to her.

She coughed again, sipped more water. The photographer seemed satisfied enough with his photos thus far that he lowered his camera and melted toward the back of the crowd.

Lia stopped coughing. A few minutes later, Zach wound up his speech. The room erupted in applause. Lia breathed deeply, relieved. Though, perhaps Zach had been in control the whole time. Perhaps he'd never needed her intervention, lame though it was.

She watched him walk toward her. People stopped him, talked to him, making his progress back to her side take quite a long time. But then he was there, and she was gazing up at him, searching his face for signs of stress.

There were none.

He gazed over her head, his attention caught by something. Just for a moment, his mouth tightened. The flash went off again and Lia whirled toward the source.

"Come, darling," Zach said, holding out his hand. "Let's get you home."

Several of the Washington elite slid sideways glances at them, but Lia didn't care. She gave Zach a big smile and put her hand in his. He helped her from her chair and then they were moving toward the exit. They were waylaid a few more times, but soon they were on the street and Lia sucked in a relieved breath. They were facing the National Mall and the street was far quieter here since it fronted the museums instead of busy Constitution Avenue.

Raoul pulled up in the Mercedes on cue. Zach didn't wait for him to come around and open the door. He yanked it open and motioned Lia inside. Then he joined her and they were speeding off into the night. Zach leaned back against the seat and closed his eyes. His palms were steepled together in his lap.

She found herself wanting to trace a finger along the hard line of his jaw. She would not do it, of course.

"Are you all right?" she asked presently.

His eyes opened. "Fine. Why?"

She fiddled with the beading on her gown. "I thought the photographer might have disturbed you."

Zach was very still. "Not at all," he said after a moment's hesitation. "It goes with the territory. I am accustomed to it."

His answer disappointed her, but she decided not to push him further. She remembered how angry he'd been in Palermo, how disgusted with himself. She'd hoped he might confide in her tonight, but she had to understand why he did not.

Still, she ached for him.

"I'm sorry those things happened to you," she said. "In the war."

He shrugged. "That's what war is, Lia. Brutal, inhumane. People get hurt and people die. I'm one of the lucky ones."

Lucky ones. He didn't sound as if he believed those words at all. And yet he was lucky. He was here, alive—and she was suddenly very thankful for that. Her chest squeezed tight as she thought of what he'd said tonight—and how very close she'd come to never knowing him at all.

"Why don't you fly anymore, Zach?" She remembered that he'd said he couldn't but she didn't know why. She'd asked him that night in Palermo, but then she'd told him not to answer when she'd thought she'd crossed a line into something too personal.

Now, however, she wanted to know. She felt like she needed to know in order to understand him better. Her heart beat harder as she waited.

He sighed. And then he tapped his temple. "Head trauma. Unpredictable headaches accompanied by vision loss. Definitely not a good idea when flying a fighter jet at thirty thousand feet."

He sounded so nonchalant about it, but she knew how much it must hurt him. "I'm sorry."

His eyes gleamed as he looked at her. "Me, too. I loved flying."

"I don't like to fly," she said. "I find it scary."

He grinned, and it warmed her. "That's because you don't understand how it works. By that, I mean the noises the plane makes, the process of flight—not to mention the fact you aren't in control. It's some unseen person up there, holding your life in his or her hands. But it's all very basic, I assure you."

"I know it's mostly safe," she said. "But you're right. I haven't flown much, and the sounds and bumps and lack of control scare me."

She'd longed for a sedative on the long flight from Sicily, but she hadn't dared take one because of the baby.

His laugh made a little tendril of flame lick through her. "A fighter jet is so much more intense. The engines scream, the thrust is incredible and the only thing keeping you from blacking out is the G suit."

Lia blinked. "What is a G suit?"

"An antigravity suit," he said. "It has sensors that tell it when to inflate. It fits tight around the abdomen and legs in order to prevent the blood draining from the brain during quick acceleration."

Lia shivered. "That sounds frightening."

He shrugged. "Blacking out would be frightening. The suit not so much. You get used to it."

"You miss flying, don't you?"

He nodded. "Every damn day."

"Then I'm sorry you can't do it anymore."

"Me, too." He put his head back on the seat and closed his eyes. She wanted to reach out and touch him, wanted to run her fingers along his jaw and into his hair. But she didn't.

She couldn't breach that barrier, no matter how much she wanted to. She didn't know what she really meant by such a gesture, what she expected. And she couldn't bear it if he turned away from her. If he rejected her.

Lia clasped her hands in her lap and turned to look at the White House as they glided by on Constitution Avenue, heading toward the Lincoln Memorial and the bridge across the Potomac. The monuments were brightly lit, glowing white in the night. Traffic wasn't heavy and they moved swiftly past the sites, across the bridge and toward Zach's house in Virginia.

Lia racked her brain for something to say, something basic and innocuous. No matter what he'd said about the photographer, she was certain he'd had trouble with the intrusiveness of the flash.

But she didn't feel she could push the subject. He'd already shared something with her when he'd told her why he could no longer fly, and how much he missed it. He had not said those things during his speech. He'd said them to her, privately, and she knew it bothered him a great deal.

She was still trying to think of something to say when Zach's phone rang. He opened his eyes and drew it from his pocket, answering only once he'd looked at the display. He spent the next fifteen minutes discussing his schedule with someone, and then the car was sliding between the gates and pulling up in front of the house.

Zach helped her out of the car and they passed inside as a uniformed maid opened the door. It was dark and quiet inside. The maid disappeared once Zach told her they needed nothing else this evening.

The grand staircase loomed before them, subtly lit with wall sconces that went up to the landing. Zach took Lia's elbow and guided her up the stairs. His touch was like a brand, sizzling into her, and her breath shortened as all her attention seemed to focus on that one spot. She didn't want to feel this heat, this curl of excitement and fear that rolled in her belly, but she couldn't seem to help it.

The way he'd touched her earlier, kissed her—

Lia swallowed. She shouldn't want him to do it again, and yet a part of her did. A lonely, traitorous part of her. She wanted him to need her, wanted him to share his loneliness with her.

He escorted her to the room she'd been shown to earlier. But he didn't push her against the wall the way he had in the museum. His hand fell away from her elbow and he took a step back.

Disappointment swirled in her belly, left her feeling hot and achy and empty. After that blazing kiss in the art museum, she'd expected something far different. And after his speech tonight, she'd wanted something far different. That was the Zach she wanted to know—the one who hid his feelings beneath a veneer of coldness, who'd watched six marines die and who would never fly again, though he loved it.

That was the Zach he buried deep, the one he'd let out in Palermo. The one she wanted again.

"You did well tonight," he said. Still so cool, so indifferent.

Lia dropped her gaze as another emotion flared to life inside her. Confusion. Maybe she was wrong. Maybe he was just very good at being what the situation required. War hero. Senator's son. Fiery lover. "Thank you."

"Good night, Lia." He leaned forward and kissed her cheek. The touch was light, almost imperceptible. His hands were in his pockets.

She blinked up at him. "Good night, Zach."

He didn't make a move to leave so she opened her door and went inside her room because she thought that was what he wanted her to do. Then she turned and pressed her ear against the door, straining to hear him as he walked away. Her heart pounded in her chest.

What if he didn't go? What if he knocked on her door instead? What if she opened it and he took her in his arms and said he needed her?

What would she do?

Maybe she should open the door. Just yank it open and confront him. Ask him why he'd kissed her like that earlier. Why he'd mentioned altering the arrangement and then acted like it never happened.

Her fingers tightened on the knob. She would do it. She would jerk it open. She would demand an answer and she wouldn't fear rejection—

Footsteps moved away down the hall. A door opened and closed.

Lia wanted to cry out in frustration. She'd waited too long. The moment was gone.

CHAPTER EIGHT

IT WAS STILL DARK when Lia woke. She lay in bed, uncertain for the first few moments where she was. And then she remembered. She was in Zach's house, in a guest room. She reached for her phone to check the time—2:00 a.m.

Lia yawned and pressed the button to open her mail. Four new messages popped into her inbox, but only one caught her attention.

From: Rosa Corretti
To: Lia Corretti
Subject: Hi

Lia's pulse thrummed as she clicked on the message. She read through it quickly, and then went back to the beginning to make sure she'd read it right the first time. Rosa was actually writing to her. There wasn't a snarky word or single insult in the entire missive. In fact, there was a word Lia had never expected to see: *Sorry.*

Rosa was sorry for snapping at her after Carmela's outburst. Not only that, but her half sister said she'd been thinking about many things and that she realized how rotten it must have been for Lia to live with Teresa and Salvatore once her father remarried and had a new family.

Rosa wouldn't know that Lia had actually been sent away

long before Benito remarried. Why would she? Until just now, Lia was pretty sure Rosa barely remembered her existence, much less thought about her in any capacity.

Still, it was nice to hear from her. Surprising, but nice.

Lia would answer her, most definitely, but she wasn't about to get her hopes up for what their relationship could be. She'd spent her entire life mostly forgotten, and she wasn't planning to stick her neck out now. She didn't really know Rosa, but she knew what kind of woman Carmela was. Hopefully her daughter was nothing like her, but Lia intended to proceed with caution.

She got out of bed and slipped on her robe. Even thinking about Carmela had the power to make her feel badly about herself. When she remembered the way Zach had left her at her door tonight, the feeling intensified. It had taken her some time, but she'd figured out what he'd been doing at the museum when he'd kissed her.

He'd been getting her under control after she'd broken out of the box he'd put her in for the night. She'd dared to show temper, and he'd managed to smooth it over and make her forget for a while. He'd tugged her into the corner he wanted her in and tied her up neatly with a bow.

She'd sat there like a good girl, smiling and applauding and worrying over him. It infuriated her to remember how compliant she'd been, and all because he'd pressed her against that wall and made her remember what it had been like between them.

Heat crawled up her spine, settled between her legs and in her core. In spite of it all, her body still wanted his. It angered her to be so out of control of her own reactions, to feel so needy around a man who clearly didn't need her.

Lia went to the French doors and pulled them open, hoping the night air would help to cool her down.

A mistake, because it was summer in Virginia and the

night air wasn't precisely cool. Oh, it was far cooler than it had been in the heat of the day, but it was still quite warm.

There was a breeze, however. Lia stepped outside and walked barefooted across the stone terrace to the railing. The strong scent of lavender rose from the pots set along the wall. She ran her fingers over the blooms, brought them to her nose. It made her think of home.

If she could add lemon to the mix, she'd be transported to Sicily. Except that Sicily didn't quite feel like home any longer, she had to admit. Since the moment she'd fallen into Zach's arms at the wedding, she'd felt a restlessness that hadn't gone away. Sicily had seemed too small to contain her, too lonely.

But coming to the States was no better. She was still alone.

She could hear the river gurgling over boulders in the distance. The moon was full, its pale light picking out trees and grass and the foaming water where it rolled over rocks.

It was peaceful. Quiet, other than the river and the sound of a distant—very distant—dog barking. She leaned against the railing and tried to empty her mind of everything but sleep.

It was difficult, considering her body was on another time zone. Not only that, but she also had a lot on her mind. She'd fled Sicily because she'd been scared of what her family would do, but she'd never considered what Zach would do. Or what her life would become once she was with him.

Was it only yesterday that she'd stood in a hotel and told him their arrangement would be in name only? And now here she was, aching for his touch, and simply because he'd kissed her tonight with enough heat to incinerate her will.

She was weak and she despised herself for it. She didn't fit in, not anywhere, and she wanted to. Zach had held out the promise of belonging on that night in Palermo—and she'd leaped on it, not realizing it had been a Pandora's box of endless heartache and trouble.

There was a noise and a crash from somewhere behind her. Lia jumped and spun around to see where it had come from. It seemed to be from farther down the terrace, from another room. Her heart was in her throat as she stood frozen, undecided whether to run into her room and close the door or go see what had happened. What if it were Zach? What if he needed her?

But then a door burst open and a man rushed through and Lia gasped. He was naked, except for a pair of dark boxer shorts. He went over to the railing and leaned on it, gulping in air. He dropped his head in his hands. His skin glistened in the night, as if he'd just gotten out of a sauna.

The moonlight illuminated the shiny round scar tissue of the bullet wound in the man's side. Zach.

As if it could be anyone else. Her heart went out to him.

"Is everything okay?" she asked softly.

He spun toward her, his body alert with tension. Briefly, she wondered if she should run. And then she shook herself. No, she would not run.

Zach wasn't dangerous, no matter that he'd told her he was in Palermo.

"You're okay, Zach," she said, moving cautiously, uncertain if he was still caught in the grips of a dream or an episode like the one in Palermo. "It's me. It's Lia."

He scraped a hand through his hair. "I know who it is," he said, his voice hoarse in the night. The tension in him seemed to subside, though she knew it was still right beneath the surface. "What are you doing outside in the middle of the night?" he demanded.

She ignored his tone. "I could ask the same of you."

He turned toward the railing again, leaned on it. It was such a subtle maneuver, but it warmed her because it meant, on some level, at least, that he trusted her. After what he'd been through in the war, she didn't take that lightly.

"I had a dream," he said. The words were clipped and tired.

Lia stepped closer, until she could have touched him if she reached out. She didn't reach out. "And it was not a good one," she said softly.

He shook his head. Once. Curtly. "No."

"Do you often dream of the war?"

He swung to look at her. "Who said I was dreaming of the war?"

She thought of the wild look in his eyes when he'd first looked at her, at the way he'd seemed to be somewhere else instead of here, and knew she was right. Just like that night in Palermo, though he had been wide awake then.

"Is it the same as what happened when I first met you? Or different?"

He didn't say anything at first. He simply stared at her. The moonlight limned his body, delineating the hard planes and shadows of muscle. She had an overwhelming urge to touch him, but she clenched her hands tightly at her sides instead.

She would not reach for him and have him push her away. She'd done that too many times in her life, when she'd reached out to family and been shunned instead.

"You don't quit, do you?" he asked.

"You can deny it if you like," she said. "But I think we both know the truth."

"Fine." He blew out a breath. "It's different than Palermo. When I dream, it's much worse."

"Do you want to talk about it?"

He laughed suddenly. A broken, rusty sound. "God, no. And you don't want to hear it, Lia. You'd run screaming back to Sicily if you did. But thanks for trying."

Lia bristled at his presumption. "I'm tougher than I look."

He shook his head. "You only think you are. Forget it, kitten."

Kitten. She didn't know whether to be insulted or warmed by that endearment. "The photographer did bother you."

"Yes."

There was a warning in his tone. But she couldn't leave it, not now.

"Why do you do these things if you're worried about your reaction?"

He growled. "Because I have no choice, Lia. I'm a Scott, and Scotts do their duty. And you'd better get used to it because soon you'll be one of us."

It suddenly made her angry. Why should people do things that hurt them just to please other people? "So you're saying I must put myself in situations that cause me stress for the sake of the Scotts?"

His eyes flashed. "Something like that."

She lifted her chin. "And if I refuse?"

"Too late to back out now, babe. I told Elizabeth Cunningham you were my fiancée. Tomorrow, the papers will be filled with you and me. The whole city will be interested in the woman who captured my heart. And you will be at my side for every damn event I have to attend. Like it or not."

A tremor slid through her. "You're no different than my grandfather was," she said bitterly. "It's all about appearances. The family. What will people think? What will they do if they know we're human, too?" Lia cursed in Italian. "We can't have that, can we? Because the family reputation is everything."

So long as you didn't shame the family, so long as you kept your mouth shut and your head down, you could stay. But, oh, don't expect them to care about you.

Don't ever expect that. She put her hand over her belly

and vowed with everything in her that her child would never for one minute think public façades were more important than feelings. It was untenable, no matter the importance of the family.

She started to turn away, but Zach gripped her arms. She tried to pull out of his hold, but he wouldn't let her go. His face was so close to hers. And, in spite of her fury, her body was softening, aching. She hated that he did that to her. Especially when she did no such thing to him in return.

"Some things are bigger than our own desires," he said. "You know that."

Lia sucked in a breath that shook with tears. "And some things are more important than appearances." She thought of him at the podium, of the way he'd looked when he'd started to fight the demons in his head, and then of the way he'd rushed out onto the terrace tonight, and she couldn't stand that he would have to face the same issue again and again, and all for the sake of his family reputation. "Maybe you should talk to someone—"

He let her go and shoved back, away from her. Then he swore. Explosively.

A second later he was back, one long finger inches from her nose. It trembled as he pointed. If not for that single detail, she would have been frightened of his temper.

"Leave it, Lia. It's none of your business," he growled. The finger dropped and he spun away, put both hands on the railing and stood there, drawing in breath after breath after breath.

She didn't know quite what to say. She hadn't thought her suggestion would cause him such pain, but clearly it had. She hated that it did. And she hated that he wouldn't share with her. That he lost his cool, but wouldn't tell her what she so desperately wanted to know to help him.

She closed her eyes and swallowed, and then closed the distance between them until she was beside him. He didn't move or speak, and neither did she.

"I'll do my duty, Zach," she said softly. "I'll be at every event you are. And I won't let them get to you."

No matter what she'd said about refusing to go along, she wouldn't leave him to face those situations alone. Not after tonight. He needed someone with him, and she would be that someone.

He turned toward her, his brows drawn down in a question.

She lifted her chin and tumbled onward. She felt silly, but it was too late to turn back.

"The photographers. The flashes. The crowds. Whatever it is, I won't let them derail you or trigger a reaction. You can count on me."

His expression didn't change, but his nostrils flared. "You're offering to protect me?"

Oh, it did sound so ridiculous when he put it like that. On impulse, she reached for his bare arm, squeezed the hard muscle encouragingly while trying to ignore the heat sizzling into her.

"Whatever it takes," she said. And then, because her cheeks were hot with embarrassment and she didn't want to hear what he might say in response, she turned and walked away.

"Lia."

She was to her door when he called out. She turned to face him, her hands at her sides, trying for all the world to seem casual and calm. "Yes?"

"Grazie, cara mia."

Her heart skipped. "You're welcome," she said. And then she stepped into her room and closed the door with a quiet, lonely click.

* * *

The day did not promise to be a good one. Zach turned up the speed on the treadmill, forcing himself to run faster. He needed to reach that Zen moment of almost total exhaustion before he could consider himself in any shape to deal with everything coming his way today.

The sun hadn't yet peeked over the horizon, and the sky was still gray and misty from the river. Soon, however, all hell would break loose.

As if the hell of his dream hadn't been enough to endure. He squared his jaw and hit the speed button. He'd been back in the trench, immobile from the drugs the medic had given him, and listening to the shouts and rat-a-tat-tats of gunfire. The marines had been cool, doing their job, but they'd known air support wasn't coming in time.

He'd wanted to help so badly. He could still see the last marine, still feel the pistol grip in his hand as the man gave him a weapon. He'd lifted it, determined to do what needed to be done—

But he always woke at the moment he pulled the trigger. Terrified. Angry. Disgusted.

Sweat poured down his face, his naked torso. He ran faster, but he knew from experience he couldn't outrun the past.

No, he had to focus on today. On what was coming his way after last night.

First, there would be the papers. Then there would be an angry phone call from his father, Senator Zachariah J. Scott, demanding to know who Lia was and what the hell was going on.

Zach almost relished that confrontation. Except he didn't want Lia hurt. He should have chosen a better way to announce her role in his life, but he'd been too angry to think straight once Elizabeth Cunningham had looked at her like she was another piece of flotsam moving across his orbit. He'd simply reacted. Not the way he'd been trained to deal with things, but too late now.

She would handle it, though. He pictured her last night when he'd cornered her before his speech. She'd been fierce, angry, determined.

Sexy.

God, she was sexy. Something about Lia's special combination of innocence and fierceness was incredibly sexy to him. Addictive.

She wasn't like the women he'd been linked with in the past. They had always been polished, smooth, ready to step in and become the perfect society wife. Oh, he'd had his flings with unsuitable women, too. Women who were wild, fun, completely inappropriate.

Lia fit none of those categories. She wasn't smooth and polished, but she wasn't inappropriate, either. He doubted she was wild, though she'd certainly been eager and willing during their two-night fling.

Zach gritted his teeth and resolved not to think about that. Not right now anyway.

But he couldn't stop thinking about last night on the terrace when she'd said she would protect him. He'd wanted to laugh—but he hadn't. It had been incongruous, her standing there in her silky pajamas, looking all soft and womanly, staring up at him and telling him she would be at his side, making sure he didn't have a meltdown because of a camera flash or a nosy reporter.

He'd been stunned and touched at the same time. Yes, he'd nearly growled at her. He'd nearly told her she was too naive and to mind her own business. But her eyes had been shining up at him and she'd looked so grave that he'd been unable to do it.

He'd realized, looking at her, that she really was serious.

That she cared, on some level, and that if he was nasty to her, she would crumple inside.

So he'd swallowed his anger and his pride and he'd thanked her. It had been the right thing to do, even if the idea of her protecting him was ridiculous.

Except that she had intervened during his speech, coughing when he'd stumbled on the words. At the time, he'd thought little of it, though he'd been grateful to have something to focus on besides the photographer.

Now he wondered if she'd done it on purpose.

Zach finished his workout, showered and dressed, and went into his office to read the papers. The phone call came at seven. He let it ring three times before he picked it up.

"Care to tell me what's going on, Zach?" His father's voice was cool and crisp, like always. They'd never had a close relationship, though it was certainly more strained since Zach had come home from the war.

He knew his father loved him, but feelings were not something you were supposed to let show. They made you weak, a target to those who would exploit them.

And there wasn't a single aspect of his father's life that hadn't been thought out in triplicate and examined from all angles—except for one.

The only thing he hadn't been able to control was falling in love with his wife. It was the one thing that made him human.

"I'm getting married," Zach said, his voice equally as cool.

He heard the rustling of the newspaper. The *Washington Post*, no doubt. "I see that. The question is why."

"Why does anyone get married?"

His father snorted softly. "Many reasons. Love, money, comfort, sex, children. What I want to know is which reason it is for you. And what we need to do on this end."

A thread of anger started to unwind inside him. It was his life they were talking about, and his father was already looking at it like it was something to be handled and packaged for the world to digest. "For the spin, you mean."

"Everything needs to be spun, Zach. You know that."

Yes, he certainly did. From the time he was a child and his father had decided to step away from Scott Pharmaceuticals and put his hat in the political ring, their lives had been one big spin job. He'd grown sick of the spin. He'd thought going into the military and flying planes would be authentic, real, a way to escape the fishbowl of his powerful family's life.

He'd been wrong. It had simply been another chance for spin. Hero. All-American. Perfect life. Doing his duty. Father so proud.

How proud would his father be if he knew Zach hated himself for what had happened out there? That he wished he'd died along with the marines sent to rescue him? That he was no hero?

"But your mother and I love you," his father was saying. "We want to know what's going on in truth."

Zach's jaw felt tight. "She's pregnant," he said, and then felt immediately guilty for saying it. As if he were betraying Lia. As if it were her secret and not his, too.

He could hear the intake of breath on the other end of the phone. No doubt his father was considering how to minimize the embarrassment of his only son making such a foolish mistake.

Except the idea it was a mistake made him angry. How could it be a mistake when there was a small life growing inside Lia now? A life that was one half of him.

"You are certain the baby is yours?"

Zach ground his teeth together. An expected question, one he'd asked, too, and yet it irritated him. "Yes."

His father blew out a breath. "All right, then. We'll do what we need to do to minimize the damage."

"Damage?" Zach asked, his voice silky smooth and hard at the same time.

And yet had he not thought the very same thing? Had he not proposed this arrangement to Lia in order to minimize the damage to their families—most specifically his?

He had, and it infuriated him that he'd thought it for even a moment. What was wrong with him?

"You know what I mean," his father said tightly.

"I do indeed. But Lia is not a commodity or a project to be managed. She's an innocent young woman, she's pregnant with my child and I'm marrying her just as soon as I get the license."

His father was silent for the space of several heartbeats. "Very well," he said softly. "Your mother and I will look forward to meeting her."

It was the same sort of cool statement his father always made when he wasn't pleased but knew that further argument would result in nothing changing. Zach felt uncharacteristically irritated by it. He knew how his father was, and yet he'd thought for the barest of moments that his parent might actually have a conversation about Lia and marriage instead of one based on how Zach's choices would impact the family.

Zach didn't bother to waste time with any further pleasantries. "If that's all, I have things to attend to," he said in clipped tones.

"Of course," his father said. "We'll be in touch."

Zach ended the call and sat at his desk for several minutes. He'd never once had a meaningful conversation with his father. It bothered him. Instead of telling the older man what kind of hell he'd been through in the war, and how it really made him feel to be treated like a returning hero, he smiled and shook hands and did his duty and kept it buried deep inside.

Because that's what a Scott did.

The gardener rolled a wheelbarrow full of something across the lawn outside. Zach watched his progress. The man stopped by a winding bed of roses and began clipping stems, pruning and shaping the bushes. He was whistling.

Two days ago, Zach had been going about his life as always, attending events, making speeches and feeling empty inside. It was the life he knew, the life he expected.

Now, oddly enough, he felt like those bushes, like someone had taken shears to him and begun to shape him into something else. They were cutting out the dead bits, tossing them on the scrap heap and leaving holes.

He felt itchy inside, jumpy. He stood abruptly, to do what he didn't know, but then Lia moved across his vision and he stopped in midmotion. She was strolling down the wide lawn in the early morning sunshine, her long hair streaming down her back, her lush form clad in leggings and a loose top.

He watched her move, watched the grace and beauty of her limbs, and felt a hard knot form in his gut. She went over to the gardener and started to talk. After a moment, the man nodded vigorously and Lia picked up a set of pruning shears. Zach watched in fascination as she began to cut branches and toss them on the pile.

He suddenly wanted to be near her. He wanted to watch her eyes flash and chin lift, and he wanted to tug her into his arms and kiss her until she melted against him the way she had last night in the art gallery.

CHAPTER NINE

"YOU DON'T NEED to do that."

Lia looked up from the rosebush she'd been pruning to find Zach watching her. She hadn't heard him approach. He stood there, so big and dark and handsome that her heart skipped a beat in response.

He was wearing faded jeans and a navy T-shirt, and his hands were shoved in his pockets. He looked...delicious. And somehow weary, too.

Lia frowned. Larry the gardener had moved farther down the row. He was whistling and cutting, whistling and cutting. If he knew Zach had arrived, he didn't show it. Except that he moved even farther away, presumably out of earshot, and she knew he was aware of his boss's presence, after all.

Lia focused on Zach again. "I know that," she said. "I want to."

Zach's gaze dropped. "You don't have any gloves. What if you scratch yourself?"

Lia glanced down at her bare hands holding the pruning shears. "I'm careful. Besides, I'm not in a race."

She thought he might argue with her, but instead he asked, "Did you work in your grandparents' garden?"

She lopped off a spent bloom and set the shears down to carefully extract it from the bush. "Yes. I enjoy growing things. I'm pretty good at it, too."

"I don't doubt that. But you shouldn't be out here. It's hot, and you're pregnant."

As if in response to his reminder about the heat, a trickle of moisture slid between her breasts. "It's hot in Sicily, too. And the doctor said I should get some exercise. It's not good to sit indoors and do nothing."

"I have a gym, and a perfectly good treadmill. You can walk on it."

"I want to be outside, Zach. I want to be in the garden."

He frowned. "All right, fine. But not more than half an hour at a time, and not after nine in the morning or before five at night."

Lia blinked at him. "Why, thank you, your majesty," she said. "How very generous of you."

"Lia." Zach reached for her hand, took it gently in his. Instantly, a rush of sensation flooded her. She would have pulled free—except that she liked the feeling. "I'm not trying to be difficult. But you aren't used to the heat here. It's oppressively muggy in the summer, and it'll get to you before you realize it. Besides, we have a busy schedule and I don't want you to exhaust yourself."

Lia reached for another bloom with her free hand, only this time she was rattled from his touch and she grasped it too low on the stem. A sharp thorn punctured her thumb and she cried out. Zach swore softly and grabbed her hand. Now, he held both her hands between his.

Blood welled in a bright round bubble on the fleshy pad of her thumb.

"It's fine," she said, trying to pull her hand away.

Zach's grip tightened. "You're coming inside and washing it."

Lia sighed. She knew she wasn't going to win this battle. Besides, it was kind of nice that he was concerned. She shook herself mentally. There was no sense reading more into his concern than there was.

"Fine."

She called to Larry, who waved and smiled after she explained why she had to go. Then she followed Zach up to the house. He led her into the kitchen and slid on the taps. When the water was hot, he poured soap in her hand and made her wash.

"It's a rosebush, Zach, not a used hypodermic needle."

"Better safe than sorry," was all he said.

She finished washing, and then frowned while Zach put a dab of antibiotic ointment on her thumb and covered it with a Band-Aid.

When she looked up at him, his dark eyes were intent on her, his brows drawn down as he studied her. Her heart skipped the way it always did. Angrily, she tamped down on the rising tide of want within her.

"Did you eat breakfast yet?"

"I had a cup of tea and some toast," she said a touch breathlessly.

Zach frowned. "That's not good enough," he muttered, turning away from her and grabbing a pan off the hanging rack. "You need protein."

Lia crossed her arms, bemused suddenly. "Are you planning to cook for me?"

He glanced up at her, still scowling. And then he grinned and she had to catch her breath at the transformation of his features. "I can, actually. I had to learn when I entered the service. The air force frowns on hired help in the bachelor officers' quarters."

A man from a rich family who'd grown up with chefs and servants suddenly having to cook for himself? What an adjustment that must have been.

"Allora," she said. "It's a wonder you didn't starve."

He winked. "I'm a quick learner."

He retrieved eggs and cheese from the refrigerator. The housekeeper came in, took one look at the pan and him and shrugged. She retrieved whatever thing she'd come for—Lia didn't pay attention—and was gone again.

Lia didn't actually think she could eat anything else right now, but she was too fascinated to stop him from cracking the eggs and whipping them.

"So why did you join the air force? Couldn't you have learned to fly planes anyway?"

His back was to her. She wasn't sure what was on his face just then, but he stiffened slightly, the fork ceasing to swirl the eggs for half a second before he started again. She berated herself for injecting a note of discord into the conversation when it had seemed to be going so well.

"I wouldn't have been able to fly fighter jets, no. I could have bought one, I suppose. The older ones come up for sale sometimes—but it's not quite the same. Besides, I wanted to serve my country."

"A noble cause."

He shrugged. "Yes." Then he stopped again, his broad shoulders tight. A moment later, he turned to her. His expression was troubled. "No, that's not why I did it," he said softly. "I joined the military because I wanted to get away from life as Zachariah J. Scott IV. I didn't want the career at Scott Pharmaceuticals, the governorship of a state, the senate run and then maybe the presidency. Those are my father's dreams, not mine. I wanted to do something that mattered."

Lia's heart felt as if it had stopped beating. Dear God, he was sharing something with her. Something important. She didn't want to screw it up.

"You seem to have done that," she said. She thought of the medal in her room and knew he'd gotten it for good reasons. But why had he thrown it away?

He sighed, his shoulders relaxing a fraction. "You'd think so, wouldn't you? But here I am, and all that my time in the military did for me was set me up for even greater success if I were to follow the path my father wants."

"I think those things matter, too, Zach. It takes a lot of sacrifice to serve your country in any manner, don't you think?"

He glanced at her. "You're right, of course. Still…"

"It's not the path you want to take," she said when he didn't finish the sentence.

He slid the pan onto the stove and added a pat of butter. Then he turned on the burner. "No, I don't."

"What do you want, then?"

He looked at her for a long minute. "I want to fly. But I don't get to do that anymore, no matter that I want to." The butter started to sizzle. Zach poured in the eggs and swirled them in the pan.

"Surely there's something else," she said softly.

His gaze was sharp. "I want to help people returning from the war. It's not easy to go back to your life after you've been through hell."

Lia swallowed. He was talking from experience. And it suddenly made something clear. "Which is why you speak at these fundraisers."

"Yeah."

Yet he wasn't comfortable doing it. That much she knew from watching the effect on him last night. Oh, he was good at it—but it took a toll on him each and every time. "That's a good thing, then. I'm sure it makes a difference."

He shrugged. "It helps fund programs to return vets to a normal life. It also keeps the public aware of the need."

The eggs set in the pan, and Zach added the cheese. Soon, he was sliding the omelet onto a plate and carrying it to the kitchen island. He turned to look at her expectantly.

"Coming?"

How could she say no? She was ridiculously touched that he'd made her an omelet, and ridiculously touched that he'd shared something private with her. She walked over to the island and hopped onto the bar stool. Zach retrieved a fork and napkin, poured her a glass of juice and sat across from her, chin on his hand as he watched her take the first bite.

The omelet was good, creamy and buttery, with just the right amount of cheese. But it was hard to eat it when he was watching her. She could feel her face growing hot as she slid a bite between her lips.

"You have to stop staring at me," she finally said when her heart was thrumming and her face was so hot that he surely must see the pink suffusing her skin.

"I want to make sure you eat it all."

"I won't be able to if you don't stop watching me."

He sighed. "Fine." He sat back on the bar stool and turned to look out the window. "Better?"

"Yes. *Grazie.*"

Though she hadn't thought she was hungry, the omelet was good enough that she took another bite. Lia glanced up at Zach, and her heart pinched in that funny way it did whenever she realized how very attractive he was. And how little she really knew him.

"Thank you," she said after a minute. "It's very good."

"Hard to mess up an omelet," he said. "But I'm glad you like it."

"I could," she said. "Mess up an omelet, that is."

He turned to look at her. "You can't cook?"

She shrugged. "Not really, no. Nonna tried to teach me, but I'm hopeless with the whole thing. I get the pan too hot or not hot enough. I either burn things or make gelatinous messes. I decided it was best to step away from the kitchen and let others do the work. Better for all involved."

"How long have you lived with your grandparents?"

"Since I was a baby," she said, her heart aching for a different reason now. The old feelings of shame and inadequacy and confusion suffused her. "My mother died when I was little and my father sent me to my grandparents. I grew up there."

"I'm sorry," he said. "I don't know what it's like to lose a mother, but I can't imagine it was easy."

Lia shrugged. "I don't remember her, but I know she was very beautiful. A movie star who fell in love with a handsome Sicilian and gave up everything to be with him. Unfortunately, it didn't work out." She moved a slice of omelet around on the plate. "My father remarried soon after she died."

She could see him trying to work it out. Why she hadn't gone to live with her father and his new wife. Why they'd left a baby with her grandparents. Bitterness flooded her then. She'd often wondered the same thing herself, until she was old enough to know why they didn't take her back. She was simply unwanted.

The words poured out before she could stop them. "My father pretended like his new family was the only family he had. He did not want me. He never sent presents or called or acknowledged me the few times he did see me. It was as if I was someone else's child rather than his."

Zach reached for her hand, enclosed it in his big, warm one. "Lia, I'm sorry that happened to you."

She sniffed. "Yes, well. Now you know why I had to tell you about the baby. I didn't have a father. I wanted one."

"Yeah," he said softly, "I understand."

Ridiculously, a tear spilled down her cheek. She turned her head, hoping he wouldn't see. But of course he did. He put a finger under her chin and turned her back again. She kept her eyes downcast, hoping that if she didn't look at him, she wouldn't keep crying. She didn't want to seem weak or emotional, and yet that's exactly how she felt at the moment.

Thinking of her childhood, and the way her father had rejected her, always made her feel vulnerable. Another tear fell, and then another.

Zach wiped them away silently. She was grateful he didn't say anything else. He just let her cry.

"I'm sorry," she said after a minute. "I don't know why…" Her voice trailed off into nothing as she swallowed hard to keep the knot in her throat from breaking free.

Zach let her go and scraped back from the island. Another moment and he was by her side, pulling her into the warm solidness of his body.

She pressed her face against his chest and closed her eyes. Her arms, she vaguely realized, were around his waist, holding tight. He put a hand in her hair, cupping her head. The other rubbed her back.

"It's okay, Lia. Sometimes you have to let it out."

She held him hard for a long time—and then she pushed away, not because she didn't enjoy being in his arms, but because she was enjoying it too much. Her life was confusing enough already.

"I haven't cried over this in years," she said, not looking at him. "I'm sure it's the hormones."

"No doubt."

She swiped her palms beneath her cheeks and wiped them on her leggings. *Dio*, how attractive she must be right now, with puffy eyes and a red nose.

"It won't happen again," she said fiercely. "I'm over it."

He lifted an eyebrow. "I wonder—do we ever get over the things that affect us so profoundly? Or do we just think we do?"

Lia sniffled. "I'd like to think so. Not that the past doesn't inform our experience, but if all we do is dwell on it, how will we ever have much of a present?"

She felt a little like a hypocrite, considering how often

she'd felt unwanted and out of sync with her family. But she didn't let it rule her. Or she was determined not to. Perhaps that was a better way of saying it. It crept in from time to time, like now, but that didn't mean it was in charge.

His eyes glittered in the morning light. "Precisely. And yet sometimes we can't help but dwell on a thing."

She knew what he meant. "Your dreams."

"That's part of it."

Lia closed her eyes for a moment. She was in over her head with this. How could what she'd been through compare to his ordeal? Shot down, injured, nearly killed, watching others be killed before your eyes. It made her shiver.

"I think maybe there's something in our psyches that won't let go," she said. "Until one day it does."

He looked troubled. "There were things that happened out there, things—"

He stopped talking abruptly, turned his head to look out the window. His jaw was hard, tight. But he swallowed once, heavily, and her heart went out to him.

"What things?" she whispered, her throat aching. When he turned back to her, his eyes were hot, burning with an emotion that stunned her. Self-loathing? It didn't seem possible, and yet…

He opened his mouth. And then closed it again. Finally, he spoke. "No," he said, shaking his head. "No."

Jesus, he was losing his mind. She'd been here for two days and he wanted to tell her everything. He wanted to take her to his bed, strip her naked and worship every last inch of her body. Which she would not allow him to do if he told her his darkest fears. His deepest secrets.

If she knew how flawed he was, she'd run far and fast in the opposite direction. She'd take that baby in her womb and get the hell away from him. Hell, she'd probably get a restraining order against him.

Her eyes were wide and blue as she sat on that bar stool and looked up at him. Innocent.

God, Lia was so very innocent. She would never understand what he'd been through, or what he'd almost done out there in that trench. Hell, he didn't understand it himself. He lived with the guilt every minute of his life and he still didn't understand it.

She was at a loss for words. He could see that. She dropped her gaze again, and he stepped away from her, breathed in air that wasn't scented with her intoxicating lavender and vanilla and lemon scent.

His body was hard. Aching. He hadn't needed a woman this much in...well, he couldn't remember. The last time had been with her. He wanted her again.

Now wouldn't be soon enough. But she was sweet and delicate and pregnant. She did not need him making sexual demands of her just yet.

Zach rubbed a hand over his head. He couldn't think straight. His entire plan had been to protect his family from scandal—but really, was that the reason? His father had been in office for over two decades now. Would the news his son had knocked up a girl really shock anyone enough that they might not vote for him if he ran for president?

But what if Zach knocked her up and abandoned her to raise the child alone? Yeah, that might raise some heads. But so what?

It was his life, not his father's. Besides, his father had people who spun these things for him. Any scandal of Zach's, unless it involved criminal activities, wasn't likely to touch his father's career—or the funding for the veterans' causes that Zach worked so hard to obtain.

His plan, such as it was, had little to do with protecting anyone, if he were truthful.

And everything to do with the odd pull Lia Corretti had on him.

He wanted her, even if his brain had had trouble figuring that out at first. He'd nearly sent her away. He could hardly credit it at this moment.

"I'm sorry," she finally said. "I shouldn't have asked."

His gaze slewed her way. She was toying with the remains of her omelet. He had a sudden, overwhelming urge to tell her what she wanted to know.

But he couldn't. How could he say the words? He'd never said them to anyone. And if he did, what would she think of him? Would she look at him with terror or pity in her expression?

He couldn't bear either.

"It's not you," he said, because he didn't want to see that hurt expression on her face. She had so much to be hurt about, he realized, now that he knew about her father and what he'd done to her.

Rotten bastard. If the man was still alive, Zach would love to get his hands on him.

He blew out a harsh breath. "It's just…I don't talk about what happened out there. Not to anyone."

"It's okay. I understand."

She wasn't looking at him. He walked over and tilted her chin up with a finger. Her eyes were liquid blue, so deep he could drown in them.

"Do you?" he asked.

"Yes." Her voice was firm. "I know what it's like to have things that hurt you. Things you can't talk about."

The idea anyone had ever hurt her made him want to howl.

She reached up and wrapped her hand around his wrist. It was a soft touch, gentle—and he felt the ricochet effect all the way down to his toes. If he kissed her now, here, would she kiss him back?

"But if you ever want to talk about it," she was saying, "I'm here."

Here. His. He lowered his mouth, brushed his lips gently across hers. Her intake of breath made a current of hot possession slide into his veins. He wanted to hold her closer, kiss her harder.

Instead, he lifted his head and walked away.

CHAPTER TEN

LIA CAREFULLY BRUSHED her hair and donned the dress she'd chosen for this afternoon's cocktail party. Her reflection in the mirror looked the same as always, but she felt as if she'd been changed somehow. Her lips tingled at the thought of Zach, at that light brush of a kiss that had not really been a kiss.

She'd wanted more. She'd wanted to reach up and pull him to her and not let him go until he'd thoroughly kissed her.

And then some.

But he'd walked away without a word. He'd had no trouble doing so. He'd left her sitting there with a half-eaten omelet and a fire inside her that wouldn't go away.

She was mortified. And angry. He might not want her, but he had no right making her want him. If he tried that again, she was going to sock him.

Because her heart couldn't take it. He smiled and laughed and fixed her an omelet, and she wanted to sigh and melt and bask in his presence.

Pitiful, Lia. Just like Carmela had accused her of being. She'd spent so many years wanting to belong to a family that shunned her, and now she was up to her same old tricks with Zach. When would she ever learn? She had her baby now, and that would have to be enough. This thing with Zach was temporary.

He'd told her as much in her hotel room, hadn't he?

Except, dear heaven, when she thought of him this morning, telling her why he'd joined the military and why he continued to book public appearances even though they were difficult for him—well, she wanted to know him. Really know him.

She didn't want this to be temporary when he said things like that. She wanted this to be real. She wanted a chance. They'd gone about it backward, no doubt, but there was something about Zach that hadn't let her have a moment's peace since the instant she'd seen him in that ballroom in Palermo.

She wanted him in her life, and she wanted him to want her.

Lia picked up her perfume and dabbed a very little behind her ears and in the hollow over her collarbone. Then she grabbed her phone to check her email one last time before slipping it into her bag.

There was another email from Rosa. She opened it and read carefully, her heart rising a bit with every line. She had, after careful deliberation, answered Rosa's initial email. Now she had a reply. One that was friendly and open and even a little curious.

Lia sighed. Just when she'd given up on ever having a relationship with any Corretti other than her grandmother, this happened. She was pleased, but she was also baffled. It was as if so long as she wanted a connection, it would always elude her. The moment she stopped caring, or stopped wanting what she wasn't going to get, it happened.

If she could force herself not to care about Zach, would he suddenly be interested?

Lia frowned. If only it worked that way. She dropped her phone into her bag and went to meet Zach. He was waiting for her in the grand living room that overlooked the lawn and the river beyond. He looked up as she walked in, his dark eyes sparking with a sudden heat that threatened to leave her breathless.

His gaze drifted over her appreciatively. Tiny flames of hunger licked at her skin wherever he looked. Then he met her eyes again. The fire in her belly spiked. For a moment, she thought he might close the distance between them and draw her into his arms.

He did not, of course. Zach was nothing if not supremely controlled. Disappointment swirled inside her as they drove to the Lattimores' cocktail party. She kept her gaze focused straight ahead, but she was very aware of Zach's big hand on the gearshift so near her knee.

It was insane to be this crazy aware of a man, and yet she couldn't help it. Zach filled her senses. The more she worked to keep it from happening, the worse it got. He was the sun at the center of her orbit when he was near, no matter how she tried to ignore him.

The event was in a gorgeous mansion in Georgetown. After leaving the car with the valet, Zach escorted her into the gathering, his hand firmly on the small of her back. Lia's stomach vibrated with butterflies. Last night, she'd simply been the woman on his arm at an event. Tonight, she was his fiancée, and the media would take a more pointed interest in her now.

She'd seen the papers in his office, and read the stories about all-American hero Zach Scott and the mystery woman he was suddenly engaged to marry. Of course there was speculation as to why. That didn't surprise her at all.

The story basically went that Zach had traveled to Palermo for a wedding, met the groom's cousin and had a whirlwind romance. They also speculated that she and Zach had conducted this affair over the phone and through email until they simply couldn't stand to be separated any longer.

It was a lovely hypothesis, though laughably far from the truth.

Zach, however, seemed determined to play his role to the hilt once they entered the party. He was the besotted fiancé. He stayed by her side, fetched her drinks, kept a hand on her arm or her waist or her shoulder. Lia took a sip of her non-alcoholic cocktail and tried to calm the racing of her heart.

Zach's touch was driving her insane.

She could hardly remember half the people she met, or half the conversations she had. Her entire focus was on Zach's hand, on his warm, large presence beside her. On the butterflies that hadn't abated. Oh, no, they kept swirling, higher and faster, each time Zach touched her.

It was all she could do not to climb up his frame in front of everyone and kiss him senseless.

Her senses were on red alert, and her body was primed for him. Only him.

It irritated her, but she couldn't stop it. She watched him as he spoke with a gray-haired woman, watched the curve of his mouth when he laughed, the sparkle in his eyes and the long, lean fingers of his hand—the one she could see—as he held his drink.

Lia closed her eyes, tried to blot out the visual of that hand tracing a sensual path over her body. It didn't work, especially since she knew precisely how it would feel.

His arm went around her and she shuddered. "Darling, are you all right?"

Lia looked up at him, into those dark beautiful eyes that seemed full of concern for her. It was an act, she told herself. An act.

Her heart didn't care. It turned over inside her chest—and then it cracked wide-open, filling with feelings she didn't want.

"I—" She swallowed and licked her suddenly dry lips. "I need to freshen up," she blurted.

Without waiting for his reply, she turned and made her way blindly through the crowd until she found an exit. It didn't take her down a hall toward the restrooms, as she'd hoped, but spilled out onto a covered patio that gave way to a manicured garden with a tall hedge. Lia walked right down the path and between the hedges before she realized it was actually a maze.

Her heart beat hard as she breathed in the clean air, hoping to calm down before she went back inside and faced all those people—and Zach—again.

What was the matter with her? Why had she come unglued like that?

Because she was Lia Corretti, that's why. Lost little girl looking for love, for a home, for someone who needed her. She'd been staring at Zach, letting her mind wander, letting her fantasies get the best of her.

And she'd realized, boom, that she felt far more than she should be feeling. That she'd let herself fantasize him right into her heart.

How could you love someone you hardly knew? How could your heart make such a catastrophic mistake?

She hadn't seen it coming. How could she? Of course, she'd thought about him for the past month, thought about their blissful nights together and the way everything between them felt so right—but that was lust, not love.

When did love enter the equation?

When he'd made her an omelet and told her he wanted to do something meaningful with his life? Or earlier, when he'd pulled her against his hard body in Palermo and told her she was beautiful?

"Lia."

She turned at the sound of his voice, her heart thrumming,

her skin flushing hot. She didn't want him here, and yet she did. He moved toward her, so tall, dark and gorgeous that he made her want to weep inside.

How had she let this happen? Panic flooded her as he approached.

But then she had a thought. Maybe—just maybe—it wasn't love, after all. Maybe it was simply a deep infatuation. Yes, she could certainly be infatuated with him. That was far less pitiful than falling in love with a man who was only marrying you because you were pregnant.

Zach came closer, his brows drawn together. "Is everything all right?"

"I needed space," she said. "The crowd was too much."

It wasn't entirely untrue. She wasn't accustomed to so many people. Her life in Sicily had rarely involved crowds or massive gatherings. Her grandparents entertained, and quite frequently, but she hadn't been expected to attend. Now she'd been to three events in as many days, and it was tiring.

"Do you feel well? Should we sit down somewhere?"

"I'm fine," she said quickly.

"Lia." He stopped in front of her, so close she could feel his heat. Her head tilted back to stare up at him. Her breath shortened in her chest as their eyes caught and held. His hands came up to settle on her shoulders, and she felt a deep throbbing note roll through her at that simple touch. "Don't lie to me, *cara mia*."

She loved it when he spoke to her in Italian.

"Fine, I will tell you," she said. "I feel overwhelmed, Zach. I feel as if I don't really know you, and I won't know you so long as we are constantly putting on a public face. I miss the man I spent time with in Palermo, the one who didn't say or do anything he didn't mean. There were no masks there, no appearances to maintain."

She dropped her gaze, focused on the buttons of his deep

blue shirt. He'd worn a gray pinstripe suit, no tie, and Italian loafers. His jacket was open, and his shirt molded to the hard muscles of his chest. It was custom fit, of course—and the effect was mind-blowing on her already addled brain. He was perfect, beautiful.

For the life of her, she still didn't know what he'd ever seen in her. Or what he ever would see.

"This is my life," he said. "The way it really is. Palermo was an anomaly."

"Yes, well, I choose not to believe that is entirely true. You were more you because you weren't worried about being Zach Scott. You were freer there. You know it's true."

His head dropped for a second. And then he was looking at her again, his gaze dark and mysterious. "Yes."

"That's it? Just yes?"

He sighed. His hands on her shoulders were burning a hole in her. He slid them back and forth, back and forth, and the tension in her body bent like a bowstring. When he slid them to her upper arms, it wasn't a relief.

"You're right. What more do you want me to say?"

She couldn't believe he'd admitted it. But it made something inside her soar that he had. "About which part?"

"That I felt freer in Sicily. I wasn't the main attraction, and I knew it. The press might hound me here, they might follow me if I make a well-publicized trip abroad, but Sicily was unexpected. And too quick to matter much, though of course, they now wish they'd pursued me."

"Why?"

He laughed softly. "Because of you, Lia. Because the confirmed bachelor went to Sicily and came back with a fiancée."

"Thank heavens they didn't," she said, imagining a photographer lurking outside the Corretti Hotel. Or, worse, somehow learning they'd spent two nights together and contriving to get a photo through the open window. Lia shuddered.

"If they had, I doubt any of this would have happened," he said, and her heart twisted in pain. She knew what he meant.

"Perhaps you wish that had been the case." She lifted her chin, trying to hide the hurt she felt deep inside. He was so close. Too close. All she could smell was his delicious scent—a hint of spice and hard masculinity. She wanted to step in, close the distance between them and wrap her arms around him.

Her body ached with the need to feel him inside her again. To be needed by him.

Dio, she was pathetic.

She expected him to agree, to step away, put distance between them and tug her toward the house and the party.

He did not do any such thing. Instead, he slid one of those electric hands up to her jaw, cupped her cheek. The other went to the small of her back, brought her that short step closer, until her body was pressed to his, until she could feel the heat and hardness of him emanating through the fabric of his clothes.

"I should wish it," he said. "But I don't."

Her head was tilted back, her eyes searching the hot depths of his. "I don't know what that means, Zach."

His gaze dropped to her mouth, lingered. And then his lips spread in the kind of wicked smile that made her heart flutter. "I think I'm about to show you, *bella mia*...."

His mouth claimed hers in a hot, possessive kiss that stole her breath and her sense. Lia threaded her arms around his neck without hesitation, melded her body to his. She could do nothing else. She simply wasn't programmed to respond any other way.

The answering hardness in his groin sent a fresh blast of desire ricocheting through her. Had it been this incendiary between them the first time? Had she felt this sweet, sweet fire raging in her belly, her brain, her core? His tongue against hers was nirvana. She couldn't get enough. She kissed him back hotly, desperately, her tongue tangling with his again and again.

He groaned low in his throat, pulling her closer, one hand splayed over her hip, the other sifting into her hair, cupping her head, holding her mouth against his.

She was being swept away on a tide of heat and deep burning feelings that ached to get out. If he kept kissing her like this, she wouldn't survive it. She would not be the same Lia Corretti when it was over.

She would be his creature, his to do with as he wanted. His slave. His, his, his…

With a cry, she pushed him away. She didn't know why, except she knew it was necessary to her sanity, her survival. She could not be any less in control of herself and her emotions than she already was. She could not allow him to own her like this when he gave her nothing of himself in return.

Because she was certain, as certain as she was breathing, that she had no claim on his heart or his emotions. It was physical, this need, nothing more.

For him anyway.

And that was a kind of servitude she did not need. She knew what it was like to be unnecessary—and she could not bear to be so in his life.

He let her go, his hands dropping to his sides. He looked angry, desperate—and then he looked cool, unperturbed. He wiped a thumb across his mouth, across that gorgeous mouth that had been pressed so hotly to hers only moments ago. Then he straightened his shirt, and she was mortified to see that she'd pushed it askew in her desire to touch him.

"Forgive me," he said coolly. "I forgot myself."

Her heart beat hard and swift, and nausea danced in her

stomach. She took a step back, collided with the hedge. Tears filled her eyes, threatening to spill free. What was wrong with her? Why was she so emotional?

"I want to go home," she said.

His head came up, his eyes glittering hard as diamonds. "Home?"

She was confused at his reaction, at the tightness in his voice. "Yes, back to my room. I have a headache, and I want to sleep...."

She wasn't quite certain, but she thought his stance softened, as if a current of tension had drained away. He seemed remote, a gorgeous automaton of a man who stared back at her with cool eyes. He stepped to the side and swept a hand toward the entrance to the maze, indicating that she should precede him.

"Then we'll go," he told her.

They returned to the house in silence. Once there, they played the game again. Lia smiled, though it shook at the corners, as they moved through the gathering. Their leave taking was tedious, but then they were outside and the valet was bringing the car around. There were people clustered together on the mansion's grand portico, waiting for their cars or simply finding another place to take the party.

The lawn was wide, sweeping and, though the property was gated, the gates were opened to the street as cars came and went. A valet pulled up in Zach's BMW while another opened the passenger door for Lia with a flourish. Zach stood by her side. Ordinarily, he would hand her into the car, but this time he didn't touch her. She reckoned he was angry with her.

She took a step toward the car when something bright flashed in her face. It took her a moment to realize they'd been photographed. At first she thought it was simply someone taking a picture they'd ended up in by accident, but when she glanced at Zach, his taut expression told her it was more than that.

He stood there a moment, fists clenched at his side, but then he started around the car when nothing else happened.

The moment he was gone, the photographer took the opportunity to approach again, this time focusing in on Lia. Zach was halfway around the car when he turned to swing back toward the photographer, his face twisted in rage. The valet tried to put himself between Lia and the other man, but the man bumped against him and the car door swung into Lia, knocking her off balance. Before she could save herself, she landed on her hands and knees on the pavement.

Zach was at her side in a second, helping her up, his face tight with fury as he pulled her into the protective embrace of his body. He held her as if he were shielding her from another onslaught. She clung to him, breathed him in, though she told herself she should push away and tell him she was perfectly fine. Her body was still so attuned to his touch that her nerve endings tingled and sparked like fireworks on a summer night.

"Madame, I am so sorry," the valet said. "I tried to stop him—"

"It's not your fault," Zach said, cutting him off abruptly.

"Is the photographer still there?" Lia asked.

"He's gone." Zach pushed her back. "Are you okay?"

Lia nodded. "I think so. My palms hurt, but…"

Zach took her hands and turned them over, revealing scrapes on the heels of her palms. His expression grew thunderous.

"If I ever get ahold of that bastard—"

"I'm fine," Lia said quickly. "It was an accident."

"Your knees," Zach growled, and Lia glanced down. Her knees were scraped and bloody. A trickle of bright red blood ran down the front of her leg.

"I'll be fine," she said. "But I need to wash up."

Zach didn't look convinced. "Maybe we should have a doctor look at you. What if something happened to the baby?"

Lia smiled to reassure him. The scrapes stung, but they weren't life-threatening. She'd had worse the time she got stung by a nest of bees while working in the garden. That could have been life threatening, had she not ran and dived into the pool. "Zach, honestly. I fell on my hands and knees. If babies were hurt by such minor accidents, no one would ever be born."

He frowned, but he ushered her back inside. Their host and hostess were mortified, of course, and they were shown to a private sitting room with an attached bath where Lia could clean up before they went home.

The photographer had disappeared as quickly as he'd arrived. No one could seem to find him. Zach paced and growled like a wounded lion while she sat in the bathroom with a warm wet towel and cleaned the bloody scrapes. He would have done it for her, but she'd pushed him out of the room and told him she could take care of herself.

Once she cleaned the scrapes and stopped the bleeding on her knees, she reemerged to find Zach prowling, his phone stuck to his ear. He stopped when he saw her. He ended the call and pocketed the phone before coming over to her. He looked angry and worried at once.

"I think we should get you to a doctor to be sure," he said.

"Zach, I fell on my hands and knees. I didn't fall off a roof."

He looked doubtful. "I think I'd feel better if someone examined you."

Lia sighed. "Then make an appointment for tomorrow. Tonight, I want to soak in a hot bath and go to bed."

He raked a hand through his hair. "Fine," he said, blowing out a frustrated breath.

This time when they went out to the car, there was no photographer lurking nearby. The gates to the property were closed, opening only when Zach rolled to a stop before them and waited for them to swing open.

It was still light out, because it was summer, but the sun threw long shadows across the road. Zach didn't say anything as they drove, and Lia turned to look at the trees and rocks as they glided down a wide parkway that could have been in the middle of nowhere rather than in a major city.

"We're leaving," Zach said into the silence, and Lia swung to look at him.

"I beg your pardon?"

He glanced at her. "We're not staying here and enduring a media frenzy. I won't have you hurt or scared."

Lia frowned. "Zach, I'm not six years old. I'm not scared, and the hurt is minor. It's annoying, and I'm angry, but I won't break."

"I should have realized this would happen. I should have taken you somewhere else and married you first, then brought you back once they'd had time to get used to it."

Lia didn't know how that would help, considering he was still a Scott and still a media target no matter where he went. "It was an accident. Celebrities get photographed every day, and rarely do any of them fall down when it happens."

Not that she was a celebrity. In fact, that was the problem. She wasn't accustomed to the attention and she hadn't reacted quicker. She'd been surprised, and she'd let her surprise catch her off guard when the valet had tried to help.

"Vegas," Zach said, ignoring her completely. "We'll marry in Vegas, and then we'll go to my house on Maui. They won't be able to get close to us there."

CHAPTER ELEVEN

ZACH DIDN'T KNOW what he was doing. It was a difficult thought to grow accustomed to. He was always sure of his choices, always in charge of his actions. Even when he didn't want to do a thing, like stand in front of a crowd and make a patriotic speech about his time in the service, he did it. And he did it because he'd made a choice. There was an end goal.

Always.

What was his end goal now?

He ran a hand over his face and tried to focus on the computer in front of him. Less than twenty-four hours ago, he'd been at the Lattimores' cocktail party, mingling and schmoozing the guests for contributions to his causes.

Now he was on a jet to Hawaii, having taken a side trip to Las Vegas where he'd stood in a seedy little chapel and pledged to love, honor and cherish Lia Corretti until death do them part.

Which, of course, was a lie.

They would not be together until death.

There was a purpose for this match, a reason they had to join forces. He was protecting her from her family's wrath, first of all. Second, he was avoiding a media scandal that would be troublesome and inconvenient were it to erupt.

Except those reasons no longer felt like the whole truth.

Zach closed the computer with a snap. He couldn't concentrate on business right now. All he could think about was Lia, asleep in the bedroom, her body curled sweetly beneath the sheets, her hair spread out in an auburn curtain he wanted to slide his fingers into.

This need for her was like a quiet, swelling tide. The more he denied it, the stronger and more insistent it grew.

And now he was taking her to a remote location, where the distractions would be minimal. How would he keep his hands off her?

Did he even need to? She'd certainly kissed him back yesterday in the garden. Until that moment when she'd pushed him away, she'd been as into the kiss as he had. He'd forgotten where they were, why he couldn't have her the way he wanted then and there. He'd been ready to lift her skirt and push her back on the grass if it gave him the release he needed.

But she'd been the one to say no. The one to remind him this wasn't normal between them.

Zach snorted. Hell, what was normal anymore? He'd left normal in the rearview the moment his plane disintegrated beneath him and he'd hit the eject button. Nothing since had been the same.

But, for a few minutes yesterday, he'd felt like it had. And, he had to admit, for those blissful few hours in Palermo, too. When he'd been with Lia, he hadn't forgotten—but he'd felt as if he could accept what had happened, what his life had become, and move on.

Why did she do that to him? Why did she make him hope for more?

Lia Corretti—Lia Scott—was a dangerous woman. Dangerous for him. It had taken time, but he'd learned how to live with himself in the aftermath of his rescue.

She threatened to explode it all in his face. To force him

to face the things he kept buried. If he told her, would she understand? Or would she recoil in horror?

He got to his feet and paced the length of the main cabin. A flight attendant appeared as if by magic.

"Did you need anything, sir?"

"Thanks, but no," he said, waving her off again. She disappeared into the galley and he was alone once more.

He was restless, prowling, his mind racing through the facts, through the possibilities. Since he'd met Lia, nothing had been the same. And now they were married, and he was feeling shell-shocked—and hungry.

Hungry for her. He'd thought he could keep it at bay, that this arrangement between them would be tidy. But he'd been wrong. So very wrong.

Soon, he had to do something about this hunger—or go mad denying it.

Maui was bright and beautiful, with a rolling blue surf—which changed from deep sapphire to the purest lapis, depending on the depth—impossibly blue sky and green palm trees that stood in tall clusters, their lush foliage fanning out from the top like a funky hairdo.

Except there were other kinds of palm trees, too, Lia noticed, palms that were short and looked like giant pineapples jutting out of the ground. The tropical flowers were colorful, exotic and so sweetly scented that she fell in love with the island's perfumed air immediately.

A car was waiting at the airport when their private jet landed, and a dark-haired woman in a brightly patterned dress greeted them with leis. Lia's was made of fragrant tuberose and plumeria, while Zach's was open on the end and made from kukui nuts and green ti leaves and tiny puka shells.

They got into the back of a Hummer limo and drove across

an island that was flat in the middle and ringed by mountains. On one side was Haleakala, the tall volcanic mountain that could boast more than one climate. At the bottom, the weather was warm and tropical, but at the top, Zach informed her, it was often windy, rainy and cloudy. It was also bare and cratered, like the surface of the moon. But, before you got that high, there was an Alpine region, with chalets and misty cool air.

It was the oddest thought when all she could see were tall jagged peaks, fields of sugarcane and ocean.

Soon, however, they were on the coast again and driving up a road that led to a stretch of beach dotted with sprawling homes. Eventually, they arrived at one and were met by a man who came and got their bags and took them into the house. Zach lead her into the house and over to the stunning floor-to-ceiling windows that were actually sliding-glass doors. Once the doors were completely open, the house gave way to a sweeping lanai, which was tiered so that part of it sat in the infinity pool. Beyond was the beach, so white and sugary and inviting.

Lia could only stare at how beautiful it was. She came from an island, but one that was completely different from this island. They were both stunning, but Maui was a new experience.

"It's gorgeous," she said when Zach came up beside her again and stood there in silence.

She glanced up at him, and her heart flipped. They were married. *Dio*, she had a husband. She could hardly credit it. Even though he'd told her only a few days ago they would marry, she'd never quite gotten accustomed to the idea it would really happen. She'd been waiting, she could admit now, for that moment when he would decide he didn't want her, after all. When he would send her back to Sicily and the wrath of the Correttis.

Her family might be angry with her when they learned the truth, but at least they would be satisfied she'd gotten married and wouldn't be bringing scandalous shame onto the family by having a baby without a husband.

She wondered if Alessandro knew about the marriage by now. She'd sent a quick email to Rosa when they'd left Las Vegas, and then she'd sent another one to her grandmother. Nonna wasn't online for endless hours, like so many people, but she was technologically proficient and would get the missive soon enough. And she would surely tell the head of the family the news.

Lia decided not to worry about it. What was done was done.

"We won't be bothered here," Zach said. "It's too far out of the way for your typical paparazzi. They'll find easier quarry to harass." He stood with his hands in his pockets—he was wearing khakis and a muted aloha shirt—and looked gravely down at her. "How are you feeling? Do you need to rest?"

He was still hung up on the fact the doctor had said she needed more rest and less stress in her life. Everything had been fine with the baby, as she'd predicted. But the doctor had given him something new to worry about.

"I slept on the plane. I'm fine."

"Then you should eat," he said. "I'll go see what we have." He started to turn away, but she put a hand on his arm to stop him. Sparks sizzled into her nerve endings, as always, when she touched him.

She wanted to melt into him, like butter in a hot pan. He looked down at where her hand rested on his arm, and she remembered that she'd meant to say something. That it was odd and awkward if she did not.

"You work so hard to avoid me," she said. "It's not necessary."

That wasn't what she'd intended to say, but it was too late

to take the words back. They hung in the air between them, hovering like candle smoke.

His eyes were dark, fathomless, as he looked at her. Studied her like something he'd never encountered before. Her pulse skittered along merrily, and she forced herself to drop her hand away from the bare skin of his arm.

"You noticed," he said softly. "And here I thought I was so subtle."

Her head snapped up as pain sliced into her. Yes, she'd known he was avoiding her—but to hear him admit it dragged on the same nerve that had made her question her worth since she was a little girl. It should not hurt so much, but it always did.

She knew her worth was not determined by others, and yet she could never quite appease that lonely little girl inside who was still looking for acceptance.

"I noticed." She dropped her gaze, swallowing against the ridiculous lump in her throat, and his fingers came up to slide along her cheek. His touch made heat leap and tangle in her veins. If this heat were a light inside her, it would glow wherever he touched her.

"You pushed me away, *cara*. I was respecting your wish."

"I—I don't know what my wish is," she said truthfully. "I just know that you confuse me."

His gaze sharpened. "Why are you confused, Lia? I think you know what I want."

It took her a minute to answer. "I do," she finally said. "But I don't know why."

He blinked. And then he laughed. The sound burst from him, loud and rich and unexpected. Lia stared at him, her cheeks heating. A tiny thread of irritation began to dance through her. She crossed her arms and stared him down.

He stopped laughing at her, but he was still smiling. "Damn, I needed that." He put his hands on her upper arms.

He didn't pull her in close like she thought he might. Like she hoped he might.

Yesterday, she'd pushed him away. Today, she wanted to pull him to her. Maybe it made no sense, but now that they were married, she felt more...secure. And her need for him had amplified since the moment he'd pushed a diamond—a large, family heirloom, it turned out—on her finger and said, "I do."

His fingers dug into her arms. Not painfully, but possessively. "Hell, Lia, you really don't know why I want you? Are you that blind?"

"I am not blind," she said defensively.

"You must be if you can't figure out what's going on here. You're beautiful, lush and perfect, and I ache with the need to touch you the way I did in Palermo."

His words made her soften, melt. Want. She wanted what they'd had in Palermo—except for the part where she woke up and he was gone.

"I..." She swallowed as her heart beat a tattoo against her rib cage. Her throat was as dry as baked sand. It was a frightening thing to say what she wanted. But he was looking at her as if he was dying to touch her, and so she took a chance. "I think I want that, too."

He made a noise of relief. Then he slid his hands down her arms and around her back, cupping her buttocks as he pulled her fully into his embrace.

"Grazie a Dio," he said then in a throaty purr, and a liquid shiver danced down her spine. Her hands went up to clutch his shirt as his head descended.

Their mouths touched and a shudder went through Lia. All those feelings she'd felt in the maze yesterday came rushing to the fore. They were almost too much, too overwhelming.

But she wouldn't push him away again. She couldn't.

He was big and hard and strong, and she pressed herself

against him, her hands running over the hard muscles of his chest and shoulders. Her body was on fire as liquid heat gathered in her core. She could feel the dampness in her panties, the instant response that she couldn't have prevented even if she'd wanted to.

This thing between them was hot and bright and uncontrollable. It was a need that had to be assuaged, or she would be as restless as a spirit condemned to roam the earth for all eternity.

"Wait," he said, pushing her back, breaking that delicious contact.

Lia's stomach fell. If he was rejecting her now...

"Not yet," he said, his voice sounding tortured enough that she relaxed infinitesimally. "We just arrived, and you need to rest first."

"I told you I slept on the plane...."

He slid a hand into her hair, cupped her head while he traced a path over her collarbone with the fingers of his other hand. "I know, but it was a long trip and the doctor said—"

Lia cursed. "I wish you would allow me to make my own decisions without all this argument! We're going to get off to a very bad start, Zachariah Scott, if you constantly tell me what I should be doing."

He looked at her for a long minute. One corner of his mouth turned up in a grin.

"What's so funny?" she asked crossly.

"You. Such a temper from a little thing."

Heat suffused her. "I am not a little thing and you know it. I'm too tall and I'm only going to get fatter—"

He put a finger over her lips, silencing her. "You are not fat, Lia. You're lush and gorgeous and you make me hard."

The tops of her ears were on fire. She didn't consider herself to be a prude by any stretch—she'd read plenty of books where people had sex, sometimes even raunchy sex—but the idea she affected him that way, and that he had no problem saying it, both embarrassed and thrilled her.

"*Allora,*" she said, resisting the urge to fan herself with both hands. "The things you say."

"Makes you hot, doesn't it?"

Lia put a hand over her eyes. "*Dio,*" she said.

Zach laughed and drew her hand away from her face. Then he took both her hands in his and held them in front of his body. "I like that you're still so innocent," he told her. "I like the idea of corrupting you."

A shiver washed over her as she imagined all the ways in which he might corrupt her. She'd had a taste of it, certainly, for two blissful days—but she knew there was more, knew they hadn't even scratched the surface of their need for each other.

"There's no time like the present," she replied, and then felt herself blushing harder than before if that were possible.

He led her through the gorgeous house with the soaring ceilings, the koa wood floors and overstuffed couches and huge open sliding doors, to a bedroom with a king-size bed and a breathtaking view of the ocean, with its white sand beaches, jagged black volcanic rocks and rolling surf.

The bed was on a platform, clothed in pristine white, and there was a television mounted on the opposite wall. She wondered who would ever want to watch television in a house like this, but then Zach stopped and tugged her into his arms again.

He kissed her softly, sweetly—too softly and sweetly to mean he was actually planning to make love to her, she realized, and then he stepped away.

"Take a bath, Lia. Have a nap. We'll have dinner on the lanai and watch the sunset. After that—" he shrugged "—anything goes."

* * *

Anything goes.

Lia couldn't get that thought out of her mind as she bathed and dressed. In spite of her insistence she'd slept on the plane, she had managed to fall into that giant king bed and drift off to sleep after she'd stared at the ocean for several minutes. It had surprised her to wake sometime later, when the sun was sliding down the bowl of the sky.

The doors to the outside were still open, and the ocean rolled rhythmically against the shore. A gentle trade wind blew through the room, bringing with it the scent of plumeria trees.

Now, Lia gazed at the ocean again as she stood in the open doors and gathered her courage before she went to meet Zach. Why, when she'd been ready earlier, did she suddenly feel as if a thousand hummingbirds were beating their wings in her belly?

Finally, she turned and strode from the bedroom, down the stairs and into the main living area. Zach wasn't on the lanai, and he wasn't in the living room. She continued to the kitchen, a huge room with koa wood cabinets and stainless-steel appliances. Zach was standing at the kitchen island, slicing fruit.

Lia blinked. It was such a domestic picture, and a surprising one. He looked up and smiled, and her body melted.

"You are fixing dinner?" she asked.

"It's nothing terribly exciting," he told her. "My repertoire is limited. But I can broil a fish, and I can make salad and cut up some fruit for dessert."

"You are a man of many talents," she said.

One eyebrow lifted. "I am indeed. I look forward to showing you some of those talents in detail."

Lia blushed and a grin spread over Zach's face. "You like embarrassing me," she said.

He walked over with a piece of pineapple and handed it to her. She popped it in her mouth, nearly moaning at the juicy sweetness.

"Not at all," he said as he went back over to the island. "I find it charming that you blush over such things."

"Charming," she repeated, as if it were a foreign word. Her family had never found her charming. They'd never thought she was anything but a nuisance. Except for Nonna, of course.

He picked up the platter. "Come out to the lanai and I'll bring everything," he told her.

"I can take the fruit."

He handed it to her and then went back for the salad. When they reached the table on the lanai—a table set with simple dishes and silverware—he set the salad down and took the fruit from her. Then he tugged her into his arms and kissed her.

"Yes, charming," he said. "I've never known anyone as innocent about such things as you are."

He let her go and pulled out her chair for her. As she sat, she looked up at him, her chest tightening at the emotions filling her. Emotions she really didn't want to spend much time analyzing. She already knew she cared too much. Did she need to know more than that?

"I don't like blushing like a nun in a locker room," she said. "It's ridiculous."

He laughed. "Like I said, charming."

He went and retrieved the rest of the food, and then they sat on the lanai with a view of the blue, blue ocean, and a big orange ball sinking into it. They ate fresh fish and talked about many things, none of them singularly important, but all important in the bigger picture of getting to know each other.

Lia learned that Zach liked to read biographies and military treatises, and that he'd defied his father by going to the

Air Force Academy rather than Harvard. She also learned that he managed his family's charitable foundation, and that he'd met Taylor Carmichael in his work supporting veterans' causes.

"Why did you drop the medal?" she asked, and then wanted to kick herself when he stiffened slightly.

But he took a sip of his wine and relaxed. "It's something the military does automatically, writing you up for medals when you've been in combat. But I didn't want it. I didn't want any of them."

Her heart pinched at the darkness in his tone. "But why?"

He kept his gaze on the ocean for a long time, and her pulse thrummed hot. She berated herself for pushing him, and yet she felt like she would never know him if she didn't ask these things. He was her husband, the father of her child, and she wanted to know who he was inside.

He turned to her, his dark eyes glittering hot. "Because six marines died saving me, Lia. Because I was drugged and I didn't do anything but lay there while they fought and died. They worked so damn hard to save me, and I couldn't help them. They died because of me."

Lia swallowed the lump that had formed in her throat. "I'm sorry, Zach," she said. She reached for his hand, squeezed it. She was encouraged when he didn't snatch it away. "But I think they died because they were doing their job, not because of you."

"You aren't the first to say that to me," he said, rubbing his thumb against her palm. "Yet I still have trouble believing it. I'm treated like a hero, and yet I haven't earned the right to be one. They were the heroes."

She hurt for him. He looked stoic, sitting there and staring out at the ocean beyond, and she wanted to wrap her arms around him and hold him tight. She fought herself, fought her natural inclination not to reach for him because of her fear of being rejected. In the end, the fear won.

"I doubt anyone thinks they weren't heroes," she said hotly, because she was angry with herself and angry with him, too. "They had jobs to do, and they did them. But they died because the enemy killed them. No other reason."

His expression was almost amused when he turned it on her. Except there was too much pain behind that gaze to ever be mistaken for amusement. "How fierce you are, *cara*. One wonders—do you have a limit? Would you, for instance, stop defending me if I crossed the line?"

CHAPTER TWELVE

SHE WAS LOOKING at him curiously, her brows drawing down over her lovely eyes. He could tell she was grappling with herself, with the things he was saying. Did she want to run? Did she want to lock herself in her room, away from him?

He almost wished she would. It would make things so much easier.

Because he was enjoying this too much, sitting here on the lanai with her and talking about their lives while they ate and watched the sun sink into the sea. He couldn't remember ever enjoying a woman's company the way he did hers. He loved women, loved sex, but companionship? He'd never thought of that before. Never cared. The old Zach changed women the way he changed clothes—frequently and as the situation dictated.

But, with Lia, he enjoyed the simple pleasures of spending time with her. It was a dangerous thing. Because she made him feel as if he could be normal again, when he knew he never could. He'd changed too much to ever go back to what he'd been before.

In the beginning, he'd thought it was possible. He'd thought the dreams would go away with time. That's what everyone said he needed: time. Time was the great healer. Time made everything better. Time, time, time.

He'd had time. More than a year's worth, and nothing was

the same. He had to accept that it never would be. He might always be plagued by dreams and fears, the same as he was plagued with unpredictable headaches. Those had changed his ability to fly forever, so why did he think time could fix the other stuff?

It couldn't. She couldn't.

"What line?" she asked, her voice soft and strong at once. As if she was challenging him. As if she didn't believe him. His chest felt tight as emotions filled him. This woman—this sweet, innocent woman—had faith in him. It was a stunning realization. And a sobering one.

He didn't want to fail her. And he didn't want to fail their child.

Another paradigm-shifting realization.

"It's nothing," he said, surprised at the trembling in his fingers as he reached for his wine. "Forget it."

She kept staring at him, her eyes large and liquid. "You are a man of integrity and honor," she said. "I do not doubt that at all."

"I tried to pay you off and send you away, Lia. Or have you forgotten?"

She picked up her glass. "I have not. But I understand why you did it."

"Because I'm an arrogant bastard with an unhealthy sense of self-importance?" He meant it to be self-deprecating, but he recognized the truth in it, too. He'd had his family consequence drummed into him from birth, after all.

"I wouldn't have put it that way," she said carefully, and he laughed.

She looked at him in confusion, and he didn't blame her. Just a moment ago, the conversation had been so serious, so dramatic. Now that it had moved away from the deeply intense and dark things residing in his soul, he could find humor in her reaction.

"Because you are too sweet," he said. He reached for her hand. The heat that sparked inside him was always surprising.

She frowned. "I don't feel particularly sweet. I feel quite cross at the moment, actually."

He brought her hand to her mouth, nibbled the skin over her knuckles. "I think I know how to change that," he murmured.

Lia's insides were melting. She didn't want to melt just yet, but she realized she had no choice in the matter. Sparks were zinging and pinging inside her like a fireworks display on New Year's eve.

She was still concerned about the things he'd said, about the self-loathing beneath his mask, but it seemed the subject was now closed. She'd been allowed a peek at the raw, tormented nature of Zach Scott, but now he was wrapped up tight again and she wasn't getting in.

She wanted to know the man who dreamed, who worked hard to make those speeches and ignore the triggers that could send him spiraling out of control. She wanted to touch the heart of him, she realized.

The way he'd touched hers.

He tugged her toward him until she got up and went to his side. Then he was pulling her down on his lap, tilting her back in his arms. His eyes gleamed with heat, and a hot wave of longing washed through her with the same kind of relentless surge of the ocean beyond.

"No more talking, Lia," he said, his fingers gliding over the skin beneath her collarbone.

When his lips replaced his fingers, her head fell back against the chair. His mouth moved over her, teasing, tormenting. The ocean pounded the shore a few yards away, and the trade winds blew, and Lia shuddered and gasped and knew she'd found heaven.

Her heart hurt with everything she felt: passion, hot and bright; fear, cold and insidious; and love, warm and glowing, like the sun as it had been right before it sank into the sea. There was a rightness about this, a rightness that felt like destiny and perfection.

She was meant to be here, and Zach was meant to be the man she shared her life with. She shivered again as he unbuttoned her shirt and peeled it back to reveal her shoulders and the soft swell of her breasts against the silk of her bra.

"Bellissimo," he said, his voice a silky purr. *"Ho bisogno di te, Lia."*

I need you.

Lia shivered again, her entire body on fire from tip to toes as his gaze raked her with that naked hunger she'd come to crave.

"Yes," she said. "Oh, yes."

His mouth came down on hers, and she was lost to anything but this molten hot fire between them. She wrapped her arms around him and shifted in his lap—and felt the hard evidence of his arousal pressing against her bottom.

His body tightened beneath her—and then all that beautiful power was lifting her, carrying her into the house while she clung to him and pressed kisses to his jaw, his neck, the delicious skin of his collarbone.

Soon, she was on her feet in the master suite. The doors were still slung open to let in the breezes, but they were completely alone out here on this remote stretch of beach. Zach stripped away her silky top and tailored trousers until she stood before him in nothing but her bra and a tiny scrap of silk that covered her sex.

His eyes darkened as they drifted over her, and a thrill shot through her.

"You look good enough to eat, Lia," he purred.

A fresh wave of heat pulsed inside her. She was wet, hot, and she wanted him.

But she couldn't move. She couldn't take those three steps to him, couldn't wrap her arms around him and be a wanton, seductive woman. Always she feared she wouldn't do it right, that he'd disapprove, or that he'd push her away and tell her she wasn't good enough, after all.

She knew better, she really did. But when you'd believed something your entire life, it was difficult to suddenly stop in a moment where every gesture, every touch, every look, set off firestorms inside. You'd do anything to keep the storm happening, anything to keep feeling the sweet heat. You would not take a risk.

He took a step toward her, his big body menacing—but in a good way. In a hard, protective, thoroughly delicious way.

"Do you want to touch me?" he asked.

She could only nod her head.

"Do it, then," he told her. "Touch me wherever you want. However you want."

"You have too many clothes on," she said, and blushed.

His laugh was deep, sexy, sinful. "Take them off, then."

She moved toward him, her fingers fumbling with the buttons of his shirt until she could finally push it free. It fell off his shoulders and landed in a pile at his feet. The shorts he'd changed into hung low on his body, revealing ridges of hard muscle and the perfect slash of hip bones.

She wanted to run her tongue along those bones. Wanted to dip it into the hollow of his abdomen, and then slide it down to the thick, hard length of his penis. But she didn't. She just stood and gaped like a kid in a candy store.

Zach swore, and then he was unbuttoning his shorts and shoving them down. His underwear went with them until he stood before her gloriously naked. His penis jutted out proudly, and his warrior's body made her mouth water.

She forgot herself. She reached for him.

But he reached for her, too, and soon they were lost in each other, kissing and touching and feeling what they'd missed for the past few weeks.

Lia wrapped herself around him until he put his hands on her bottom and lifted her. Her legs scissored around his waist as he carried her the few steps to the bed and tumbled her backward onto it.

"I wanted to seduce you slowly. But I can't wait, Lia," he managed finally, the hard ridge of his erection riding against the silk of her panties.

"Me, neither," she said—panted, really.

He rose up above her, jerked her panties down her legs and discarded them—and then he was back, pushing inside her until they were joined completely.

This, she thought, eyes closed, back arched, this utter perfection of his body so deeply within hers. This was what she wanted. What she needed.

His mouth fused to hers as he began to move. He wound his fingers into hers, pushed her arms above her head and proceeded to devastate her utterly with his lovemaking.

Days passed. Glorious sex- and sun-drenched days. They didn't talk about the military again, didn't talk about Zach's dreams. He slept with her at night, though she hadn't believed he would. The first night, when they'd made love and she was so thoroughly languid that she couldn't have moved if her life depended on it, he'd alarmed her by climbing from the bed and gathering his clothes.

When she'd asked him where he was going, he'd informed her he was going to his room. She'd sat up, the sheet tucked around her still-naked and glowing body, and wanted to cry. He'd told her it was best for them both, and that it wasn't her. It was him. She knew what he meant, but it still hurt to see him willing to walk away when she would have gladly walked across a room of broken glass just to be by his side.

He'd left her alone, and she'd turned to stare out at the ocean glowing beneath a full moon. The waves crashed against the shore, broke against the jagged rock cliffs that dotted the shoreline, and she felt as if her heart was broken and jagged, too.

Fifteen minutes later, Zach had returned. When he'd slipped into bed with her, she'd been unable to contain the small cry that erupted from her. He'd pulled her close, his mouth at her throat, and told her he wanted to try to stay with her.

She'd put her arms around him, threaded her fingers into that silky hair and nearly wept with relief and fierce joy.

They had not slept. Not at first. No, within minutes, Zach was inside her again, his body taking hers to heights that made the peak of Mount Everest look like an afternoon trek up a tiny foothill.

Finally, they crashed to the bottom again and fell asleep, entangled in each other's arms.

The days began to pass, each one as perfect and heartbreaking as the last. They spent hours making love, hours in the sunshine—floating in the pool, lying on the beach—and didn't leave the house to go anywhere. A service did the shopping and cleaning for them, so all they had to worry about was fixing their meals.

Zach did a great job at that, so there was nothing lacking in their self-imposed isolation. He'd been right, too, about the paparazzi. There were none on this lonely stretch of beach. They were opportunists, and opportunity was easier elsewhere.

The papers were filled at first with news of their hasty marriage and tropical honeymoon. Zach merely laughed and said it had all gone perfectly to plan. Eventually, though they were still news, they weren't on the front pages of the gossip rags anymore. Some Hollywood starlet and her latest drunk-driving conviction were taking center stage at the moment.

Lia spoke with her grandmother. The older woman seemed happy for her, though sad as well that she hadn't been at the wedding. Lia gave her some story about wildly beating hearts and true love being impatient, and her grandmother accepted it. Her cousin, apparently, was currently preoccupied with his own issues and wasn't inclined to worry about her fate at all.

She'd married a rich, influential man and that was good enough for the family. As for Rosa, Lia had been emailing back and forth with her sister quite frequently. They were both still wary, but there was a budding relationship that Lia thought might eventually grow into something she cherished.

Right now, however, she cherished Zach. She looked up from her book and let her gaze slide over him where he stood in the infinity pool, having just emerged from his swim. He was so very beautiful, hard and lean and fit in ways that made her mouth water.

And virile. She couldn't forget that one. The man did not tire out in the bedroom, or not until he'd exhausted himself pleasing her.

It was a good trait in a husband, she thought wickedly.

She was growing bolder in her experiments with his body. At first, she'd been afraid to try anything, afraid she would get it wrong and he'd not tell her because he didn't want to hurt her feelings.

But if she was getting it wrong, then he was a superb actor, because his gasps and groans and urgent touches and kisses spurred her to even greater experiments.

Like last night, when she'd taken him in her mouth as they sat out here on the lanai in the dark and listened to the ocean.

"Lia," he'd gasped as she'd freed him and then swirled her tongue around the head of his penis. And then he'd grabbed fistfuls of her hair and held her gently but firmly while she took him into her mouth. Her heart had beat so hard, so loud in her ears, but she could still hear him making those sounds of pleasure in his throat.

Before he'd orgasmed, however, he'd pulled her up and made her straddle him. She'd been wearing a silken nightie, no panties, and she'd sunk down on him while he held her hips and guided her.

She didn't remember much after that, except for the frantic way she'd ridden him until they'd both collapsed on the chaise longue. Much later, he'd carried her to bed and repeated the performance.

"What are you reading?" he said now, arraying his splendid form on the lounge beside her.

She held up her book. "I'm learning about the flowering plants of Hawaii. And how they make leis. Quite fascinating."

He groaned. "Please don't let me find you out pruning the plumeria one morning, searching for the perfect blooms."

Lia looked across at the single plumeria tree near the side of the house. It was tall, at least twenty feet, and filled with blooms whose perfume wafted over to her even now. "Don't be ridiculous," she said. "It's huge, and I'd need a ladder."

"You are definitely not getting on a ladder," he growled.

She laughed. "Of course not. I wouldn't dream of it."

His expression softened, his gaze raking over her. She got that warm glow inside that she always did. The words she'd not yet said to him welled behind her teeth, threatened to burst out into the open if she didn't work to contain them.

How could she tell him she loved him when that would be the ultimate soul-baring act she could perform? She'd be naked before him, naked in a way she could never take back. And he would have the ability to crush her. A single word. A single look.

He could crush her beneath his well-shod heel and she'd never recover.

Dio.

His brows drew down. "Are you feeling all right?" he asked. "Do you need to see a doctor?"

Lia rolled her eyes. It was a screen to cover all her raw, exposed feelings, but it was also a true reaction. He was incessantly worried about her health, which was sweet, but also managed to exasperate her.

"Zach, I'm fine. I have an appointment with the doctor on Oahu next week, remember?"

He continued to study her like she was a bug under a microscope. "Would you tell me if you were unwell? Or would you hide it?"

She blinked. "Why on earth would I hide such a thing?"

He looked at her for a long minute. And then he shrugged. "I have no idea. I just get the feeling that sometimes you aren't being completely honest about what you're feeling."

Her heart skipped a beat. Wow, he'd nailed it in one. But not for the reason he supposed. She reached out and grasped his hand. His skin was still cool from the pool. "I'm not used to sharing my life with anyone," she said truthfully. "I'm used to being self-reliant in many ways, but if I felt truly ill, I would tell you. I don't want anything to happen to this baby."

"Or you," he said, and her heart seemed to stop beating in her chest. A moment later, it lurched forward again, beating in triple time. She told herself not to read anything into that statement, but, oh, how her heart wanted to.

He turned away and reached for his tablet computer while her pulse surged and her heart throbbed. She wanted what he'd said to mean something. Wanted it desperately. But he sat there scrolling through his tablet so casually, and she knew that it hadn't meant a thing. Oh, he didn't want her to hurt herself, certainly.

But not because he didn't know what he'd do if she weren't here. Not because the air he breathed would suddenly grow stale without her. Not because his life would cease to be bright if she were not in it.

Lia turned away from him, her eyes pricking with tears, and picked up the virgin mai tai he'd fixed for her before he slipped into the pool. The trade winds blew so gently across her skin, and the sun was bright in the azure sky above. It was so perfect here, and she'd let herself be lulled by it.

But she had to remember there was nothing about this situation that was permanent. It could all end tomorrow, if he so chose. Lia shivered and tried not to imagine what would happen when it did.

In the end she didn't need to imagine a thing.

There was a storm in the middle of the night. It was a rare occurrence on Maui, because the trade winds and the air pressure didn't usually allow for it, but tonight there was thunder and jagged lightning sizzling over the ocean.

Lia woke with a jerk when a crack of thunder sounded close by. Zach was beside her, sitting up, his eyes wide.

"Zach?"

He didn't move. She reached for him. He jerked, then spun and pinned her to the bed. His eyes were wild, his skin damp. He growled something unintelligible.

"Zach, *caro*, it's me," she said. "It's Lia."

He was very still. "Lia?"

"Yes."

The tension in his body collapsed. He rolled away from her with a groan and lay on his back, an arm thrown over his eyes. "Jesus," he breathed. "I could have hurt you."

She propped herself on an elbow and leaned over him. "You wouldn't," she said, utterly convinced.

The arm fell away and his dark eyes gleamed at her as he drew in deep lungfuls of breath. "How can you be so sure? I'm a mess, Lia." He choked out something unintelligible. "A damn mess."

Fear was beginning to dance along the surface of her psyche. He frightened her, but not physically. "I don't believe that."

He laughed bitterly. "You're too damn trusting. Too naive. You have no idea what goes on in this world."

He threw the covers back and got out of bed while she sat there with her heart pinching and her chest aching. He yanked on a pair of shorts and stalked outside, onto the balcony, oblivious to the rain coming down.

Lia's first instinct was to stay where she was, to let him cool off. But she couldn't do it. She loved him too much, and she hated when he was hurting.

She climbed from the bed and put on her robe. Then she went to stand in the open door and look at him.

The rain washed over him, soaking his hair, running in rivulets down his chest. He looked lonely and angry and her heart went out to him. She knew what it was like to be lonely and angry. She wanted nothing more than to fix it for him.

"Zach, please talk to me."

He spun to look at her. "You don't want to hear what I have to say."

She took a step toward him.

He held a hand up to stop her. "Don't come out here. You'll get wet."

"It doesn't seem to be hurting you," she said, though she stopped anyway, folding her arms around her body. "And you're wrong. I do want to hear what you have to say."

He shoved his wet hair back from his face, but he didn't

make a move to come inside. Thunder rolled in the distance. A flash of lightning zipped along the sky, slicing it in two for a brief moment.

"I should have known better," he said. "I should have known it was a mistake to think this could work between us."

Her chest filled with chaotic emotion, tightening until she thought she wouldn't be able to breathe. But she held herself firmly, arms crossed beneath her breasts, and refused to let him see how much he hurt her. He thought she was naive, trusting. Unworthy.

It stung. But, worse, the idea she was a mistake threatened to make her fold in on herself.

"You can't mean that," she said tightly, though her brain gibbered at her to be quiet. To detach. To roll into a ball and protect herself. "These past couple of weeks have been perfect."

"Which is why it was a mistake," he snapped. "There's no such thing as perfect, not where I'm concerned."

"Because you don't deserve those medals?" she threw back at him, anger beginning to grow and spin inside her belly. "Because you have bad dreams and think you're so terrible?"

He took a step toward her, stopped. His hands clenched into fists at his side. He was close enough he could have reached out and touched her. But he didn't.

"You want to know the truth? I'll tell you," he grated. "The whole, sorry story."

He turned his back on her, walked over to the railing. The rain was lessening, but it was still coming down. When he turned back to her, his expression was tight.

"You've heard part of it. I broke my leg during the ejection. It hurt like hell, and I couldn't move much. But I'd landed near a protected ravine and hunkered down to wait.

I expected the enemy to find me first. But they didn't. The marines did. Only the enemy wasn't far behind."

Lia imagined him alone like that, imagined him waiting, and fear crawled up her throat, no matter that she'd heard him say this part before. She wanted to go to him, but she knew he didn't want her to. It made her desperate inside, but all she could do was listen.

"The medic drugged me," he said. "And I couldn't help them defend our position when they most needed me. Hell, I think I drifted in and out of consciousness. I have no idea how long it went on, but it seemed to take forever. They hit us with grenades, small-arms fire. It was ceaseless, and air support wasn't coming no matter how many times the marines called for it. One by one, the enemy picked off the marines, until it was one sergeant and me."

He didn't keep going, but she knew he wasn't finished. He turned away again, and she could see the tightness in his jaw, his shoulders. Zach was on edge in a way she'd only ever seen him when he was in the grips of a dream.

"Zach?"

He turned his head toward her. "Here's the part you don't know. The part no one knows. He gave me a pistol. Put it in my hand and removed the safety. And then he told me it was my choice when the enemy came. Shoot them, or shoot myself."

"No," she breathed as horror washed over her.

Zach's gaze didn't change, didn't soften. "Obviously," he said, "I didn't shoot myself. I didn't shoot anyone. Sometime in the night, the last marine died. And I wanted to shoot myself. I wanted it pretty badly."

"Oh, Zach…" Her eyes filled with tears.

"What you need to know, Lia, is that I tried to do it. I put the gun under my jaw." He put his finger just where he would have stuck the gun. Her heart lurched at the thought of him lying helplessly like that with so much death and destruction all around him. "But I couldn't pull the trigger."

The words hung in the air between them, like poison.

"I'm glad you didn't," Lia said fiercely, her throat a tight, achy mess. How close had he come? How close had she been to never, ever knowing him? It didn't bear thinking about.

"I can't forget that night. I can't forget how they all died, and how I could do nothing about it. I can't forget that I should have died with them."

Lia put a hand over her belly without conscious thought. "You weren't meant to die, Zach. You were meant to live. For me. For our baby."

His laugh was bitter, broken. "God, why would you think that? Why, after everything I just said to you, after the way I attacked you tonight, would you want me within a thousand miles of a child?"

She was starting to quake deep inside. Something was changing here. Something she couldn't stop. She was losing him. She'd begun to believe, over the past couple of weeks, that something was happening between them. Something good. She'd let herself be lulled by the sun and sea and the fabulous sex. Hadn't she had a glimmering of it earlier today by the pool?

"You didn't attack me. I startled you, but you have to remember that you let me go."

"What if I hadn't? You can't trust me, Lia. I can't trust myself."

"Then get some help!" she yelled at him. "Fight for me. For us."

He was looking at her, his chest rising and falling rapidly, and her hopes began to unfurl their wings. He could do this.

"It's not that easy," he said between clenched teeth. "Don't you think I've tried?"

"Then try again. For us."

He looked almost sad for a moment. "Why are you so stubborn, Lia? Why can't you just accept the truth? I told you I couldn't be a husband or a father. Now you know why."

Fear and fury whipped to a froth inside her. "Because I—" *I love you.*

But she couldn't say the words. They clogged her throat, like always, the fear of them almost more than she could bear. She'd worked hard not to love people who wouldn't love her back. She'd hidden inside her shell and shut everyone out.

Until Zach. Until he'd walked into her life and opened her up, exposing her soft underbelly. He'd made her love him. He'd made her vulnerable to this horrible, shattering pain again.

"Because what?" he said.

Lia swallowed the fear. She had to say the words. If she expected him to face his fear, then she had to face her own.

"Because I love you," she said, the words like razor blades. They weren't supposed to hurt. But they did.

Raw emotion flared in his eyes. And then his face went blank. He was shutting down, pulling up the cold, cool, untouchable man who lived inside him. She wanted to wail.

"That," he finally said, his voice so icy it made her shiver, "is a mistake."

"I don't believe that," she said on a hoarse whisper. "I refuse to believe that."

He came over to stand before her. She wanted to touch him, but she knew better than to try. Not now. Not when he was pushing her away. Not when her heart was breaking in two.

He put a finger under her chin and lifted until she had to look him in the eye. What she saw there eroded all her hopes.

"You're a good woman, Lia. You deserve better than this." His throat moved as he swallowed.

She feared what he would say, feared the look in his eyes. "Zach, no…"

He put his finger over her lips to silence her. "That's why I'm letting you go."

CHAPTER THIRTEEN

SICILY WAS JUST as Lia had left it, though she was not the same as she'd been when she'd left Sicily. She was bitterly angry. Hurt.

But one thing she was not, not ever again, was pitiful. She'd told her grandmother about the baby, because she couldn't hide it for much longer—and because she was no longer afraid of her family's reaction. Yes, it helped that she'd married the father. But she was still having this baby alone, regardless of what her family thought about that.

Far from being scandalized, Teresa had been thrilled to have a great-grandchild on the way. If the head of the family was upset about it, Lia didn't know it. Nor did she care.

Lia snipped lavender from the garden and dropped it into the basket sitting on the ground beside her. Then she wiped the back of her hand across her brow to remove the sweat before it could drip into her eyes. It was hot outside, crackling. Perhaps she should be inside, but she was going a little crazy just sitting there and reading books.

She was still in her cottage on her grandparents' estate, but she was in the process of purchasing an apartment of her own in Palermo. Once she'd returned to Sicily a month ago, she'd marched right into the family lawyer's office and told him she wanted her money. He'd blinked at her in a slow, lazy way that she feared meant he was about to deny her request or refer her to Alessandro, but instead he'd turned to his computer and began bringing up the family accounts.

She'd discovered that she had far more money than she'd thought. She would not need Zach's money to take care of their baby. It wasn't a fortune, but it would do.

It gave her great satisfaction to refuse a meeting with Zach's local attorney when he'd called to say he'd set up a bank account for her and needed her signature on some papers.

She would not take a dime of Scott money. Not ever.

The thought of Zach still had the power to make her feel as if someone had stabbed her with a hot dagger. She was so angry with him. So filled with rage and hate and—

No, not hate. Bitter disappointment. Hurt.

Her worst nightmare had come true when she'd given him her heart and he'd flung it back at her. He'd rejected her, just as she'd always been rejected by those to whom she wanted to mean something.

And it hadn't killed her. That was the part she'd found amazing, once she stopped crying and feeling sorry for herself.

She was hurt, yes, but she was here. Alive. And she had a life growing inside her, a tiny, wonderful life that she already loved so much. Her child would have everything she had not had. Friends, love, acceptance.

But not a father, she thought wistfully. Her baby would not have a father. Oh, Zach didn't want a divorce. He'd been very clear that she was still a Scott for as long as she wanted to be one, and that their child would have his name.

She'd met Zach's parents before she'd left. They'd been nice, if a bit formal, and they'd told her they wanted to be involved in their grandchild's life. So, her baby might not have a father, but he or she would have grandparents. She had agreed to return to the United States at least once a year, and they had indicated they would come to Sicily as often as she would allow it.

It had seemed far enough in the future that she figured she would have learned how to deal with her memories of Zach by then. She kept seeing him as he'd been that last night in Hawaii. Dark, tortured, dripping wet and so stubborn she wanted to put her hands around his throat and squeeze until he would listen to sense.

But there was no talking to Zach when he made up his mind. And, in his mind, he was a dangerous, damaged man who had no hope for the future. They'd boarded a jet the next morning after the storm on Maui. By nightfall they'd been back in D.C and then he'd disappeared.

Finally, on the fifth day, she'd decided she'd had enough. She'd made travel arrangements to Sicily and then she'd informed Raoul when she was leaving for the airport.

Zach had appeared very quickly after that. It had been an awkward meeting in which he'd told her he didn't want a divorce and that he would support her and their child. She'd sat through it silently, fuming and aching and wanting to throw things.

In the end, she'd left because it hurt too much to stay. Before she'd walked out the door the final time, she'd gone into his office and dropped the medal on his desk. He wasn't there, but she'd known he would see it. If it made him angry, so be it. It was the final tie she needed to cut if she was to move on with her life.

Apparently, her leaving hadn't fazed him in the least. It had been a month and she'd heard nothing from Zach, though she'd heard plenty from his local attorney. A man who was beginning to leave increasingly strident messages. Messages she had no intention of returning.

She clipped off some rosemary a little more viciously than necessary and dropped it in the basket. Then she got to her feet and put her hand in the small of her back. Her back ached quite a lot these days, but the doctor said everything was normal. She hadn't really started to show yet, though she'd had to get expansion bands for her pants and wear clothing that was loose around the middle. Soon, it would be time for maternity wear, but right now her maxi dress and sandals did just fine.

In the distance, the sea sparkled sapphire. It looked nothing like Maui, but it made her wistful nevertheless. She often found herself sitting on her little secluded terrazzo and gazing at the sea. She thought that if she did it enough, she would anesthetize herself to the pain.

So far, it hadn't worked. It was like reopening a wound each and every time.

She turned to make her way back to her cottage. The grounds sloped upward and the walk in this heat made her heart pound until she began to feel light-headed. She stopped for a moment, the basket slung over her arm, and wiped her forehead again. Her vision was growing spotty and her belly was churning. She groped in the basket for her water and came up with an empty bottle.

She could see her destination, see the terrazzo through the pencil pines and bougainvillea—and a man standing with his back to her. He had dark hair and wore a suit, and a swift current of anger shot through her veins, giving her the impetus she needed to keep putting one foot in front of the other.

She'd told Zach's lawyer that she didn't want to meet him. Yet he'd dared to come anyway, no doubt to try and force her to sign the documents that would make her the owner of a bank account with far too much money in it. She was not about to let Zach assuage his guilt that way. Let him choke on his millions for all she cared.

The man should not have made it through the estate's security, but he'd obviously sweet-talked his way inside. A red mist of rage clouded her vision as she trod up the lawn. Her stomach churned and her vision swam, but she was determined to make it. Determined to tell this man to take his briefcase full of papers and shove them where the sun didn't shine.

He might have sweet-talked Nonna into letting him onto the estate, but he wasn't sweet-talking her.

She stepped onto the tiles, her heart pounding with the effort. "How dare you," she began—but he turned around and the words got stuck in her mouth.

Her vision blurred and started to grow dark at the edges as bile rose in her throat. Too late, she recognized what was happening. Then everything ceased to exist.

Zach was miserable. He paced the halls of the local hospital where Lia had been taken. Her grandmother had promised to let him know what was happening, but she'd disappeared into the room with Lia and the doctor and hadn't come out again.

Zach shoved a hand through his hair and contemplated bursting through the door to Lia's room. This was not at all what he'd expected when he'd arrived today. He cursed himself for not being more cautious, for not calling her first. If he'd caused any harm to Lia or the baby, he would never forgive himself.

He stood with his fists clenched at his sides. He'd been such a fool, and now he couldn't shake the feeling he'd come too late.

That night, when he'd stood in the rain and told Lia about what had really happened—what had nearly happened—in that trench, he'd felt like the lowest kind of bastard. The kind who didn't deserve a sweet wife and a happy ending. He'd hated himself for turning on her during the storm—and earlier, in Palermo. He couldn't control the beast inside him, the slavering animal that reacted blindly, lashing out in fear and fury.

When he'd shoved her back on the bed, he'd known he couldn't take that risk ever again. He hadn't hurt her, as she'd pointed out, but he didn't trust that he was incapable of hurting her. He'd known then that he had to end it between them, and he had to do it immediately.

Letting her go had been the hardest thing he'd ever done. For days after she'd left, he'd walked around his house like a ghost, looking at the places she'd been, imagining her there within reach. Dying to touch her again and aching so hard because he couldn't.

He told himself he'd done the right thing. He was a beast, a monster, a man incapable of tenderness and love. He'd sacrificed himself for her safety, her happiness, and he'd felt honorable doing it.

But he'd also been miserable. And once he'd walked into his office and found the medal she'd left, he'd had a sudden visceral reaction that had left him on his knees, his gut hollow with pain, his throat raw with the howl that burst from him.

That's when he realized what he'd done. He'd sent her away, the greatest gift to come into his miserable life. In that moment, he knew what the hollowness, the despair, deep inside him was. He was in love with his wife. And he'd sent her away.

He'd wanted to go to her immediately, to beg her forgiveness—but he couldn't. He had to get himself straight first. He had to work on the things he'd shoved down deep. She'd told him to fight for her, and he'd been a coward.

Well, no more. He wasn't ready to quit. He wasn't going to quit. He'd done everything he could to come to her a changed man. Everything he could to deserve her.

He stared at the door to her room, ready to burst through

it and see if she was all right. It was taking too long and he was about to go crazy with fear. But then the door opened and the doctor came out.

"How is she?"

The man looked up from the chart he was holding. "Signora Scott will be fine. But she needs rest, *signore*. A woman in her condition should not be working outside in the heat of the day." He shook his head, then consulted the chart again. "She is dehydrated, but the fluids will take care of that. I want to keep her for observation, because of the baby, but she should be able to go home again in a few hours if all remains stable."

Shuddering relief coursed through him, leaving his knees weak. He put a hand on the wall to hold himself upright. He was about to ask if he could see her when Teresa Corretti came out of the room. She was an elfin woman, but she had a spine of steel. He'd seen that the instant he'd met her. Right now, she was looking at him with a combination of fury and concern.

"She will see you," she said. "But don't you dare upset her, young man. If you do, I will not be responsible."

He took her meaning quite well, especially since it was accompanied by a hard look that said she'd like to rip his balls off and feed them to him if he harmed a hair on her granddaughter's head.

She jerked her head toward the door. "Go, then. But remember what I said."

"Sì, signora," he replied. Then he took a deep breath and went inside.

His heart turned over at the sight of Lia in a hospital bed. She was sitting up, but her normally golden skin was pale, and her head was turned away from him as she gazed through the window at the parking lot beyond.

"Lia." His throat was tight. His chest ached. He'd been

through so much this past month, so many emotions. He hadn't thought seeing her again would be so hard, but he should have known better. He'd done his best to destroy her feelings for him, hadn't he?

"Why are you here, Zach?" she asked, still not looking at him.

He went over to the bed and sat in the chair beside it. He did not touch her, though he desperately wanted to. "To say I'm sorry."

Her head turned. Bright blue-green eyes speared into him. "You have come all this way to say you are sorry? For what? Breaking my heart? Abandoning your baby?" She waved a hand as if to dismiss him. "Take your apologies and leave. I do not need them."

His chest was so tight he thought he might start to hyperventilate at any moment. But he swallowed the fear and looked at her steadily. He could do this. He *would* do this.

"I'm ready to fight," he said.

She blinked. "Fight? I don't want to fight, Zach. Go away."

He took her hand this time. He had to touch her, needed to touch her. She flinched but did not try to pull away. Currents of heat swirled in the air between them, like always. It gave him hope.

"No, I want to fight for you. For us."

She turned her head away again, and his heart felt as if someone had put it in a vise and turned the screws. Her lip trembled, and something like hope began to kindle again inside his soul. If she was affected by his words, maybe it wasn't too late.

But it was a fragile hope. He'd done too much to her to deserve a second chance. He'd taken her love and thrown it away. He knew what kind of life she'd had, how she'd been deserted by her father and ignored by her family, and he'd pushed her away just the same as they had.

He'd discarded her when he should have fought for her. He'd figured it out finally. He just hoped it wasn't too late.

"You come here now and say this to me," she said, her voice thready. "Why should I believe you? What has changed in the past month? Do you dare to tell me you realized you cannot live without me?"

She'd turned back to him then, her voice gaining in intensity until he could feel the heat of her anger blistering through him. Her eyes flashed and her red hair curled and tumbled over her shoulders and he was suddenly unsure what to say. What if he got it wrong? What if she sent him away?

He couldn't let that happen. He'd do anything to prevent it.

"Yes," he said firmly. "That is exactly what I intend to say."

Lia's chest ached, and not from her fainting episode. She'd gotten overheated, her grandmother had told her. She'd fainted on her terrazzo, though Zach had caught her before she'd hit the hard marble. And then he'd carried her up to the house and ordered someone to call an ambulance.

Now she was here, feeling like a fool for getting too hot and fainting. She was also getting flustered by Zach's presence. By the words she could hardly believe he'd uttered.

They made her heart sing. But she was also afraid.

"I want you to come home," he said. "I want to be with you."

Lia swallowed. "I'm not sure I can do that," she said softly.

His expression was stark. Terrified.

"Leaving was hard," she continued, resolutely ignoring the ache in her heart, "but I've started to live my life without you. And if you drag me back, if you pull me into your life and then decide you can't handle a wife and child, I'm not sure I will survive that heartbreak a second time."

"I went to see a doctor," he told her quietly. His hand was

still wrapped around hers, and she felt the tremor shake him as he said those words.

"Oh, Zach." There was a lump in her throat.

"I can't guarantee I won't have dreams. I'm pretty sure I will have them. But I know how to deal with them now."

He stood, moved until he was so close she could reach up and touch him if she wanted to.

He pressed her hand to his heart. It beat hard and fast beneath her palm.

"I told the doctor about the gun and how I couldn't pull the trigger. And I'm taking medicine, Lia. It helps with the fear and anger. I didn't want to take it before. I thought I could handle it myself. But the truth is I can't. No one can. We aren't meant to handle these things alone."

Her vision blurred again, but this time it was due to the moisture in her eyes. "I'm glad you got help, Zach. Really glad." She turned her hand in his and squeezed. "But I'm still not sure coming back is the right thing. You hurt me when you sent me away, and I can't be hurt like that again. I can't let our baby be hurt, either."

He looked suddenly uncertain, as if he'd come across a roadblock he hadn't expected.

"And if I said I love you?"

Her heart went into free fall before soaring again. She told herself to be realistic, practical. To not simply accept what he said at face value because she'd wanted it for so long. She'd been disappointed so many times by her need to be loved. She would not let it rule her now.

"Why do you love me, Zach? Why now?"

He sank onto the chair beside the bed again. His eyes were intense, burning, as they caught hers and held.

"I love you because you give me hope. Because you see the good in me instead of the bad. Because you believe in me. Because you made me believe in myself." He sucked in a breath, his nostrils flaring. His voice, when he spoke again, was fierce. "I'm glad I lived, Lia. I'm glad I'm here with you, and even if you send me away, even if you never let me back in your life again, I won't regret a single moment I spent with you."

She felt a tear spill free and slide down her cheek. She dashed her hand over her face, as if she could hide her tears from him.

But he saw them, of course.

"It kills me when you cry," he said softly. "And it kills me to think I caused it."

Her heart squeezed. "I'm not crying because I'm unhappy. I'm hormonal."

It wasn't the truth, of course, but she stubbornly didn't want to admit she was crying because of him. She'd cried too much over him this past month already.

"I love you, Lia. I don't want you to cry. I want to make you happy. Always."

She was trembling hard now, but she turned away from him and tried to focus on the cars moving in the parking lot outside. How could she cross this bridge again? How could she make herself vulnerable once more to all the vicissitudes of a relationship with this man?

"I—I want to believe you. But I'm not sure I can."

"You can," he said. "I know you can. Isn't that what you said to me?"

She dropped her chin to her chest and sucked in a huge breath. She had said that to him. She'd said it and she'd been angry when he hadn't listened. When he'd denied it and sent her away.

How could she do the same thing to him? How could she be a coward, when he ultimately had not? He was facing his fears, finally. How could she be any different?

"I will try," she said softly. "That's the best I can do."

* * *

She left the hospital that evening. She'd thought she was going back to her grandmother's house, but when Zach turned a different direction, she could only look at him. He glanced over at her.

"I'm taking you to our home," he said. "It will be more private for us."

She lifted an eyebrow. "I wasn't aware we had a home in Sicily."

He shrugged. "Actually, it's a rental. If you like it, I'll buy it for you. And if you don't, I'll buy you another one somewhere else."

A little thrill went through her, in spite of her resolve to take this slowly and carefully. She'd agreed to try to believe he loved her, and that this could work between them, but she hadn't actually thought about what that would entail. Of course they would go to a home they shared. And of course they would be alone together.

So much for her resolve when her pulse picked up at the thought.

Zach took her to a large, beautiful villa with a view of the sea. She could tell because the lights of homes carpeting the island below them gave way to a vast inky darkness. The lights of a ship moved alone on that black surface, isolated from civilization.

She stood on the balcony and let the sea breeze ruffle her hair, feeling like that ship, adrift on an immense sea of uncertainty and fear.

"You should be sitting," Zach told her. "You've had a rough day."

"In more ways than one," she replied.

"Yes."

She felt bad for saying it then, for making him quietly accept her lingering animosity. But it was the only thing standing between her and complete capitulation, so she nursed it in wounded silence. Until it burst from her, like now.

"I'm sorry," she said, turning to him. He stood so near, hands in pockets, dark eyes trained on her.

"Don't be. I deserve it."

She sighed. "No. I'm just afraid, Zach. Afraid it won't be real."

"Maui," he said, his voice so quiet, and her heart pinched because he knew.

"Yes, Maui." She took a deep breath. "We had such a perfect time there. I thought there was something between us, and then it stormed and you became a stranger to me. You showed me that I didn't matter, that nothing we'd shared mattered."

"I'm more sorry for that than you know. But I was damaged, Lia, and I was afraid of that damage somehow spilling over onto you. You, the sweetest, most innocent woman I've ever known. How could I tarnish that brightness of yours with my darkness?"

"You can't be undamaged now," she said, shaking her head. "Not in a month. Not ever. So how do you propose to reconcile what you think of as damage—which I think of as life, by the way—with our relationship now? Will the first dream or episode send you running again?"

He sighed. "I deserve every bit of your condemnation. No, I am not undamaged. But none of us are, are we? I'm learning to cope with that." He paused for a moment. "I found the medal you left behind. I put it with the others. And they're in my desk drawer at home, where I see them every day when I open it. I earned them with my blood and sweat and tears. And I owe it to those who gave their lives for me to honor their memories by not running from my own."

A chill slid down her spine as he spoke. And she knew, deep in her heart, that what he said was true. That he'd turned a corner somewhere in his journey and he was finally on the way to healing.

She took a step toward him, reached up and caressed the smooth skin of his jaw. "Zach," she said, her heart full.

He turned his face into her palm and kissed it. "I love you, Lia Corretti Scott. Now and forever. You saved me."

A dam burst inside her then. She went into his arms with a tiny cry, wrapped herself around him while he held her tight. This was what it meant to love and be loved. To belong.

"No, I think we saved each other."

"Does this mean you still love me?" he asked, his voice warm and breathless in her ear.

She leaned back so she could see his face. His beautiful, beloved face. "I never stopped, *amore mio*. I never could."

"Grazie a Dio," he said. And then he kissed her as a full moon began to rise from the sea, lighting their world with a soft, warm glow.

EPILOGUE

LIA WOKE IN the middle of the night. She sat up with a start, certain she'd heard a cry. It was raining outside, a typical summer storm. A jagged bolt of lightning shot across the sky, followed by a crack of thunder.

The bed beside her was empty, the sheets tossed back. She grappled on the nightstand for the baby monitor, but it was gone. Sighing, she climbed from bed and put on her robe. Then she padded out the door and down the hallway to the nursery.

Zach looked up as she entered. He was sitting in the rocking chair, cradling their son in his arms while the baby cooed and yawned. Zach smiled, and her heart lurched with all the love she felt for the two men in her life.

"I believe it was my turn," she said tiredly.

"I was awake," he said, shrugging.

"A dream?" she asked, thinking of the storm and worrying for him.

"I was dreaming, yes," he said. "But not about the war."

"You weren't?"

He looked down at their baby, his sexy mouth curling in a smile. "No. I dreamed I was flying. And then I dreamed I was on a beach with you."

"What happened then?"

"I could tell you," he said, slanting a look up at her. "But I'd far rather show you."

Heat prickled her skin, flooded her core. "I'll look forward to it," she said softly.

"Give me a few minutes." His gaze was on his son again.

Lia pulled a chair next to the rocker and sat down beside him. Zach reached out and took her hand in his, and they sat there with their baby until his little eyes drifted shut. Gently, Zach placed him in his crib—and then he took Lia by the hand and led her back to their bedroom.

Later, as she lay in his arms and drifted off to sleep, she knew she'd gotten everything she ever wanted.

Love. Family. Belonging.

* * * * *

A SCANDAL IN
THE HEADLINES

CAITLIN CREWS

CHAPTER ONE

"WHAT THE HELL are you doing on my boat?"

Elena Calderon froze in the act of polishing the luxurious teak bar in the yacht's upper lounge. The low growl of the male voice from across the room was laced with a stark and absolute authority that demanded instant obedience. And she knew exactly who he was without looking up. *She knew.*

She felt it slam into her, through her, like a sledgehammer.

Alessandro Corretti.

He wasn't supposed to be here, she thought wildly. He hadn't used this boat in over a year! He usually rented it out to wealthy foreigners instead!

"I'm polishing the bar," she managed to say. She kept her tone even because that was how a stewardess on a luxury yacht spoke to the guests. To say nothing of the owner himself. But she still couldn't bring herself to look at him.

He let out harsh kind of laugh. "Is this some kind of joke?"

"It's no joke." She tapped her fingers on the bar before her. "It's teak and holly, according to the chief steward."

She'd told herself repeatedly that what had happened during that one mad dance six months ago had been a fluke. More to do with the wine and the music and the romantic ballroom setting than the man—

But she didn't quite believe it. Warily, she looked up.

He was half-hidden in the shadows of the lounge's entryway, with all of that bright Sicilian sun blazing behind him—but she recognized him. A bolt of sensation sizzled over her skin, then beneath it, stealing her breath and setting off a hum deep and low inside.

Alessandro Corretti. The man who had blown her life to bits with one single dance. The man she knew was bad no matter how intensely attractive he was and no matter how drawn she was to him, against her will. The man who was even worse than her lying, violent, criminally inclined ex-fiancé, Niccolo.

Elena hadn't dared go to the *polizia* when she'd fled from Niccolo, fearing his family's connections. Alessandro's family, however, made those connections seem insubstantial, silly. They were the Correttis. They were above the law.

And yet when Alessandro stepped farther into the lounge, out of the shadows, Elena's chest tightened in immediate, helpless reaction—and none of it terror. Her breath caught. Her heart sped up. She yearned, just as she had six months ago, as if her body believed he was good. Safe.

"Was that an attempt at levity?" There was nothing in the least bit safe about his hard voice, or that look in his eyes. "Hilarious, I'm sure. But you still haven't answered my question, Elena."

Today the usually breathtakingly sophisticated eldest heir to and current CEO of Corretti Media and its vast empire looked…rumpled. Uncharacteristically disheveled, from his thick, messy dark hair to his scuffed shoes. His tall, muscled strength was contained in a morning suit with the torn jacket hanging open over his lean, hard chest. He had a black eye, scrapes and cuts that only accentuated his aristocratic cheekbones, a slightly puffy lip, even scraped knuckles. And that famous, cynical mouth of his was set in a grim line while his too-dark green eyes were ferociously narrowed. Directly at her.

What was truly hilarious, Elena thought then, was that she'd actually convinced herself he wouldn't recognize her in the unlikely event that they ran into each other on this yacht she'd been repeatedly assured he hardly used. She'd told herself that he had world-altering interactions like the one she wanted to forget with every woman he'd ever clapped eyes on. That it was simply what he did.

And if some intuitive, purely feminine part of her had whispered otherwise, she'd ignored it.

"I'm not trespassing," she said with a calm she wished she felt. "I work here."

"Like hell you do."

"And yet here I am." With a wave of her hand she indicated the smart tan-colored skirt she wore, the pristine black T-shirt tucked in at the waist, the sensible boat shoes. "Uniform and all."

His dark eyes were trained on her, hard and cold. She remembered the fire in them that night six months ago, the impossible longing, and felt the lack of both as a loss.

"You are…what, exactly? A maid?" His voice managed to be both incredulous and fierce at once, and she ordered herself not to react as he began to walk toward her, all impeccable male lines and sheer masculine poetry despite the beating he'd obviously taken.

Damn him. How could he still affect her like this? It disgusted her. She told herself what she felt now was *disgust*.

"I'm a stewardess. Cleaning is only one of my duties."

"Of course. And when you found yourself possessed

of the urge to trade in designer gowns and luxury cars for actual labor, I imagine it was pure coincidence that made you choose this particular yacht—my yacht—on which to begin your social experiment?"

"I didn't know it was yours." Not when she'd answered the original advert, when she'd decided waitressing at the tourist restaurants along the stunning Sicilian coast was too risky for someone who didn't want to be found. And now she wished she'd heeded her impulse to keep running when she'd discovered the truth. Why hadn't she? "When I found out, I'd already been working here a week. I was told you rarely, if ever, used it."

If she was honest, she'd also thought he owed her, somehow. She'd liked the idea that Alessandro had been paying her, however indirectly. That he was affected in some way by what that dance had put into motion, no matter if he never knew it. It had felt like a kind of power, and she needed every hint of that she could find.

"What a curious risk to take for so menial a position," he murmured.

He was even closer now, right there on the other side of the bar, and Elena swallowed hard when he put his hands down on the gleaming surface with the faintest hint of a sensual menace she didn't want to acknowledge. If she'd been on the same side he was, he would have been caging her between them. She couldn't seem to shake the image— or perhaps it was that the barrier seemed flimsy indeed when the way he was looking at her made something coil inside of her and pull taut.

"It's an honest job."

"Yes." His dark green gaze was laced through with something she might have called grief, were he anyone else. "But you are not an honest woman, are you?"

Elena couldn't hide the way she flinched at that, and she

wasn't sure what she hated more—that he saw it, or that she obviously cared what this man thought about her. When he didn't know anything about her. When all he'd ever known about her was that shocking, overwhelming explosion of awareness between them at that long-ago charity ball.

He couldn't know how bitterly she regretted her own complicity in what had happened that night, how her reaction to him still shamed her. He couldn't know what Niccolo had planned, what she'd very nearly helped him do. He knew how blind she'd been, sadly, but he couldn't know the truth....

But Alessandro was just like Niccolo, she reminded herself harshly then, no matter her physical reaction to him. Same kind of man, same kind of "family business," same kind of brutal exploitation of whoever and whatever he could use. She'd had a lot of time to read about Alessandro Corretti and the infamous Corretti family in her six months on the run. There was no telling what he might know about his rival Niccolo Falco's broken engagement and missing fiancée, or how he might use that information.

She had to be careful.

"I already know what you think of me," she said, keeping her voice cool. Unbothered. "And anyway, people change."

"Circumstances change." There was no denying the bitterness in his voice then, or stamped all over that battered, arrogant face. She told herself it didn't move her at all, that she didn't feel the insane, hastily checked urge to reach over and cover his hand with hers. "People never do."

Sadly, she knew he was right. Because if she'd changed at all—if she'd learned anything from these months of running and hiding—she wouldn't have found this man compelling in the least. She would have run screaming in the opposite direction, flung herself from the side of the boat and swum for the Palermo shoreline they'd left more than ninety minutes ago.

"If you don't want me here—"

"I don't."

She swallowed, fighting to remain calm. She couldn't afford to lose her temper, not when he could ruin everything with a single telephone call. It would take no more than that to summon Niccolo from that villa of his she'd nearly moved into outside of Naples. Alessandro would probably even enjoy throwing her back into that particular fire. Why not? The Correttis had been at bitter odds with Niccolo's family for generations. What was one more bit of collateral damage?

Especially when Alessandro already thought she was the sort of woman who aspired to be a pawn in the kind of games men like him played.

Think, she ordered herself. *Stop reacting to him and think about how best to play this!*

"Then I'll go, of course." Given what she knew he believed about her, he must imagine she'd be impervious to threats. Which meant she had to be exactly that. She smiled coolly. "But we're out at sea."

He shifted then, only slightly, and yet a new kind of danger seemed to shimmer in the air of the lounge, making Elena's pulse heat up and beat thick and wild beneath her skin. His dark green eyes gleamed.

"Then I certainly hope you can swim."

"I never learned," she lied. She tilted her head, let her smile flirt with him. "Are you offering me a lesson?"

"I suppose I can spare a lifeboat," he mused, that gleam in his eyes intensifying. "You'll wash up somewhere soon enough, I'm sure. The Mediterranean is a small sea." One corner of his battered mouth quirked up. "Relatively speaking."

She didn't understand how she could still find this man so beautiful, like one of the old gods sent down to earth again. Savage and seductive, even as he threatened to set her adrift. But she knew better than to believe her eyes, her traitorous body, that awful yearning that moved in her like white noise, louder by the second…. She knew what and who he was.

She shouldn't have had to keep reminding herself of that. But then, she couldn't understand why she wasn't afraid of him the way she'd come to be afraid of Niccolo, when she also knew Alessandro was far more dangerous than Niccolo could ever be.

"You're not going to toss me overboard," she said with quiet certainty.

A different kind of awareness tightened the air between them, reminding her again of that fateful dance. The way he'd held her so close, the things she'd simply *known* when she'd looked at him. That curve in his hard mouth deepened, as if he felt it, too. She knew he did, the way she'd known it then.

"Of course not," he said, those dark eyes much too hot, something far more alarming than temper in them now. Memories. That old longing. She had to be careful. "I have staff for that."

"Alternatively," she said, summoning up that smile again, forcing herself to stand there so calmly, so carelessly, "though less dramatically, I admit—you could simply let me go when we arrive at the next port."

He laughed then, and rubbed his hands over his bruised face. He winced slightly, as if he'd forgotten he was hurt.

"Maybe I'm not making myself clear." When he lowered his hands his gaze burned fierce and hot. She remembered that, too. And it swept through her in exactly the same way it had before, consuming her. Scalding her. "Niccolo

Falco's woman is not welcome here. Not on this boat, not on my island, not anywhere near me. So you swim or you float. Your choice."

"I understand," she said after a moment, making it sound as if he bored her. She should have been racked with panic. She should have been terrified. Instead, she shrugged. "You must have your little revenge. I rejected you, therefore you have to overreact and throw me off the side of a yacht." She rolled her eyes. "I understand that's how it works for men like you."

"Men like me," he repeated quietly, as if she'd cursed at him. He sounded tired when he spoke again, and it made something turn over inside of her. But she kept on.

"You're a Corretti," she said. "We both know what that means."

"Petty acts of revenge and the possibility of swimming lessons?" he asked dryly, but there were shadows in that dark gaze, shadows she couldn't let herself worry about, no matter that strange sensation inside of her.

"It also means you are well known to be as cruel and occasionally vicious as the rest of the crime syndicate you call your family." Her smile was brittle. "How lucky for me that I've encountered you on two such occasions."

"Ah, yes," he said, his dark gaze hard as his cynical mouth curved again, and something about that made her legs feel weak beneath her. "I remember this part. The personal attacks, the insulting comments about my family. You need a new topic of conversation, Elena."

He didn't move but, even so, she felt as if he loomed over her, around her, and she knew he was remembering it even as she did—those harsh words they'd thrown at each other in the middle of a ballroom in Rome, the wild flush she'd felt taking over her whole body, the way he'd only looked at her and sent that impossible, terrifying fire roaring through her. She felt it again now. Just as hot. Just as bright.

And just like then, it was much too tempting. She wanted to leap right into the heart of it, burn herself alive—

She shoved it aside, all of it, her heart pounding far too hard against her ribs. There was so much to lose if she didn't handle this situation correctly—if Niccolo found her. If she forgot what she was doing, and why. If she lost herself in Alessandro Corretti's dark, wild fire the way she still wanted to do, all these months later, despite what had happened since then.

"Far be it from me to stand in the way of your pettiness," she said, jerking her gaze from his and moving out from behind the bar. She headed for the doorway to the deck and the sunshine that beckoned, bright and clear. "It's a beautiful day for a swim, isn't it? Quite summery, really, for May. I'm sure I won't drown in such a small sea."

"Elena. Stop."

She ignored him and kept moving.

"Don't make me put my hands on you," he said then, almost conversationally, but the dark heat in it, the frank sensual promise, almost made her stumble. And, to her eternal shame, stop walking. "Who knows where that might lead? There are no chaperones here. No avid eyes to record our every move. No fiancé to watch jealously from the side of the dance floor. Which reminds me, are congratulations in order? Are you Signora Falco at last?"

Elena fought to breathe, to keep standing. To keep herself from telling this man—this dangerous, ruinous man— the truth the way every part of her screamed she should. She hardly knew him. She couldn't trust him. She didn't know what made her persist in thinking she could.

She thought of her parents—her loving mother and her poor, sick father—and what they must believe about her now, what Niccolo must have told them. The pain of that shot through her, taking her breath. And on some level, she knew, she deserved it. She thought about the unspoiled little village she'd come from, nestled on a rocky hill that ran along the sea, looking very much the same as it had hundreds of years ago. She needed to protect it. Because she was the only one who could. Because her foolishness, her selfishness and her vanity, had caused the problem in the first place.

She'd chosen this course when she'd run from Niccolo. She couldn't change it now. She didn't know what it was about Alessandro, even as surly and forbidding as he was today, that made her want to abandon everything, put herself in his hands, bask in that intense ruthlessness of his as if it could save her.

As if he could. Or would.

"No," she said. She cleared her throat. She had to be calm, cool. The woman he thought she was, unbothered by emotion, unaffected by sentiment. "Not yet."

"You've not yet had that *great honor*, then?"

She didn't know what demon possessed her then, but she looked back over her shoulder at him as if his words didn't sting. He was lounging back against the bar, gazing at her, and she knew what that fire in his eyes meant. She'd known in Rome, too. She felt the answering kick of heat deep in her core.

"I can't think of a greater one," she said. Lying through her teeth.

He watched her for a long, simmering moment, his gaze considering.

"And because you feel so honored you have decided to take a brief sabbatical from your engagement to tour the world as a stewardess on a yacht? My yacht, no less? When Europe is overrun by yachts this time of year, swarming like ants in every harbor, and only one of them belongs to me?"

"I always wished I'd taken a gap year before university," she said airily. Careless and offhanded. "This is my chance to remedy that."

"And tell me, Elena," he said, his voice curling all around her, tangling inside of her, making her despair of herself for all the ways he made her weak when she should have been completely immune to him, when she *wanted* to be immune to him, "what will happen when this little journey is complete? Will you race back into the *great honor* of your terrible marriage, grateful for the brief holiday? Docile and meek, as a pissant like Niccolo no doubt prefers?"

She didn't want to hear him talk about Niccolo. About the marriage he'd warned her against in such stark terms six months ago. It made something shudder deep inside of her, then begin to ache, and she didn't want to explore why that was. She never had.

This is not about you, she snapped at herself then, reminding herself how much more she had to lose this time. *And it's certainly not about him.*

"Of course," she said with an air of surprise, as if he really might believe that Niccolo Falco's fiancée was acting as a stewardess on a yacht simply to broaden her horizons before her marriage. As if she did. "I think that's the whole point."

"I've witnessed more than my share of terrible marriages," he said then, a bleakness beneath his voice and moving in his too-dark eyes as he regarded her. It made her shiver, though she tried to hide it. "I was only yesterday jilted at the start of one myself, as a matter of fact. My blushing bride was halfway down the aisle when she thought better of it." His mouth curved, cynical and hard.

"And yet yours, I guarantee you, will be worse. Much worse."

She didn't want to think about Alessandro's wedding, jilted groom or not. Much less her own. Once again, she fought back the strangest urge to explain, to tell him the truth about Niccolo, about her broken engagement. But he was not her friend. He was not a safe harbor. If anything, he was worse than Niccolo. Why was that so hard to keep in mind?

"I'm sorry about your wedding." It was the best she could do, and she was painfully aware that it wasn't even true.

"I'm not," he said, and she understood the tone he used then, at last, because she recognized it. *Self-loathing.* She blinked in surprise. "Not as sorry as I should be, and certainly not for the right reasons."

Alessandro straightened then, pushing away from the bar. He moved toward her—stalked toward her, if she was precise—and she turned all the way around to face him fully. As if that might dull the sheer force of him. Or her wild, helpless reaction to him that seemed to intensify the longer she was in his presence.

It did neither.

He stopped when he was much too close, that marvelous chest of his near enough that if she'd dared—if she'd taken leave of her senses entirely, if she'd lost what small grip she had left on what remained of her life—she could have tipped her head forward and pressed her mouth against that hard, beautiful expanse that she shouldn't have let herself notice in the first place.

"Tell me why you're here," he said in a deceptively quiet voice that made her knees feel like water. "And spare me the lies about gap-year adventures. I know exactly what kind of woman you are, Elena. Don't forget that. I never have."

There was no reason why that comment should have felt like he'd slapped her, when she already knew what he thought of her. When she was banking on it.

"You're hardly one to talk, are you? Remember that I know who you are, too."

"Wrong answer."

Elena sighed. "You were never meant to know I was here. Let me off when we reach port—any port—and it will be like I was never on this boat at all."

And for a moment, she almost believed he would do it.

That he would simply let it drop, this destructive awareness that hummed between them and the fact she'd turned up on his property. That he would shrug it off. But Alessandro's mouth curved again, slightly swollen and still so cynical, his eyes flashed cold, and she knew better.

"I don't think so," he said, his gaze moving from hers to trace her lips.

"Alessandro—" she began, but cut herself off when his gaze slammed back into hers. She jumped slightly, as if he'd touched her. She felt burned straight through to the core, as if he really had.

"I've never had someone try to spy on me so ineptly before," he told her in a whisper that still managed to convey all of that wild heat, all of that lush *want*, that she felt crackling between them and that would, she knew, be the end of her if she let it. The end of everything. "Congratulations, Elena. It's another first."

"Spy?" She made herself laugh. "Why would I spy on you?"

"Why would you want to marry an animal like Niccolo Falco?" He shrugged expansively, every inch an Italian male, but Elena wasn't fooled. She could see the steel in his gaze, that ruthlessness she knew was so much a part of him. Something else that reminded her of that dance. "You are a woman of mystery, made entirely of unknowables and impossibilities. But you can rest easy. I have no intention of letting you out of my sight."

He smiled then, not at all nicely, and Elena's heart plummeted straight down to her feet and crashed into the floor.

She was in serious trouble.

With Alessandro Corretti.

Again.

It was not until he propped himself up in the decadent outdoor shower off his vast master suite that Alessandro allowed himself to relax. To breathe.

The sprawling island house he'd built here on the small little spit of land, closer to the coast of Sicily than to Sardinia, was the only place he considered his true home. The only place the curse of being a Corretti couldn't touch him.

He shut his eyes and waited for the hot water to make him feel like himself again.

He wanted to forget. That joke of a wedding and Alessia Battaglia's betrayal of the deal they'd made to merge their high-profile families—and, of course, of him. To say nothing of his estranged cousin Matteo, her apparent lover. Then the drunken, angry night he hardly remembered, though the state of his face—and the snide commentary from the *polizia* this morning when he'd woken in a jail cell, hardly the image he liked to portray as the CEO of Corretti Media—told the tale eloquently.

His head still echoed with the nasty, insinuating questions from the paparazzi surrounding his building in Palermo when his brother, Santo, had taken him there this morning, merging with his leftover headache and all various agonies he was determined to ignore.

Did you know your fiancée was sleeping with your cousin? Your bitter rival?

Can the Corretti family weather yet another scandal?

How do the Corretti Media stockholders feel about your very public embarrassment—or your night in jail?

He wanted to forget. All of it. Because he didn't want to think about what a mess his deceitful would-be bride and scheming cousin had left behind. Or how he was ever going to clean it up.

And then there was Elena.

Those thoughtful blue eyes, the precise shade of a perfect Sicilian summer afternoon. The blond hair that he'd first seen swept up behind her to tumble down her back, that she'd worn today in a shorter tail at the nape of her neck. Her elegant body, slender and sleek, as enchanting in that absurd yachting uniform as when he'd first found himself poleaxed by the sight of her in that ballroom six months ago.

Then, she'd worn a stunning gown that had left her astonishingly naked from the nape of her neck to scant millimeters above the swell of her bottom. All of that silken skin *just there.*

His throat went dry at the memory, while the rest of his body hardened as it had the moment he'd laid eyes on her at that charity benefit in Rome. He didn't remember which charity it had been or why he'd attended it in the first place; he only remembered Elena.

"Careful," Santo had said with a laugh, seconds after Alessandro had caught sight of her standing only a few feet away in the crush of the European elite. "Don't you know who she is?"

"Mine," Alessandro had muttered, unable to pull his gaze away from her. Unable to get his bearings at all, as if the world had shuddered to a halt—and then she'd turned.

She'd looked around as if she'd been able to feel the heat of his gaze on her, and then her eyes had met his.

Alessandro had felt it like a hard punch in the gut. Hard, electric, almost incapacitating. He'd felt it—her—everywhere.

His.

She was supposed to be his.

He hadn't had the smallest doubt. And the fact that he'd acquiesced to his grandfather's wishes and agreed to a strategic, business-oriented marriage some two months before had not crossed his mind at all. Why should it have? The woman he was engaged to was as mindful of her duty and the benefits of their arrangement as he was. This, though—this was something else entirely.

And then he'd seen the man standing next to her, a possessive hand at her waist.

Niccolo Falco, of the arrogant Falco family that had given Alessandro's grandfather trouble in Naples many years before. Niccolo, who fancied himself some kind of player when he was really no more than the kind of petty criminal Alessandro most despised. Alessandro had hated him for years.

It was impossible that this woman—*his woman*—could have anything to do with scum like Niccolo.

"The rumor is her father has some untouched land on the Lazio coast north of Gaeta," Santo had said into his ear, seemingly unaware of the war Alessandro was fighting on the inside. "He is also quite ill. Niccolo thinks he's struck gold. Romance the daughter, marry her, then develop the land. As you do."

"Why am I not surprised that a pig like Niccolo would have to leverage a woman into marrying him?" Alessandro had snarled, jerking a drink from a passing waiter's tray and draining it in one gulp. He hadn't even tasted it. He'd seen only her. Wanted only her.

"Apparently that's going around," Santo had muttered.

Alessandro had only glared at him.

"Are you really going to marry that Battaglia girl in cold blood?" Santo had asked then, frowning, his dark green eyes so much like Alessandro's own. "Sacrifice yourself to one of the old man's plots?"

Santo was the only person alive who could speak to him like that. But Alessandro was a Corretti first, like it or not. Marrying a Battaglia was a part of that. It made sense for the family. It was his responsibility. He would marry for duty, not out of deceit.

Alessandro was not Niccolo Falco.

"I will do my duty," he had said. He'd tapped his empty glass to his brother's chest, smiling slightly when Santo took it from him. "A concept you should think about yourself, one of these days."

"Heaven forbid," Santo had replied, grinning.

The orchestra had started playing then, and Alessandro had ordered himself to walk away from the strange woman—*Niccolo Falco's woman*—no matter how bright her eyes were or how that simple fact made his chest ache. There was no possibility that he could start anything with a woman who was embroiled with the Falcos. It would ignite tempers, incite violence, call more attention to the dirty past Alessandro had been working so hard to put behind him.

Walking away had been the right thing to do. The only reasonable option.

But instead, he'd danced with her, and sealed his fate.

CHAPTER TWO

AND NOW SHE was here.

Alessandro had thought he was hallucinating when he'd first seen her on the yacht. He'd thought the stress was finally getting to him—that or the blows to his head. *You've finally snapped,* he'd told himself.

But his body had known better. It knew *her.*

He could still feel the heat of her when he'd touched her all those months ago, when he'd pulled her close to dance with her, when his fingers had skimmed that tempting hollow in the small of her back and made her breath come too fast. He still remembered her sweet, light scent, and how it had made him hunger to taste her, everywhere.

He still did. Even though there was no possible way that he could have ignored his responsibilities back then and pursued her, even if she hadn't been neck-deep in a rival family, engaged to one of the enemies of the Corretti empire. He'd told himself that all he'd wanted after that charity ball was to forget her, and he'd tried. God help him, but he'd tried. And there'd certainly been more than enough to occupy him.

There'd been the pressure of managing his grandfather's schemes, the high-profile wedding and the docklands regeneration project the old man had been so determined would unite the warring factions of the Corretti family.

"You will put an end to this damned feud," Salvatore had told him. "Brother against brother, cousins at war with one another. It's gone too far. It's no good."

It was still so hard to believe that he'd died only a few weeks ago, when Alessandro had always believed that crafty old Salvatore Corretti would live forever, somehow. But then again, it was just as well he'd missed that circus of a wedding yesterday.

And if Alessandro had woken from a dream or two over the past few months, haunted by clever eyes as blue as the sky, he'd ignored it. What he'd felt on that dance floor was impossible, insane.

The truth was, he'd never wanted that kind of mess in his life.

His late father, Carlo, had always claimed it was his intensity of emotion that made him do the terrible things he'd done—the other women, the shady dealings and violently corrupt solutions. Just as his mother, Carmela, had excused her own heinous acts—like the affair she'd confessed to yesterday that made Alessandro's adored sister, Rosa, his uncle's daughter—by blaming it on the hurt feelings Carlo's extramarital adventures had caused her.

Alessandro wanted no part of it.

He'd viewed his calm, dutiful marriage as a kind of relief. An escape from generations of misery. He was furious enough that Alessia Battaglia had left him at the altar—what would he have done if he had *felt* for her?

He'd felt far too much on a dance floor for a woman he couldn't respect. Far more than he'd believed he could. Far more than he should have. It still shook him.

Alessandro turned the water off and reached for a towel, letting the bright sun play over his body as he walked into his rooms. He didn't want to think about the wedding-that-wasn't. He didn't want to think about the things Santo had told him this morning en route to the marina—all the business implications of losing that connection with Alessia's father, the slimy politician who held the Corretti family's future in his greedy hands. He didn't want to think at all. He didn't want to feel those things that hovered there, right below the surface—his profound sense of personal failure chief among them.

And luckily, he didn't have to. Because Elena Calderon had delivered herself directly into his hands, the perfect distraction from all of his troubles.

He didn't care that she was almost certainly on some kind of pathetic mission from Niccolo and the Falco family, who had been openly jealous of the Corretti empire for decades. He didn't care why she was here. Only that she was when he'd thought her lost to him forever.

And he still wanted her, with that same wild ferocity that had haunted him all this time.

He'd had every intention of doing his duty to his family, to his grandfather's final wishes, and it had exploded in his face. Maybe it was time to think about what *he* wanted instead.

Maybe it was time to stop worrying about the consequences.

He found her in one of the many shaded, open areas that flowed seamlessly from inside to outside, making the whole house seem a part of the sea and the sky above. She was frowning out at the stretch of deep blue water as if she could call back the yacht he'd sent on its way with the force of her thoughts alone. He'd pulled on a pair of linen trousers and a soft white T-shirt, and he ran his fingers through his damp hair as she turned to him.

That same kick, hard to the gut and low. That same wildfire, that same storm.

His.

She looked almost vulnerable for a moment. Something about the softness of her full mouth, the shadows in her beautiful eyes. The urge to protect her roared through him, warring with the equally strong impulse to tear her open, learn her secrets—to figure out how she could want that jackass Niccolo, to start, and fail to see what kind of scum he was. How she could have felt what Alessandro had felt on that dance floor and turned her back on it the way she had.

How she did this to him when no other woman had ever got beneath his skin at all.

And there were no prying eyes here on his island. No whispers, no gossip. No one had to know she'd ever been here. There would be no business ramifications if he finally put his mouth on her. No ancient feuds to navigate, no humiliating scenes in public with his shareholders and the world looking on. Whatever game she and Niccolo were playing, it wouldn't affect Alessandro at all if he didn't let it.

No consequences. No problems. No reason at all not to do exactly as he wished.

At last.

"I told you to change into something more comfortable," he said, jerking his chin at that dowdy little uniform she still wore, not that it concealed her beauty in the least. Not that anything could. "Why didn't you?"

Clear blue eyes met his, and God, he wanted her. That same old fist of desire closed hard around him, then squeezed tight.

"I don't want to change."

"Is that an invitation?" he asked silkily, enjoying the way her cheeks flushed with the same heat he could feel climb in him. "Don't be coy, Elena. If you want me to take off your clothes, you need only ask."

* * *

His mocking words scalded her, then shamed her.

Because some terrible part of her wanted him to do it—wanted him to strip her right here in the sea air and who cared what came afterward? Some part of her had always wanted that, she acknowledged then. From the first moment their eyes had met.

Elena remembered what it had been like to touch this man, to feel his breath against her cheek, to feel the agonizingly sweet sweep of his hand over the bared skin of her back. She remembered the heat of him, the dizzying expanse of those shoulders in his gorgeous clothes, the impossible beauty of that hard mouth so close to hers.

It lived in her like an open flame. Like need.

She remembered what it had been like between them. For those few stolen moments, the music swelling all around them, making it seem preordained somehow. Huge and undeniable. Fated.

But look where it had led, that careless dance she knew even then she should have refused. Look what had come of it.

"No?" Alessandro looked amused. That sensual gleam in his dark green gaze tugged at her. Hard. "Are you sure?" His amusement deepened into something sardonic, and it didn't help that he looked sleek and dark and dangerous now, the pale colors he wore accentuating his rich olive skin and the taut, ridged wonder of his torso. "You look—"

"Thank you," she said, cutting him off almost primly. "I'm sure."

He really did smile then.

Alessandro sauntered toward her with all the arrogant confidence and ease that made him who he was, and that smile of his made it worse. It made him lethal. His shower had turned the evidence of his misspent night, all those cuts and bruises, into something very nearly rakish. Almost charming.

No one man should be this tempting. No other man ever was.

She had to pull herself together. The reality that she was trapped here, with Alessandro of all people, on this tiny island in the middle of the sea, had chipped a layer or two off the tough veneer she'd developed over the past few months. She was having trouble regaining her balance, remembering the role she knew she had to play to make it through this.

You will lose everything that matters to you if you don't snap out of this, she reminded herself harshly. *Everything that matters to the people you love. Is that what you want?*

He stopped when he stood next to her at the finely wrought rail that separated them from the cliff and the sea below. He was much too close. He smelled crisp and clean, and powerfully male. Elena could feel the connection between them, magnetic and insistent, surrounding them in its taut, mesmerizing pull.

And she had no doubt that Alessandro would use it against her if he could, this raging attraction. That was the kind of thing men like him did without blinking, and she needed to do the same. It didn't matter who she really was, how insane and unlike her this reaction to him had been from the start. It didn't matter what he would think of her—what he already did think of her. What so many others thought of her, too, in fact, or what she thought of herself. And while all of that was like a deep, black hole inside of her, yawning wider even now, she had to find a way to do this, anyway. All that mattered was saving her village, preserving forever what she'd put at risk in the first place.

What was her self-respect next to that? She'd given up her right to it when she'd been silly and flattered and vain enough to believe Niccolo's lies. There were consequences to bad choices, and this was hers.

"I should tell you," he said casually, as if he was commenting on the weather. The temperature. "I have no intention of letting you go this time. Not without a taste."

That was not anticipation that flooded through her then. And certainly not a knife-edge excitement that made her pulse flutter wildly in response. She wouldn't allow it.

"Is that an order?" she asked, her voice cool, as if he didn't get to her at all.

"If you like." He laughed. So arrogant, she thought. So sure of her. Of this. "If that's what gets you off."

"Because most people consider a boss ordering his employee to 'give him a taste' a bit unprofessional." She smiled pure ice at him. She did not think about what *got her off*. "There are other terms for it, of course. Legal ones."

He angled himself so he was leaning one hip against the rail, looking down at her. A faintly mocking curve to his mouth. Bruised and bad, head to foot. And yet still so terribly compelling. Why couldn't what she *knew* rid her of what she *felt*?

"Are we still maintaining that little bit of fiction?" He shrugged carelessly, though his gaze was hot. "Then consider yourself fired. Someone will find another stewardess for my yacht. You, however." His smile then made her blood heat, her traitorous body flush. "You, I think, have a different purpose here altogether."

Elena had to fight herself to focus, to remember. Alessandro Corretti was one of the notorious Sicilian Correttis. More than that, he was the oldest son of his generation, the heir to the legend, no matter how they'd split up the family fortune or the interfamily wars the press reported on so breathlessly. He was who Niccolo aspired to become—the real, genuine article. Corrupt and wicked to the marrow of his bones, by virtue of his blood alone.

He should have disgusted her to the core. He should have terrified her. It appalled her that he didn't. That nothing could break this hold he had on her. That she still felt this odd sense of safety when she was near him, despite all evidence to the contrary.

"Oh, right," she said now. "I forgot." She sighed, though her mind raced as she tried to think of what she would do if she really was the woman he thought she was. If she was that conniving, that amoral. "You think I'm a spy."

"I do."

No man, she thought unsteadily, should look that much like a wolf, or have dark green eyes that blazed when he looked at her that way. It turned her molten, all the way through.

"And what do you think spying on you would get me?"

"I know it will get you nothing. But I doubt you know that. And I'm sure your lover doesn't."

That he called Niccolo her lover made her skin crawl. That she'd had every intention of marrying Niccolo—and probably would have, had fate and this man and Niccolo's own temper not intervened—made her want to curl up into a ball and wail. Or tear off her own skin. But she tacked on a little smile instead, and pretended.

She got better at it all the time.

"You've caught me," she said. "You've unveiled my cunning master plan." She lifted her eyes heavenward. "I'm a spy. And I let myself be caught in the act of…stewardessing. Also part of my devious mission! What could I possibly want next?"

He looked amused again, which only made the ferocity he wore like a shield around him seem that much more pronounced.

"Access," he said easily. "Though I should warn you now, my computers require several layers of security, and if I catch you anywhere near them or near me when I'm having a private conversation, I'll lock you in a closet. Believe that, Elena, if nothing else."

He said that so casually, almost offhandedly, that smile playing around his gorgeous, battered mouth—but she believed him.

"You've clearly given my imaginary career in espionage a great deal of thought," she said carefully, as if she was appeasing a raving lunatic. "But ask yourself, why would I risk this? Or imagine you'd let me?"

His expression of amusement edged over into something else, something voracious and dark, and her pulse jumped beneath her skin.

"Your fiancé was not blind, all those months ago," he said softly. She felt him everywhere, again, as if he was touching her the way she knew he wanted to do. The way she couldn't help but wish he would. "Nor was I."

For a moment, she forgot herself. His dark green eyes were so fierce on hers then, searing into her. Challenging her. The world fell away and there was nothing but him and all the things she couldn't—wouldn't—tell him. All the things she shouldn't want.

And despite herself, she remembered.

Six months ago...

"Tell me your name," he demanded, sweeping her into his arms without even asking her if she'd like to dance with him.

Elena had seen the way he looked at her. She'd *felt* it, like a brand, a claim, from halfway across the room. She told herself that Niccolo, who had gone to fetch her a drink, wouldn't mind *one dance*. They were in full view of half of Rome. It was all perfectly innocent.

She knew she was lying. And yet, somehow, she didn't care.

He was stunning. Overwhelmingly masculine, impossibly attractive and, she thought with a kind of dazed amazement, *hers*. Somehow hers. He looked at her and set her alight. He touched her, and her whole body burst into a hectic storm of sensation, like being dropped headfirst into freezing cold water at the height of summer.

"Your name," he urged her. His hands were on her, hard and hot, making her shiver uncontrollably. His dark head was bent to hers, putting that mesmerizing mouth of his much too close. Tempting her almost past endurance.

"Elena," she whispered. "Elena Calderon."

He repeated it, and made it into something else. A kind of song. It swelled in her, changing her. It hung there between them, like a vow.

"I am Alessandro," he said, and then they'd danced.

He swept her along, every step perfect, his attention on Elena as if she was the only woman in the room. The only woman alive. Lightning struck everywhere they touched, and everywhere they did not, and some shameless, heedless part of her gloried in it, as if she'd been made for this. For only this. For him.

She felt him in the treacherous ache of her breasts, the unmistakable hunger low in her belly and the glazed heat that held her in its relentless grip as surely as he did. She *felt him*—and understood that what she was doing was wrong. Utterly, indisputably wrong.

She understood that she would have to live with this. That this was a defining moment. That her life would be divided into before and after this scorching hot dance, and that she would never again be the person she'd believed she was before this stranger pulled her against him. But his eyes were locked to hers, filled with wonder and fire, and she didn't pull away. She didn't even try—and she understood she'd have to live with that, too.

And then he made it all so much worse.

"You cannot marry him," he said, those dark green eyes so fierce, his face so hard.

It took her longer than it should have to clear her head, to hear him. To hear an insult no engaged woman should tolerate. It was that part that penetrated, finally. That made her fully comprehend the depths of her betrayal.

"Who are you?" she demanded. But she still let him hold her in his arms, like she was something precious to him. Or like she wished she was. "What makes you think you can say something like that to me?"

"I am Alessandro Corretti," he bit out. She stiffened, and his voice dropped to an urgent, insistent growl. "And you know why I can say that. You feel this, too."

"Corretti…" she breathed, the reality of what she was doing, the scope of her treachery, like concrete blocks falling through her one after the next.

He saw it, reading her too easily. His dark eyes flashed.

"You cannot marry him," he said again, some kind of desperation beneath the autocratic demand in his voice. As if he knew her. As if he had the right. "He'll ruin you."

Elena would never know what might have happened then, had she not jerked her gaze away from Alessandro's in confusion—and seen Niccolo there at the side of the dance floor, glaring at the two of them with murder in his black eyes.

Elena was amazed that it was possible to hate herself so much, so fully. And that the shame didn't kill her where she stood.

"How dare you?" she ground out, all her horror at her

own appalling actions in her voice. "I know who you are. I know *what* you are."

"What *I* am?" As if she'd stabbed him.

"Niccolo's told me all about you, and your family."

Something like a laugh. "Of course he has."

"The Correttis are nothing but a pack of violent thugs," she threw at him desperately, quoting Niccolo. "Criminals. One more stain on our country's honor."

"And Niccolo is the expert on honor, I suppose?" His face went thunderous, but his voice stayed cool. Quiet. Somehow, it made him that much more formidable. And it ripped into her like a knife.

"Do you think this will work?" she demanded, furious, and she convinced herself it was all directed at him. All *because* of him. "Do you really think you'll argue me into agreeing with you that *my fiancé*, the man I *love*, is some kind of—"

"You don't strike me as naive," he interrupted her, that fierce, dark edge in his voice, his gaze, even in his hands as he held her. "You must know better. You must."

He shook his head then, and she watched as bitter disappointment washed over him, turning his dark green eyes black. Making that fascinating mouth hard, nearly cruel. Making him look at her as if there had never been that fire between them, as if she couldn't still feel the flames, licking over her skin.

And she would never forgive herself, but she *ached.* She ached.

"Unless you like the money, the cars, the houses and the jewelry." His gaze was a jagged blade as it raked over her, and she bled. "The fancy dresses. Why ask where any of it comes from? Why face so many unpleasant truths?"

"Stop it!" she hissed at him.

"Ignorance is the best defense, I'm sure," he continued in that withering tone. "You can't be a stain on Italy's honor if you're careful not to know any of the sordid details, can you?"

None of this should be possible. A look, a dance, a few words with a total stranger—how could it *hurt?* How could she feel as if her whole world was ripping apart?

"You don't know what kind of woman I am," she told him, desperate to reclaim herself. To fix this. "And you never will. I have standards. I can't wait for Niccolo to do me the great honor of marrying me—to make me a Falco, too. I would never lower myself to Corretti scum like you. *Never.*"

He looked shattered for a moment, but only a moment. Then contempt moved over his fine, arrogant face, and made her stomach twist in an agony she shouldn't feel. He led her to the edge of the floor, gazed at her for one last, searing moment and then walked off into the crowd.

Elena told herself that wasn't grief she felt then, because it couldn't be. Not for a stranger. Not for a dance.

Not for a man she'd been so sure she'd never see again.

"I don't really remember," Elena said now in desperation, standing out on his terrace with only the sea to hear her lies. "It was a long time ago."

Alessandro only watched her, that wolf's smile sharp-edged, digging deep into her and leaving marks. He was much too close, and she hadn't forgotten a thing. Not a single thing.

"Then why are you blushing?" he asked, a knowing look on that battered, somehow even more attractive face—and her heart kicked hard against her ribs.

"I'm not spying on you," she gritted out, trying to break through the tension that gripped her. Trying to pretend he

CHAPTER THREE

HOT. WILD.

She was his.

And she kissed him back as if she wanted to devour him, too.

As if he'd set her on fire and this was how they'd burn, together, in this tumult of heat and glory, and her perfect mouth he couldn't taste enough.

She was better—this was better—than Alessandro had dared imagine in the middle of a hundred nights, when he'd pictured this in stark detail. When the dark fury that she could bewitch him as she had and be so much less of a person than he'd hoped didn't matter.

It didn't matter now, either. Need stormed through him, making him closer to desperate than he'd ever been before.

He wanted her skin against his, slick and sweet. He wanted his hands on those tempting breasts, her enchanting curves. He wanted to lick between her legs and stay there until she screamed. He wanted deep inside of her. *He wanted.* And every kiss, every taste, every little way she moved against him, only drove him higher.

"More," he said, and he picked her up again, yanking that damned skirt up and over her hips.

Deep masculine elation pounded through him when she lifted her legs and wrapped herself around him. And then he was there. Hard and hot against her melting heat, separated only by his trousers and the slightest wisp of material she wore. A delicate shudder moved through her, and for a moment he thought he might lose control.

But Alessandro wanted her too much, and had for too long. He took her mouth again, thrilled when she met him with a passion he could taste. She arched against him, her arms wrapped around his neck, and it wasn't enough.

It would never be enough.

He carried her to one of the loungers scattered about the terrace, then set her down. She was unsteady on her feet, her blue eyes wide and dazed, bright with need, and he wanted her more than he'd ever wanted anyone else. More than he'd imagined it was possible to want.

"Please," Elena said, her voice ragged with desire. The most beautiful thing he'd ever heard. "Don't stop."

Her hands were still on his chest, and he could feel each touch, each caress, directly in his sex. He kissed her again, deep and demanding, ravaging her mouth, and she thrilled him by returning it in kind.

Out of control. So good it hurt. Again. And again.

"These clothes need to come off," he muttered, pulling his mouth away from hers.

Alessandro moved to tug her T-shirt over her head, then hissed out a breath when he threw it aside and she stood there before him, bared to the waist. No bra to block him from her perfect breasts, small and round, with nipples like hard, ripe points. Lovely beyond reason. He nearly shook as his hands went to her skirt, working the zipper and then grabbing on to her panties as he tugged all of it down over her hips and out of his way.

And then Elena was naked. Gloriously, beautifully naked, and she was real and *here* and his. Finally his.

For a moment he only stared at her, a kind of awe sweeping through him as his body went wild, so desperate for her he could hardly bear it. He swept her up and then took her down with him, splaying her out above him as he lay back on the chaise.

Elena twisted against him, and then her frantic hands were on the hem of his T-shirt and he sat up slightly to peel it off. He brushed her hands out of the way to rid himself of his trousers, kicking them aside. And when he pulled her back into place they both sighed in something like reverence. And then she was like silk against him, all over him, soft and naked and hot.

Finally.

Alessandro's heart pounded. He was so hard it bordered on the painful, and then she rolled her hips and moved all of that slick, wet heat against the length of him, and he groaned. He traced the line of her spine down to her bottom, and then bent to take one of those achingly perfect nipples into his mouth. She made a wild, greedy sort of noise, and he couldn't wait. He couldn't take another moment of this magnificent torture.

It had been too long already. It had been forever.

He sat up, holding her against him, her soft thighs falling on either side of his. She knelt astride him, her hands moving from his chest to his shoulders, then burying themselves in his hair. Alessandro reached down between them, sinking his fingers deep inside the molten core of her.

She cried out, and he loved it. He tested her slickness, learned her lush shape, his palm hard against the center of her need. He watched her pretty face flush, felt her hips buck against his hand, and he returned to her breasts, sucking a taut nipple into his mouth and then biting down. Just hard enough.

She broke apart in his arms with a wordless cry, hot and wet in his hand, her head falling forward until her face was pressed into his neck. He lifted her in his arms while she still shook and shuddered, and then he thrust hard and deep inside her.

At last.

She was scalding hot, so deliciously soft, and still in the grips of her climax when he began to move. Alessandro held her hips in his hands and guided her into the rhythm he wanted. Slow, but demanding, catching the fire that was tearing her apart and building it up again with every stroke.

Higher. Hotter. Hungrier.

He heard her breath catch again, felt her stiffen, heard the shocked sound she made in his ear. She gripped his shoulders tight and shook all around him again, just as he wanted. He watched her arch back into the sunlight—so painfully, perfectly beautiful. This woman, *his woman*, lost to her pleasure, mindless and writhing against him, while he moved hard and deep inside of her.

He rolled them over on the lounger, coming on top of her and deeper into her. Alessandro let his head drop down next to hers, and then her arms wrapped around him, her hips meeting his in a wild, uncontrollable dance.

He felt her move beneath him, heard her gasp anew, and each hitch in her breath, each mindless cry, made him want her more. He was so deep inside of her, and they moved together like a dream—like a dream he'd had a thousand times, only much slicker, much hotter, much better.

And this time, when she began to break apart around him, when she threw her head back once more and arched up against him, Alessandro called out her name like the incantation it was and fell right along with her.

Elena came back to herself slowly. Painfully.

She was tucked up against Alessandro's side. He was sprawled out on the lounger beside her, one arm thrown over his head, looking for all the world like some kind of lazy, sated god. There was no reason he should be so appealing, even now, with his dark lashes closed, his arrogant features with the marks of the previous night's violence stamped into his skin. And yet...

She sat up gingerly, surprised her body still felt at all like her own when he'd made it his—made her his—with such devastating completeness. Her body still hummed with pleasure. So much pleasure Elena could hardly believe she'd survived it, that she was still in one piece.

Then again, perhaps she wasn't.

He shifted, and she felt his hand on her back, smoothing its way down to curl possessively over her hip. Impossibly, she felt something in her catch anew. A spark where there should have been nothing but ash and burned-out embers.

Surely this was the end of it. Succumbing to what had burned so bright between them had to have destroyed it, didn't it? But his fingers traced a lazy alphabet across her skin, spreading that fierce glow deep into her all over again, making her realize this wasn't over at all.

Elena had made a terrible mistake, she understood then. There were many ways to pay, and she'd just discovered a brand-new one. Perhaps, on some level, she'd held out the hope that what had surged between them was all smoke, no fire. That indulging it would defeat it.

Now she knew better. Now she knew exactly how hot they burned. She would have to live with that, too.

"Come here," he said, and she felt his voice move in her like magic, making her chest feel tight.

Despite herself, she turned. She looked down at him, bracing herself for a smug expression, a cocky smile—but that hard gaze of his was serious when it met hers. Almost contemplative. And that was worse, because she had no defense against it.

He reached up and traced a lazy line from her collarbone down over the upper swell of her breasts, and there was a dangerous gleam in his eyes when she caught his hand in hers and stopped him.

"Alessandro..." she began, but she didn't know what to say.

He didn't respond. Instead, he tugged her back down beside him, surrounding her once again with all that warm male strength. As if she were safe, she thought in a kind of despair. As if she'd finally come home.

When she knew perfectly well neither one of those things were true.

His gaze darkened as he watched her. He slid a hand around to the nape of her neck, but she was the one who closed the distance between them, pressing her mouth to his, spurred on by a great wealth of emotion she didn't want to understand.

This time, there should have been no wild explosion, no impossible heat. This time, she should have been more in control of herself, of all these things she didn't want to feel.

But his mouth moved on hers and something incandescent poured through her, lighting her up all over again. She felt that spark ignite, felt that same fire grow again inside of her. His kiss was tender, something like loving, and it ripped her into pieces.

She kissed him back, desperately, letting her hands learn his fascinating body all over again, letting herself disappear into this madness that she knew perfectly well would destroy her. It was only a matter of time.

And this time when he slid into her it was a different kind of fire. Slow, deliberate. It stripped her bare, made her eyes fill with tears, battered what was left of her defenses, her carefully constructed veneers. He gazed down at her as he moved inside of her, his dark eyes grave and something more she didn't want to name, as he spun this wicked fire around them.

As he wrecked her totally, inside and out, and she loved every second of it.

And then he pushed them both straight over the edge of the world.

When she woke a second time, the sun was beginning to sink toward the sea, bathing the sky in peaches and golds, and Alessandro wasn't next to her. Elena sat up in confusion, only realizing as she almost let it slide from her that she was draped in something deliciously silky. A robe, she discovered when she frowned down at it.

She pulled it on as she stood, belting it around her waist, and when she looked up she saw him.

He sat at a nearby table in the gathering dusk, a wineglass in one hand, his gaze trained on her. He hadn't bothered with his shirt. A quick glance assured her he was wearing those loose, soft trousers, low on his narrow hips. That lean, smoothly muscled body was even more beautiful from a distance and now, of course, she knew what he could do with it. *She knew.* She snapped her attention back to his face—and went still.

He was watching her with an expression that made her breath catch in her throat. She recognized that look. This was the Alessandro Corretti she remembered, brooding and dark.

And it seemed he'd remembered that he hated her.

Elena steeled herself. It was better this way. This was what she'd wanted. She ran her hands down the front of the silk robe, but then stopped, not wanting him to see any hint of her agitation.

"Sit down," he said, indicating the table before him and the selection of platters spread out across its inlaid mosaic surface. His voice was cold. Impersonal. A slap after what they'd shared, and she was sure he knew it. "You must be hungry."

The moment he said it she realized she was ravenous, and she told herself that was the only reason she obeyed him and sat. Alessandro seethed with a dark menace, lounging there with such studied carelessness, watching her with a slight curl to his lip.

She'd expected this, she reminded herself. She'd known sleeping with him would make him despise her, would confirm his low opinion of her, when he believed her still engaged to Niccolo and all manner of other, horrible things. But it shocked her how much it hurt to see it, how it clawed into her, threatening to spill out of her eyes. She blinked it away.

And then she settled herself in the seat across from him as if she hadn't a care in the world, and gazed down at the food spread out before her. A plate of plump, ripe cheeses, tangy cured meats and an assortment of thick, lush spreads—an olive tapenade, a fragrant Greek-style taramasalata—next to a basket of fresh, golden semolina bread. A serving dish piled high with what looked like an interesting take on the traditional Sicilian caponata, a cooked aubergine salad laden here with succulent morsels of seafood, rich black and green olives and sweet asparagus spears.

Elena took the wine he poured for her, a rich and hearty red, and sipped at it, letting the mellow taste wash over her, wash her clean. She tried to match his seeming insouciance, leaning back in her chair and holding her glass airily, as if she spent most of her evenings with her various lovers in their magnificent island estates. As if this—as if he—was nothing but run of the mill.

"It's quite good," she said, because she thought she should say something.

Not for the first time, she was painfully aware of how deeply unsophisticated she really was—how categorically unsuited to playing in these deep, dark waters with men like him. Niccolo had dressed her up and taught her how to play the part, but here, now, she was forcefully reminded that she was only Elena Calderon, a nobody from a remote village no one had ever heard of, descended from a long line of mostly fishermen. She was out of her league, and then some.

Alessandro only watched her. Something about that cold regard, that dark, silent fury, made her feel raw. Restless.

"Alessandro Corretti with nothing to say?" She attempted a smile. "Shocking."

"Tell me," he said in that calm, easy way that only emphasized the deadly edge beneath. "When you run back to your fiancé and tell him what you did here, how detailed a picture will you paint for him? When you tell him you slept with a man he loathes, will you also tell him how many times you screamed my name?"

Elena paled, even though she knew she shouldn't—that she should have expected this. That she *had* expected this. Her fingers clenched hard on the stem of her glass.

"Or perhaps that's how he likes it. Perhaps he enjoys picturing his woman naked and weeping with ecstasy in another man's arms." His eyes were like coals, hot and black. "Perhaps this is a game the two of you play, and I am only the latest in a long line of targets. Perhaps you are the bullet he aims at his enemies, then laughs about it later."

Elena congratulated herself on achieving precisely what she'd set out to achieve, and in spades. She told herself his opinion of her didn't matter. That the worse it was, the better. The less he thought of her, the less he'd feel compelled to betray her to Niccolo. She took another nonchalant sip of her wine, and ordered herself to enjoy her curiously bitter-tasting triumph.

"Niccolo is a man of many passions," she said, and was perversely satisfied by the flash of temper in his gaze.

"Never mind what that makes you."

She glared at him, determined not to let him see he'd landed a blow. She reminded herself that she could only be used as a bargaining chip if he believed she had some worth.

"Are you calling me a whore?" she asked softly. *This is good,* she assured herself. *This is what you want.*

But even the air seemed painful, shattering all around her. As if it was as broken as she felt.

"Is this some kind of twisted retribution for Rome?" he asked after long moments passed, no hint of green in those dark eyes of his.

"I'm not the one who started this," Elena threw at him before she had time to consider it. Not that he was the first man to think she was a whore, not that Niccolo hadn't covered the same ground extensively—but somehow, this didn't feel anything like the triumph it should have been. It hurt. "I was perfectly happy on that boat. But you had to sweep in and ruin everything, the same way you did—"

She cut herself off, appalled at what she'd nearly said. Her heart was rioting in her chest, and she was afraid to look at him—afraid of what she'd see. Or what he would.

"By all means," he invited her, his voice silk and stone. "Finish what you were saying. What else did I ruin?"

She would never know how she pulled herself together then, enough to look at him with clear eyes and something like a smile on her mouth.

"That was the first ball I'd ever attended, my first night

in Rome," she said, light and something like airy, daring him to refute her. "I felt like a princess. And you ruined it."

"You have no comprehension whatsoever of the damage you do, do you?" He shook his head. "You're like an earthquake, leaving nothing but rubble in your wake."

It's like he knows, a little voice whispered, directly into that dark place inside of her where she hated herself the most. *Like he knows what you nearly let happen.*

She set her glass back down on the table with a sharp click. "I don't know what you want from me."

"I would have thought that much was clear," he replied, a self-mocking curve to that hard mouth she knew too well now. Far too well. "If nothing else. I want you, Elena. Then. Now. Still. God help us both."

Elena clenched her hands together in her lap, everything inside of her seeming to squeeze tight and *ache.* Something deep and heavy sat over the table as the sun disappeared for good, and soft lights came on to illuminate the terrace. She could feel it pressing down on her, into her, and the way he was looking at her didn't help.

"No clever reply to that?" His voice then was quiet, yet no less lethal, and it sliced into her like a jagged blade. "I don't know what lies you tell yourself. I can't imagine. But I know you want me, too."

She shook her head as if that might clear it, pulling in a breath as if that might help. When she looked at him again, she wasn't playing her part. She couldn't.

"I want you," she said in a low voice, letting all of the ways she loathed herself show, letting it all bleed out between them, letting it poison him, too. "I always have. And I'll never forgive myself for it."

She thought he looked shaken then, for the briefest moment, but he blinked it away. And he was too hard again, too fierce. She told herself she'd seen only what she wanted to see. He sat forward, those dark, cruel eyes fixed on her, and she reminded herself that nothing shook this man. Nothing could. Especially not minor little earthquakes like her.

"Congratulations, Elena," he said, his voice a sardonic lash. "I believe that's the first honest thing you've said to me since you told me your name."

She had to wrench her gaze away from his then, while she ordered herself to stay calm. To tamp down the chaotic emotions that surged inside of her, taking her over, making her want nothing more than to sob—once again—for something she could never have. Something she never should have wanted in the first place.

Unbidden, images of what they'd done together, here on this very same terrace, skated through her mind. His mouth, those hands. The wild heat of him, his impossible strength and his ruthless, intense possession—

Something occurred to her then, slamming through her as hard and as vicious as if he'd punched her in the gut. He might as well have. It couldn't have been worse.

She had been on birth control pills throughout her relationship with Niccolo, but the past six months had been so hectic. She'd run away and run out of the pills, and she hadn't wanted to leave any kind of record of where she'd been—so no doctors. She hadn't imagined it would be an issue. And then, today, she'd simply forgotten she wasn't protected.

She'd forgotten.

"We didn't use anything," she gasped out, so appalled she could hardly get the words past her lips. She felt numb with horror.

Alessandro went still. Too still. And for the first time in their brief, impossible acquaintance, she couldn't read a thing in the narrow, considering gaze he aimed at her. She could only see the darkness.

"I'm clean," he said. Cool and concise. And nothing more.

And the caustic slap of that helped her, strangely. It reminded her who she was, what she was doing here. Why she'd decided to give in to her desire for him in the first place.

"You think I'm a liar and I know very well you are," she said, trying for a calm tone. "You'll excuse me if I have no particular reason to believe you."

Temper streaked across that arrogant face of his. "You know I'm a liar, do you?" His deceptively gentle tone made her skin prickle. "And how exactly do you know that?"

She laughed, deliberately callous. "Because I know your name."

A deep blackness flashed through his dark green eyes and over his face then, old and resigned, with the faint hint of some kind of pain, and Elena fought off a sharp stab of regret. She shouldn't care if she hurt this man's feelings. He certainly didn't care if he hurt hers. So why couldn't she stave off the bizarre urge to apologize? To trust him the way that insane part of her urged her to do?

But even as she opened her mouth to do exactly that, she stopped herself. Because their carelessness had changed everything. She knew enough about him to know that he would never send her back to Niccolo if he thought she might be carrying his baby. Not a proud man like Alessandro. Not when the blood between the Falcos and the Correttis had been notoriously bad for generations.

Which meant, after all of this, she really was as safe as she'd always felt with him.

It should have felt something more than hollow.

But she had to keep going no matter how it felt. She had

to push this to its logical extreme. This was her chance to stay hidden away in a place Niccolo could never find her. In a place he'd never dream or dare to look.

"I could be pregnant," she said, steeling herself to the look on his face then, to her own intense horror at what she was doing. But she had no other option. There was so little time left, and she couldn't let Niccolo find her. She would do anything to keep that from happening, even this.

"I'm familiar with the risks," Alessandro bit out, temper still dark on his face, in his eyes, shading his firm mouth. "Why the hell aren't you protected?"

Elena eyed him across the table. "I wasn't aware that the sole responsibility for protection fell to me. Were you not equally involved?"

He muttered a harsh, Sicilian word beneath his breath, and she was perfectly happy she couldn't understand the dialect even after her time there.

She reached out to one of the platters, scooping up some of the olive tapenade with a piece of the fragrant bread and settling back to nibble at it as if she hadn't a care in the world.

"It will be fine, I'm sure," she said. She met his gaze and allowed herself a callous smirk. "Niccolo will never know the difference."

Alessandro actually jerked in his chair. His face went white.

"Over my dead body will you pass off a child of mine as his," he said hoarsely, so furious he nearly lit up the night with it. "Over my dead body, Elena—or yours."

She smiled. It didn't matter that he looked at her as if she revolted him completely. It didn't matter that she hated herself, that she thought she might be sick from this terrible manipulation. It didn't even matter that she really might be pregnant, which she couldn't let herself consider. It only mattered that she kept herself safe, one way or another, for this little while longer. Whatever the cost.

And the truth was, she knew somehow Alessandro would never hurt her. Hate her, perhaps, but never hurt her, and after all these months that was the same thing as safe. And it was a far better bargain than being with a man like Niccolo, who had pretended to love her and would likely put her in the hospital if he caught up with her.

"Then we'll count a month from today," she said smoothly, as if she'd never had any doubt that it would end this way. That she would get what she wanted. "Plus an extra ten days or so, as these things are so inexact. And we'll see if any dead bodies are necessary, won't we?"

His jaw was tight and hard, his gaze like bullets. "Forty days. On my island. Alone. With me."

He stared at her for a long moment, and she made herself look back at him, shameless and terrible, the woman he'd always believed she was and far worse than he'd imagined. This was her protection. This brazen, horrible creature she'd become, this calculated act. This was how she'd save herself, and the things she held dear.

"Or I could text you," she offered.

His face was drawn, that serious mouth grim. And his eyes were like the night around them, haunted and destroyed. This was what she'd done. This was what security looked like.

This was one more thing she'd have to live with when all of this was done.

"Just remember," he said, threat and promise laced through that low voice, bright in his dark eyes. "You asked for this."

CHAPTER FOUR

IT WAS WORSE now that he knew, Alessandro thought days later.

Worse now that he'd touched her, tasted her, held her. Lost himself inside her. There was no unknowing her exquisite heat, her lithe body wrapped around his as if she'd been created for that alone. For him. There was no forgetting it.

Alessandro didn't understand how he could know what he knew and still want her. How she could have used their carelessness as leverage, making him wonder if it had been carelessness on her part at all—and yet, he still wanted her.

He sickened himself.

"You don't need to look at me like that," she'd said the other morning out by the pool, not looking up from the glossy English magazine he assumed one of his unfailingly efficient staff had provided for her. Better to focus on that than what she looked like in a scalding red bikini hardly big enough to lick over the curves it displayed. Better to ignore how much he wanted to lick those curves himself. "I'm aware of what you think of me. The dark and terrible glare is overkill."

"This glare is the only thing between you and my temper," he'd replied, making no attempt to cushion her from the thrust of that temper in his voice. "I'd be more grateful for it, were I you."

"And what will you do if you lose it?" Elena had asked, sounding bored. She'd angled a look at him then over the rims of her dark glasses. "Hate me even more? By all means. Try."

It had taken everything he had not to cross over to her then and there and teach her exactly where his temper would lead. Exactly where it would take them both. The hot glory of the way they could burn each other alive. Only the fact that he wanted it too badly, and was furious at himself for that shocking deficiency in his character, kept him from it.

Alessandro stood up on one of the terraces now, looking out over the sweep of land that made up the rest of the island behind his house. On the far side of the tennis court was the small meadow that ran down to the rocky shore, late-spring grasses and early-summer flowers preening beneath the June sun. Scrappy pines and elegant palm trees scraped the sky. Stout fruit trees displayed their wares— lemons and oranges and leafy almonds. Seagulls floated in the wind, calling out their lonely little songs. And in the center of all that natural beauty was Elena.

Elena. Always Elena.

He'd been so furious that first night he was glad she'd removed herself shortly after dropping her little bombshell about her possible pregnancy—and her intention to stay here, with him. He'd drunk his way into what passed for sleep and had woken the next morning determined to regain the upper hand he never should have yielded in the first place.

She wanted to stay on his island to further some twisted agenda of her own? She wanted to play this game of consequences with him? *Va bene.* Then she would have to deal with what she'd put into action. And she'd have to face him while she did it.

"I'll expect you at dinner," he'd told her that first morning. "Every night."

She'd been walking into the cheerful breakfast room then, its floor-to-ceiling glass windows pulled back to let the morning in. She'd hardly looked at him as she'd helped herself to the carafe of the strong Indonesian coffee he preferred to the more traditional, milky cappuccinos.

"Your expectations are your own, Alessandro," she'd said almost sweetly when she'd turned back from the simple, wood-carved sideboard to face him, balancing her coffee cup in her hands.

She'd worn a huge, shapeless sundress, swaddling herself in cheery turquoise from her neck to her toes, and topped off with one of those flimsy, gauzy wrap things that served no discernible purpose at all but to conceal her figure.

He'd liked the idea that she'd felt she had to hide herself from him. That he'd got at least that far beneath her treacherous skin, that he hadn't been the only one feeling battered that morning.

"If you want to hold me captive on my own island for forty days, that's the price."

"The price is too high."

He'd smiled. "You really won't like my alternate plan. Trust me."

"I told you I'd be happy to go my merry way and let you know what happens," she'd replied, her expression cool but her blue eyes a shade darker than usual. "You were the one who started ranting on about dead bodies. I don't see why I should have to subject myself to more of the same over dinner."

"Afraid you won't be able to control yourself?" he'd

taunted her. "Will I be forced to fend off your advances over pasta alla Norma, Elena? Defend what remains of my virtue over the soup?"

Her blue eyes had blazed. "Unlikely."

"Then I fail to see the problem," he'd said, still smiling, though his gaze had been a challenge and demand on hers.

Her mouth had curved slightly then, that cool slap of a smile he'd already come to loathe.

"Also unlikely," she'd replied.

He'd lounged there in his chair and looked at her for a moment, enjoying himself despite the pounding in his head, the stark disillusionment in his heart. Despite what he knew about her now. Despite his own weakness for her that even her distasteful manipulations couldn't erase.

"I warned you," he'd said softly. Deliberately. "You wanted this."

"I wanted—" But she'd thought better of whatever she'd been about to say, and had pressed her lips together.

"Be careful what you wish for next, *cara,*" he'd advised her silkily. "You might get that, too."

Alessandro moved farther out on the terrace now, frowning down at her. That exchange had been days ago. He'd spent a good hour this morning working out his weakness in his pool, swimming lap after lap and still not managing to shift this thing off him that made him want her like this. That made him hunger for her no matter how little he liked her.

That made him *long* and *yearn* and *wish*, like he was someone else entirely.

Or as if she was.

She sat out in his sweet-smelling meadow on a bright orange blanket, her eyes closed and her head tipped back, soaking in the sunshine like some kind of flower. Like something utterly innocent, clean and pure. His mouth twisted. She wore a short, flirty dress in a pale yellow color that left her golden-skinned arms and legs bare, then tucked in at her delectable waist to highlight the unmistakable elegance of her lean, slender form.

He let his gaze trace the beautiful lines of her face, that perfectly lush mouth and the loose waves of the blond hair that she hadn't pulled back again since that first night. It danced around her in the ocean breeze, the color of country butter with hints of white-blond, as well, and he hated that she could be so pretty, so effortlessly lovely, when he knew the sordid truth about her.

She was engaged to Niccolo Falco, and she'd slept with him, anyway.

He couldn't understand why that alone wasn't the end of this pitched battle inside of him. Why that simple fact didn't end this need for her that still burned him up and kept him from his sleep. It should have been all he needed to dismiss her from his thoughts entirely. He was not the kind of man who enjoyed poaching, unlike his cousin Matteo. He got no pleasure from finding himself in the middle of other people's relationships. Life was complicated enough, he'd always thought, and his own parents' squalid legacy had seemed to confirm it. Why cause himself more trouble?

After all, he had more than his share already. It was his birthright.

He'd spent the bulk of the morning fuming over his voice mail and most of his text and email messages, sending his beleaguered assistant increasingly terse instructions to deal with whatever came up as best he could, and not to bother Alessandro with any of it unless it was an emergency. An objectively dire one. The various pleas and attempts to draw him out from friends and family he deleted without a reply—all except for Santo, who got a terse line indicating that Alessandro was alive, and only because his messages had focused on Alessandro's well-being instead of the family.

His goddamned family.

He wasn't coming home to sort out the cursed business deal his aborted wedding had left in tatters. He didn't want to know that his illegitimate half-brother, Angelo, ignored all his life by their father and understandably furious about it, was making his move at last. He wasn't interested in what the latest Corretti family scandal was now that he'd removed himself. He didn't want to hear his mother's pathetic excuses for the way she'd savaged his sister, Rosa, in earshot of most of Palermo society, dropping the truth of her parentage on her like a loud, drunken guillotine. He didn't care where his runaway bride had gone and he certainly didn't want to join in the speculation about whether or not his cousin Matteo had gone with her.

He wanted to be numb. He wanted to encase himself in ice and steel and feel nothing, ever again. No useless sense of duty. No pathetic compulsion to play the rescuer, the hero, for his endlessly needy family members, none of whom ever quite appreciated it. No useless longing for a woman who neither deserved it nor wanted it.

No wondering what it was in him that was so twisted, so ruined and corrupt and despicable, that the bride he'd carefully arranged and contracted abandoned him at the altar and the beautiful stranger he'd fallen for so disastrously at a glance wanted nothing more than to use him for her own ends.

He wanted to be numb.

But if he couldn't be numb, he decided then, staring down at her luxuriating in all of that sunlight, he might as well explore that darkness inside of him that he'd fought his whole life.

Elena wanted to play her games with him. Dangerous games, because she thought she was dealing with another brutish thug like her fiancé. Maybe he should give her what she wanted. Maybe he should bring out the whole of his arsenal in return.

Maybe it was finally time to be who he was: a Corretti, callous and selfish, destined for nothing but depravity from the moment of his birth.

Just like all the rest of them. Just like the father he'd always despised.

"I want to be inside you," Alessandro said casually. He was standing at the windows, his back to her. "Now."

Elena froze in her seat. She set her fork down carefully.

She'd grown used to these long, fraught meals they shared each night, prodding each other for weaknesses. She'd come to enjoy the strange exhilaration she got from matching wits with him, so different from meals with Niccolo—who had done the talking while she'd sat there adoringly, grateful for her good luck.

She'd grown used to the dark looks he sent her way whenever he saw her, cold condemnation and a banked fury, a far cry from the flat coldness she'd once seen in Niccolo's eyes, moments before he'd showed her who he really was. She'd told herself she was used to this by now. To Alessandro himself. To all this forced exposure to the man who had chased her through dreams for six long months.

"I gave in to that urge once already," she murmured. "And look what's happened."

She hadn't thought to worry about sex.

She hadn't imagined it would be an issue, after that first day. He'd looked at her as if he'd rather die than touch her again, and she'd told herself she was glad of it.

Of course she was.

"I might be pregnant," she reminded him now, though she tried to think of it as little as possible. It was too much to take in. She kept that faintly amused note in her voice. "And we are trapped here, strangers who think the worst of each other. I'll pass on a reprise, thank you."

"This table will do well enough," he continued as if she hadn't spoken, turning so she could see his starkly sensual expression. And that passion in his dark green eyes. Elena's heart gave a hard kick to her ribs, and she felt much too warm, suddenly. "All you need to do is bend over."

The image exploded through her, too vivid, too real. It didn't take much effort at all to imagine him behind her, deep inside her—

"You've obviously had too much to drink," she said. She pressed her napkin to her mouth, more to check that she wasn't trembling than to wipe anything away. She had to stay calm, focused. She had to remember why she was here, why she was doing this.

"Does it make you feel better to think so?" He smiled, and the heat of it catapulted her back to that night in Rome. That dance. The way he'd looked at her, smiled at her, as if she was precious to him. "I haven't. But I want you either way."

She forced a cool smile, and tried to force the past from her head. "You can't have me."

"Why not?" He looked amused, his face carved in those fiercely sensual, powerfully masculine lines, his dark eyes gleaming. Elena fought to restrain her shivery reaction, to ignore that melting, pulling sensation low in her belly. "You've already betrayed your fiancé. What does it matter now how many times you do it?"

She was shocked by how easily he could hurt her, when he should never have had that kind of power in the first place. She should have been pleased that he hated her so openly, that he disdained her so completely. She'd gone out of her way to make sure he did. Instead, it hurt. *It hurt.*

But she couldn't show him that. She could only show him what he wanted to see—what he already saw. A cold, hard woman. Brazen and base.

"I don't like to repeat myself," she said, holding his gaze. "It's boring."

She expected the lash of his temper, but Alessandro laughed. It made the green in his eyes brighten, and worse, made everything inside of her seem to squeeze tight. Breath, belly, core. Even her traitorous heart.

"But you're the one in control, are you not?" he asked, too arrogant, too confident, to believe what he was saying. "Your wish is my command. If you're bored, you need only demand that I relieve it and I will." His smile took on that wolfish edge. "I'm very inventive."

She had a sinking sensation then, as if she'd somehow strayed into quicksand and was moments away from being sucked under. *Think*, she ordered herself in a panic. *Turn this around!*

"And that's all it takes?" She arched her brows high in disbelief. "I need only click my fingers and you'll serve my every whim?"

"Of course." The amusement on his ruthless face did nothing to ease the fierceness of it. And the lie on his lips was laced with laughter. "I am powerless in the face of your machinations, Elena."

Her pulse was wild in her veins, and she felt like prey— like he was stalking her when he hadn't moved. He only stood there, his hands thrust deep in his pockets, and she felt as if she was running hard and scared with his hot breath *right there* on the back of her neck—

"Somehow," she managed to say, her voice cool and dry

rather than panicked, though it cost her, "I have trouble seeing you as *quite* that submissive."

"But this is what you want," he replied in that soft, taunting way, his dark eyes alight. "Isn't that why we're here at all? You demanded it. I obeyed."

Elena had to leave. Now. She had to shut this down before she betrayed herself, before she gave in to the need blazing through her. She would lock herself inside her room, ignore the emptiness and yearning inside of her, and pretend she was locking him out rather than keeping herself in. All she had to do was walk away from him.

She stood in a rush, aware she gave herself away with the speed of it, the total lack of grace. His hard mouth moved into that devastating curve that seemed to curl into the very core of her, making her soften. Ache. She couldn't trust herself to stay, to try to act her way through this. She wanted to run for the door, but she made herself walk instead. As if she was making a simple choice to leave. As if she didn't already feel pursued when he still hadn't moved a muscle.

"I'm not going to chase you through the house, Elena." His voice slid over her, dark and insinuating. Finding its way into her deepest, blackest, most secret corners, far away from any light. Deep into the places she pretended weren't there. "Unless you ask nicely. Is that what you need? Permission to scream *no* at the top of your lungs and know I'll take you, anyway? No responsibility, no regrets?"

The shudder that worked through her then was fierce and deep, involuntary, and she couldn't pretend it had anything to do with revulsion. She felt weak. Weak and desperate. She had to stop walking, had to reach out and hold on to the wall near the wide, arching doorway. She had to fight to keep from revealing how tempted she was, how twisted that made her. She had to keep from confirming what he already seemed to know.

"I don't—" she began desperately, but he sighed impatiently, cutting her off.

"No more lies. Not about this."

Alessandro was leaning back against one of the windows when she turned to look at him again, but nothing about him was languid. She could see his coiled strength, his seething power. He was dressed all in white tonight, and should have looked relaxed. Casual. But he looked more to her like a warrior king, surveying the field of battle and entirely too confident of his own impending victory.

He smiled again, and she felt it bloom inside of her, almost like pain. That low, impossible almost-pain that never entirely left her and that pulsed now, bright and demanding and hungry. Between her legs. In the fullness of her breasts. Even behind her eyes.

"I didn't realize you wanted to play games," she said stiffly, because she had to say something, and she was rapidly forgetting all the reasons why she couldn't simply throw herself at him and worry about it later.

"Of course you did." Laughter lurked in his voice again, gleamed in those dark, knowing eyes. "You want to play them, too."

"I don't." But what if she did? She flushed red hot, imagining.

You are truly shameless, a cold voice hissed inside her, condemning her anew.

Alessandro only crooked his index finger at her then, ordering her to come to him. To admit the things she wanted—to surrender herself to them. To him.

And she wanted that almost more than she could bear.

"No," she said too loudly, and she knew she was talking to herself. To remind herself of who she was, before she did something else she'd bitterly regret.

He wasn't safe, no matter how much that insane part of her insisted otherwise. He wasn't. And she was too afraid that giving in to him, to this, would make her believe she could trust him with the truth. She couldn't.

No matter how hard that was to remember.

"Stop pretending, Elena," he said then, that darker edge in his voice curling around her, drawing her in, calling her out that easily. "You're halfway to desperate. Up all night, tormented and needy. Longing for more but too afraid to ask for it."

That wolf's smile, challenging her. Daring her. Seeing all the things in her she wanted desperately to keep hidden away in the dark. Making her realize that she'd underestimated him, completely. And that he knew that, too.

"I said no," she managed to get out, but her voice was too thick, and it shook, and his smile only deepened.

"I won't even make you beg." He didn't have to do anything but look at her, predatory and sure, and she wanted everything she couldn't have, everything she couldn't risk. She wanted him more than her next breath. "All you have to do is own it. This. Ask and you will receive, *cara.*"

It should have been easy to ignore Alessandro. To shrug off the darkly stirring things he said to her, the fantasies he brought to life within her with so little effort. It should have been simple to concentrate on these weeks of reprieve, and what it meant not to have to look over her shoulder after all these months, not to have to run.

Elena didn't understand why she couldn't seem to do it.

"It's only a matter of time," he'd said in his devastating way that night, when she'd finally turned to go. "Inevitable."

"Nothing is inevitable," she'd bit out over her shoulder, fully aware that he'd been throwing that word back in her face. Remembering exactly when she'd whispered it to him, what she'd felt when she did.

He'd laughed at her. "Keep telling yourself that."

So she did—fervently and repeatedly—but it didn't seem to work.

The nights were long and precarious. Each night she lay awake for hours, trying desperately to think of anything but him, and losing herself in need-infused fantasies instead. Or worse, reliving what had already happened.

Every touch. Every sigh. Every telling whisper.

Even if she managed to fall asleep, there was no relief. She would dream only of him and then wake, heart pounding and mouth dry, her body screaming for his touch. Memories of his possession hot and red in her head, branded into her.

The days were no better. No matter what she did, or where she went in his rambling house or the surrounding grounds, he found her. He was always there. Always watching her with those dark, hungry eyes of his, that wicked smile on his cynical mouth. Always, she understood, a word from her away from catapulting them both straight back into that glorious, terrifying fire that was never quite banked between them.

And all the while, she had to play her role. Cool, sometimes amused, forever teetering on the edge of boredom. The kind of hard, amoral woman Alessandro thought she was. And maybe, she was forced to acknowledge, he wasn't far off.

She could be pregnant—*pregnant*—and all she thought about was the way he'd touched her. While he—the man who might even now be the father of her child—believed she'd sought him out deliberately for sordid reasons of her

she couldn't argue with him without giving herself away, and the fact that she still wanted to explain this to him, that she still so desperately wanted him to know who she really was, horrified her. She eyed him. "What about you?"

"My childhood was significantly less idyllic."

He might as well have been an unyielding, forbidding wall as he gazed back at her. And yet she felt that twist inside of her again.

That poor child, she thought, unable to keep herself from it. *Growing up with those people.*

His eyes narrowed as if he could sense her softening.

"Have we covered enough ground?" he asked, the hint of impatience in his voice, his gaze. "Are you ready to stop playing this game?" His eyes were so dark, so knowing. "I beg of you," he whispered. But he wasn't really begging. He wasn't a man who begged. "Say the word."

But she couldn't let herself do that. She might trust him on some primitive level that defied all reason, that she didn't even understand—but she didn't trust herself. It was much too risky. She shook her head slowly, not looking away from him.

"Don't tell me this is your version of misplaced loyalty," he said, his dark gaze moving over her face. "Once was business, but twice is a betrayal of your beloved Niccolo?"

"Business?" she asked in confusion, but then she remembered. She sighed. "Yes, because I'm spying on you. Over decadent gourmet meals. So far the only thing I've discovered, Alessandro, is that you employ a fantastic chef."

He shook his head, as if she'd disappointed him. "He doesn't deserve your loyalty. He never did."

"Enough about Niccolo," she said, pretending she didn't feel his disappointment like a blow. Pretending she wasn't clamoring to share everything with this man who was wise enough to hate Niccolo. She forced a smile, aware that it was brittle. "Why don't we talk about your fiancée, for a change?"

"What about her?" he asked, as if he'd forgot he ever had a fiancée in the first place. He laughed. "She's hardly worth mentioning. In truth, she never was."

CHAPTER FIVE

"WHAT A LOVELY sentiment," Elena said dryly. "No wonder she left you."

Something desolate moved over his face then, though he hid it almost the very second she saw it. The lump in her throat stayed where it was.

I hate this, she thought furiously. *I hate* me *like this.*

"Alessia Battaglia had exactly one promise to keep," Alessandro said, no sign of any desolation whatsoever in his hard voice, as if she'd imagined it. "Only one. And she not only failed to keep it, she did so in the most public way possible—designed, I can only assume, to cause me the maximum amount of embarrassment professionally and personally. Which she achieved." His lips twitched. "What is worth mentioning about that?"

"Sometimes people fall out of love," she offered. She was such a fool. She wanted that bleakness she'd seen in his eyes to mean something. His dark green gaze was contemplative as he studied her, and it took everything she had not to look away.

"It was a business arrangement, Elena. Love had nothing to do with it."

An odd sensation worked its way through her then, blooming up from the darkest part of her and uncurling, and it took her long moments to understand that it was a fierce, unwarranted satisfaction. As if the fact he had not loved his fiancée, did not care that she'd left him as much as the fact he'd been left, was not more evidence that he was the worst kind of man—but instead something to celebrate. She despaired of herself.

"And you're surprised she changed her mind?" she asked. That strange feeling hummed in her, making it hard to sit still, to keep her voice so smooth. "Why would anyone subject themselves to an arranged marriage in this day and age? That sounds like the perfect recipe for a lifetime of misery."

"As opposed to what?" He laughed. "The great benefits romance brings to the equation? The jealousy, the emotional manipulation, the very real possibility that at any moment, as you say, people could fall out of it? What makes you think that's the kind of security rational people should build a life on?"

"Because if it's not entirely rational, at least it's honest," she blurted out before she could think better of it. "It's real."

"So is a contract." His voice was dry. Amused. "Which has the added benefit of being tangible. Inarguably rational. And enforceable by law."

"Maybe you were no more than collateral damage." Elena didn't know why she couldn't stop. Why did she care why this man's fiancée had abandoned him? He was Alessandro Corretti. Surely that was reason enough for anyone. "Maybe it wasn't about you at all."

"I was the only one standing at the altar," he said, tilting his head slightly as he gazed at her. "Do you imagine she objected to the priest her father chose? Palermo's great basilica itself? Hundreds of her closest friends and family members?"

"Maybe—" Elena began.

"I don't want to speculate about Alessia Battaglia's tangled, self-serving motives," he said impatiently. "All that matters are her actions. If you want to psychoanalyze a doomed engagement, why not focus on your own?"

"I don't want to talk about Niccolo again." Or that doom he mentioned. Especially not that.

"Then let's talk about you." He lounged there so casually, but Elena knew better. He was still picking at her resistance, over platters of grilled fish and bottles of wine. Over flickering candles and glistening crystal glasses. Over her own objections. "Since you won't let me do what I want to do."

She could almost hear the music they'd danced to, lilting somewhere inside of her. Back when he had looked at her as if she was miraculous, not a battle to be won. Back when he had held her close for such a little while and made her name into a song.

"Fine," she said. Anything to stop the memories, the emotions, that threatened to break her. The lump in her throat returned, and she had to breathe past it. "What do you want to know?"

"The man is a toad." Flat. Certain. Daring her to argue with his characterization. She didn't. "Less than a toad. Yet you agreed to marry him, and for all your faults of character, you don't strike me as the kind of woman you would have to be to overlook such things." Alessandro shifted in his chair, looking even more relaxed, but Elena knew better. She could sense what roared there beneath his skin, powerful and predatory. She could feel it. "Why did you?"

"Because I love—" She caught herself. Barely. She'd almost said *loved*. "I love him." She watched his eyes flash, and enjoyed the fact he didn't like hearing that any more than she liked saying it. "And not because he drove a pretty car or promised me a villa somewhere." She held his gaze, and told the truth. "He was sweet."

"Sweet." Alessandro looked appalled.

"He told me that once he'd seen me, his life could never be the same," she said, letting herself remember when Niccolo had been no more than a handsome, smiling stranger on an otherwise wholly familiar street. "He brought me flowers he picked himself from the hills above the village. He begged me to let him take me to dinner, or even simply take a walk with him near the water. It was the easiest thing in the world to fall for him. He was— He's the most romantic man I've ever met."

"It sounds like a con."

It wasn't as if she didn't agree, but she couldn't show him that. Or admit how ashamed she was of herself for falling for it, head over heels, so easily. Like the little fish she supposed she had been, reeled right into Niccolo's net.

She sniffed. "Says the man who thinks a chilly business contract is a solid basis for a marriage."

"But I am not a toad," he pointed out, dark amusement lurking in his gaze, in the corner of his mouth. "And she did not agree to marry me because I was *sweet.* She agreed to marry me because her father wished it, and because the life I would have given her was generous and comfortable." Again, a lift of those sardonic brows. "That is called practicality. Our situations are not at all similar."

"True." She aimed her smile at him. "But I don't expect Niccolo will leave me at the altar, either."

He stared at her for a long moment, that dark gaze baleful. She shivered, the intensity emanating from him sliding over her skin like a kind of breeze, kicking up goose bumps, though she tried to hide it. Then, not taking his eyes from hers, he threw his napkin on the table and rose.

Liquid and graceful. Powerful and male.

Elena ordered herself to run. But she couldn't seem to move.

Alessandro rounded the table, and then he was behind her, and she thought the heat that exploded through her then might kill her. It hurt when she breathed. It hurt when she held it instead. His hands came down to rest on her shoulders, light and something like innocuous, so nearly polite, and yet she was sure that he could feel the heat of her skin. The bright hot flame she became whenever he touched her.

Remember—an urgent voice cried, deep inside her. *Remember*—

But he was touching her again, he was finally touching her, and she couldn't hold on to a single thought but that.

"Fall for me, then," he said, bending down to speak softly into her ear, his breath tickling her even as it triggered that volcanic need she'd tried too hard to deny. "I'll pick you flowers from the meadow if that's all it takes."

"Stop it," she said, but her voice was so insubstantial. Little more than a whisper, and she knew it told him exactly how affected she was. How little resistance she had left.

"I'll lay you down beneath the moon," he continued as if she hadn't spoken, one clever hand moving beneath her hair to caress the sensitive skin at her nape, and she couldn't contain her shiver then—couldn't hide it from him. "And I'll demonstrate the only kind of love that isn't a sentimental story. The only kind that's real."

He meant sex. She knew he meant sex. And still, *that word*.

That word with his hands on her. *That word* in his low voice, wreaking its havoc as it sunk its claws into her. As it left deep marks that made a mockery of every lie she'd told herself since he'd found her on that boat. Every lie she'd told herself so desperately since that fateful night in Rome.

"I promise you, Elena," he said then, quoting Niccolo, wielding those same words like his own weapon—and a far more deadly one. "Your life will never be the same."

Her heart slammed against her ribs, so hard she worried they might crack. Once. Then again. Elena was lost. Held securely in his hands and unable to think of a single reason why she should extricate herself. Why she should do anything at all but let herself fall into this magnificent fire and burn herself away until there was nothing left of her but smoke. And him.

His hands dropped to her chair to pull her back from the table, and by the time she stood on her trembling legs, by the time she turned to look at his beautiful face made no less arrogant by the heat stamped across it, she remembered. If not herself, not entirely, than some tiny little spark of self-preservation that reminded her what was at stake. What there was left to lose.

His clever eyes moved over her face, and he frowned, reaching out again to take her upper arms in his hands. His thumbs moved over the skin the sleeveless empire-cut top she wore left bare, sending his personal brand of electricity arrowing straight into her core.

Where she ached. And melted. And ached anew.

"Don't," he said, urgency making his voice harsh. "Don't walk away again."

"I have to," she replied, but she couldn't look away from him. She couldn't move.

"There's no one on this island but you and me and the people I pay exorbitantly to keep my secrets," he said, all temptation and demand, and she could feel him, feel *this*, feel the dizzying intensity in every cell of her body. In every breath. In the way her heart beat and her pulse pounded. "No one to see what you do. No one to know. No one to contradict you if you lie about it later."

"I'll know," she said quietly.

And knew immediately, when his expression changed, that she'd made a critical mistake. For a moment she didn't understand, though the air between them seemed to burst into flames. His face lit with a dark, almost savage triumph, and his hard mouth curved.

"Yet we both know where your moral compass points, don't we?"

"Away from you," she said hurriedly, but it was too late.

"Another lie is as good a word as any, Elena," he said then, more wolf in that moment than man. "I accept."

Alessandro pulled her to him with that ruthless command that undid her—that thrilled her no matter how she wished it didn't. And her body simply obeyed. She knew she should resist this. She knew she needed to push him away, to wrench herself out of his arms before—

But she didn't.

She didn't even try.

He took her mouth, masterful and merciless at once, inevitable, and Elena melted against him, went up on her toes, and met him.

Finally.

His mouth was on her again, at last, and it wasn't enough. Her taste flooded him, driving him wild. Her tongue was an exquisite torture against his, her head tilting at the slightest touch of his hand for that perfect, slick fit he craved. He pulled her even closer, bending her back over his arm, kissing her as if both their lives depended on it.

Mine, he thought, with a ferocity that shook through him and only made him want her that much more.

She was pliant and beautiful, graceful in his arms, her luscious body plastered against him. He could feel her breasts against his chest, her hips pressed to his, and he was fervently grateful she was the sort of woman who wore shoes with wicked heels so gracefully. It made it that much easier to haul the delectable place where her legs met against the hardest part of him, right where he wanted her.

God, how he wanted her.

He lost his head. He forgot what he'd planned, what he'd intended here—he tasted her and the whole world fell away, narrowed down to one specific goal. To thrust himself inside her, again and again. To make them both shatter into a thousand pieces.

To take them both home.

He reached down and pulled her black top up over those fantastic breasts she never covered with any kind of bra, muttering words he hardly understood in Sicilian as well as Italian. He ran his fingers over her taut nipples, watched her bite her lip against the pleasure of it, her head falling back to give him better access.

But it wasn't enough, so he backed her up against the table and set her there, leaning down to lick his way from one delicious crest to the other. To lose himself in the softness of her warm skin, the scent of it, and those small, high cries she made when he took a nipple deep into his mouth.

She was gripping the edge of the table, her breath coming in hard, quick bursts, and she was so beautiful he thought he might die if he couldn't bury himself in her. If he couldn't feel her tremble all around him, screaming out his name. If he couldn't drive so deep into her he'd forget all about who he'd once imagined she was. Who she should have been.

Who she wasn't, damn her.

He remembered the stark, sensual picture he'd drawn for her at that dinner weeks back and smiled then, against the delicate skin beneath one of her breasts. He straightened, tugged her to her feet and found himself distracted by the glaze of passion in her bright summer eyes, the color high on her cheeks. He held her face between his hands, his thumbs sweeping from her temples to those elegant cheekbones that drove him mad, and plundered her mouth.

Taking, tasting. Exulting in this, in her. Making her his the only way he could.

He tore his mouth from hers, then spun her around. He felt her tremble against him as he leaned her forward, spreading her before him over the table, using one hand to push a forgotten serving dish, piled high with the remains of fluffy, fragrant rice, out of her way.

"Alessandro..." she whispered as she bent there, offering him the perfect, delectable view. A prayer. A vow. So much more than simply his name.

He smoothed his hands down her back, the sensual shape of her making him harder, making him desperate. But he didn't rush. He reached around beneath her to flatten his hands against the delectable curve of her belly.

He held his hands there for a moment, savoring the fine, low tremor that shuddered through her. Letting her absorb the heat of his hands. And then he moved lower, pulling open the button fly of her trousers with one hand as the other slid inside to cup her scalding heat in his palm.

She was panting now, leaning her forehead against the table, and he held her femininity in his hand, hot and damp and swollen with desire. And then he squeezed.

Elena bucked against him, against the table, and he did it again. Then again.

Slowly, deliberately, he built up a rhythm. Teasing her. Seducing her. Pressing against her urgent center with every stroke. Her breath grew ragged, her heat bloomed into his hand, and only then—only when she was mindless before him, stretched out breathless and boneless and his to command—did he pull his hand away.

Leaving her trembling right there on the edge.

She sobbed something incoherent into the arm she had thrown up near her head and then let out a moan as Alessandro tugged on her trousers, peeling them over her hips and shoving them down her legs to her knees. He left her panties where they were, an electric blue thong that beautifully framed then disappeared between the perfect twin curves of her pert bottom.

She was restless, shifting her weight from one foot in its high wedged sandal to the other, her hips swaying in an age-old invitation that speared into him like a new heat, mesmerizing him for a moment. Her shoes lifted her to him, making her arch her back slightly as she sprawled there before him, mindless and moaning. His in every way.

He loved it. He thought he could die in this moment a happy man at last, this woman his own, perfectly crafted feast—and he intended to eat every bite. He traced over her thong with a lazy finger, then ran his hands over her bottom, vowing that one day he would learn every millimeter of her with his mouth. Every hollow. Every mark. With his teeth. His tongue.

But not now. His need was like a wild storm in him, pounding in his blood, making his chest tight and his vision narrow.

He freed himself from his trousers and quickly rolled on the protection he'd carried in his pocket, then bent over her, shoving her thong down and out of his way. She was still trembling, still breathing hard and fast, and her eyes were shut tight. He braced himself on one arm, his hand flat against the table near her shoulder.

"Alessandro," she said again, her voice strangled, but she lifted her hips when he slid a hand beneath her, pressing her face against the table as if it was a pillow.

He reached down and pressed hard against her center even as he shifted his position and drove straight into her.

She came apart beneath him, sobbing and wild.

He had to grit his teeth as she shuddered, as her fingers pressed into the table's hard surface as if she could find some hold. He let her ride it out, waiting hot and hard and deep inside of her, her perfect bottom snug against him, almost more enticement than he could bear.

When she started to come back to him, he began to move.

He wasn't gentle. She made that small, highly aroused noise in the back of her throat, the sweetest sound he'd ever heard, and met him, thrust for thrust. She was sinuous and lithe, arched there before him with her black top flowing all around her as she moved with him, like some kind of erotic dance.

It was almost too much for him. He reached out and held the nape of her neck in his hand, making her shudder, then keeping her still.

And then he simply took her.

He ravaged. He savored. *He took.*

And all the while she cried out her pleasure, her hips wild against his, her eyes shut tight and her cheeks stained red with all of that desperate, delicious heat.

It was perfect. She was perfect.

"You are mine," he ground out from between his teeth, his hips hard against hers, riding her, devouring her. *"Mine."*

When he couldn't hold on any longer he slid a hand beneath her once more, finding the heart of her hunger and rubbing hard against it, making her jerk against him.

"Again," he ordered her, his voice so deep, so guttural, he hardly recognized it. And he didn't care, his own climax roaring toward him. "Now."

She obeyed him with a beautiful scream, her feet leaving the ground as she shattered into a flare of white hot heat around him, catapulting over that edge once more.

And finally, *finally,* he followed.

Alessandro didn't know how long it was before he caught his breath. Before he was himself again, and not just a handful of scattered fragments thrown to every corner of this island. Of the globe.

Elena still lay beneath him, her cheek pressed against the tabletop, and he could feel every breath she took. He angled himself back and off her, regretting that he had to pull out of her soft heat.

She didn't move, or open her eyes. Alessandro rid himself of the protection he'd used, fastened his trousers, and still she lay there. Making a perfectly debauched, impossibly lovely picture. Her trousers and thong were a tangle at her knees, her sweet bottom and the feminine secrets beneath on display as she bent there over his table so obediently, her mouth slightly ajar as she breathed and her slender arms thrown out before her as if in total surrender.

Desire coiled within him again, and he rubbed his hands over his face as if that might make sense of this hunger. Nothing eased it. Not even the one thing that should have.

He wondered, then, if it would ever leave him. If he would ever be free of it. Of her.

Is that what you want? a voice queried from a place inside of him he preferred to ignore, and he shoved it away.

"Elena."

She stirred then, her eyes fluttering open, and Alessandro watched as she slowly peeled herself up from the table, then reached down to pull her panties and her trousers into place, all without looking his way. All a bit shaky, a bit too careful, as if she wasn't sure her legs would hold beneath her. Her hair was a wanton tangle around her face but she ignored it, not even pushing it out of her way as she buttoned up her denim trousers.

So he did it for her, tucking a silken blond sheaf behind one ear.

"Are you all right?"

Her gaze flicked to his, then away.

"Yes," she said. Her voice was rough and she coughed. "Of course."

But there was a defenseless cast to her jaw as she said it, and he reached over to tilt up her chin, forcing her to look at him. Her blue eyes were stormy, and there was something somehow bruised about the way she stared back at him. He felt cold.

"Are you?" he asked again, his tone serious. Gruff.

She knocked his hand away. He let her.

"Please don't patronize me." She looked around as if in search of something, but only hugged herself instead. As if, he thought, she was very small. The cold in him grew wider, deeper. "I said I was fine."

He studied her, battling the strangest urge to pull her into his arms, to hold her against him. To warm them both. It was ridiculous.

And then he did it anyway, not understanding himself at all.

She fit beneath his chin and securely against his chest, and he couldn't have said what he felt then. It didn't make sense. He didn't recognize it—or himself. And yet he held her, he listened to her breathe, and he hated it when she pulled away from him.

"Stop this," she said in a low voice, her gaze dark and troubled. "I don't need your backhanded form of comfort."

He didn't understand any of this. Why was he having this conversation in the first place? He didn't tolerate scenes like this. He avoided even the faintest hint of what he saw swimming there in all of that summer blue. So why was he still standing here?

"Elena," he began.

She blew out a breath. "I asked you to stop," she whispered.

Alessandro felt profoundly off balance. Uneven down into his soul. He scowled.

"So I can take you any way I please," he said in a less pleasant voice than he might have, had he been able to make this strange feeling disappear. Had any of this made sense to him. "I can bend you over a table and make you scream and shake, and you'll submit to that happily. Greedily."

Her face paled, but that didn't stop him. And whatever was happening inside of him shifted, turned furious. At himself, at her—he couldn't tell the difference. He just needed this feeling to stop. Now.

"There is nothing I couldn't make you beg me to do to you, is there?" He folded his arms across his chest. "Nothing at all."

"Does this make you feel better?" she asked, lifting her head, her eyes flashing.

"I'm not the one who has convenient pretensions of modesty, Elena," he bit out. "But only when it suits."

He watched her shake that off, a quick jerk of her smooth shoulders, and wondered that it even hurt her.

"I know you don't respect me, Alessandro," she said, and her voice wasn't angry. It was something else. Something that worked in him like shame, oily and thick. "I know exactly what you think of me. You've told me repeatedly. You don't have to act it out again now."

"You don't respect yourself!" he threw at her. How did she dare?

"But you should." She shook her head, then he saw to his horror that her eyes were full. Though she didn't cry. She only looked at him with tears bright in her gaze and he felt small. Mean. "Shouldn't you? What kind of man does the things you do with me, revels in them, and yet has no respect for me at all?"

"Elena," he began, but there was too much inside of him. It was too big and too dangerously unwieldy, and it had something to do with that way she looked at him. As if she thought he was a better man. That he ought at least to try. And that vulnerability in the way she held herself, as if she knew what he'd long suspected—that, deep down, he wasn't. And never had been.

"You call me a whore and then you call me yours," she said quietly. "Am I the one who doesn't respect myself or is that you?"

He felt buffeted by wild, treacherous storms—but yet he stood still, and there was only that way she gazed at him, as if she saw through all of his darkness and saw what lay there on the other side of it. Something he refused to name.

Something that could not exist. He wouldn't allow it.

"It's like you're two different women," he told her when he was sure he could keep his balance. When he'd beat back the storms as best he could. "One I know all too well. One who would marry a man like Niccolo Falco and defend that choice, call it romantic."

She looked away from him then. In shame? In some kind of triumph that he cared this much, so much more than he should, than he even admitted to himself?

How could he still not know?

"But the other, Elena." He dropped his voice, and saw her eyes close against it, as if it tempted her beyond endurance, or hurt her. As if he did. "The other..."

Was the woman he'd imagined she was when he'd met

her. The woman he'd wanted so desperately he'd ignored
her association with Niccolo to dance with her, to hold
her. The woman he'd called his before he knew her name.
The woman he sometimes saw in her still—like now....

That woman doesn't exist, he reminded himself harshly.
She hadn't then and she never would.

"People are complicated," she said after a moment, a
bleakness making her blue gaze gray when she looked at
him again. "You can't shove them into little boxes. And
you can't really know them unless they let you."

"Or they show you," he agreed. "As you have."

She swallowed, and then her head bowed forward, only
slightly, but Alessandro saw it. He knew defeat when it
stood before him. That should mean he'd won, that he was
victorious in this—whatever this was. It should mean he
felt triumph at the very least. And instead what he felt
was empty.

"The show's over, Alessandro," she whispered, and he
couldn't make sense of what he saw on her face then.

Perhaps because he couldn't, he didn't stop her when
she turned and walked away from him, again, leaving him
there alone in the quiet room, the echoes of the passion
they'd shared seeming to cling to the walls like rich, wild
tapestries.

And still he tried to work out what he'd seen on her elegant features before she'd left. Temper, certainly. The lingering trace of that powerful desire that, it seemed, never
truly left either one of them. A kind of weary resignation.

And sadness.

It was like a punch to the gut.

Elena was sad. And he'd made her that way.

She had looked at him like he was a monster. Worse,
as if she knew he'd chosen to become exactly that. As if
she knew he'd vowed he would never become this kind of

man—a man of cruelty and dark impulse like his father—no matter the provocation, and then had gone ahead and done it, anyway.

As if she knew.

He wasn't sure he could live with it. He wasn't sure he could bear being this much of a disappointment to himself, this much of a bastard.

But he didn't know how to stop.

CHAPTER SIX

"I WANT YOU in my bed," he said curtly later that same night, appearing in the doorway of her bedchamber.

Elena was curled up in the blue-and-white armchair near one of the sweeping, open windows, staring out at the dark sea and the silver pathway that rippled there, stretching toward the swollen orange moon hanging low on the horizon. She'd been thinking about resistance. About surrender.

About how to use this uncontrollable passion for her own ends before it swallowed her whole.

"I knew I meant to lock that door," she murmured, dropping her mask into place as she turned to look at him.

"Tonight," Alessandro told her in that same clipped, commanding tone, the slight narrowing of his fierce eyes the only indication he'd heard her. "And for good. This particular game is over and I think we both know you lost."

He'd showered. She could smell the faint scent of his soap, fresh and clean. His thick hair lay in damp waves on his head, and he no longer looked the way he had when she'd left him in the dining room. Bereft, she might have said, if he were a smaller creature, a lesser man.

He expected her to resist him. Still. Again. Elena could see it in the way he held himself, the fine lines of his powerful body taut. She could see it in the way his dark green gaze was hooded, yet tracked her every breath.

So what if you lose a little bit more of yourself? she asked herself briskly, shoving aside what felt like a kind of despair, concentrating instead on that ravenous hunger for him she couldn't seem to escape. That was what she had to exploit. The possibility of a pregnancy had brought her this far—passion would do the rest. It had to. *There are worse things to lose—and far worse fates.*

"All right," she said.

The moment stretched out. He cocked his head slightly to one side, eyes narrow and jaw hard. "What did you say?"

"I'm agreeing with you, Alessandro." She swung her feet off the chair, pressing her bare toes into the polished wood floor beneath her. Like that would keep her grounded. Like anything could. "You win."

There was a tense, shimmering silence. Elena kept her gaze trained down at her bare feet, on the toes she'd painted a bright pink in some attack of hopefulness when she'd still worked on his yacht—but then, she didn't have to look at him to feel the way he was glaring at her. The fire and the force of him like a wild heat against her skin. A dark magic inside of her, changing her. Ruining her.

Only if I let it, she assured herself. She might lose a bit of herself, but it was worth it, wasn't it? She was safe here, and she needed to stay that way. And he would lose interest in her all the quicker once she ceased to be a challenge, because that was how men like him operated—so this would ensure that when their forty days were up, he would wash his hands of her. Discard her, happily, without bothering to inform on her to Niccolo. She would be free, and Niccolo would have lost her trail completely.

This was insurance, plain and simple.

"And what," he asked, his low voice threaded with seductive, sensual menace, "do I win, Elena? Be specific."

She lifted her head. His expression was deeply cynical, his stance tense, and yet that same passion burned in him, bright and hot, as obvious to her as if it was tattooed across his face.

"Whatever you like," she told him.

She raised her brows as he only stood there in the doorway and did no more than continue to study her, as if she was a code he intended to break. A trickle of apprehension worked its way down her spine—because she couldn't let him do that. He could have her, but not all of her. And never the truth.

"Isn't this what you want?" she asked, taunting him. Distracting him. She smiled, cool and challenging. "My complete and total surrender, entirely on your terms? Well, here it is. This is what it looks like. You should be pleased, surely."

"Is that meant to shame me?" he countered, a dark gleam in his eyes then, and Elena had to fight back an involuntary shiver. "I think you'll find I'm far past that. Nothing can. Certainly not you."

"Then you have nothing to fear." She stood, smoothing her hands down the front of the silk-and-lace chemise she wore, in a soft champagne shade that she knew made her eyes that much bluer. "I found this on the end of the bed, like all the rest of the clothes I've found waiting for me since I got here. It's as if you make them all yourself in some secret workshop in the night."

"Not me." There was a sardonic curve to his mouth, but his dark eyes burned as he watched her walk toward him. Possessive. Hungry. "My cousin Luca runs a fashion house. We may not be close, but the clothes speak for themselves."

Elena didn't say anything. She wasn't sure she could, now that she was really going through with this. It was one thing to decide to surrender herself to this man, at least in bed. It was something else again to *do* it.

It might very well shred her into tiny little pieces she wasn't sure she'd ever manage to put back together. But she knew this was the only way.

And she couldn't deny the fact that it excited her. That he did. That the idea of sharing his bed made her shiver with need, no matter what price she'd end up paying.

She walked toward him, holding his gaze. Letting her hips sway beneath the silken embrace of the fabric that clung to her. Letting him watch, wait. She could see the stamp of hunger across his face. She could see the blaze of it in his eyes.

And felt more powerful in this moment than she had in a very long time. Since she'd looked up from her life to find a shockingly beautiful man watching her as if she was a goddess come down to earth. She felt it hum in her like an electrical current.

She stopped when she was no more than a breath away and stood there. She waited. He tensed, but he didn't move. His hands were thrust deep into the pockets of his loose black trousers as if he was perfectly at ease, but she knew better.

"Do you think this will work, Elena?" he asked, his voice hoarse. "This suspicious capitulation, this attempt at seduction, coming so soon on the heels of your deep concerns about respect?"

"You should ask yourself," she said, her tone light, though her gaze was hard on his, "why even when I do what you say you want, you accuse me of something. Anything."

"Because it won't," he said, answering his own question. His mouth twisted. "Not the way you imagine. I don't care how you come to me. I don't care how I have you. I don't care at all, so long as I do. Are you prepared for that?"

"I told you," she said softly. "You win." She held out

her arms like some kind of supplicant, but she smiled like a queen. "To the victor go the spoils—isn't that what they say?"

"They do."

He reached over and traced a deceptively lazy trail from the wildly fluttering pulse in her throat to the hollow between her breasts. All of his ruthlessness, all of his simmering power, in that one fingertip.

"You should be afraid of me," he told her then, and his voice moved in her, threat and promise, sex and demand, and something even darker in his eyes. "Why aren't you?"

"I'm terrified," she whispered, but she wasn't. And she could see he knew it.

"I wish I knew which one of us is the greater fool," he replied in the same harsh whisper, and it made her throat constrict.

"Someone once told me you should be careful what you wish for, Alessandro," she said, because it was better to taunt him. It was better to push. Safer. "You just might get it, and then what will you do?"

Her heart beat like a hammer in her chest, in her breasts, between her legs, and she could swear he heard it, too, because his hard mouth curved, not a trace of cynicism to be seen. Only desire.

And that was all the warning she got.

He hauled her up into the air, then threw her over one shoulder like she weighed nothing at all. Like the warrior king she'd imagined him. Claiming her that easily—that completely.

She gasped—but his hand came down on her bottom, his big, hard palm holding her fast and warning her, and she gulped her own words down.

His shoulder was wide and hard against her belly as he moved through the house; his hand was a hot brand of fire against the exposed skin of her behind, the backs of her thighs. She caught a glimpse of herself as they passed a mirror, hanging down his strong back, her hair wild and her face flushed, and it made her breath go shallow. She couldn't stop trembling, and it still wasn't fear.

Surrender, she told herself. *It's the only way to save everything else that matters.* But what scared her wasn't the act of surrendering to him. It was that it was so easy. That it felt so good.

Alessandro tossed her down in the center of his bed, and she had only a quick impression of bold colors, dark woods and arching windows wide open to let the night inside. Then her gaze fixed on him, and stayed put. He stood by the side of the wide bed for a moment, looking down at her as she sprawled there, and she couldn't quite read the intense look in his eyes, on his hard face.

But she trembled. And wanted. And melted into liquid fire.

He didn't ask. He didn't ply her with more of those lethal, sensual promises of his, those half terrifying and half intriguing things he'd said he would do to her, with her, if only she'd ask.

He simply took.

And she gloried in that, too.

This is exactly what you wanted, Elena reminded herself a week or so later as she stood in that gorgeous shower room built outside to take in the sunlight and the crisp sea air.

She tilted her face up into the spray, and let the heat work its way into her as she considered her success. Her delicious, dangerous surrender.

There was no part of her body Alessandro hadn't claimed. No millimeter of skin he hadn't investigated with his fingers, his mouth, his wicked tongue. He took her with a ferocity and a kind of desperation she understood too well, because it was in her, too, this terrible hunger. It was never satisfied. It never dimmed.

No matter how many times he tore her apart, no matter how often she screamed his name and then held him close as he collapsed against her, it was still there. Moving within her. Ripping her open. Making her fear it would be impossible to ever really leave this man, that this kind of hunger would mark her, scar her....

But she'd returned the favor. She'd thrown herself head-first into that fire, and who cared what burned? She'd pushed him down on that same dinner table and climbed on top of him, using her mouth and hands to make him groan. She'd learned what made him burst into flame, what made him roll her over and take control, what made him laugh in the dark as they explored each other. She'd teased him, taken him, taunted him—and then slept wrapped up against him, held close against that powerful chest of his, lulled into sleep by the steady beat of his heart.

This is what success feels like, she told herself now. *You should be happy.* But instead, she pictured them dancing, around and around in that ballroom, all of that wonder and delight between them. It glowed in her still, even here. Even now.

What they could have been. What they should have been.

She shouldn't let herself dream about such things, because it only hurt her. She shouldn't let herself imagine what it would be like if none of what had happened on this island had that darker undertone, if this wasn't one more game they played. If it really meant something when he kissed her face and smiled at her, when she held him close and whispered his name.

If it meant what she'd seen back then, glimmering between them, just out of reach—

Snap out of the daydream, she ordered herself now, annoyed at herself and that gnawing ache in her chest that made her feel so hollow. *You're here to be the whore he thinks you are. Nothing more.*

It turned out, she was good at that.

She shut off the water and reached for her towel, and he was there when she opened her eyes. Her stomach still clenched. Her heart still jumped. He was still so impossibly beautiful, fierce and male, standing in the open door between his suite and the open shower area, his arms crossed over his bare chest.

"How long have you been there?" she asked. She had to fight to make her voice smooth, and she didn't know why. It should have been easy after all this practice. It should have been second nature by now.

"Not long."

"Weren't you going for a run?"

"I was." He smiled. "I did."

"I must have spent more time in the shower than I realized."

She wanted to sound light. Easy. She couldn't understand why that raw, hollow place inside of her still bled into everything. As if it mattered how close this all was to what it should have been, yet wasn't.

And won't ever be, she reminded herself.

"Do you think you're pregnant?" he'd asked one afternoon, the sun pouring in through the windows, bathing them both in white light as they moved together on his bed. He'd run his hands over her belly, his gentle touch at distinct odds with his gruff voice. It had been too much. There'd been that look in his eyes, so close to a kind of yearning. It had torn her up inside.

She'd been straddling him, and she'd twisted her hips to take him deep inside of her. Sex was better than emotion. Easier. He'd hissed out a breath, his dark eyes narrowing.

"We'll find out soon enough," she'd said, reminding him who they were, moving against him to make her point. "And then we can stop pretending there's anything more to this than sex."

He'd reached up to pull her mouth down to his, and he'd whispered something against her lips. It had only been later, when they'd collapsed again, breathless and destroyed, that she'd realized what he'd said. *Damn you.*

She walked toward him now, wrapping the towel around her, and he stepped back to let her pass. She made her way into his bedroom and over toward the massive bed that dominated the far wall, angled for the best view out of the many windows.

None of this was what she'd thought it would be. He wasn't the man she'd believed he was. He was nothing like Niccolo, and she didn't know how to process that. She'd expected the fire to dissipate the more she indulged herself in him, showing her what horrors lay beneath. But Alessandro wasn't made of Niccolo's brand of bright surface charm to hide the bully within, or if he was, he was better at concealing it. He was gruff and hard, ruthless and demanding—but he was also surprisingly thoughtful. Caring in ways that made it hard for her to breathe, much less throw out the next, necessary barb. As likely to take the hairbrush from her hand and brush her hair, making her tremble with something far different from lust when he met her eyes in the mirror, as he was to throw her up against the nearest wall and let the raging fire consume them.

He's like Niccolo. He's worse than Niccolo. She chanted it at herself. *You might not be able to see it, but it's there. It has to be there.*

Because if he wasn't like Niccolo, if she'd been that terribly wrong about him, then she had no reason not to trust him the way she wished she could. She might feel oddly safe with him, still. He might thrill her in ways she was afraid to admit to herself. But she'd been running for too long, and there was as much to lose now as there had been when she'd started.

More, perhaps, if she counted her foolish heart, and the way it beat for him.

"What's the matter?" he asked from behind her, that combination of perception and kindness in his tone that was uniquely his. It undid her.

But she couldn't cry. She couldn't betray herself like this, when she'd come so far and given up so much.

Elena turned to face him. She met his dark gaze, saw the concern there that she couldn't acknowledge, that she couldn't let herself accept. Alessandro's mouth crooked in one corner, and that was all it took for her to melt. To want. To topple over into that stark, demanding need.

"Come here," she said, her voice husky with the things she couldn't say, the truths she couldn't tell.

And he obeyed, this fierce predator of a man, his dark eyes bright and fixed on her with that same hunger. She waited until he was close and then she dropped the towel, and he laughed.

"You'll be the death of me," he said in that low voice that made her skin prickle, and then his hands were on her skin, lifting her and pushing her back onto the bed, coming down on top of her with that delicious weight of his, smooth muscle and dangerous man.

"I'll sing the elegy at your funeral," she promised him, and his smile deepened in a way that made her ache everywhere, hot and greedy for him.

"I won't die alone." He buried his hands in her wet

hair, pulling her mouth to within a breath of his. "I promise you that."

Their gazes tangled, held, as she reached between them and pulled him free from his running shorts. As she reached for the side table, then rolled protection down over the hard, smooth length of him. As she guided him to her entrance.

"Elena," he whispered. "I—"

But words were even more dangerous than he was. She couldn't have it. She couldn't risk it. She moved her hips against him, inviting him in. Making him groan. Keeping him quiet.

Being the whore he thought she was, or she thought she was, or this situation had made her. She told herself it didn't matter anymore. She only knew she had to see it through.

He pushed inside of her, and they both sighed. That perfect, impossible fit. That slick, wild fire. That coil of desire, tight and hot, that only seemed stronger every time.

This was killing them, she thought then, her gaze locked to his, lost in his, truths shimmering between them that she refused to voice. He knew things he shouldn't know, the way he always had, and they might as well be dancing still, around and around, as familiar and as lost to each other as ever.

But he moved in her then, commanding and powerful and hers—hers despite everything as he had been from that first glance, that very first touch of their hands—and she forgot again, the way she always did.

For a little while.

Alessandro stalked out of the house.

He moved across the terrace toward the pool, where Elena sat on one of the loungers, whiling away another summer morning. She looked perfectly at ease, while he was still boiling over with all the frustration he'd unloaded on his assistant over the past few hours. He made a mental note to increase the man's annual bonus.

"One more week, Giovanni," he'd snapped when yet another Corretti family crisis had been trotted out as if it was a critical business issue that required his immediate attention. Because Alessandro was expected to care, to be responsible. To handle everyone else's mess. "I'm on holiday. Tell them to sort it out themselves, or wait."

"But, sir…" His assistant had cleared his throat. "They grow more insistent by the hour!"

"Then I suggest you earn your outrageous salary," Alessandro had growled, ending the call. But it hadn't done much for the restless agitation that still coursed through him, making him feel edgy.

He slowed as he drew closer to Elena, tucked up in the shade of an umbrella, paging through foreign magazines with every outward appearance of lazy contentment. For some reason, that flipped a kind of switch in him.

One more week to forty days. One more week until he and Elena were finished—or bound together in a way he'd tried not to think about too closely. One more week, and he wasn't ready.

He didn't want the life he'd left behind when he'd fled Sicily a month ago. He didn't want to slip back into that same old role that had brought him nothing but grief for the whole of his adult life. He didn't want to dance to the tune of a dead man, or fight these losing battles against his family's bad reputation. He was as tired of it as he'd been the day he'd left.

Just as he was fed up with Elena's stubborn determination to keep him at arm's length.

He knew what she was doing, with her mysterious smiles and the sex she doled out as if she was nothing more than a sensual buffet and he a mindless glutton. She was giving him what she thought he wanted. Soothing the savage beast.

But he knew there was more to her, and he wanted it. He was so damned tired of half measures, of *almost*. He wanted everything she had. Every last secret. He wanted to know her better than he knew himself.

He wanted *her*.

Alessandro was sick and tired of settling for less.

"It's been thirty-three days, Elena," he said when he reached her side. He waited until she looked up from her magazine, and then smiled. "Does that mean we already have our answer?"

"Good morning to you, too," she said in her usual way, arch and arid, but this time he sensed her temper beneath it. And he couldn't have said why he wanted to see it so much, so badly. "And no. There are a few days left before I'd jump to any conclusions."

For a moment, they only gazed at each other, and he could feel what flowed between them. That wild electricity, as always, but there was something else beneath it. Something real. He was sure of it.

She shifted position, and smiled in a way she knew by now was guaranteed to poke at his hunger. Her fingers plucked at the ragged hem of the denim shorts she wore beneath an open-necked, nearly sheer shirt that flowed all around her in bright reds and deep blues, hinting at the delectable curves beneath. Her smooth legs went on forever, sun-kissed and shaped so beautifully. She patted the lounger beside her, and it caused him physical pain not to put his hands on her. Not to wrap those legs around his waist, throw them over his shoulders, revel in all the ways he wanted her.

But it wasn't enough, and he didn't care that she wanted

it that way. That she was using their explosive chemistry to hide in. He couldn't allow it any longer.

"I wonder what would happen if we kept our clothes on," he said then, quietly, and her eyes widened. "What then, Elena? What do you think we'd discover?"

"That we are perfect strangers," she replied coolly, but her clear eyes darkened. "Who never should have met in the first place."

"I'm not convinced." He held her gaze, saw the hint of panic in hers. "What are you hiding?"

He was sure he saw her flinch, then control it. Almost too fast to track.

"What could I possibly be hiding?" she retorted. "You've taken everything. You know everything. There's nothing left."

"I've taken your body, yes," he agreed. "I know it very well, just as you intended. But what about the rest of you?"

He watched her struggle, one emotion after the next moving across her face, and he knew he was right. She shook her head, her blue eyes cloudy.

"What do you care?" she asked quietly. "You have what you want."

"I want everything," he said, raw and intense, and smiled when she jerked back against the lounger.

And everything might not be enough, a voice whispered deep inside of him. He might have been a ruined thing, twisted and dark all the way through, but he needed this. He needed her. He didn't care why. He only knew he did.

He watched her pull in a breath, then another, and she curled her hands into tight fists on her thighs. He forced himself to wait. She looked away for a long, tense moment, and when her eyes met his again, he saw her. *Her.*

At last.

"I knew it," he said with deep satisfaction. "I knew you were right there, simmering beneath the surface."

"What do you want, Alessandro?" she asked, and her voice was neither cool nor amused, for the first time in a very long while. "We only have a few days left here. Why ruin them with this?"

"I want the woman I met in Rome," he told her. "I don't want a damned sex toy."

She let out a short, derisive laugh. "Of course you do. Men like you always do."

He felt that same familiar darkness in him expanding, rising, sweeping through him, reminding him how ruined and twisted he was and always had been, since the day he was born. *Men like you.* Would he never escape his name? Was he doomed to be exactly like his father, no matter how hard he'd struggled against it?

"I don't care if you hate me, Elena," he gritted out. "But whatever else this is, whatever happens, I want it to be real."

Because one thing in his life had to be. Just one thing.

"'Real,'" she repeated in a flat tone. "You. That's almost funny. What do you know about *real*?" Her face heated as she spoke, her temper flooding in like a rising tide and as beautiful to him, however perverse that was. "You almost married a woman for what? A business expense?"

"Duty," Alessandro corrected her, and she laughed.
She laughed.

"The reality, Alessandro, is that you are not a good man," she said with an awful, deliberate finality, staring straight at him, deliberate and pointed. "How could you be? You're a Corretti."

Condemnation and curse, all wrapped up in his name. His damned name. She said it as if it was the vilest word imaginable. As if the very saying of it blackened her tongue. He felt something crack open inside of him.

Because, of course, he wasn't simply a Corretti. He was the one his family was happy to sacrifice to serve their own ends. He was the one who was expected to do his duty, because he always had. His own parents had used him as a pawn. His grandfather had manipulated him. His "business expense" had walked out on him. Then Elena had crashed into his life like a lightning bolt, illuminating all of his darkest corners in that single, searing, impossible dance, but she hated him—he'd made sure of it. He had never been anything but a dark, ruined thing, masquerading as a man.

"Your conscience will be your undoing, boy," Carlo had jeered at him more than once. "It makes you weak."

As long as it didn't make him Carlo, he thought now, bitterly. Perhaps that was the most he could hope for.

Elena had no clue what she was dealing with. No possible clue what he held in check. "You don't have the slightest idea who I am."

"The entire world knows who you are," she retorted, glaring at him as if he'd never been anything but a monster, and he couldn't stand it. Not any longer. Not from her. "You're—"

"I am so tired of paying for the sins of others," he gritted out. He slashed a hand through the air when she opened her mouth and she shut it again, sinking back against the lounger, her hands in fists at her sides. "I've spent my life doing nothing but the right thing, and it still doesn't matter. Yes, I was going to marry that girl." He raked a hand through his hair. "Because it was my grandfather's dying wish and I am many things, Elena, none of them as polluted or as vile as you seem to believe, but I could not defy my own grandfather."

"Your grandfather—" she began, her eyes flashing, and he knew what she was about to say. The stories she was about to tell. His twisted family history in all its corrupt glory.

"Was no saint," he interrupted her. "I know. But he was my *grandfather*, Elena, and whatever else I might think of the way he lived his life, I have him to thank for mine. How do you repay that kind of debt?"

"Selling yourself off to the highest bidder is an interesting answer to that question."

"You're one to talk," he retorted, and she sucked in a breath, her face going white, then flushing deep red.

He hated himself for that, but that was nothing new, so he kept going—as if he could explain himself to her. As if she might understand him, somehow. How sad was that? How delusional? But he couldn't seem to stop.

"The docklands project that the wedding was supposed to secure would have done what years of struggle on my part couldn't—assure the Corretti family's legacy into the future, legitimately. Bring all the warring factions of the family together." He searched her face. "How could I refuse to do something so important? Why would I? I was prepared to do my duty to my family, and I can't say I wouldn't do it again."

But she was shaking her head, and she even let out another laugh that seemed to pierce him through the chest, leaving only an icy chill in its wake.

"I've heard all of this before," she said, shrugging. "The struggle to be a good man, the weight of the family name, the call to duty. It's like a song and I know all the words." Her gaze slammed into his, and he was amazed to find it felt as if she'd used a fist instead. "But when Niccolo said it, I believed him."

CHAPTER SEVEN

NICCOLO FALCO. AGAIN. Always.

"Your beloved Niccolo is a liar and a crook," Alessandro said through his teeth. "He wouldn't know the right thing to do if it attacked him on the streets of Naples, and he certainly wouldn't do it. Don't kid yourself."

She got to her feet then, stiff and jerky, as if she thought she might break apart where she stood. "I would never lower myself to a Corretti scum like you," she'd hissed at him on that dance floor, and he'd believed her then.

He didn't know why he wanted so badly not to believe her now.

"Is this what you meant by *real,* Alessandro?" she asked in a harsh whisper, her bright eyes ablaze. "Are you satisfied?"

"It would be so much easier to simply give in," he threw at her, his voice unsteady. As if he'd lost control of himself, which was unacceptable, but he couldn't stop. "To simply be the man everyone thinks I am, anyway, no matter what I do. Even you, who shouldn't dare to throw a single stone my way for fear of what I could throw back at you. *Even you.*"

She sucked in a breath, as if he really had thrown something at her.

"Because there could be no one lower in all of Italy."

Something in the way she said it ripped at him, or maybe that was the way she looked at him, as if he'd finally managed to crush her—and he detested himself anew. "Not one person lower than me. Yet you can't keep your hands off me, can you?"

"You know exactly what kind of man Niccolo is," he said then, because he couldn't handle what her voice did to him. What that look in her eyes made him feel. "You're here at his bidding, to do whatever dirty work he requires. And it's certainly been dirty, hasn't it? But you sneer at *my* name?"

"I am here," she threw back at him, her voice still so ragged and her eyes so dark, too dark, "until we discover whether or not our recklessness results in a pregnancy neither one of us wants. We risked bringing a brand-new life into all of this bitterness and hate. That's the kind of people we are, Alessandro."

"Why don't you teach me," he said then, his gaze on hers, hot and hurt and too many other things he couldn't define and wasn't sure he wanted to know, though he could feel them all battering at him.

"Teach you what? Manners? I think we're past that."

"You're the expert on *men like me,*" he said, fascinated despite himself when she blanched at the way he said that. "You know all about it, apparently. Teach me what that means. Show me. Help me be as bad as you think I am already."

Something shifted in the air between them. In her gaze. The way her blue eyes shone with unshed misery, and the way she suddenly looked so small then, so vulnerable. So shattered.

And all he felt was…raw. Raw and ruined, all the way through to his bones.

Or maybe that was the way she looked at him.

"Let me guess what makes me the perfect teacher," she said, her voice cracking.

"You tell me, Elena," he said, his own voice a low, dark growl. "You're the one in bed with the enemy."

And she swayed then, as if he'd punched her hard in the gut. He felt as if he had, a kind of hot, bitter shame pouring over him, almost drowning him. But she steadied herself, and one hand crept over her heart, as if, he realized dimly, it ached. As if it ached straight up through her ribs, enough for her to press against it from above.

"I can't do this anymore."

Her voice was thick and unsteady, and he had the impression she didn't see him at all, though she stared right at him. Her eyes were wide and slicked with pain, and he watched in a kind of helpless horror as they finally overflowed.

"I don't..." She shook, and she wept, and it tore him apart. And then her uneven whisper smashed all the pieces. "I don't know what I'm doing here."

Alessandro reached for her then because he didn't know what else to do. Elena threw her free hand out to stop him, to warn him. Maybe even to hit him, he thought—and he'd deserve it if she did. He did yet another thing he couldn't understand, reaching out and lacing his fingers through hers, the way he had on that dance floor long ago. She shuddered, then drew in a harsh breath.

But she didn't pull away, and something in him, hard and desperate, eased.

"I can't breathe anymore," she whispered, those tears tracking down her soft cheeks. He felt the tremor in her hand, saw it shiver over her skin. "I can't breathe—"

He pulled her to him, cradling her against his chest as if she was made of glass, the need to hold her roaring in him, loud and imperative and impossible to ignore. She bowed her head into him and he felt the hand she'd held against her own heart ball into a fist against the wall of his chest.

He ran his free hand down the length of her spine and then back up. Again and again. He found himself murmuring words he didn't entirely comprehend, half-remembered words from the long-ago nannies who had soothed his nightmares and bandaged his scrapes as a boy. He bent his head down close to hers and rested his cheek on top of her head.

She shook against him, silent sobs rolling hard through her slender body, and he held her. He didn't think about how little sense this made. He didn't think about what this told him about himself, or how terrified he should be of this woman and the things she made him feel. And do. He simply held her.

And when she stopped crying and stirred against him, it was much, much harder than it should have been to let her pull away. She stepped out of his arms and dropped his hand, then scrubbed her palms over her face. And then she looked up at him, tearstained and wary with a certain resolve in her brilliant blue eyes, and something flipped over in his chest.

"I'm not a whore," she said, something naked and urgent moving over her face and through her remarkable eyes as they met his. "I'm not engaged to Niccolo. I ran out on him six months ago after he hit me, and I've been hiding from him ever since."

He only stared at her. The world, this island, his house, even he seemed to explode, devastating and silent, leaving nothing but Elena and the way she looked at him, the faint dampness against his chest where she'd sobbed against him and what she'd said. What it meant.

She was not engaged. She was not a whore. She wasn't a spy.

It beat in him, louder and louder, drowning out his own heartbeat.

"I'm risking everything I care about to tell you this," she continued, and he heard the catch in her voice, the tightness. *The fear,* he thought. *She's afraid. Of me.* "The only things I have left. So please…" She choked back a sob and it made him ache. It made him loathe himself anew. "Please, Alessandro. Prove you're who you say you are."

"A Corretti?" He hardly recognized his own voice, scratchy and rough, pulled from somewhere so deep in him he hadn't known he meant to speak.

She crossed her arms, more to hold herself than to hold him off, he thought. She took a deep breath. Then her chin lifted and her blue eyes were brave and somber as they held his, and he felt everything inside of him shift. Then roll.

"Be the man who does the right thing," she said, her voice quiet. And still it rang in him, through him, like a bell. Like a benediction he couldn't possibly deserve. "Who does his duty and would again. If that's who you are, please. Be you."

"Come," Alessandro said in a hushed voice Elena had never heard before.

She was so dazed, so hollowed out by what had happened, what she'd done, that she simply followed where he led. He ushered her out onto a small nook of a terrace that jutted out over the water, settling her into the wide, swinging chair that hung there, swaying slightly in the soft breeze.

"Wait here," he told her, and then walked away.

She couldn't have moved if she'd wanted to, she realized. She drew her knees up onto the bright white seat and leaned back. The chair swung, gently. Rocking her. Soothing her the way his hand had, warm and reassuring along her back as she'd cried. Down below, the rocky cliff fell steeply into the jagged rocks, and the sea sparkled and danced in the afternoon sun, as if everything was perfectly fine. As if none of this mattered, not really.

But Elena knew better.

She'd betrayed her family and her village and every last thing she'd clung to across all of these months, and yet somehow she couldn't seem to do anything but breathe in the crisp air, the scent of sweet flowers and cut grass in the breeze.

Almost as if she really believed she was safe. Almost as if she thought *he* was, the way she always had. When she suspected the truth was that she was simply broken beyond repair.

Alessandro returned with a damp cloth in his hand and when he squatted down before her his hard face was so serious that it made her chest feel tight. She leaned forward and let him wash the tears from her face. He was extraordinarily gentle, and it swelled in her like pain.

He pulled the cloth away and didn't move for a moment. He only looked up at her, searching her face. She had no idea what he saw.

"Tell me," he said.

It was an order as much as it was a request, and she knew she shouldn't. Her mind raced, turning over possibilities like *tavola reale* game pieces, looking for some way out of this, some way to fix what she'd done, what she'd said, what she'd confessed....

But it was too late for that.

This was the price of her foolishness, her selfishness. First Niccolo had tricked her, and then this man had hurt her feelings, and she was too weak to withstand either. Now that her tears were dry, now that she could breathe, she could see it all with perfect, horrifying clarity. She hadn't kept her village or her family's legacy safe the first time, and given the opportunity to fix that, she'd failed.

Because he thought too little of her, and she couldn't stand it.

She was more than broken, she thought then. She was a disgrace.

"Tell me what happened to you," he said then, carefully, again so very gentle that her throat constricted. "Tell me what he did."

He rose and then settled himself on the other end of the swinging chair, one leg drawn up and the other anchoring them to the floor. His hard mouth was in a firm line as he gazed at her, his dark green eyes grave. For a moment she was thrown back to that ballroom in Rome, when she'd looked up to see a stranger looking at her, exactly like this. As if the whole world hinged on what might happen next.

Which she supposed it had then. Why not again?

"I'm from a long line of very simple fishermen," she said, pushing past the lump in her throat, concentrating on her hands instead of him. "But my great-grandfather eloped with the daughter of a rich man from Fondi. Her parents begged her to reconsider, but she refused, and they decided it was better their daughter live as a rich fisherman's wife than a poor one's. They gave my great-grandfather her dowry. It was substantial."

She pulled up her knees, then wrapped her arms around her legs, fully aware that this was as close to the fetal position as she could get while sitting up. And she fought off her sense of disloyalty, the fact that she should be protecting this legacy, not handing it over to man who was perfectly capable of destroying it. On a whim.

But she didn't know what else to do.

"He was a proud man and he didn't want their money," she continued, swallowing back the self-recrimination.

"But my great-grandmother convinced him to put it toward a big stretch of land along the coast, so her family need not be as dependent on the whims of the sea as the rest of the village. And the land has been handed down ever since, from eldest son to eldest son."

She looked past him then, out toward the water, as if she could squint hard and see all the way across the waves to the remote little village she was from, tucked up in its rocky hills so far away. She could imagine every rock, every blade of grass, every tree, as if she was standing there now. She knew every house that clung to the hillside, every boat in the harbor. And most of the faces, too.

"It must," Alessandro said quietly, "be worth a great deal more now than it was then."

Elena should have thanked him, she thought, her eyes snapping back to his, for reminding her where she was. And who he was. She wasn't sharing this story with him—she was gambling everything on the slim possibility he was a better man than she thought he was. She nodded.

"It is," she said. "And my parents had only me."

"So the land is yours?" he asked, his brows lifting.

"My father is a traditional man," Elena said, looking down the sweep of her legs, staring at her feet against the bright white cushions. Anywhere but at Alessandro. "When he dies, if I'm not married, the land will be held in trust. Once I marry it will transfer to my husband. If I'm already married when he dies, my husband will get the land on our wedding day."

"Ah," Alessandro said, a cynical twist to his lips when she looked at him again. "You must have been Niccolo's dream come true."

"Last summer my father was diagnosed with a brain tumor," she told him, pushing forward because she couldn't stop now. "There was no possible way to operate." So matter-of-fact, so clinical. When it had cast her whole world into shadow. It still did. "The doctors said he had a year to live, if he was lucky."

"A year?" His dark green gaze felt like a touch. The long arm he'd stretched out along the back of the seat moved slightly, as if he meant to reach for her but thought better of it. That shouldn't have warmed her. "It's nearly July."

She hugged herself tighter, guilt and shame and that terrible grief flattening her, making it hard to breathe.

"About a month after we got the news, I was walking home one evening when a handsome stranger approached me, right there in the street," she said softly.

Alessandro's lips thinned, and he muttered something guttural and fierce in Sicilian. He looked furious again, dark and powerful, like some kind of vengeful god only pretending to sit there so civilly. Only waiting.

"Do you want to hear this?" she asked then, lifting a hand to rub at the pressure behind her temple and only then realizing that she was shaking. "All of it?"

"I told you," he said, a kind of ferocity in his voice, all that ruthlessness and demand gleaming in his dark green eyes. He touched her then, reaching over to tuck a wayward strand of her hair behind her ear, that hard mouth curving when goose bumps rose along her neck, her shoulder. "I want everything."

And Elena understood then that she was open and vulnerable to this man in ways she'd never been before. This really was everything. This was all she had left inside of her, all she'd had left to hold, laid out before him because she'd finally given in. She'd finally let go. This was everything lost, her whole world ruined, and nothing left to hope for but the possibility of his mercy.

This was surrender. Everything else had been games.

"I didn't think I was particularly naive," she said then,

because he was looking at her in that too-incisive way of his, and she was afraid of what he might see. And of what he might do when she was finished. "I'd been to university. I have a law degree. I was starting to take on all the duties and responsibilities of the family business. The land. The money. The constant development proposals." She shook her head, scowling at her own memories. Her own stupidity. "I wasn't just some silly village girl."

And that was the crux of it. She felt new tears prick at the backs of her eyes, and hurriedly blinked them back. She'd thought she was better than where she came from. She'd thought very highly of herself indeed. She'd been certain she *deserved* the handsome, wealthy stranger who had appeared like magic to sweep her off her feet.

Such vanity.

She only realized she'd said it out loud when Alessandro said something else in his brash Sicilian, so little of which she understood even after her time there. He shifted in his seat, making it swing with him as he did.

"I told you before," he said. "It was a con."

"I believed him," Elena said simply, shame and regret in her voice, moving in her veins like sludge. She felt it all over her face, and had to stop looking at him before she saw it on his, too. "I believed every single thing he told me. All of his big dreams. All of his plans. That he and I were a team." Her voice cracked, but she kept going. "That he loved me. I believed every word."

"Elena," he said in a voice she'd never heard him use before. She had to close her eyes briefly against it. As if her name was an endearment she couldn't believe a man so hard even knew. "You were supposed to believe him. He set you up."

She didn't know why she wanted to weep then, again.

"I knew you were lying to me in Rome," she said

fiercely, hugging her knees tight, keeping her eyes trained on the sea, determined to hold the tears back. "About everything. You had to be lying, because Niccolo couldn't possibly be the man you described, and because, of course, you were a Corretti."

"Of course." His tone made her wince. She didn't dare look at his expression.

"I went looking for things to prove you were a liar. One night while Niccolo slept, I got up and decided to search the laptop he took everywhere with him."

She heard Alessandro's release of breath, short and sharp, but she still couldn't look at him. Especially not now.

"He caught me, of course, but not until after I read far too many emails that explained in detail his plans for my family's land." She frowned, as horrified now as she had been then. "He wanted to build a luxury hotel, which would transform my forgotten village into a major tourist destination. We're fishermen, first and foremost. We don't even have a decent beach. We like to visit Amalfi, but we don't want to compete with it."

She shook her head, remembering that night in such stark detail. She'd only thrown on a shirt of Niccolo's and a pair of socks, and had snuck down to the kitchen to snoop on his computer while he snored. It had been cold in his villa, and she remembered shivering as she sat on one of the stools, her legs growing chillier the longer she sat there.

And she remembered the way her stomach had lurched when she'd looked up to see him in the doorway.

He hadn't asked her what she was doing. He'd only stared at her, his black eyes flat and mean, and for a terrifying moment Elena hadn't recognized him.

She'd told herself she was only being fanciful. It had been well after midnight and she hadn't heard him approach. But he was still her Niccolo, she'd assured herself.

He was in love with her, he was going to marry her, and while they were probably going to fight about his privacy and all these emails she couldn't understand, it would all be fine.

She'd been so sure.

"I asked him what it meant, because I was certain there had to be a reasonable explanation." She let out a hollow laugh. "He knew we wanted to conserve the land, protect the village. He'd spent hours talking to my father about it. He'd promised."

"I imagine he did not have a satisfying explanation," Alessandro said darkly.

"He slapped me." Such a funny, improbable word to describe it. The shock of the impact first, then the burst of pain. Then she'd hit the cold stone floor, and that had hurt even more.

Alessandro went frighteningly still.

Elena's heart raced, and she felt sick. Her knuckles were white where she gripped her own legs, and she still wanted to curl up further, disappear. But it didn't matter if he believed her, she told herself staunchly. Her own parents hadn't believed her. It only mattered that she told this truth, no matter what he thought of it.

"He slapped me so hard he knocked me down. Off my stool. To the floor." She made herself look at Alessandro then, burning there in his quiet fury, his dark green eyes brilliant with rage.

Directed at Niccolo, she understood. Not at her. And maybe that was why she told him something she'd never told anyone else. Something she'd never said out loud before.

"He called me a whore," she told him quietly. "Your whore, in fact."

Alessandro swore, and his hand twitched along the back

of the swing as if he wanted to reach through her memories, through her story, and respond to Niccolo in kind.

"When was this?" he asked, his voice hoarse.

"A few days after the ball," she said. "After…"

"Yes," he said in a low voice with too many deep currents. "After."

She let go of her iron grip on her legs before her hands went numb, and used them, shaky and cold, to scrape her hair back from her face.

"He said it was bad enough he had to marry me to get the land, but now he had to do it after I'd made him a laughingstock with his sworn enemy?" She didn't see the sea in front of her then. She only saw Niccolo's face, twisted in a rage. She saw the way he'd stood over her, so cruel, so cold, while she lay there too stunned to cry. "He told me that if I knew what was good for me, I'd shut my mouth and be thankful the land was worth more than I was. And then he walked out of the villa and left me there on the floor."

"Elena."

But she had to finish. She had to get it out or she never would, and she didn't want to think about why it was suddenly so important to her that the man she'd never thought she'd see again know every last detail. Every last way she'd made such a fool of herself.

"I left, of course," she said, ignoring the wobble in her voice and the constriction in her throat. And all of his heat and power beside her. "But I didn't really mean it. I thought there was some kind of misunderstanding. He couldn't have meant to hit me, to say those things to me. Maybe he'd been drinking. I went home to my parents, as I always did." She swallowed, hard. "And they hugged me, and told me that they loved me, and then they told me they blamed themselves that I'd turned out so spoiled, so high-strung. So selfish."

She shook her head when he started to speak and he stilled, frowning.

"They were so *kind*. Niccolo was going to be my husband, they told me, and marriages took work. Commitment. I was going to have to grow up and stop telling terrible stories when I didn't get my way." She laughed again, and it sounded broken to her own ears. "Niccolo was a good man, they said, and I believed them. I *wanted* to believe them. It was easier to believe that I'd made up the whole thing than that he was the person I'd seen that night."

Alessandro shifted, and put his arm around her, then gathered her close to his side. Holding her again. Holding her close, as if he could fight off all her demons that easily. She wondered if he could, if he even wanted to bother, and her eyes slicked over with a glaze of heat.

"He laughed when I rang him," she whispered. "He told me that I was a stupid bitch. A whore. He told me I had twenty-four hours to get back to the villa and if I didn't he'd come get me himself, and I would really, truly regret it. That he didn't care if he had to marry me in a wheelchair."

Alessandro's arm tightened around her, and she allowed herself the comfort of his heat, his strength, even though she knew it was fleeting at best. That it wasn't hers, no matter how much it felt as if it was. That he was far more dangerous to her now, armed with all of the knowledge she'd given him, even if he really was the man he claimed he was.

Neither one of them spoke for a long while. His hand moved over her hair, stroking her as if she was something precious to him. She accepted that she wished she was. That she always had. That she'd wanted too much from him from the start, and had been paying for it ever since.

"And that time," she said when she could speak again, giving him everything he'd asked for, everything she'd been hiding, *everything,* "I believed him."

* * *

Alessandro stood on the balcony outside his bedroom long after midnight, staring out into the dark.

He couldn't sleep. He could hardly think straight. Once again, she'd shoved his world off its axis, and he was still reeling.

"Why didn't you tell me sooner?" he'd asked her as the light began to change, still holding her on the swinging chair, pulling her closer as the wind picked up.

"You would never have believed me."

"Perhaps," he'd said, but she'd only smiled. "Perhaps, in time, I might have."

But she'd been right. He would have thought it was another game. He would have laughed at her. Hated her all the more. He would have treated her exactly the same—worse, even. He couldn't pretend otherwise.

He balled his hands into fists against the rail now, scowling.

He should have known. He had been too busy concentrating on the darkness in him, too busy nursing his wounded pride. The truth had always been there, staring him in the face. In every kiss, every touch. In the way she'd given herself to him so unreservedly.

In what he'd known about her the moment he'd seen her in Rome.

He should have tried to reach her then. Instead, he'd stormed off that dance floor and left her to be brutalized. He'd put her through hell all on his own. And he couldn't blame his family for that. That had been all him.

He was no different from them at all. He couldn't imagine how he'd ever believed otherwise.

He sensed her behind him a moment before she stepped to the rail beside him, hugging herself against the cool night air.

"I didn't mean to wake you," he said.

She smiled, but she didn't look at him. "You didn't."

He watched her, feeling something work through him, something powerful and new and all about that tilt to her jaw, that perfect curve of her hip, the way she squared her shoulders as she stood there. Her lovely strength. Her courage.

He didn't have the slightest idea what to do with any of it. Or with her.

Alessandro couldn't help but touch her then, his hands curving over her bare shoulders and turning her to face him. She was as beautiful in the shadows as she was in the light, though the wariness in her gaze made his chest ache. He wanted to protect her, to keep her safe. From Niccolo. From the world.

Even from himself.

He stroked his fingers down her lovely face, and felt the way she shivered, heard the way she sighed. He thought of that first touch, so long ago now, that glorious heat. He thought of that marvelous glow between them. That easy, instant perfection.

And all of it was true.

Everything he'd felt. Everything he'd imagined. Everything he'd wanted then, and thought impossible.

"What happens now?" she asked softly, her eyes searching his.

He smiled then, over the rawness inside of him, the dangerous, insidious hope.

"Now?" he asked, his voice gruff. As uneven as he felt. "I apologize."

And then he kissed her, gently, and she melted into him. Like the first time all over again. Better.

Real.

Elena woke in his wide bed, safe and warm.

She lay on her side and gazed out at the morning light,

the blue sky, and the previous afternoon came back to her slowly, drip by drip. Then the night. The way he'd picked her up so gently and carried her back to bed. The way he'd moved over her, worshipping every part of her, taking his time and driving her into a sweet, wild oblivion, before curling around her and holding her close as they fell asleep together.

It had been so different, Elena thought now. She smiled to herself. It had felt like—

But she pushed that thought away, afraid to look at it too closely. Her stomach began to ache, and she cursed herself. Things were precarious enough already. There were any number of ways Alessandro could use what she'd told him against her. No need to tangle her emotions any further. No need to make it that much worse.

No need to walk straight into another disaster as blindly as she had the first.

She climbed from the bed and started for the bathroom, aware with each step that she didn't feel well—as if her body was finally taking all of the past weeks' excesses out on her. As if it was punishing her. She had a slight headache. Her stomach hurt. Even her breasts ached. And she felt heavy, all the way through. Almost as if—

She stopped in her tracks and, for a moment, was nothing at all but numb. Then she walked into the bathroom, confirmed her suspicion and had only just come back out again and pulled on the first thing she could find—the long-sleeved shirt he'd been wearing the night before, as it happened—when Alessandro walked through the bedroom door.

He had his mobile phone clamped to his ear, a fierce scowl on his beautiful face, and Elena simply stood there, helplessly, and stared. Everything had changed. Again.

She didn't have any idea how this would go, or what might happen next.

And he still made her heart beat faster when he walked into a room. He still made her knees feel weak. All this time, and she hadn't grown used to him at all. All of these weeks, and if anything, she was even more susceptible to him than she had been at the start.

She didn't dare think about what that meant, either. She was terribly afraid she already knew.

"I don't care," he growled into the phone. He raked an impatient hand through his hair. "I'm running out of ways to tell you that, Mother, and I ran out of patience ten minutes ago. None of this has anything to do with me."

He hung up, then tossed the phone on the bed. His dark green eyes narrowed when they found hers. He stilled, that restlessness she could see written all over him fading.

"Has something happened?" Elena asked, and she could hear the nerves in her voice. The panic. His gaze sharpened, telling her he did, too.

"Just one more scandal linked to the Corretti name, though this time, happily, not mine," he said. "Or not entirely mine, though it gives rise to all sorts of speculation I should probably care about." His focus was on Elena, his dark green eyes speculative as they swept over her face. "Alessia Battaglia is pregnant."

Elena swallowed. "Oh," she said.

She wished she wasn't wearing only his shirt. It was like déjà vu. The last time she'd worn a man's shirt— But she couldn't let herself think that way. It would only make this harder.

"Well," she said lamely. She had to clear her throat. "I…am not."

For a long moment, there was only the sound of her heartbeat, loud in her ears. And the way he looked at her across the expanse of his bed, that fierce and arrogant face of his unreadable.

"You're sure?" he asked.

Her throat was dry. "I am."

She didn't know what she expected. But it wasn't the way his face changed, the way his eyes darkened—a brief, searing flash. It wasn't the way that pierced her, straight to the bone.

Regret.

That was what she saw on his face, in his dark gaze. For a dizzying moment, she couldn't breathe.

Because she felt it, too, like a newer, deeper ache. As if they'd lost something today. As if they should grieve this instead of celebrate it, and that didn't make any kind of sense at all.

"All right," he said then. "That's good news, isn't it?"

She nodded, because she didn't trust her voice.

"We must be lucky," he said quietly. But his smile was like a ghost, and it hurt her.

It all hurt.

And she knew why, she thought then, in dawning understanding and a surge of fear. This hadn't been about the games they played, or any of the things she'd been telling herself so fiercely for so long. The lust and the hurt and the wild, uncontrollable passion had been no more than window dressing, and she'd been desperately ignoring what lay beyond all of that since the moment she'd laid eyes on this man in Rome.

Because it shouldn't have happened like that. It shouldn't have happened at all. Love at first sight was nonsense; it belonged in poems, songs. Sentimental films. Real people made choices, they didn't take one look at a stranger on a dance floor and feel the world shift around them, a key turning in a lock.

Elena had been telling herself that for months, and here she was anyway, not carrying his child and as absurdly upset about it as if they'd been trying to get pregnant instead of simply unpardonably reckless.

She was in love with him, God help her. *She was in love with him.*

It rang in her, long and low and deep. And it wasn't new. It had been there from that very first glance. It had happened that fast, that irrevocably, and she simply hadn't wanted to accept that it could be true. But it was.

And now she simply had to figure out how to survive the end of her time with him, the end of these months that had changed her life forever, without giving him that last, worst weapon to use against her.

"Yes," she agreed, aware he was watching her with those clever eyes of his and she knew he saw too much, the way he always did. "Very lucky."

CHAPTER EIGHT

THE FORTIETH DAY dawned with no less than three emails
from his assistant detailing the precise time the helicopter
would arrive to transport him back to Sicily, and Alessandro still wasn't ready.

He'd run out of excuses. He had to return home or risk
damaging Corretti Media in a way he might not be able
to fix, and despite his attempts to cut off the part of him
that cared about that, he knew he couldn't let it happen.
He was the CEO, and he was needed. And he had to deal
with his family before they all imploded, something his
mother's daily, increasingly hysterical voice-mail messages
suggested was imminent.

He had to go back to his life. His attempt to leave it behind had only ever been a temporary measure, a reaction
to that cursed wedding. It wasn't him. Duty, responsibility—they beat in him still, and grew louder by the day.

But he couldn't leave Elena. Not now that he'd discovered she was the woman he'd believed she was from the
start. Not now that everything had changed.

He didn't know what she wanted, however, and the uncertainty was like a fist in his gut. It had been hard enough
to convince her to remain on the island once she'd discovered she wasn't pregnant.

"There's no reason to stay here any longer." She'd at-

tempted that calm, cool smile he hated and he'd taken pleasure in the fact she couldn't quite pull it off, sitting there
so primly in the sitting area of his bedchamber, dressed
only in one of his shirts and all of the smooth, bare flesh
of her legs on display. "Our arrangement was based entirely around waiting to find out—"

"That arrangement was based on the premise that you
were still engaged to Niccolo Falco," he'd said, cutting her
off. "Working for him, in fact. A spy." He'd smiled. "You
are none of those things, *cara.*"

"Most importantly, I'm not pregnant," she'd argued,
with a stubborn tilt to her chin. "What you thought about
me until yesterday is irrelevant, really."

"Do you think he's still searching for you?" he'd asked
calmly when he'd wanted nothing more than to put his
mouth on her—to remind her how they were anything but
irrelevant. And despite that black punch of murderous rage
that slammed into him at the thought of Niccolo.

"I know he is," she'd said with a shrug. "He sends me
an email every week or so, to make sure I never forget it."
She'd smiled then, but it was far too bitter. "It was a good
thing I stopped waitressing and took the yacht job. He was
in Cefalù only a few days behind me."

He'd had to force his violent fury down, shove it under
wraps, before he'd been able to say another word—and
even then, the dark pulse of his temper was in every clipped
syllable.

"Do you really believe I will simply let you go like
this?" he'd asked. "Wash my hands of you and go about
my business while that bastard runs you into the ground?
What makes you think that's a possibility?"

Something he hadn't been able to identify chased over
her face then, but had echoed in him all the same.

"It's not your decision," she'd said after a moment. "It's mine."

They'd stared at each other for a long while.

"You must know I can keep you here," he'd said quietly. "No one comes or goes from this place without my permission."

"You won't do something like that," she'd replied with conviction, her eyes meeting his. Holding. "You're better than that."

And, damn her, he'd wanted to be.

He'd reached over to take her hands in his, threading his fingers through hers, then pulling their joined hands up to his mouth. She'd sighed, her eyes filling with all of that heat and passion that had delivered them here in the first place. And he'd willed her to relent. To bend. To yield.

To want to hold on to him the way he needed to hold on to her.

"You're the one who wanted forty days," he'd said, searching her face, trying to see what he needed to see written there. "There's almost a whole week left."

She'd shaken her head. "Playtime is over, Alessandro."

"Forty days," he'd repeated, because he hadn't known what else to say, how else to convince her. She couldn't leave. This wasn't over—it had only just begun.

"Alessandro..."

"Elena. Please." He hadn't recognized his own voice, much less what coursed through him as he'd said it. "Stay."

He'd begged. There was no other word for it.

But she'd looked up at him then and he hadn't cared at all that he'd bent in a way he'd previously believed impossible. He'd only cared that it worked.

"I'll give you forty days," she'd said when he'd begun to lose hope, her eyes changing from blue to gray. "But that's it. This can't go on any longer than that."

He'd only moved closer to her, and then he'd taken her mouth with his, answering her as best he could.

It had all gone by too quickly, he thought now, glaring out his window at the sea as if it had betrayed him. As if nature and time had conspired against him. He sensed her come into the master suite before he heard her, that familiar spark of lightning down his spine and straight into his sex—and that fist in his gut seemed to burrow deeper.

"Are you ready?" he asked without turning around. He had to fight to keep his voice level, to keep his temper under control, and it was much harder than it should have been. How could he lose her when he'd just found her? "The helicopter will be here any moment."

"Of course," Elena said, back to that smooth voice he loathed. "I packed everything that's mine."

"And my staff packed everything else," he said evenly. "What use do you imagine I have for the clothes you wore while you were here?"

She didn't answer. He shoved his hands into his pockets so she wouldn't see that he'd balled them into fists. He knew she was still standing there—he could feel her—but the silence stretched out between them, sharp and treacherous. He didn't know what to do, or say.

He only knew he couldn't stand this.

Alessandro heard the unmistakable sound of his helicopter then, roaring toward the meadow for its landing. Coming down fast to hasten this unacceptable ending.

Too late, he thought. *It's always too late.*

He turned then, abruptly, and caught the look on her face. Resolute. Miserable. Brave and determined. He concentrated on *miserable*.

"Stay with me," he bit out. An order this time, with no silk or seduction or even begging to sweeten it.

"Stay?" she echoed, as if she didn't understand the word.

"Here?" She shook her head, sketched that airy smile. "You can't keep hiding away here, Alessandro. It's time to go home."

She was dressed for the outside world. No flowing dress, no tiny shorts, no skimpy bikini. She wore those white denim trousers that made him uncomfortably hard, another pair of wicked heels and a peach-colored top that flirted with her curves beneath a cream-colored scarf looped lazily around her neck. Her hair was slicked back into a sleek ponytail, and she had sunglasses perched on her head, ready to slide over her eyes. She looked casually fashionable, impenetrably lovely, and he knew it was armor.

He hated it.

"Come to Palermo with me," he threw out without thinking, but it didn't matter. He didn't care how complicated that could become. He didn't care if it started a damned war with the Falco family. He'd fight it with his own bare hands if he had to. He didn't care about anything but her.

And if an alarm sounded deep inside of him then, he ignored it.

"You know that's impossible," she said fiercely. As if he'd finally struck a nerve. "You know I have to go."

Alessandro remembered that night, so long ago now, when he'd told her he would chase her through the house if she wanted him to do it. That he would let her abdicate any responsibility for what happened between them, let it all be on him, if that was what it took. Was that what she needed?

But he couldn't do it.

"I won't hold you against your will. I won't even beg." His voice was low, but all of their history was in it. That dance. This island. All the truths they'd finally laid bare. "Come with me anyway."

"This isn't fair," she whispered, and he shouldn't have

taken it as a kind of harsh victory that she sounded as ago-
nized as he felt. As torn apart. "We agreed."

"Just this once," he said fiercely, "just this one time,
admit what's happening here. What's always been happening here. For God's sake, Elena—come with me because
you can't bear to leave me."

Whole worlds moved through her gaze then, and left
the overbright sheen of tears in their wake. And it wasn't
enough, that he knew she wanted him, too, that he knew
exactly how stark her need was. That he could feel it inside of him, lighting up his own. That he knew he could
exploit it, with a single touch.

He needed her to admit it. To say it. He needed all of this
to matter to her. And the fact that he was uncomfortable
with the intensity of that need—that it edged into territory
he refused to explore—didn't make it any less necessary.

A moment dragged by, too sharp and too hard. Then
another.

"I'm not a good person," she said finally. Her hands
opened and closed fitfully, restlessly, at her sides. "And
neither are you. A good person would never have allowed
what happened between us in Rome to happen at all. I was
engaged. And you knew I was with Niccolo when you approached me." Her gaze slammed into his. "All we do is
make mistakes, Alessandro. Maybe that's all this is. Maybe
that's what we should admit."

He started toward her, watching her face as he drew
closer. He had never been so uncertain of anything or anyone in his life, and yet so oddly sure of her at the same
time. So sure of *this.* He didn't understand it. But like everything with Elena, from that very first glance, it simply
was. Undefinable. Undeniable. But always and ever *his.*

"I know that you don't trust me," he said when he
reached her, looking down into her troubled blue gaze. "I

know what the name Corretti means to you. I know you think all manner of terrible things about me, and I know you're waiting for the next blow." He reached over to trace the vulnerable curve of her mouth with his thumb, making her tremble. "Come to Palermo. Have faith."

He read the storms in her eyes, across her pretty face. And he forced himself to do nothing at all but wait it out. Wait her out.

"I don't believe in faith anymore." A great cloud washed over her, across her face and through those beautiful eyes, and left them shadowed. She pulled in a deep, long breath, then let it out. "But I'll do it," she said finally, as if the words were wrenched from her. "I'll come with you."

Satisfaction and intense relief ripped through him, making him feel bigger. Wilder. Edgy with a ferocious kind of triumph.

But he wasn't finished.

"Tell me why."

Her eyes darkened, and she started to shake her head, started to retreat from him. He slid his hand along her jaw, and held her like that, forcing her to look at him. Keeping her right there in plain sight. Her lips parted slightly, and her breath came hard, as if she was running away the way she no doubt wished she was.

"Tell me," he said quietly. "I need to hear you say it."

She gazed back at him. He could feel her pulse against his hand, could see it wild and panicked in her throat. "Because..." she began, and had to stop, as if her throat closed in on her. Her eyes were filled with heat and damp. She swayed on her feet as if there was a great wind howling around them, and it threatened to knock her flat.

But she didn't fall.

He brushed the knuckles of his other hand over her soft cheek, her distractingly elegant cheekbone.

"Say it," he whispered.

"Because I can't leave you," she said finally, in a broken, electrifying rush. He felt it from the top of his head to the bottom of his feet, as if he'd been struck by lightning, by her, all over again. As if she'd shone that bright light into all of that darkness within him, chasing it away at last. "Not yet."

The helicopter ride was bumpy and noisy, despite the bulky headphones she'd been given to wear, but Elena was happy enough to stay silent while Alessandro and the assistant who'd flown out to meet him discussed Corretti Media business concerns. She soaked in the beckoning Mediterranean blue far below, and pretended the only thing in her head was the sea. The golden sun. The lovely view.

But it didn't work. The enormity of what she'd done was like iron in her chest, making it harder and harder to breathe. It had been one thing to hand over her body, another still to offer up her story to his mercy, such as it was. But she was very much afraid that, today, Alessandro had demanded she give him her soul.

And she'd done it.

She couldn't believe she'd actually done it.

Too soon, the helicopter was making its way through the Palermo skyline, and then setting down on the roof of the landmark Corretti Media tower. Elena climbed out slowly, staying behind Alessandro and the assistant who hadn't stopped talking in all this time, trying to pretend she was not in the least bit overwhelmed. That she gave away her soul like it was little more than a trinket every day of the week. That she was in control of this.

"Signorina Calderon and I are going to eat something," Alessandro said then, breaking into his assistant's stream of chatter in a steely tone she'd never heard before. It brought Elena back to the present with a jolt.

"But, sir," his assistant said in a rush. "Since you've been gone, your family..." His voice trailed off as Alessandro glared at him, but he visibly rallied. "The Battaglia situation is only getting more heated, and time is nearly up for the new docklands proposal—"

"I will come into the office later, Giovanni," Alessandro said with wintry finality.

Elena's stomach twisted. He was cold, harsh, commanding—but with none of that dark fire she knew so well beneath it. This must be Alessandro, the much-feared and much-respected CEO. Alessandro, the eldest Corretti heir. No wonder people spoke of him in such awed, cowed tones. He was terrifying.

"My apologies," his assistant said smoothly, inclining his head. "Of course, that is perfect. We will expect you after lunch."

"If you want me to sign those papers," Alessandro continued in an impatient tone, stalking across the rooftop toward the entrance to the building, "I suggest you do it in the elevator. Quietly."

Elena walked faster as Alessandro's assistant got on his mobile, ordering the car brought around and demanding that someone make sure that Alessandro's favorite table was waiting for him. She reminded herself to breathe as she stepped into the shiny, gold-plated elevator where Alessandro waited, looking for all the world like a surly, caged animal. Dangerous and unpredictable.

The elevator started its descent. Alessandro signed the papers his assistant handed him on a hardbacked folder, one after the next. Without bothering to read them, Elena thought in some surprise—but then he scowled down at one of them.

"These terms are unacceptable. As both you and Di Rossi are well aware."

"He insisted that you had caved," his assistant said mildly, as if he heard that tone from Alessandro every day.

"Send it back," Alessandro ordered. "If he has a problem with it, tell him he can take it up with me personally."

His assistant's brows rose. That was obviously a threat.

The elevator stopped smoothly, discharging Alessandro's assistant on one of the higher floors, and then the doors swished shut and they were alone again. Elena told herself there was no reason at all to be so nervous. Alessandro lounged against the far wall of the car, looking deceptively languid in what was clearly a bespoke suit, the way it marveled over every fine line of his physique. The bright golden walls seemed to shrink into her as the car kept moving. His dark green eyes found hers, and Elena's heart picked up speed.

"Second thoughts?" he asked softly. A challenge.

"You're a very formidable man," she said. "Do you enjoy it?"

He only watched her, that arrogant face a study in careless, encompassing masculine power. His dark brows rose in query.

"Wielding that kind of authority like that," she said. "Making that poor man jump through your hoops without even the faintest pretense of politeness."

Dark green eyes lit with amusement. "Are you calling me rude, Elena? Or just a bad boss?"

"If that's how you treat your employees, I shudder to think how you treat your enemies." She smiled coolly. "Oh, but wait. I already know."

Alessandro's mouth crooked. "Point taken," he said gruffly, surprising her. "I apologize."

"Your assistant is very likely weeping in the toilet,"

she continued, her tone dry, burying her confusion. Alessandro? Apologizing? "Don't feel you have to apologize to *me*."

"For the record," he said, laughter in his voice, "'that poor man' comforts himself with a new Maserati every fiscal year. He's certainly not weeping as he cashes his paycheck."

"If you say so."

"Come here." His voice dropped, became something else. Something that wound through her like honey, golden and slow, making it hard to remember that he even had an assistant, or why on earth she cared.

"You're at your place of business," she said primly, but she went to him, anyway. "Smiting down every assistant in your path, apparently. All in a day's work, no doubt."

He slid a hand around to the back of her neck and then tugged her off balance so she sprawled against his chest.

This was familiar, finally. His scent, his heat. That gleam in his eyes. Her immediate reaction, molten and hot. And only as it washed through her did she understand how much she'd needed the reminder. That it didn't matter how formidable he might seem here. How distant. That this was still theirs, this electric current. This need.

It was why she was here.

"Ah, Elena," he murmured, simply holding her there against the wall of his chest, his thumb moving against her nape, his expression so intent it made her knees feel like water. "What am I going to do with you?"

"Do you mean in general or in this elevator?" she asked, aware of the breathlessness in her voice, the pounding desire that she had no doubt he could see all over her, the way he always did.

His mouth curved. "I already know what I'm going to do to you in this elevator," he told her, his other hand wrapping around her hip and pulling her against him, letting her feel how much he wanted her. His voice lowered to that sexy growl that lit her up, heating her blood, making her melt. "It might be acrobatic, but I think you can handle it."

Elena heard the *ping* that announced they'd arrived at the ground floor, but Alessandro didn't move. Her hands were pressed against the fascinating muscles of his perfect torso as she arched into him. It wasn't enough, and she didn't care where she was. This was his company—let him care. She lifted herself up on her toes and moved her mouth so close to his that if she licked her lips, she'd taste him.

"Go ahead, then," she whispered, daring him. "Show me some acrobatics."

On some level she was vaguely aware of the elevator doors sliding open, but all that mattered was Alessandro. That dark, consuming green gaze. That familiar fire, still so devastating and far too hot. As if he blacked out everything else.

He laughed, sex and heat and delicious challenge, and she shivered in anticipation, because she knew that sound, she knew its sensual promise—

And everything exploded.

Flashing lights, shouting. The press of too many bodies, the harsh slap of all that noise—

It took her too long to make sense of it—to understand that a scrum of paparazzi crowded into the open elevator door, cameras snapping and tape rolling, while Elena was still plastered against Alessandro's chest, clinging to him, announcing their relationship in stark, unmistakable terms.

But then she understood, and that was worse.

It was the end of the world as she knew it, right there and then.

Elena couldn't stop pacing.

Alessandro's penthouse spread out over the top of the

Corretti Media tower, three stories in all. It was magnificent. Glass, steel and granite, yet decorated with a deep appreciation of color and comfort. Lush Persian carpets stretched in front of fireplaces and brightened halls. Stunning, impressive art hung on the high walls, all bold colors and graceful lines. He favored deep chairs, dark woods, and all of it somehow elegant and male. Uniquely him.

And she couldn't enjoy any part of it. She could hardly see it through her panic.

"Of course he'll see the pictures," she said, not for the first time, worrying her lower lip with her fingers as she stared out the great windows. "You can count on it."

Alessandro was sprawled on one of his couches, a tablet computer in his hand. He shot a dark, unreadable look in her direction, but he didn't answer. But then, Elena was really only talking to herself.

He'd dealt with the paparazzi as best he could. He'd stepped in front of her, concealing her from view. He'd alerted his security, then whisked her up to his penthouse and hidden her away from any more cameras.

"Jackals," he'd snarled when the elevator doors finally closed again, leaving them in peace once more. "Nothing but scavengers."

But it was too late. The damage was already done.

Elena's head had spun wildly. She'd let him lead her out of the elevator bank and into his opulent home, and as soon as he'd closed that heavy penthouse door behind them she'd grabbed hold of the nearest wall and sunk down to the floor. Six months of fear and adrenaline and grief had coalesced inside of her and then simply…broken open. Flooding her.

"Don't you understand?" she'd cried. "Niccolo will see those pictures! He'll know exactly where I am! It will take him, what? A matter of *hours* to get to Palermo?"

Alessandro had gazed down at her, an enigmatic expression on his hard face.

"He won't go through me to get at you," he'd said. "He's a coward."

"I'm thrilled for you that you don't have to take him seriously," she'd thrown at him. "But I do. Believe me, Alessandro. *I do.*"

"Elena."

She'd hated the way he said her name then, the way it coiled in her, urging her to trust he'd somehow make this go away. To *have faith.*

"You can't make this disappear simply because you command it," she'd told him, caught between weariness and despair. "You have no idea how devious he is, or how determined."

"If you must insult me," Alessandro had said then, "please spare my security detail. Aside from today's disaster, they're very good at their jobs."

"For how long?" she'd demanded. "A week or two? Another forty days? When will you tire of this—of me?" She'd stared up at him, daring him to contradict her. Daring him to argue. "Because when that day comes, as we both know it will, Niccolo will be waiting. If I have faith in anything, it's that."

Alessandro's expression had shuttered, but he'd only held her gaze for a strained moment before turning on his heel, murmuring something about unavoidable paperwork and walking out. Leaving her there on his floor to drive herself out of her head with worry and the cold, hard fear that had spurred her on all this time.

The fear she'd set aside when she'd been on Alessandro's island. When she'd been safe.

She had to leave, she thought now, frowning out the towering windows at the coming dark. She had to run while she still could. That was the obvious conclusion she'd been circling around and around, not wanting to admit it was the only thing that made sense.

Because he'd been right. She didn't want to leave him. She loved him. It was that simple and that complicated. It always had been.

She turned to look at him then. He was so impossibly, powerfully beautiful. He'd stunned her from the start. And now she knew how that proud jaw tasted. She could lose herself for hours in his hard, cynical mouth. She knew what he could do with those elegant hands of his, with every part of his lean, hard frame. She knew that he felt deeply, and darkly, and that there were mysteries in him she desperately wanted to solve. She knew he'd comforted her, soothing something in her she'd thought ripped forever raw. She knew what it was like when he laughed, when he teased her, when he told her stories. She wanted all of this to be real, for him to be the man she so desperately wanted to believe he was.

She wanted to have faith. She wanted to stay.

God, how she wanted to stay.

He'd thrown off his jacket when he'd returned to the penthouse, lost his tie and loosened the top buttons of his shirt. He looked like what he was. The infinitely dangerous, ruthless and clever CEO of Corretti Media. A man of great wealth and even greater reach. The man who'd taken her body, her painful history, her heart and even her soul. And would take much more than that, she had no doubt. If she let him. If she stayed.

But he didn't love her. She didn't kid herself that he ever would. He spoke only of *want*.

This was sex. Need. A shockingly intense connection mixed with explosive chemistry. Clear all of that away and Elena was as on her own as the day she'd realized even her parents' home wasn't safe for her, and had gone on the run. The past forty days had been nothing but consuming lust, blinding fireworks, and all of it a distraction from that ugly little truth.

He looked up then, his dark green eyes searing and too incisive.

"They've been posted," he said without inflection.

That was it, then. The paparazzi pictures were online. The clock had started ticking. She had to assume Niccolo was on his way even now. Which meant she was standing here on borrowed time.

"I have to go," she said, quick and fierce, before she could talk herself out of it. Before he could. "I have to leave immediately."

"And may I ask where you plan to go?" That cool CEO's voice. It felt like nails against her skin. "Do you have a plan or are you simply…running away? Again?"

"It doesn't matter where I go," she said, trying so hard to keep all of her feelings out of this. They could only hurt her—and so could Niccolo. It was better to think of him, and run. "So long as it's far from here."

Alessandro tossed his tablet to one side. He gazed at her for a long while, as if he'd never seen her before. As if he saw too much.

Elena repressed an involuntary shiver, and found she couldn't breathe.

"I think you should marry me," he said.

CHAPTER NINE

HER HEART STOPPED in her chest.

Elena stared at him. She couldn't move. She certainly couldn't speak.

Alessandro shrugged, as if what he'd said was as casual as an invitation to coffee, though his dark green eyes were shrewd. They didn't leave her face.

"It's the only way to beat Niccolo at his own game," he said. So matter-of-fact. So calm, so controlled. As if this was nothing but one more contract that required his signature, and not one he needed to read all that closely. "Running from him hasn't worked. How else can this end?"

"It will end when my father dies," she said, though her tongue felt as numb as the rest of her. She was dimly surprised it worked at all. "I'm the executor of the trust. Obviously, he won't be able to manipulate me the way he's manipulated my father."

"He told you he would put you in a wheelchair if necessary," Alessandro reminded her with an edge in his voice and too much dark in his eyes. "He's not going to stop. In fact, he's likely to club you over the head and marry you while you're in a coma."

Elena couldn't think. The room had started revolving around her, whirling in lopsided, drunken circles. She was afraid she might fall over. She ignored the kick of hard, fierce joy inside her, because this wasn't real. It couldn't be real. And if it was? Then it was simply one more game. It wasn't something she should be joyful about.

But it only kicked harder.

"I don't think the solution is to marry you instead," she managed to say.

"Yes, of course," he said then with definite edge that time. "Because you are opposed to marrying for practical reasons, if memory serves. Or is it that you'd prefer to be dragged to the altar by your hair, to the delightful wedding music of Niccolo's abusive threats?"

"This isn't practical" was all she could think of to say.

"He won't touch you if you're my wife," Alessandro replied, steel and fire in his gaze. "The impetus to do so would disappear the moment we said our vows. If you're married, the land is no longer in any dispute. It becomes mine, and your problem is solved."

"On our wedding day," Elena heard herself say from somewhere far away. She couldn't make sense of the words. Or anything else.

His dark eyes gleamed. Something male and primitive moved over his face, then was gone. *Hidden,* something inside of her whispered, but what could he have to hide? He shrugged again, then reached beside him for the tablet, dismissing her.

As if none of this mattered to him, either way. As if this was a minor favor he'd thought he might do her, nothing more.

"Do you really think I'll let you go like this?" he'd asked a week ago on the island, so fiercely. "Wash my hands of you?"

She'd wanted to believe that he wouldn't—that he couldn't. She still did.

"Your choice, Elena."

He wasn't even looking at her. As if this conversation, his proposal of marriage, hardly maintained his interest. But she didn't believe that, either. He was not a man who begged, and yet he had. Surely that meant something. Didn't it have to mean something?

"I know you have strong feelings about the Corretti name," he said in the same offhanded way, "but all you have to do is take it and this insanity ends. It's simple."

It wasn't simple, she thought in a wash of something like anguish. It was anything but simple.

But even as she opened her mouth to refuse him—to do the sane thing and leave him, leave Sicily, save herself the only way she knew how—Elena knew she wouldn't do it. She would take him any way she could have him, even marry him under these questionable circumstances, knowing he would never feel the way she felt.

Nothing had changed. She was the same selfish, foolish girl she'd ever been. She wanted yet another man to love her when she knew that no matter what she'd thought she glimpsed in him now and again, this was nothing more than a game to him, and she no more than another piece on a chessboard he controlled. Eventually, he would grow tired of her. He would leave her.

And yet some part of her was still vain enough to think he might change his mind, that *she* might change it. Still silly enough to risk everything on that slim, unlikely chance.

She hadn't learned a thing in all this time.

"By all means," he said then, languidly scrolling down a page on his tablet, "take your time agonizing over the only reasonable choice available to you. I'm happy to wait."

Could she do it? Could she surrender the most important thing of all—the one thing even Niccolo had never got his hands on? The entire future of her village. Her family's heritage. The land. All because she so desperately hoped that Alessandro was different. That he really would do the right thing.

Because she loved him.

Idiot. The voice in her head was scathing.

Elena jerked herself around and stared out his impressive windows at the lights of the city spread out before her, but what she saw were her parents' faces. Her poor parents. They deserved so much better than this. Than her.

"What a romantic proposal." She shut her eyes. She hated herself. But she couldn't seem to stop the inevitable. She was as incapable of saving herself now as she'd been on that dance floor. And as guilty. "How can I possibly refuse?"

Late that night, Alessandro stood in the door of his bedroom and watched Elena sleep. She was curled up in his bed, and the sight of her there made the savage creature in him want to shout out his triumph to the moon. He almost did. He felt starkly possessive. Wildly victorious.

He could wake her, he knew. She would turn to him eagerly—soft and warm from sleep, and take him inside of her without a word. She would sigh slightly, sweetly, and wrap herself around him, then bury her face in his neck as he moved in her.

She'd done it so many times before.

But tonight was different. Tonight she'd agreed to become his wife.

His wife.

He hadn't known he'd meant to offer marriage until he had. And once he had, he'd understood that there was no other acceptable outcome to this situation. No alternative. She needed to be his, without reservation or impediment.

It had to be legal. It had to last. He didn't care what trouble that might cause.

There were words for what was happening to him, Alessandro knew, but he wasn't ready to think about that. Not until he'd secured her, made her his. He turned away from the bed and forced himself to head down the stairs.

Down in his home office, he sat at his wide, imposing desk and frowned down at all of the work Giovanni had prepared for his review. But he didn't flip open the top report and start reading. He found himself staring at the photo that sat on the corner of his desk instead.

It was a family shot he'd meant to get rid of ever since his grandmother had given it to him years ago. All of the Correttis were gathered around his grandmother, Teresa, at her birthday celebration eight years ago. Canny old Salvatore was smirking at the camera, holding one of Teresa's hands in his, looking just as Alessandro remembered him—as if death would never dare take him.

Alessandro's father and uncle, alive and at war with each other, stood with their wives and children on either side of Teresa, who had long been the single unifying force in the family. Her birthday, at her insistence, was the one day of the year the Correttis came together, breathed the same air, refrained from spilling blood or hideous secrets and pretended they were a real family.

Alessandro sighed, and reached over to pick up the photograph. His uncle and four cousins looked like some kind of near mirror image of his own side of the family, faces frozen into varying degrees of mutiny and forced smiles, all stiffly acquiescing to the annual charade. They were all the same, in the end. All of them locked into this family, their seedy history, this bitter, futile fight. Sometimes he found himself envious of Angelo, the only family member missing from the picture, because at least he'd been spared the worst of it.

His sister, Rosa—because he couldn't think of her any other way, he didn't care who her father was—smiled genuinely. Alessandro and Santo stood close together, looking as if they were biting back laughter, though Alessandro could no longer remember what about. His father glared, as haughty and arrogant as he'd been to his grave. And his mother looked as she always did: ageless and angry. Always so very, very angry.

"You should never have stayed away so long," she'd seethed at him earlier today. "It looks like weakness. As if you've been off licking your wounds while your cousin has stolen your bride and made our side of the family the butt of every joke in Palermo!"

"Let him," Alessandro had retorted.

"Surely you don't plan to let the insult stand?" Carmela Corretti had gasped. "Our family's honor demands—"

"Honor?" Alessandro had interrupted her icily. "Not the word I'd choose, Mother. And certainly not if I were you."

She'd sucked in a breath, as if he'd wounded her.

But Alessandro knew the woman who'd raised him. He knew her with every hollow, bitter, blackened part of his Corretti soul. She was immune to hurt. And she always returned a slap with cannon fire.

"You're just like your father," she'd said viciously. And it had speared straight through him, hitting its mark. "All of that polish and pretense on the surface, and rotten to the core within. And we know where that leads, don't we?"

He was so tired of this, he thought now. Of this feud that rolled on and on and did nothing but tear them all apart. Of the vitriol that passed for family communication, the inevitability of the next fight. Would they all end up like his father and uncle, burned on their mysterious funeral pyre, while the whole world looked on sagely and observed that they'd brought it upon themselves? Violent lives, desperate acts—it all led to a terrible end. The cycle went on and on and on.

And was Alessandro really any different? Carlo Corretti had never met a person he wouldn't exploit for his own purposes. He'd never been honest when he could cheat, had never used persuasion when violence worked instead, and he'd never cared in the least that his hands were covered in blood.

"Right and wrong are what I say they are," he'd told Alessandro once, after ten-year-old Alessandro had walked in on him with one of his mistresses. There hadn't been the slightest hint of conscience in his gaze as he'd sprawled there in the bed he shared with Carmela. Right there in the family home. "Are you going to tell me any different, boy?"

Alessandro had hated him. God, how he'd hated him.

He looked up as if he could see Elena through the floors that separated them. She deserved better than this, and he knew it. She wasn't the Battaglia girl, auctioned off by her father to the highest bidder and fully aware of what joining the Corretti family meant—even if, as it turned out, she'd preferred a different Corretti. Elena had already escaped Niccolo Falco and whatever grim fate he'd had in store for her.

If he was any kind of man, if he was truly not like his viciously conniving father, he would set her free immediately.

Instead, he'd manipulated her, and he'd done it deliberately. She didn't have to marry him to be safe; he had teams of lawyers who could help her and her village. Who could deal with the likes of Niccolo Falco in the course of a single morning.

His mother was right. He was following in his father's

footsteps. He couldn't pretend any differently. But in the end, even that didn't matter. He wanted her too much, too badly, to do what he knew was right.

He would do his penance instead, as small as it was in the grand scheme of things. He would keep his hands off her until he married her. He would torture himself, and pretend that made this all right. That it made him something other than what he was: his father's son.

Alessandro simply didn't have it in him to let her go.

Four days later, by a special license she hadn't asked how he'd managed to obtain, Elena married Alessandro Corretti in a small civil ceremony.

It was 10:35 in the morning, in a small village outside of Palermo that Elena had never heard of before. But then, she didn't know the name of the man who married them, either, though he had introduced himself as the local mayor. Nor did she know either of the two witnesses who stood with them, both happy to take handfuls of Alessandro's euros for so little of their time.

It took all of twenty minutes.

In the private antechamber even more of Alessandro's money had secured for them, Elena stared at herself in the room's small mirror and ran her fingers down the front of the dress she wore. It was a rich, deep cream. It had delicate sleeves and fell from a pretty scooped neck into a flattering A-line that ended at her knees. Her hair was twisted back into a sophisticated chignon, and she wore a single strand of stunning pearls around her throat to match the diamond-and-pearl clusters at her ears. She looked elegant and chic. Polished. Smart.

She looked nothing at all like herself.

And why should you? a caustic voice inside her demanded. Elena Calderon was no more. She was Alessandro's wife now. *Signora Elena Corretti.*

She swallowed against the tide of emotion she didn't dare examine here, and chanced a look in Alessandro's direction. He was her husband. *Her husband.*

But he didn't love her.

Better to deal with the repercussions of that sooner rather than later, she thought, bracing herself. Better to ensure she didn't fall prey to her own imagination, her own precarious hopes. And what better place to make everything between them perfectly clear than the lounge of a town hall in a sleepy village, fitted with two ugly chairs and a desperate-looking sofa arranged around a cracked wood floor?

Congratulations on your hasty and secretive wedding, Signora Corretti, she mocked herself. *No expense or luxury was spared for your happy day!*

Alessandro stood near the closed door, on his mobile. The phone had beeped some thirty seconds after they'd signed the register. He'd announced he needed to take the call, and had waved her back into the antechamber she'd used before the ceremony.

She was almost positive she'd seen pity on the mayor's face before Alessandro had closed the door behind them.

"When do you think we should divorce?" she asked briskly when he ended his call, looking out through the small windows at the Sicilian countryside. Proud mountains with vineyards etched into the lower slopes. Red-roofed houses clinging to green hillsides. Olive groves and ancient ruins. All of it piercingly, hauntingly lovely. There was no reason at all it should have made her chest ache. "Did you have a particular time frame in mind?"

When he didn't respond, Elena turned away from the window—

And found him staring at her in amazement.

"We have been married for ten minutes, Elena," he said in a voice that made her skin pull tight. "Possibly fifteen. This conversation seems a trifle premature."

"This was the only reasonable choice I had, as you pointed out, and a convenient way to fix the Niccolo problem." She was suddenly too aware of the rings he'd slid onto her finger—a trio of flawless diamonds set in platinum on the drive over, and a diamond-studded platinum band during the ceremony, such as it was. It occurred to her that she was, in fact, deeply furious with him. She'd wanted this to mean something. She'd wanted it to matter. She was an idiot. "Nothing more than that. What does it matter if we discuss it now?"

He went incandescent. She actually saw him catch fire. His dark eyes were ferocious, his mouth flattened, and she was certain she could hear his skin sizzle with the burn of his temper from across the tiny room.

And it didn't scare her. She welcomed it. It was a happy alternative to the icy cold CEO who'd taken Alessandro's place since they'd returned to Sicily. Since the paparazzi had found them and plastered their faces across every gossip magazine and website in Europe. Since he'd shocked her with his proposal. He'd been distant. Controlled. He hadn't laid a finger on her, and there'd been nothing but winter in his dark green eyes.

She preferred this Alessandro. She knew this Alessandro.

No matter how tight and close it felt suddenly, in such a small room, with him blocking the only exit.

"I suggest you drop this subject," he advised her, hoarse with the force of his temper. There was that glitter of high passion, furious desire, in his too-dark eyes, and she exulted in it. She needed it.

"Oh," she said brightly, unable to help herself. "Were you thinking an annulment would work better?"

He laughed. It was a hard, male sound, primitive and stirring. It coursed through her, made her shiver with the heat of it. Made her ache. And the look he turned on her then melted her bones.

"I did warn you," he said.

He reached behind him and locked the door, and Elena felt it like a bullet. Hard and true, straight into her core. He crossed the room in a single stride, hauled her to him and then pulled her down with him as he sat on the sad, old sofa. Then he simply lifted her over his lap.

He hiked her dress up over her hips, ripped her panties out of his way with a casual ferocity that made her deliciously weak, then stroked two long fingers into the melting furnace of her core. Elena gasped his name. He laughed again at the evidence of how much she wanted him, all of her molten desire in his hand. She braced her hands on the smooth lapels of his wedding suit, another stunning work of art in black, and not half as beautiful as that mad hunger that changed his face, made him that much starker. Fiercer.

Hers.

Alessandro didn't look away from her as he reached between them and freed himself. He didn't look away as he ripped open a foil packet with his teeth and rolled protection on with one hand. And he didn't look away as he thrust hard into her, pulling her knees astride him, gripping her bottom in his hard hands to move her as he liked.

"An annulment is out of the question," he told her, his voice like fire, roaring through her. "And in case you're confused, this is called consummation."

Elena's head fell back as she met his thrusts, rode him, met his passion with every roll of her hips. She felt taken and glorious and his.

Completely his.

He changed the angle of her hips, moving her against him in a wicked rhythm, and she felt herself start to slip toward that edge. That easily. That quickly. Still fully dressed. Still wearing her wedding shoes and the pearls he'd presented her this morning. Still madly in love with this hard, dangerous man who was deep inside of her and knew exactly how to make her blind with desire. This man who was somehow her husband.

Whatever that meant. However long it lasted. Right then, she didn't care.

"You are mine, Elena," he whispered fiercely, his voice dark and sinful, lighting her up like a new blaze. "You are my wife."

It was that word that hurled her over, sent her flying apart in his arms, forced to muffle her cries with her own hand as he muttered something hot and dark and then followed right behind her.

When she came back to herself, he was watching her face, and she wondered in a surge of panic what he might have seen there. What she might have revealed.

"Don't talk to me about divorce," he said in a low voice, his dark green eyes hot. "Not today."

He shifted forward, setting her on her feet before him. She felt unsteady. Utterly wrecked, yet a glance in the mirror showed he hadn't disturbed a single hair on her perfectly coiffed head. She smoothed her dress back down into place, her hands trembling slightly. Alessandro tucked himself back into his trousers and then reached down to scoop up the lace panties he'd torn off her.

Because he'd been too desperate, too determined to get inside her, to wait another instant. She didn't know why that should make her feel more cherished, more precious to him, than all twenty strange minutes of their wedding ceremony.

She held out her hand to take the panties back. His hard mouth curved, his dark eyes a sensual challenge and something far more intense, and then he tucked them in his pocket.

"A memento of our wedding day," he said, mocking her, she was sure. "I'll treasure it."

She smiled back at him, cool and sharp.

"An annulment it is, then," she said. "This has been such a useful, rational discussion, Alessandro. Thank you."

He laughed again then, almost beneath his breath, and then he was on his feet and striding for the door, as if he didn't trust himself to stay locked in this room with her a moment longer. She allowed herself a small, satisfied smile.

"We can argue about this in the car," he said over his shoulder. "I have a one o'clock meeting I can't miss."

Because, of course, the CEO of Corretti Media didn't stop doing business on his wedding day, not when the wedding meant so little to him. Her smile vanished. It was a brutal reminder of reality. Of her place. It didn't matter how hot they burned. It didn't matter how desperate he'd been. Elena clenched her hands into fists and felt the bite of the unfamiliar bands around her finger like one more slap.

And then followed him, anyway.

His mobile beeped again as they walked. He answered it, slowing down as he talked. Elena heard the words *docklands, cousin* and *Battaglia.* Alessandro pushed open the glass doors at the entrance of the village hall, and nodded her through, almost as if he had a chivalrous bone in that powerful body of his.

"Wait for me in the car," he said, and then turned back toward the interior of the hall. Dismissing her.

The door swished shut behind her as she stepped

through it, and Elena pulled in a long, deep breath. The morning was still as bright and cheerful as it had been when she'd walked inside. A lovely July day in the rolling hills of Sicily. The perfect day for a wedding.

She had to figure out how to handle this, to enjoy it while it lasted, or she'd never survive it. And she had to do it fast.

Elena kept her eyes on the stairs below her as she climbed down the hall's steps, her legs still so shaky and the heels she wore no help at all, so she had to hold tight to the bannister as she went. Cracking her head open on the pavement would hardly improve matters.

She made it to the bottom step in one piece, and started to walk around the man who stood there, his back to the hall. Alessandro's sleek black sports car was parked near the fountain in the center of the pretty village square, the convertible top pulled back, reminding her of how silly she'd been on the drive over—glancing at the way the ring sparkled on her hand, allowing herself to yearn for impossibilities.

"Excuse me," she murmured absently as she navigated her way around the man, glancing at him to smile politely—

But it was Niccolo.

All of the blood drained out of her head. Her stomach contracted in a sickening lurch, and she was sure her heart dropped out of her body and lay at her feet on the pavement.

"Niccolo..." she whispered in disbelief.

Niccolo, like all of the nightmares that had kept her awake these past months. Niccolo, his arms folded over his chest and his black eyes burning mean and cold as he soaked in her reaction.

Niccolo, who she'd thought she loved until Alessandro

had walked into her life and showed her how pale that love was, how small. Niccolo, who she'd trusted. Who she'd laughed with, thinking they were laughing together. Who she'd dreamed with, thinking they were planning a shared future. Niccolo, who had hunted her across all these months and the span of Italy, and was looking at her now as if that slap in his villa was only the very beginning of what he'd like to do to her.

She couldn't believe this was happening. Today. Here. Now.

"Elena," he said, his voice almost friendly, but she could see that nasty gleam in his eyes. She could see exactly who he was. "At last."

CHAPTER TEN

ELENA NEEDED TO say something, *do* something.

Scream for help, at the very least. Kick off her shoes and run. She needed to get as far away from Niccolo as possible, to distance herself from that vicious retribution she saw shining in his black eyes and all across his boyishly handsome face.

But she couldn't seem to move a single muscle.

His lip curled. "Did you really think you could outrun me forever?"

She threw a panicked glance back up the stairs. Alessandro was still there, on the far side of the glass door, but he had his back turned to the square. To what was happening. To her.

Elena didn't know why she'd believed he could save her from this, even for an instant. Hadn't she always known she would have to handle it herself?

Niccolo looked up at Alessandro, then back at her, and his expression grew uglier.

"You've never been anything but a useless little whore, Elena," he said, his black eyes bright with malevolence. "I took you out of that fishing boat you grew up in. I made something out of you. And this is how you repay me?"

Elena straightened. Pulled in a breath. He was shorter than she remembered. Thicker and more florid. The ob-

didn't have to run. Alessandro had given her that much. As she looked up at Niccolo now, Elena finally accepted that even if Niccolo had been who he'd pretended to be, it still would have been over between them.

It had been over the moment she'd met Alessandro.

Even if she'd never seen him again after that night in Rome, she would have known the truth: that she'd loved a stranger for the duration of a dance far more than she'd loved her fiancé. It would have ended her engagement one way or another. Maybe, she thought then, she'd actually been lucky that dance had forced Niccolo to reveal himself. It would have been much, much harder to leave the man she'd thought he was.

"But then," Niccolo was saying, "he doesn't care about you, does he? He wants the land. Do you think he would trouble himself to marry you otherwise?"

He shook her, and that hurt, too, but she didn't try to pull away. She didn't defend Alessandro's motives or worry that she didn't know what they were. She didn't cry or protest. She stared at him, memorizing this, so she would never forget what it felt like the moment she'd not only stopped being afraid of Niccolo Falco, but stopped feeling guilty about how this had all happened in the first place.

Inevitable, something whispered inside of her. *This was all inevitable.*

"I never would have married you," she said then, her voice smooth and strong. "Alessandro only expedited things. You would have shown your true face sooner or later. And I would have left you the moment I saw it."

"Look at where you are," Niccolo ground out, his fingers digging into her arm. "This tiny town, all alone. Have you really convinced yourself that a man like Alessandro Corretti, who invited half of Europe to his last wedding, cares about a nobody like you?" He laughed. "Wake up,

Elena. The only difference between Alessandro Corretti and me is that he has enough money to be a better liar."

Elena would have to think about that, she knew. She would have to investigate the damage he'd caused with that hard, low blow. But not now. Not here.

"You don't need to concern yourself with that land," she said, ignoring the rest of it. She let him see how little she feared him, let him see she wasn't shaking or cowering. "It will never be yours. You lost it the moment you thought you could hit me."

His face flushed even redder, even angrier than before. He yanked her closer to him, shoving his face into hers, trying to intimidate her with his size and strength. He was a petty man, a vicious one. But she still wasn't afraid.

"I'm not scared of you anymore, Niccolo," she said very distinctly, tilting her head back to look him full in the face. Not hiding. Not running. Not afraid. "And that means you need to let go of my arm. Now."

Whatever he saw in her face then made him drop her arm as if she'd turned into a demon right there in front of him. And Elena smiled, a real and genuine smile, because she was free of him.

After all this time, she was finally free of him.

"Step away from my wife, Falco."

Alessandro's icily furious voice cracked like a whip, startling Elena. Better, it made Niccolo move back. Alessandro was beside her then, his hand stroking down her back, as if he was reassuring himself that she still stood in one piece.

Or, the cynical part of her whispered, *marking his territory.*

"Give us a minute."

It took Elena a moment to realize that Alessandro was

His father would have simply kicked in one of Niccolo's kneecaps, the better to drag him off and beat the life out of him in a more private place. Alessandro had seen Carlo do exactly that when he was fourteen.

"Men deal with problems like men, boy," Carlo had told him, clearly disappointed that Alessandro hadn't reacted better. "Take that scared look off your face. You're a Corretti. Act like one."

And Alessandro had never felt more like a Corretti, with all of the blood and graft and misery that implied, than he did right now.

Retribution. Revenge. Finally, he understood both.

"Be very careful," Alessandro said through his teeth, trying to push back the red haze that obscured his vision. "You're talking about my wife."

Niccolo's neck was flushed. His black eyes were slits of rage, and his thick hands were in fists. Alessandro knew he'd used one of those meaty hands on Elena, once before and once today, and had to battle back the urge to break the both of them.

He had no doubt at all that he could. He hadn't fought in over forty days now—but he wasn't drunk this time.

"I had her first," Niccolo threw at him, a sly look in his eyes. "In every possible—"

"I won't warn you again."

It would be so easy. To simply end this man, as he richly deserved. He was nothing but a parasite, a lowlife. Alessandro didn't even have to get his hands dirty, the way his father had so enjoyed. He knew which former associates of his father's he could call to "handle" this. It was part and parcel of his blackened family legacy. It would take a single phone call.

This was who he was. Just as his mother had told him.

Just as Elena had accused him. Just as he had always feared.

But this would be justice, that seductive darkness whispered. *Simple. Earned.*

Alessandro had to force air into his lungs. All the choices his father and uncle and grandfather had made, all the blood that stained their hands as they'd built this family up from nothing and punished whoever dared stand in their way—he'd always looked down on them for it.

He'd never understood how easy it might be to step across that line. He'd never understood the temptation. Or that it could seem not only right to exterminate a cockroach like Niccolo Falco, but inarguably just.

Necessary.

That darkness in him didn't even seem particularly dark to him today as he stared at the bastard who'd terrorized Elena. It seemed like a choice. The right choice.

But.

But Elena had cried in his arms, and then she'd trusted him when he didn't deserve it at all. When he'd given her no reason to trust him. She'd married him. He couldn't understand why she'd done it. He wasn't sure he ever would.

But it burned in him. It lived in him, bright like hope.

"Be the man who does the right thing," she'd said once. And her eyes were the perfect blue of all his favorite summers, and she'd looked at him as if he could never be a man like his father.

As if she had some kind of faith in him, after all.

"Why take her at all?" Niccolo demanded, stepping even closer, tempting fate. "Because she was mine?"

Alessandro smiled at him, cold and vicious. "Because I can."

Niccolo snorted. "You're nothing but a thug in fancy clothes, aren't you?"

Alessandro was done then. With Niccolo, with all of this. With who he'd nearly become. With that dark spiral he'd almost lost himself in today, that he could still feel inside of him.

But Elena was like light, and he wanted her more.

"Don't let me see you again, Falco. Don't even cross into my line of sight. You won't like what happens." He leaned closer then, pleased in a purely primitive way that he was bigger. Taller. That there was that flicker of fear in the other man's eyes. "And stay the hell away from my wife. That goes for you and your entire pathetic family. You do not want to go to war with me, I promise you."

Niccolo recoiled, the angry flush on his face and neck bleeding into something darker. Nastier.

"Don't worry," he said, ugly and flat. "Once I'm finished with a whore—"

Alessandro shut him up. With his fist.

He felt the crunch of bone that told him he'd broken Niccolo's nose, heard the other man's bellow of pain as he crumpled to the ground. Where he lay in a cowardly heap, clutching at his face.

And Alessandro wasn't his father, he would never be his father, but he was still Corretti enough to enjoy it.

"Next time," he promised, "I won't be so kind."

And then he walked away and left Niccolo Falco bleeding into the ground.

But alive.

"I'm sorry I let him touch you," Alessandro said gruffly when he swung into the car. Elena sat there so primly in the passenger seat, looking perfect. Untouchable. Her face smooth and her eyes hidden away behind dark glasses. "It won't happen again."

"He didn't hurt me," she said. Far too politely. When he

only frowned at her, searching her face for some sign, she shifted slightly in her seat. "Don't you have a meeting?"

He reminded himself that he had her torn panties in his pocket. That if he reached over and touched her, he could have her moaning out his name in moments. But he started the car instead, and pulled out onto the small country road that led away from the village and back toward Palermo.

He'd told her Niccolo wouldn't come for her, and he had. She had every right to be afraid, even angry. To blame him.

He could handle that. He could handle anything—because she'd married him, and they had nothing now but time. The rest of their lives, rolling out before them. There was nowhere to hide. Not for long.

They drove in silence, the warm summer day rushing all around them, sunshine and wind dancing in and around the car. The hills were green and pretty and off in the distance the sea beckoned. She was his wife, and he wasn't his father.

It might not be perfect, Alessandro thought. It might take some work yet. But it was good.

"Why did you hit him?" she asked as they started to make their way into the city sprawl, and the wind no longer prohibited conversation.

"I should have killed him," Alessandro replied shortly. "I wanted to kill him."

But he hadn't.

He hadn't.

"I didn't say he didn't deserve it," she replied in that cool way that he still hated, even now. "I only wondered what horrible thing he might have said to tip you over that edge."

Alessandro eyed her as he stopped at a traffic light. He considered telling her about real edges, and what lay on the other side of them, but refrained. There would be time enough to introduce her to all the poison and pain that was his birthright, to tell her what had happened back there and what he'd finally rejected once and for all.

"He called you a whore."

"Ah," she said. She sat there so elegantly. So calmly. Her hands folded in her lap, her legs neatly crossed. She smiled, and it scraped at him. "So it's only okay when you do it?"

Alessandro pulled in a breath through his teeth.

"Damn it, Elena," he began, but she turned to face the front again, and nodded toward the road with every appearance of serenity.

"The light's changed."

He swore in Sicilian as well as Italian, and then he drove with more fury than skill through the city, screeching to a halt at the valet in front of the Corretti Media tower.

Elena let herself out of the car before he had the chance to come around and get her, starting toward the building's entrance as if she didn't care one way or the other if he followed her. Gritting his teeth, he did.

She said nothing as they walked through the marble lobby. She only slid her dark glasses onto the top of her head and let him guide her into the elevator when it arrived.

"Is there anything else you plan to throw at me today?" he asked, tamping down on his temper as the doors slid shut. "Do we need to have another discussion like the one we had about divorce?"

Elena stared straight ahead, her gaze fixed on the far wall and the flashing numbers that announced each floor, though a faint flush spread across her cheeks.

"There's nothing else," she said. He didn't recognize that voice she used, the way she held herself. But he knew she was lying. "I'm sorry. I don't know why I said that."

"Are you sure he didn't hurt you?" he asked quietly.

She looked at him then, and her blue eyes were shadowed. Dark.

"No." There was something there then. Something making her voice catch, her mouth take on that hint of vulnerability that killed him. "I told you."

"Elena," he said. "You have to know—"

But his mobile beeped. She blinked, then looked away, and when she glanced at him again her face was that smooth mask. He couldn't stand it.

"Tell me what's wrong," he urged her. "Tell me what happened."

"You should answer that," she said, much too calmly, when his phone kept beeping. "I'm sure it's important."

He pulled out the phone to look at the screen, and wasn't surprised at the number he saw flashing there.

"It's my family," he started, not knowing how to compress the history of the Corretti feuds into something coherent. Not knowing how he felt about any of it, now that he'd pulled himself back from the abyss that had stalked him all these years. "There are all these divisions, these petty little wars—"

"I read the papers, Alessandro," she said gently. "I know about your family." She nodded at his mobile. "You should take the call."

"I always take the call," he gritted out. "And it never helps. Whenever there's a possibility of ending this nonsense, we make sure to destroy it." He shook his head. "I'm beginning to believe we always will."

She looked at him for a long moment, and he had the sense she was weighing something behind those stormy eyes he couldn't read. She reached over and hit one of the elevator buttons, making his main office floor light up.

"Then you should fix it," she said. She even smiled, and it was almost real. He almost believed she meant it. "Isn't that what you do?"

"No," he said shortly, his gaze searching hers. "Obviously not."

Her eyes were much too dark, and it ate at him. Something flared between them in the small space, a different kind of fire, and he had the awful sense that he'd already lost her. That she had already disappeared.

But she was right here, he reminded himself sternly. She had married him slightly more than an hour ago. She was his.

"What's the right thing?" she asked, her voice too quiet. "Do that, even if it hurts. Your family deserves it."

"And if they don't?"

After all these bitter years. After all the pain, the blood.

He thought he saw compassion in her gaze, or maybe he only wanted that. Maybe he was simply desperate for something he recognized, something to ease the gnawing sensation inside of him.

The elevator doors slid open, and she looked away, out toward the hushed executive level of Corretti Media.

His phone beeped again. Insistent. Annoying. He heard Giovanni's voice from the office floor, the valet no doubt having informed him that Alessandro had returned.

"Your family might not deserve it, Alessandro. But you do."

"Me?" He hardly made a sound. He hardly breathed. "I fear I deserve it least of all."

The moment stretched between them, taut and shimmering with all the things he did not, could not, feel, except for her. He said her name again. His favorite incantation. His only remaining prayer.

"Go," she whispered.

And it wasn't until the elevator door had closed on her, and he was striding toward his responsibilities the way he always did, that he realized what he'd seen flash in her eyes then was a deep, dark sadness.

Elena took an early-afternoon flight out of Palermo's Falcone Borcellino Airport, headed for Naples and the car she'd hired for the drive back to her village. She settled into the economy-class seat she'd bought with the money she'd earned waitressing and on Alessandro's yacht, not the money he—or, more likely, his staff—had left for her in the penthouse in a folder with her name on the front and a selection of credit cards and cash within.

And when the plane took off and soared into the air above Sicily, she didn't let herself look back.

"Because I can," he'd said to Niccolo. That was why he'd danced with her. That was why he'd done all of this. Married her. Just as she'd suspected, it was all a game. Because he could.

She hadn't thought she'd hear him admit it.

And as she'd sat in his car in the sun-drenched village square, twisting all of those diamonds around and around on her finger, Niccolo's harsh words circling in her head, she'd had to face the facts she'd been avoiding for far too long.

She'd been so sure that she, Elena Calderon, *deserved* what Niccolo had represented. That she *should* be the one chosen from all the girls in the village to swan off into a posh life, dripping in gowns and villas.

Alessandro had been right to accuse her of that, but wrong about why—and around him it was even worse. He was the most powerful man she'd ever met. His ruthlessness was equal parts intimidating and exciting. He was beautiful and lethal, and he'd wanted her as desperately as she'd wanted him.

Some part of her obviously believed that she deserved

no less than the CEO of one of the most successful media corporations in Europe. That she deserved rings made of diamonds, private islands and a three-story penthouse perched over Palermo like an opulent aerie.

How remarkably conceited she was.

She remembered then, as the plane winged across the blue sea, one of the last nights they'd spent on the island. They'd sat together on the beach, watching the sunset. He'd been behind her, letting her sprawl between his legs and against his chest.

He'd played with her hair and she'd watched the sun sink toward the horizon. She'd felt so filled with hope. So unreasonably optimistic.

Until she'd recalled the last time she'd felt that way.

It had been the night of that fateful charity ball. She'd finished dressing in the new, beautiful gown Niccolo had chosen for her, and she'd been unable to stop staring at herself in the mirror of their hotel suite. She'd looked so glamorous, so sophisticated. And she'd felt the same sense of well-being, of happiness, roll through her.

This is exactly how my life should be, she'd thought then.

On the beach with Alessandro, she'd shivered.

"What's the matter?" he'd asked, tugging gently on her hair so she'd look back at him. The reds and golds of the setting sun cast him in bronze, once again like a very old god, perfect and deadly.

"Nothing," she'd lied, and she'd wanted it to be nothing. Just an odd coincidence. No reason at all for that sudden hollow pit in her stomach.

He'd smiled, and kissed her, then he'd wrapped his arms around her like a man in love and had tucked her under his chin in that way she adored, and she'd known without a shadow of a doubt that it was no coincidence. That it had been a sign, and she'd do well to heed it.

That when the forty days were up she had to leave him. *She had to.*

And she'd gone ahead and married him, anyway.

But then, she thought now, shifting in her narrow seat, every decision she'd made for more than half a year she'd made out of fear.

Fear of what Niccolo would do to her. Fear of her parents' disappointment. Fear of losing Alessandro—a man who had insulted her upon their first meeting, thought the very worst of her even as he slept with her, and had even married her in undue, secretive haste in a sleepy little village where no one knew him.

Niccolo was a disgusting creep, but he'd had a point.

And the truth was, though she never would have phrased it the way he had, she would always smell of fish and hard, thankless work like the people she came from. No matter what airs she tried to put on, what gowns or jewels she wore, she was a village girl. She had no place with a man like Alessandro.

More than that, he was a Corretti.

Maybe Alessandro really was the man he claimed he was, a man who strove to do what was right no matter what his family name. She thought of that painful conversation in the elevator and she ached—because she wanted so badly to believe him. To believe that the darkness she'd seen in him today was an aberration, not the true face he'd kept from her the way Niccolo had.

Maybe.

But she had to accept that it was just as likely that he was exactly who Niccolo had told her he was. Exactly who she'd believed he was.

It was time to go home. It was time to stop playing at games she hardly understood. It was past time.

Elena needed to face up to what she'd done. She needed

to beg for her parents' forgiveness—not for calling off one wedding, not for marrying yet another man who might very well ruin everything, but for not trusting them enough. For not staying and fighting the lies Niccolo had told. For not believing that they could love her enough to overcome their disappointment in her. For running away instead.

It had solved nothing. It had been a selfish, scared act. It had hurt the people who loved her. And it had broken her heart.

The land was out of her hands, she thought now, her eyes easing closed as she accepted that bitter reality. As she acknowledged her own failure. In the end, it was only land. Dirt and stones and trees. It wasn't worth all of this suffering.

Elena had to believe that.

She closed the window shade beside her so she wouldn't give in to the temptation to look back, shut her eyes tight and prayed she'd make it home in time.

CHAPTER ELEVEN

ALESSANDRO SAT ALONE in his office on the executive floor of the Corretti Media tower. His mobile beeped insistently at him, but he ignored it. Just as he ignored the new proposal Giovanni had drafted for him, comprising Alessandro's bid for the cursed docklands regeneration project. All he needed to do was sign it.

And then, of course, persuade Alessia Battaglia's grasping, two-faced father to honor the commitment he'd made back when Alessandro and Alessia had agreed to marry.

But instead he'd cleared his office.

The proposal was one more gauntlet thrown down in this same old war. It cut out his cousins completely, following right along in Carlo's footsteps, adhering to the same script his father and uncle had written in their blood decades back.

Alessandro pushed back from his desk and roamed restlessly around his great office, a suitable corporate celebration of a man of his wealth, power and position. It was a space meant to intimidate. To assert in no uncertain terms the full weight and heft of Corretti authority.

That goddamned name.

He walked to the windows, and looked out over the city of his birth. Palermo basked before him in the summer sun, corrupt and decaying, beautiful and serene. A mass of contradictions imprinted with the fingerprints of history, this place; streets marked with violence surrounding ancient green squares of breathtaking loveliness. Byzantine churches, leftover city walls, influences ranging from the Phoenicians to the Mafia. And it was inside of him. It was home. Unlike his brother, he had never wanted to live abroad. Sicily sang in his blood. Palermo was the key to who he was.

And who he was, who he had always been, was a Corretti.

But he was no longer sure what that meant.

He could have become his father at any time in all these years. He could have stepped all too easily into Carlo's shoes today. He'd finally felt what that would mean. He'd wanted it. He'd even thought Niccolo Falco deserved it.

But the woman who'd told him that he deserved what was right, whatever that was, deserved better than a violent criminal as her husband. And it made him question not only himself, but this whole notion of who the Correttis were. If it was a curse, this name—or it was merely one more choice they all kept making.

Today Alessandro had chosen not to take the easy way, the corrupt and criminal way. His father's way. He'd spent his life believing he did what was right, that he did his duty.

Now it was time to prove it.

He walked back over to his desk and shoved the proposal out of his way, picking up his mobile to make two calls he should have made years ago. To offer, if not an olive branch, a start. A fresh, clean start.

His duty to his family should be about the living, not the dead. The Corretti name should not be forever synonymous with the actions of those long buried.

Because the past didn't matter. What mattered were the choices they made now. He, his half-brother, Angelo, and his cousin Matteo shouldn't have to follow along in the footsteps of monsters, simply because those monsters were their fathers. And they certainly didn't have to become them.

Surely, he told himself, they could simply…stop this.

His cousin Matteo picked up the phone, and Alessandro braced himself for a necessary, if excruciatingly awkward, conversation.

It was only as dark as they allowed it to be, he thought. And it was long past time for the light.

Elena let herself out of her parents' house high up on the rocky hillside, and pulled the door closed behind her quietly, so as not to disturb her father's rest. It was a gray, foggy morning, the air thick and cool against her skin. She pulled her old jacket tighter around her, and set off down the slanting street.

She felt turned inside out. Rubbed entirely raw. Her parents had done nothing but love her since her return yesterday afternoon. Her mother had wept. Her father had smiled as if she was a blessing from on high. Elena was humbled. Grateful.

And she'd still been unable to sleep, her mind and her body torturing her with memories of Alessandro. Images of Alessandro. All of that heat and light, fire and need.

She'd learned nothing.

The sloping streets and ancient stone stairs that led the way down the hillside were second nature to her. Each house, each alley, each clothesline hanging naked in today's weather, was like its own separate greeting. This was home. It had always been home. She was made to smell of the sea, the salt and the sun and the bounty they provided. There was no shame in that.

Yet today she felt out of place in a way she never had before.

It will come, she assured herself as she came to the bottom of the steep hill that led into the main square. *You've been away for a long time.*

Everything seemed different in the thick mist. Sounds were muffled, and strange echoes seemed to nip at her heels. She narrowly avoided one of the village's biggest gossips, darting around the far side of the great statue that sat in the center of the square, and was so busy looking back over her shoulder to be sure she'd escaped that she ran right into someone.

Elena opened her mouth to apologize, but she knew that rock-hard chest. She knew the strong hands that wrapped around her upper arms and righted her.

It seemed to take a thousand years to lift her gaze to his, to confirm what she already knew.

What her body was already celebrating, with an insistent ache in her heart and core alike.

"What are you doing here?" she gasped out.

Alessandro's wicked brows rose in arrogant amazement. "You left me."

"I had to come home," she blurted out in a rush, the strangest urge to apologize to him, to offer him comfort, working its way through her. Proving, she thought, her terrible weakness. "And what does it matter to you?"

"You left me," he said again, each word distinct and furious.

Elena ignored the things that clamored in her then, all of that fear and despair that she'd lost him, all of her desperate, foolish love for a man she couldn't have. Not really. Not the way she wanted him.

"Is this about the land?" she asked baldly. "Because you

didn't have to come all the way here for that. You don't have to pretend anymore."

His eyes blazed, so lethally hot she took a step back, and then cursed herself for it. Alessandro was a lot of things, but he wasn't Niccolo. She knew he would never hurt her—not like that.

"It turns out," Alessandro bit out, betrayal and accusation in those dark green eyes, "that I am sick and tired of being discarded on my wedding day."

Elena paled, then reddened.

"Not here," she managed to get out.

She ducked into one of the ancient passageways that wound around behind a few of the shops and deposited them on a lonely stretch of the rocky cliffs overlooking the small harbor. And then she faced him.

He stood there, dark and furious, dressed in one of those impossibly sleek suits that made him look terrifying and delicious all at once, a symphony of powerful, wealthy male beauty. It reminded her that she was only a village girl in old clothes and messy hair, no doubt smelling again of fish.

"What exactly are you doing, Elena?" he asked, his voice clipped.

"This is where I belong," she said defiantly. "This is who I am."

He only watched her, his dark green eyes narrow and fierce.

"I brought you something," he said after a moment. He reached into an inside pocket of his suit jacket and she was sure, for a dizzy moment, that he was going to pull out those torn panties and then what would she do? But instead, he handed her a thick envelope.

Elena took it, her fingers acting of their own accord, a

miserable, sinking sensation washing through her, from her throat to her heart to her belly.

"Is this—?" Her throat was so dry she could hear the words scrape as she formed them. "Are these divorce papers?"

This was what she wanted, she tried to tell herself. This was a good thing. But she wanted only to curl up somewhere and cry.

His hard mouth curved into something far too angry to be a smile.

"It's a legal document," he said, his eyes never leaving hers. "It relinquishes any claim I might have had to your family's land, and hands it back to you." Elena made a small noise, her fingers clutching almost convulsively at the envelope. "And I suggest you take note of the date. It was signed three days ago."

Meaning, it took her a confused moment to understand, that he had signed the land over to her before their wedding.

"I don't..." she whispered.

"In case there is any lingering confusion," he said in that deadly way of his, "I never wanted the goddamn land. I wanted you."

Which meant he really was the man she'd wanted him to be—but Elena couldn't process that. There was nothing but a roar of thunder inside her, loud and overwhelming.

He didn't love her, she reminded herself then, cutting through all the noise. No matter what kind of man he was.

The envelope shook in her hand. "I don't know what to say."

"What a surprise." His voice was cool, but his eyes burned hot, and she burned with them. "And here I thought your silent defection was so eloquent."

He reached out for her other hand, taking it in his, and Elena watched in stunned silence—as if it was not her hand at all, as if it was connected to someone else—as he reached into a different pocket and slid the rings she'd left in the penthouse back onto her finger.

"I don't want those," she croaked out. His hand closed around hers then, and she felt that electric charge sizzle all the way up her arm.

"They're yours," he bit out, his dark eyes flashing. "Just like the clothes you left behind. If you don't want them, fine. Sell them. Burn them in your back garden. But I won't take them back."

She yanked her hand away, as if her palm was on fire. It felt like it was. It felt like she was.

But Alessandro was a dream and it was time to wake up. She had to stop prostrating herself to impossibilities. She had to stop dreaming about what she thought she ought to have, and concentrate instead on what she did have. And that wasn't him.

"I appreciate this more than I can say," she said in a low voice, stepping back from him and tucking the envelope in the pocket of her jacket.

"All I asked was that you have a little faith," he gritted out. "Was that really so hard, Elena? Did it warrant you running away from me mere hours after our wedding?"

"We have sex," she said evenly, because it was time to accept reality. "That's all it is, Alessandro. That's all it ever was."

"You're still such a liar," he said in a kind of wonder.

"It's not real," she continued, determined to make him see reason. "It's chemical. It fades."

"We do not *just* have sex," he said, moving toward her then. "What we have, Elena, is extraordinary. It was there from the moment we met."

He reached over and slid his palm along her jaw, her cheek, anchoring his fingers in her hair. That same fire roared in her, that easily. That same old connection that had caused all this trouble. And he knew it. His mouth curved.

"You can't—" she began, but he only pressed a finger over her lips and she subsided, her heart pounding.

"And if you want something real," he said in a low, stirring voice that did nothing to conceal his temper and seemed to echo in her bones, her veins, her core, making something like shame twist in her, low and deep, "then you're going to have to treat me like I'm real, too. Not something you have to bend and contort to get around. Just a man, Elena. Nothing more or less than that."

That thudded into her, hard. She wrenched herself back, away from his touch. She fought for breath.

"You're a man, yes," she threw at him. "I know that. But your only form of communication is in bed—"

"Do not," he interrupted her furiously, "*do not* claim I can't *communicate* when your version of a discussion involves sneaking off for a plane ride and two hours' drive."

"You don't understand!" She hardly knew what she was saying. She was panicked. Cornered. "I loved you so much I was willing to do anything. I wrecked my engagement. I betrayed my family. I lost myself—anything to have you. But that's not love, Alessandro." She shook her head wildly. Desperately. "It's an addiction. *It's just sex.*"

"Thank you," he said grimly, "for using the past tense. Keep sticking your knife in, Elena. Twist it, why don't you."

But she couldn't stop. It was as if something else had taken control of her.

"We never should have met," she told him. "We were never *meant* to meet. It was a complete disaster at first sight."

"It was love at first sight," Alessandro snapped at her. "And you know it."

That was like a deep, terrible rip, so far inside her she didn't think she could survive it.

"Don't you dare say that!" she hurled at him. "Don't you dare pretend!"

"I love you!" he thundered, the words ricocheting from the stone walls of the village, the rocky cliffs, the thick fog and the water below.

Or maybe that was only in her head. Maybe that was her heart.

Alessandro found her gaze, held it. Frustration and determination gleamed there in all of that dark green, along with something else.

Sincerity, she thought, from some stunned distance. *He meant it.* She heard a small noise, a kind of gasp, and only dimly realized she'd made it.

"I love you, Elena," he said, his voice serious. Certain. "Since the moment I saw you, I've never been the same."

"You…" But she couldn't seem to speak.

"There were no contracts," he said then, fiercely. "No discussions about assets or settlements. No prenuptial agreement. I simply married you, because I can't be without you. I can't let you leave me." His dark eyes flashed. *"I can't."*

She tried to say his name, formed the syllables of it with her mouth, but no sound came out.

"I have a great darkness in me," he said then, intently. "I can't pretend I don't. But it's not going to win. It can't, if I have you."

She shook her head, as if she could shake this off. As if she could push him back into those neatly labeled boxes she'd set out for him. She had to do it, or she might die where she stood. She didn't question that—she simply knew it.

"We were always destined to burn ourselves out, Alessandro," she said when she could speak. "This was doomed from the start."

He closed the distance between them then, and took her shoulders in his hands. Kind and gentle. Heartbreakingly firm.

"Do you want me to convince you?" he asked roughly, a broken look in his dark eyes. "Is that what this is? Because we both know I can."

"What?" Her ears were ringing, louder by the second. "No, I—"

"Tell me what you *want*, Elena," he said, all of his ferocity and all of the desolation she'd sensed in him right there between them, suddenly. Alive in the damp air. "Do you *want* me to hunt you down, make you accept what's between us? Do you *want* me to leave you alone? You need to choose. You need to *fight*."

He dropped his hands then, stepped back, and the distance between them was unbearable. It made her shake.

"You can't put this all on me," he continued, his voice low but with the ring of a kind of finality that made everything inside of her twist tight in anguish.

"I don't know what I want," she lied, and the look in his eyes then shamed her. Destroyed her. Because he knew she was lying. He always knew.

"I loved you before I knew your name," he said then. "I love you more now, even when you lie to my face. All you have to do is own this, Elena."

She shuddered. She couldn't do it. She couldn't—

"I do," she said desperately. "I love you."

"I know you do," he replied, a slight curve to that hard mouth, but it wasn't enough. "But that's not the issue, is it? It never has been."

And something in her finally broke then. Pride, fear. Selfishness and vanity. All the things she'd been accused of, all the accusations she'd levied at herself. It all simply cracked into pieces and washed over her.

"I left because I couldn't bear to be so stupid," she told him in a rush. "To make such a terrible mistake again." Her eyes filled with tears, spilled over, wetting her cheeks. "But I married you because I wanted to marry you. I wanted you."

She wiped at her eyes, then focused on him, and he took up the whole world. Commanding and strong. But waiting to hear what she'd say next. What she'd decide. As if she was the one with the power, after all.

"I still do, Alessandro," she whispered. "I want you more than I've ever wanted anything else. I can't fight that. I tried."

"You don't have to fight that," he said, his dark green eyes so fierce on hers she trembled. "You don't have to fight me. Just fight *for* this, Elena. Don't run away. Don't hide."

She made a wordless sort of sound, far past the ability to speak, and he pulled her close and let her cry.

"I'm not your enemy," he murmured into her hair.

"I know," she whispered into his strong, warm chest. "I know you're not."

She shuddered against him, and then he kissed her. Sweet, sure. Hot. Like a promise. Like hope. And when he drew back she saw the future she'd been too afraid to imagine, right there in his dark eyes, that curve of his perfect mouth.

"Come back to Sicily with me," he said. "And stay this time. Stay for good."

Elena nodded, too overwhelmed to speak. And this wasn't surrender, she realized. She wasn't losing a thing. She was gaining Alessandro—she was gaining *them*.

She was trading in something broken, something ruined and outgrown, for a shared set of wings and the whole bright sky to call their own.

"I want you to meet my parents," she whispered. "My father. He's not well, but…I think he'll like you."

"That is exceedingly unlikely," he said quietly. "I'm a Corretti."

And it was Elena's turn to kiss him then, to press her mouth against his and set him free with all of that fire that was always, only theirs. To love him with nothing held back, nothing hidden. To bask in that terrible, impossible, extraordinary love that had slammed into them with no warning, changing them both. Changing everything.

"He'll love you," she told him. She looped her arms around his neck and adored the way he smiled down at her. "Because I love you. That's how it works."

He was shadow and light. Ruthless and kind. Dark green eyes and that wild, hot heat when he looked at her.

And all of him hers, as he had been from the start. From that single glance across a crowded room.

"I will always be a Corretti," Alessandro said. It was a warning. Or, she thought, a promise.

Elena smiled. "So will I."

* * * * *

A HUNGER FOR
THE FORBIDDEN

MAISEY YATES

CHAPTER ONE

ALESSIA BATTAGLIA ADJUSTED her veil, the whisper-thin fabric skimming over the delicate skin of her neck. Like a lover's kiss. Soft. Gentle.

She closed her eyes, and she could feel it.

Hot, warm lips on her bare flesh. A firm, masculine hand at her waist.

She opened her eyes again and bent down, adjusting the delicate buckles on her white satin heels.

Her lover's hands on her ankle, removing her high heels. Leaving her naked in front of him, naked before a man for the first time. But there was no time for nerves. There was nothing more than the heat between them. Years of fantasy, years of longing.

Alessia swallowed and took the bouquet of bloodred roses from the chair they were resting on. She looked down at the blossoms, some of them bruised by the way she'd laid them down.

Brushing her fingertips over the crushed velvet petals brought another wave of memory. A wave of sensation.

Her lover's mouth at her breast, her fingers woven through his thick dark hair.

"Alessia?"

Her head snapped up and she saw her wedding coordinator standing in the doorway, one hand covering her headset.

"Yes?"

"It's time."

Alessia nodded, and headed toward the doorway, her shoes loud on the marble floor of the basilica. She exited the room that had been set aside for her to get ready in, and entered the vast foyer. It was empty now, all of the guests in the sanctuary, waiting for the ceremony.

She let out a long breath, the sound loud in the empty, high-ceilinged room. Then she started her walk toward the sanctuary, past pillars inlaid with gold and stones. She stopped for a moment, hoping to find some comfort, some peace, in the biblical scenes depicted on the walls.

Her eyes fell to a detailed painting of a garden. Of Eve handing Adam the apple.

"Please. Just one night."

"Only one, cara mia?*"*

"That's all I have to give."

A searing kiss, like nothing she'd ever experienced before. Better than any fantasy.

Her breath caught and she turned away from the painting, continuing on, continuing to the small antechamber outside of the sanctuary.

Her father was there, his suit crisp and pressed. Antonioni Battaglia looked every inch the respectable citizen everyone knew he was not. And the wedding, so formal, so traditional, was another statement of his power. Power that he longed to increase, with the Corretti fortune and status.

That desire was the reason she was here.

"You are very much like your mother."

She wondered if there was any truth to the words, or if it was just the right thing to say. Tenderness was something her father had never seemed capable of.

"Thank you," she said, looking down at her bouquet.

"This is what's right for the family."

She knew it was. Knew that it was the key to ensuring

that her brothers and sisters were cared for. And that was, after all, what she'd done since her mother died in child- birth. Pietro, Giana, Marco and Eva were the brightest lights in her existence, and she would do, had done, what- ever she could to ensure they had the best life possible.

And still, regret settled on her like a cloak, and memory clouded the present. Memories of her lover. His hands, his body, his passion.

If only her lover, and the man waiting behind the doors to the sanctuary, waiting to marry her, were the same.

"I know," she said, fighting against the desolation in- side of her. The emptiness.

The double doors parted, revealing an impossibly long aisle. The music changed, everyone turned to look at her— all twelve hundred guests, who had come to watch the union of the Battaglia family and their much-hated rivals, the Correttis.

She held her head up, trying to breathe. The bodice of her dress threatened to choke her. The lace, which formed a high collar, and sleeves that ended in a point over her hands, was heavy and scratched against her skin. The yards of fabric clung to her, heat making her feel light-headed.

It was a beautiful dress, but it was too fussy for her. Too heavy. But the dress wasn't about her. The wedding wasn't about her.

Her father followed her into the sanctuary but didn't take her arm. He had given her away when he'd signed his agreement with the late Salvatore Corretti. He didn't need to do it again. He didn't move to take a seat, either, rather he prowled around the back of the pews, up the side of the church, his steps parallel to hers. That was Antonioni Battaglia all over. Watching proceedings, ensuring all went well. Watching her. Making sure she did as she was told.

A drop of sweat rolled down her back and another flash of memory hit her hard.

His sweat-slicked skin beneath her fingertips. Her nails digging into his shoulders. Her thighs wrapped around lean, masculine hips...

She blinked and looked up at Alessandro. Her groom. The man to whom she was about to make her vows.

God forgive me.

Had she not been holding the roses, she would have crossed herself.

And then she felt him. As though he had reached out and put his hands on her.

She looked at the Corretti side, and her heart stopped for a moment. Matteo.

Her lover. Her groom's enemy.

Matteo was arresting as ever, with the power to draw the breath from her lungs. Tall and broad, his physique outlined to perfection by his custom-made suit. Olive skin and square jaw. Lips that delivered pleasure in beautiful and torturous ways.

But this man standing in the pews was not the man who'd shared her bed that night a month ago. He was different. Rage, dark and bottomless, burned from his eyes, his jaw tight. She had thought, had almost hoped, that he wouldn't care about her being promised to Alessandro. That a night of passion with her would be like a night with any other woman.

Yes, that thought had hurt, but it had been better than this. Better than him looking at her like he hated her.

She could remember those dark eyes meeting hers with a different kind of fire. Lust. Need. A bleak desperation that had echoed inside of her. And she could remember them clouded by desire, his expression pained as she'd touched him, tasted him.

She looked to Alessandro but she could still feel Matteo watching her. And she had to look back. She always had to look at Matteo Corretti. For as long as she could remember, she'd been drawn to him.

And for one night, she'd had him.

Now…now she would never have him again.

Her steps faltered, her high heel turning sideways beneath her. She stumbled, caught herself, her eyes locking with Matteo's again.

Dio, it was hot. Her dress was suffocating her now. The veil too heavy on her head, the lace at her throat threatening to choke her.

She stopped walking, the war within her threatening to tear her to pieces.

Matteo Corretti thought he would gag on his anger. Watching her walk toward Alessandro, his cousin, his rival in business and now, because of this, his enemy.

Watching Alessia Battaglia make her way to Alessandro, to bind herself to him.

She was Matteo's. His lover. His woman. The most beautiful woman he had ever seen in his life. It wasn't simply the smooth perfection of her golden skin, not just the exquisite cheekbones and full, rose-colored lips. It was something that existed beneath her skin, a vitality and passion that had, by turns, fascinated and confused him.

Her every laugh, every smile, every mundane action, was filled with more life, more joy, than his most memorable moments. It was why, from the first time he'd sneaked a look at her as a boy, he had been transfixed.

Far from the monster he'd been made to believe the Battaglias were, she had been an angel in his eyes.

But he had never touched her. Never breached the unspoken command issued by his father and grandfather. Because she was a Battaglia and he a Corretti, the bad blood between them going back more than fifty years. He had been forbidden from even speaking to her and as a boy he had only violated that order once.

And now, when Salvatore had thought it might benefit him, now she was being traded to Alessandro like cattle. He tightened his hands into fists, anger, anger like he hadn't felt in more than thirteen years, curling in his gut. The kind of rage he normally kept packed in ice was roaring through him. He feared it might explode, and he knew what happened when it did.

He could not be held responsible for what he might do if he had to watch Alessandro touch Alessia. Kiss her.

And then Alessia froze in place, her big, dark eyes darting from Alessandro, and back to him. Those eyes. Those eyes were always in his dreams.

Her hand dropped to her side, and then she released her hold on her bouquet of roses, the sound of them hitting the stone floor loud in the sudden silence of the room.

Then she turned, gripping the front of her heavy lace skirt, and ran back down the aisle. The white fabric billowed around her as she ran. She only looked behind her once. Wide, frightened eyes meeting his.

"Alessia!" He couldn't stop himself. Her name burst from his lips, and his body burst from its position in the pews. And he was running, too. "Alessia!"

The roar of the congregation drowned out his words. But still he ran. People were standing now, filing into the aisle, blocking his path. The faces of the crowd were a blur, he wasn't aware of who he touched, who he moved out of his way, in his pursuit of the bride.

When he finally burst through the exterior doors of the basilica, Alessia was getting into the backseat of the limo that was waiting to carry her and her groom away after the ceremony, trying to get her massive skirt and train into the vehicle with her. When she saw him, everything in her face changed. A hope in her eyes that grabbed him deep in his chest and twisted his heart. Hard.

"Matteo."

"What are you doing, Alessia?"

"I have to go," she said, her eyes focused behind him now, fearful. Fearful of her father, he knew. He was gripped then by a sudden need to erase her fears. To keep her from ever needing to be afraid again.

"Where?" he asked, his voice rough.

"The airport. Meet me."

"Alessia…"

"Matteo, please. I'll wait." She shut the door to the limo and the car pulled out of the parking lot, just as her father exited the church.

"You!" Antonioni turned on him. "What have you done?"

And Alessandro appeared behind him, his eyes blazing with fury. "Yes, cousin, what have you done?"

Alessia's hands shook as she handed the cash to the woman at the clothing shop. She'd never been permitted to go into a store like this. Her father thought this sort of place, with mass-produced garments, was common. Not for a Battaglia. But the jeans, T-shirt and trainers she'd found suited her purpose because they were common. Because any woman would wear them. Because a Battaglia would not. As if the Battaglias had the money to put on the show they did. Her father borrowed what he had to in order to maintain the fiction that their power was as infinite as it ever was. His position as Minister for the Trade and Housing department might net him a certain amount of power, power that was easily and happily manipulated, but it didn't keep the same flow of money that had come from her grandfather's rather more seedy organization.

The shopgirl looked at her curiously, and Alessia knew

why. A shivering bride, sans groom, in a small tourist shop still wearing her gown and veil was a strange sight indeed.

"May I use the changing room?" she asked once her items were paid for.

She felt slightly sick using her father's money to escape, sicker still over the way she'd gotten it. She must have been quite the sight in the bank, in her wedding gown, demanding a cash advance against a card with her father's name on it.

"I'm a Battaglia," she'd said, employing all the self-importance she'd ever heard come from Antonioni. "Of course it's all right for me to access my family money."

Cash was essential, because she knew better than to leave a paper trail. Having a family who had, rather famously, been on the wrong side of the law was helpful in that regard at least. As had her lifelong observation of how utter confidence could get you things you shouldn't be allowed to have. The money in her purse being a prime example.

"Of course," the cashier said.

Alessia scurried into the changing room and started tugging off the gown, the hideous, suffocating gown. The one chosen by her father because it was so traditional. The virgin bride in white.

If he only knew.

She contorted her arm behind her and tugged at the tab of the zip, stepping out of the dress, punching the crinoline down and stepping out of the pile of fabric. She slipped the jeans on and tugged the stretchy black top over her head.

She emerged from the room a moment later, using the rubber bands she'd purchased to restrain her long, thick hair. Then she slipped on the trainers, ruing her lack of socks for a moment, then straightened.

And she breathed. Feeling more like herself again. Like

Alessia. "Thank you," she said to the cashier. "Keep the dress. Sell it if you like."

She dashed out of the store and onto the busy streets, finally able to breathe. Finally.

She'd ditched the limo at the bank, offering the driver a generous tip for his part in the getaway. It only took her a moment to flag down a cab.

She slid in the back, clutching her bag to her chest. "Aeroporto di Catania, *per favore*."

"*Naturalmente.*"

Matteo hadn't lingered at the basilica. Instead, he'd side-stepped his cousin's furious questions and gotten into his sports car, roaring out of the parking lot and heading in the direction of the airport without giving it any thought.

His heart was pounding hard, adrenaline pouring through him.

He felt beyond himself today. Out of control in a way he never allowed.

In a way he rarely allowed, at least. There had been a few breaks in his infamous control, and all of them were tied to Alessia. And they provided a window into just what he could become if the hideous cold that lived in him met with passionate flame.

She was his weakness. A weakness he should never have allowed and one he should certainly never allow again.

Dark eyes clashing with his in a mirror hanging behind the bar. Eyes he would recognize anywhere.

He turned sharply and saw her, the breath pulled from his lungs.

He set his drink down on the bar and walked across the crowded room, away from his colleagues.

"Alessia." He addressed her directly for the first time in thirteen years.

"Matteo." *His name sounded so sweet on her lips.*

It had been a month since their night together in New York City, a chance encounter, he'd imagined. He wondered now.

A whole month and he could still taste her skin on his tongue, could still feel the soft curves of her breasts resting in his palms. Could still hear her broken sighs of need as they took each other to the height of pleasure.

And he had not wanted another woman since.

They barely made it into his hotel room, they were far too desperate for each other. He slammed the door, locking it with shaking fingers, pressing her body against the wall. Her dress was long, with a generous slit up the side, revealing her toned, tan legs.

He wrapped his fingers around her thigh and tugged her leg up around his hip, settling the hardness of his erection against her softness.

It wasn't enough. It would never be enough.

Matteo stopped at a red light, impatience tearing at him. Need, need like he had only known once before, was like a beast inside him, devouring, roaring.

Finally, she was naked, her bare breasts pressing hard against his chest. He had to have her. His entire body trembling with lust.

"Ready for me, cara mia?*"*

"Always for you."

He slid inside of her body, so tight, much more so than he'd expected, than he'd ever experienced. She cried out softly, the bite of her nails in his flesh not due to pleasure now.

A virgin.

His. Only his.

Except she had not been his. It had been a lie. The next morning, Alessia was gone. And when he'd returned to Sicily, she'd been there.

He'd been invited to a family party but he had not realized that all branches of the Corretti family would be present. Had not realized it was an engagement party. For Alessandro and Alessia. A party to celebrate the end of a feud, the beginning of a partnership between the Battaglias and the Correttis, a chance to revitalize the docklands in Palermo and strengthen their family corporation.

"How long have you and Alessia been engaged?" he asked, his eyes trained on her even as he posed the question to Alessandro.

"For a while now. But we wanted to wait to make the big announcement until all the details were finalized."

"I see," he said. *"And when is the blessed event?"*

"One month. No point in waiting."

Some of the old rage burned through the desire that had settled inside of him. She had been engaged to Alessandro when he'd taken her into his bed. She'd intended, from the beginning, to marry another man the night she'd given herself to him.

And he, he had been forced to watch her hang on his cousin's arm for the past month while his blood boiled in agony as he watched his biggest rival hold on to the one thing he wanted more than his next breath. The one thing he had always wanted, but never allowed himself to have.

He had craved violence watching the two of them together. Had longed to rip Alessandro's hands off her and show him what happened when a man touched what belonged to him.

Even now, the thought sent a rising tide of nausea through him.

What was it Alessia did to him? This wave of possessiveness, this current of passion that threatened to drown him, it was not something that was a part of him. He was a man who lived in his mind, a man who embraced logic and fact, duty and honor.

When he did not, when he gave in to emotion, the danger was far too great. He was a Corretti, cut from the same cloth as his father and grandfather, a fabric woven together with greed, violence and a passion for acquiring more money, more power, than any one man could ever need.

Even with logic, with reason, he could and had justified actions that would horrify most men. He hated to think what might happen if he were unleashed without any hold on his control.

So he shunned passion, in all areas of life.

Except one.

He pulled his car off the road and slammed on his breaks, killing the engine, his knuckles burning from the hard grip he had on the steering wheel, his breath coming in short, harsh bursts.

This was not him. He didn't know himself with Alessia, and he never had.

And nothing good could come from it. He had spent his life trying to change the man he seemed destined to be. Trying to keep control, to move his life in a different direction than the one his father would have pushed him into.

Alessia compromised that. She tested it.

He ran his fingers through his hair, trying to catch his breath.

Then he turned the key over, the engine roaring to life again. And he turned the car around, heading away from the airport, away from the city.

He punched a button on his dashboard and connected himself to his PA.

"Lucia?"

"Si?"

"Hold my calls until further notice."

It had been three hours. No doubt the only reason her father and his men hadn't come tearing through the airport was that they would never have imagined she would do something so audacious as to run away completely.

Alessia shifted in the plastic chair and wiped her cheek again, even though her tears had dried. She had no more tears left to cry. It was all she'd done since she'd arrived.

And she'd done more since it had become clear Matteo wasn't coming.

And then she'd done more when she'd suddenly had to go into the bathroom and throw up in a public stall.

Then she'd stopped, just long enough to go into one of the airport shops and pick up the one thing she'd avoided buying for the past week.

She'd started crying again when the pregnancy test had resulted in two little pink, positive, yes-you're-having-a-baby lines.

Now she was wrung out. Sick. And completely alone.

Well, not completely alone. Not really. She was having a baby, after all.

The thought didn't comfort her so much as magnify the feeling of utter loneliness.

One thing was certain. There was no going back to Alessandro. No going back to her family. She was having the wrong man's baby. A man who clearly didn't want her.

But he did once.

That thought made her furious, defiant. Yes, he had. More than once, which was likely how the pregnancy had happened. Because there had been protection during their times in bed, but they'd also showered together in the early hours of the morning and then…then neither of them had been able to think, or spare the time.

A voice came over the loudspeaker, the last call for her flight out to New York.

She stood up, picked up her purse, the only thing she

had with her, the only thing she had to her name, and handed her ticket to the man at the counter.

"Going to New York?" he asked, verifying.

She took a deep breath. "Yes."

CHAPTER TWO

HE'D NEVER EVEN opened the emails she'd been sending him. She knew, because she'd set them up so that they would send her a receipt when the addressee opened her message, but she'd never gotten one.

He didn't answer her calls, either. Not the calls to his office, not the calls to his mobile phone, not the calls to the Palazzolo Corretti, or to his personal estate outside Palermo.

Matteo Corretti was doing an exceptional job of ignoring her, and he had been for weeks now while she'd been holed up in her friend Carolina's apartment. Carolina, the friend who had talked her into a New York bachelorette party in the first place. Which, all things considered, meant she sort of owed Alessia since that bachelorette party was the source of both her problems, and her pregnancy.

No, that wasn't fair. It was her fault. Well, a lot of it was. The rest was Matteo Corretti's. Master of disguise and phone-call-avoider extraordinaire.

She wished she didn't need him but she didn't know what else to do. She was so tired. So sad, all the time. Her father wouldn't take her calls, either, her siblings, the most precious people in her life were forbidden from speaking to her. That, more than anything, was threatening to burn a hole in her soul. She felt adrift without them around her. They'd kept her going for most of her life, given her a sense of purpose, of strength and responsibility. Without them she just felt like she was floundering.

She'd had one option, of course. To terminate the pregnancy and return home. Beg her father and Alessandro for forgiveness. But she hadn't been able to face that. She'd lost so much in her life already and as confused as she was about the baby, about what it would mean for her, as terrified as she was, she couldn't face losing the tiny life inside of her.

But she would run out of money soon. Then she would be alone and penniless while Matteo Corretti spent more of his fortune on sports cars and high-rise hotels.

She wasn't going to allow it anymore. Not when she'd already decided that if he didn't want to be a part of their baby's life he would have to come tell her to her face. He would have to stand before her and denounce their child, verbally, not simply by ignoring emails and messages. He would have to make that denouncement a physical action.

Yes, she'd made the wrong decision to sleep with him without telling him about Alessandro. But it didn't give him the right to deny their child. Their child had nothing to do with her stupidity. He or she was the only innocent party in the situation.

She looked down at the screen on her phone. She had her Twitter account all set up and ready to help her contact every news outlet in the area.

She took a breath and started typing.

@theobserver @NYTnews @HBpress I'm about to make an important announcement re Matteo Corretti & the wedding scandal. Luxe Hotel on 3rd.

Then she stepped out of the back of the cab and walked up to the front steps of Matteo's world-renowned hotel, where he was rumored to be in residence, though no one would confirm it, and waited.

The sidewalks were crowded, people pushing past other people, walking with their heads down, no one sparing her a glance. Until the news crews started showing up.

First there was one, then another, and another. Some from outlets she hadn't personally included in her tweet. The small crowd drew stares, and some passersby started lingering to see what was happening.

There was no denying that she was big news. The assumption had been that she'd run off with Matteo but nothing could be further from the truth. And she was about to give the media a big dose of truth.

It didn't take long for them to catch the attention of the people inside the hotel, which had been a key part of her plan.

A sharply dressed man walked out of the front of the hotel, his expression wary. "Is there something I can help you with?"

She turned to him. "I'm just making a quick announcement. If you want to go get Matteo, that might help."

"Mr. Corretti is not in residence."

"That's like saying someone isn't At Home in a Regency novel, isn't it? He's here, but he doesn't want anyone to know it."

The reporters were watching the exchange with rapt attention, and the flash on one of the cameras started going, followed by the others.

"Mr. Corretti is not—"

She whirled around to face him again. "Fine, then if Mr. Corretti is truly not in residence you can stand out here and listen to what I have to say and relay it to your boss when you deliver dinner to the room he is not in residence in."

She turned back to the reporters, and suddenly, the official press release she'd spent hours memorizing last night seemed to shatter in her brain, making it impossible to piece back together, impossible to make sense of it.

She swallowed hard, looking at the skyline, her vision filled with concrete, glass and steel. The noise from the cars was deafening, the motion of the traffic in front of her making her head swim. "I know that the wedding has been much talked about. And that Matteo chasing me out of the church has been the headline. Well, there's more to the story."

Flashes blinded her, tape recorders shoved into her face, questions started to drown out her voice. She felt weak, shaky, and she wondered, not for the first time, if she was completely insane.

Her life in Sicily had been quiet, domestic, one surrounded by her family, one so insular that she'd been dependent upon imagination to make it bearable, a belief of something bigger looming in her future. And as a result, she had a tendency to romanticize the grand gesture in her mind. To think that somehow, no matter how bleak the situation seemed, she could fix it. That, in the end, she would make it perfect and manage to find her happy ending.

She'd done it on the night of her bachelorette party. New York was so different than the tiny village she'd been raised in. So much bigger, faster. Just being there had seemed like a dream and so when she'd been confronted with Matteo it had seemed an easy, logical thing to approach him, to follow the path their mutual attraction had led them down. It was a prime example of her putting more stock in fantasy, in the belief in happy endings, over her common sense.

This was another.

But no matter how well planned this was, she hadn't realized how she would feel, standing there with everyone watching her. She wasn't the kind of woman who was used to having all eyes on her, her aborted wedding being the exception.

"I'm pregnant, and Matteo Corretti is the father of my baby." It slipped out, bald and true, and not at all what she'd been planning to say. At least she didn't think it was.

"Mr. Corretti—" the employee was speaking into his phone now, his complexion pallid "—you need to come out here."

She released a breath she hadn't realized she'd been holding.

"When is the baby due?"

"Are you certain he's the father?"

"When did you discover you were pregnant?"

The questions were coming rapid-fire now, but she didn't need to answer them because this was never about the press. This was about getting his attention. This was about forcing a confrontation that he seemed content to avoid.

"I'll answer more questions when Matteo comes to make his statement."

"Did the two of you leave the wedding together, or are you estranged? Has he denied paternity?" one of the reporters asked.

"I…"

"What the hell is going on?"

Alessia turned and her heart caught in her throat, making it impossible to breathe. Matteo. It felt like an eternity since she'd seen him, since he'd kissed her, put his hands on her skin. An eternity.

She ached with the need to run to him, to hold on to him, use him as an anchor. In her fantasies, he had long been her knight in shining armor, a simplistic vision of a man who had saved her from a hideous fate.

But in the years since, things had changed. Become more complex, more real. He was her lover now. The father of her child. The man she had lied to. The man who had left her sitting alone in an airport, crying and clutching a positive pregnancy test.

For a moment, the longing for those simple, sun-drenched days in Sicily, when he had been nothing more than an idealized savior, was so sharp and sweet she ached.

"Mr. Corretti, is this why you broke up the wedding?"

"I didn't break up anyone's wedding," he said, his tone dark.

"No, I ran out of the wedding," she said.

"And is what why I broke up the wedding?" he asked, addressing the reporter, stormy eyes never once looking at her.

"The baby," the reporter said.

Matteo froze, his face turning to stone. "The baby." Color drained from his face, but he remained stoic, only the change in his complexion a clue as to the shock that he felt.

He didn't know. She felt the impact of that reality like a physical blow. He hadn't even listened to a single message. Hadn't opened any emails, even before she'd started tagging them to let her know when he opened them.

"Is there more than one?" This from another reporter.

"Of course not," Matteo said, his words smooth, his eyes cold like granite. "Only this one."

He came to stand beside her, his gaze still avoiding hers. He put his arm around her waist, the sudden contact like touching an open flame, heat streaking through her veins. How did he manage to affect her this way still? After all he'd done to her? After the way he'd treated her?

"Do you have a statement?"

"Not at this point," he bit out. "But when the details for the wedding are finalized, we will be in touch."

He tightened his hold on her waist and turned them both around, away from the reporters, leading her up the steps and into the hotel. She felt very much like she was being led into the lion's den.

"What are you doing?" she asked, wishing he would move away from her, wishing he would stop touching her.

"Taking you away from the circus you created. I have no desire to discuss this with an audience."

If he wasn't so angry with her, she might think it was a good idea. But Matteo Corretti's rage was like ice-cold water in a black sea. Fathomless, with the great threat of pulling her beneath the waves.

His hold tightened with each step they took toward the hotel, and her stomach started to feel more and more unsettled until, when they passed through the revolving door and into the hotel lobby, she was afraid she might vomit on the high-gloss marble floors.

A charming photo to go with the headlines.

He released her the moment they were fully inside. "What the hell is the meaning of this?" he asked, rounding on her as his staff milled around very carefully not watching.

"Should we go somewhere more private?" she asked. Suddenly she felt like she'd rather brave his rage than put on a show. She was too tired for that. Too vulnerable. Bringing the press in was never about drawing attention to herself, it was about getting information to Matteo that he couldn't ignore. Giving the man no excuse to say he didn't know.

"Says the woman who called a bloody press conference?"

"You didn't answer my calls. Or return my messages. And I'm pretty sure now that you didn't even listen to any of them."

"I have been away," he said.

"Well, that's hardly my fault that you chose this moment to go on sabbatical. And I had no way of knowing."

He was looking at her like she'd grown an extra head. "Take me to your suite," she said.

"I'm not in the mood, Alessia."

"Neither am I!" she shot back. "I want to talk."

"It's just that last time we were in this hotel, talking was very much not on the agenda."

Her face heated, searing prickles dotting her skin. "No. That's very true. Which is how we find ourselves in this current situation."

"Communication seems to be something we don't do well with," he said. "Our lack of talking last time we were here together certainly caused some issues."

"But I want to talk now," she said, crossing her arms beneath her breasts.

He cocked his head to the side, dark eyes trained on her now with a focus he'd withheld until that moment. "You aren't afraid of me."

"No."

"A mistake, some might say, *cara mia*."

"Is that so?"

"You won't like me when I'm angry."

"You turn green and split your pants?"

"Perhaps taking this somewhere private is the best idea," he said, wrapping his fingers around her arm, just above her elbow, and directing her toward the elevator.

He pushed the up button and they both waited. She felt like she was hovering in a dream, but she dug her fingernails into her palms, and her surroundings didn't melt away. It was real. All of this.

The elevator doors slid open and they both stepped inside. And as soon as they were closed into the lift, he rounded on her.

"You're pregnant?" His words were flat in the quiet of the elevator.

"Yes. I tried to tell you in a less public way, but it's been two months and you've been very hard to get ahold of."

"Not an accident."

"Oh, no, I know. It was far too purposeful to be accidental. You never even opened my emails."

"I blocked your address after you sent the first few."

"Uh," she said, unable to make a more eloquent sound.

"I see it offends you."

"Yes. It does offend me. Didn't it occur to you that I might have something important to tell you?"

"I didn't care," he said.

The elevator stopped at the top floor and the doors slid open. "Is there a point in me going any further, then? Or should I just go back to my friend Carolina's apartment and start a baby registry?"

"You are not leaving."

"But you just said you didn't care."

"I didn't care until I found out you were carrying my child."

She was both struck, and pleased, by his certainty that the child was his. She wouldn't have really blamed him if he'd questioned her at least once. She'd lied about her engagement to Alessandro. By omission, but still. She knew she wasn't blameless in the whole fiasco.

"What did you think I was trying to contact you for? To beg you to take me back? To beg you for more sex? Because that's what we shared that night, that's all we shared." The lie was an acid burn on her tongue. "I would hardly have burned my pride to the ground for the sake of another orgasm."

"Is that true? You would hardly be the first person to do it."

"If you mean you, I'm sure it cost you to take a Battaglia to your bed. Must have been some epic dry spell."

"And not worth the price in the end, I think."

His words were designed to peel skin from bone, and they did their job. "I would say the same."

"I can see now why you ran from the wedding."

A wave of confusion hit her, and it took her a moment to realize that she hadn't told him the order in which the events had occurred. Wedding abandonment, then pregnancy test, but before she could correct him he pressed on.

"And how conveniently you've played it, too. Alessandro would, of course, know it wasn't his child as you never slept with him. I hope you're pleased with the way all of this unfolded because you have managed to ensure that you are still able to marry a Corretti, in spite of our little mistake. Good insurance for your family since, thanks to your abandonment, the deal between our family and yours has gone to hell."

"You think I planned this? You aren't even serious about marrying me, are you?"

"There is no other choice. You announced your pregnancy to the whole world."

"I had to tell you."

"And if I had chosen not to be a part of the baby's life?"

"I was going to make you tell me that to my face."

He regarded her closely. "Strange to think I ever imagined you to be soft, Alessia."

"I'm a Battaglia. I've never had the luxury of being soft."

"Clearly not." He looked at her, long and hard. "This makes sense, Alessia." His tone was all business now. Maddeningly sure and decisive. "It will put to rest rumors of bad blood, unite the families."

"You didn't seem to care about that before."

"That was before the baby. The baby changes everything."

Because he wanted to make a family? The idea, so silly and hopeful, bloomed inside of her. It was her blessing and curse that she always found the kernel of hope in any situation. It was the thing that got her through. The thing that had helped her survive the loss of her mother, the cold detachment from her father, the time spent caring for her siblings when other girls her age were out dating, having lives, fulfilling dreams.

She'd created her own. Locked them inside of her. Nurtured them.

"I… It does?" she asked, the words a whisper.

"Of course," he said, dark eyes blazing. "My child will be a Corretti. On that, there can be no compromise."

CHAPTER THREE

MATTEO'S OWN WORDS echoed in his head.

My child will be a Corretti. On that there can be no compromise.

It was true. No child of his would be raised a Battaglia. Their family feud was not simply a business matter. The Battaglias had set out to destroy his grandfather, and had they succeeded they would have wiped out the line entirely.

It was the hurt on her face that surprised him, and more than that, his response to it.

Damn Alessia Battaglia and those dark, soulful eyes. Eyes that had led him to ruin on more than one occasion.

"Because you won't allow your child to carry my name?" she asked.

"That's right."

"And what of my role in raising my child?"

"You will, of course, be present."

"And what else? Because more than mere presence is required to raise a child."

"Nannies are also required, in my experience."

"In your experience raising children, or being raised?"

"Being raised. I'm supremely responsible in my sexual encounters so I've never been in this situation before."

"Supremely responsible?" she asked, cheeks flushing a gorgeous shade of rose that reminded him of the blooms in his Sicilian palazzo. "Is that what you call having sex with your cousin's fiancée with no condom?"

Her words, so stark and angry, shocked him. Alessia had always seemed fragile to him. Sweet. But tangling with her today was forcing him to recognize that she was also a woman capable of supreme ruthlessness if the situation required it.

Something he had to reluctantly respect.

"I didn't know you were engaged to be married, as you withheld the information from me. As to the other issue, that has never happened to me before."

"So you say."

"It has not," he said.

"Well, it's not like you were overly conscious of it at the time."

Shame cracked over his insides like a whip. He had thought himself immune to shame at this point. He was wrong. "I knew. After."

"You remembered and you still didn't think to contact me?"

"I did not think it possible." The thought hadn't occurred to him because he'd been too wrapped up in simply trying to avoid her. Alessia was bad for him, a conclusion he'd come to years ago and reaffirmed the day he'd decided not to go after her.

And now he was bound to her. Bound to a woman who dug down far too deep inside of him. Who disturbed his grasp on his control. He could not afford the interruption. Could not afford to take the chance that he might lose his grip.

"Why, because only other people have the kind of sex that makes babies?"

"Do you always say what comes to your mind?"

"No. I never do. I never speak or act impulsively, I only think about it. It's just you that seems to bring it out."

"Aren't I lucky?" Her admission gripped him, held him. That there was something about him that brought about a change in her…that the thing between them didn't only shatter his well-ordered existence but hers, too, was not a comfort. Not in the least.

"Clearly, neither of us are in possession of much luck, Alessia."

"Clearly," she said.

"There is no way I will let my child be a bastard. I've seen what happens to bastards. You can ask my cousin Angelo about that." A cousin who was becoming quite the problem. It was part of why Matteo had come to New York, why he was making his way back into circulation. In his absence, Angelo had gone and bought himself a hefty amount of shares for Corretti Enterprises and at this very moment he was sitting in Matteo's office, the new head of Corretti Hotels. He'd been about to go back and make the other man pay. Wrench the power right back from him.

Now, it seemed there was a more pressing matter.

"So, you're doing this to save face?"

"For what other reason? Do you want our child to be sneered at? Disgraced? The product of an illicit affair between two of Sicily's great warring families?"

"No."

Matteo tried not to read the emotion in her dark eyes, tried not to let them pull him in. Always, from the moment he'd seen her, he'd been fascinated. A young girl with flowers tangled in her dark hair, running around the garden of her father's home, a smile on her lips. He could remember her dancing in the grass in her bare feet, while her siblings played around her.

And he had been transfixed. Amazed by this girl who, from all he had been told, should have been visibly evil in some way. But she was a light. She held a brightness and joy like he had never seen. Watching it, being close enough to touch it, helped him pretend it was something he could feel, too.

She made him not so afraid of feeling.

She'd had a hold on him from day one. She was a sorceress. There was no other explanation. Her grip on him defied logic, defied every defense he'd built inside of himself.

And no matter how hard he tried, he could read her. Easily. She was hurt. He had hurt her.

"What is it?" he asked.

She looked away. "What do you mean?"

"Why are you hurt?"

"You've just told me how unlucky we both are that I'm pregnant—was I supposed to look happy?"

"Don't tell me you're pleased about this. Unless it was your plan."

"How could I have…planned this? That doesn't make any sense."

He pushed his fingers through his hair and turned away from her. "I know. *Che cavolo*, Alessia, I know that." He turned back to her.

"I just wanted to tell you about the baby."

He felt like he was drowning, like every breath was suffocating him. A baby. She was having his baby. And he was just about the last man on earth who should ever be a father. He should walk away. But he couldn't.

"And this was the only way?"

Her eyes glittered with rage. "You know damn well it was!"

He did. He'd avoided her every attempt at contacting him. Had let his anger fuel the need for distance between them. Had let the very existence of the emotion serve as a reminder. And he had come back frozen again. So he'd thought. Because now Alessia was here again, pushing against that control.

"Why didn't you meet me at the airport?" she asked, her words a whisper.

"Why didn't I meet you?" he asked, his teeth gritted. "You expected me to chase after you like a dog? If you think you can bring me to heel that easily, Alessia, you are a fool."

"And if you think I'm trying to you're an idiot, Matteo Corretti. I don't want you on a leash."

"Well, you damn well have me on one!" he said, shouting for the first time, his tenuous grip on his control slipping. "What am I to do after your public display? Deny my child? Send you off to raise it on your own? Highly unlikely."

"How can we marry each other? We don't love each other. We barely like each other right now!"

"Is that so bad? You were prepared to marry Alessandro, after all. Better the devil you know. And we both know you know me much better than you knew him."

"Stop it," she said, the catch in her voice sending a hot slash of guilt through his chest. Why he was compelled to lash out at her, he wasn't sure.

Except that nothing with Alessia was ever simple. Nothing was ever straightforward. Nothing was ever neat or controlled.

It has to be.

"It's true, though, isn't it, Alessia?" he asked, his entire body tense now. He knew for a fact he was the first man to be with her, and something in him burned to know that he had been the only man. That Alessandro had never touched her as he had. "You were never with him. Not like you were with me."

The idea of his cousin's hands on her... A wave of red hazed his vision, the need for violence gripping his throat, shaking him.

He swallowed hard, battled back the rage, fought against

images that were always so close to the surface when Alessia was around. A memory he had to hold on to, no matter how much he might wish for it to disappear.

Blood. Streaked up to his elbows, the skin on his knuckles broken. A beast inside of him unleashed. And Alessia's attackers on the ground, unmoving.

He blinked and banished the memory. It shouldn't linger as it did. It was but one moment of violence in a lifetime of it. And yet, it had been different. It had been an act born of passion, outside of his control, outside of rational thought.

"Tell me," he ground out.

"Do you honestly think I would sleep with Alessandro after what happened?"

"You were going to. You were prepared to marry him. To share his bed."

She nodded wordlessly. "Yes. I was."

"And then you found out about the baby."

"No," she said, her voice a whisper.

"What, then?"

"Then I saw you."

"Guilt?"

"We were in a church."

"Understandable."

"Why didn't you meet me?" she asked again, her words holding a wealth of pain.

"Because," he said, visions of blood washing through his brain again, a reminder of what happened when he let his passions have control, "I got everything I wanted from you that night. Sex. That was all I ever wanted from you, darling."

She drew back as though he'd struck her. "Is that why you've always watched me?"

"I'll admit, I had a bit of an obsession with your body, but you know you had one with mine."

"I liked you," she said, her words hard, shaky. "But you never came near me after—"

"There is no need to dredge up the past," he said, not wanting to hear her speak of that day. He didn't want to hear her side of it. How horrifying it must have been for a fourteen-year-old girl to see such violence. To see what he was capable of.

Yet, she had never looked at him with the shock, the horror, he'd deserved. There was a way she looked at him, as though she saw something in him no one else did. Something good. And he craved that feeling. It was one reason he'd taken her up on her invitation that night at the hotel bar.

Too late, he realized that he was not in control of their encounter that time, either. No, Alessia stole the control. Always.

No more, he told himself again.

Alessia swallowed back tears. This wasn't going how she'd thought it would. Now she wasn't sure what she thought. No, she knew. Part of her, this stupid, girlish, optimistic part of her, had imagined Matteo's eyes would soften, that he would smile. Touch her stomach. Take joy in the fact that they had created a life together.

And then they would live happily ever after.

She was such a fool. But Matteo had long been the knight in shining armor of her fantasies. And so in her mind he could do no wrong.

She'd always felt like she'd known him. Like she'd understood the serious, dark-eyed young man she'd caught watching her when she was in Palermo. Who had crept up to the wall around her house when he was visiting his grandmother and stood there while she'd played in the garden. Always looking like he wanted to join in, like he wanted to play, but wouldn't allow himself to.

And then…and then when she'd needed him most, he'd

been there. Saved her from…she hardly even knew what horror he'd saved her from. Thank God she hadn't had to find out exactly what those two men had intended to use her for. Matteo had been there. As always. And he had protected her, shielded her.

That was why, when she'd seen him in New York, it had been easy, natural, to kiss him. To ask him to make love to her.

But after that he hadn't come to save her.

She looked at him now, at those dark eyes, hollow, his face like stone. And he seemed like a stranger. She wondered how she could have been so wrong all this time.

"I don't want to dredge up the past. But I want to know that the future won't be miserable."

"If you preferred Alessandro, you should have married him while you had him at the altar with a priest standing by. Now you belong to me, the choice has been taken. So you should make the best of it."

"Stop being such an ass!"

Now he looked shocked, which, she felt, was a bit of an accomplishment. "You want me to tell you how happy I am? You want me to lie?"

"No," she said, her stomach tightening painfully. "But stop…stop trying to hurt me."

He swore, an ugly, crude word. "I am sorry, Alessia, it is not my intent."

The apology was about the most shocking event of the afternoon. "I…I know this is unexpected. Trust me, I know."

"When did you find out?" he asked.

"At the airport. So…if you had met me, you would have found out when I did."

"And what did you do after that?"

"I waited for you," she said. "And then I got on a plane

and came to New York. I have a friend here, the friend that hosted my little bachelorette party."

"Why did you come to New York?"

"Why not?" She made it sound casual, like it was almost accidental. But it wasn't. It had made her feel close to him, no matter where he might have been in the world, because it was the place she'd finally been with him the way she'd always dreamed of. "Why did you come to New York?"

"Possibly for the same reason you did," he said, his voice rough. It made her stomach twist, but she didn't want to ask him for clarification. Didn't want to hope that it had something to do with her.

She was too raw to take more of Matteo's insults. And she was even more afraid of his tenderness. That would make her crumble completely. She couldn't afford it, not now. Now she had to figure out what she was doing. What she wanted.

Could she really marry Matteo?

It was so close to her dearest fantasy. The one that had kept her awake long nights since she was a teenager. Matteo. Hers. Only hers. Such an innocent fantasy at first, and as she'd gotten older, one that had become filled with heat and passion, a longing for things she'd never experienced outside of her dreams.

"And if…" she said, hardly trusting herself to speak "… if we marry, my family will still benefit from the merger?"

"Your father will get his money. His piece of the Corretti empire, as agreed upon."

"You give it away so easily."

"Because my family still needs the docklands revitalization. And your father holds the key to that."

"And it will benefit Alessandro, too."

"Just as it would have benefitted me had he married you."

Those words, hearing that it would have benefitted him

for her to marry someone else, made her feel ill. "So a win all around for the Correttis, then?"

"I suppose it is," he said.

There was a ruthless glint in his eyes now. One she had never seen directed at her before. One she'd only seen on one other occasion.

"What if I say no?" she asked, because she had to know. She wasn't sure why she was exploring her options now. Maybe because she'd already blown everything up. Her father likely hated her.... Her siblings...they must be worried sick. And she wondered if anyone was caring for them properly.

Yes, the youngest, Eva, was fourteen now and the rest of them in their late teens, but still, she was the only person who nurtured them. The only person who ever had.

The life she'd always known, the life she'd clung to for the past twenty-seven years, was changed forever. And now she felt compelled in some ways to see how far she could push it.

"You won't say no," he said.

"I won't?"

"No. Because if you do, the Battaglias are as good as bankrupt. You will be cared for, of course our child will be, too. I'm not the kind of man who would abandon his responsibility in that way. But what of your siblings? Their care will not be my problem."

"And if I marry you?"

"They'll be family. And I take care of family."

A rush of joy and terror filled her in equal parts. Because in some ways, she was getting just what she wanted. Matteo. Forever.

But this wasn't the Matteo she'd woven fantasies around. This was the real Matteo. Dark. Bitter. Emotionless in a way she'd somehow never realized before.

He'd given her passion on their night together, but for

the most part, the lights had been off. She wondered now if, while his hands had moved over her body with such skill and heat, his eyes had been blank and cold. Like they were now.

She knew that what she was about to agree to wasn't the fantasy. But it was the best choice for her baby, the best choice for her family.

And more fool her, she wanted him. Still. All of those factors combined meant there was only ever one answer for her to give.

"Yes, Matteo. I'll marry you."

CHAPTER FOUR

THE HUSH IN the lobby of Matteo's plush Palermo hotel was thick, the lack of sound more pronounced and obvious than any scream could have been.

It was early in the day and employees were milling around, setting up for a wedding and mobilizing to sort out rooms and guests. As Matteo walked through, a wave of them parted, making room for him, making space. Good. He was in no mood to be confronted today. No mood for questions.

Bleached sunlight filtered through the windows, reflecting off a jewel-bright sea. A view most would find relaxing. For him, it did nothing but increase the knot of tension in his stomach. Homecoming, for him, would never be filled with a sense of comfort and belonging. For him, this setting had been the stage for violence, pain and shame that cut so deep it was a miracle he hadn't bled to death with it.

He gritted his teeth and pulled together every last ounce of control he could scrape up, cooling the anger that seemed to be on a low simmer in his blood constantly now.

He had a feeling, though, that the shock was due only in part to his presence, with a much larger part due to the woman who was trailing behind him.

He punched the up button for the elevator and the doors slid open. He looked at Alessia, who simply stood there, her hands clasped in front of her, dark eyes looking at everything but him.

"After you, *cara mia*," he said, putting his hand between the doors, keeping them from closing.

"You don't demand that a wife walk three paces behind you at all times?" she asked, her words soft, defiant.

"A woman is of very little use to me when she's behind me. Bent over in front of me is another matter, as you well know."

Her cheeks turned dark with color, and not all of it was from embarrassment. He'd made her angry, as he'd intended to do. He didn't know what it was about her that pushed him so. That made him say things like that.

That made him show anything beyond the unreadable mask he preferred to present to the world.

She was angry, but she didn't say another word. She simply stepped into the elevator, her eyes fixed to the digital readout on the wall. The doors slid closed behind them, and still she didn't look at him.

"If you brought me here to abuse me perhaps I should simply go back to my father's house and take my chances with him."

"That's what you call abuse? You didn't seem to find it so abhorrent the night you let me do it."

"But you weren't being a bastard that night. Had you approached me at the bar and used it as a pickup line I would have told you to go to hell."

"Would you have, Alessia?" he asked, anger, heat, firing in his blood. "Somehow I don't think that's true."

"No?"

"No." He turned to her, put his hand, palm flat, on the glossy marble wall behind her, drawing closer, drawing in the scent of her. *Dio.* Like lilac and sun. She was Spring standing before him, new life, new hope.

He pushed away from her, shut down the feeling.

"Shows what you know."

"I know a great deal about you."

"Stop with the you-know-me stuff. Just because we slept together—"

"You have a dimple on your right cheek. It doesn't show every time you smile, only when you're really, really smiling. You dance by yourself in the sun, you don't like to wear shoes. You've bandaged every scraped knee your brothers and sisters ever had. And whenever you see me, you can't help yourself, you have to stare. I know you, Alessia Battaglia, don't tell me otherwise."

"You knew me, Matteo. You knew a child. I'm not the same person now."

"Then how is it you ended up in my bed the night of your bachelorette party?"

Her eyes met his for the first time all morning, for the first time since his private plane had touched down in Sicily. "Because I wanted to make a choice, Matteo. Every other choice was being made for me. I wanted to…I wanted to at least make the choice about who my first lover should be."

"Haven't you had a lot of time to make that choice?"

"When? With all of my free time? I've spent my life making sure my brothers and sisters were cared for, really cared for, not just given the bare necessities by staff. I spent my life making sure they never bore the full brunt of my father's rage. I've spent my life being the perfect daughter, the hostess for his functions, standing and smiling next to him when he got reelected for a position that he abuses."

"Why?" he asked.

"Because of my siblings. Because no matter that my father is a tyrant, he is our father. We're Battaglias. I hoped… I've always hoped I could make that mean something good. That I could make sure my brothers and sisters learned to do the right things, learned to want the right things. If

I didn't make sure, they would only have my father as a guiding influence and I think we both know Antonioni Battaglia shouldn't be anyone's guiding influence."

"And what about you?"

"What about me?"

The elevator doors slid open and they stepped out into the empty hall on the top floor.

"You live your whole life for other people?"

She shook her head. "No. I live my life in the way that lets me sleep at night. Abandoning my brothers and sisters to our father would have hurt me. So it's not like I'm a martyr. I do it because I love them."

"But you ran out on the wedding."

She didn't say anything, she simply started walking down the hall, her heels clicking on the marble floor. He stood and watched her, his eyes drifting over her curves, over that gorgeous, heart-shaped backside, outlined so perfectly by her pencil skirt.

It looked like something from the Corretti clothing line. One thing he might have to thank his damn brother Luca for. But it was the only thing.

Especially since the rumor was that in his absence the other man was attempting to take Matteo's share in the Corretti family hotels. A complete mess since that bastard Angelo had his hands in it, as well.

A total mess. And one he should have anticipated. He'd dropped out of the dealings with Corretti Enterprises completely since the day of Alessia and Alessandro's aborted wedding. And the vultures had moved in. He should try to stop them, he knew that. And he could, frankly. He had his own fortune, his own power, independent of the Corretti machine, but at the moment, the most pressing issue was tied to the tall, willowy brunette who was currently sauntering in the wrong direction.

"The suite is this way," he said.

She stopped, turned sharply on her heel and started walking back toward him, past him and down the hall.

He nearly laughed at the haughty look on her face. In fact, he found he wanted to, but wasn't capable of it. It stuck in his throat, his control too tight to let it out.

He walked past her, to the door of the suite, and took a key card out of his wallet, tapping it against the reader. "My key opens all of them."

"Careful, *caro*, that sounds like a bad euphemism." She shot him a deadly look before entering the suite.

"So prickly, Alessia."

"I told you you didn't know me."

"Then help me get to know you."

"You first, Matteo."

He straightened. "I'm Matteo Corretti, oldest son of Benito Corretti. I'm sure you know all about him. My criminal father who died in a fire, locked in an endless rivalry with his brother, Carlo. You ought to know about him, too, as you were going to marry Carlo's son. I run the hotel arm of my family corporation, and I deal with my own privately owned line of boutique hotels, one of which you're standing in."

She crossed her arms and cocked her hip out to the side. "I think I read that in your online bio. And it's nothing I don't already know."

"That's all there is to know."

She didn't believe that. Not for a moment. She knew there was more to him than that. Knew it because she'd seen it. Seen his blind rage as he'd done everything in his power to protect her from a fate she didn't even like to imagine.

But he didn't speak of it. So neither did she.

"Tell me about you," he said.

"Alessia Battaglia, Pisces, oldest daughter of Antonioni. My father is a politician who does under-the-table dealings with organized-crime families. It's the thing that keeps him in power. But it doesn't make him rich. It's why he needs the Correttis." She returned his style of disclosure neatly, tartly.

"The Correttis are no longer in the organized-crime business. In that regard, my cousins, my brothers and I have done well, no matter our personal feelings for each other."

"You might not be criminals but you are rich. That's why you're so attractive. In my father's estimation at least."

"Attractive enough to trade us his daughter."

She nodded. She looked tired suddenly. Defeated. He didn't like that. He would rather have her spitting venom at him.

"You could walk away, Alessia," he said. "Even now you could. I cannot keep you here. Your father cannot hold you. You're twenty-seven. You have the freedom to do whatever you like. Hell, you could do it on my dime since I'll be supporting my child regardless of what you do."

He didn't know why he was saying it, why he was giving her the out. But part of him wished she would take it. Wished she would leave him alone, take her beauty, the temptation, the ache that seemed to lodge in his chest whenever she was around, with her. The danger she presented to the walls of protection he'd built around his life.

She didn't say anything. She didn't move. She was frozen to the spot, her lips parted slightly, her breath shallow, fast.

"Alessia, you have the freedom to walk out that door if you want. Right now."

He took a step toward her, compelled, driven by something he didn't understand. Didn't want to understand. The beast in him was roaring now and he wanted it to shut up. Wanted his control back.

He'd had a handle on it again. Had moved forward from

the events of his past. Until Alessia had come back into his life, and at the moment all he wanted was for her to be gone, and for his life to go back to the way it had been.

He cupped her chin, tilted her face up so that her eyes met his. "I am not holding you here. I am not your father and I am not your jailer."

Dark eyes met his, the steel in them shocking. "No, you aren't. But you are the father of my baby. Our baby. I'm not going to walk away, Matteo. If you want an out, you'll have to take it yourself. Don't think that I will. I'm strong enough to face this. To try to make this work."

"It would be better if you would."

"Do you really think that?"

"You think I will be a hands-on father? That I will somehow…be an influence in our child's life?" The very thought made him sick. What could he offer a child but a legacy of violence and abuse? But he couldn't walk away, either. Couldn't leave Alessia on her own. But he feared his touch would only poison a child. His baby would be born innocent, unspoiled by the world, and Matteo was supposed to hold him? With his hands? Hands that were stained with blood.

"You think you won't be?"

"How can you give what you never had?"

"I hardly remember my mother, Matteo, but I did a good job with my brothers and sisters."

"Perhaps I find that an absence of a good parent is not the same as having bad ones. What lessons shall I teach our child, *cara*? The kind my father taught me? How to find a man who owes you money? How to break his knee-caps with efficiency when he doesn't pay up? I think not."

He had thought she would look shocked by that, but she hardly flinched, her eyes never wavering from his. "Again you underestimate me, Matteo. You forget the family I come from."

"You are so soft," he said, speaking his mind, speaking his heart. "Breakable. Like a flower. You and I are not the same."

She nodded slowly. "It's easy to crush a flower. But if it's the right kind of flower, it comes back, every year, after every winter. No matter how many times you destroy the surface, it keeps on living underneath."

Her words sent a shot of pain straight to his chest, her quiet strength twisting something deep inside of him. "Don't pretend you were forced into this," he said softly. "You were given your choice."

"And you were given yours."

He nodded once and turned away from her, walked out of the room ignoring the pounding in his blood, ignoring the tightness in his chest. Trying to banish the image of his hand closing around a blossom and crushing the petals, leaving it completely destroyed.

Alessia looked around the lavish, now empty, suite that she was staying in until…until she didn't know when. Weeks of not being able to get ahold of Matteo, not knowing what she would do if she didn't, and now he was suddenly in her life like a hurricane, uprooting everything, taking control of everything.

She really shouldn't be too surprised about it. That was one thing she did know about Matteo Corretti, beyond that stupid ream of noninformation he'd given her. He was controlled. Totally. Completely.

Twice she'd seen him lose that control. Once, on a sunny day in Sicily while he was staying at his grandparents' rural estate. The day that had cemented him in her mind as her potential salvation.

And their night in New York. There had been no control then, not for either of them.

She pictured him as he'd been then. The way he'd

looked at her in the low light of the bar. She closed her eyes and she was back there. The memory still so strong, so painfully sweet.

"What brings you to New York, Alessia?"

"Bachelorette party." It was easy enough to leave out that it was for her. If he didn't know about Alessandro, then she wouldn't tell him.

"Did you order any strippers?"

Her cheeks heated. "No, gosh, why? Are you offering to fill the position?"

"How much have you had to drink?" he asked, a smile on his face. It was so rare for her to see him smile. She couldn't remember if she ever had.

"Not enough."

"I could fix that, but I think I'd like a dance and if you're too drunk you won't be able to keep up."

"Why are you talking to me?" she asked. She'd known there was a chance he could be here. He owned the hotel, after all. Part of her had hoped she'd catch a glimpse of him. A little bit of torture, but torture that would be well worth it.

"What do you mean?"

"You haven't spoken to me since—" something flashed in his eyes, a strange unease, and she redirected her words "—in a long time."

"Too long," he said, his voice rough.

Her heart fluttered, a surge of hope moving through her. She tried to crush it, tried to stop the jittery feelings moving through her now.

"So, do you have a dance for me?" he asked. "For an old friend?"

"Yes." She couldn't deny him, couldn't deny herself.

She left her friends in the corner of the bar, at their table with all of their fruity drinks, and let Matteo lead her away from them, lead her to the darkened dance floor. A jazz quartet was playing, the music slow and sensual.

He wrapped his arms around her waist and pulled her against his body. Heat shot through her, heat and desire and lust.

His eyes locked with hers as they swayed in time to the music, and she was powerless to resist the desire to lean in and press her lips to his. His tongue touched the tip of hers, a shot of need so sharp, so strong, assaulting her she thought it would buckle her knees then and there.

She parted her lips for him, wrapping her arms around his neck, tangling her fingers in his hair. Years of fantasies added fuel to the moment.

Matteo Corretti was her ultimate fantasy. The man whose name she called out in her sleep. The man she wanted, more than anything. And this was her last chance.

Panic drove her, made her desperate. She deepened the kiss, her movements clumsy. She didn't know how to make out. She'd never really done it before. Another thing that added fuel to the fire.

She'd never lived. She'd spent all of her life at the Battaglia *castello*, taking care of her siblings, making sure her family didn't crumble. Her life existed for the comfort of others, and she needed a moment, a night, to have something different.

To have something for her.

Matteo pulled away from her, his chest rising and falling heavily with each indrawn breath. "We cannot do that here."

She shook her head. "Apparently not." The fire between them was burning too hot, too fast, threatening to rage out of control.

"I have a suite." A smile curved his lips. "I own the hotel."

She laughed, nervous, breathless. She flexed her fingers, where her engagement ring should be. The engagement ring she hadn't put on tonight as she'd gotten ready for the party.

"Please. Just one night," she said.

"Only one, *cara mia*?"

"That's all I have to give."

"I might be able to change your mind," he said, his voice rough. He leaned in and kissed her neck, his teeth scraping her delicate skin, his tongue soothing away the sting.

Yes. She wanted to shout it. *Yes, forever. Matteo,* ti amo.

Instead, she kissed him again, long and deep, pouring everything out, every emotion, every longing that had gone unanswered for so long. Every dream she knew would never be fulfilled. Because Matteo might be hers tonight, but in just a month, she would belong to another man forever.

"Take me to your room."

Alessia shook her head, brought herself back to the present. Everything had been so perfect that night. It was the morning that had broken her heart. The cold light of day spilling over her, illuminating the truth, not allowing her to hide behind fantasy any longer.

She could remember just how he'd looked, the sheets tangled around his masculine body, bright white against his dark skin. Leaving him had broken her.

She'd wanted so badly to kiss him again, but she hadn't wanted to chance waking him.

Somehow that night she'd let her fantasies become real, had let them carry her away from reality, not just in her imagination but for real. And she couldn't regret it, not then, not now.

At least, she hadn't until recently. The way Matteo looked at her now...she hated it. Hated that he saw her as a leash.

But it was too late to turn back now. The dutiful daughter had had her rebellion, and it had destroyed everything in its path.

"You don't go halfway, do you, Alessia?" she asked the empty room.

Unsurprisingly, she got no answer.

CHAPTER FIVE

"YOU CANNOT SIMPLY take what is mine without paying for it, Corretti."

Matteo looked at Antonioni Battaglia and fought a wave of rage. The man had no idea who he was dealing with. Matteo was a Corretti, the capability to commit hideous acts was a part of his DNA. More than that, Matteo had actually done it before. Had embraced the violence. Both with cold precision, and in the heat of rage.

The temptation to do it again was strong. Instead, he leaned forward and adjusted a glass figurine that his grandmother had had commissioned for him. A perfect model of his first hotel. Not one of the Corretti Hotels, the first hotel he'd bought with his own personal fortune.

"And what exactly is that?" Matteo asked, leaning back in his office chair.

"My daughter. You defiled her. She's much less valuable to me now, which means you'd better damn well marry her and make good on the deal I cut with your grandfather, or the Correttis won't be doing any trading out of Sicily."

"My mistake, I thought Alessia's body belonged to her, not you."

"I'm an old-fashioned man."

"Be that as it may, the law prevents you from owning anyone, which means Alessia does not belong to you." He gritted his teeth, thought of Alessia's siblings, of all she'd given up to ensure they would be cared for. "However, at my fiancée's request, I have decided to honor the agreement." He paused for a moment. "What are your other children doing at the moment?"

"I've arranged for the boys to get a job in the family business."

Matteo gritted his teeth. "Is that what they want?"

"You have to take opportunity where it exists."

"And if I created a different opportunity?" He turned the figurine again, keeping his hands busy, keeping himself from violence.

"Why should I do any more business with a Corretti than necessary?"

"Because I hold your potential fortune in the palm of my hands. Not only that, I'll be the father of your first grandchild. Mainly, though, because you'll take what I give you, and no more. So it's by my good grace that you will have anything."

Antonioni's cheeks turned red. It was clear the old man didn't like being told what to do. "Corretti, I don't have to give your family rights to—"

"And I don't have to give you a damn thing. I know you're making deals with Angelo. And you know how I feel about Angelo, which puts you in my bad book right off. I may, however, be willing to overlook it all if you do as I ask. So I suggest you take steps to make me happy. Send your children to college. I'm paying for it."

"That's hardly necessary."

He thought of Alessia, of all she'd sacrificed for them. "Listen to me now, Battaglia, and remember what I say. Memorize it. Make a nice little plaque and hang it above your fireplace if need be: If I say it is necessary, then it is. So long as you do what I say, you'll be kept well in the lifestyle you would like to become accustomed to."

The other man nodded. "It's your dime, Corretti."

"Yes, and your life is now on my dime. Get used to that concept."

Had Alessia's father not said what he had, had he not acted as though her virginity, her body, was his bargaining tool, Matteo might not have taken such joy in letting the other man know his neck was, in effect, under his heel.

But he had. So Matteo did.

"I paid for one wedding," Battaglia said. "I'm not paying for another."

"I think I can handle that, too." Matteo picked up the tiny glass hotel, turning it in front of the light. "You're dismissed."

Battaglia liked that last order least of all, but he complied, leaving Matteo's office without another word.

Matteo tightened his hold on the small, breakable representation of his empire, curling his fingers around it, not stopping until it cracked, driving a shard deep into his palm.

He looked down, watched the blood drip down his wrist. Then he set the figurine back on his desk, examined the broken pieces. Marveled at how easy it was to destroy it with his anger.

He pulled the silk handkerchief out of the pocket of his jacket and wrapped the white fabric around his hand, pressing it hard, until a spot of crimson stained the fabric.

It was so easy to let emotion ruin things. So frighteningly easy.

He gritted his teeth, pushed the wall up around himself again. Control. He would have it, in all things. Alessia Battaglia was not allowed to steal it from him. Not anymore.

Never again.

"I've secured the marriage license, and we will have the wedding at my palazzo." His inheritance after the death of his father. A piece of his childhood he wasn't certain he wanted. But one he possessed nonetheless.

"Not at your family home?"

"I have no use for that place," he said, his tone hard. "Anyway, it has all been arranged."

Alessia stood up from the plush bed, crossing her arms beneath her breasts. "Really? And what shall I wear? How shall I fix my hair? Have you written my vows for me?"

"I don't care. Who gives a damn? And didn't someone already take care of writing vows for weddings hundreds of years ago?"

She blinked, trying to process his rapid-fire response. "I… Don't you have… I mean, don't I need to conform to some sort of image you're projecting or…something?"

"This will be a small affair. We may provide the press with a picture for proof. Or perhaps I'll just send them a photocopy of the marriage license. Anyway, you can wear what you like. I've never seen you not looking beautiful."

The compliment, careless, offhanded, sent a strange sensation through her. "Oh. Well. Thank you."

"It's the truth."

"Well, thank you again."

She wasn't sure what to do, both with him being nice and with him giving her a choice on what to wear to the wedding. Such a simple thing, but it was more than her father had given her when it came to Alessandro.

"As long as it doesn't have lace," she said.

"What?"

"The wedding dress."

"The dress for your last wedding was covered in it."

"Exactly. Hellish, awful contraption. And I didn't choose it. I didn't choose any of that."

"What would you have chosen?"

She shook her head and looked down. "Does it matter?"

"Why not? You can't walk down the aisle naked and

we have to get married somewhere, so you might as well make the choice."

"I would wear something simple. Beautiful. And I would be barefoot. And it would be outside."

He lifted his hand and brushed it over his short hair. "Of course. Then we'll have it outside at the palazzo and you may forego shoes." He lowered his hand and she saw a slash of red on his palm.

She frowned and stepped forward. "What did you do?"

"What?" He turned his hand over. "Nothing. Just a cut."

"You look like you got in a fight."

His whole body tensed. "I don't get in fights."

"No, I know. I wasn't being serious." Tension held between them as they both had the same memory. She knew that was what was happening. Knew that he was thinking of the day she'd been attacked.

But she wanted to know what he remembered, how he remembered it, because it was obvious it was something he preferred to ignore. Not that she loved thinking about it except…except as horrible as it had been to have those men touching her, pawing at her, as awful as those memories were, the moment when they'd been wrenched from her, when she'd seen Matteo…the rush of relief, the feeling of absolute peace and certainty that everything would be okay, had been so real, so acute, she could still feel it.

She'd clung to him after. Clung to him and cried. And he'd stroked her cheek with his hand, wiping away her tears. Later she'd realized he'd left a streak of blood on her face, from the blood on his hands. Blood he'd shed, spilled, for her.

He'd been her hero that day, and every day since. She'd spent her whole life saving everyone else, being the stopgap for her siblings, taking her father's wrath if they'd been too noisy. Always the one to receive a slap across the face, rather than allow him near the younger children.

Matteo was the only person who'd ever stood up for her. The only one who'd ever saved her. And so, when life got hard, when it got painful, or scary, she would imagine that he would come again. That he would pull her into impossibly strong arms and fight her demons for her.

He never did. Never again. After that day, he even stopped watching her. But having the hope of it, the fantasy, was part of what had pulled her through the bleakness of her life. Imagination had always been her escape, and he'd added a richer texture to it, given a face to her dreams for the future.

He'd asked if she always spoke her mind, and she'd told him the truth, she didn't. She kept her head down and tried to get through her life, tried to simply do the best she could. But in her mind…her imagination was her escape, and always had been. When she ran barefoot through the garden, she was somewhere else entirely.

When she went to bed at night, she read until sleep found her, so that she could have new thoughts in her head, rather than simply memories of the day.

So that she could have better dreams.

It was probably a good thing Matteo didn't know the place he occupied in her dreams. It would give him too much power. More than he already had.

"I'm not like my father," he said. "I will never strike my wife."

She looked at him and she realized that never, for one moment, had she believed he would. Her father had kept her mother "in line" with the back of his hand, and he'd done the same with her. But even having grown up with that as a normal occurrence, she'd never once imagined Matteo would do it.

"I know," she said.

"You know?"

"Yes."

"And how is it you know?"

"Because you aren't that kind of person, Matteo."

"Such confidence in me. Especially when you're one of the very few people who has actually seen what I'm capable of."

She had. She'd seen his brute strength applied to those who had dared try to harm her. It had been the most welcome sight in all of her life. "You protected me."

"I went too far."

"They would have gone further," she said.

He took a step away from her, the darkness in his eyes suddenly so deep, so pronounced, it threatened to pull her in. "I have work to do. I'll be at my downtown office. I've arranged to have a credit card issued to you." He reached into his pocket and pulled out a black card, extending his hand to her.

She took it, not ready to fight with him about it.

"If you need anything, whatever you need, it's yours." He turned away and walked out of the room, closing the door behind him.

She'd done the wrong thing again. With Matteo it seemed she could do nothing right. And she so desperately wanted to do right by him.

But it seemed impossible.

She growled, the sound releasing some of her tension. But not enough. "Matteo, why are you always so far out of my reach?"

This was Alessia's second wedding day. Weird, because she'd never technically had a boyfriend. One hot night of sex didn't really make Matteo her boyfriend. *Boyfriend* sounded too tame for a man like Matteo, anyway. Alessia finished zipping up the back of her gown. It was light, with flutter sleeves and a chiffon skirt that swirled around her ankles. It was lavender instead of white. She was a pregnant bride, after all.

There weren't many people in attendance, but she liked that better. Her father, her brothers and sisters, Matteo's grandmother, Teresa, and his mother, Simona.

She took the bouquet of lilacs she'd picked from the garden out of their vase and looked in the mirror. Nothing like what the makeup artist had managed on The Other Wedding Day, but today she at least looked like her.

She opened the guest bedroom door and tried to get a handle on her heart rate.

She was marrying Matteo Corretti today. In a sun-drenched garden. She was having his baby. She repeated that, over and over, trying to make it feel real, trying to hold on to the surge of good feelings it gave her. Because no matter how terrifying it was sometimes, it was also wonderful. A chance at something new. A chance to have a child, give that child the life that had been denied her. The life that had been denied Matteo.

The stone floor was cool beneath her bare feet, the palazzo empty, everyone outside waiting. She'd opted to forego shoes since that was how he said he knew her.

Barefoot in the garden. So, she would meet him as he remembered her. Barefoot in the garden, with her hair down. Maybe then they could start over. They were getting married today, after all, and in her mind that meant they would have to start trying to work things out. They would at least have to be civil.

She put her hands on the rail of the curved, marble staircase, still repeating her mantra. She walked through the grand foyer, decorated in traditional, ornate furniture that didn't remind her one bit of Matteo, and she opened the door, stepping out into the sun.

The music was already playing. A string quartet. She'd

forgotten to say what she wanted for music but this was perfect, simple.

And in spite of what Matteo had said, there was a photographer.

But those details faded into the background when she saw Matteo, standing near the priest, his body rigid, his physique displayed to perfection by a custom-made gray suit.

There was no aisle. No loud click of marble beneath her heels, just grass beneath her feet. And the guests were standing, no chairs. Her father looked like he was ready to grab her if she decided to run. Eva, Giana, Pietro and Marco looked worried, and she didn't blame them. She had been their stability for most of their lives, their surrogate mother. And she hadn't told them she was marrying Alessandro for convenience, which meant her disappearance, subsequent reappearance with a different groom and a publicly announced pregnancy must seem a few steps beyond bizarre to them.

She gave them her best, most confident smile. This was her role. To show them it was all okay, to hold everything together.

But her eyes were drawn back to Matteo. He made her throat dry, made her heart pound.

But when she reached him, he didn't take her hand. He hardly looked at her. Instead, he looked at the priest. The words to the ceremony were traditional, words she knew by heart from attending hundreds of society weddings in her life.

There was nothing personal about them, nothing unique. And Matteo never once met her eyes.

She was afraid she was alone in her resolve to make things work. To make things happy. She swallowed hard. It was always her job to make it okay. To smooth it over. Why wasn't it working?

"You may kiss the bride."

They were the words she'd been anticipating and dreading. She let her eyes drift shut and she waited. She could feel his heat draw near to her, and then, the brush of his lips on hers, so soft, so brief, she thought she might have imagined it.

And then nothing more.

Her breath caught, her heart stopped. She opened her eyes, and Matteo was already turning to face their small audience. Then he drew her near to him, his arm tight around her waist. But there was no intimacy in the gesture. No warmth.

"Thank you for bearing witness," Matteo said, both to her father and his grandmother.

"You've done a good thing for the family, Matteo," his grandmother said, putting a hand over his. And Alessia wondered just how much trouble Matteo had been in with his family for the wedding fiasco.

She knew the media had made assumptions they'd run off together. Too bad nothing could be further from the truth.

Still, her father, his family, must think that was the truth. Because now they were back in Sicily, she was pregnant and they were married.

"Perhaps we should go inside for a drink?" her father suggested.

"A good plan, Battaglia, but we don't talk business at weddings."

Simona begged off, giving Matteo a double kiss on the cheeks and saying she had a party to get to in the city. Matteo didn't seem the least bit fazed by his mother's abandonment. He simply followed her father into the house.

She watched him walk inside, her heart feeling heavy.

Teresa offered her a smile. "I'll see that Matteo's staff finds some refreshments to serve for us. I'll only be a moment." The older woman turned and went into the house, too, leaving Alessia with her siblings.

It was Eva, fourteen and emotional, who flung herself into Alessia's arms. "Where did you go?"

"New York," Alessia said, stroking her sister's hair.

"Why?"

"I had to get away...I couldn't marry Alessandro."

"Then why did you agree to the engagement?" This from Marco, the second oldest at nineteen.

"It's complicated, Marco, as things often are with Father. You know that."

"But you wanted to marry Corretti? This Corretti, I mean," asked sixteen-year-old Pietro.

She nodded, her throat tight. "Of course." She didn't want them to be upset. Didn't want them to worry. She maybe should have thought of that before running off to New York, but she really hadn't been able to consider anyone else. For the first time, she'd been burned out on it and she'd had to take care of herself.

"They're having a baby," Giana said drily. "I assume that means she liked him at least a little bit." Then she turned back to Alessia. "I'm excited about being an aunt."

"I'm glad," she said, tugging on her sister's braid.

They spent the rest of the afternoon out in the garden, having antipasti, wine for the older children and Teresa, and lemonade for her and younger kids. Her siblings told her stories of their most recent adventures, which ended up with everyone laughing. And for the first time in months, Alessia felt at ease. This was her family, her happiness. The reason she'd agreed to marry Alessandro. And one of the driving reasons behind her decision to marry Matteo.

Although she couldn't deny her own desire where he was concerned. Still, *happy* wasn't exactly the word that she would use to describe herself at the moment. Anxiety-ridden? Check. Sick to her stomach? That a little bit, too.

The sun was starting to sink behind the hills, gray twilight settling on the garden, the solar lights that were strung across the expanse of the grass illuminating the growing darkness.

Their father appeared on the balcony, his arms folded across his chest, his eyes settled on her siblings.

"I guess we have to go," Marco said.

"I know. Come back and stay with us anytime," she said, not even thinking to ask Matteo if it was okay. As soon as she had the thought, she banished it. If she was going to be married to the man, then she wasn't going to ask his permission to breathe in their shared home. It wasn't only his now and he would have to get used to it.

Her father was the unquestionable head of their household, but she was the heart of it. She'd kept it running, made sure the kids got their favorite meals cooked, remembered birthdays and helped with homework. Her role in their lives didn't end with her marriage, and she wasn't equipped to take on a passive role in a household, anyway.

So, on that, Matteo would just have to learn to deal.

She stopped and kissed her brothers and sisters on the head before watching them go up to where their father stood. All of them but Marco. She held him a bit longer in her embrace. "Take care of everyone," she said, a tear escaping and sliding down her cheek.

"Just like you always did," he said softly.

"And I'm still here."

"I know."

He squeezed her hand before walking up to join the rest of the family.

"And I should leave you, as well," Teresa said, standing. "It was lovely to see you again, my dear."

Teresa hadn't batted an eye at the sudden change of groom, had never seemed at all ruffled by the events.

"You care for him," she said, as if she could read Alessia's internal musings.

Alessia nodded. "I do."

"That's what these men need, Alessia. A strong woman to love them. They may fight it, but it is what they need." Teresa spoke with pain in her eyes, a pain that Alessia felt echo inside of her.

Alessia couldn't speak past the lump in her throat. She tried to avoid the *L* word. The one that was stronger than *like*. There was only so much a woman could deal with at once. So instead, she just nodded and watched Teresa walk back up toward the house.

Alessia stayed in the garden and waited. The darkness thickened, the lights burning brighter. And Matteo didn't come.

She moved into the house, walked up the stairs. The palazzo was completely quiet, the lights off. She wrapped her arms around herself, and made her way back to the bedroom Matteo had put her in to get ready.

She went in and sat on the edge of the bed and waited for her husband to come and claim his wedding night.

CHAPTER SIX

MATTEO DIDN'T GET DRUNK as a rule. Unfortunately, he had a tendency to break rules when Alessia Battaglia—or was she Alessia Corretti now?—was involved.

Damn that woman.

Even after his father's death he hadn't gotten drunk. He'd wanted to. Had wanted to incinerate the memories, destroy them as the fire had destroyed the warehouses, destroyed the man who had held so much sway over his life.

But he hadn't. Because he hadn't deserved that kind of comfort. That kind of oblivion. He'd forced himself to face it.

This...this he couldn't face.

He took another shot of whiskey and let it burn all the way down. It didn't burn as much at this point in the evening, which was something of a disappointment. He looked down at the shot glass and frowned. Then he picked it up and threw it against the wall, watching the glass burst.

Now that was satisfying.

He chuckled and lifted the bottle to his lips. *Dio*, in his current state he almost felt happy. Why the hell didn't he drink more?

"Matteo?"

He turned and saw Alessia standing in the doorway. Alessia. He wanted her. More than his next breath. He wanted those long legs wrapped around his waist, wanted to hear her husky voice whispering dirty things in his ear.

He didn't think she'd ever done that, whispered dirty things in his ear, but he could imagine it, and he wanted it. *Dio*, did he want it.

"Come here, wife," he said, pushing away from the bar, his movements unsteady.

"Are you drunk?"

"I should be. If I'm not...if I'm not there's something very wrong with this whiskey."

Her dark eyes were filled with some kind of emotion. Something strong and deep. He couldn't decipher it. He didn't want to.

"Why are you drunk?"

"Because I've been drinking. Alcohol. A lot of it."

"But why?"

"I don't know, could be because today I acquired a wife and I can't say I ever particularly wanted one."

"Thank you. I'm so glad to hear that, after the ceremony."

"You would have changed your mind? You can't. It's all over the papers, in the news all over the world. You're carrying a Corretti. You, a Battaglia. It's news, *cara*. Not since Romeo and Juliet has there been such a scandal."

"I'm not going to stab myself for you just because you've poisoned your damn self, so you can stop making those parallels anytime."

"Come to me, Alessia."

She took a step toward him, her movements unsteady, her lips turned down into a sulky frown. He wanted to kiss the expression off her face.

"You left your hair down," he said, reaching out and taking a dark lock between his thumb and forefinger, rubbing the glossy strands. "You're so beautiful. An angel. That was the first thing I thought when I saw you."

She blinked rapidly. "When?"

"When we were children. I had always been told you Battaglias were monsters. Demons. And I couldn't resist the chance to peek. And there you were, running around your father's garden. You were maybe eleven. You were dirty and your hair was tangled, but I thought you looked like heaven. You were smiling. You always smile." He frowned, looking at her face again. "You don't smile as much now."

"I haven't had a lot of reasons to smile."

"Have you ever?"

"No. But I've made them. Because someone had to smile. Someone had to teach the children how to smile."

"And it had to be you?"

"There was no one else."

"So you carry the weight of the world, little one?"

"You should know something about that, Matteo."

He chuckled. "Perhaps a little something." He didn't feel so much like he was carrying it now.

He took her arm and tugged her forward, her dark eyes wide. "I want you," he said.

Not waiting for a response, he leaned in and kissed her. Hard. She remained immobile beneath his mouth, her lips stiff, her entire body stiff. He pulled her more firmly against him, let her feel the evidence of his arousal, let her feel all of the frustration and need that had been building inside of him for the past three months.

"Did he kiss you like this?" he asked, pressing a heated kiss to her neck, her collarbone.

She shook her head. "N-no."

"Good. I would have had to kill him."

"Stop saying things like that."

"Why?" he asked. "You and I both know that I could, Alessia. On your behalf, I could. I might not even be able to stop myself." He kissed her again, his heart pounding hard, blood pouring hot and fast through his veins.

"Matteo, stop," she said, pulling away from him.

"Why? Are you afraid of me, too, Alessia?"

She shook her head. "No, but you aren't yourself. I don't like it."

"Maybe I am myself, and in that case, you're wise not to like it."

He released his hold on her. And he realized how tight his grip had been. Regret, the kind he usually kept dammed up inside of himself, released, flooding through him. "Did I hurt you?"

She shook her head. "No."

"Don't lie."

"I wouldn't."

Suddenly, he was hit with a shot of self-realization so strong it nearly buckled his knees. He had done it again. He had let his defenses down with Alessia. Let them? He didn't allow anything, with her it was just total destruction, a sudden, real demolition that he didn't seem to be able to control at all.

"Get out," he said.

"Matteo…"

"Out!" he roared, images flashing before his eyes. Images of violence. Of bones crushing beneath his fists, of not being able to stop. Not being able to stop until he was certain they could never hurt her again.

And it melded with images of his father. His father beating men until they were unconscious. Until they didn't get back up again.

"What did they do?"

"They didn't pay."

"Is that all?"

"Is that all? Matteo, you can't let anyone disrespect you, ever. Otherwise, it gets around. You have to make them an

*example. Whatever you have to do to protect your power,
you do it. And if people have to die to secure it, so be it.
Casualties of war, figlio mio."*

No. He wasn't like that.

But you were, Matteo. You are.

Then in his mind, it wasn't his father doing the beating. It was him.

"Out!"

Alessia's dark eyes widened and she backed out of the room, a tear tracking down her cheek.

He sank down into a chair, his fingers curled tightly around a bottle of whiskey as the edges of his vision turned fuzzy, darkened.

Che cavolo, what was she doing to him?

Alessia slammed the bedroom door behind her and tore at the back of her wedding dress, such as it was, sobbing as she released the zipper and let it fall to the floor. She'd wanted Matteo to be the one to take it off her. She hadn't realized how much until now.

Instead, her groom was off getting drunk rather than dealing with her.

"It's more than that," she said out loud. And she knew that it was. He was getting drunk instead of dealing with a whole lot of things.

Well, it was unfair because she couldn't get drunk. She was pregnant with the man's baby, and while he numbed the pain of it all, she just had to stand around and endure it.

There was nothing new to that. She had to smile. Had to keep it all moving.

She sat down on the edge of the bed, then scooted into the middle of it, lying down, curling her knees into her chest. Tonight, there was no fantasy to save her, no way to avoid reality.

Matteo had long been her rescue from the harsh reality

and pain of life. And now he was her harsh reality. And he wasn't who she'd believed he was. She'd simplified him, painted him as a savior.

She'd never realized how much he needed to be saved. The question was, was she up to the challenge? No, the real question was, did she have a choice?

There wasn't a word foul enough to help release the pain that was currently pounding through Matteo's head. So he said them all.

Matteo sat upright in the chair. He looked down at the floor, there was a mostly empty whiskey bottle lying on its side by the armchair. And there was a dark star-shaped whiskey stain on the wall, glass shards gathered beneath.

He remembered…not very much. The wedding. He was married now. He looked down at the ring on his left hand. Yes, he was married now.

He closed his eyes again, trying to lessen the pain in his head, and had a flash of lilac memory. A cloud of purple, long dark hair. He'd held her arm and pulled her against him, his lips hard on hers.

Dio, what had he done? Where had it stopped? He searched his brain desperately for an answer, tried to figure out what he'd done. What she'd done.

He stood quickly, ignoring the dizziness, the ferocious hammering in his temples. He swore again as he took his first step, he legs unsteady beneath him.

What was his problem? Where was his control? He knew better than to drink like that, knew better than to allow any lowered inhibitions.

The first time he'd gotten that drunk had been the night following Alessia's rescue. He hadn't been able to get clean. Hadn't been able to get the images out of his head. Images of what he was capable of.

The stark truth was, it hadn't been the attack that had

driven him to drink. It had been what his father had said afterward.

"You are my son."

When Benito Corretti had seen his son, blood-streaked, after the confrontation with Alessia's attackers, he'd assumed that it meant Matteo was finally following in his footsteps. Had taken it as confirmation.

But Matteo hadn't. It had been six years after that night when Benito had said it to him again. And that night, Matteo had embraced the words, and proven the old man right.

He pushed the memories away, his heart pounding too hard to go there.

He knew full well that he was capable of unthinkable things, even without the loss of control. But when control was gone…when it was gone, he truly became a monster. And last night, he'd lost control around Alessia.

He had to find her.

He walked down the hall, his heart pounding a sick tempo in his skull, his entire body filled with lead.

He went down the stairs, the natural light filtering through the windows delivering a just punishment for his hideous actions.

Coffee. He would find coffee first, and then Alessia.

He stopped when he got to the dining room. It turned out he had found both at the same time.

"Good morning," Alessia said, her hands folded in front of her, her voice soft and still too loud.

"Morning," he said, refusing to call it good.

"I assume you need coffee?" she asked, indicating a French press, ready for brewing, and a cup sitting next to it.

"Yes."

"You know how that works, right?" she asked.

"Yes."

"Good."

She didn't make a move to do it for him, she simply sat in her seat, drinking a cup of tea.

He went to his spot at the expansive table, a few seats away from hers, and sat, pushing the plunger down slowly on the French press.

He poured himself a cup, left it black. He took a drink and waited a moment, letting the strong brew do its magic.

"Alessia," he said, his voice rusty, the whiskey burn seeming to linger, "last night...did I hurt you?"

"In what way?" she asked, leaning back in her chair, her dark eyes unflinching.

"Physically."

"No."

The wave of relief that washed over him was profound, strong. "I'm pleased to hear it."

"Emotionally, on the other hand, I'm not sure I faired so well."

"Why is that?"

"Well, let's see, my husband got drunk on our wedding night instead of coming to bed with me. What do you think?"

"I'm sorry if I wounded your pride," he said, "that wasn't my intention." What he'd been after was oblivion, which he should have known wasn't a safe pursuit.

"Wouldn't your pride have been wounded if I'd done the same?"

"I would have ripped the bottle out of your hand. You're pregnant."

There hadn't been a lot of time for him to really pause and think through the implications of that. It had all been about securing the marriage. Staying a step ahead of the press at all times. Making sure Alessia was legally bound to him.

"Hence the herbal tea," she said, raising her cup to him. "And the pregnancy wasn't really my point."

"Alessia…this can't be a normal marriage."

"Why not?" she asked, sitting up straighter.

"Because it simply can't be. I'm a busy man, I travel a lot. I was never going to marry…I never would have married."

"I don't see why we can't have a normal marriage anyway. A lot of men and women travel for business, it doesn't mean they don't get married."

"I don't love you."

Alessia felt like he'd slapped her. His words were so bald, so true and unflinching. And they cut a swath of devastation through her. "I didn't ask you to," she said, because it was the only truth she could bring herself to speak.

"Perhaps not, but a wife expects it from her husband."

"I doubt my father loved my mother, and if he did, it wasn't the kind of love I would like to submit to. What about yours?"

"*Obsession,* perhaps, was a better word. My father loved Lia's mother, I'm sure of that. I'm not certain he loved mine. At least, not enough to stay away from other women. And my mother was—is, for that matter—very good at escaping unpleasant truths by way of drugs and alcohol." His headache mocked him, a reminder that he'd used alcohol for the very same reason last night.

"Perhaps it was their marriages that weren't normal. Perhaps—"

"Alessia, don't. I think you saw last night that I'm not exactly a brilliant candidate for husband or father of the year."

"So try to be. Don't just tell me you can't, Matteo, or that you don't want to. Be better. That's what I'm trying to do. I'm trying to be stronger, to do the right thing."

"Yes, because that's what you do," he said, his tone dry. "You make things better, because it makes you feel better, and as long as you feel good you assume all is right with your world. You trust your moral compass."

"Well, yes, I suppose that's true."

"I don't trust mine. I want things I shouldn't want. I have already taken what I didn't have the right to take."

"If you mean my virginity, I will throw this herbal tea in your face," she said, pregnancy hormones coming to the rescue, bringing an intense surge of anger.

"I'm not so crass, but yes. Your body, you, you aren't for me."

"For Alessandro? That's who I was for?"

"That isn't what I meant."

"The hell it's not, Matteo!" she shouted, not caring if she hurt his head. Him and his head could go to hell. "You're just like him. You think I can't make my own decisions? That I don't know my own mind? My body belongs to me, not to you, not to my father, not to Alessandro. I didn't give myself to you, I took you. I made you tremble beneath my hands, and I could do it again. Don't treat me like some fragile thing. Don't treat me like you have to protect me from myself."

He stayed calm, maddeningly so, his focus on his cup of coffee. "It's not you I'm protecting you from."

"It's you?"

A smile, void of humor, curved his lips. "I don't trust me, Alessia, why should you?"

"Well, let me put you at ease, Matteo. I don't trust anyone. Just because I jumped into bed with you doesn't mean you're the exception. I just think you're hot." She was minimizing it. Minimizing what she felt. And she hated that. But she was powerless to do anything to stop the words from coming out. She wanted to protect herself, to push him back from her vulnerable places. To keep him from hurting her.

Because the loss of Matteo in her fantasies…it was almost too much to bear. As he became her reality, she was losing her escape, and she was angry at him for taking it. For not being the ideal she had made him out to be.

"I'm flattered," he said, taking another drink of his coffee.

"How do you see this marriage going, then?"

"I don't want to hurt you."

"Assume it's too late. Where do we go from here?"

He leaned forward, his dark eyes shuttered. "When exactly are you due?"

"November 22. It was easy for them to figure out since I knew the exact date I conceived."

"I will make sure you get the best care, whatever you need. And we'll make a room for the baby."

"Well, all things considered, I suppose our child should have a room in his own house."

"I'm trying," he bit out. "I'm not made for this. I don't know how to handle it."

"Well, I do. I know exactly how much work babies are. I know exactly what it's like to raise children. I was thirteen when my mother died. Thirteen when my baby sister and the rest of my siblings became my responsibility. Babies are hard work. But you love them, so much. And at the same time, they take everything from you. I know that, I know it so well. And I'm terrified," she said, the last word breaking. It was a horrible confession, but it was true.

She'd essentially raised four children, one of them from infancy, and as much as she adored them, with every piece of herself, she also knew the cost of it. Knew just how much you poured into children. How much you gave, how much they took.

And she was doing it again. Without ever finding a place for herself in the world. Without having the fantasies she'd craved. True love. A man who would take care of her.

You've had some of the fantasies.

Oh, yes, she had. But one night of passion wasn't the sum total of her life's desires.

"All of this," he said. "And still you want this child?"

"Yes, Matteo. I do. Because babies are a lot of work. But the love you feel for them…it's stronger than anything, than any fear. It doesn't mean I'm not afraid, only that I know in the end the love will win."

"Well, we can be terrified together," he said.

"You're terrified?"

"Babies are tiny. They look very easily broken."

"I'll teach you how to hold one."

Their eyes met, heat arching between them, and this time her pregnancy hormones were making her feel something other than anger.

She looked back down at her breakfast. "How's your head?"

"I feel like someone put a woodpecker in my skull."

"It's no less than you deserve."

"I will treat you better than I did last night. That I promise you. I'm not sure what other promises I can make, but that one…that one I will keep."

She thought of him last night. Broken. Passionate. Needy. She wondered how much of that was the real Matteo. How much he kept hidden beneath a facade.

How much he kept from escaping. And she knew just how he felt in some ways. Knew what it was like to hide everything behind a mask. It was just that her mask was smiling, and his hardly made an expression at all.

"Will you be faithful to me?" she asked, the words catching in her throat.

Matteo looked down into his coffee for a moment, then stood, his cup in his hand. "I have some work to see to this morning, and my head is killing me. We can talk more later."

Alessia's heart squeezed tight, nausea rolling through her. "Later?"

"My head, Alessia."

My heart, you jackass. "Great. Well, perhaps we can have a meeting tonight, or something."

"We're busy tonight."

"Oh. Doing what?"

"Celebrating our marriage, quite publicly, at a charity event."

"What?" She felt far too raw to be in public.

"After what happened with Alessandro, we have to present a united front. Your not-quite wedding to him was very public, as was your announcement of your pregnancy. The entire world is very likely scratching their heads over the spectacle we've created, and now it's time to show a little bit of normal."

"But we don't have a normal marriage—I mean, so I've been told."

"As far as the media is concerned we do."

"Why? Afraid of a little scandal? You're a Corretti."

"What do you want our child to grow up and read? Because thanks to the internet, this stuff doesn't die. It's going to linger, scandal following him wherever he goes. You and I both know what that's like. To have all the other kids whisper about your parents. For our part, we aren't criminals, but we've hardly given our child a clean start."

"So we go out and look pretty and sparkly and together, and what? The press just forgets about what happened?"

"No, but perhaps they will continue on in the vein that they've started in."

"What's that?" She'd, frankly, spent a lot of energy avoiding the stories that the media had written about the wedding.

"That we were forbidden lovers, who risked it all to be together."

It wasn't far from the truth, although Matteo hadn't truly known the risk they'd been taking their night together. But she had. And she'd risked it all for the chance to be with him.

Looking at him now, dealing with all the bruises he'd inflicted on her heart, she knew she would make the same choice now. Because at least it had been her choice. Her mistake. Her very first big one. It was like a rite of passage in a way.

"Well, then, I suppose we had better get ready to put on a show. I'm not sure I have the appropriate costume, though."

"I'm sure I can come up with something."

CHAPTER SEVEN

"SOMETHING" TURNED OUT to be an evening gown from the Corretti fashion line. It was gorgeous, and it was very slinky, with silky gold fabric that molded to her curves and showed the emerging baby bump that she almost hadn't noticed until she'd put on the formfitting garment.

Of course, there was no point in hiding her pregnancy. She'd announced it on television, for heaven's sake. But even so, since she hadn't really dealt with it yet, she felt nervous about sharing it with the public like this.

She put her hand on her stomach, smoothing her palm over the small bump. She was going to be a mother. Such a frightening, amazing thing to realize. She'd been tangled up in finding Matteo, and then in the days since—had it really only been days?—she'd been dealing with having him back in her life. With marrying him. She hadn't had a chance to really think of the baby in concrete terms.

Alessia looked at herself in the mirror one more time, at her stomach, and then back at her face. Her looks had never mattered very much to her. She was comfortable with them, more or less. She was taller than almost every other woman she knew, and a good portion of the men, at an Amazonian six feet, but Matteo was taller.

He managed to make her feel small. Feminine. Beautiful.

That night they were together he'd made her feel especially beautiful. And then last night he'd made her feel especially undesirable. Funny how that worked.

She turned away from the mirror and walked out of the bedroom. Matteo was standing in the hall waiting for her, looking so handsome in his black suit she went a little weak-kneed. He was a man who had a strong effect, that was for sure.

"Don't you clean up nice," she said. "You almost look civilized."

"Appearances can be deceiving," he said.

"The devil wore Armani?"

"Something like that." He held his hand out and she hesitated for a moment before taking it and allowing him to lead her down the curved staircase and into the foyer. He opened the door for her, his actions that of a perfectly solicitous husband.

Matteo's sports car was waiting for them, the keys in the ignition.

Alessia waited until they were on the road before speaking again. "So, what's the charity?"

He shifted gears, his shoulders bunched up, muscles tense. "It's one of mine."

"You have charities?"

"Yes."

"I didn't realize."

"I thought you knew me."

"We're filled with surprises for each other, aren't we? It's a good thing we have a whole lifetime together to look forward to," she said drily.

"Yes," he said, his voice rough, unconvincing.

And she was reminded of their earlier conversation in the dining room. She'd asked him point-blank if he would be faithful, and he'd sidestepped her. She had a feeling he was doing it again.

She gritted her teeth to keep from saying anything

more. To keep from asking him anything, or pressing the issue. She had some pride. She did. She was sure she did, and she was going to do everything she could to hold on to her last little bit of it.

"Well, what is your charity for, then?"

"This is an education fund. For the schools here."

"That's...great," she said. "I didn't get to do any higher education."

"Did you want to?"

"I don't know. I don't think so. I mean...I didn't really have anything I wanted to be when I grew up."

"Nothing?"

"There weren't a lot of options on the table. Though I did always think I would like to be a mother." A wife and a mother. That she would like to have someone who loved her, cherished her like the men in her much-loved books cherished their heroines. It was a small dream, one that should have been somewhat manageable.

Instead, she'd gone off and traded it in for a night of wild sex.

And darn it, she still didn't regret it. Mainly.

"Mission accomplished."

"Why, yes, Matteo, I am, as they say, living the dream."

"There's no need to be—"

"There is every need to be," she said. "Don't act like I should thank you for any of this."

"I wasn't going to," he said, his tone biting.

"You were headed there. This is not my dream." But it was close. So close that it hurt worse in some ways than not getting anywhere near it at all. Because this was proving that her dream didn't exist. That it wasn't possible.

"My apologies, *cara*, for not being your dream." His voice was rough, angry, and she wanted to know where he got off being mad after the way he'd been treating her.

"And my apologies for not being yours. I imagine if I

had a room number stapled to my forehead and a bag of money in my hand I'd come a little closer."

"Now you're being absurd."

"I don't think so."

Matteo maneuvered his car through the narrow city streets, not bothering with nice things like braking before turning, and pulled up to the front of his hotel.

"It's at your hotel," she said.

"Naturally." He threw the car into Park, then got out, rounding to the passenger side and opening the door for her. "Come, my darling wife, we have a public to impress."

He extended his hand to her and she slowly reached her hand out to accept it. Lighting streaked through her, from her fingertips, spreading to every other part of her, the shock and electricity curling her toes in her pumps.

She stood, her eyes level with his thanks to her shoes. "Thank you."

A member of the hotel staff came to where they were and had a brief exchange with Matteo before getting into the car and driving it off to the parking lot. Alessia wandered to the steps of the hotel, taking two of them before pausing to wait for her husband.

Matteo turned back to her, his dark eyes glittering in the streetlamps. He moved to the stairs, and she advanced up one more, just to keep her height advantage. But Matteo wasn't having it. He got onto her stair, meeting her eyes straight on.

"There are rules tonight, Alessia, and you will play by them."

"Will I?" she asked. She wasn't sure why she was goading him. Maybe because it was the only way in all the world she could feel like she had some power. Or maybe it was because if she wasn't trying to goad him, she was longing for him. And the longing was just unacceptable.

A smile curved his lips and she couldn't help but wonder if he needed this, too. This edge of hostility, the bite of anger between them.

Although why Matteo would need anything to hold her at a distance when he'd already made his feelings quite clear was a mystery to her.

"Yes, my darling wife, you will." He put his hand on her chin, drawing close to her, his heat making her shiver deep inside. It brought her right back to that night.

To the aching, heart-rending desperation she'd felt when his lips had finally touched hers. To the moment they'd closed his hotel room door and he'd pressed her against the wall, devouring, taking, giving.

He drew his thumb across her lower lip and she snapped back to the present. "You must stop looking at me like that," he said.

"Like what?"

"Like you're frightened of me." There was an underlying note to his voice that she couldn't guess at, a frayed edge to his control that made his words gritty.

"I'm not."

"You look at me like I'm the very devil sometimes."

"You act like the very devil sometimes."

"True enough. But there are other times…"

"What other times?"

"You didn't used to look at me that way."

"How did I look at you?" she asked, her chest tightening, her stomach pulling in on itself.

"When you were a girl? With curiosity. At the hotel? Like you were hungry."

"You looked at me the same way."

"And how do you think I look at you now?"

"You don't," she whispered. "When you can help it, you don't look at me at all."

He moved his other hand up to cup her cheek, his thumb still stroking her lower lip. "I'm looking at you now."

And there was heat in his eyes. Heat like there had been their night together, the night that had started all of this. The night that had changed the course of her life.

"Because you have to," she said. "For the guests."

"Oh, yes, the guests," he said.

Suddenly, a flash pierced the dim light, interrupting their moment. They both looked in the direction of the photographer, who was still snapping pictures in spite of the fact that the moment was completely broken.

"Shall we go in?" he asked. Any evidence of frayed control was gone now, the rawness, the intensity, covered by a mask. And now her husband was replaced with a smooth, cool stranger.

She'd love to say it wasn't the man she'd married, but this was exactly the man she'd married. This guarded man with more layers of artifice than anyone she'd ever met. She had been so convinced she'd seen the man behind the fiction, that the night in the hotel she'd seen the real Matteo. That in those stolen glances they'd shared when they were young, she'd seen the truth.

That in the moment of unrestrained violence, when he'd put himself in harm's way to keep her from getting hurt, she'd seen the real man.

Now she realized what small moments those were in the entirety of Matteo's life. And for the first time, she wondered if she was simply wrong about him.

A feeling that settled sickly in her stomach, a leaden weight, as they continued up the stairs and into the entrance to the hotel's main ballroom.

There were more photographers inside, capturing photographs of the well-dressed crème de la crème of Sicilian society. And Alessia did her best to keep a smile on her face. This was her strength, being happy no matter what was going on. Keeping a smile glued to her face at whatever event she was at on behalf of her father, making sure she showed her brothers and sisters she was okay even if she'd just taken a slap to the face from their father.

But this wasn't so simple. She was having a harder time finding a place to go to inside of herself. Having a harder time finding that false feeling of hope that she'd become so good at creating for herself to help preserve her sanity.

No one could live in total hopelessness, so she'd spent her life creating hope inside of herself. She'd managed to do it through so many difficult scenarios. Why was it so hard now? So hard with Matteo?

She knew she'd already answered that question. It was too hard to retreat to a much-loved fantasy when that much-loved fantasy was standing beside you, the source of most of your angst.

Though she couldn't blame it all on Matteo. The night of her bachelorette party was the first night she'd stopped trying to find solace in herself, had stopped just trying to be happy no matter what, and had gone for what she wanted, in spite of possible consequences.

She spent the night with Matteo's arm wrapped around her waist, his touch keeping her entire body strung tight, on a slow burn. She also turned down champagne more times than she could count. Was she normally offered alcohol so much at a party? She'd never been conscious of it when she was allowed to drink it. Right now it just seemed a cruelty, since she could use the haze, but couldn't take the chance with her baby's health.

Anyway, for some reason it all smelled sour and spoiled to her now. The pregnancy was making her nose do weird things.

Although Matteo smelled just as good as he ever had. The thought made her draw a little closer to him, breathe in the scent of him, some sort of spicy cologne mingling with the scent of his skin. She was especially tuned into the scent of his skin now, the scent of his sweat.

Dio, even his sweat turned her on. Because it reminded her of his bare skin, slick from exertion, her hands roaming over his back as he thrust hard into her, his dark eyes intent on hers. And there were no walls. Not then.

She blinked and came back to the present. She really had to stop with the sexual fantasies, they did her no good.

A photographer approached them. "Smile for me?" he asked.

Matteo drew her in close to his body, and she put her hand on his chest. She knew her smile looked perfect. She had perfected her picture smile for events such as these, to put on a good front for the Battaglia family. She was an expert.

Matteo should have been, as well, but he looked like he was trying to smile around a rock in his mouth, his expression strained and unnatural.

"A dance for the new bride and groom?" the photographer asked while taking their picture, and she was sure that in that moment her smile faltered a bit.

"Of course," Matteo said, his grin widening. Was she the only one who could see the totally feral light in his eyes, who could see that none of this was real?

The photographer was smiling back, as were some of the guests standing in their immediate area, so they must not be able to tell. Must not be able to see how completely disingenuous the expression of warmth was.

"Come. Dance with me."

And so she followed him out onto the glossy marble dance floor, where other couples were holding each other close, slow dancing to a piece of piano music.

It was different from when they'd danced in New York. The ballroom was bright, crystal chandeliers hanging overhead, casting shimmering light onto caramel-colored walls and floors. The music was as bright as the lighting, nothing darkly sensual or seductive.

And yet when Matteo drew her into his hold, his arms tight, strong around her, they might as well have been the only two people in the room. Back again, shrouded in darkness in the corner of a club, stealing whatever moments together they could have before fate would force them to part forever.

Except fate had had other ideas.

She'd spent a lot of her life believing in fate, believing that the right thing would happen in the end. She questioned that now. Now she just wondered if she'd let her body lead her into an impossible situation all for the sake of assuaging rioting hormones.

"This will make a nice headline, don't you think?" he asked, swirling her around before drawing her back in tight against him.

"I imagine it will. You're a great dancer, by the way. I don't know if I mentioned that…last time."

"You didn't, but your mouth was otherwise occupied."

Her cheeks heated. "Yes, I suppose it was."

"My mother made sure I had dance lessons starting at an early age. All a part of grooming me to take my place at the helm of Benito's empire."

"But you haven't really. Taken the helm of your father's empire, I mean."

"Not as such. We've all taken a piece of it, but in the meantime we've been working to root out the shadier elements of the business. It's one thing my brothers and I do not suffer. We're not criminals."

"A fact I appreciate. And for the record, neither is Alessandro. I would never have agreed to marry him otherwise."

"Is that so?"

"I've had enough shady dealings to last me a lifetime. My father, for all that he puts on the front of being an honorable citizen, is not. At least your father and your grandfather had the decency to be somewhat open about the fact that they weren't playing by the rules."

"Gentleman thugs," he said, his voice hard. "But I'll let you in on a little secret—no matter how good you are at dancing, no matter how nicely tailored your suit is, it doesn't change the fact that when you hit a man in the legs with a metal cane, his knees shatter. And he doesn't care what you're wearing. Neither do the widows of the men you kill."

Alessia was stunned by his words, not by the content of them, not as shocked as she wished she were. People often assumed that she was some naive, cosseted flower. Her smile had that effect. They assumed she must not know how organized crime worked. But she did. She knew the reality of it. She knew her father was bound up so tightly in all of it he could hardly escape it even if he wanted to.

He was addicted to the power, and being friendly with the mob bosses was what kept him in power. He couldn't walk away easily. Not with his power, possibly not even with his life.

And yet, the Correttis had disentangled themselves from it. The Corretti men and women had walked away from it.

No, it wasn't the content of his words that had surprised her. It was the fact that he'd said them at all. Because Matteo played his cards close to his chest. Because Matteo preferred not to address the subject of his family, of that part of his past.

"You aren't like that, though."

"No?" he asked. "I'm in a suit."

"And you wouldn't do that to someone."

"Darling Alessia, you are an eternal optimist," he said, and there was something in his words she didn't like. A hard edge that made her stomach tighten. "I don't know how you manage it."

"Survival. I have to protect myself."

"I thought that was where cynics came from?"

"Perhaps a good number of them. But no matter how I feel about a situation, I've never had any control over the outcome. My mother died in childbirth, and no amount of feeling good or bad about it would have changed that. My father is a criminal, no matter the public mask he wears, who has no qualms about slapping my face to keep me in line." They swirled in a fast circle, Matteo's hold tightening on her, something dangerous flickering in his eyes. "No matter how I feel about the situation, that is the situation. If I didn't choose to be happy no matter what, I'm not sure I would have ever stopped crying, and I didn't want to live like that, either."

"And why didn't you leave?" he asked.

"Without Marco, Giana, Eva and Pietro? Never. I couldn't do it."

"With them, then."

"With no money? With my father and his men bearing down on us? If it were only myself, then I would have left. But it was never only me. I think we were why my mother stayed, too." She swallowed hard. "And if she could do it for us, how could I do any less?"

"Your mother was good to you?"

"So good," Alessia said, remembering her beautiful, dark-haired mother, the gentle smile that had always put her at ease when her father was in the other room shouting. The sweet, soothing touch, a hand on her forehead to help her fall asleep. "I wanted to give them all what she gave to me. I was the oldest, the only one who remembered her very well. It seemed important I try to help them remember. That I give them the love I received, because I knew they would never get it from my father."

"And in New York? With me?"

"What do you mean?"

"You toed the line all of your life, Alessia. You were

prepared to marry to keep your brothers and sisters safe and cared for. Why did you even chance ruining it by sleeping with me?" His hold tightened on her, his voice getting back that rough edge. That genuine quality it had been missing since they'd stepped inside the hotel.

It was a good question. It was *the* question, really.

"Tell me, *cara*," he said, and she glimpsed something in his eyes as he spoke. A desperation.

And she couldn't goad him. Couldn't lie to him. Not now.

"Did you ever want something, Matteo, with all of yourself? So much that it seemed like it was in your blood? I did. For so many years. When we were children, I wanted to cross that wall between our families' estates and take your hand, make you run with me in the grass, make you smile. And when I got older...well, I wanted something different from you, starting about the time you rescued me, and I don't want to hear about how much you regret that. It mattered to me. I dreamed of what it would be like to kiss you, and then, I dreamed of what it would be like to make love with you. So much so that by the time I saw you in New York, when you finally did kiss me, I felt like I knew the steps to the dance. And following your lead seemed the easiest thing. How could I not follow?"

"I am a man, Alessia, so I fear there is very little romance to my version of your story. From the time you started to become a woman, I dreamed of your skin against mine. Of kissing you. Of being inside you. I could not have stopped myself that night any more than you could have."

"That's good to know," she said, heat rushing through her, settling over her skin. It made her dress, so lovely and formfitting a few moments ago, feel tight. Far too tight.

"I don't understand what it is you do to me."

"I thought... I was certain that I must not be so different from all your other women."

"There weren't that many," he said. "And you are different."

It was a balm to her soul that he felt that way. That she truly hadn't been simply one in a lineup. It was easy for her, she realized, to minimize the experience on his end. It had been easy for her to justify being with him, not being honest with him, giving him a one-night stand, because she'd assumed he'd had them before. It had been easy to believe she was the only one who'd stood to be hurt or affected, because she was the virgin.

That had been unfair. And she could see now, looking into his eyes, that it wasn't true, either.

"Kiss me," he said, all of the civility gone now.

She complied, closing the short distance between them, kissing him, really kissing him, for the first time in three months. Their wedding kiss had been nothing. A pale shadow of the passion they'd shared before. A mockery of the desire that was like a living beast inside of them both.

She parted her lips for him, sucked his tongue deep inside of her mouth, not caring that it would be obvious to the people around them. Matteo was hers now, her husband. She wouldn't hide it, not from anyone. Wouldn't hide her desire.

He growled low in his throat, the sound vibrating through his body. "Careful, Alessia, or I will not be responsible for what happens."

"I don't want you to be responsible," she said, kissing his neck. Biting him lightly. There was something happening to her, something that had happened once before. A total loss of control. At the hands of Matteo Corretti.

It was like she was possessed, possessed by the desire to have him, to take him, make him hers. Make him understand what she felt. Make herself understand what she felt.

"We can't do this here," he said.

"This sounds familiar."

"It does," he said. He shifted, pulled her away from his body, twining his fingers with hers. "Come with me."

"Where?"

"Somewhere," he said.

He led her out of the ballroom, ignoring everyone who tried to talk to them. A photographer followed them and Matteo cursed, leading them a different way, down a corridor and to the elevators.

He pushed the up button and they both waited. It only took a moment for the elevator doors to slide open, and the moment they did, she was being tugged inside, tugged up against the hard wall of his chest and kissed so hard, so deep, she was afraid she would drown in it.

She heard the doors slide closed behind them, was dimly aware of the elevator starting to move. Matteo shifted their positions, put her back up against the wall, his lips hungry on hers.

"I need you," he said, his voice shaking.

"I need *you*," she said.

Her entire body had gone liquid with desire, her need for him overshadowing everything. Common sense, self-protection, everything. There was no time for thought. This was Matteo. The man she wanted with everything she had in her, the man who haunted her dreams. This was her white knight, but he was different than she'd imagined.

There was a darkness to him. An edge she'd never been able to imagine. And she found she liked it. Found she wanted a taste of it. She didn't know what that said about her, didn't know what it meant, but at the moment, she didn't care, either.

"This is a beautiful dress," he said, tracing the deep V of the neckline with his fingertip, skimming silk and skin with the movement. Her breath hitched, her entire body on edge, waiting for what he would do next. Needing it more than she needed air. "But it is not as beautiful as you. And right now, I need to see you."

He reached around, tugging on the zipper, jerking it down.

"Careful," she said, choking on the word. "You'll snag the fabric."

"I'll tear it if I have to," he said.

The top fell around her waist, revealing her breasts, covered only by a whisper-thin bra that showed the outline of her nipples beneath the insubstantial fabric.

He lifted his hand and cupped her, slid his thumb over the tightened bud. "Hot for me?" he asked.

"Yes."

"Wet for me?" He put his other hand on her hip, flexed his fingers.

She couldn't speak, she just nodded. And he closed his eyes, his expression one of pained relief like she'd never seen before.

She put her hand between her breasts, flicked the front clasp on her bra, letting it fall to the elevator floor. He looked at her, lowering his head, sucking her deep into his mouth. An arrow of pleasure shot from there down to her core. She tightened her fingers in his hair, then suddenly became conscious of the continued movement of the elevator.

"Hit the stop button," she said, her voice breathless.

"What?" he asked, lifting his head, his cheeks flushed, his hair in disarray. Her heart nearly stopped. Matteo Corretti undone was the most amazing thing she'd ever seen.

"The elevator," she said.

He cursed and turned around, hitting the red button on the wall, the elevator coming to a halt. He cursed again and reached into his pocket, taking out his cell phone. "Just a second."

"You better not be texting," she said.

He pushed a few buttons, his eyes not straying to her. "Not exactly." He turned the screen toward her and she saw him. And her. And her breasts.

"Oh."

He pushed a few more buttons. "I have disabled the security camera now. Unless you like the idea of being on film."

She had to admit, she had a certain amount of curiosity as to what it looked like when Matteo Corretti made love to her. It was a video she wouldn't mind owning, in all honesty. But she didn't want it on security footage, either.

"Not in the mood to provide security with any early-evening jollies."

"No worries, I have now deleted that little stretch of footage. There are advantages to being a control freak. Having an app on your phone that lets you see all the security at your hotels, and do as you please with the cameras, is one of them."

He discarded his suit jacket and tie then, throwing them onto the floor of the elevator, tossing his phone down on top of them.

"Have you used that trick before?" she asked, before he lowered his head to kiss her again.

"With a woman?"

"Yes."

"Jealous?"

"Hell, yes," she said, not worried if he knew it. She wanted this moment, this desperation that was beyond anything she'd known, to be as foreign to him as it was to her.

"No, I haven't." He kissed her again, his tongue sliding against hers, and she forgot her lingering concerns.

Forgot about everything but what it felt like to have Matteo kissing her. Caressing her.

"Later—" he kissed the hollow of her throat "—I will do this right—" lowered his head and traced the line of her collarbone with his tongue. "I'll taste every inch of you. Take time to savor you. Take your clothes off slowly. Look at those gorgeous curves." He kissed her neck, bit her lightly like she'd done to him earlier. "Now, though… now I just need to be inside you."

He started to gather her skirt up in his hands, the slippery fabric sliding up her legs easily. "Take your panties off," he said.

She complied, her hands trembling as she worked her underwear down, kicking them to the side with her heels. He pushed her dress up around her hips, his hand hot on her thigh. He tugged her leg up around his, her back pinned against the wall of the elevator.

He tested her with his other hand, teasing her clitoris, sending streaks of white heat through her body with each pass his fingers made through her slick folds. "You didn't lie," he said. "You do want me."

"Yes," she said.

"Tell me," he said.

"I want you."

"My name."

"I want you, Matteo."

He abandoned her body for a moment, working at his belt, shoving his slacks and underwear down, just enough to free his erection so that he could sink into her. It was a shock, all those weeks without him, and she'd forgotten just how big he was. Just how much he filled her. She let her head fall back against the wall of the elevator, pleasure building deep inside her, her internal muscles tightening around his length.

And then there was no more talking. There was nothing but their ragged breathing, Matteo moving hard and fast inside her, blunt fingertips digging into her hips as he held her steady, thrusting into her.

He lowered his head, capturing her nipple in his mouth

again. A raw sound of pleasure escaped her lips and she didn't even care. She wasn't embarrassed at all.

Because this was Matteo. The man she'd always wanted. Wanted enough to break out of what was expected of her for the first time in her life. The man who had saved her, the man who made her angry and hurt her, the man who made her feel things she'd never felt before.

Matteo scared her. He confused her. He made her feel more than anyone else ever had.

And right now he was driving her to a point she'd never even imagined, to the edge of a cliff so high she couldn't see the bottom of the chasm below.

She was afraid to fall, afraid to let the pleasure that was building in her break, because she didn't know what would greet her on the other side. Didn't know what would happen. And something *would* happen. Something would change. There was no question. None at all.

And then he looked at her, those dark eyes meeting hers, and she saw him. Not the mask, the man. Raw need, desperation and a fear that mirrored her own.

He lowered his head, his lips pressing against her neck, his thrusts losing their measured rhythm. And something in her broke, released. And she was falling, falling into that endless chasm. But she wasn't afraid anymore.

Release rolled through her in waves, stealing every breath, every thought, everything but the moment.

And when she finally did reach bottom, Matteo was there, his strong arms around her. He was breathing hard, too, sweat on his brow, the back of his shirt damp, his heartbeat raging, so hard that, with his body pressed so tightly against hers, she could feel it against her own chest.

He stepped away from her slowly, running his hand over his hair, erasing the evidence that she'd ever speared her fingers through it. That she'd messed with his well-ordered control.

He adjusted his pants. Bent and collected his jacket, putting his phone back into his pocket. And she just stood there, her back to the wall, her dress still pushed partway up around her hips, the top resting at her waist, her underwear on the floor by her feet.

Matteo put his tie around his neck and started straightening it, too, before he looked at her. "Get dressed," he said.

"What?"

"Get dressed," he said. "We have to go back to the party."

"W-we do?"

"It's my charity," he said. "I have a speech to make." He checked his wristwatch. "And it seems I'm not too late for it so I really should try to manage it."

"I…"

"Turn around," he ordered, his voice harsh.

She did as he asked. He put her straps back into place, zipped the dress back up.

"My bra…"

"You don't need it," he said.

"What should I do with it?"

He opened up his jacket and indicated his inner pocket. She bent and scooped up her bra and panties and handed them to him, and he put both tiny garments into his pocket.

"Solved," he said.

She looked down at her chest, cupped her breasts for a moment. "I'm sagging."

"You are not."

He hit the button on the elevator and it started moving again, the doors sliding open. Then he hit the button for the first floor and they waited for the doors to close again.

Alessia felt…used. No, not even that. She just felt sad. Angry, because he was able to do that with her and then go back to his purely unruffled self.

Maybe she'd been making more out of them, and the sex, than she should have. Maybe she was wrong. Maybe it didn't mean anything to him. Nothing more than just sex, anyway, and a man like Matteo surely had it quite a bit.

They rode in silence, and the doors opened again. The photographer was still out there, wandering the halls. Looking for a photo op, no doubt.

Matteo put his arm around her waist and led her through the hall, that false smile back on his face. They started back toward the ballroom and she had the strangest feeling of déjà vu. Like they were back at the beginning of the night. Like their interlude in the elevator hadn't happened at all. But it had. She knew it had.

The photographer snapped a picture. And Alessia didn't bother to smile.

CHAPTER EIGHT

MATTEO WASN'T SURE how he managed to get up and speak in front of the large crowd of people. Not when he could see Alessia in the audience, her face smooth, serene, her dark eyes the only window to the storm that lurked beneath.

A storm he was certain would boil over and onto him once they were alone.

He found he didn't mind. That he welcomed the chance to take her on because it was better than the overwhelming, biting need to take her back to the elevator and have her again. To let the elevator continue up to his suite where he would have her again. And again. Tasting her this time, truly savoring her.

Yes, fighting was infinitely better than that. He would rather have her yelling at him than sighing his name in his ear.

Because he didn't know what to do with her, what to do about his desire for her.

It wasn't what he was used to. Wasn't normal in any way.

Sex was simply a need to be met, like eating or breathing. Yes, he liked some food better than he liked others, but he wasn't a slave to cravings. He believed in moderation, in exercising control in all areas of life.

Alessia was the one craving he didn't seem to be able to fight, and that meant he had to learn how.

Anything else was inexcusable.

"Thank you all for coming tonight, and for your generous donations. I am happy to announce that I am personally matching all of the donations given tonight. And that thanks to your generosity, it is now possible for the Corretti Education Foundation to branch out into college grants. It is my belief that a good education can overcome any circumstance, and it is my goal that every person be given that chance. Thank you again, enjoy the rest of the evening."

He stepped down from the podium, not paying attention to the applause that was offered up for his speech. He could hardly hear anything over the roar of blood in his ears. Could hardly see anything but Alessia. Which was one reason he allowed himself to be pulled to the side by some of the guests, interrupted on his way back to where his wife was standing.

He stopped and talked to everyone who approached him, using it as a tactic to keep himself from having to face Alessia without his guard firmly back in place. Cowardly? Perhaps. But he found he didn't care. Not much, at least.

Alessia didn't make a move to approach him; instead, she made conversation with the people around her. And every so often she flicked him a glare with those beautiful eyes of hers, eyes that glittered beneath the lights of the chandeliers. Eyes that made promises of sensual heaven, the kind of heaven he could hardly risk trying to enter again.

Every time he touched Alessia, she tore down another piece of the wall, that very necessary wall of control he'd built around himself.

People started to disperse, and as they both went along the natural line of people that wanted to converse with them, the space between them started to close. Matteo's blood started to flow hotter, faster, just getting nearer to Alessia.

No matter there were still five hundred people in the room. No matter that he'd had her against a wall an hour earlier. Still she challenged him. Still she made him react like a teenage boy with no control over his baser urges.

Yes, think about that. Remember what that looks like.

Blind rage. Two young men, still and unmoving, blood everywhere. And then a calm. A cold sort of emptiness. If he felt anything at all it was a kind of distant satisfaction.

And then he'd looked at Alessia. At the terror in her eyes.

And he'd done what he'd sworn he would never do.

He'd wrapped his arms around her and pulled her into his chest, brushing away her tears. He'd made her cry. Horrified her, and he couldn't blame her for being horrified. It wasn't the kind of thing a girl of fourteen, or any age, should ever have to see.

When he pulled away, when he looked down at her face, her cheeks were streaked with blood. The blood from his hands. Not the only blood he had on his hands.

He breathed in sharply, taking himself back to the present. Away from blood-soaked memories.

Except it was still so easy to see them when he looked at Alessia's face. A face that had been marred with tears and blood. Because of him.

The gap between them continued to shrink, the crowd thinning, until they met in the middle, in the same group. And there was no excuse now for him not to pull her against his side, his arm wrapped around her waist. So he did.

Alessia's body was stiff at his side, but her expression was still relaxed, her smile easy. A lie. Why had he never noticed before that Alessia's smile wasn't always genuine?

He'd assumed that it was. That Alessia displayed and felt emotion with ease and honesty. Now he wondered.

The last of the guests started to file out, leaving Alessia and Matteo standing in the empty ballroom.

He looked around, at the expansive room. This was his hotel, separate from his family dynasty, and often, looking at it, at the architecture, the expanse of it, filled him with a sense of pride. He had hotels all over the world, but this one, back in Sicily, a hotel that belonged to him and not to his family in any part, had always filled him with a particular amount of satisfaction.

Now it just seemed like a big empty room.

He picked up his phone and punched in a number. "Delay cleaning until further notice, I require the ballroom for personal use for a while."

Alessia looked at him, her dark eyes wide. "What do you need the ballroom for?"

He shrugged. "Anything I want." He walked over to the edge of the stage and sat, gripping the edge. "It is my hotel, after all."

"Yes, and you're a man who takes great pride in the ownership of whatever he can possess," she said.

"And why not?" he asked, loosening his tie, trying not to think of Alessia's fingers on the knot, trying not to imagine her fingers at the buttons of his dress shirt as he undid the collar. "That's what it's always been about in my family. I go out of town—" and off the grid "—and my bastard cousin has taken over my office. My younger brother has managed to charm his way into the top seat of the fashion houses for Corretti. So you see? In my family, ownership is everything. And if you have to stab someone to get it, all the better."

"Metaphorical stabbing?" she asked, wrapping her arms around her waist, as if holding herself together. He hated that. Hated that he might cause her pain in any way.

"Or literal stabbing. I told you, my family has a colorful history."

"You said you and your brothers weren't criminals."

"We're not. Not convicted, anyway," he added, not sure why. Maybe because, in his heart, he knew he was one.

Knew he could be convicted for assault several times over if evidence was brought before a court.

"Why are you saying this?"

"What do you mean, why am I saying this? I'm telling you the truth. Was what I did that day near your father's gardens legal? Answer me," he said, his words echoing in the empty room.

"You saved me."

"Maybe."

"They would have raped me," she said.

He remembered it so clearly. And yet so differently.

Because he remembered coming upon Alessia, backed up against a tree, a stone wall behind her, two men in front of her, pressing her back to the tree, touching her, jeering at her. They had her shirt torn. They were pushing her skirt up. And he'd known what they intended to do. The evil they meant for his angel.

And then he remembered seeing red.

He pushed off from the stage, standing and pacing, trying to relieve the restless energy moving through him. Trying to ease the tightness in his chest.

He hadn't simply stopped when he'd gotten those men away from Alessia. Hadn't stopped when they quit fighting back. He hadn't stopped until Alessia had touched his back. And then he'd turned, a rock held tightly in his hand, ready to finish what he'd started. Ready to make sure they never got up again, ready to make sure they could never hurt another woman again. Any other woman, but most especially Alessia.

But then he'd looked into her eyes. Seen the fear. Seen the tears.

And he'd dropped his hand back to his side, letting the rock fall to the ground. Letting the rage drain from his body.

That was when he'd realized what he had done. What he had been about to do. And what it had done to Alessia to see it. More than that, it confirmed what he'd always known. That if he ever let himself go, if he ever allowed himself more than his emotionless existence, he would become a man he hated.

"I did more than save you," he said. "A lot more."

"You did what you had to."

"You say it as if I gave it some thought. I didn't. What I did was a reaction. Blind rage. As I was, if you were not there, I wouldn't have ended it until they were dead."

"You don't know that."

"That's the thing, Alessia, I do know that. I know exactly what my next move was going to be, and trust me, it's not something people get back up from."

"I wish you could see what I saw."

"And I wish like hell you hadn't seen any of it," he said, his voice rough.

"You were...I thought...I thought they were going to get away with it. That no one would hear me scream. No one would stop them. I thought that they would do it. And then you came and you didn't let them. Do you have any idea what that meant to me? Do you know what you stopped?"

"I know what I stopped."

"Then why do you regret it so much?"

"I don't regret it, not like you mean." He could remember his father's face still, as he'd administered punishment to men in his debt. The calm. The absolute calm. But worse, he could remember his father's face when someone

had enraged him. Could remember how volatile, how beyond reason, he became in those situations.

And always, the old man had a smug sense that he had
done what must be done. Full and complete justification
for every action.

Just as Matteo had felt after Alessia's attack. How he
had felt after the fire.

"To me you were just a hero," she said, her words soft.

They hit him hard, like a bullet, twisted inside of him,
blooming outward and touching him everywhere, scraping his heart, his lungs. For a moment, he couldn't breathe.

"It's so much more complicated than that," he said.

"Not to me. Not to the girl you rescued. You were like...
You were every unfulfilled dream from my entire life,
showing up when I needed you most. How can you not
understand that?"

"Maybe that," he said, "is our problem now. You know
a dream, a fantasy, and I am not that man. I'm not the hero
of the story."

She shook her head. "You were the hero of my story
that day. And nothing will change that."

Coldness invaded him. "Is that what led you to my bed
that night?"

She didn't look away. "Yes."

He swore, the word loud in the empty expanse of the
ballroom. "So that was my thank-you?"

"No!" she said, the exclamation reverberating around
them. "It's not like that at all. Don't make it into something like that it's... No."

"Then what, Alessia? Your fantasy of a knight?" Her
cheeks turned pink and then she did look away. "*Dio*, is
that what it is? You expected me to be your chivalrous
knight in shining armor? What a disappointment this must
be for you. You would have likely been better off with
Alessandro."

"I didn't want Alessandro."

"Only because you lied to yourself about who I am."

"Who are you, then?" she asked. "You're my husband. I think you should tell me."

"I thought we went over this already."

"Yeah, you gave me that internet bio of a rundown on who you are. We told each other things we already knew."

"Why do we have to know each other?"

"Because it seems like we should. We're…married."

"Not really."

"You took me into an elevator and had me against the wall—what would make it more real for you?" she asked, the words exploding from her, crude and true, and nothing he could deny.

"That's sex, Alessia, and what we have is great, explosive sex. But that kind of thing isn't sustainable. It's not meant to be. It's not good for it to be."

"And you know this because you're constantly having spontaneous, explosive sex with strangers?"

"No."

"Then how do you know?"

"There's no control in it. No sense. We nearly let it get filmed, nearly let the elevator go to the next floor. Neither of us think when sex is involved."

"Maybe you think too much."

"And maybe you don't think enough. You feel, and look where all of that feeling has gotten you."

Her lip curled into a sneer. "Don't you dare blame this on me! Don't you dare act like it was me and my girlish feelings that led us here. That's far too innocent of a take on it, first of all. Yes, I might have built you up as a hero in my head, but what I wanted that night in New York had nothing to do with you being some kind of paragon and everything to do with me wanting you as a woman wants a man. I didn't want hearts and flowers, I wanted sex. And that was what I got. That wasn't led by my feelings," she said, her words cold, "that was led by my body and I was quite happy with the results."

"Too bad the price was so steep."

"Wasn't it?"

Alessia looked at Matteo and, for a moment, she almost hated him. Because he was fighting so hard, against her, against everything. Or maybe she was the one fighting. And she was just mad at him for not being who she'd thought he was.

And that wasn't fair, not really. He couldn't help it if he didn't line up with the fantasy she'd created about him in her head. It wasn't even fair to expect him to come close.

But no one in her life had ever been there for her, not since her mother. It had all been about her giving. And then he'd been there, and he'd put it all on the line for her, he'd given her all of himself in that moment. And yes, what he'd done had been violent, and terrifying in a way, but it was hard for her to feel any sadness for the men who would have stolen her last bit of innocence from her.

She'd grown up in a house with a criminal father who lied and stole on a regular basis. She knew about the ugliness of life. She'd lost her mother, spent her days walking on eggshells to try to avoid incurring any of her father's wrath.

But in all that time, at least, no one had forced themselves on her sexually, and considering the kind of company her father kept, it had always seemed kind of an amazing thing.

And then someone had tried to take that from her, too. But Matteo had stopped it.

"Do you understand how much of my life has been decided for me?" she asked.

"Yes," he said slowly, obviously unwilling to admit to not understanding something.

"I don't think you do. I spent my days mothering my siblings, and I don't regret it, because it had to be done, but that meant I didn't go away to school. It meant I stayed at home when a lot of girls my age would have been moving out, going to university. I went to events my father wanted me to go to, hosted parties in dresses he deemed appropriate. That day…that day on the road, those two men tried to take another choice from me. They tried to choose how I would learn about sex, how I would be introduced to it. With violence and pain and force. They tried to take something from me, and I don't just mean virginity, I mean the way I saw myself. The way I saw men. The way I saw people. And you stopped them. So I'm sorry if you don't want to have been my hero, but you were. You let me hold on to some of my innocence. You let me keep some parts of life a fantasy. I know about how harsh life can be. I know about reality, but I don't need to have every horrible thing happen to me. And it was going to." Her voice was rough, raw with tears she needed to shed.

She turned away from him, trying to catch her breath.

"And then my father told me that I was going to marry Alessandro. And I could see more choices being taken from me but this time I didn't see a way out. Then my friend Carolina said she would host a bachelorette party for me. And for once my father didn't deny me. I didn't know you would be there. And Carolina suggested we go to your hotel and I…well, then I hoped you'd be there. And you were. And I saw another chance to make a choice. So don't ask me to regret it."

His eyes were black, endless, unreadable. "I won't ask you to regret it, because then I would have to regret it, and I don't. When I found out I was your first…I can't tell you how that satisfied me, and I don't care if that's not the done thing, if I shouldn't care, because I did. I still care. I'm still glad it was me."

"I am, too," she said, her voice a whisper. The honesty cost them both, she knew.

His eyes met hers, so bleak, so filled with need. And she hoped she could fill it. Hoped she could begin to understand the man that he was and not just the man she'd created a fiction about in her head.

She nearly went to him then. Nearly touched him. Asked him to lie her down on the cold marble of the ballroom floor and make love to her again. But then she remembered. Remembered the question he hadn't answered. The one she'd been determined to get the answer to before she ever let him touch her again.

She'd messed up earlier. She hadn't been able to think clearly enough to have a conversation with him. But now, she would ask now. Again. And she would get her answer.

"Will you be faithful to me?" she asked.

He pushed his fingers through his hair. "Why do you keep asking me this?"

"Because it's a simple question and one I deserve the answer to. I'm not sleeping with you if you won't promise I'm the only woman in your life."

"I can't love you," he said, the words pulled from him. Not *I don't love you*, like he'd said earlier, but *I can't*.

"I'm not asking you to love me, I'm asking you to not have sex with other women."

His jaw tightened, his hands clenching into fists at his sides. "To answer that question, I would have to know how I planned on conducting our relationship, and I do not know the answer to that yet."

"Were you planning on asking me?"

He shook his head. "I already told you we won't have a normal marriage."

"Why?" She knew she shouldn't ask, not in such a plaintive, needy tone, but she couldn't help herself, couldn't hide the hurt that was tearing through her. How was it she'd managed to get her dream, only to have it turn to ash the moment her fingers touched it?

"Because I cannot be a husband to you. I can't. I won't love you. I won't… I can't give what a husband is supposed to give. I don't know where to begin. I have an empire to run, my hotels, plus I have my bastard cousin installed in my offices at the family corporation, with his ass in my chair, sitting at my desk like he's the one who worked so hard for any of it. I don't have time to deal with you. If you took me on as a husband you would have me in your bed and nowhere else. And I'm not sure I want to put either of us through that."

"But you are my husband. Whether or not you want to be doesn't come into it at this point. You are my husband. You're the father of my baby."

"And our baby has the protection of my name, the validity of having married parents. I'm able to strike the deal for the docklands with your father thanks to this marriage and your siblings will be cared for. I'm sending them all to school, I don't think I told you."

Her throat closed, her body trembling. "I… No, you didn't."

"My point is, regardless of what happens behind closed doors, our marriage was a necessity, but what we choose to do in our own home rests squarely on us. And there are decisions to be made."

Decisions. She'd imagined that if she married Matteo her time for decision making would be over before it ever started. But he was telling her there was still a chance to make choices. That them legally being husband and wife didn't mean it was settled.

In some ways, the opportunity to make decisions was a heady rush of power she'd only experienced on a few occasions. In other ways…well, she wanted him to want to be married to her, if she was honest.

You're still chasing the fantasy when you have reality to contend with.

She had to stop that. She had to put it away now, the haze of fantasy. Had to stop trying to create a happy place where there wasn't one and simply stand up and face reality.

"So…if I say I don't want to be in a normal marriage, and if you can't commit to being faithful to me, does that mean that I have my choice of other lovers, too?"

Red streaked his cheekbones, his fists tightening further, a muscle in his jaw jerking. "Of course," he said, tight. Bitter.

"As long as there are no double standards," she said, keeping her words smooth and calm.

"If I release my hold on you, then I release it. We'll have to be discreet in public, naturally, but what happens behind closed doors is no one's business but our own."

"Ours and the elevator security cameras," she said.

"That will not happen again."

"It won't?"

"An unforgivable loss of control on my part."

"You've had a few of those recently."

She'd meant to spark an angry reply, to keep the fight going, because as long as they were fighting, she didn't ache for him. Wasn't so conscious of the tender emotions he made her feel. And she wasn't so overwhelmed by the need to be skin to skin to him when they were fighting. But she didn't get anger. Instead, she got a bleak kind of pain that echoed in her soul, a hopelessness in his dark eyes that shocked her.

"Yes," he said. "I have. Always with you."

"I don't know how you are in other areas of your life. I only know how you are with me," she said.

His eyes grew darker. "A pity for you. I'm much more pleasant than this, usually."

"I make you misbehave."

He chuckled, no humor in the sound. "You could say that. We should go home."

She nodded. "Yes, we should."

They were in an empty ballroom, and she really would have loved a romantic moment with him here. The chance to dance as the only two people in the room. To go up to his suite and make love. To share a moment with each other that was out of time, apart from reality.

But they'd had their fantasy. Reality was here now, well and truly.

She still didn't want to leave.

Matteo picked up his phone and dialed. "Yes, you can send in the crew now."

She swallowed hard, feeling like they'd missed a key moment. Feeling like she'd missed one.

"Let's go," he said. There was no press now, no one watching to see if he would put his arm around her. So he didn't. He turned and walked ahead, and she followed behind him, her heart sinking.

Matteo didn't know what he wanted. And she didn't, either.

No, that was a lie, she knew what she wanted. But it would require her to start dealing with Matteo as he was, and at some point, it would require him to meet her in the middle, it would require him to drop his guard.

She wasn't sure if either of them could do what needed to be done. Wasn't sure if they ever had a hope of fixing the tangled mess that they'd created.

She wasn't even sure if Matteo wanted to.

CHAPTER NINE

MATTEO WAS TEMPTED to drink again. He hated the temptation. He hated the feeling of temptation full stop. Before
Alessia there had been no temptation.

No, that was a lie. The first temptation had been to
break the rules and see what the Battaglias were really
like. And so he had looked.

And from there, every temptation, every failing, had
been tied to Alessia. She was his own personal road to
ruin and there were some days he wondered why he bothered to stay off it.

At least he might go up in flames in her arms. At least
then heat and fire might be connected with her, instead of
that night his father had died.

Yes, he should just embrace it. He should just follow to
road to hell and be done with it.

And bring her with you. Bring the baby with you.

Porca miseria. The baby.

He could scarcely think of the baby. He'd hardly had
a moment. He felt a little like he was going crazy sometimes, in all honesty. There was everything that was happening with Corretti Enterprises, and he had to handle
it. He should go in and try to wrench the reins back from
Angelo, should kick Luca out of his position and expose
whatever lie he'd told to get there because he was sure the
feckless playboy hadn't gotten there on merit alone.

Instead, Matteo was tied up in knots over his wife. Bewitched by a dark-haired vixen who seemed to have him in a death grip.

She was the reason he'd left, the reason he'd gone up to a remote house he owned in Germany that no one knew about. The reason he hadn't answered calls or returned emails. The reason he hadn't known or cared he was being usurped in his position as head of his branch of the family business.

He had to get a handle on it, and he had no idea how. Not when he felt like he was breaking apart from the inside out.

The business stuff, the Corretti stuff, he could handle that. But he found he didn't care to, and that was the thing that got to him.

He didn't even want to think about the baby. But he had to. Didn't want to try to figure out what to do with Alessia, who was still sleeping in the guest bedroom in the palazzo, for heaven's sake.

Something had to be done. Action had to be taken, and for the first time in his life, he felt frozen.

He set his shot glass down on the counter and tilted it to the side before pushing the bottom back down onto the tile, the sound of glass on ceramic loud and decisive. He stalked out of the bar and into the corridor, taking a breath, trying to clear his head.

Alcohol was not the answer. A loss of control was not the answer.

He had to get a grip. On his thoughts. On his actions. He had a business to try to fix, deals to cement. And all he could think about was Alessia.

He turned and faced the window that looked out on the courtyard. Moonlight was spilling over the grass, a pale shade of gray in the darkness of night.

And then he saw a shadow step into the light. The brightness of the moon illuminated the figure's hair, wild and curling in the breeze. A diaphanous gown, so sheer the light penetrated it, showed the body beneath, swirled around her legs as she turned in a slow circle.

An angel.

And then he was walking, without even thinking, he was heading outside, out to the courtyard, out to the woman who woke something deep in his soul. Something he hadn't known existed before she'd come into his life.

Something he wished he'd never discovered.

But it was too late now.

He opened the back door and stepped out onto the terrace, walking to the balustrade and grasping the stone with his hands, leaning forward, his attention fixed on the beauty before him.

On Alessia.

She was in his system, beneath his skin. So deep he wondered if he could ever be free of her. It would be harder now, all things considered. She was his wife, the mother of his child.

He could send her to live in the *palazzolo* with his mother. Perhaps his mother would enjoy a grandchild.

He sighed and dismissed that idea almost the moment it hit. A grandchild would only make his mother feel old. And would quite possibly give her worry lines thanks to all the crying.

And you would send your child to live somewhere else?

Yes. He was considering it, in all honesty.

What did he know about children? What did he know about love? Giving it. Receiving it. The kind of nurturing, the father-son bond fostered by his father was one he would just as soon forget.

A bond forged, and ended, by fire.

He threw off the memories and started down the steps that led to the grass. His feet were bare and in that moment he realized he never went outside without his shoes.

A strange realization, but he became conscious of the fact when he felt the grass beneath his feet.

Alessia turned sharply, her dark hair cascading over her shoulder in waves. "Matteo."

"What are you doing out here?"

"I needed some air."

"You like being outdoors."

She nodded. "I always have. I hated being cooped up inside my father's house. I liked to take long walks in the sun, away from the...staleness of the estate."

"You used to walk by yourself a lot."

"I still do."

"Even after the attack?" The words escaped without his permission, but he found he couldn't be sorry he'd spoken them.

"Even then."

"How?" he asked, his voice rough. "How did you keep doing that? How did you go on as if nothing had changed?"

"Life is hard, Matteo. People you love die, I know you know about that. People who should love you don't treat you any better than they'd treat a piece of property they were trying to sell for a profit. I've just always tried to see the good parts of life, because what else could I do? I could sit and feel sorry for myself, but it wouldn't change anything. And I've made the choice to stay, so that would be silly. I made the choice to stay and be there for my brothers and sisters, and I can't regret it. That means I have to find happiness in it. And that means I can't cut out my walks just because a couple of horrible men tried to steal them from me."

"And it's that simple?"

"It's not simple at all, but I do it. Because I have to find a way to live my life. My life. It's the only one I have. And I've just learned to try to love it as it is."

"And do you?" he asked. "Do you love it?"

She shook her head. "No." Her voice was a whisper. "But I'm not unhappy all the time. And I think that's something. I mean, it has to count for something."

"What about now? With this?"

"Are you happy?"

"Happiness has never been one of my primary goals. I don't know that I've ever thought about it too closely."

"Everybody wants to be happy," she said.

Matteo put his hands into his pockets and looked over the big stone wall that partitioned his estate from the rest of the world, looked up at the moon. "I want to make something different out of my family. I want to do something more than threaten and terrorize the people in Palermo. Beyond that…does it matter?"

"It does matter. Your happiness matters."

"I haven't been unhappy," he said, and then he wondered if he was lying. "What about you, Alessia?"

"I made a decision, Matteo, and it landed me in a situation that hasn't been entirely comfortable. It was my first big mistake. My first big fallout. And no, not all of it has been happy. But I can't really regret it, either."

"I'm glad you don't regret me."

"Do you regret me?"

"I should. I should regret my loss of control more than I do—" a theme in his life, it seemed "—but I find I cannot."

"What about tonight? In the elevator? Why did you just walk away?"

"I don't know what to do with us," he said, telling the truth, the honest, raw truth.

"Why do we have to know what we're doing?"

"Because this isn't some casual affair, and it never can be." Because of how she made him feel, how she challenged him. But he wouldn't say that. His honesty had limits, and that was a truth he disliked admitting even to himself. "You're my wife. We're going to have a child."

"And if we don't try, then we're going to spend years sniping at each other and growing more and more bitter, is that better?"

"Better than hurting you? I think so."

"You've hurt me already."

"I did?"

"You won't promise to be faithful to me, you clearly hate admitting that you want me, even though as soon as we touch…Matteo, we catch fire, and you can't deny that. You know I don't have a lot of experience with men, but I know this isn't just normal. I know people don't just feel this way."

"And that's exactly why we have to be careful."

"So we'll be careful. But we're husband and wife, and I think we should try…try for the sake of our child, for our families, to make this marriage work. And I think we owe it to each other to not be unhappy."

"Alessia…"

"Let's keep taking walks, Matteo," she said, her voice husky. She took a step toward him, her hair shimmering in the dim light.

He caught her arm and pulled her in close, his heart pounding hard and fast. "I can't love you."

"You keep saying."

"You need to understand. There is a limit to what we can share. I'll have you in my bed, but that's as far as it goes. This wasn't my choice."

"I wasn't your choice?"

Her words hit him hard, and they hurt. Because no, he hadn't chosen to marry her without being forced into it. But it wasn't for lack of wanting her. If there was no family history. If he had not been the son of one of Sicily's most notorious crime bosses, if there was nothing but him and Alessia and every other woman on earth, he would choose her every time.

But he couldn't discount those things. He couldn't erase what was. He couldn't make his heart anything but cold, not just toward her, but toward anyone. And he couldn't afford to allow a change.

Alessia had no idea. Not of the real reasons why. Not the depth he was truly capable of sinking to. The man underneath the iron control was the very devil, as she had once accused him of being. There was no hero beneath his armor. Only ugliness and death. Only anger, rage, and the ability and willingness to mete out destruction and pain to those who got in his way.

If he had to choose between a life without feeling or embracing the darkness, he would take the blessed numbness every time.

"You know it wasn't."

She thrust her chin into the air. "And that's how you want to start? By reminding me you didn't choose me?"

"It isn't to hurt you, or even to say that I don't want you. But I would never have tied you to me if it wasn't a necessity, and that is not a commentary on you, but on me, and what I'm able to give. There are reasons I never intended to take a wife. I know who I am, but you don't."

"Show me," she said. And he could tell she meant it, with utter conviction. But she didn't know what she was asking. She had no way of knowing. He had given her a window into his soul, a glimpse of the monster that lurked beneath his skin, but she didn't know the half of it.

Didn't know what he was truly capable of. What his father had trained him for.

And what it had all led to seven years ago during the fire that had taken Benito's and Carlo's lives.

That was when he discovered that he truly was the man his father had set out to make him. That was when he'd discovered just how deep the chill went.

He was cold all the way down. And it was only control that held it all in check.

There was only one place he had heat. Only one way he could get warm. But it was a fine line, because he needed the cold. Needed his control, even with it...even with it he was capable of things most men would never entertain thoughts of. But without it he knew the monster would truly be unleashed. That it would consume him.

"I know what I'd like to show you," he said, taking a step toward her, putting his hand on her cheek. She warmed his palm. The heat, the life, that came from her, pouring into him. She shivered beneath his hand, as though his touch had frozen her, and he found it oddly appropriate.

If he kissed her, if he moved nearer to her now, he was making the choice to drag her into the darkness with him. To take what he wanted and use her to his own selfish ends.

He could walk away from her now and he could do the right thing. Protect her, protect their child. Give them both his name and a home, his money. Everything they would need.

She didn't need him in his bed, taking his pleasure in her body, using her to feel warm.

To court the fire and passion that could burn down every last shred of his control. It would be a tightrope walk. Trying to keep the lusts of his body from turning into a desire that overwhelmed his heart.

If he wanted Alessia, there was no other choice.

It was easy with her, to focus on his body. What he wanted from her. Because she called to him, reached him, made him burn in a way no other woman ever had.

With her, though, there was always something else. Something more.

He shut it down. Severed the link. Focused on his body. The burn in his chest, his gut. Everywhere. He was so hard it hurt. Hard with the need for her. To be in her. To taste her.

He could embrace that, and that only. And consign her to a life with a man who would never give her what she deserved.

In this case, he would embrace the coldness in him. Only an utter bastard would do this to her. So it was a good thing that was what he was.

He bent his head and pressed his lips to hers. It wasn't a deep kiss, it was a test. A test for him. To see if he could touch her without losing his mind.

She was soft. So soft. So alive. A taste of pure beauty in a world so filled with ugliness and filth. She reached into him and shone a light on him. On the darkest places in him.

No. He could not allow that. This was only about sex. Only about lust.

"Only me," she said when they parted.

"What?"

"You either have only me, or every other woman you might want, but before you kiss me again, Matteo, you have to make that decision."

His lips still tasted of her skin. "You." It was an easy answer, he found.

She put her hands on his face and drew up on her tiptoes. Her kiss was deep. Filled with the need and passion that echoed inside of his body. He wrapped his arm around her waist and relished every lush detail of holding her. Her soft curves, those generous breasts pressed against his chest. He slipped his hand over her bottom, squeezed her tightly. She was everything a woman should be. Total perfection.

She kissed his jaw, her lips light on his skin, hot and so very tempting. She made him want more, stripped him of his patience. He had always been a patient lover, the kind of lover who worked to ensure his partner's pleasure before taking his own. Because he could. Because even if he took pleasure with his body, his actions were dictated by his mind.

But she challenged that. Made him want so badly to lose himself. To think of nothing but her. Alessia. He was hungry for her in a way he had never hungered for anyone or anything.

He slid his hands over the bodice of her nightgown, cupped her breasts through the thin fabric and found she had nothing on underneath. He could feel her nipples, hard and scarcely veiled by the gauzy material.

He lowered his head and circled one of the tightened buds with his tongue, drew it deep into his mouth. It wasn't enough. He needed to taste her.

Her name pounded through his head in time with the beat of his heart. His need a living, breathing thing.

He gripped the straps of her gown and tugged hard, the top giving way. It fell around her waist, exposing her to him. He smoothed his hand over her bare skin, then lowered his head again, tasting her, filling himself with her.

He dropped to his knees and took the fabric in his hands, tugging it down the rest of the way, ignoring the sound of tearing fabric.

"I liked that nightgown," she said.

"It was beautiful." He kissed her stomach. "But it was not as beautiful as you are."

"You could have asked me to take it off."

"No time," he said, tracing a line from her belly button down to the edge of her panties. "I needed to taste you."

Her response was a strangled "Oh."

"Everywhere." He tugged at the sides of her underwear and drew them down her legs, tossing them to the side. He kissed her hip bone and she shuddered. "I think you should lay down for me, *cara*."

"Why is that?"

"All the better to taste you, *cara mia*."

"Can't you do it from where you are?"

"Not the way I want to."

She complied, her movements slow, shaky. It was a sharp reminder of how innocent she still was.

You let me hold on to some of my innocence.

Her words echoed in his mind as she sank to the ground in front of him, lying back, resting on her elbows, her legs bent at the knees.

No, he would not allow himself to be painted as some kind of hero. He might have saved her innocence then, but he had spent the past months ensuring that what remained was stripped from her. And tonight, he would continue it.

Keeping her bound to him would continue it.

It was too late to turn back now. Too late to stop. He put his hand on her thigh and parted her legs gently, sliding his fingers over the slickness at the entrance of her body. "Yes," he said, unable to hold the word back, a tremor of need racking his body.

He lowered his head to take in her sweetness, to try to satiate the need he felt for her. A need that seemed to flow through his veins along with his blood, until he couldn't tell which one was sustaining him. Until he was sure he needed both to continue breathing.

He was lost in Alessia. Her flavor, her scent.

He pushed one finger deep inside her while he continued to lavish attention on her with his lips and tongue. She arched up against him, a raw cry escaping her lips. And he took it as her approval, making his strokes with mouth and hands firmer, more insistent.

She drove her fingers deep into his hair, tugging hard, the pain giving him the slight distraction he needed to continue. Helping him hold back his own need.

He slipped a second finger inside of her and her muscles pulsed around him, her body getting stiff beneath him, her sound of completion loud, desperate. Satisfying to him on a level so deep he didn't want to examine it too closely.

He didn't have time to examine it because now he needed her. Needed his own release, a ferocity that had him shaking. He rose up, pausing to kiss her breasts again, before taking possession of her mouth.

He sat up and tugged his shirt over his head, shrugging his slacks down as quickly as possible, freeing his aching erection.

"Are you ready?" he asked. He needed the answer to be yes.

"Yes."

He looked at her face, at Alessia, and as he did, he pushed inside the tight heat of her body. He nearly lost it then, a cold sweat breaking out over his skin, his muscles tense, pain coursing through him, everything in him trying to hold back. To make this last.

"Matteo."

It was her voice that broke him. Her name on his lips. He started to thrust hard into her, and no matter how he told himself to take it slow, take it gentle, he couldn't. He was a slave to her, to his need.

Finesse was lost. Control was lost.

She arched against him every time he slid home, a small sigh of pleasure on her lips. He lowered his head, buried his face in her neck, breathing her in. Lilacs and skin. And the one woman he would always know. The one woman who mattered.

Sharp nails dug into the flesh on his shoulder, but this time, the pain didn't bring him back. He lost himself, let his orgasm take him over, a rush of completion that took him under completely. He was lost in a wave, and burning. Burning hot and bright, nothing coming to put him out. To give him any relief. All he could do was hang on and weather it. Try to survive a pleasure so intense it bordered on destructive.

And when it was over, she was there, soft arms wrapped around him, her scent surrounding him.

"Will it always be like this?" Alessia's voice was broken with sharp, hard breaths.

He didn't have an answer for her. He couldn't speak. Couldn't think. And he hoped to God it wouldn't always be like this because there was no way his control could withstand it. And at the same time he knew he couldn't live with her and deny himself her body.

He would keep it under control. He would keep his heart separate from his body. He'd done it with women all his life. He'd done it when his father had asked him to learn the family business. The night his father had forced him to dole out punishment to a man in debt to the Corretti family.

He had locked his heart in ice and kept himself from feeling. His actions unconnected to anything but his mind.

He could do it again. He would.

"We should go inside," he said, sitting up, his breathing still ragged.

"Yeah. I'm pretty sure I have grass stains in…places."

He turned to her, a shocked laugh bursting from him. A real laugh. He couldn't remember the last time he'd laughed and meant it. "Well, you should be glad I made quick work of your gown, then."

"You tore it," she said, moving into a standing position and picking up her shredded garment.

"You liked it."

He could see her smile, even in the dim light. "A little."

There was a strange lightness in his chest now, a feeling that was completely foreign to him. As though a rock had been taken off his shoulders.

"I'm hungry," she said.

She started walking back toward the house, and he kept

his eyes trained on her bare backside, on the twin dimples low on her back. She was so sexy he was hard again already.

He bent and picked his underwear up from the ground, tugging the black boxer briefs on quickly and following her inside. "Do you want to eat?" he asked.

"Yes, I do." She wandered through the maze of rooms, still naked, and he followed.

"And what would you like?"

"Pasta. Have you got an apron?"

"Have I got an apron?"

"You have a cook, yes?"

"Yes."

"Does he have an apron?"

"She." He opened the pantry door and pulled a short red apron off a hook.

Alessia smiled and slipped the apron over her head, tying it tight. She was a lot taller than the little round woman he'd hired to cook his meals. The apron came down just to the tops of her thighs and it tied in the back, exposing her body to him from that angle.

"Dinner and a show," he said.

She tossed him a playful glare, then started riffling through the cabinets. "What kind of pasta have you got?"

"Fresh in the fridge," he said.

She opened up the stainless-steel fridge and bent down, searching for a few moments before popping up with a container that held pappardelle pasta and another that had marinara sauce.

She put a pan of water on the stove, then put the sauce in another pan to reheat, and leaned back against the counter, her arms crossed beneath her breasts.

"Didn't you ever hear that a watched pot never boils?"

"No. Who says that?"

"People do," he said.

"Did your mom say it to you?"

"No. A cook we had, I think."

"Oh. It's the kind of thing my mother probably would have said to me someday. If she had lived."

"You miss her still."

"I always will. But you lost your father."

Guilt, ugly, strangling guilt, tightened in his chest. "Yes."

"So you understand."

He shook his head slowly. "I'm not sure I do."

"You don't miss him?"

"Never."

"I know your father was hard to deal with. I know he was...I know he was shady like my father but surely you must—"

"No," he said.

"Oh."

"Will you miss your father?"

"I think so. He's not a wonderful man, but he's the only father I have."

"I would have been better off without one than the one that I had."

Alessia moved to put the pasta into the pan. "You say that with a lot of certainty."

"Trust me on this, Alessia."

They stood in silence until the pasta was done. Matteo got bowls out of the cupboard and set them on the counter and Alessia dished them both a bowl of noodles and sauce.

"Nothing like a little post...you know, snack," she said, lifting her bowl to her lips, her eyes glued to his chest. "You're barely dressed."

"You should talk," he said.

She looked down. "I'm dressed."

"Turn around." She complied, flashing her bare butt to him. "That's not dressed, my darling wife."

"Are you issuing a formal complaint?"

"Not in the least. I prefer you this way."

"Well, the apron is practical. Don't go tearing it off me if you get all impatient." She took a bit of pasta and smiled, her grin slightly impish. It made it hard to breathe.

There was something so normal about this. But it wasn't a kind of normal he knew. Not the kind he'd ever known. He wasn't the sort of man who walked barefoot in the grass and then ate pasta at midnight in his underwear.

He'd never had a chance to be that man. He wondered again at what it would be like if all the things of the world could simply fall away.

"Matteo?"

"Yes?"

"I lost you for a second. Where were you?"

"Just thinking."

"Mmm." She nodded. "I'm tempted to ask you what about but I sort of doubt you'd want to tell me."

"About my father," he said, before he could stop himself.

"You really don't miss him?"

"No." A wall of flame filled his mind. An image of the warehouse, burning. "Never."

"My father has mainly ignored my existence. The only time he's ever really acknowledged me is if he needs something, or if he's angry."

Rage churned in Matteo's stomach. "Did he hit you?"

"Yes. Not beatings or anything, but if I said something that displeased him, he would slap my face."

"He should feel very fortunate he never did so in front of me."

Alessia was surprised at the sudden change in Matteo's demeanor. At the ice in his tone. For a moment, they'd actually been getting along. For a moment, they'd been connecting with clothes on, and that was a rarity for the two of them.

He was willing to try. He'd told her that. And he would be faithful. Those were the only two promises she required from him. Beyond that, she was willing to take her chances.

Willing to try to know the man she'd married. Past her fantasy of him as a hero, as her white knight, and as the man he truly was. No matter what that might mean.

"I handled it," she said.

"It was wrong of him."

She nodded. "I know. But I was able to keep him from ever hitting one of the other kids and that just reinforced why I was there. Yes, I bore the brunt of a lot of it. I had to plan parties and play hostess, I had to take the wrath. But I've been given praise, too."

"I was given praise by my father sometimes, too," Matteo said. There was a flatness to his tone, a darkness in his words that made her feel cold. "He spent some time, when I was a bit older, teaching me how to do business like a Corretti. Not the business we presented to the world. The clean, smooth front. Hotels, fashion houses. All of that was a cover then. A successful cover in its own right, but it wasn't the main source of industry for our family."

"I think…I mean, I think everyone knows that."

"Yes, I'm sure they do. But do you have any idea how far-reaching it was? How much power my father possessed? How he chose to exercise it?"

She shook her head, a sick weight settling in her stomach. "What did he do, Matteo? What did he do to you?"

"To me? Nothing. In the sense that he never physically harmed me."

"There are other kinds of harm."

"Remember I told you I wasn't a criminal? That's on a technicality. It's only because I was never convicted of my crimes."

"What did he do to you, Matteo?" Her stomach felt sick now, and she pushed her bowl of food across the counter, making her way to where Matteo was standing.

"When I was fifteen he started showing me the ropes. The way things worked. He took me on collection calls. We went to visit people who owed him money. Now, my father was only ever involved on the calls where people owed him a lot of money. People who were in serious trouble with him. Otherwise, his men, his hired thugs, paid the visits."

"And he took you on these...visits?"

Matteo nodded, his arms crossed over his bare chest. There was a blankness in his eyes that hurt, a total detachment that froze her inside.

"For the first few weeks I just got to watch. One quick hit to the legs. A warning. A bone-breaking warning, but much better than the kind of thing he and his thugs were willing to do."

"*Dio.* You should never have... He should never have let you see..." She stopped talking then, because she knew there was more. And that it was worse. She could feel the anxiety coming off him in waves.

She took a step toward him, put her hand on his forearm. It was damp with sweat, his muscles shaking beneath her touch.

"One night he asked me to do it," he said.

His words were heavy in the room, heavy on her. They settled over her skin, coating her, making her feel what he felt. Dirty. Ashamed. She didn't know how she was so certain that was what he felt, but she was.

"What happened?" She tried to keep her voice steady, tried to sound ready to hear it. Tried to be ready to hear it. Because he needed to say it without fear of recrimination from her. Without fear of being told there was something wrong with him.

She knew that as deeply, as innately, as she knew his other feelings.

"I did it," he said. "My father asked me to break a man's legs because he owed the family money. And I did."

CHAPTER TEN

MATTEO WAITED FOR the horror of his admission to sink in.
Waited for Alessia to turn from him, to run away in utter
terror and disgust. She should. He wouldn't blame her.

He also desperately wanted her to stay.

"Matteo..."

"These hands," he said, holding them out, palms up,
"that have touched you, have been used in ways that a man
should never use his hands."

"But you aren't like that."

He shook his head. "Clearly I am."

"But you didn't enjoy it."

"No. I didn't enjoy it." He could remember very vividly
how it had felt, how the sweat had broken out on his skin.
How he had vomited after. His father's men had found that
terribly amusing. "But I did it."

"What would your father have done to you if you
hadn't?"

He shook his head. "It doesn't matter."

"Yes, it does, Matteo, you were a boy."

"I was a boy, but I was old enough to know that what
my father did, what he was, was wrong."

"And you were trapped in it."

"Maybe. And maybe that would be an acceptable excuse for some people, but it's not for me."

"Why not? You were a boy and he abused you. Tell me,

and be honest, what did he say he would do to you if you didn't do it?"

Matteo was afraid for one moment that his stomach might rebel against him. "He told me if I couldn't do it to a grown man, there were some children in the village I might practice on."

Alessia's face contorted with utter horror. "Would he have done that?"

"I don't know. But I wasn't going to find out, either."

"He made you do it."

"He manipulated me into doing it, but I did it."

"How?" she asked, her voice a whisper.

"It's easy to do things, anything, when you can shut the emotion down inside yourself. I learned to do that. I learned that there was a place inside of myself as cold as any part of my father's soul. If I went there, it wasn't so hard to do." It was only after that he had broken. In the end, it was both the brokenness, and the cold, that had saved him.

His father had decided he wasn't ready. Didn't want his oldest son, the one poised to take over his empire, undermining his position by showing such weakness.

And after, the way he'd dealt with the knowledge that he'd lived with a monster, the way he'd dealt with knowing that he was capable of the very same atrocities, was to freeze out every emotion. He would not allow himself to want, to crave power or money in the way his father did. Passion, need, greed, were the enemy.

Then he'd seen Alessia. And he had allowed her a place inside him, a place that was warm and bright, one that he could retreat to. He saw happiness through her eyes when he watched her. His attraction to her not physical, but emotional. He let a part of himself live through her.

And that day when he'd seen those men attacking her, the monster inside him had met up against passion that had still existed in the depths of him, and had combined to create a violence that was beyond his control. One that frightened him much more than that moment of controlled violence in his father's presence had.

More even than that final act, the one that had removed his father from his life forever.

Because it had been a choice he'd made. It had been fueled by his emotion, by his rage, and no matter how deserving those men had been…it was what it said about himself that made him even more certain that it must never happen again. That he must never be allowed to feel like that.

"Do you see?" he asked. "Do you see what kind of man I am?"

She nodded slowly. "Yes. You're a good man, with a tragic past. And the things that happened weren't your fault."

"When I went back home the day of your attack, there was still blood all over me. I walked in, and my father was there. He looked at me, saw the evidence of what had happened. Then he smiled, and he laughed," Matteo spat. "And he said to me, 'Looks like you're ready now. I always knew you were my son.'"

That moment was burned into his brain, etched into his chest. Standing there, shell-shocked by what had happened, by what he had done. By what had nearly happened to Alessia. And having his father act as though he'd made some sort of grand passage into manhood. Having him be proud.

"He was wrong, Matteo, you aren't like him. You were protecting me, you weren't trying to extort money out of those men. It's not the same thing."

"But it's the evidence of what I'm capable of. My father had absolute conviction in what he did. He could justify it. He believed he was right, Alessia, do you understand that? He believed with conviction that he had a right to this money, that he had the right to harm those who didn't pay what he felt he was owed. All it takes is a twist of a man's convictions."

"But yours wouldn't be…"

"They wouldn't be?" He almost told her then, but he couldn't. The words he could never say out loud. The memory he barely allowed himself to have. "You honestly believe that? Everyone is corruptible, *cara*. The only way around it is to use your head, to learn what is right, and to never ever let your desire change wrong to right in your mind. Because that's what desire does. My father's desire for money, your father's desire for power, made them men who will do whatever it takes to have those things. Regardless of who they hurt. And I will never be that man."

"You aren't that man. You acted to save me, and you did it without thought to your own safety. Can't you see how good that is? How important?"

"I don't regret what I did," he said, choosing his words carefully. "I had a good reason to do it. But how many more good reasons could I find? If it suited me, if I was so immersed in my own needs, in my own desires, what else might I consider a good reason? So easily, Alessia, I could be like Benito was."

"No, that isn't true."

"Why do you think that?"

"Because you're…good."

He laughed. "You are so certain?"

"Yes. Yes, Matteo, I'm certain you're good. Do you know what I remember from that day? The way you held me after. Do you know how long it had been since someone had tried to comfort me? Since someone had wiped away my tears? Not since my mother. Before that, I had done all of the comforting, and then when I needed someone? You were there. And you told me it would be okay.

More than that, you made it okay. So don't tell me you aren't good. You are."

He didn't believe her, because she didn't know the whole truth. But he wanted to hold her words tightly inside of him, wanted to cling to her vision of him, didn't want her to see him any other way.

"I got blood on your face," he said, his voice rough. "That day when I wiped your tears."

She looked at him with those dark, beautiful eyes. "It was worth it." She took a step toward him, taking his hand in hers. "Come on. Let's go to bed."

And he was powerless to do anything but follow her.

Alessia woke the next morning with a bone-deep feeling of contentment. She noticed because she'd never felt anything like it before. Had never felt like things were simply right in the world. That there wasn't anything big left to accomplish. That she just wanted to stay and live in the moment. A moment made sweeter by the fact that there was nothing pressing or horrible looming in the future.

Then she became conscious of a solid, warm weight at her back, a hand resting on her bare hip. And she was naked, which was unusual because she normally slept in a nightgown.

A nightgown that was torn.

A smile stretched across her face and she rolled over to face Matteo. Her lover. Her husband. He was still sleeping, the lines on his forehead smoothed, his expression much more relaxed than it ever was when he was awake.

She leaned over and kissed his cheek, the edge of his mouth. She wanted him again. It didn't matter how many times he'd turned to her in the middle of the night, she wanted him again. It didn't matter if they had sex, or if he just touched her, but she wanted him. His presence, his kiss, him breathing near her.

This moment was one she'd dreamed of for half of her life. This moment with Matteo Corretti. Not with any other man.

She'd woken up next to him once before, but she hadn't been able to savor it. Her wedding had been looming in the not-too-distant future and guilt and fear had had her running out the door before Matteo had woken up.

But not this morning. This morning, she would stay with him until he woke. And maybe she would share his bed again tonight. And every night after that. He was her husband, after all, and it only seemed right that they sleep together.

They were going to try to make a real marriage out of a legal one.

He'll never love you.

She ignored the chill that spread through her veins when that thought invaded her mind. It didn't matter. She wouldn't dwell on it. Right now, she had a hope at a future she could be happy with. Matteo in her bed. In her life.

And she was having his baby. At some point, that would sink in and not just be a vague, sort of frightening, sort of wonderful thought.

But right now, she was simply lingering in the moment. Not wondering if Matteo's feelings would ever change, not worrying about changing diapers.

He shifted then, his eyes fluttering open. "Good morning," he said. So much different than his greeting the morning after their wedding.

"Good morning, handsome."

"Handsome?"

"You are. And I've always wanted to say that." *To you.*

"Alessia…you are something."

"I know, right?" Matteo rolled over onto his back and she followed him, resting her breasts on his chest, her chin propped up on her hands. "Last night was wonderful."

He looked slightly uncomfortable. Well, she imagined she wasn't playing the part of blasé sophisticate very well, but in her defense…she wasn't one. She was a woman with very little sexual experience having the time of her life with a man who'd spent years as the star attraction in her fantasies. It was sort of hard to be cool in those circumstances.

He kissed her, cupping her chin with his thumb and forefinger. She closed her eyes and hummed low in her throat. "You're so good at that," she said when they parted. "I feel like I have a post-orgasm buzz. Is that a thing?"

He rolled onto his side again and moved into a sitting position, not bothering to cover himself with the blankets.

"I don't know," he said. "I can't say I've ever experienced it."

"Oh." That hurt more than it should have. Not because she wanted him to have experienced post-orgasm buzz with anyone else, but because she wished he'd experienced it with her.

"What is it, *cara*?"

"Nothing." She put her palm flat on his chest and leaned in, her lips a whisper from his. Then his phone started vibrating on the nightstand.

"I have to take that," he said, moving away from her. He turned away from her and picked it up. "Corretti." Every muscle in his back went rigid. "What the hell do you want, Alessandro?"

Alessia's stomach rolled. Alessandro. She would rather not think about him right at the moment. She felt bad for the way things had ended. He'd been nice enough to her, distant, and there had been no attraction, but he'd been decent. And she'd sort of waited until the last minute to change her mind.

She got out of bed and started hunting for some clothes.

There was nothing. Only a discarded red apron that she knew from last night didn't cover a whole lot.

"I'm busy, you can't just call a meeting and expect me to drop everything and come to you like a lapdog. Maybe you're used to your family treating you that way, but you don't get that deference from me."

Alessia picked the apron up and put it on. It was better than nothing.

Matteo stood from the bed, completely naked, pacing the room. She stood for a moment and just watched. The play of his muscles beneath sleek, olive skin was about the sexiest thing she'd ever seen.

"Angelo?" The name came out like a curse. "What are you doing meeting with that bastard?" A pause. "It was a commentary on his character, not his birth. Fine. Noon. Salvatore's."

He pushed the end-call button and tossed the phone down on the bed, continuing to prowl the room. "That was Alessandro."

"I got that."

"He wants me to come to a meeting at our grandfather's. With Angelo, of all people."

"He is your cousin. He's family, and so is Alessandro."

"I have enough family that I don't like. Why would I add any more?"

"You don't even like your brothers?"

"No."

"Why don't you like your brothers?"

"Because if I ever do seem to be in danger of being sucked into the Corretti mind-set it's when we start playing stupid business games."

"But they're your family."

"My family is a joke. We're nothing but criminals and selfish assholes who would sell each other out for the right price. And we've all done it."

"So maybe someone needs to stop," she said, her voice soft.

"I don't know if we can."

"Maybe you should be the first one?"

"Alessia…"

"Look, I know I'm not a business mind, and I know I don't understand the dynamics of your family, but if you hate this part of it so much, then end it."

"I need to get dressed."

"I'll go make breakfast," she said. "I'm dressed for it."

"You might give my staff a shock."

"Oh—" her cheeks heated "—right, on second thought I might go back to my room."

"That's fine. And after that, you can ask Giancarlo if he would have your things moved into the master suite."

"You want me to move in?"

"Yes. You tramping back to your room in an apron is going to get inconvenient quickly, don't you think?"

Alessia felt her little glow of hope grow. "Yeah. Definitely it would be a little bit inconvenient. I would love to move into your room."

"Good." He leaned in and dropped a kiss on her lips. "Now, I have to get ready."

When Salvatore had been alive, Matteo had avoided going to his grandparents' home as often as he could. The old man was a manipulator and Matteo was rarely in the mood for his kind of mind games.

Still, whenever his grandmother had needed him, he had been there. They all had. This had long been neutral ground for that very reason. For Teresa. Which made it a fitting setting for what they were doing today.

Matteo walked over the threshold and was ushered back toward the study. He didn't see his grandmother, or any of the staff. Only a hostile-looking Alessandro, and Angelo sitting in a chair, a drink in hand.

"What was so important that you needed to speak to me?"

"Sorry to interrupt the blissful honeymoon stage with your new bride. I assume she actually went through with your wedding," Alessandro said.

"She did," he said.

Angelo leaned back in one of the high-backed chairs, scanning the room. "So this is what old Corretti money buys. I think I prefer my homes."

"We all prefer not to be here," Matteo said. "Which begs the question again, why are we?"

"You married Alessia, I can only assume that means you've cut a deal with her father?"

"Trade in and out of Sicily is secured for the Correttis and the docklands are ours. The revitalization project is set to move forward."

"Handy," Angelo said, leaning forward, "because I secured a deal with Battaglia, as well." Angelo explained the details of the housing development he was working on, eased by Battaglia's connections.

"And what does that have to do with us?"

"Well," Angelo continued, "it can have a lot to do with you. Assuming you want to take steps to unify the company."

"We need to unify," Alessandro said, his tone uncompromising. "Otherwise, we'll just spend the next forty years tearing everything apart. Like our fathers did."

Matteo laughed, a black, humorless sound. "You are my cousin, Alessandro, but I have no desire to die in a warehouse fire with you."

"That's why this has to end," Alessandro said. "I have a proposal to make. One that will see everyone in the family with an equal share of power. It will put us in the position to make the company, the family, strong again. Without stooping to criminal activity to accomplish it."

Alessandro outlined his plan. It would involve everyone, including their sisters, giving everyone equal share in the company and unifying both sides for the first time.

"This will work as long as this jackass is willing to put some of the extra shares he's acquired back into the pot," Alessandro said, indicating Angelo.

"I said I would," Angelo responded, his acquiescence surprising. Equally surprising was the lack of venom and anger coming from the other man. Or maybe not. Matteo had to wonder if Angelo had met a woman. He knew just the kind of change a woman could effect on a man.

"There you are," Alessandro said. "Are you with us?"

Matteo thought of the fire. Of the last time he'd seen his father. Of all that greed had cost. This was his chance to put an end to that. To start fresh. The past could never be erased, it would always be there. But the future could be new. For him. For Alessia. For their child.

He had too many other things in his life, good things, to waste any effort holding on to hatred he didn't even have the energy to feel.

He extended his hand and Alessandro took it, shaking it firmly. Then Matteo extended his hand to Angelo and, for the first time, shook his hand. "I guess that means you're one of us now," he said to Angelo. "I don't know if you should be happy about that or not."

"I'll let you know," Angelo said. "But so far, it doesn't seem so bad."

"All right, where do I sign?"

CHAPTER ELEVEN

MATTEO WAS EXHAUSTED by the time he got around to driving back to his palazzo. Dealing with Alessandro, going to his grandfather's house, had been draining in a way he had not anticipated. And yet, in some ways, there was a weight lifted. The promise of a future that held peace instead of violence. The first time his future had ever looked that way.

And he had Alessia to go home to. That thought sent a kick of adrenaline through him, made him feel like there was warmth in his chest. Made him feel like he wasn't so cold.

He left the car parked in front of his house with the keys in the ignition. One of his staff would park it for him later. And if not, he didn't mind it being there in the morning. But he couldn't put off seeing Alessia, not for another moment. He needed to see her for some reason, needed affirmation of who he was. To see her face light up. To have someone look at him like they didn't know who and what he was.

Alessandro and Angelo didn't know about his past, but they knew enough about the family to have an idea. Alessandro certainly hadn't escaped a childhood with Carlo without gaining a few scars of his own.

But Alessia looked at him like none of that mattered. Like she didn't know or believe any of it.

That isn't fair. She should know.

No, he didn't want her to know. He wanted to keep being her knight. To have one person look and see the man he might have been if it weren't for Benito Corretti.

He would change what it meant to be a Corretti for his child. He would never let them see the darkness. Never.

A fierce protectiveness surged through him, for the first time a true understanding of what it meant for Alessia to be pregnant.

A child. His child.

He prowled through the halls of the palazzo and found Alessia in a sitting room, a book in her hands, her knees drawn up to her chest. She was wearing a simple sundress that had slid high up her thighs. He wanted nothing more than to push it up the rest of the way, but he also found he didn't want to disturb her. He simply wanted to look.

She raised her focus then, and her entire countenance changed, her face catching the sunlight filtering through the window. Her dark eyes glittered, her smile bright. Had anyone else ever looked at him like that?

He didn't think they had.

"How did the meeting go?"

"We called each other names. Insulted each other's honor and then shook hands. So about as expected."

She laughed. "Good, I guess."

"Yes. We've come up with a way to divide Corretti Enterprises up evenly. A way for everyone to get their share. It's in everyone's best interests, really. Especially the generation that comes after us. Which I now have a vested interest in."

She smiled, the dimple on her left cheek deepening. "I suppose you do. And…I'm glad you do."

He moved to sit on the couch, at her feet, then he leaned in. "Can you feel the baby move yet?"

She shook her head. "No. The doctor said it will feel like a flutter, though."

"May I?" he asked, stretching his hand out, just over the small, rounded swell of her stomach.

"Of course."

He swallowed hard and placed his palm flat on her belly. It was the smallest little bump, but it was different than it had been. Evidence of the life that was growing inside her. A life they'd created.

She was going to be the mother of his child. She deserved to know. To really understand him. Not to simply look at him and see an illusion. He'd given her a taste of it earlier, but his need for that look, that one she reserved just for him, that look he only got from her, had prevented him from being honest. Had made him hold back the most essential piece of just why he was not the man to be her husband.

The depth to which he was capable of stooping.

Because no matter how bright the future had become, the past was still filled with shadows. And until they were brought into the sunlight, their power would remain.

"There is something else," he said, taking his hand from her stomach, curling it into a fist. His skin burned.

"About the meeting?"

"No," he said. "Not about the meeting."

"What about?"

"About me. About why…about why it might not be the best idea for you to try to make a marriage with me. About the limit of what I can give."

"Matteo, I already told you how I feel about what happened with your father."

"By that you mean when he took me on errands?"

"Well…yes."

"So, you don't mean what happened the night of the warehouse fire that killed him and Carlo."

"No. No one knows what happened that night."

"That isn't true," he said, the words scraping his throat raw. "Someone knows."

"Who?" she asked, but he could tell she already knew.

"I know."

"How?"

"Because, *cara mia*, I was there."

"You were there?"

He nodded slowly. Visions of fire filled his mind. Fire and brimstone, such an appropriate vision. "Yes. I was there to try to convince my father to turn over the holdings of Corretti to me entirely. I wanted to change things. To end the extortion and scams. All of it. But he wouldn't hear it. You see, at the time, he was still running criminal schemes, using the hotels, which I was managing, to help launder money. To help get counterfeit bills into circulation, into the right hands. Or wrong hands as the case may have been. I didn't want any part of it, but as long as my father was involved in the running of the corporation, that was never going to end. I wanted out."

"Oh," Alessia said, the word a whisper, as if she knew what was coming next. He didn't want her to guess at it, because he wanted, perversely, for her to believe it impossible. For her to cling to the white-knight image and turn away from the truth he was about to show her.

"I don't know how the fire started. But the warehouse was filled with counterfeiting plates, and their printing presses. That's one way to make money, right? Print your own."

He looked down at his hands, his heart pounding hard, his stomach so tight he could hardly breathe. "The fire spread quickly. I don't know where Carlo was when it broke out. But I was outside arguing with my father. And he turned and…and he looked at the blaze and he started to walk toward it."

Matteo closed his eyes, the impression of flames burning bright behind his eyelids. "I told him if he went back into that damned warehouse to rescue those plates, I would leave him to it. I told him to let it burn. To let us start over. I told him that if he went back, I would be happy to let him burn with it all, and then let him continue to burn in hell."

"Matteo...no." She shook her head, those dark eyes glistening with tears. She looked horrified. Utterly. Completely. The light was gone. His light.

"Yes," he said, his voice rough. "Can you guess what he did?"

"What?" The word was scarcely a whisper.

"He laughed. And he said, 'Just as I thought, you are my son.' He told me that no matter how I dressed it up, no matter how I pretended I had morals, I was just as bloodthirsty as he was. Just as hungry for vengeance and to have what I thought should be mine, in the fashion I saw fit. And then he walked back into the warehouse."

"What did you do?"

Matteo remembered the moment vividly. Remembered waiting for a minute, watching, letting his father's words sink in. Recognizing the truth of them. And embracing them fully. He was his father's son. And if he, or anyone else, stood a chance of ever breaking free, it had to end.

The front end of the warehouse had collapsed and Matteo had stood back, looking on, his hand curled around his phone. He could have called emergency services. He could have tried to save Benito.

But he hadn't. Instead, he'd turned his back, the heat blistering behind him, a spark falling onto his neck, singeing his flesh. And then he'd walked away. And he hadn't looked back, not once. And in that moment he was the full embodiment of everything his father had trained him to be.

He'd found out about Carlo's and Benito's deaths over the phone the next day. And there had been no more denial, no more hiding. No more believing that somewhere deep down he was good. That he had a hope of redemption.

He had let it burn in the warehouse.

"I let him die," he said. "I watched him go in, watched as the front end of the building collapsed. I could have called someone, and I didn't. I made the choice to be the man he always wanted me to be. The man I always was. I turned and I walked away. I did just as I promised I would do. I let him burn, with all of his damned money. And I can't regret the choice. He made his, I made mine. And everyone is free of him now. Of both of them."

Alessia was waxen, her skin pale, her lips tinged blue. "I don't know what to say."

"Do you see, Alessia? This is what I was trying to tell you. What you need to understand." He leaned forward, extending his hand to her, and she jerked back. Her withdrawal felt like a stab to the chest, but it was no less than he deserved. "I'm not the hero of the story. I am nothing less than the villain."

She understood now, he could see it, along with a dawning horror in her eyes that he wanted to turn away from. She was afraid. Afraid of him. He wasn't her knight anymore.

"I think maybe I should wait a few days to have my things moved into your room," she said after a long moment of silence.

He nodded. "That might be wise." Pain assaulted him and he tried to ignore it, tried to grit his teeth and sit with a neutral expression.

"I'll talk to you later?"

"Of course." He sat back on the couch and watched her leave. Then he closed his eyes and tried to picture her smile again. Tried to recapture the way she'd looked at him just a few moments before. But instead of her light, all he could see was a haunted expression, one he had put there.

* * *

Alessia was gasping for breath by the time she got to her bedroom. She closed the door behind her and put her hand on her chest, felt her heart hammering beneath her palm.

Matteo had let Benito and Carlo die.

She sucked in a shuddering breath and started pacing back and forth, fighting the tears that were threatening to spill down her cheeks.

She replayed what he had said again in her mind. He hadn't forced Benito or Carlo back into the burning building. Hadn't caused them harm with his own hands.

He had walked away. He had washed his hands and walked away, accepting in that moment whatever the consequences might be.

Alessia walked over to her bed and sat on the edge of it. And she tried to reconcile the man downstairs with the man she'd always believed him to be.

The man beneath the armor wasn't perfect. He was wounded, damaged beyond reason. Hurting. And for the first time she really understood what that meant. Understood how shut down he was. How much it would take to reach him.

And she wasn't sure if she could do it. Wasn't sure she had the strength to do it.

It had been so much easier when he was simply the fantasy. When he was the man she'd made him be in her mind. When he was an ideal, a man sent to ride to her rescue.

She'd put him in that position. From the moment she'd first seen him. Then after he had rescued her, she'd assigned him that place even more so.

The night of her bachelorette party…

"Damn you, Alessia," she said to herself.

Because she'd done it then, too. She'd used Matteo as part of her fantasy, as part of the little world she'd built up in her mind to keep herself from crumbling. She had taken him on her own terms, used him to fill a void, and never once had she truly looked into his. Never once had she truly tried to fill it.

Being there for Matteo, knowing him, meant knowing this. Meant knowing that he had faced down a terrible decision, and that he had made a terrible choice.

The wrong choice, at least in traditional terms of right and wrong.

Very few people would hold it against him that he hadn't raced into the burning building after his father, but to know that he had also not called for help. That he had meant what he'd said to his father. That he would let him, and all of it, burn. In flame. In greed. And he had.

Her lover, her Matteo, had a core of ice and steel. Getting through it, finding his heart, might be impossible. She faced that, truly faced it, for the first time.

Matteo might never love. The ending might not really be happy. The truth was, she lived her life in denial. The pursuit of contentment at least, at all costs, and if that required denial, then she employed it, and she'd always done it quite effectively.

Walking down the aisle toward Alessandro had been the first time she'd truly realized that if she didn't do something, if she didn't stop it, it wouldn't stop itself.

She wrapped her arms around herself, cold driving through her. She had another choice to make. A choice about Matteo. And she wouldn't make it lightly.

There was no sugarcoating this. No putting on blinders. It was what the wives of these Corretti men, of the Battaglia men, had always done. Looked the other way while their husbands sank into destruction and depravity, but she wouldn't do that.

If she was going to be Matteo's wife, in every sense, then she would face it all head-on.

It was empty to make a commitment to someone if

you were pretending they were someone they weren't. It was empty to say you loved someone if you only loved a mirage.

Love. She had been afraid of that word in connection to Matteo for so long, and yet, she knew that was what it was. What it had always been. At least, she'd loved what she'd known about him.

Now she knew more. Now she was going to have to figure out whether she loved the idea, or the man.

Matteo lay in bed. It was past midnight. Hours since he'd last seen Alessia. Hours since they'd spoken.

His body ached, a bleeding wound in his chest where his heart should be. The absence of the heart was nothing new, but the pain was. He had lived in numbness for so long, and Alessia had come back into his life.

Then things had started to change. He'd started to want again. Started to feel again. And now he felt like he was torn open, like the healed, scarred-over, nerveless pieces of himself had been scrubbed raw again. Like he was starting over, starting back at the boy he'd been. The one who had been taken into his father's hands and molded, hard and cruel, into the image the older man had wanted to see.

He felt weak. Vulnerable in a way he could never recall feeling at any point in his life.

Alessia had walked away from him, and he couldn't blame her. In a way, it comforted him. Because at least she hadn't simply blithely walked on in her illusion of who she wanted him to be. She had heard his words. And she'd believed them.

He should be completely grateful for that. Should be happy that she knew. That she wasn't committed to a man who didn't truly exist.

But he couldn't be happy. Selfishly, he wanted her back.

Wanted the light and heat and smiles. Wanted one person to look at him and see hope.

"Matteo?"

He looked up and saw Alessia standing in the doorway, her dark hair loose around her shoulders.

"Yes?" He pushed into a sitting position.

"I felt like I owed it to you to really think about what you said."

"And you owed it to you."

She nodded. "I suppose I did."

"And what conclusion have you come to?"

"You aren't the man I thought you were."

The words hit him with the force of a moving truck. "No. I'm sure in all of your fantasies about me you never once dreamed that I was a killer."

She shook her head. "I didn't. I still don't think you're that. I don't think you're perfect, either, but I don't think it was ever terribly fair of me to try to make you perfect. You had your own life apart from me. Your own experiences. My mistake was believing that everything began and ended during the times our eyes met over the garden wall. In my mind, when you held me after the attack, you went somewhere hazy, somewhere I couldn't picture. I didn't think about what you did after, not really. I didn't think of the reality of you returning home, covered in blood. I didn't think about what your father might have said to you. I knew Benito Corretti was a bad man, but for some reason I never imagined how it might have touched you. I only ever pictured you in the context of my world, my dreams and where you fit into them. It was my mistake, not yours."

"But I wouldn't have blamed you if you never imagined that. No one did. Not even my family, I'm certain of that."

"Still, I wasn't looking at you like you were a real person. And you were right to make me see."

"Alessia, if you want—"

"Let me finish. I see now. I see you, Matteo, not just the fantasy I created. And I don't want to walk away. I want to stay with you. I want to make a family with you."

"You trust me to help raise your child after you found out what I'm capable of?"

"That night of your life can't live in isolation. It's connected to the rest of your life, to all of it. To who your father was, the history of what he'd done to other people, to what he'd done to you."

"He never did anything to me, he just—"

"He forced you to do things you would never have done. He made you violate your conscience, over and over again until it was scarred. He would have turned you into a monster."

"He did, Alessia. That's the point. He did."

She shook her head. "You put a stop to it."

"I had to," he said, his voice rough. "I had to because you don't just walk away from the Correttis. It's not possible. My father would not have released his hold."

"I know. I understand."

"And you absolve me?"

"You don't need my absolution."

"But do I have it?" he asked, desperate for it, craving it more than his next breath.

She nodded. "If I have yours."

"For what?"

"For what I did. For not telling you about Alessandro. For agreeing to marry him in the first place. For trapping you in this marriage."

"You didn't trap me."

"You said—"

"Alessia, I have been manipulated into doing things far worse than marrying you, and I have done it with much greater coercion. A little news piece on what a jerk I am for not making your child legitimate was hardly going to force my hand."

"Then why did you do it?"

"To cement the deal. To give our child my name. All things I could have walked away from."

"Then forgive me, at least, for lying to you. For leaving you in the hotel room."

"I do. I was angry about it, but only because it felt so wrong to watch you walking toward him. To know that he would have you and not me. If I had known that there was a deal on the table that could be secured by marriage to you I would have been the one volunteering for the job."

A ghost of a smile touched her lips. "When my father first told me about the deal with the Correttis, that it would be sealed by marriage, I said yes immediately. I was so sure it would be you. And when it was Alessandro who showed up at the door to talk terms the next day I thought...I thought I would die."

"Waiting for your knight to rescue you?"

"Yes. I was. But I've stopped doing that now. I need to learn to rescue myself. To make my own decisions."

"You've certainly been doing that over the past couple of months."

"I have. And some of them have been bad, ill-timed decisions, but they've been mine. And I want you to know that I've made another decision."

"What is that?"

"You're my husband. And I'll take you as you are. Knowing your past, knowing the kind of man you can be. I want you to understand that I'm not sugarcoating it, or glossing over the truth. I understand what you did. I understand that...that you don't feel emotion the same way that I do. The same way most people do."

"Do you really understand that? I keep it on a leash for

a reason, Alessia, a very important reason, and I won't compromise it."

She nodded. "I know."

"And still you want to try? You want to be my wife? To let me have a hand in raising our child?"

"Yes. No matter what, you're the father of my child, Matteo, and there is no revelation that can change that. I don't want to change that."

"How can you say that with such confidence?"

"Because no matter what you might have done, you aren't cruel."

She leaned in and he took a strand of her hair between his thumb and forefinger. Soft like silk. He wanted to feel it brushing over his skin. Wanted to drown out this moment, drown out his pain, with physical pleasure.

"Am I not?" he asked.

"No."

"You're wrong there," he said. "So very wrong. I am selfish, a man who thinks of his own pleasure, his own comfort, above all else. No matter how I pretend otherwise."

"That isn't true."

"Yes, it is. Even now, all I can think about is what your bare skin will feel like beneath my hands. All I want is to lose myself in you."

"Then do it."

His every muscle locked up, so tight it was painful. "Alessia, don't."

"What?"

"Don't sacrifice yourself for me!" he roared. "Don't do this because you feel sorry for me."

"I'm not." She took a step toward him. "I want this because I want to be close to you. To know you. To be your wife in every way." A smile tugged at the corners of her lips. "I'm also not opposed to the orgasms you're so good at giving me. This is by no means unselfish on my part, trust me."

His skin felt like it was burning. Or perhaps that was the blood beneath his skin. Either way, he felt like he would be consumed by his need. His desire. Passion he swore he would never allow himself to feel.

Emotion he swore he would never feel.

But in this moment with Alessia, her eyes so bright and intense, so honest, he could hold back nothing. Deny her nothing. Least of all this.

She knew the truth, and still she wanted him. Not as a perfect figure, a knight in shining armor, but as the man he was. It was a gift he didn't deserve, a gift he should turn away, because he had no right to it.

But he had spoken the truth. He was selfish. Far too selfish to do anything but take what was on offer.

"Show me you want me." His words were rough, forced through his tightened throat. "Show me you still want me." Those words echoed through his soul, tearing through him, leaving him raw and bleeding inside.

Alessia wrapped one arm around his neck, her fingers laced in his hair, and put the other on his cheek. She pressed a kiss to his lips, soft, gentle. Purposeful. "Always."

There was no hope of him being noble, not now, not tonight. But then, that shouldn't be a surprise. He didn't do noble. He didn't do selfless. And it wouldn't start now.

He kissed her, deep and hard, his body throbbing, his heart raging. He wrapped his arms around her and pulled her in close, reveling in the feel of her. Touching Alessia was a thrill that he didn't think would ever become commonplace. He had hungered for her touch, for her closeness, for so many years, and he knew his desire for it would never fade.

If anything, it only grew.

He slid his hands down her waist, over her hips, her thighs, and gripped her hard, tugging her up into his arms, those long, lean legs wrapping around his waist as he walked them both to the bed.

Alessia started working on the knot on his tie, her movements shaky and clumsy and all the sexier for it. He sat on the bed, and Alessia remained on top of him, now resting on her knees. She tugged hard on the tie and managed to get it off, then started working at the buttons on his shirt.

He continued to kiss her, deep and desperate, pushing her dress up, past her hips, her waist, her breasts, and over her head. Her lips were swollen from kissing, her face flushed, her hair disheveled from where he'd run his fingers through it.

She looked wild, free, the most beautiful thing he'd ever seen. But then, Alessia had been, from the moment he'd seen her, the most beautiful sight he'd ever beheld. And then, when his vision of her had been one of innocence, protectiveness, it had been all about that glow that was inside of her.

He could see it, along with the outer beauty that drove him to madness. Now that their lives, their feelings, had no more innocence left, he could still see it. Still feel it deep inside of him, an ache that wouldn't ease.

She pushed his shirt off his shoulders, the buttoned cuffs snagging on his hands. A little growl escaped her lips. He wrapped one hand around her waist to hold her steady and lay back on the bed, leaving her perched over him, then he undid the buttons as quickly as possible and tossed the shirt to the side.

Alessia moved away from him, standing in front of the bed, in front of him. She met his eyes, and put her hands behind her back, her movement quick. Her bra loosened, then fell, baring her breasts to him. His stomach tightened, he could barely breathe.

She smiled, then hooked her fingers into the sides of her panties and tugged them off.

He wanted to say something. To tell her how beautiful she was, how perfect. But he couldn't speak. He could only watch, held completely under her spell.

She approached the bed, her fingers deft on his belt buckle, making quick work of his pants and underwear, and leaving him as naked as she was.

"You're so much more…just so much more than I ever imagined," she said. "I made fantasies about you, but they were a girl's fantasies. I'm not a girl, though, I'm a woman. And I'm glad you're not only that one-dimensional imagining I had of you. I'm glad you're you."

She leaned in, running the tip of her finger along the length of his rock-hard erection. Every thought ran from his head like water, his heart thundering in his ears.

Lush lips curved into a wicked smile and she leaned in, flicking her tongue over the head of his shaft. "I've never done this before. So you have to tell me if I do it wrong."

"You couldn't possibly do it wrong," he said, not sure how he managed to speak at all. It shouldn't be possible when he couldn't breathe.

And she proved him right. Her mouth on him hot, sweet torture that streaked through his veins like flame. But where other flames destroyed, this fire cleansed. He sifted his fingers through her hair, needing an anchor. Needing to touch her, to be a part of this. Not simply on the receiving end of the pleasure she was giving him.

He needed more. Needed to taste her, too.

"Get on the bed," he growled.

She complied, not abandoning her task as she got up onto the bed, onto her knees. He sat up and she raised her head, her expression confused. Then he grasped her hips and maneuvered her around so that she was over him, so that he could taste her like she was tasting him.

She gasped when his tongue touched her.

"Don't stop," he said, the command rough, firmer than he'd intended it to be, but she didn't seem to mind.

He slipped a finger inside of her while he pleasured her with his tongue, and she gasped again, freezing for a moment before taking him fully into her mouth. His head fell back, a harsh groan on his lips.

"I can't last much longer," he said.

"Neither can I," she panted, moving away from him, returning a moment later, her thighs on either side of his. She bent down and pressed a kiss to his lips. "Ready?" she asked.

"More than."

She positioned her body so that the head of his erection met with her slick entrance, then she lowered herself down onto him, so slowly he thought he would be consumed utterly by the white heat moving through him.

She moved over him, her eyes locked with his. He grasped her hips, meeting each of her thrusts, watching her face, watching her pleasure.

He moved his hand, pressed his palm flat over her stomach, then slid it upward to cup one of her breasts. He liked the view. Liked being able to see all of her as she brought them both to the brink.

She leaned forward, kissing his lips, her breath getting harsher, faster, her movements more erratic. He lowered his hand back to her hip and strengthened his own movements, pushing them farther, faster.

They both reached the edge at the same time, and when he tipped over into the abyss, all he could do was hold on to her as release rushed through him like a wave, leaving no part of him untouched. No part of him hidden.

When the storm passed, Alessia was with him.

She rested her head on his chest, her breath hot on

his skin. He wrapped his arms tight around her, held her to him.

He would keep her with him, no matter what.

Yes, he was a selfish bastard.

But in this moment, he couldn't regret it. If it meant keeping Alessia, he never would.

CHAPTER TWELVE

ALESSIA WOKE UP a few hours later, feeling cold. She wasn't sure why. It was a warm evening, and she had blankets, and Matteo, to keep her warm.

Matteo.

He made her heart feel like it was cracking apart. She wanted to reach him. Wanted to touch him. Really touch him, not just with her hands on his skin, but to touch his heart.

This was so close to what she wanted. A baby. The man she loved. *Dio*, she loved him so much. It made her hurt. Not just for her, but for him. For what she knew they could have that he seemed determined to wall himself off from.

A tear slipped down her cheek and she sat up, getting out of bed and crossing to the window. Now she was crying. She wasn't really sure why she was crying, either.

But she was. Really crying. From somewhere deep inside of herself. From a bottomless well that seemed to have opened up in her.

Why did she never get what she wanted? Why was it always out of reach?

Her mother's love had been there, so briefly, long enough for her to have tasted it, to know what it was. Just so she could feel the ache keenly when it was gone? And then there was Matteo. The man she'd wanted all her life. Her hero. Her heart's desire.

And when her father said she would marry a Corretti, of course it was Matteo who had come to mind. But she'd been given to Alessandro instead. And then, one more chance, Matteo at the hotel. And she'd managed to mess that up.

In the end, she'd gotten Matteo, but in the clumsiest, most dishonest way imaginable. Not telling him she was engaged, announcing to the world she was pregnant, forcing him to marry her, in a sense.

And now there was this…this heat between them that didn't go deeper than skin on his side. This love that was burning a hole through her soul, that he would never, ever be able to return.

"Alessia?" She turned and saw Matteo sitting up, his voice filled with concern. "Are you okay? Did I hurt you?"

"No." She shook her head. And he hadn't. She'd hurt herself. "I was just…thinking." There was no point in hiding the tears. Her voice was wobbly, watery. Too late to bother with the fiction that she was fine.

"About what?"

She bit her lip. Then opted for some form of honesty. "I've been pretending."

"What do you mean?"

"My whole life. I thought if I pretended to be happy, if I made the best of what I had, that I would be okay not having it all. That if I smiled enough I would get past my mother being gone. That my father's most recent slap to my face hadn't hurt me deeper than I wanted to admit. I had to, because someone had to show my brothers and sisters that you made a choice about how you handled life. We only had what we had, and I didn't want them…I didn't want them to be sad, or to see me sad. So I protected them from what I could. I made sure they didn't know how hard it was. How bad it was. I've been carrying around the burden of everyone's happiness and just trying to make what

I had work. But I'm not happy." It burst from her, truer than any words she'd ever spoken. "I don't want to smile about my childhood. It was horrible. My father was horrible. And I had to care for my siblings and it was so hard." She wiped at a tear on her cheek, tried to stop her hands from shaking. But she couldn't.

She couldn't stop shaking.

"I love them, so much, so I hate to even admit this but...I was willing to give everything for them. And no one...no one has ever given even the smallest thing for me. And I'm sorry if that makes me a bad person but I want someone to care. I want someone to care about me."

"Alessia..."

"I'm sorry," she said, wiping at more tears. "This is... probably hormones talking."

"Is it?"

She nodded, biting her lip to keep a sob from escaping. "I'm feeling sorry for myself a little too late."

"Tell me what you want, Alessia."

It was a command, and since he was the first person to ever ask, she felt compelled to answer.

"I wish someone loved me."

"Your brothers and sisters do."

She nodded. "I know they do."

Matteo watched Alessia, her body bent in despair, her expression desolate, and felt like someone was stabbing him.

Her admission was so stark, so painful. He realized then that he had put her in a position, as his angel, his light, and he had never once sought out whether or not she needed something.

He was taking from her instead. Draining her light. Using it to illuminate the dark and void places in himself. Using her to warm his soul, and he was costing her.

Just another person intent on taking from her for his own selfish needs.

"It's not the same as what you mean, though, is it?" he asked slowly.

"It's just…I can't really be myself around them," she said. "I can't show them my pain. I can't…I can't let my guard drop for a moment because then they might know, and they'll feel like they're a burden, and I just…don't want them to carry that. It's not fair."

"But what about you?"

"What about me?"

Matteo felt like someone had placed a rock in his stomach. Only hours ago, he had been content to hold Alessia tight against him. Content to keep her because she had accepted who he was, hadn't she?

But he saw now. He saw that Alessia accepted far less than she should. That she gave at the expense of herself. That she would keep doing it until the light in her had been used up. And he would be the worst offender. Because he was too closed off, too dark, to offer anything in return.

Sex wouldn't substitute, no matter how much he wanted to pretend it might. That as long as he could keep her sleepy, and naked and satisfied, he was giving.

But they were having a baby, a child. She was his wife. And life, the need for support, for touch, for caring, went well outside the bedroom. He knew that, as keenly as he knew he couldn't give it.

"I have to go," he said, his words leaden.

"What?"

"I have to go down to my offices for a few hours."

"It's four in the morning."

"I know, but this cannot wait."

"Okay," she said.

Damn her for accepting it. Damn him for making her. He bent down and started collecting his clothes, running his fingers over his silk tie, remembering how she'd undone it only hours before with shaking fingers. How she'd kissed him. How she'd given to him.

He dressed quickly, Alessia still standing by the window, frozen, watching him.

He did the buttons on his shirt cuffs and opened his closet, retrieving his suit jacket. Then he took a breath, and turned his back on Alessia.

"I should be back later today. Feel free to go back to bed."

"In here?"

"Perhaps it would be best if you went back to your room. You haven't had your things moved, after all."

"But I made my decision."

"Perhaps I haven't made mine."

"You said you had earlier."

"Yes, I did, and then you decided you needed more time to think about it. Now I would like an extension, as well. That seems fair, doesn't it?"

He took his phone off the nightstand and curled his fingers around it. A flashback assaulted him. Of how it had been when he'd turned his back on the burning warehouse, leaving the people inside of it to deal with the consequences of their actions without his help.

But this was different. He was walking away for different reasons. It wasn't about freeing himself. This was about freeing her.

And when he returned home later in the day, perhaps he would have the strength to do it. To do what needed to be done.

Alessia didn't go back to sleep. Instead, she wandered around the palazzo like a zombie, trying to figure out why she'd exploded all over Matteo like that. And why he'd responded like he had.

It was this love business. It sucked, in her opinion.

Suddenly she'd felt like she was being torn open, like she was too full to hold everything in. Like she'd glossed over everything with that layer of contentment she'd become so good at cultivating.

She wanted more than that, and she wasn't sure why. Wasn't sure why she couldn't just keep making the best of things. She had Matteo. That should be enough.

But it wasn't.

Because you don't really have him.

She didn't. She had his name. She was married to him. She was having his baby, sharing his bed and his body, but she didn't really have him. Because the core of him remained off-limits to her. Not just her, but to everyone.

She wanted it all. Whether she should or not. Whether it made sense or not. But that was love. Which brought her back around to love sucking. Because if she could just put on a smile and deal with it, if she could just take what he was giving and not ask for any more, she was sure there could be some kind of happiness there.

But there wouldn't be joy. There wouldn't be anything deep and lasting. And she was tired of taking less than what she wanted to keep from making waves. She was so tired of it she thought she might break beneath the strain of it.

"Buongiorno."

Alessia turned and saw Matteo standing in the doorway, his hair a mess, as though he'd run his fingers through it a few too many times, his tie undone, his shirt unbuttoned at the collar. His jacket had been discarded somewhere else.

"Hello, Matteo. Did you have a good day at work?"

"I didn't go to work," he said.

His admission hit her hard. "You didn't?"

"No. I was running again. Like I did the day of your first wedding. That was what I did, you know. You asked me to go to the airport, and I nearly went. But in the end I was too angry at you. For lying. For being ready to marry him. So I went to my house in Germany, mainly because no one knows about it. And I did my best to be impossible to reach, because I didn't want to deal with any accusations. I didn't want to hear from my family. And I didn't want to hear from you, because I knew you would be too much of a temptation for me to resist. That if I read your emails or listened to your messages, I would want you back. That I would come back to you."

"So you hid instead?"

"It was easier. And today I thought I might do the same thing. Because I don't like to see you cry. I don't like seeing you sad, knowing that it's my fault."

"It's not your fault."

"Mainly I just drove," he said, as if she hadn't spoken. "A little too fast, but that's what a Ferrari is for."

"I suppose so."

"I've come to a decision."

"Wait, before you say anything, I want to say something."

"Why is it your turn?"

"Because you left this morning before I could finish. All right, not really, I didn't know what I was going to say then. But I do now."

"And what are you going to say?"

"I love you, Matteo. I think, in some ways, I always have. But more over the past months, more still when you told me your story. I am in love with you, and I want you to love me back. I'm tired of not having everything, and I think you and I could have everything. But you have to let us."

"Alessia…I can't."

"You can, you just have to… you have to…"

"What? I have to forget a lifetime of conditioning? I

have to ignore the fact that my losing control, that my embracing emotion, might have horrible, devastating consequences, not just for you, but for our child? I have to ignore what I know to be true about myself, about my blood, and just…let it all go? Do you want me to just forget that I'm the sort of man who walked away and left his father to die in a burning warehouse? To just take that off like old clothes and put on something new? It wouldn't work. Even if it did it would be dangerous. I can't forget. I have to keep control."

"I don't believe you," she said.

"You don't believe me? Did you not listen to what I told you? Did you not understand? All of that, breaking that man's legs, leaving my father, that was what I am capable of when I have the most rigid control of myself. What I did to those men who attacked you? That blind rage? I didn't know what I was doing. I had no control, and if you hadn't stopped me…I would have killed them. I would have killed them and never felt an ounce of guilt for it."

"So you would have killed rapists, am I supposed to believe that makes you a bad, horrible, irredeemable person? That you would have done what you had to do to save a young girl?"

"That isn't the point," he said. "As long as I control it…as long as I don't feel, I won't do something I regret. I won't do something beyond myself. Even with control, do you see what I can do? What I have done? I can never afford to let it go. I can't afford—"

"I don't believe it. That isn't it. You're running scared, Matteo. You aren't afraid of losing control, you're afraid that if you feel you're going to have to face the guilt. The grief. You're hiding from the consequences of your actions. Hiding behind this blessed wall of cold and ice, but you can't live there forever."

"Yes, I can."

"No, you can't. Because at least for the sake of our child, our baby, Matteo, you have to break out of it."

"Has it ever once occurred to you that I don't want to?" he roared. "I don't want to feel, Alessia, I damn well don't. I don't want to face what I've done. To feel the full impact of my life. Of what was done to me. I don't want it. I don't need it. And I don't want you."

She stepped back, her body going numb suddenly. Shock. It must be that. Her body's defense because if it allowed her to feel the pain, she would collapse at his feet.

"You don't want me?" she asked.

"No. I never did. Not outside the bedroom. I told you that if you didn't expect love we would be fine. It was the one thing I told you could never be. I said no love. I promised faithfulness, a place in my home, my bed, what more did you want? I offered everything!"

"You offered me nothing," she said, her voice quivering, a slow ache starting to break through the numbness, shards of pain pushing through. "None of that means anything if you're withholding the only thing I really want."

"My love is so important? When has love ever given you anything but pain, Alessia?"

"I don't know because I've never had it for long enough to see."

"Then why make it so important?"

"Because I deserve it!" She broke then, tears spilling down her cheeks. "Don't I deserve it, Matteo?"

Matteo's face paled, and he took a step back. "Yes."

She didn't take it as a sign that she had gotten what she wanted. No, Matteo looked like someone had died.

She didn't say anything. She just waited.

"You deserve that," he said finally. "And you won't get it from me."

"Can't you just try?"

He shook his head. "I can't."

"Stop being so bloody noble. Stop being so repressed. Fight for us. Fight for this."

"No. I won't hold you to me. I won't hold you to this. That is one thing I will do for you, one thing I'll do right."

"You really think removing yourself is the only way to fix something? Keeping yourself distant?" It broke her heart. More than his rejection, it was his view of himself that left her crippled with pain.

"It's a kindness, Alessia. The best thing I've ever done. Trust me."

He turned and walked out of the room, left her standing there in the massive sitting area by herself. She couldn't cry. Couldn't bring herself to make the sound of pain that was building inside her. Endless. Bereft.

She wanted to collapse. But she couldn't. Because she had to stand strong for her child. Matteo might have walked away, but it didn't change the fact that they were having a baby. Didn't change the fact that she would be a mother in under six months.

It didn't change the fact that, no matter what, she loved Matteo Corretti with everything she had in her.

But she would never go back and demand less. Would never undo what she'd said to him. Because she had a right to ask for more. Had a right to expect more. She was willing to give to Matteo. To love him no matter who he was. No matter what he had done.

But she needed his love in return. Because she wasn't playing at love, it was real. And she refused to play at happiness, to feign joy.

She sank into one of the plush love seats, the pain from her chest spreading to the rest of her body.

She had a feeling there would be no happiness, fake or genuine, for a very long time.

CHAPTER THIRTEEN

MATTEO DIDN'T BOTHER with alcohol this time. He didn't deserve to have any of the reality of the past few hours blunted for his own comfort. He deserved for it to cut him open.

He shifted into Fifth and pushed harder on the gas pedal. Driving always helped him sort through things. And it helped him get farther away from his problems while he did it. But Alessia didn't feel any farther away.

She was with him. In him. Beneath his skin and, he feared, past his defenses.

Those defenses he had just given all to protect.

You aren't afraid of losing control, you're afraid that if you feel you're going to have to face the guilt.

That was just what he was. Afraid. To his very core.

He was scared that if he reached a hand out and asked for redemption it would truly be beyond his reach. He was afraid that if he let the door open on his emotions there would be nothing but pain, and grief, and the unending lash of guilt for all he had done, both under his father's influence, and the night of the fire.

He was afraid that he would expose himself, let himself feel it all, and he would still fall short for Alessia. That he wouldn't know how to be a real husband, or a real father.

He was afraid to want it. Afraid to try it.

She wanted him to fight for them. Nothing good came from him fighting.

Except the time you saved her.

Yes, there was that. He had always held that moment up as a banner displaying what happened when he lost control. A reminder that, as dangerous as he was in general, it was when he felt passion that he truly became a monster.

He pulled his car over to the side of the road, heart pounding, and he closed his eyes, let himself picture that day fully.

The fear in Alessia's eyes. The way those men had touched her. The rage that had poured through him.

And he knew one thing for certain in that moment. That no matter how blinded he was by anger, he would never hurt Alessia. He would never hurt his child. No, his emotions, not his mind, told him emphatically that he would die before he let any harm come to them.

That he would give everything to keep them safe.

He had been so certain, all this time, that his mind would protect him, but it had been his heart that had demanded he do whatever it took to save Alessia Battaglia from harm. It had been his heart that had demanded he spend that night in New York with her.

And it was his heart that was crumbling into pieces now. There was no protecting his defenses, because Alessia had slipped in beneath them years ago, before they had fully formed, and she was destroying them now from the inside out.

Matteo put his head on the steering wheel, his body shaking as pain worked its way through him, spreading through his veins like poison.

Something in him cracked open, every feeling, every desire, every deep need, suddenly acute and sharp. It was too much. Because it was everything all at once. Grief for the boy he'd been, for the man his father had become and what the end had done to both of them. Justification because he'd done what he had for his whole family. To free everyone. To free himself. Guilt, anguish, because in some ways he would always regret it.

And a desperate longing for redemption. A desperate wish he could go back to the beginning, to the start of it all, and take the path that would form him into Alessia's white knight. So that he could truly be the man she'd seen.

Alessia. He thought of her face. Her bright smile. Her tears.

Of meeting her eyes in the mirror at a bar, and feeling a sense of certainty, so deep, so true, he hadn't even tried to fight it.

And he felt something else. A light, flooding through his soul, touching everything. Only this time, it wasn't brief. Wasn't temporary. It stayed. It shone on everything, the ugly, the unfinished and the good. It showed him for what he was, what he could be.

Love. He loved Alessia. He had loved her all of his life.

And he wasn't the man that she should have. He wasn't the man he could have been if things had gone differently.

But with love came hope. A hope that he could try. A hope for redemption. A hope for the future.

For every dirty, broken feeling that he'd unleashed inside of him, he had let loose the good to combat it.

He had never imagined that. Had never believed that there was so much lightness in him.

It was Alessia. His love for her. His hope for their future.

He might not be the man she'd once imagined. He might not be the man he might have been in different circumstances. But that man was the one that Alessia deserved and no less.

So he would become that man. Because he loved Alessia too much to offer her less.

Matteo picked up his phone, and dialed a number he rarely used if he could help it. But this was the start. The start of changing. He was too tired to keep fighting, anyway. Too tired to continue a rivalry he simply didn't want to be involved in. A rivalry created by his father, by Alessandro's father. They both hated those bastards so what was the point of honoring a hatred created and fostered by them?

No more. It had to end.

"Corretti."

"It's Matteo."

"Ah, Matteo." Alessandro didn't sound totally thrilled to hear from him.

"How is everything going? In terms of unifying the business?"

"Fine."

"Great. That's not exactly why I called."

"Why did you call, then? I'm a little busy."

"I called because I want to make sure that as we unify the company, we unify the family, as well. I…I don't want to keep any of this rivalry alive. I've been holding on to some things for far too long that I need to let go. This is one of them."

"Accepting my superiority?"

"If that's what it takes."

Alessandro paused for a moment. "You aren't dying, are you?"

"It feels like it. But I think it will pass." It had to. "I don't want to carry things on like Carlo and Benito did, and I don't just mean the criminal activity. If we have a problem, I say we just punch each other in the face and get it over with, rather than creating a multigenerational feud."

"That works for me."

"Good. See you at the next meeting." He hung up. It wasn't like he needed to hug it out with his cousin or anything, but he was ready to start putting things behind him. To stop shielding himself from the past and embrace the future.

A future that would include Alessia.

Alessia looked up when the Ferrari roared back onto the grounds. She was standing in the garden, doing her best to at least enjoy the waning sunlight. It was better than the whole dissolving-into-never-ending-tears bit.

Matteo left the car in the middle of the drive and strode into the yard, his eyes fixed on hers. When he reached her, he pulled her into his arms, his expression fierce. Then he lowered his head and kissed her. Long. Deep. Intense.

She wrapped her arms around his neck and kissed him back, her face wet, tasting salt from tears. She didn't know whose. She didn't care.

She didn't want to ask questions now, she just wanted to live in this moment. When they parted, Matteo buried his face in her neck and held her tight. And she held him, too. Neither of them moved, neither of them spoke.

Emotion swelled in her chest, so big she wasn't sure she could stand it. Wasn't sure she could breathe around it.

"I love you," he said. "I have never said it before, Alessia. Not to anyone. Not to a woman, not to family. So when I say it, I mean it. With everything I have, such as it is. I love you."

A sob broke through her lips and she tightened her hold on him. "I love you, too."

"Still?"

"Always."

"You were right. I was afraid. I'm still afraid. But I can't hide anymore. You made it impossible. I want to be the man worthy of that look you used to give me. I want to be everything for you, I don't just want to take from you. I was content to just take that light you carry around in you, Alessia. To let it warm me. But you deserve more than that. So I'll be more than that. I'm not everything I should be. I'm broken. I've done things that were wrong. I've seen things no man should have to see. But I will give you everything that I have to give, and then I'll reach deep and find more, because you're right, you deserve it all. And I want you, so that means I have to figure out a way to be it all."

"Matteo, no, you don't. You just have to meet me in the middle. And love will cover our shortcomings."

"Just meet you in the middle?"

"Mainly, I just need you to love me."

"That I can do, Alessia Corretti. I've been doing it for most of my life."

"You might not believe this, Matteo, but as you are, you're my knight in shining armor. You are flawed. You've been through unimaginable things, and you love anyway. You're so strong, so brave, so utterly perfect. Well, not perfect, but perfect for me. You're the only man I've ever wanted, the only man I've ever loved. And that will never change."

"How is it that you see me, all of me, and love me, anyway?"

"That's what love is. And you know what? It's not hard to love you. You're brave, honorable. You were willing to cut off any chance at having your own happiness to try to protect the people around you. To try to do right. You're the most incredible man I've ever known."

"Quite the compliment coming from the most amazing woman. Your bravery, your willingness to love, in spite of all you've been through, that's what pulled me out of the darkness. Your light won. Your love won."

"I'm so glad it did."

He put his hand on Alessia's stomach. "This is what I want. You, me, our baby. I was too afraid before to admit how much I wanted it. Too afraid I didn't deserve it, that I would lose it. I'm still afraid I don't deserve it, but I want it so much." He leaned in and kissed her lips. "I'm not cold anymore."

"Never again," she said.

He wrapped his arms tight around her and spun them both in a circle. She laughed, and so did he. Genuine. Happy. Joy bloomed inside of her. Joy like she'd never felt before. Real, true. And for her. Not to keep those around her smiling.

"We agreed on one night. This is turning into a lot longer than one night," he said when they stopped spinning.

"It is," she said. "All things considered, I was thinking we might want to make it forever."

"Forever sounds about right."

EPILOGUE

THE CORRETTIS WERE all together. But unlike at the funerals that had been the most common reason for them to come together in the past, unlike Alessia and Alessandro's wedding-that-wasn't, there was no veiled animosity here at the celebration of Teresa's birthday. And not just Teresa's birthday, but the regeneration of the docklands. The culmination of a joint family effort. Of them coming together.

After the big ceremony down at the docklands, they'd returned to the family estate.

They had all sat down to dinner together. They had all talked, business and personal, and not a single punch had been thrown. And it wasn't only Correttis. Some of the Battaglias, Alessia's siblings, were there, as well.

Matteo considered it a resounding success.

After dinner, they all sat in the garden, lights strung overhead, a warm breeze filtering through. And Matteo felt peace.

"Hey there." Alessia walked away from where she'd been talking to his sister Lia and came to stand beside him, their daughter, Luciana Battaglia-Corretti, on her hip.

"The most beautiful women here have graced me with their presence. I am content," he said, brushing his knuckles over Alessia's cheek and dropping a kiss onto Luciana's soft head.

Matteo looked at his wife and daughter, at his family,

all of them, surrounding him. That word meant something new now. The Correttis were no longer at war.

He bent down and extracted Luciana from her mother's arms, pulling his daughter close, the warm weight of her, her absolute trust in him, something he would never take for granted.

Alessia smiled at him, her eyes shining, her face glowing. "The way you look at me," he said. "Like I'm your knight in shining armor."

"You are," she said. "You saved me, after all."

Matteo looked around one more time, at all of the people in his life. People that he loved. "No, Alessia. You saved me."

* * * * *

'I want my son to grow up in Spain—'

'Well, you can't always have what you want,' Jemima pointed out flatly.

Alejandro strolled across the floor towards her. 'I gave this matter serious thought last night. I can give you a choice…'

Her spine went rigid, her eyes flying wide with uncertainty. 'What sort of a choice?'

'Option one: you return to Spain and give our marriage another chance. Or option two: I take you to court over Alfie and we fight for him.' As Jemima lost colour and a look of disbelief tautened her delicate pointed features, Alejandro surveyed her with unblemished cool. 'From my point of view it's a very fair offer, and more than you deserve.'

SECRETLY PREGNANT

With this ring, I claim my baby!

The amazing new trilogy
by best-selling Modern™ Romance author

Lynne Graham

The charming and pretty English village of
Charlbury St Helens is home to three young women
whose Cinderella lives are about to be turned upside
down…by three of the wealthiest, most handsome and
impossibly arrogant men in Europe!

Jemima, Flora and Jess aren't looking for love,
but all have babies very much in mind.
Jemima already has a young son,
Flora is hoping to adopt her late half-sister's
little daughter, and Jess just longs to be a mum.

But whether they have or want a baby,
all the girls must marry ultimate alpha males
to keep their dreams… And Alejandro,
Angelo and Cesario are not about to be tamed!

SECRETLY PREGNANT

NAÏVE BRIDE, DEFIANT WIFE:
Jemima and Alejandro's story

FLORA'S DEFIANCE:
Flora and Angelo's story

JESS'S PROMISE:
Jess and Cesario's story

NAÏVE WIFE, DEFIANT BRIDE

BY
LYNNE GRAHAM

First published in Great Britain 2010
Harlequin Mills & Boon Limited,
Eton House, 18-24 Paradise Road, Richmond, Surrey TW9 1SR

© Lynne Graham 2010

ISBN: 978 0 263 21545 8

Harlequin Mills & Boon policy is to use papers that are natural, renewable and recyclable products and made from wood grown in sustainable forests. The logging and manufacturing process conform to the legal environmental regulations of the country of origin.

Printed and bound in Great Britain
by CPI Antony Rowe, Chippenham, Wiltshire

NAÏVE WIFE, DEFIANT BRIDE

CHAPTER ONE

ALEJANDRO NAVARRO VASQUEZ, the Conde Olivares, sat on his superb black stallion in the shade of an orange grove and surveyed the valley that had belonged to his ancestors for over five hundred years. On this fine spring morning, below a clear blue sky, it was a gorgeous view encompassing thousands of acres of fertile earth and woodland. He owned the land as far as the eye could see, but his lean, darkly handsome features were grim as they had often been since the breakdown of his marriage almost two and a half years earlier.

He was a landowner and wealthy, but his family—which every Spaniard cherished far beyond material riches—had been ripped asunder by his imprudent marriage. For a male as strong, proud and successful as Alejandro, it was a bitter truth that undermined his every achievement. He had followed his heart and not his head and he had married the wrong woman, a very expensive mistake for which he was still paying the price. His half-brother, Marco, had taken a job in New York, cutting off all contact with his mother and siblings. Yet if Marco, whom Alejandro had helped to raise after their father's premature death, had appeared before him at that moment could he have forgiven the younger man and urged him back to his childhood home with sincerity and warm affection?

Alejandro swore under his breath as he pondered that merciless question and the less than acceptable negative answer that he would have had to give it. However, when it came to *Jemima*, there was no forgiveness in his heart, only outrage and aggression. He nursed a far from charitable desire for vengeance against the wife and the brother who had together betrayed his trust and his love. Ever since Jemima had walked out on their marriage and disappeared, defying his wishes to the last, Alejandro had burned with a desire for justice, even while his keen intelligence warned him that there was no such thing when it came to affairs of the heart.

His mobile phone vibrated and, suppressing a groan of impatience, for it was always a struggle to protect his rare moments of leisure, he tugged it out. His ebony brows rose when he learned that the private detective he had hired to find Jemima had arrived to see him. He rode swiftly back to the castle, wondering impatiently if Alonso Ortega had finally managed to track down his estranged wife.

'My apologies for coming to see you without an appointment, Your Excellency,' the older man murmured with punctilious good manners and a promising air of accomplishment. 'But I knew you would want to hear my news as soon as possible. I have found the Condesa.'

'In England?' Alejandro questioned and, having had that long-held suspicion confirmed, he listened while Ortega furnished further details. Then, unfortunately, at that point his mother, the dowager countess, entered the room. A formidable presence, Doña Hortencia settled acid black eyes on the private detective and demanded to know if he had finally fulfilled the purpose of his hire. At the news that he had, a rare smile of approval lightened her expression.

'There is one more fact I should add,' Ortega revealed in a reluctant tone of voice, evading the uncomfortably intense scrutiny of his noble hostess. 'The Condesa now has a child, a little boy of around two years of age.'

Alejandro froze and a yawning silence greeted the detective's startling announcement.

The door opened again and his older sister, Beatriz, entered with a quiet apology to her brother for the interruption. She was hushed into silence by her domineering mother, who said glacially, 'That wanton English witch who married your unlucky brother has given birth to a bastard.'

Horrified at such an announcement being made in front of Alonso Ortega, Beatriz shot her brother an appalled glance and hastened to offer the detective refreshments in an effort to change the subject to one less controversial. His discomfited sister, Alejandro appreciated, would quite happily sit and discuss the weather now while he, her more primitive brother, was strongly tempted to seize hold of Ortega's lapels and force every single fact from the man without further ado. But, possibly sensing his employer's impatience, the detective handed Alejandro a slim file and hastily excused himself.

'A…child?' Beatriz gasped in shock and consternation the instant the door had closed on the detective's departure. 'But *whose* child?'

His profile set like granite, Alejandro answered his sister only with a dismissive shrug. It was certainly not his child, but for him that had to be the biggest badge of ignominy he had ever endured. Yet another metaphorical nail in Jemima's coffin, he conceded bitterly. Jemima, he had learned the hard way, knew exactly how best to put a man through an emotional and physical wringer. *Dios mio*, another man's child!

'If only you had listened to me,' Doña Hortencia lamented. 'The instant I met that wicked young woman I knew she was wrong for you. You were one of the biggest matrimonial prizes in Spain and you could have married anyone—'

'I married Jemima,' Alejandro pointed out tersely, for he had never had much time for the older woman's melodrama.

'Only because she mesmerised you like the shameless hussy she is. One man was never going to be enough for her. Thanks to her, my poor Marco is living on the other side of the world. That she could have given birth to an illegitimate child while still bearing our name is the most disgusting thing I ever—'

'*Enough!*' Alejandro incised with crushing force to close out that carping voice. 'There is no point to such recriminations now. What is done is done.'

Doña Hortencia, her lined face full of anger and malice, rested accusing eyes on his lean strong visage. 'But it is *not* done yet, is it? You still haven't begun divorce proceedings.'

'I will travel to England and see Jemima as soon as the arrangements can be made,' Alejandro pronounced grittily.

'Send the family lawyer! There can be no need for you to make a personal trip to England,' his mother protested with vigour.

'There is every need,' Alejandro contradicted with all

the quiet, unhesitating assurance of his rich, well-educated and extremely aristocratic background. 'Jemima is still my wife.'

As Doña Hortencia broke into another barrage of loud objections Alejandro lost patience. 'I inform you of my intentions only as a matter of courtesy. I do not require either your permission or your approval.'

Alejandro retired to the privacy of his study and poured himself a stiff brandy. A child? Jemima had had a child. He was still in shock at that revelation, not least because he could hardly forget that his wife had miscarried *his* baby shortly before she'd left him. That was how he knew beyond any shadow of doubt that this child, which she had given birth to since, then could not possibly be his. So, was the boy Marco's baby? Or some other man's? Such speculation was sordid, he acknowledged with a distaste that slivered through his lean powerful frame like a knife blade.

He leafed through the file but the facts were few. Jemima was now living in a Dorset village where she ran a florist's shop. For a moment as he allowed himself to think about his estranged wife memories threatened to overwhelm him, but he shut them out, utilising the fierce intelligence and self-discipline that were second nature to him. Yet where had either trait been when he got involved with Jemima Grey in the first place?

He could make no excuses for his behaviour because he had freely acknowledged the huge and irrefutable differences between them even before he married her. Of course, what had mesmerised him then—to borrow his mother's expression—was Jemima's superlative sex appeal. Like many men, he had been more vulnerable to that temptation than he had ever realised he might be.

Possibly life prior to that point had spoiled him with too many easy female conquests. His failure to keep a lid on his fierce sexual desire to possess Jemima's pale slim body had proved to be his fatal weakness, he assured himself with grim conviction. Fortunately, however, the passage of time and the process of hard disillusionment he had experienced during his short-lived marriage had obliterated Jemima's desirability factor entirely.

His ill-judged marriage had, after all, virtually destroyed his family circle. But in the short term, Jemima had no family support of her own and she was still his legal wife; regardless of his feelings on that score she remained *his* responsibility. As did her child, whom the law would deem to be his child until a divorce was finalised, Alejandro conceded, irate at that demeaning fact. He had to go to England.

No Conde Olivares since the fifteenth century had ever been known to act as a coward or to shirk his duty, no matter how unpleasant it might be. Even in the most trying circumstances, Alejandro expected no less of himself. He reckoned that Jemima was fortunate to be a twenty-first-century woman, for his medieval ancestors would have locked an unfaithful wife up in a convent or killed her for inflicting such a stain on the family honour. Though at least his less civilised ancestors had possessed the power of retaliation, he reflected broodingly.

While Jemima wrapped the bouquet in clear, decorative cellophane, Alfie peered round the corner of the shop counter, his big brown eyes dancing with mischief. ''Ello,' he said chirpily to the waiting customer, shyness not being one of Alfie's personality traits.

'Hello. He's a beautiful child,' the woman remarked, smiling down at Alfie as the toddler looked up at her with his irrepressible grin.

It was a compliment that often came Alfie's way, his mother conceded as she slotted the payment in the till, while wondering what age her son would reach before that particular description embarrassed him. But like father like son, she thought ruefully, and in looks Alfie was very much a product of his Spanish father's genes, with gorgeous dark brown eyes, olive-tinted skin and a shock of black silky hair. All he had inherited from his less exotic mother was her rampant curls. On the inside, however, Alfie had all the easy warmth of his mother's essentially optimistic nature and revealed only the occasional hint of his father's infinitely darker and more passionate temperament.

With a slight shiver, Jemima pushed that daunting thought back out of her mind again. With Alfie playing with his toy cars at her feet, she returned to fashioning a flower arrangement requested by a client who had photographed a similar piece of floral art at a horticultural show. Pure accident had brought Jemima to the village of Charlbury St Helens at a crisis point in her life and she had never regretted staying on and laying the foundations for her new future there.

The only work she'd been able to find locally while she'd been pregnant was as an assistant at a flower shop. She had needed to earn back her self-respect by keeping busy and positive. Discovering that she had a very real interest in floristry, she had found more than a job to focus on and had since studied part-time for formal qualifications. By the time her employer decided to retire, owing to ill health, Jemima had had the courage and vision to take over the business and expand it by taking on occasional private projects that encompassed small weddings and other functions.

She was so proud of running her own business that sometimes she had to pinch herself to believe that she could have come so far from her humble beginnings. Not bad for the daughter of a violent, criminal father who had never worked if he could help it, and a downtrodden, alcoholic mother, who had died when her husband crashed a stolen car. Jemima had never dared to develop any aspirations as a teenager. Nobody in her family tree had ever tried to climb the career or social ladders.

'Those kinds of ideas aren't for the likes of us. Jem needs to get a job to help out at home,' her mother had told the teacher who'd tried to persuade the older woman that her daughter should stay on at school to study for her A-level exams.

'You're like your mother—dumb as a rock and just about as useful!' her father had condemned often enough for that label to have troubled Jemima for many year afterwards.

With lunch eaten, she walked Alfie down to his session at the playgroup in the village hall, wincing when her son bounded boisterously through the door calling his friends' names at the top of his voice. Alfie, named for his great-grandfather on Jemima`s mother's side of the family, was very sociable and full of energy after spending the morning cooped up at the shop with his mother. Although Jemima had created a play corner in the backstore room for her child, there really wasn't enough space to house a lively little boy for long. With the help of a childminder, she had often contrived to keep Alfie with her during working hours, but now that he was of an age to join the playgroup in the afternoons and she no longer attended floristry classes she needed a lot less childcare. Considering that her close friend and former childminder, Flora, was now often too busy with her bed-and- breakfast operation to help out as much, Jemima was grateful for that fact.

It was a pleasant surprise therefore when Flora came into the shop an hour later and asked Jemima if she had time for a coffee. Brewing up in the small kitchen, Jemima eyed her red-headed friend and read the other woman's uneasiness with a frown. 'What's up?'

'It's probably nothing. I meant to come over and tell you at the weekend, but a whole family booked in with me on Saturday and I was run off my feet,' Flora groaned. 'Apparently some guy in a hire car was hanging around the village last Thursday and someone saw him taking a picture of your shop. He was asking questions about you in the post office as well.'

Jemima stilled, dark blue eyes widening while her heart-shaped face paled below her cloud of wildly curling strawberry-blonde hair and the stance of her tiny slender figure screamed tension. Just an inch over five feet in height, she had reminded the more solidly built Flora of a delicate blown-glass angel ornament when they'd first met, but she had later appreciated that nobody as down-to-earth and quirky as Jemima could be seen for long in that improbable light. However, her friend was unquestionably beautiful in an ethereal way and if men could be equated to starving dogs, Jemima was the equivalent of a very juicy bone, for the male sex seemed to find her irresistible. Locals joked that the church choir had been on the brink of folding before Jemima had joined and a swell of young men had soon followed in her wake, not that any of them had since got anywhere with her, Flora reflected wryly. Badly burned by her failed marriage, Jemima preferred men as friends and concentrated her energies on her son and her business.

'What sort of questions?' Jemima prompted sickly, the cold chill of apprehension hollowing out her stomach.

'Whether or not you lived around here, and what age Alfie was. The guy asking the questions was young and good-looking. Maurice in the post office thought he was playing cupid…'

'Was the man Spanish?'

Flora shook her head and took over from her anxious friend at the kettle to speed up the arrival of the coffee. 'No, a Londoner according to Maurice. He probably just fancied trying his chances with you—'

'I don't remember *any* young good-looking men coming in here last week,' Jemima pointed out, her concern patent.

'Maybe he lost interest once he realised you were a mother.' Flora shrugged. 'I wouldn't have told you about him if I had known you would get wound up about it. Why don't you just get on the phone and tell…er…what's his name, your husband?'

'Alejandro,' Jemima supplied tautly. 'Tell him what?'

'That you want a clean break and a divorce.'

'Nobody gets away with telling Alejandro what to do. He's the one who does the telling. It wouldn't be that simple once he found out about Alfie.'

'So you go to a solicitor and say what a lousy husband he was.'

'He didn't drink or beat me up.'

Flora grimaced. 'Why should such extremes be your

only yardstick? There are other grounds for divorce, like mental abuse and neglect—and what about the way he left you at the mercy of his horrible family?'

'It was his mother who was horrible, not his brother or his sister,' Jemima pointed out, wanting as always to be fair. 'And I don't think it's right to say I was mentally abused.'

Flora, whose temper was as hot as her hair, regarded the younger woman with unimpressed eyes. 'Alejandro criticised everything you did, left you alone all the time and got you pregnant before you were ready to have a kid.'

Jemima reddened to the roots of her light-coloured hair and marvelled that she could have been so frank with Flora in the early weeks of their friendship, sharing secrets that she sometimes wished she had kept to herself, although not, mercifully, the worst secrets of all. Of course, back then, she had been as steamed up as a pressure cooker of emotions and in dire need of someone to talk to. 'I just wasn't good enough for him…' She spoke the truth as she saw it, as lightly as she could.

Growing up, Jemima had never been good enough for either of her parents and the ability to search out and focus on her own flaws was second nature to her. Her mother had entered her in juvenile beauty contests as a young child but Jemima, too shy to smile for the photos and too quiet to chatter when interviewed, had not shone. Bored out of her mind as she was as a daydreaming teenager, she had done equally poorly at the office-skills course her mother had sent her on, shattering her mother's second dream of her becoming a high-powered personal assistant to some millionaire who would some day fall madly in love with her daughter. Her mother had pretty much lived in a fantasy world, which, along with the alcohol, had provided her with her only escape from the drudgery and abuse of a bad marriage.

Jemima's father, whose only dreams related to making pots of money without ever getting up off the sofa, had wanted Jemima to become a model, but she failed to grow tall enough for fashion work and lacked the bountiful curves necessary for the other kind. After her mother's death, her father had urged her to become a dancer at a club run by his mate and had hit her and thrown her out of the family home when she'd refused to dress up in a skimpy outfit and attend an audition. It was years before she saw her father again and then in circumstances she preferred to forget. Yes, Jemima had learned at an early age that people always expected more from her than she ever seemed able to deliver and, sadly, her marriage had proved no different. It was for that reason that making her own way in life to set up and run her business had added greatly to her confidence; for once she had surpassed her own expectations.

Yet when she had first met Alejandro and he had swept her off her feet, he had seemed to be *her* every dream come true, which in retrospect seemed laughable to her. But love had snatched her up like a tornado and made her believe in the impossible before it flung her down again. Somehow, and she had no idea how, she had truly believed that she could marry a rich, educated foreigner with a pedigree as long as her arm and make a go of it. But in practice the challenges and the disparities had proved insurmountable. Her background had come back to seriously haunt her, but her biggest single mistake had been getting too friendly with her brother-in-law, Marco. Although, she reasoned defensively, had

Alejandro been around more and made more effort to help her come to terms with her new life in Spain she wouldn't have been so lonely and wouldn't have jumped at the offer of Marco's company. And she had *adored* Marco, she acknowledged abstractedly, recalling how wounded she had felt when even after her marriage broke down he had made no attempt to get in touch with her again.

'You were *too* good for that husband of yours,' Flora told Jemima with strong emphasis. 'But you really should tell Alejandro about Alfie instead of staying in hiding as if you have something to be ashamed of.'

Jemima turned her head away, her cheeks colouring as she thought, *If only you knew...* Telling the whole unvarnished truth would probably turn her closest friend off her as well, she reckoned painfully.

'I honestly believe that if Alejandro found out about Alfie, he would go to any lengths to get custody of him and take him back to Spain to live,' she replied heavily. 'Alejandro takes his responsibilities towards the family very seriously.'

'Well, if you think there's a risk of Alfie being snatched by his father, you're wise keeping quiet about him,' Flora said, although there was an uncertain look on her face when she voiced that opinion. 'But you can't keep him quiet for ever.'

'Only, for now, it's the best option,' Jemima declared, setting down her coffee to attend to a customer as the shop bell on the door sounded.

Soon afterwards, she went out to deliver a floral arrangement for a dinner party to one of the big houses outside the village. On the way home she collected Alfie, his high energy dissipated by a couple of hours of horseplay. The tiny terraced cottage she rented on the outskirts of the village enjoyed a garden, which she had equipped with a swing and a sandpit. She was proud of her small living space. Although the little house was inexpertly painted and furnished cheaply with flat-pack furniture, it was the first place she had ever been able to make feel like her home since childhood.

Sometimes it seemed like a dim and unbelievable fairy tale to recall that after she had married Alejandro she had lived in a castle. *Castillo del Halc*ón, the Castle of the Hawk, built by his warrior ancestors in a mix of Islamic and European styles and filled with history, luxury and priceless artefacts. Moving the furniture or the pictures around had been forbidden and redecorating equally frowned on because the dowager countess, Doña Hortencia, could not bear any woman to interfere in what she still essentially saw as her home. Living there, Jemima had often felt like a lodger who had outstayed her welcome, and the formal lifestyle of changing into evening clothes for dinner, dealing with servants and entertaining important guests had suited her even less.

Had there been any redeeming features to her miserable marriage? she asked herself, and instantly a picture of Alejandro popped up unbidden inside her head. Her spectacularly gorgeous husband had initially felt like a prize beyond any other she had ever received, yet she had never quite been able to stifle the feeling that she didn't deserve him and he deserved better than her. It crossed Jemima's mind that most of the best things that had happened to her in life had occurred seemingly because of blessed accidents of fate. That description best covered Alfie's unplanned conception, her car choosing to break down in Charlbury St Helens after she had run away from Spain, her marriage, and ironically it even covered her first meeting with Alejandro...

He had knocked her off her bike in a car park or, rather, his driver's overly assertive driving style had done so. She had been on her day off from the hotel where she was working as a receptionist and riding a bicycle was a necessity when she was employed in a rural business and buses were scarcer than hens' teeth. The opulent Mercedes had ground to a halt and Alejandro and his chauffeur had emerged to check out the damage done while she was struggling to blink back tears from the pain of her skinned knees and bruised hip. Before she had known what was happening to her, her damaged bike was stacked in the local repair shop and she was ensconced in the luxury Mercedes, being swept off to the nearest hospital A and E department by the most gorgeous-looking guy she had ever met in her life. It was a shame that she really hadn't noticed that day just how domineering and deaf to all argument Alejandro could be, for he had refused to listen when she declared that she did not require any medical attention. No, she had been X-rayed, cleaned up, bandaged and bullied within an inch of her life all because Alejandro's dazzling smile had cast a spell over her.

Love at first sight, Jemima labelled with an instinctive frown of antipathy while she shifted about restlessly in her bed that night. She had never believed in love at first sight, indeed had grown up promising herself that she would never allow any man to wield the kind of power over her that her father had always exercised over her mother. But despite the hard lessons she had believed she had learned at her mother's knee, Jemima had taken one look at Alejandro Navarro Vasquez and fallen as hard and as destructively for him as a brick thrown from a major height. And the *real* lessons she had learned she had picked up from Alejandro himself, only she had failed to put what she learned to sensible use.

Long before Alejandro had shocked her with his proposal of marriage, he had put her through months of dating hell by not phoning when he said he would, by cancelling meetings last minute and by seeing other women and getting photographed with them. Even before she'd married him he had battered her heart and trodden her pride deep in the dirt. But she had understood even then why he was giving her the runaround. He was, after all, a Spanish count, while she worked for peanuts at a little hotel that he considered to be a dump. He had known she was not his equal on any level and the disparity had bothered him deeply from the outset of their acquaintance. Six months after that first encounter, however, Alejandro had seemed to shed that attitude…

'*Sol y sombre*…sun and shade, *querida mia*,' Alejandro had murmured then as he compared the pale skin of her slender arm to the bronzed vibrancy of his darker colouring. 'You cannot have one without the other—we belong together.'

But they had mingled as badly as oil and water, Jemima conceded with the dulled pain of acceptance that she had learned she had to live with, and she finally dropped off to sleep around two in the morning by dint of trying to forget the delivery she had to get up for the next morning.

There was hardly any floor space left in the shop once

she had loaded the fresh blooms into the waiting containers. Her fingers numbed by the brisk spring morning temperature and too much contact with wet stems and water, Jemima rubbed her hands over her slim jeans-clad hips and tried not to shiver, because she knew that one shiver would only lead to another half-dozen and that in the end she would only feel colder. After all, winter or summer, the shop was always cool. It was an old building with poor insulation and she was always quick to remind herself that too much heat would only damage her stock. She went into the back room and dragged a black fleece jacket off the hook in the wall and put it on. Alfie was out in the little backyard playing on his trike while making loud motoring noises and she smiled at the sight of his innocent enjoyment, which took no account of the early hour he had been dug out of his cosy bed or the chilly air.

'Jemima...'

It was a voice she had hoped never to hear again: rich, melodic, dark and deep, and so full of accented earthy male sexiness it sent little quivers down her sensitive spine. She shut her eyes tight, refusing to turn round, telling herself wildly that her mind had somehow slipped dangerously back into the past and that she was imagining things...

Imagining waking up in bed with Alejandro, all tousled black hair, stubble and raw male sensual appeal... Alejandro, who could ignite her hunger with one indolent glance from his stunning black-fringed dark-as-the-night-sky eyes and seal it by simply saying her name... But even as a steamy burst of imagery momentarily clouded her brain and interfered with her breathing, she was instead recalling the emptiness of her bed once she had fallen pregnant and the wounding anguish of that physical lack of interest in her rapidly swelling body. As a chill slid through her slender length she spun round.

And there he was, Alejandro Navarro Vasquez, her husband, who had taught her to love him, taught her to need him and who had then proceeded to torture her with deprivation for her weakness. She was shocked, deeply, horribly shocked, her dazed violet-blue eyes widening to roam slowly over him as if she could not credit what she was seeing. Thick blue-black hair swept back from his brow, a fitting overture to the splendour of high patrician cheekbones bisected by a strong arrogant nose and punctuated by a sensually shaped and perfect masculine mouth. He was a staggeringly handsome man and fabulously well turned out in a dark business suit of faultless cut and polished handmade shoes. He always looked immaculate…except in bed, she recalled dully, when her hands had disarranged his hair and her nails had inflicted scratch marks down the long golden expanse of his flawless back. And she wanted to scream against the recollections that would not leave her alone, that were uniting with her sense of panic to destabilise her even more.

'What are you doing here?' she exclaimed breathlessly…

CHAPTER TWO

'WE HAVE unfinished business,' Alejandro intoned softly, his keen gaze wandering slowly over her small figure.

And Jemima went from cold to hot as if he had turned a blowtorch on her. She flushed because she knew she looked less than her best with her hair loose round her to keep her ears warm and only a touch of mascara and lip gloss on her face, not to mention the worn jeans, fleece jacket and shabby low-heeled boots that completed her practical outfit. And even though it was bloody-minded—for she wanted nothing between them to be as it had once been, when she'd had no control over her responses—she deeply resented his cool stare and businesslike tone: it was the ultimate rejection. She leant against the door frame, her slender spine taking on an arch that enhanced the small firm curves below the neat fit of wool and denim, her head lifting so that the pale foaming ringlets of her eye-catching strawberry-blonde hair rippled back across her shoulders.

An almost infinitesimal tightening hardened Alejandro's darkly handsome features, his sculpted jaw line clenching, his brilliant gaze narrowing and brightening. Then Jemima knew he had felt the challenge from her as stridently and clearly as though she had used a loud hailer. Suddenly the atmosphere was seething with tension. At that point, she suffered a dismaying reduction in courage and veiled her gaze, drawing back a step while being terrifyingly aware of the swelling tightness of her nipples inside her bra and the twisting slide of sexual awareness low in her pelvis. It shocked her that a man she now hated as much as she had once loved him could still have such a powerful effect on her body.

'Always the temptress,' Alejandro drawled with a roughened edge to his dark deep voice that vibrated through her like a jamming wireless signal and made her rigidity give way to a trembling vulnerability. 'Do I really look that desperate?'

The fierce chill of his rejection might have cut her like a knife had she not been more aware of the way his strikingly beautiful eyes lingered on her. As she tore her attention from the lean, strong face that haunted her dreams and her gaze dropped she could not help noticing the distinctive masculine bulge that had disturbed the perfect fit of his trousers. Her cheeks flamed as hot as a kettle on the boil as she was both mollified by that reaction and burned by it at the same time.

'What are you doing here?' she demanded for the second time.

'I want a divorce. I need an address for you to obtain it,' Alejandro spelt out in a driven undertone. 'Or didn't that occur to you? Your staging a vanishing act was selfish and immature.'

That fast Jemima wanted to lift one of the buckets of flowers and upend it over him. 'You forced me to behave like that,' she told him heatedly.

'How?' Alejandro growled, striding forward to brace

his lean, well-shaped hands on the counter, clearly more than ready for an argument.

'You wouldn't listen to a word I said. We had reached stalemate and there was nothing more I could do.'

'I told you that we would work it out,' Alejandro reminded her in a tone of galling condescension.

'But in the whole of our marriage you never did work anything out with me. How could you when you wouldn't talk to me? When I told you how unhappy I was what did you ever do to make anything better?' Jemima demanded, her violet eyes shimmering with pain and condemnation as she remembered the lavish gifts he had given her instead of more concrete and meaningful things like his time and his attention.

Straight away, anger flared in Alejandro, his stunning eyes flaming bright gold with heat just as the bell on the shop door rang to herald the arrival of Jemima's assistant, Sandy. The silence inside the shop was so deep and so tense it could have filled a bank vault and as she came in the dark-haired, neatly dressed older woman shot Jemima a look of dismay. 'Am I late? Were you expecting me to start early today?'

'No, no,' Jemima hastened to reassure her employee. 'But I'm afraid I have to go back home for an hour, so you'll be in charge.'

Without even looking in Alejandro's direction, Jemima went out to the backyard to retrieve Alfie, hoisting him into her arms and hurrying back indoors to say in a frazzled aside to Alejandro, 'I live a hundred yards down the road at number forty-two.'

But before she could reach the door a broad-shouldered young man with cropped fair hair strolled through it brandishing a bag. 'Fresh out of the bakery oven,

Jemima!' he exclaimed with satisfaction. 'Cherry scones for our elevenses…'

'Oh, Charlie, I totally forgot you were coming today!' Jemima gasped in dismay. She had made the arrangement the previous week when she'd last seen Charlie at choir practice. 'Look, I have to go out for a little while, but first I'd better show you that electrical socket that's not working.'

Anchoring Alfie more firmly to her hip, Jemima dived back behind the counter with Charlie close behind her and pointed out the socket that had failed the previous week.

Full of cheerful chatter, Charlie rested appreciative eyes on her delicate profile. 'If it would suit you better I can come back tomorrow when you're here.'

'No, that's fine, Charlie. Today is perfect,' Jemima insisted, turning back to head for the door where Alejandro waited in silence, his shrewd gaze pinned to the hovering electrician, who was making no attempt to hide his disappointment that she was leaving. 'Sandy will look after you.'

Jemima stepped out into the fresh air, hugely conscious of Alejandro's presence by her side but also perplexed, because if he had even looked at Alfie for ten seconds he had contrived to hide the fact from her. 'I'll see you at the house,' she said flatly, setting Alfie down and grasping his hand because he was too heavy for her to carry any further.

'I'll give you a lift,' Alejandro drawled.

'No, thanks.' Without any further ado, Jemima crossed the road and began to walk away fast with Alfie tottering along beside her. Outside working hours she used the van to get around, but when the shop was open it was needed to deliver orders.

She had only gone twenty yards before a neat, dark saloon car pulled in beside her and the driver's door opened. Then a tall man in a business suit climbed out. 'Going home?' Jeremy prompted. 'Get in. I'll drop you off.'

'Thank you, Jeremy, but I'm so close it's easier just to walk,' she declared breezily, though all her thoughts were miles away, lodged back on Alejandro and his assurance that he wanted a divorce.

Had he already met someone else? Some well born beauty from a moneyed background, much more suitable than she had been? She wondered how many other women he had been with since she had left him and it made a tiny shudder of agonising emotional pain arrow through her tender heart. She didn't want Alejandro back, no, she definitely didn't, but she didn't want any other woman to have him either. Where he was concerned, she was a real dog in the manger. But it would be foolish to imagine that he might have been celibate since her departure, for that high-voltage libido of his required frequent gratification…or at least it had until he was faced with her enlarged breasts and thickening waistline and it had become painfully, hurtfully obvious that he'd found his pregnant wife's body about as attractive as a mud bath. So how could she possibly care what he had done and with whom since then?

Jeremy yanked open the passenger door of his car. 'Get in,' he urged. 'You're both getting soaked.'

Belatedly appreciating that it had started raining while she'd stood there, Jemima scooped up her son and clambered in. Jeremy pulled in just ahead of the sleek sports car already waiting outside her home. He vented a low whistle of appreciation as he studied the opulent model. 'Who on earth does that beauty belong to?'

'An old friend of mine,' she replied as she stepped out of his car. 'Thanks.'

As she attempted to turn away Jeremy strode round the bonnet to rest a staying hand on her arm. 'Eat out with me tonight,' he urged, his blue eyes pinned hopefully to her face. 'No strings, no big deal, just a couple of friends getting together for a meal.'

Turning pink, Jemima stepped back from his proximity, awesomely conscious that just feet away from them Alejandro was listening to the exchange. 'I'm sorry, I can't,' she answered awkwardly.

'I'll keep on asking,' Jeremy warned her.

Jemima almost winced at that unnecessary assurance, as she had already discovered that Jeremy, the local estate agent and a divorcee in his early thirties, had the hide of a rhinoceros when it came to taking a polite hint that a woman wasn't interested. Since the day she had signed the rental agreement on her cottage, he must have asked her out at least a dozen times.

Aware of the glacial cool of Alejandro's scrutiny, Jemima hastened to slot her key into the lock on the front door.

'Why didn't you just tell him that you were married?'

'He already knows that. Everybody knows that,' Jemima fielded irritably, making a point of flexing the finger that bore her wedding ring as she pushed open the door. 'But he also knows that I'm separated from my husband.'

'There's nothing official about our separation,'

Alejandro countered, crowding her with his presence in the tiny hall before he moved on into the small living room. 'But I am surprised that you're still wearing the ring.'

Jemima shrugged a slight shoulder and made no reply as she unbuttoned Alfie's jacket and hung it up beside her fleece.

'Juice.' Alfie tugged at her sleeve.

'Please,' Jemima reminded him.

'Peese,' Alfie said obediently.

'Do you want coffee?' Jemima asked Alejandro grudgingly. He had taken up a stance by the window and his height and wide shoulders were blocking out a good deal of the light.

'*Sí*,' Alejandro confirmed.

'Peese,' Alfie told him helpfully. 'Say peese.'

'*Gracias,*' Alejandro pronounced in his own tongue, stubborn to the last and barely sparing the attentive toddler a glance.

Once again Jemima was taken aback by that pronounced lack of interest in her child. She had expected Alejandro to be stunned by Alfie's existence and, at the very least, extremely curious. 'Haven't you got any questions to ask me about him?' she enquired, her attention resting pointedly on Alfie's dark curly head as he crouched down to take his beloved cars out of the toy box and line them up in a row.

Alfie liked things organised and tidy, everything in its place. She had a sudden disconcerting recollection of Alejandro's immaculately neat desktop at the castle and wondered if there were other similarities that she had simply refused to see.

'When the family lawyer engages a solicitor here

to represent my interests, they can ask the questions,' Alejandro responded very drily.

'So, you're already convinced he's not yours,' Jemima breathed in a very quiet tone, her lips sealing over her gritted teeth like a steel trap.

Luxuriant black lashes swept up on Alejandro's gorgeous dark golden eyes, his handsome mouth taking on a sardonic cast. 'How could he be?'

Seething frustration filled Jemima. For a crazy instant, she wanted to jump on him and kick him and punch him, batter him into a state where he would be forced to listen to her. But she wasn't a violent woman and if he didn't listen to her, or believe in her, or even trust her, and he never had, at this stage of their relationship he probably never would. Wasn't that another good reason as to why she had walked out on their marriage? The conviction that she was beating her stupid head up against a brick wall? Not to mention the sheer impossibility of staying married to a man who was utterly convinced that she had had an affair with his brother?

While she waited on the kettle in the galley kitchen, she reached a sudden decision and lifted the wall phone to call Flora, asking her friend if it would be possible for her to look after Alfie for an hour. 'Alejandro is here,' she explained stiffly.

'Give me five minutes—I'll come down and pick Alfie up,' Flora promised.

Jemima set a china mug of coffee down near Alejandro. She knew what she had to do next but she just didn't want to. Been there, done that, got the T-shirt and the scars. Flora arrived very quickly, bridging the awkward silence with her chatter while Jemima fed Alfie into his coat again.

'Alejandro...Flora,' Jemima performed the introduction stiffly.

'I've heard so much about you,' Flora said brightly to Jemima's husband. 'None of it good.'

Alejandro sent Jemima a censorious look of hauteur and she reddened, wishing that the other woman had kept quiet rather than revealing how much she knew about her friend's marital problems.

The silence left after Flora's departure spread like a sheet of black ice waiting to entrap the unwary. Jemima straightened her slight shoulders, her blue eyes so dark with strain they had the glimmer of purple against her skin. 'I hate that I have to say this again, but you don't give me much choice—I did *not* sleep with your brother.'

Alejandro shot her a grim dark-eyed appraisal. 'At least he had the courage not to deny the charge—'

'Oh...right,' Jemima sliced in, rage bubbling and pounding through her like a waterfall that had been dammed up inside her. 'Marco didn't deny it, so therefore I have to be lying!'

'My brother has never lied to me but you have,' Alejandro pointed out levelly.

Jemima's hands clenched into fists. 'What lies? What are you talking about?'

'You went through thousands and thousands of pounds while we were still living together, yet you had nothing to show for your extravagance and could not even cover your own expenses in spite of the generous allowance I gave you. Somewhere in that financial mess, when I asked you for an explanation, there must have been lies,' he concluded.

Jemima had turned white as milk, for those were

charges she could not deny. She *had* got through a terrifying amount of money, although she hadn't spent it
on herself. Sadly, she had had nothing to show for it,
however, and she had found herself in the embarrassing
position of not being able to pay bills during the last
weeks of their marriage. All her sins had come home to
roost by then, all because of the one seemingly harmless
and seemingly even sensible little lie that she had told
him when they'd first met.

'Did you give all that money to Marco?' Alejandro
asked her abruptly, his voice harsh. 'He often overspent
and I was afraid that he might have approached you for
a loan.'

For a split second, Jemima was tempted to tell another lie to cover herself and then shame pierced her and
she bent her head, refusing to look at him. Although,
while on one level she was still angry with Alejandro's
brother for dropping her in the mire by refusing to deny
the allegations of an affair, she still retained enough
fondness for the younger man not to seek revenge and
to tell the truth. 'No, Marco never once asked me for
money.'

Alejandro's lean, powerful body had tautened. He
flicked her a narrowed glance so sharp that she was
vaguely surprised it didn't actually cut her. 'I assume
that you are still in contact with my brother?'

That comment startled her. 'No, I'm not. I haven't
talked to Marco since I left Spain.'

Alejandro made no attempt to hide his surprise at
that news. 'I'm amazed, when you were so intimate.'

Her teeth clenched at that crack. Not for the first time
she was tempted to give way and simply tell him the
truth. Unfortunately the repercussions threatened to be

too great. Furthermore she had once faithfully promised Marco that she would never betray him. After all, she had seen for herself and on more than one occasion why the younger man was quite so determined to keep that particular secret from his family. Unfortunately, Marco's selfishness did not release her from her pledge of silence. In any case, she reminded herself ruefully, it was not solely Marco's fault that her marriage to his brother had broken down.

'Marco has been working in New York at our art gallery for the past couple of years. You haven't had any contact with him at all?' Alejandro persisted in a silky smooth tone, his accent growling along the edges of every syllable.

'But presumably he is supporting his child?'

'Alfie is not his bloody child!' Jemima raked at him furiously.

'There is no need to swear,' Alejandro murmured smooth as glass.

Jemima trembled and struggled to master a temper that was threatening to overwhelm her. Two years ago when she walked out on her marriage she had been exhausted and worn down to the bone by the weight of her secrets, but since then she had made a strong recovery. 'Alfie is not Marco's son,' she pronounced flatly.

'Your child is only the smallest bone of contention between us,' Alejandro intoned in a driven undertone, his stunning eyes full of condemnation bright as sunlight in his lean, saturnine face.

'Is that so?' Jemima asked tightly, ridiculously annoyed that he could so easily dismiss Alfie's existence as an unimportant element.

Alejandro bit out an unamused laugh. 'You know

surprisingly little about men,' he breathed roughly. 'I'm much more interested in what you *did* in my bed with my brother and why you felt the need to do it.'

In one comprehensive sentence, he tore down the deceptive veil of civility and confronted her with the reality of his convictions and she was shocked into silence by that direct attack. The experience also reminded her that she had never found Alejandro's moods or actions easy to predict and had often failed to identify the whys and wherefores that drove that hot-blooded temperament of his.

'Did you *have* him in our bed?' Alejandro gritted, lean brown hands clenched so hard by his side that she could see the white of bone over his knuckles. Intimidated, she stepped away, which wasn't easy to do in that small room and her calves pressed back against the door of the pale modern cupboard unit behind her.

In the inflammable mood he was in she didn't want to engage in another round of vehement denials, which he had already heard and summarily dismissed two years earlier. 'Alejandro...' she murmured as quietly as she could, trying to ratchet down the tension in the explosive atmosphere.

He flung his dark head back, his brilliant gaze splintering over her so hard that she would not have been surprised to see a shower of sparks light up the air. For a timeless moment and without the smallest warning she was entrapped by his powerfully sexual charisma and it was like looking into the sun. She remembered the hum of arousal and anticipation that had once started on the rare nights he was home on time for dinner, when she knew he would join her in their bedroom and take her to a world of such joyous physical excitement that she would briefly forget her loneliness and unhappiness.

'Is my need to know such sordid details too raw for you? Did you ever once stop to think of what it might be like for me to be forced to picture my wife in my brother's arms?' Alejandro ground out wrathfully.

'No,' she admitted, and it was the truth because she had never been intimate with Marco in that way and had wasted little time wondering how Alejandro's offensive and unfounded suspicions might be making him feel. Angry with her? Disillusioned? She had already been much too familiar with the knowledge that he had to be experiencing such responses while she failed to live up to the steep challenge of behaving like a Spanish countess.

'No, why should you have?' Alejandro growled, his accent thick as treacle on that rhetorical question. 'Marco was simply a sacrifice to your vanity and boredom, a destructive, trashy way of hitting back at me and my family—'

'That's absolute nonsense!' Jemima flailed back at him furiously.

'Then why did you ever let him touch you? Do you think I haven't wondered how it was between you?' Alejandro slung back bitterly. 'Do you think it didn't hurt to imagine you naked with him? Sobbing with gratification as he pleasured you? Crying out as you came?'

'Stop it!' Jemima launched at him pleadingly, her face hot with mortification at the pungent sexual images he was summoning up. 'Stop talking like that right now!'

'Does it strike too closely for you?' Alejandro hissed

fiercely. 'You got off lightly for being a faithless, lying slut, so stop staring at me with those big shocked eyes. I won't fall for the little-fragile-girl act this time around— I *know* you for what you are.'

Disturbed by the implicit threat in those hard words, Jemima spun away and walked past him to the window, fighting to get a grip on the turmoil of her emotions. He had shocked her, he had shocked her very deeply, for it had not until that moment struck her that his belief in her infidelity could have inflicted that much damage. Two years back when he had confronted her about Marco, he had been cold, controlled, behaving almost as though he were indifferent to her. By then she had believed that Alejandro felt very little for her and might even be grateful for a good excuse to end their unhappy alliance. Only now did she recognise that she had been naïve to accept that surface show from a male as deep and emotional as he could be.

'I'm not a slut because I didn't have an affair with your brother,' Jemima muttered heavily, slowly turning back round to face him. 'And you should know now that my son, Alfie, is your son.'

'Is that supposed to be a joke?' Alejandro demanded with a look of angry bewilderment. 'I'm well aware that you suffered a miscarriage before you left Spain.'

'We *assumed* I had had a miscarriage,' Jemima corrected with curt emphasis. 'But when I finally went to see a doctor here in the UK, I discovered that I was still pregnant. He suggested that I might have initially been carrying twins and lost one of them, or that the bleeding I experienced was merely the threat of a miscarriage rather than an actual one. Whatever,' she continued doggedly, her slender hands clenching tightly in on themselves beneath his incredulous appraisal, 'I was still very much pregnant when I arrived in England and Alfie was born just five months later.'

Alejandro dealt her a seething appraisal, his disbelief palpable. 'That is not possible.'

Jemima yanked open a drawer in the sideboard and leafed through several documents to find Alfie's birth certificate. In one sense she could not credit what she was doing and yet in another she could not see how she could possibly do anything else. Her son was her husband's child and that was not something she could lie about or leave in doubt because she had to take into account how Alfie would feel about his parentage in the future. It was a question of telling the truth whether she liked it or not. Emerging with the certificate, she extended it to Alejandro.

'This has to be nonsense,' Alejandro asserted, snatching the piece of paper from her fingers with something less than his usual engrained good manners.

'Well, if you can find some other way of explaining how I managed to give birth to a living child by that date and it not be yours, I'd like to hear it,' Jemima challenged without hesitation.

Alejandro stared down at the certificate with fulminating force and then glanced up, golden eyes bright as blades and as dangerous. 'All this proves is that you must still have been pregnant when you walked out on our marriage. It does not automatically follow that the child is mine.'

Jemima shook her fair head and expelled her breath in a slow hiss. 'I know it doesn't suit you to hear this news now and I really didn't want to tell you. Too much water has gone under the bridge since we split up and now we lead separate lives. But the point is, I can't lie to you about it. Some day Alfie may want to look you up and get acquainted.'

Alejandro studied her with brooding dark ferocity. 'If what you have just told me is the truth, if that little boy does prove to be mine, it was vindictive and extremely selfish of you to leave me in ignorance!'

Jemima had paled. 'When I left you I had no idea that I was still pregnant,' she protested.

'Two years is a long period of time, yet you made no attempt to inform me that I might be a father,' he fielded harshly. 'I will want DNA tests to confirm your claim before I make any decision about what I want to do.'

Jemima compressed her lips hard at the reference to the testing. Once again Alejandro was insulting her with the assumption that she had been an unfaithful wife and that, for that reason, there could be doubt over who had fathered her child. 'Do as you like,' she told him curtly. '*I* know who Alfie's father is and there has never been any doubt of his identity.'

'I will make arrangements for the tests to be carried out and I will see you again when the result is available,' Alejandro drawled, with lashings of dark Spanish masculine reserve emanating from his forbidding demeanour and cool taut intonation.

'I'll contact a solicitor and start the divorce,' Jemima proffered in turn, determined not to leave him with the impression that he was the only one of them who could act and make decisions.

Alejandro frowned, dark eyes unlit by gold narrowing in a piercing scrutiny that made her uncomfortable. 'It would be foolish to do anything before we have that DNA result.'

'I disagree,' Jemima flashed back at him angrily. 'I should have applied for a divorce the minute I left you!'

Cool as ice water, Alejandro quirked an ebony brow. 'And why didn't you?'

Jemima dealt him a fulminating glance but said nothing, merely moving past him to yank open her front door in a blunt invitation for him to leave. She was shaken to register that she was trembling with temper. She had forgotten just how angry and frustrated Alejandro could make her feel with his arrogant need to take charge and do exactly what he wanted, regardless of other opinions.

'I'll be in touch,' he delivered on the doorstep.

'I'd appreciate some warning the next time.' Jemima lifted a business card off the table and gave it to him. 'Phone and tell me when you're coming.'

Anger shimmering through her, she slammed the door in his wake and peered out from behind the shelter of the curtains to watch him swing into his fancy car and drive off.

Nothing had changed, she reflected unhappily. Even being in the same room again as Alejandro revived all the doubts, insecurities and regrets she had left behind her when she gave up on being his wife…

CHAPTER THREE

JEMIMA left her teenaged babysitter in charge of the house and closed the front door as quietly as she could behind her. Thursday nights she and Flora went to choir practice and enjoyed a convivial evening in the company of friends. As a rule she looked forward to getting out. But, recently, Jemima had been in a thoroughly bad mood and indeed was still stiff with the angry resentment that she had been struggling to suppress for two long weeks.

'Cheer up,' Flora urged as the two women walked in the direction of the quaint little medieval stone church and village green that made Charlbury St Helens so pretty a village. 'You're letting this whole DNA-testing business eat you alive and it's not healthy for you.'

Jemima flung her friend an apologetic glance. 'I can't help feeling as though I've been publicly humiliated by it,' she confessed ruefully.

'Both the notary and the GP are bound by rules of confidentiality,' Flora reminded her with a reassuring glance. 'I seriously doubt that either will discuss your private business with anyone, particularly if it may end up in a civil courtroom.'

Unconvinced, but recognising her friend's generous

attempt to offer comfort, Jemima compressed her lips, not wanting to be a bore on the subject, even though the DNA tests had proved to be an exercise in mortification in which she felt that her anonymity and privacy had been destroyed. When such tests were required for a case that might end up in a court they had to be done in a legal and formal manner. A snooty London solicitor acting on Alejandro's behalf had phoned her to spell out the requirements. Jemima had had to make an affidavit witnessed by a public notary as well as have photos taken to prove her identity before she could have the tests for her and Alfie done by her own GP. The actual tests had been swabs taken from the mouth and completed in seconds, but Jemima had writhed in mortification over the simple fact that both the notary and the doctor were being made aware of the fact that her husband doubted that Alfie was his child. She knew that she would never, ever forgive Alejandro for forcing her to undergo that demeaning process, all because he was convinced that she had broken her marriage vows.

Yet how could she have refused the tests when refusal would have been viewed as a virtual admission of wrongdoing? she asked herself as she moved into the comparative warmth of the church and greeted familiar faces with a wave and a determined smile. Common sense told her that it was essential that Alfie's father should know the truth; for Alfie's sake there should be absolutely no doubt on that score in anyone's mind. Those were the only reasons why she had agreed to the tests being carried out.

The effort of raising her voice in several rousing choruses and then singing a verse solo in her clear sweet soprano took Jemima's mind off her combative feelings.

She was definitely feeling more relaxed by the time she helped to stack the chairs away. Fabian Burrows, one of the local doctors and a very attractive male in his mid-thirties, reached for her jacket before she did and extended it for her to put on.

'You have a really beautiful voice,' he told her.

'Thanks,' she said, her cheeks warming a little beneath his keen appraisal.

He fell into step beside her and Flora. 'Are you going for a drink?' he asked, a supportive hand settling to her spine as she stumbled on the way down the church steps.

'Yes.'

'Fancy trying The Red Lion for a change?' he suggested, coming to a halt by the church gate while other members of the choir crossed the road to the usual hostelry.

'Thanks, but I'm with Flora,' Jemima told him lightly.

'You're both very welcome to keep me company,' he imparted while Jemima tried frantically to interpret the frowning meaningful expression on her friend's face. Did that look mean that Flora wanted to take up the invitation or that she didn't?

'I'm afraid this isn't a good night,' Flora remarked awkwardly, turning pointedly to look out onto the road.

Jemima saw the sports car parked there a split second before she saw the tall dark male sheathed in a cashmere overcoat leaning up against the bonnet and apparently waiting for her. Dismay gripped her and then temper ripped through her tiny frame like a storm warning. After all, she had specifically asked Alejandro to give her notice of his next intended visit. How dared he just turn up again without giving her proper notice of his plans?

But somehow the instant her attention settled on

Alejandro an uninvited surge of heat shimmied over her entire skin surface and sexual awareness taunted her in tender places. His dangerous sensuality threatened her like the piercing tip of a knife. Scorching dark golden eyes set in a lean dark-angel face assailed her and suddenly it was very hard to breathe because, no matter how angry she was with him, Alejandro was still drop-dead gorgeous and sinfully sexy. Even the lean, well-balanced flow of his powerful body against his luxurious car was elegant, stylish and fluid with grace. She wanted to walk past him and act as if he were invisible while the compelling pull of his attraction angered her almost as much as his unexpected appearance.

'How did you know where I was?'

'The babysitter,' Alejandro told her softly. 'My apologies if I'm intruding on your evening.'

'Who is this?' Fabian demanded loftily.

'Oh, I'm just her husband,' Alejandro drawled in a long-suffering tone that made Jemima's teeth grind together in disbelief.

The other man stiffened in discomfiture and muttered something about seeing Jemima the following week at practice. Turning to address Flora, who was also hovering, Fabian escorted her away.

'How *dare* you say that and embarrass him?' Jemima hissed like a spitting cat at Alejandro.

Alejandro, very much in arrogant Conde Olivares mode, gazed broodingly down at his diminutive wife. 'It is the truth. Every time I come here you're knee-deep in drooling men and flirting like mad.'

'You don't have the right to tell me how to behave any more.' Jemima threw those angry words back at him in defiance of the manner in which he was looking down at her.

Alejandro closed lean, strong hands over her shoulders and, dark eyes glittering like polished jet in the moonlight, he hauled her close and his wide sensual mouth plunged down on hers in an explosion of passion that blew her defences to hell and back. She hadn't been prepared, hadn't even dreamt that he might touch her again, and she was so taken aback that she was totally vulnerable. Her legs wobbled below her as the fiery demand of his mouth sent a message that hurtled through her slight body like a shriek alarm and awakened the desire she had shut out and denied since Alfie's birth.

In an equally abrupt movement, Alejandro straightened, spun her round and pinned her between his hard muscular length and the car. A gasp of relief escaped her as he pressed against her for, at that moment, pressure was exactly what her body craved; indeed, in the grip of that craving she had no shame. Her breathing was as ragged as the crazy pulse pounding in her throat while he ground his hips into her pelvis and heat and moisture burned between her thighs.

'*Dios mio! Vamonos*…let's go,' Alejandro urged raggedly, pulling back from her to yank open the car door. He almost lifted her nerveless body into the leather passenger seat and with a sure hand he protected the crown of her head from a painful bump courtesy of the roof.

'Let's go,' he said. Let's go where? she almost shouted back in response. But she hid from that revealing question to which she already knew her own answer while being fully, painfully aware of what her body longed for. She shrank into the seat as he clasped the seat belt round her and then bent her buzzing head, her hands closing over her knees to prevent them from visibly shaking in his presence.

She had trained herself to forget what that desperate, yearning, wanting for him could feel like and she did not want to remember. But the taste of him was still on her lips, just as the phantom recall of his hands on her still felt current while the slow burn pain of his withdrawal of contact continued to shock-wave through her and leave her cold.

'We really shouldn't touch in public places,' Alejandro intoned soft and low.

Jemima clenched her teeth together, hating herself for not having pushed him away. How dared he just grab her like that? How dared he prove that he could still make her respond to him? Of course, had she known what he was about to do she would have rejected him as he deserved, yes, she definitely would have, she reasoned stormily. But back when she had still been living with him, she had *always* wanted him. Need had been like a clawing ache inside her whenever she looked at him and the only time she had felt secure was when she was in his arms and she could forget everything else. Hugging that daunting memory to her, she hauled a stony shell of composure round her disturbed emotions, determined not to let him see how much he had shaken her up.

'You still haven't told me what you're doing here,' Jemima complained as he followed her to her front door.

'We'll talk inside.'

Jemima had to swallow back a sharp-tongued comment. In every situation Alejandro assumed command and that he rarely got it wrong only annoyed her more. She went in to her babysitter and paid her. Audra lived only two doors down from her and the arrangement suited both of them.

'Do you make a habit of leaving a child in charge of a child?' Alejandro enquired.

'No, I don't,' Jemima countered curtly. 'And though Audra may look immature, she's eighteen years old and training to be a nurse.'

Alejandro did not apologise for his misapprehension. Jemima hung up her jacket and hovered, her face burning as she remembered the heat of that extravagant kiss.

'It's a little late for a social call,' she remarked flatly, avoiding any visual contact with him, refusing to knuckle down and play hostess.

'I wanted to see my son,' Alejandro confided in a roughened undertone.

The import of that admission engulfed her like a tidal wave. So the DNA testing had delivered its expected result and backed up her claims, and thanks to that he now had to accept that she had not been lying to him yet he had not opened the subject with the fervent apology that he owed her. Her chin came up at a truculent angle. 'Alfie's asleep.'

'I don't mind looking at him while he sleeps,' Alejandro confessed in a not quite steady rush, his excitement at even that prospect unconcealed.

For a split second that look on his face softened something inside her but she fought it. 'But you didn't believe me when I told you he was yours—'

'Let's not get into that. I know the truth now. I know he is my child. I only got the news this morning. This is the soonest I could get here.'

His eagerness to see Alfie dismayed her, even while

she tried to tell herself that his reaction was only to be expected. He had just found out that he was a father. Naturally he was much more interested in Alfie than he had been when he had assumed that her son was some other man's. 'I'll take you upstairs,' she offered, striving to take control of the situation.

Alejandro moved quietly into the bedroom in Jemima's wake and studied the sleeping child in the wooden cot. Black curls tousled, with his little sleep-flushed face, Alfie looked peaceful and utterly adorable to his besotted mother's eyes. Alejandro closed a strong hand over the cot rail and stared down, spiky black lashes screening his gaze from her.

Without warning Alejandro looked across the cot at her, brilliant dark eyes brandishing a fierce challenge. 'I want to take him home to Spain.'

That announcement hit her like a bucket of icy water, shocking her and filling her with fear for the future. She backed away to the door and watched Alejandro award his son an undeniably tender last glance. Yes, he could be tender when he wanted to be but it wasn't a notion that took him very often, she conceded painfully. He had looked at her the same way the day they learned that she had conceived and his initial unconcealed pleasure in the discovery that she was pregnant had made her swallow back and conceal her own very different feelings on the same score. Yet how could she recall those confusing reactions now when Alfie had since become the very centre of her world? Given the chance she would never have turned the clock back to emerge childless from her failed marriage, but it was already beginning to occur to her that a childfree marriage would have been easier to dissolve.

I want to take him home to Spain. That frank declaration raced back and forth inside her head as she led the way back downstairs. It was only natural that Alejandro would want to show Alfie off to his family while ensuring that Alfie learnt about the magnificent heritage and ancestry that he had been born into on his father's side, she reasoned, eager not to overreact to his announcement.

'What did you mean when you said you wanted to take him back to Spain?' Jemima heard herself ask abruptly.

Alejandro took off his heavy cashmere overcoat and draped it on a dining chair by the table that filled the small bay window in the living room. His elegant charcoal-grey business suit accentuated his height. His classic profile was cool and uninformative when he turned back to her but his stunning dark eyes were bright gold chips of challenge.

'I cannot allow you to have full custody of my son,' Alejandro spelt out without apology. 'I don't believe that you can offer him what he needs to thrive in this environment. I wish I could say otherwise. I have no desire to fight you for custody of our child but I do not see how I can do anything else without betraying my duty to him.'

'How...*dare*...you?' Jemima threw back at him in a fiery temper of disbelief, her heart racing as if she were running a marathon. 'I gave birth to your precious son alone and unsupported and I've been on my own ever since. Alfie is a very happy and well-adjusted little boy and you know nothing about him, yet the minute you find out he exists you assume that I am an unfit parent!'

'Does he even know he has a father or a family in Spain? Is he learning to speak Spanish? What kind of stability can you give him? You are not a responsible person.'

'What gives you the right to say that to me?' Jemima interrupted thinly, her hands clenching into defensive fists by her side.

His lean, darkly handsome face tautened into censorious lines. 'Look at the way you dealt with our marriage, your debts, your affair with my brother—'

'For the last time, I did not have an affair with your brother!'

'You don't deal with problems, you run away,' Alejandro condemned without hesitation. 'How could you possibly raise our child properly and teach him what he needs to know?'

'I don't have to stand here putting up with being criticised by you any more. We're separated,' Jemima rattled out, her voice brittle. 'I want you to leave.'

Alejandro grabbed up his coat. 'It's impossible to talk to you,' he vented in a driven undertone of frustration.

'You call threatening to take my child away from me *talking*?' Jemima exclaimed with incredulous force. 'How did you expect me to respond to a threat?'

'A threat is something that may not happen, but I will most assuredly fight you for custody of my son,' Alejandro extended grittily, refusing to back down.

Jemima breathed in deep and slow to calm her jangling emotions and studied him with angry, anxious eyes. 'What can I do or say to convince you that I am a good mother?'

Having donned his coat, Alejandro shrugged a broad shoulder as if she was asking him the unanswerable.

Jemima's thoughts were already ploughing ahead to reach several fear-inducing conclusions. If a custody battle went to court, Alejandro had the wealth to hire the very best lawyers and nobody representing her interests would be able to compete. The very fact that she had kept quiet about Alfie's existence for the first two years of his life would weigh against her. And how much importance might a judge lay on the truth that Alfie would one day be an influential member of the Spanish aristocracy in charge of a massive country estate and a very successful string of international family businesses? Such a background and his father's ability to prepare his son for those responsibilities could not be easily ignored.

'You can't do this to me,' Jemima protested. 'I love Alfie and he loves and needs me.'

'Perhaps it is my turn to be a parent for a change,' Alejandro said drily, tugging open the front door to facilitate his departure with an alacrity that was ironically no longer welcome to her. 'When it comes to sharing one little boy a divorce will leave few, if any, equitable solutions possible. We will both have to compromise.'

Jemima reached out in an ill-considered movement to thrust the door he had opened closed again before sliding between it and him like an eel. Violet eyes dark with strain in her pale heart-shaped face, she stared up at him and muttered tightly, 'We need to discuss this *now*!'

Alejandro sent her a sardonic glance. '*Madre mia*, you change direction with the wind. You told me to leave...'

Jemima gritted her teeth. 'Possibly I was a little hasty. I wasn't expecting you to already be making plans for Alfie. You annoyed me earlier. Why did you kiss me?'

Alejandro took a small step forward that trapped her between the wooden door and his lean, powerful body. 'Because I wanted to, *mi dulzura*.'

He called her 'sweetness' and she ran out of breath and rationality in the same instant. Awareness ran like a river of red-hot lava through her trembling length, her nipples swelling and blossoming like fire flowers while the tender flesh at the very heart of her burned and ached. The atmosphere was explosive and she couldn't fight the hunger stabbing at her. She studied the full curve of his sensual lower lip, reliving the taste of him, and slowly tipped her head back to meet hot golden eyes.

'Ask me to stay the night,' Alejandro urged thickly, pushing her back against the door, letting her feel the hard, promising power of his erection through his well-cut trousers. Air scissored through her lungs in a breathless surge, sexual heat uniting with dismay to hold her there.

'You want to stay?' Jemima whispered, already visualising closing a hand into the expensive fabric of his overcoat to haul him down to her, already imagining the taste and passion of him that drew her like a fire on a winter day. Desire had her in the fiercest of holds.

A long brown finger skimmed along the quivering line of her white throat, pausing to flick the tiny pulse flickering wildly above her collarbone. 'It's what you want too—'

'No,' Jemima gasped strickenly, feeling her self-discipline shatter like glass in the ambience and below it the roar of need she had resisted for so long.

'Liar,' Alejandro countered without hesitation, his confidence in his own powers of seduction absolute.

Her slender body vibrating with awareness, she still managed to tear free of him and step back. It hurt like hell. She couldn't think; she could only fight the craving that she recognised as a dangerous weakness. 'Leave,' she urged again, wanting to hug herself in consolation for the rush of cold and disappointment enveloping her.

'Call me when you come to your senses,' Alejandro drawled, hooded dark golden eyes undimmed by rejection as he tossed a business card down on the little shelf in the hallway.

And in a moment he was gone and she was left in a disturbing mess of conflicting emotions and regrets. She was furious with herself because she hadn't sorted out anything. Sex had got in the way and had only exacerbated the tensions between them. But she should have risen above the challenge to concentrate on Alfie and on Alejandro's threats. He had wanted to stay the night with her. He had wanted to share a bed with her again. The blood ran hot below her fair skin. For just a moment he had been as vulnerable as she to the powerful attraction that could still flare between them. She adjusted that thought the instant she thought it. No, Alejandro had *not* been vulnerable. If she had let him he would have slept with her again but it wouldn't have meant anything to him or led anywhere. He believed she had slept with Marco and he hated her for it. She lifted his business card and threw it down on the dining table in a fever of self-loathing. Alejandro was calling the shots again and she didn't like that at all.

Yet over three years earlier when they were dating

she had liked the way Alejandro had automatically taken charge and looked after her and had revelled in his masculine protective instincts. Looking back with hindsight, she marvelled at the way he had made her feel and how much maturity had changed her. Of course, she had been a virgin when they'd first met. As a result she had been far too quick to idealise Alejandro and believe that they had something special together. She had not even recognised him for the womaniser he was until one of the hotel maids had slid an old newspaper beneath her nose, pointed to a photo and said, 'Isn't that that Spanish guy you're seeing?'

And there Alejandro had been, pictured at some snobby London party with a beautiful blonde in an evening dress. The accompanying prose had made it clear that he enjoyed the reputation of a heartbreaker who always had more than one woman in tow. She hadn't wanted to believe the evidence even though Alejandro had already proved to be anything but a devoted boyfriend, cancelling dates as he did at the last minute and rarely phoning when he said he would. When she'd questioned him, however, Alejandro had been commendably frank.

'I'm not looking for a serious relationship,' he had told her without apology. 'I'm not interested in being tied down.'

Feeling stupid and hurt over the assumptions she had made and grateful that she had, at that stage, stayed out of his bed, Jemima had put the brakes on her feelings for him and had begun going out socialising again with her friends. Before very long she too was dating someone else, a local accountant who was flatteringly keen to offer her an exclusive relationship. But when Alejandro had realised that she was seeing another man, he had had a furious row with her, which had made it perfectly clear that, while he expected her to share him, he was not prepared to share her. For a few weeks they had split up and, although she was heartbroken at losing him at the time, she had thought it was the only option left.

Barely a month later, though, Alejandro had come back to her and had said that he would stop seeing other women. Jemima had been overjoyed and their relationship had entered a far more intense second phase. Head over heels in love with him as she had been, she had plunged straight into a passionate affair. He had rented a house not far from the hotel where she worked and they had spent every spare minute there together. In her entire life she had never known such happiness as she had known then, during the romantic weekends he'd shared with her. The demands of business and family, not to mention the fact that he lived in Spain, had often kept them apart when they wanted to be together, and on her twentieth birthday Alejandro had asked her to marry him. He had not said he loved her; he had *never* told her he loved her. He had merely said that he could not continue spending so much time in England with her. He had made marriage sound like a natural progression.

But he had not invited her to meet his family before they took that crucial final step. No doubt he had known how much his relatives would disapprove of his ordinary English bride, who had so little to offer on their terms. Within weeks of his proposal they had married in a London church with only a couple of witnesses present. She had had no idea at all of what his life in Spain would be like. In fact she had been a lamb to the slaughter in her ignorance.

Dragging herself free of wounding memories that still rankled, Jemima lifted her head high. That silly infatuated and insecure girl was dead and gone. This time around she was in control of her own destiny and, with that in mind, she snatched up her phone and rang Alejandro.

'We have to meet to talk about Alfie,' she told him urgently.

'Couldn't you have decided that while I was still with you?' Alejandro enquired drily.

'I'm not like you. I don't plan everything,' she reasoned defensively.

He suggested that she and Alfie meet him the following afternoon at his London apartment.

'I know you want to see Alfie again, but he would be better left out of it tomorrow—we'll probably argue.'

Having agreed a time and won his agreement on the score of Alfie, Jemima put down the phone again and wondered anxiously what rabbit she could possibly pull out of the hat that might persuade him that their son was better off living with his mother in England...

CHAPTER FOUR

THE London apartment was not the same one that Jemima remembered. The new one was bigger, more centrally located and sleek and contemporary in style, while the previous accommodation had been knee deep in opulent antiques and heavy drapes, a home-from-home backdrop for a family accustomed to life in a medieval castle.

A manservant showed her into a huge elegant reception room with the stark lines and striking impact of a modern artwork, again a very appropriate look for a family that owned a famous chain of art galleries.

She caught her reflection in the glass of an interior window and decided that, even though she was wearing the smartest outfit in her wardrobe, she looked juvenile in her knee-length black boots, short black skirt and red sweater. But her lifestyle no longer required dressy clothing and she preferred to plough her profits either back into the shop or into her savings. Having survived a childhood in which cash was often in very short supply, Jemima only felt truly safe now when she had a healthy balance in her rainy day account.

In the act of putting away a mobile phone, Alejandro emerged from an adjacent room to join her. His elegant black pinstripe suit and blue shirt fitted him with the expensive fidelity of the very best tailoring and the finest cloth, outlining broad shoulders, narrow masculine hips and long, long, powerful legs. Her attention locked to his lean dark features, noting the blue black shadow round his handsome jaw line, and for a split second she was lost in the memory of the rasp of stubble against her skin in the mornings. She could feel a guilty blush envelop her from her brow to her toes. His black hair still damp and spiky from the shower, Alejandro was the most absolutely beautiful man she had ever seen and her heart was jumping inside her as if the ground had suddenly fallen away beneath her feet.

'Is your friend looking after Alfie?' he enquired.

'Yes, but he attends a playgroup in the afternoons,' she explained.

She turned down an offer of refreshments and hovered while Alejandro helped himself to strong black coffee that scented the air with its unmistakeable aroma. Memories she didn't want were bombarding her again. He had taught her to grind coffee beans and make what he called 'proper' coffee. There had been so many things she didn't know about that he took for granted. He had even been a better cook than she was and right from the start she had been captivated by his knowledge and sophistication. But before their marriage—when things had gone wrong between them—he had scooped her up into his arms and swept her off to bed and she had been so ecstatic that she wouldn't have cared if the roof had fallen in afterwards. But once their sex life had ground to a halt, they'd had no means of communication at all and it had seemed natural to her that their marriage had then fallen apart. He had just lost interest in her, a development she had seen as being only a matter of time from the outset of their acquaintance.

'I couldn't sleep last night,' Jemima admitted in a sudden nervous rush, her eyes violet as pansies in the sunlit room. 'I was worrying about what you said about Alfie.'

'You named him Alfonso after my father. That was a pleasant surprise,' Alejandro remarked.

'He was named in memory of my grandfather, Alfred, as well,' Jemima advanced, not choosing to admit that the kindly vegetable-growing maternal grandfather she recalled had probably been the only presentable member of her former family circle, in that he had worked for a living and had stayed on the right side of the law. 'That's why I call him Alfie, because that was how my grandpa was known.'

Alejandro studied her with stunning dark golden eyes ringed and enhanced by black inky lashes. His charismatic appeal was so powerful that she couldn't take her attention off him and her mouth ran dry.

'We can't reasonably hope to share a child when we're living in different countries,' he told her.

Jemima tensed and smoothed her skirt down over her slight hips with moist palms. 'Other people manage it—'

'I want my son to grow up in Spain—'

'Well, you can't always have what you want,' Jemima pointed out flatly.

Alejandro set down his empty cup and strolled across the floor towards her. 'I too gave this matter serious thought last night. I can give you a choice...'

Her spine went rigid, her eyes flying wide with uncertainty. 'What sort of a choice?'

'Option one: you return to Spain and give our marriage another chance. Or, option two: I take you to court over Alfie and we fight for him.' As Jemima lost colour and a look of disbelief tautened her delicate pointed features Alejandro surveyed her with unblemished cool. 'From my point of view it's a very fair offer and more than you deserve.'

As an incendiary response leapt onto Jemima's tongue she swallowed it back and welded her lips closed, determined not to say anything before she had thought it through. But sheer shock was ricocheting through her in wave after wave. Alejandro was asking her to go back to him and live with him as his wife again? She was totally stunned by that proposition and had never dreamt that he would consider making it. 'That's a crazy idea,' she said weakly.

'If you take into account our son's needs, it's a very practical idea,' Alejandro contradicted levelly.

Jemima breathed in slowly and tried to concentrate her mind solely on her son's best interests, even though her brain was in a total fog at what he had just suggested. Many children might be more contented with two parents rather than one but that wasn't the end of the story. 'If we're not happy together, how could Alfie possibly be happy? I don't understand why you're even discussing the idea of us living together again.'

'Are you really that naïve?' His intent gaze was semi-screened by lush sooty lashes to a hot glitter of gold while the muscles in his strong jaw line clenched hard. 'I still want you. If I didn't I wouldn't be offering you this alternative.'

The heat of that look welded Jemima to where she stood and colour ran in scarlet ribbons into her cheeks.

Once again he had taken her by surprise. 'Are you saying that you're able to forgive me for the past?'

Alejandro loosed a harsh laugh of disagreement. 'No, I couldn't go that far. I'm saying that if I get you back into my bed, I will make the effort to overlook your past transgressions.'

Her bosom swelled with wounded pride and resentment as she drew in a very deep and steadying breath. 'Fortunately for me, I haven't the slightest desire to be married to you again. You may have considered it an honour the first time around, but for me it was more like living in purgatory.'

Alejandro dealt her a stony look that chilled her to freezing point and she knew that she had angered him. She recognised that he believed that he was making an enormously generous concession in offering her—an unfaithful wife—the opportunity to live with him again. She even recognised that lots of women would bite off his hand in their eagerness to accept such an offer. After all, he was drop-dead gorgeous, amazing in bed and open-handed with money…as long as you could tell him what you'd done with it, she completed inwardly and suppressed a shiver, flinching from her bad memories. But at heart Alejandro was as flint-hard and unyielding as his centuries-old castle. He believed she had betrayed him and he was not the forgiving type and would never come round to seeing or understanding her side of the story. He thought she was a slut and even if she lived with him for another twenty years he would die thinking that she was a slut.

'I've made a life for myself now in the village and I enjoy my life there,' Jemima responded in a stiff tone of restraint that did not come naturally to her. 'I was miserable in Spain and you didn't seem any happier with me as a wife. Why would you want to revisit the past?'

'Only because we have a son.' Alejandro gave her a sardonic appraisal. 'And this time around life could be much more straightforward.'

'How?' Jemima prompted baldly, wanting every detail of his thoughts even though she had no intention of accepting his offer.

'I know you for who you are now. I would have no false expectations, no sentimental ideas. Our marriage would merely be a convenient agreement for Alfie's benefit. All I would require from you would be the superficial show—'

'And sex,' Jemima added in a tight-mouthed undertone, because she felt demeaned that he had dared to include that aspect.

'Be grateful that you still have that much appeal, *mi dulzura*. Without the pull of that angle, I wouldn't even have considered taking you back.'

Clashing unwarily with hot golden eyes, Jemima experienced a deeply mortifying sliding sensation low in her pelvis. It infuriated her that she could still react to him that way when so much else was wrong between them. Her body took not the smallest account of her brain or even of common sense, for being attracted to Alejandro was destructive and stupid and likely to get her into serious trouble. It occurred to her that maybe he felt the same way about her and that was such a novel suspicion that she stared at him, wondering if he too could be fighting the same rearguard action against his own natural inclinations.

'You don't like the fact that you still find me attractive,' Jemima commented, daringly taking a stab in the dark.

'But I can handle it. Familiarity breeds contempt— isn't that what they say?' His brilliant eyes were lit by a sensual golden glimmer that as his gaze wandered over her seemed to burn over her skin like a tiny point of flame. 'I believe that this arrangement will give me a healthy chance of working you right out of my system.'

Jemima could not resist the sensual temptation of imagining what it would be like to be put to that kind of work in the marital bedroom. The more responsive parts of her treacherous body hummed with enthusiasm until shame and pride combined to suppress her facetious thoughts. She had never been able to escape the fear that wanting and loving any man as much as she had once loved and wanted Alejandro was weak and pathetic. It had inspired her into making numerous attempts to play it cool with him, most of which had blown up in her silly face as she had lacked both subtlety and good timing. She had acted all cool, for instance, once he'd stopped sleeping with her while she was pregnant; rather a case of closing the barn door after the horse had already bolted, she recalled impatiently. Those final weeks of their marriage he hadn't seemed to notice her at all and his increasing indifference and long working days had made her feel invisible and insignificant.

'I couldn't just go back to Spain,' she told him again. 'I've worked hard to build up my business. I don't want to lose it—'

'I'm willing to cover the cost of a manager for several months. That would give you the time and space to come up with a more permanent solution.'

Cut off at the knees by that unexpectedly practical proposal, Jemima muttered, 'I couldn't live with you again.'

'That decision is yours to make.' Alejandro shifted a broad shoulder in a fluid and fatalistic shrug, his lean, strong face full of brooding dark Spanish reserve and pride. 'But I've already missed out on two years of my son's life and I don't want to waste any more time. My English lawyer is waiting to hear whether or not I wish to proceed with a custody claim.'

That assurance hit Jemima like a bucket of snow thrown across unprotected skin. Every anxious cell in her body plunged into overload. 'Are you simply expecting me to make up my mind about this here and now?' she gasped.

Alejandro quirked an ebony brow. 'Why not? I'm not in the mood to be patient or understanding. I doubt that you suffered many sleepless nights while you were denying me the chance to get to know my son.'

In receipt of that shrewd comment on her attitude, Jemima turned almost as red as her sweater. It was true. She had pretty much celebrated her escape from Spain. She had regretted her failed marriage and cried herself to sleep many nights but she had blamed him entirely for that failure. Now sufficient time had passed for her to be willing to acknowledge that she, too, had made serious mistakes that had undoubtedly contributed to their break-up. She had certainly kept far too many secrets from him, had spent a lot of money, but that did not mean that she was prepared to have another go at their marriage. But she did, however, love her son very much and she did appreciate how much she had denied

Alejandro when she chose not to inform him that he was a father.

'I could come and stay in Spain for a few weeks,' she suggested limply as an alternative.

'A temporary fix of that nature would be pointless.'

'I couldn't possibly sign up to return to our marriage for the rest of my life. That's an appalling idea. Even convicts get time lopped off their sentences for good behaviour!' Jemima pointed out helplessly. 'Maybe I could consider coming out to Spain for a trial period, like, say…three months.'

Alejandro frowned. 'And what would that achieve?' he derided.

'Well, by then we would know if such an extraordinary arrangement was sustainable and I would still have a life to return to in the village if it wasn't working,' she argued vehemently. 'I'm not saying I will do it, but you would also have to give me a legal undertaking that you would not try to claim custody of Alfie while he was still in Spain because that would give you an unfair advantage.'

'The exact same advantage that you would have as an Englishwoman applying for custody in an English court,' Alejandro traded drily.

Her eyes fell before his at that response. 'But we just couldn't do it…*live* together again,' she protested in an enervated rush, folding her arms and walking round the room in a restive circle.

'There has never been a divorce in my family!'

'That's nothing to boast about. We're not living in the Dark Ages any more. People don't have to live with a mistake for ever.'

'But you think it's all right for our son to suffer all the disadvantages of coming from a broken home?'

Jemima groaned out loud in frustration, all shaken up at the very idea of reliving any part of their brief marriage. 'We can't make everything perfect for Alfie.'

'No, but it is our responsibility to give him the best of ourselves, even if that means making personal sacrifices. I respect that,' Alejandro intoned with insistent bite.

'You're always so superior. I want the best for Alfie too.'

'Yet you didn't see a problem bringing him up without a father,' Alejandro lashed back soft and low.

Her face flamed.

'If you truly do want the best for our son, come back to Spain.'

It was blackmail whichever way she looked at it: emotional blackmail, moral blackmail. He knew which buttons to push. He knew how to make her conscience writhe. He was too clever for her, she thought worriedly. If her best hadn't been good enough two years back, how much worse would she fare now with him? But had she ever really given him her best? a little voice asked her doggedly and the abstracted look in her gaze deepened. She was older and wiser and more confident, she reminded herself fiercely. Would it do her so much harm to give their marriage another shot? Of course it went without saying that it wouldn't work out and that both the trial and the subsequent break-up would hurt her again, but wouldn't agreeing give her the satisfaction of knowing that she had tried every option and made the best effort she could?

In the heat of that last inspiring thought, Jemima

turned back to focus on her tall, darkly handsome husband. 'All right. I'll come back to Spain but initially I'm only agreeing to stay for three months,' she extended, nervous tension rippling through her in a quivering wave as she realised what she was giving her consent to.

Alejandro stared back at her with brooding dark eyes, revealing neither satisfaction nor surprise at her surrender. 'I will accept that.'

Jemima gazed back at him, suddenly horrified at what she had allowed herself to be persuaded into. He had the silver tongue of the devil, she decided wildly. He had made her feel that any decent mother would have another go at being married for her child's sake. He had studied her with those smouldering dark golden eyes and told her that he *still* wanted her. Not only had she liked that news very much but her body had burned and her brain had shrivelled while she'd thought that truth through to its natural conclusion.

'Have you had lunch?' Alejandro asked.

Jemima backed away a step like a drug addict being offered a banned substance. 'No, but I'm not hungry. I think I should get back to the shop.'

'Of course, you'll have a lot of arrangements to put in place. I'll instruct a recruitment agency to find you a manager,' Alejandro imparted smooth as ice, gleaming dark golden eyes raking over her with a subdued heat that she felt as deep as the marrow of her bones. 'I don't want this to take too long. I also want to see Alfie.'

'Will you still be here over the weekend?' At his nod of assent, Jemima added breathlessly, 'Then come down and see him tomorrow.'

'How soon will you come to Spain?' he prompted.

'Just as soon as I can get it organised.'

'I should take you home,' Alejandro murmured before she got as far as the hall.

'No. I'm used to getting the train…'

'I'll take you to the station, *mi dulzura.*'

The immediate change in his attitude to her made a big impression on Jemima. All of a sudden he believed it was his job to look after her again and it felt seriously strange to have someone expressing concern on her behalf. She accompanied him down to the basement car park and climbed into his shiny car. As she clasped the seat belt Alejandro reached for her, a lean hand tugging up her chin so that his beautiful mouth could crash down on hers without anything getting in the way. It was like plugging her fingers into an electric socket or walking out unprepared into a hurricane. As he plundered her readily parted lips her hand rose and her fingers speared into his luxuriant black hair, holding him to her. The passionate pressure of his mouth on hers was a glorious invitation to feel things she hadn't felt in too long and the plunge of his tongue stoked a hunger she had never managed to forget.

'Dios mio! Te deseo.' He told her he wanted her in a voice hoarse with desire and it sparked a flame at the heart of her and made her shiver with shock. That fast, he had contrived to turn the clock back.

As Jemima drew back from him, breathless with longing and self-loathing, his brilliant gaze scanned her flushed face. 'If you stayed, I would give you so much pleasure.'

Jemima tore her stricken eyes from his, shame sitting inside her like a heavy rock because she was tempted. 'I'll see you on Saturday,' she said tightly.

All the way home on the train she was picturing his lean, strong features inside her head and tearing herself apart over what she had agreed to do. He might as well have hypnotised her! Sandy picked her up in the shop van and dropped her at Flora's cottage.

Twenty minutes later, Jemima was sitting at the island in her friend's kitchen with Alfie cradled half asleep on her lap from his afternoon exertions. Flora was studying her with wide and incredulous green eyes. 'Tell me you're not serious...I thought you hated your ex.'

Jemima shifted her hands in an effort to explain a decision that felt almost inexplicable even to her. 'What Alejandro said about giving our marriage another go for Alfie's sake made sense to me,' she confided ruefully. 'When I walked out on him I didn't know I was still pregnant and I'm not sure I would've gone if I'd known.'

Her friend's face was troubled. 'You were a bag of nerves when I first met you and you had no self-esteem. It's not my place to criticise your husband but if that's what being married to him did to you, something was badly wrong.'

'Several things were badly wrong then, but not everything was his fault.' Alfie snuggled into his mother's shoulder with a little snuffle of contentment and she rearranged his solid little body for greater comfort. 'Marco's living in New York now and another...er... problem I had, well, it's gone too,' she continued, her expressive eyes veiled as she thought back reluctantly to those last stressful months in Spain, which had been, without a doubt, the most distressing and nerve-racking period of her life.

'You want to give your marriage another chance,'

Flora registered in a tone of quiet comprehension. 'If that's what you really do want, I hope it works out the way you hope. But if it doesn't, I'll still be here to offer support...'

CHAPTER FIVE

FROM her stance on the edge of the small adventure playground, Jemima watched Alejandro park his sumptuous vehicle. Halston Manor estate lay a few miles outside the village and its grounds were open to the public the year round and much used by locals. Jemima had arranged their meeting with care, choosing an outdoor location where Alfie could let off steam and where all interaction between his parents would have to be circumspect.

Alejandro was dressed with unusual informality in a heavy dark jacket, sweater and jeans. Black hair ruffled by the breeze and blowing back from his classic bronzed features, he looked totally amazing and every woman in the vicinity awarded his tall ,well-built figure a lingering look. Jemima tried very hard not to stare and, shivering a little in the cool spring air, she dug her hands into the pockets of her red coat and focused on Alfie, who was climbing the steps to the slide, his big dark eyes sparkling with enjoyment.

'The family resemblance is obvious,' Alejandro remarked with husky satisfaction. 'He is very much a Vasquez, though he has your curls and there is a look of you about his eyes and mouth.'

'I've told him about you,' Jemima informed him.

'How did he take it?'

'He's quite excited about the idea of having a father,' she confided. 'But he doesn't really understand what a father is or what one does.'

In receipt of that news, Alejandro gave both Jemima and Alfie an immediate demonstration, striding forward to intervene when a bigger boy pushed his way past Alfie on the slide steps and the toddler nearly fell. Jemima watched as Alejandro grabbed her son and steadied him. Alfie laughed and smiled up at Alejandro, who spoke to him before stepping back to applaud Alfie's energetic descent of the slide.

Her attention glued to man and child, Jemima hovered. Father and son did look almost ludicrously alike from their black hair and olive-tinted skin to their dark eyes and the brilliance of their smiles. Alfie shouted at her to join them at the swings and she went over, her small face taut, her eyes wary. She could barely speak to Alejandro, yet they'd had a child together: it was an unsettling thought. She pushed Alfie on the swing and watched him show off for his father's benefit. Then her son jumped off the swing before it came to a halt and fell, bursting into tears of over-excitement.

Alejandro scooped him up and took him straight over to another piece of equipment to distract him and Alfie quickly stopped crying. Jemima hadn't expected Alejandro to be as assured at handling a young child as he so obviously was. She watched him crouch down to wipe Alfie's tear-wet face, and tensed as Alfie suddenly flung his arms round Alejandro and hugged him with the easy affection that was so much a part of him. She saw Alejandro's expression as well: the sudden blossoming warmth in his dark eyes, the tightening of his fabulous bone structure that suggested that he was struggling to hold back his emotions and the manner in which he vaulted upright to unashamedly hug Alfie back.

Set down again and in high spirits, Alfie scampered over to his mother and grabbed her hand. 'Ducks... ducks,' he urged and, turning his head, he called, *'Papa...Papa!'* in Spanish as if he had been calling Alejandro that all his life.

'Now we go and feed the ducks,' Jemima explained to Alejandro.

Alfie tearing ahead of them, they walked along the wide path by the lake.

'He's a wonderful little boy,' Alejandro commented abruptly, his dark, deep accented drawl low pitched and husky. 'You've done well with him.'

Jemima shot him a surprised glance and met gleaming dark golden eyes with an inner quiver. 'Thanks.'

'Only a happy, confident child could accept a stranger so easily.'

Warmed by that approval, Jemima felt less defensive and she leant back against a tree and relaxed while Alfie fed the ducks and talked to Alejandro about them. A lot of what the little boy said was nonsense-talk because he only had a small vocabulary, but Alejandro played along. Alfie stretched out a trusting hand to hold his father's and Alejandro began to tell his son about the lake at the Castillo del Halcón and the ducks that lived there.

'The recruitment agency got in touch yesterday and have promised to send me a couple of CVs by midweek,' she told him.

'*Estupendo!* Marvellous,' Alejandro pronounced,

studying her from below the dense black fringe of his lashes, eyes a glinting gold provocation that sent colour winging into her cheeks.

He looked at her and she could barely catch her breath. Her nipples were taut, distended buds beneath her clothing and her thighs pressed together as though to contain the rise of the hot, sensitised heat there. She swallowed hard, struggling to shut out the fierce sexual awareness that was racing through her veins like an adrenalin rush.

'Tell me,' Alejandro murmured in a lazy undertone as he towered over her, one lean brown hand braced against the tree, and there was absolutely no forewarning of what he was about to say. 'What did you get from Marco that you couldn't get from me?'

Jemima recoiled from him as though he had stuck a knife in her and moved away several steps, her face flushing, her eyes evasive and full of discomfiture.

'Naturally I want to know,' Alejandro added curtly. *So beautiful and so treacherous,* he reflected darkly. It was a fact he could not afford to forget.

Jemima threw her head up, her eyes purple with strong emotion. 'He talked to me, he took me places, he introduced me to his friends… He wanted my opinions and my company, which is more than you ever did!'

In receipt of that recitation of his brother's deceptive talents, Alejandro dealt her a forbidding appraisal. 'Primarily, Marco used you to get at me. He's a player and you found that out for yourself, didn't you? Did you or did you not tell me that you hadn't heard from my brother since you left Spain?'

At that retaliatory crack, furious mortification gripped Jemima for, of course, he was correct in that assumption. Put under pressure, Marco's friendship had lacked strength, permanence and true affection. Refusing to respond in kind, however, she set her teeth together and for what remained of Alejandro's visit she spoke mainly to Alfie and only when forced to his father.

A month later, a four-wheel-drive driven by an estate worker collected Jemima and Alfie from their flight to Spain. Jemima had hoped that Alejandro might pick them up personally but she was not surprised when he failed to appear. As she had learned when they were first married, Alejandro was always very much in demand and, as his wife, she was usually at the foot of his priorities list.

It was a recollection that could only annoy Jemima on the day that she had had to leave behind both the home and the business that she cherished. An excellent manager had taken over the shop. Jemima had put most of her possessions in storage so that the older woman could also rent her house. But all the work she had put into training as a florist, growing her client base for the shop and decorating her home now seemed pointless. On the other hand, she *had* only agreed to a three-month sojourn in Spain, Jemima reminded herself bracingly. Surrendering to Alejandro's blackmail had cost her dear but retaining custody of the little boy securely strapped in the car seat beside her was much, *much* more important to her.

The Castle of the Hawk sat on rocky heights above a lush wooded valley in the remote Las Alpujarras mountains, the last outpost of the Moors in Spain. Little villages with white flat-roofed houses and steep roads adorned the mountainsides while olive, orange and almond groves, grapevines and crops grown for biofuels flourished in the fertile soil. The Vasquez family had ruled their hidden valley like feudal lords for centuries and anyone seeing Alejandro, the current Conde Olivares, being greeted by deferential locals soon appreciated just how much weight that heritage still carried.

Agriculture alone, however, had proved insufficient to keep Alejandro's family in the style to which they had long been accustomed. His father had opened an art gallery in Madrid, but it had taken Alejandro—an astute businessman with the guts to take risks and an infinitely more ruthless edge—to turn that initial purchase into a hugely profitable and influential chain of international galleries. A hotel group and several financial enterprises had also been acquired by Alejandro and between the demands of his business empire and the running of the family estate Alejandro had very little time to spare.

He had always tried to maintain a low profile with the media at home and abroad. However, not only was he very photogenic and the bearer of an ancient title, but he had also, prior to his marriage, enjoyed a love life that was very newsworthy. Those facts, allied with his growing visibility in the business world, had ensured that he could no longer pass undetected and both their wedding and their break-up had, to Alejandro's intense annoyance, attracted newspaper coverage. For that reason, Jemima felt she should have been better prepared when she'd found cameras waiting at the airport earlier that day to record their departure for Spain, but she had been out of the limelight for so long that the appearance of the paparazzi had taken her completely by surprise.

Jemima would also have liked to have known how on earth word of her apparent reconciliation with her Spanish Count and the fact that they now had a child had reached the public domain. She did have very good reason to dread renewed media exposure. Indeed, just thinking about how those photos might cause trouble for her again made Jemima feel sick with apprehension. She was praying that the bad luck that had overtaken her some years earlier and trapped her between a rock and a hard place would not reappear to cause her and those connected with her even more damage and distress.

Endeavouring to bury her worries and control her nerves, Jemima drank in the beauty of the picturesque landscape while the heavy vehicle climbed a familiar road girded by a forest of oaks and chestnuts. The car finally pulled into a courtyard ringed by ornamental trees in giant pots that bore the family coat of arms. Alfie stared out with rounded eyes at the towering thirteenth century stone fortress that now surrounded them on three sides. Her youthful figure slender in casual jeans and a tangerine T-shirt, Jemima left Alfie in the car and rattled the knocker on the giant studded front door.

The door was opened by the middle-aged housekeeper, Maria, but she stepped back to give precedence to a stout older woman with greying hair who carried herself with a ramrod straight spine, her hard black eyes glinting with outrage.

'How dare you come back to my home?' Doña Hortencia erupted, barring the doorway.

Her daughter, Beatriz, hurried into view and twisted her hands together in an ineffectual protest. 'Jemima, how lovely to see you again… *Mamá*, please, *please*… we must respect Alejandro's wishes.'

Her sister-in-law's anxious, embarrassed face was painful to behold. That her loyalties were tearing her in two was obvious.

The driver carted over two suitcases while Beatriz stared out at the child she could see peering through the window of the estate vehicle. 'Oh, is that Alfie, Jemima? May I go and see him?'

For once impervious to her mother's mood, Beatriz hurried out to the car. The driver hefted up the luggage and stepped past Doña Hortencia with a subservient dip of his head.

'Good afternoon, Doña Hortencia,' Jemima said stoically, following the driver indoors with her flight bag on her shoulder. She was determined not to react in any way to the dirty looks she was receiving and believed that she was a good deal less likely to be bullied than she had been two years earlier. The older woman would certainly make the attempt but Jemima had learned to care less about the impression she made.

Aglow with satisfaction, Beatriz returned holding Alfie's little hand in hers. '*Mamá*, look at him,' she urged with enthusiasm.

Doña Hortencia gazed down at her first grandchild and her forbidding stare softened for an instant before she shot a grim glance at her daughter-in-law. 'This little boy, Alejandro's son and heir, is the one and only thing you have got right.'

Swallowing back the urge to retaliate in kind, Jemima said nothing. What was there to say? Alejandro's mother would never like her or accept her as an equal. Her son had married an ordinary working woman and a foreigner, rather than the wealthy Spanish aristocrat whom the older woman had thought his due, and Doña Hortencia was too stubborn, arrogant and prejudiced to revise her attitude. When Jemima had first come to the castillo, the Spanish woman had done everything possible to ensure that her daughter-in-law's daily life was as miserable as she could make it. This time around, however, Jemima had no plans to accept victimhood.

Beatriz accompanied Jemima up the carved staircase and made small talk as if her life depended on it. Dark gloomy oil portraits of Alejandro's ancestors lined the hall and landing walls. Serious though Alejandro so often was, Jemima reflected helplessly, he was a positive barrel of laughs when she compared him to his predecessors.

'Alejandro has engaged a nanny to help you with Alfie,' Beatriz announced.

'How very thoughtful of your brother,' Jemima remarked after a noticeable pause.

'Placida is the daughter of one of our tenants and a very able girl,' her companion extended anxiously.

Jemima did not want to make Beatriz feel uncomfortable. 'I'm sure she's perfect for the job.'

'This is the room I chose for Alfie,' Beatriz announced with pride, throwing wide the door on a fully furnished nursery complete with a cot, a junior bed and piles of toys. 'Of course, you may prefer to choose another.'

'This is lovely. Did you organise all the toys?'

Beatriz laughed. 'No, that was my brother. Can you believe that Alejandro went shopping for his son?'

'I wouldn't have believed it if you hadn't told me,' Jemima admitted, as Alejandro's dislike of shopping was well known. Bitter as she was about finding herself back in Spain, she could only be touched by the effort he had made on Alfie's behalf. Equally quickly, however, her thoughts travelled in the opposite direction. Of course, wouldn't Alejandro's actual presence mean more than the purchase of expensive toys? In fact wasn't Alfie receiving his first dose of the same benign neglect that Jemima had once endured as Alejandro's wife?

Undisturbed by such deep and troubled mental ruminations, Alfie pelted across the room to grab a toy car with an eager hand. His aunt watched him, entranced. 'You must be so proud,' Beatriz remarked.

Not for the first time, Jemima felt sorry for Beatriz, who was only thirty-five years old but very much on the shelf of her mother's making, for no young man capable of winning Doña Hortencia's approval had ever come along. A dutiful daughter to the last, Alejandro's older sister lived the sedate life of a much older woman.

Placida, the small dark-haired nanny, came to be introduced. After chatting for a while, Jemima left Alfie with Placida and Beatriz and crossed the corridor. The elaborate suite of tower rooms in which she had lived with Alejandro before her pregnancy had brought all sharing to an end was unrecognisable to Jemima at first glance. All the furniture had been changed and a pale yellow colour scheme had banished the dark ornate wallpaper that she had once hated, but that Doña Hortencia had informed her was hand-painted, exceedingly rare and there for eternity. A maid was already busily unpacking her cases and putting her clothes away in the dressing room.

A weird and worrying sense of déjà vu was now settling over Jemima. Alejandro's non-appearance at the airport had first ignited the suspicion that she was about to discover that nothing had changed in the marriage she had left behind. He had also just demonstrated his engrained habit of taking authoritarian charge of anything and everything that came within his radius. In hiring Placida over her head, Alejandro had shown that only his opinion mattered and Jemima did not appreciate being made to feel superfluous in her child's life.

Once the maid had gone, Jemima went for a shower and padded through to the dressing room to extract fresh clothes. It was a shock to open the closets and find that they were already stuffed full of brand-new garments and the drawers packed with equally new lingerie, all of it in her size. Her own small collection of clothes looked shabby in comparison. Evidently, Alejandro, the guy who hated to shop even for himself, had ordered her a new wardrobe. Such generosity was very much his trademark but it made Jemima feel uncomfortable. Perhaps he didn't trust her to dress smartly enough. Perhaps her lack of formal fashion sense had once embarrassed him. Maybe that was why he had gone shopping for her...

Yet the prospect of dining with her haughty mother-in-law garbed like a poor relation in more humble clothing had surprisingly little appeal and Jemima succumbed to the temptation of the new clothes. She selected an elegant sapphire blue dress and slid her feet into delicate sandals before hurriedly going to check on Alfie. He was playing happily in the bath while Placida watched over him. Using her slightly rusty Spanish, Jemima established that Alfie had already eaten his evening meal and she returned to the bedroom.

While she was combing her rebellious hair into a less tumbled style the door opened and she froze. Alejandro, already in the act of removing his tie, appeared. His immaculate grooming was, for once, absent. Indeed, in the bright light of the sunset flooding into the room through the windows, his tailored suit looked crumpled and almost dusty, his black hair tousled, while a dark shadow of stubble heavily accentuated his angular jaw line. But, even with all those flaws taken into consideration, he *still* looked spectacular, awesomely masculine and awesomely sexy. As she studied him, her body reacting with treacherous enthusiasm even as her pride rejected those earthy responses, hot, heady anger threatened to consume her.

'I told Maria we would dine alone next door tonight. Give me ten minutes for a shower,' Alejandro urged her carelessly, but the scorching golden eyes that raked over the mane of strawberry-blonde curls framing her heart-shaped face, before roaming down to the pouting curves defined by the fine fabric of her dress, were in no way casual. That appraisal was so hot she was vaguely surprised that her body didn't start smoking and if anything that bold, sensually appreciative appraisal only increased her resentment.

'Where do you get the nerve to look at me like that?' Jemima launched at him in furious condemnation of that familiarity and the evident plan for a romantic meal for two. It would take a great deal more than that one tiny effort to turn her into the compliant wife he so obviously wanted and expected.

His well-shaped ebony brows drew together as he shed his jacket and embarked on the buttons of his shirt. 'You're too eye-catching to ignore,' he told her teasingly

Jemima was fighting to hang onto her temper. She

didn't need a crystal ball to tell her that it was never cool to rail at a man for keeping his distance and even less cool to complain of a lack of attention. So she spun away and glowered at her own frustrated reflection in a tall cheval mirror. Why should she give him the satisfaction of knowing that she had been disappointed when he failed to show up at the airport? Or when he didn't even take the trouble to phone to make a polite excuse for his absence from home? Yet that lack of consideration for her feelings was so familiar from the past that she couldn't help wanting to scream and shout in complaint.

'I'm such an idiot!' she suddenly exclaimed, unable to hold back her seething emotions and keep her tongue glued to the roof of her mouth any longer. 'Somehow I thought it would be different…that you'd make more of an effort to make this work this time—'

'What are you talking about?' Alejandro demanded in the act of shedding the shirt to reveal a superb bronzed muscular chest sprinkled with dark curling hair and a hard, flat stomach that easily met the attributes of the proverbial six-pack.

Jemima spun back to face him. A pulse was beating so fast at the foot of her throat that it was a challenge to find her voice. With every fibre in her body she was blocking out and refusing to respond to his mesmeric physical appeal. 'I arrived here a couple of hours ago. What did you think it would be like for me to be confronted with your mother before I even saw you again? Obviously it didn't occur to you that for once in your life you should have been here for me!'

'I left a message with my mother for you. Are you

saying that you didn't receive it?' Alejandro prompted in a tone of hauteur that only set her teeth on edge more.

'Your mother hates me like poison. Are you still so naïve that you think she would take the trouble to pass on a message to me?' Jemima fired back at him.

'If you didn't get the message, I can only apologise for the oversight,' Alejandro drawled smooth as glass, casting off the remainder of his clothes with incredible cool and strolling into the bathroom as lithe and strikingly naked as a sleek bronzed god.

That non-committal and reserved response made Jemima so mad, she was vaguely surprised that the top of her head didn't blow off. 'Don't pull that aristocratic indifference act on me to try and embarrass me into silence!' she hissed, stalking after him into the bathroom.

'Since when has it been possible to embarrass you into silence?' And with that cutting comeback Alejandro switched on the shower and forced her to swallow back her ire as she assumed that he could no longer hear her above the noise of the water beating down on the tiles.

But Jemima was so irate she still couldn't shut up. The suave assurance with which Alejandro had stripped off in front of her and calmly entered the shower had acted like an electric shock on an already raw temper. 'I hate you when you treat me like this!' she yelled.

While Alejandro showered, Jemima paced in the doorway, all recollection of her past unhappiness as his wife returning then and there to haunt her. Not for anyone would she go through that experience again! And yet hadn't she just signed up again for a rerun on Alfie's behalf? How could it benefit Alfie that she wanted to kill his father in cold blood?

The water switched off and the fleecy white towel on the tiled wall was snatched off the rail. Jemima was trembling and she wrapped her arms round herself. Alejandro reappeared with the towel knotted round his narrow hips, his damp black hair slicked back from his brow and his big powerful body still beaded with drops of moisture. He surveyed her with infuriating, deeply offensive assurance.

'You don't hate me. Of course you don't,' he told her drily.

'And how do you make that out? By the time that I walked out on our marriage, I couldn't *stand* you!'

Alejandro moved towards her and she backed into the bedroom. 'But why?' he queried in the most reasonable of voices. 'Because I had realised what you were up to with Marco? Because I asked you to explain what happened to all that money? Any man would have demanded answers from you.'

'First and foremost I left you because you wouldn't believe a word I said, but I *did* have lots of other good reasons,' Jemima flung, her eyes bright as violet stars below her fine brows as she challenged him.

Alejandro frowned darkly. 'I'm hungry. I want to get dressed and eat. I don't want to get into a big scene right now.'

Such a surge of rage shot through Jemima's tiny frame that she genuinely felt as though she had grown physically taller. 'Alejandro…there's never a right time with you. But I suggest that for once you look at what you did to contribute to the breakdown of our marriage and stop blaming me for everything that went wrong—'

'Leave the past behind us.'

'Don't you dare say that to me when you continually throw everything I did back at me!' Jemima hissed.

Alejandro groaned out loud. 'So, say what you have to say in as few words as you can manage.'

'You forced me to live under the same roof as your mother—'

'The castle is very large. Such living arrangements are common in Spain—'

'It was never that simple. Doña Hortencia loathes me and she made my life a misery the last time I was here. What did you ever do to stop her?' she condemned fiercely.

'You always exaggerate. How was your life made a misery?' Alejandro countered in a discouraging tone of disbelief.

'If I asked any of the staff to do anything they had to run it by your mother first because she insisted that she was still the mistress of this household. Usually, whatever I wanted I didn't get and I found that humiliating. She criticised everything I did, refused to speak to me at mealtimes when you weren't there and insulted me to my face in front of visitors. Ask your sister. Beatriz avoids trouble like the plague but she won't tell you any lies if you ask the right questions.'

Alejandro had screened his brilliant gaze and his wide sensual mouth was compressed by the time she had finished speaking. 'I'll check it out.'

Jemima knotted her hands into fists. 'So, you can't take my word on that either?'

'Since it looks as though I am destined to go hungry tonight, what else do I stand accused of?' Alejandro enquired with sardonic bite.

His derisive intonation made Jemima's teeth grind

together. She was shivering with temper and her gaze locked accusingly to his. 'It's your fault that I fell pregnant with Alfie!'

Alejandro studied her in obvious bewilderment. 'You love our son. You can scarcely hold his conception against me.'

'I did when I first discovered that I was pregnant. You chose to be careless with contraception but I paid the price for it,' she challenged, flushing as she recalled the passionate bout of lovemaking in the shower that had led to her unplanned pregnancy. 'We had only been married a few months and I was still quite young for motherhood. I didn't feel ready for a baby and being so sick while I was carrying him didn't help. It made me feel more trapped than ever here but you didn't understand how I felt, did you?'

'No, I didn't, but then you didn't tell me at the time,' Alejandro countered levelly. 'Naturally I realised that you were unhappy but I assumed that was because you were unwell. I would've thought that by now you would have put any bitterness behind you on that score.'

Jemima regarded him with seething resentment. 'So *you* get a clean slate while *I* get reminded of my every mistake?'

'Alfie is *not* a mistake, Jemima. He is most probably the best thing that ever happened to either of us,' Alejandro proclaimed in an undertone of driven emotion that was rare for him, his stunning golden eyes unusually eloquent.

Her eyes suddenly stung with prickling tears. 'I didn't mean that *he* was a mistake...'

'Then what *did* you mean?'

'You see, there you go again...thinking the very worst

of me!' Jemima launched accusingly, the swimming moisture in her eyes overflowing.

'No, I don't.' Alejandro reached for her slim shoulders in a sudden movement that took her by surprise and he pulled her up against his lean, powerful body. 'But it's hard for me to understand how you can love Alfie but still regret his conception.'

Jemima quivered with awareness as the heat of him penetrated her dress. 'I don't regret it any more.'

'Yet you're still blaming me for a moment's forgetfulness when you could equally well blame yourself.' His stunning dark golden eyes flamed over her upturned face.

As she met his gaze head-on a kind of crazy lethargy gripped Jemima. She could feel the slow pound of her blood through her veins, the racing beat of her heart in her ears and in the pit of her stomach the pull of that electrifying, shockingly strong craving that only he could ignite. He lowered his head and kissed her with unashamed hunger, his lips demanding, his tongue probing with ravishing skill, his teeth nipping at the soft underside of her generous lower lip in a way that made her release a long, shuddering moan of helpless response.

He kissed her until her heart hammered, until she was breathless and hot and no longer thinking straight. She *felt* the zip of her dress going down. She felt the garment shimmy down her arms and simply slide to her feet. As he lifted her up she kicked off her shoes and let him bring her down on the bed. She loved his strength, his unhesitating self-assurance. She knew that she couldn't pretend that she was being seduced against her will. She knew she wouldn't be able to tell herself that he had caught her in a weak moment. What was driving her was the almost painful clawing heat of sheer sexual hunger and the awareness shocked her.

'We shouldn't,' she told him weakly, even as her hand rose to his face and her fingers traced the splendid angle of one high cheekbone, her thumb stroking along the edge of his beautiful mouth, which was capable of giving her so much pleasure.

'Let's not go back to the games we used to play before we got married, *mi dulzura*,' Alejandro husked in sensual reproof.

Utterly bewildered by that comment, Jemima dropped her hand and stared up at him. 'What are you trying to imply...?'

CHAPTER SIX

'NO COMMITMENT, no sex,' Alejandro paraphrased huskily. 'You utilised the most basic feminine weapon of all.'

'That wasn't a game or a weapon!' Jemima protested in a pained voice, wounded that he could even think that of her. From the moment she'd realised just how strong a hold Alejandro had on her heart, she had tried her best to protect herself. Saying no to sex while he still had other women in his bed had seemed to be common sense rather than a form of manipulation.

'Why pretend?' Alejandro murmured, lowering his handsome dark head and letting his jaw line rasp softly along the extended line of her throat before he followed that trail with his mouth, lingering in places that became erogenous just through his touch and laughing when she squirmed beneath him. 'It was highly effective. In the end I wanted you, *only* you. I wanted you so much that having you began to seem like winning the top prize. And I have to admit, you more than lived up to your promise in my bed.'

Her cheeks flushed. 'But it wasn't a game. It might've been for you, it wasn't for me. I was a virgin, for goodness' sake!'

'And I was duly appreciative of the fact. I married you,' Alejandro reminded her doggedly.

But Jemima had just had an unsettling glimpse into how he viewed those months prior to their marriage. Evidently he had always believed that it was the power of lust for her long-withheld body that had stoked his desire to the point where he offered her a wedding ring so that she was always around, always available. With that shallow basis, was it any wonder that their relationship had failed? There was nothing lasting about lust, she told herself, even as she lifted her hips in a helpless circling motion beneath the pressure of his weight on hers, every skin cell singing with eagerness.

Alejandro shimmied down her body to let his mouth travel across the pale hillocks of her breasts encased in turquoise silk and lace cups. He released the catch on her bra and tugged her up against him to enjoy the warm soft weight of the sensitive flesh that spilled into his hands. She gasped as he entrapped the straining peaks between thumb and finger, rubbing the swollen pink tips until she leant back into him with an uninhibited moan of response.

'I love your breasts,' he husked. 'Such a delightfully lush surprise on that tiny frame of yours.'

Jemima strained back against him, her spine arching as the feeling of pressure and awareness low in her pelvis increased. He twisted her round and down again and found the delicate rosy buds he had already massaged into prominence with his devouring mouth. It was as though her breasts were a hotline to her groin, for the surge of heat and moisture between her thighs was instantaneous. A finger stroked along the taut damp band of fabric at her crotch and she flinched, letting her head fall back as a low moan of encouragement was wrenched from her throat. She wanted him so much it hurt to wait.

'Have you any idea how often I've fantasised about this moment in the last few weeks?' Alejandro asked her thickly, peeling off her panties and using a knee to part her legs. His dark golden eyes glowed with sexual heat over the naked expanse of her delicate curves.

Jemima was trembling. The temptation to revel in the depth of his desire had died on the reflection that lust had no longevity and lying willingly naked for his appraisal only made her all the more conscious of the things she didn't like about her body. She had always thought that her legs were too short and the extra weight she carried at breast and hip too much for her height. As she began to curl away from him he bent down and crushed her lips under his with a passionate urgency that burned through her like a flaming brand. The plunge of his tongue affected her like a chain of firecrackers sparking through her taut length and her hips rose pleadingly, her whole body singing with sharp urgent need.

'Oh, *please*,' she said shakily, impatient, needy, wanting more than she could bear.

'I want to enjoy you first...I want to wait,' Alejandro framed with ragged ardour, playing with the delicate pearly folds between her thighs while he worked his skilful passage down over her quivering body, watching her expressive face as she fought to stay in control.

'Don't watch me,' she urged unevenly, suffering sweet torment from the hunger he was stoking.

He touched her with such infinite finesse, knowing the perfect spot, the exact amount of pressure, the ideal pace. She cried out loud, eyelashes sliding down to screen her eyes as the pleasure raced and screamed through her twisting length. He licked the skin of her inner thigh, following the trail to a more intimate place and dallying there with sensual expertise until she thought she might pass out with the intensity of her response. Her climax took her like a roaring storm, demanding every ounce of her energy and throwing her up to a breathless height of excruciating pleasure as she writhed in sobbing satisfaction.

He pulled back from her when she wanted him to hold her close. The world was a thousand miles away from her at that moment when she was still lost in the cocoon of all that breathtaking pleasure. Then she heard the slide of a drawer, the sound of foil tearing and a moment later he was back with her. After what she said earlier, she registered that he would not risk her falling pregnant again.

Jemima felt wanton, because when he came back to her he was hugely aroused and her body thrilled anew for she could hardly wait for that final act of possession. Orgasm hadn't satisfied that deep driving need to be with him again in the most basic way of all. He slid over her and she lifted to him at the first probing thrust of his bold shaft. He felt so big, so good when he plunged into her long and hard and deep and she gasped, violet eyes flying wide, raw excitement licking through her like flames.

'You *really* want me,' Alejandro growled with all-male satisfaction, surging into her receptive body with sudden driving urgency.

It was like being caught in the eye of a hurricane. A kind of stormy wildness pulsed through her to stoke the rising rush of crazy excitement already leaping high with her anticipation. Alejandro settled on a potent pagan rhythm. He was rampant, irresistible and her heartbeat thumped faster and faster in tune with his strong movements. Gasping, she rose under him, her body moving of its own accord as the feverish, hot, stimulating delight of his possession gave her ever-increasing pleasure. Somewhere towards the end of that ravenous ride she screamed, writhing as the ecstatic convulsions of a second climax seized hold of her. The sheer intensity of the experience almost made her black out and she lay shell shocked in the aftermath.

'*Dios mio*. That was amazing,' Alejandro husked above her head, his arms still anchored round her to keep her close. 'To think that I was afraid I might not be able to get it up with you because of Marco. You deliver such an erotic buzz I would have to be made of stone to resist you.'

Jemima tensed and stiffened defensively. Her lips parted and almost simultaneously a long brown forefinger nudged against her mouth.

'No more denials, *querida*. Every time you deny what you did I get angry again and it has been a very long and difficult day,' Alejandro admitted heavily.

Prevented from stating her case by his wall of entrenched disbelief and distrust, Jemima suffered an immediate sense of alienation and she pulled free of his embrace to roll over into a cooler spot in the bed. She lay on her side and looked back at him, her violet eyes bright with antagonism below her wildly tumbled strawberry-blonde curls. He looked so relaxed, black hair tousled by her fingers above his bold bronzed profile. Her fair skin was tingling and probably pink from the burn of the stubble he hadn't got to shave off before taking her to bed, but deep down inside her there was a well of indescribable physical satisfaction that had been running on empty ever since she had left Spain previously. Their marriage had always been a blazing success in the bedroom. But she knew it would be a long time before she got over the embarrassment of having revealed just how much she had craved his touch.

Alejandro turned his handsome head on the pillow to look at her with spectacular dark brown eyes semi-veiled by lush ebony lashes. 'Surely you can see that we cannot make a success of living together again without an honest acceptance of the past?'

Her generous mouth took on a mutinous slant. He had already travelled from refusing to believe her to refusing even to *listen* to her denials so what hope of exoneration did that give her for the future? His belief in her infidelity was unshakable.

'Shower, then dinner,' Alejandro instructed arrogantly in the smouldering silence, closing a stubborn hand over hers to drag her across to his side of the bed while he tossed back the sheet and vaulted upright.

'Where were you today? What happened that you had to leave a message for me?' Jemima asked abruptly as he propelled her into the spacious bathroom with him.

'Pepe, one of the vineyard workers, had a tractor accident. He was badly hurt,' Alejandro told her, his mouth compressing into a bleak line. 'I stayed at the hospital to support his wife. Their only child lives abroad and the other relatives are elderly. I'm afraid Pepe didn't make it and by the time I got his wife home again and offered my condolences to the rest of the family...'

Jemima was aghast at what he was telling her. 'Yes,

I can imagine how awful it must have been. I'm sorry, if I'd known I wouldn't have said anything—'

'But you didn't know so you were entitled to complain.' The speed with which he dismissed the matter told her that he didn't want to discuss it further. He had not exaggerated when he had said what a difficult day he'd had.

In the spacious tiled shower with the water streaming down over his big bronzed body he leant back against the wall for a moment or two, his eyes closing, and she finally appreciated just how tired he was. Her conscience smote her and she resented that feeling because when they were first married Alejandro had often contrived to make her feel that way. So often he'd had something more important, serious or meaningful to do with his time than be with her. She had often felt guilty, undeserving or selfish for just wanting to see more of him. Pepe's wife and family, however, would have found his presence a source of great comfort and support because he was that kind of a guy: strong and reliable in times of crisis.

Knowing that, she had often wondered why he had let her down so badly when she needed him. Or as his unsuitable and unhappy wife had she simply been yet another burden and source of worry for him, one he'd been relieved to be free of again? It would be foolish for her to forget that he had only taken her back so that he could have his son living with him in his home in Spain.

She didn't bother getting dressed again. Clad in a blue nightdress and satin wrap, she joined Alejandro in the reception room adjoining their bedroom where a meal was served in spite of the late hour. Casually clad in jeans and a black T-shirt, he looked younger and more approachable as well as heart-stoppingly handsome. A big vase of fresh white daisies adorned the round table and she remembered how his mother had once summarily dumped one of Jemima's own amateur floral arrangements. In those days she had been naïve, easily hurt and upset. She had barely had the maturity to be a wife, never mind a mother, and she had made more than one stupid decision, opting for the wrong choices and what had seemed like the easy way out when life got tough.

Alejandro studied his reclaimed wife intently across the table. Even with her pale hair in an untidy riot of curls and without a scrap of make-up, she was so beautiful with her fragile features, flawless skin and unusually coloured eyes that she commanded and held his full attention. The sex might be even more amazing than he recalled but he wasn't yet fully convinced that he had her where he wanted and needed her to be. The memory of her three-month proviso outraged his sense of justice. His polar opposite, she was impulsive, capricious and, as he had cause to know, wildly extravagant. It would be a challenge to predict her next move.

Once again he was at war with himself, Alejandro recognised angrily. It was a familiar predicament where Jemima was concerned. How could he have so compromised his convictions that he took back an unfaithful wife? Moreover, an unfaithful wife who still refused to admit her guilt? And an unrepentant gold-digger who had undoubtedly only survived in England for so long without his financial support because she had already carefully bled him dry of thousands of euros before she'd left him. Her escape fund? What else? It was a galling suspicion for a male once accustomed to female adulation and pursuit. Only his wife had run in the other direction.

But what right had he to the moral high ground? He had used their toddler son as a weapon and blackmailed her into returning yet, amazingly, he didn't feel guilty about what he had done. Had he not acted in his son's best interests? Dealing with such a woman demanded extraordinary measures.

He sipped his wine, savouring the vintage while his keen intelligence continued to present him with truths he would have preferred to ignore. Jemima might make him burn with desire but she was bad news for him. A man should aspire to a decent woman with standards, not stoop to the level of a dishonourable and deceitful one. But the instant he'd been subjected to the sight of the men panting after her skirts in that little English village his libido and territorial instincts had flamed to unmanageable heights. The prospect of leaving her free to take such men to her bed in his place had sentenced him to sleepless nights and repeated cold showers, for his blood ran hot.

Jemima was *his* and, undeniably, a weakness. Every man could afford an indulgence as long as he practised damage control, Alejandro ruminated, his lean, strong face hard with self-discipline. And she couldn't hurt him because he didn't love her. He had never been in love and was proud of the fact, he reminded himself with innate pride. Men in love were fools with women while a man in lust knew exactly what he was doing and why he was doing it.

Uncomfortable with the lingering silence, Jemima finally spoke up. 'There were reporters and cameras at the airport when I arrived for my flight out here today. They seemed to be waiting for Alfie and me, expecting us…'

Alejandro was frowning with annoyance. 'Someone

must have tipped them off. How else would they have known you would be there?'

'Well, it wasn't me—'

'Are you sure of that?' Alejandro prompted cynically.

Her eyes widened in surprise and consternation. 'But why would I tip off the paparazzi?'

'Either because you were paid for the information or because you revel in the attention of the press.' Alejandro tossed his napkin down and rose to his full impressive height. His devastatingly handsome features were grave. 'Whichever it is, be warned: I don't like that kind of publicity.'

'Where are you going?' Jemima pressed tautly, already reeling from the accusation he had just made.

'To bed. I'll look in on Alfie first. *Buenas noches, querida.*'

A faint surge of pink illuminated her delicate bone structure. Her hands clenched into fists of restraint below the level of the table but she passed no further comment. After their passionate lovemaking in what had once been the marital bed his departure for the night to a separate room was like a slap in the face. It was a reminder that appearances were deceptive and that neither the expensive gift of a new wardrobe nor the meal eaten *à deux* meant that they were engaged in a genuine reconciliation.

'I didn't tell the paps that we were getting back together,' Jemima declared loudly.

'Someone did.' Unimpressed dark golden eyes clashed with hers, his strong jaw line at an aggressive angle.

'You know, I didn't appreciate you taking on a nanny without discussing it with me first,' she confided abruptly, deciding that she might as well confront that issue.

'We can discuss that tomorrow,' Alejandro fielded impatiently and a moment later he was gone, leaving her still seated with her dessert sitting untouched in front of her.

Minutes later, the maid arrived with a trolley to clear the table and Jemima went to check on her son, finding him sound asleep in his cot. For a moment she envied the contentment etched in Alfie's peaceful little face. A strange cot in an unfamiliar room and new faces all around him? No problem. Alejandro's son had rolled with the punches and he saw no reason to stay awake and on guard. And why shouldn't her son feel that way? There could be no comparison between his childhood and the one his mother had endured, which had marked her all her life with fear and anxiety. Alfie's world had always been safe and his needs had always been met. He had never been denied love. He had never known violence or malice. And Jemima was quietly proud of the fact that she had done much more for him than her parents had ever done for her.

Back in the bedroom she slid into bed and put on the television, finally tuning into a music channel before resting back against the pillows.

She had no idea what time it was when a sound wakened her and she half sat up, pushing her hair out of her eyes and blinking as Alejandro flicked the remote control at the television to switch it off. The bedside lamp was still lit. 'I must've fallen asleep,' she mumbled drowsily, wondering if the noise from the set had disturbed him, for he was barefoot and wearing only his jeans with the top button undone. A silky black furrow of hair ran down over his stomach and disappeared below the waistband. Suddenly she felt hot.

Alejandro sent her a brooding look from glittering dark eyes. 'I'm sleeping here tonight,' he informed her with a hostile stare-you-down cool stamped on his lean dark features as though he expected her to argue with him.

Jemima was startled by that announcement. After all, it was already three in the morning according to the digital display on the clock by the bed. Lips parting slowly in surprise, Jemima watched as he shed his jeans. A lean, powerfully muscular silhouette—he was wearing, it transpired, not a stitch below the denim and he was...well, he *was* sporting a rampant erection. There was really no avoiding that fact. Hot colour washed her face and a melted-honey sensation curled low in her pelvis. She was his object of desire and he couldn't hide it and she liked that. The separate-bedroom concept had bitten the dust at remarkable speed.

'I should be too tired for this, *querida*,' Alejandro growled as he came down on the bed beside her, his every fluid movement full of virile masculine promise. 'But I can't sleep for wanting you.'

Jemima lay back like Cleopatra reclining on a ceremonial barge, ever ready to be admired. She gazed up at him in sultry invitation and with hot golden eyes he crushed her soft full mouth under his with an erotic savagery that sent desire lancing through her slim length in an arrow of fire. She closed her hand round him and he shifted against her with a guttural sound while she teased the silky sleek heat of his sex over its iron-hard core. With an eagerness that thrilled her, he wrenched her free of the nightdress, his hands finding the white globes of her breasts and then the swollen damp flesh between her thighs. Every sense on high alert, her body went wild as the pounding throb of heat and hunger pulsed through her tender body, racking her with a stark storm of need.

'*Por Dios*, I can't wait,' Alejandro framed hungrily through a welter of passionate and devouring kisses that only left her gasping for more.

And dimly Jemima wondered what was happening to her because, somehow, even though she had been satiated he had set her alight again and the balance of power was no longer hers. Alejandro had never felt more necessary to her as he turned her on her side and plunged into her tight hot core, stretching her, filling her with a sweet, dominant force she could not resist. Delirious excitement powered through her quivering body in wave after wave when he rubbed her swollen nipples and teased the tiny bud of pleasure below her mound. He pounded into her at an enthralling pace until the ache and the burn combined into a fiery explosion. She reached a shattering release, convulsive spasms of delight roaring through her sobbing, shaking length until at last she lay still in his arms, weak and utterly spent.

Alejandro turned her round and pressed a kiss to her cheek before stretching up to douse the lights. 'Nobody but you has ever given me pleasure like that.'

And in receipt of that accolade, Jemima went from warm and reassured into a place of wounding self-doubt. Nothing had changed. It was always all about sex as far as Alejandro was concerned. He had never loved her yet, even though she had never believed she was the wife he really wanted, he had still married her. That had never made sense to her. But even so, Jemima was all too used to not making the grade with those she loved. Her mother would have loved and valued her daughter more had Jemima been the baby boy she had wanted to please her husband. Her father had never loved her, nor had he ever pretended to. There had been boyfriends but no one serious before Alejandro and she had fallen so hard for him that the sheer pain of having once loved and lost him still had the power to wound her.

She lay awake in the darkness, reassured by his continuing presence. It might only be sex that kept him there but that was better than nothing, wasn't it? She could walk away from him again without getting hurt, she told herself soothingly. She didn't love him any more; she had got over that nonsense. Once she had believed that Marco's obvious pleasure in her company might magically make his big brother view his wife with newly appreciative eyes. Instead Alejandro had simply assumed that her close friendship with Marco was based on sex. When that was the only tie he himself acknowledged with her, how could he have understood that she and Marco had bonded on quite another level?

Suppressing a regretful sigh over her tangled and unhappy past, Jemima finally drifted off to sleep...

CHAPTER SEVEN

JEMIMA only awoke when china rattled on a tray and the curtains were trailed noisily back. Sunlight drenched the bed in a shower of warm golden brilliance and she sat up with a sleepy sigh. She was immediately conscious of the stiffness of her limbs and the intimate ache at the heart of her. X-rated memories of how she had celebrated the breaking of the dawn assailed her. It was little wonder she had slept like a log afterwards, not even stirring when Alejandro got up.

She stared in disbelief at her watch, for the day was in full swing and it was comfortably past noon. The maid set down the tray on a side table and settled Jemima's wrap down on the bed for her use while asking her whether she wanted to eat in the room next door or outside on the roof terrace. Self-conscious at being naked, with her nightdress lying in a heap in the middle of the floor where Alejandro had hurled it, Jemima fought her way into the wrap while contriving to stay mostly covered by the sheet.

'Thanks. I'll eat outside,' she said, sliding out of bed and pushing her feet into mules to follow the maid through the door and up the little narrow curving staircase in the corner and out onto the roof terrace of the tower. Once it had been her favourite place in the castle, safe from all intruders and prying eyes. Warm, all-encompassing heat curled round her lightly clad frame when she stepped out into the fresh air to enjoy the magnificent view she remembered. It stretched as far as the eye could see right up to the snow-capped Sierra Mountains that girded the valley.

Far below in the gardens she heard a child's laughter and she stood at the battlements from where she espied Alfie, who was playing ball on an immaculate green lawn with a small figure she assumed to be Placida. Some mother she had proved to be since her arrival at the castle, she reflected ruefully. Resolving to spend the rest of the day with him, Jemima sat down at the shaded table and quickly embarked on the delicious lunch on the tray. She was really hungry and ate with appetite before taking the tray back downstairs, laying out white cropped knee-length trousers and a green T-shirt from her own store to wear and heading straight for the shower.

Her hair in damp ringlets, she was coming down the main staircase when she heard a female voice raised in shrill argument. Indeed the voice might almost have been described as being at screaming pitch and it was matched by the deep bass notes of a clipped male voice. The racket was emanating from the imposing salon on the ground floor. In the main hall two of the domestic staff were stationed outside the service door to the kitchens and clearly engaged in eavesdropping. Her face flushed and miserable, Beatriz emerged abruptly from the room and the staff slipped hurriedly through the service door and out of sight.

'What's going on?' Jemima asked baldly.

'*Mamá* is very offended with Alejandro,' Beatriz told her uncomfortably.

'Oh…' Stifling her curiosity because she thought it wiser not to get involved in a family matter, Jemima walked right past the door of the salon. 'I'm going out to the garden to join Alfie and Placida.'

Alejandro's sister accompanied her, clearly keen to escape the bad feeling on the domestic front. 'Alejandro has asked Doña Hortencia to move into a house on the estate,' she revealed.

Startled by that news, Jemima turned to look at her companion with wide eyes of enquiry. 'My goodness, that's very sudden!'

'Her belongings are already being packed,' Beatriz declared in a dazed undertone. '*Mamá* is very shocked. I have never seen Alejandro so angry or so resolute. She is to move into a hotel until the house is fully prepared for her.'

'That must have been some argument.' Jemima did not have the hypocrisy to pretend regret at the prospect of Doña Hortencia moving out of the castle, but she was very much surprised by the development.

'I will miss my nephew,' Alejandro's sister admitted heavily.

'But surely you're not moving out as well?' Jemima exclaimed.

'*Mamá* will expect me to accompany her.'

'But I don't and I'm sure Alejandro won't either,' Jemima stated, because she knew that Alejandro was very fond of his sister and troubled by the restricted life she led with their mother. 'This has always been your home, Beatriz.'

The tall, full-figured brunette lifted worried eyes to hers. 'Are you sure that you and Alejandro wouldn't mind if I stayed on?'

'Of course, we wouldn't. I would be glad of your company, particularly when Alejandro is away on business.'

'My stepmother would never forgive me for deserting her...' Beatriz looked shocked at the concept of the new way of life she was clearly envisaging. 'I'm not sure I *could* go against her wishes and do it—'

Her brow pleating, Jemima had come to a sudden halt. 'Did you just refer to Doña Hortencia as your "stepmother"? Or did I get that wrong?'

In her turn, Beatriz frowned uncertainly at the smaller blonde woman. 'Didn't you know?' she queried somewhat abstractedly, her mind clearly still focused on her future living arrangements. 'Of course we have always had to call her *Mamá*. I was only three years old and Alejandro a newborn baby when our own mother died.'

Jemima stifled the curious questions ready to spring to her lips. It was typical that Alejandro had not chosen to enlighten her as to that salient fact. It did at least explain why Doña Hortencia had always seemed very cold towards her elder son while seeming almost dotingly fond of his younger brother, Marco. 'But Marco is?'

'Marco was born four years after Doña Hortencia married our father,' Beatriz confirmed quietly. '*Mamá* was very upset when she realised that Marco could not inherit a larger portion of what our father left in his will because it would have meant splitting up and selling the estate.'

Alfie ran across the lawn to throw himself at his mother when he saw her approaching. Laughing and cuddling his solid little body, Jemima hugged her son close and urged his nanny to take a break. Beatriz played ball with her nephew and Jemima found herself hoping that her sister-in-law would have the courage to break free of her stepmother's suffocating control and stay on at the castle.

Almost an hour later, Alejandro strolled out to join them. Sheathed in lightweight khaki chinos with the sleek lines of a designer fit and a short-sleeved shirt, he looked gorgeous. When his spectacular black spiky-lashed golden gaze sought hers, Jemima went pink as she recalled the intimacies they had shared so freely during the night hours. Alfie beamed at his father and gave him the ball while Beatriz excused herself, saying that she ought to go and see if she could assist Doña Hortencia.

Jemima stood by containing her intense curiosity while Alejandro and Alfie fooled about with the ball. When they had both had enough, Alejandro suggested taking Alfie down to the lake and loaded them into an estate vehicle.

'I didn't realise until Beatriz mentioned it that Doña Hortencia was actually your stepmother.'

Alejandro compressed his lips. 'She's the only mother I can remember. My own died from eclampsia within hours of my birth.'

'That was a tragic loss for all of you,' Jemima remarked.

'My father remarried months after her death. Hortencia, not my mother, was the true love of his life,' Alejandro explained flatly. 'He worshipped the ground she walked on and he came close to bankrupting the estate in his determination to give her the very best of everything.'

Jemima was suddenly beginning to revise her once sunny assumptions about Alejandro's childhood. 'Was it a happy marriage?'

'*He* was happy, but I don't think she has ever been satisfied in her life with what she had. When my father was dying, however, he became very concerned about Hortencia's future—I believe she had shared her fears with him—and he begged me to always treat her as though she was my birth mother. It was his last wish. I gave my word and I have respected it ever since. Until today it did not occur to me that in tolerating her excesses I had been unfair to you.'

'Why?' Jemima questioned. 'What happened today?'

'Had you let me know how my stepmother was treating you when we were first married I would have stopped it then. You should have been honest with me,' Alejandro murmured in a tone of reproach rather than censure, his striking eyes troubled. 'This was your home and as my wife it is your right to take charge of the castle and the staff—'

'I'm not sure I could have coped with the responsibility in those days,' Jemima cut in lightly, realising that for some inexplicable reason all she wanted to do at that moment was make him feel better rather than add another weight to his conscience.

His lean, strong face clenched hard. 'But you never had the opportunity to *try*. Had you not been hampered by Hortencia's spite you would have managed perfectly well. You are a capable young woman.'

'Did your sister say that she was spiteful?' Jemima prompted in surprise, for Beatriz virtually never had a bad word to say about anyone. They were walking down towards the lake that gleamed through a grove of silvery olive trees like a reflective mirror on the valley floor.

A brooding expression darkened Alejandro's features. 'There was no need for her to do so. The manner in which my stepmother spoke of you today was sufficient for me to appreciate the level of malice which I was dealing with. The only possible solution was for her to move out—'

'Do you regret that?'

'How could I?' Alejandro confided with a harsh laugh that acknowledged the older woman's challenging temperament. 'Although Beatriz and I had no choice but to treat her as our mother, she had no maternal love to give us. She sent both of us off to boarding school as soon as she could. And after Marco was born, she resented my position as the eldest son and ensured that I had little contact with my father.'

'Then you were kinder to her than she deserved,' Jemima pronounced feelingly.

'But I can't forgive myself for not appreciating how she was treating you when I first made this your home.' Alejandro stared down at her with intent eyes and reached for her hand in a warm gesture of encouragement that took her by surprise. 'I hope you can move past that bad beginning now and learn to love this place and its people as I do, *querida*.'

That he wanted things to change for her benefit and that he had already made a bold first move towards that end pleased Jemima a great deal. But it was the eloquent expression in those beautiful eyes the colour of rich malt whisky in sunlight that affected her the most. He really did want their marriage to work this time around and, even though that might be primarily because they now had a child to consider, his determination and his caring about what it would take to make her happy in

Spain impressed her. It was a beginning, and a better beginning than they had made together when they first married...

A slight figure in an emerald-green silk skirt suit that was bright against her fair complexion and wealth of strawberry-blonde hair, Jemima stepped up to the podium with a heart beating as fast as a drum. She set her little prompt card down where it could catch her eye if she forgot what she had to say. As this was her first ever public speech, she had kept it short and succinct and had rehearsed it thoroughly with Beatriz beforehand.

In spite of those precautions, though, perspiration still dampened her short upper lip and her nerves were bouncing about like jumping beans. At a nod of readiness from the charity director, Jemima began to speak about the need for the sanctuary for female victims of domestic violence being provided by the shelter. The fund-raising benefit was aimed at providing new purpose-built premises where women and children could stay in safety and begin to rebuild their lives.

At the back of function room, she was conscious of Alejandro watching her. Beatriz was by her brother's side and smiling encouragement, but it was less easy to tell what Alejandro was thinking. She was pleased enough that he had rescheduled a business trip so that he could accompany her to the evening event. Jemima returned to their table, quietly content that she had contrived to control her nerves. It was thanks to Beatriz, who had long had an interest in the charity, that Jemima had got involved. Although it was not a fact that she would have shared with her husband, she had felt a great sense of empathy with the frightened women and children she had met and talked to at the shelter.

'You were terrific, *esposa mia*.' Alejandro regarded her with frank approbation and she reached for his hand to squeeze it. He had just called her his wife in a tone of pride and affection that went a long way towards healing the still raw wounds inflicted in the past.

But then, over the past couple of months Jemima had seen a different side to Alejandro's brooding temperament. As he turned his handsome head and stood up to politely acknowledge the greeting of a local businessman she was wearing a warm smile. Somehow they had put the past away, although sometimes she feared that putting those troubles untouched into a locked box was more of a shortcut than a long term solution. Marco was never, ever mentioned and neither, fortunately, she felt, was the disturbing question of all the money she had once contrived to run through.

On the other hand, she and Alejandro were enjoying an accord that they had never had in the past when he worked such long hours that she was constantly left to her own devices and deprived of a social life. It was that isolation that had made her so grateful for Marco's friendliness. But over two years on Alejandro had learned how to make time for her and Alfie and he had made the effort to introduce them to his world. He had taken them over every inch of the valley, showing them over his various businesses and introducing them to the tenants and the employees, so that for the first time Jemima felt as though the estate and the castle were her home as well.

An opening day for the public to view the castle had given Jemima the excuse to do several floral arrangements. Family, friends and relations, who had attended a dinner party that same evening, had been hugely impressed and Jemima had already received several requests to act as a floral consultant at local events. Having acted as an advisor at a couple now, she wasn't yet sure that she wanted to embark on what promised to be another business. No longer subject to Doña Hortencia's withering asides and cutting put-downs, Jemima was comfortable entertaining guests at the castle and had discovered that just being herself was sufficient.

Day by day, Alfie was blossoming; his days were much more active and varied than they had been in Charlbury St Helens and there were far more people around to give him attention. In fact, for a while, all that admiring attention had rather gone to Alfie's head and he had become too demanding; a solid week of toddler tantrums had ensued whenever he'd been subjected to the word no. Jemima had been amused by the discovery that Alejandro, so tough in other ways, had had to steel himself to be firm with his son when the little boy had thrown himself on the ground and sobbed with a drama that she was convinced came from his father's side of the family. It was a new relationship for Alejandro, who had never been allowed to enjoy the same close ties with his own father as a boy.

And so far Alejandro had shown every sign of being a brilliant dad. He had put a lot of effort into building a good relationship with his little son. Alfie adored him and raced to greet him the minute he heard his footsteps or his voice. Jemima had been impressed by the time and trouble Alejandro had taken to get to know Alfie and find out what he enjoyed. She had only to see father and son together to know that she had made the right decision in coming back to Spain.

Jemima was also happy in a way she had never thought she could be again, although sometimes she felt as if she were floating in a deceptively calm sea while wilfully ignoring the dangerous undertow and the concealed rocks. The next day, Alejandro took her on a long drive through the mountains to a sleepy town with an amazing little restaurant that served astonishingly good food. As they were getting back into the car Alejandro asked without the smallest warning, 'Did Marco ever bring you up here?'

And caught unawares with her defences down, she felt her face freeze, wasn't able to help that strong reaction to a name that was never voiced. 'No, he didn't. I would have said,' she murmured stiffly.

Clearly unimpressed by that claim, Alejandro gave her a hard dark appraisal, which warned her that though the body of her supposed infidelity might have been buried it was still at great risk of being disinterred. He hadn't forgotten or forgiven her imaginary betrayal and, for several taut seconds while she gazed stonily back at him, she bristled with an amount of resentment and rancour that would go a fair way to destroying any marital reconciliation. It was a struggle to keep the lid on her emotions.

'I shouldn't have asked,' Alejandro conceded tautly, the two of them momentarily enclosed by the suffocating sweaty heat of the car before the air conditioning could kick in and cool the interior.

'I'm surprised you did—Marco has urban tastes. He prefers clubs and culture to the countryside,' Jemima reminded him, staring fixedly out through the windscreen but seeing nothing, wondering why she had said that, why she had extended the dialogue instead of dropping it cold.

'And you always did like dancing,' Alejandro quipped, his intonation stinging like a sharp needle jabbed in the arm.

'After we were married, when did you ever take me?' Jemima countered defiantly, ready and looking for a fight now, all patience at an end.

Brilliant dark golden eyes alight with scorching rebuke at that tart gibe, Alejandro closed long brown fingers round her hand to tug her closer and he brought his mouth hotly and hungrily down on hers in retribution. For an instant her hand skimmed down over one high olive cheekbone in an unintended caress and then she dropped her hand and her fingers closed into the front of his jacket and clenched there instead, because the burning stream of desire he had unleashed fired her up as fiercely as her disturbed emotions. Her breasts were taut nubs below her clothing, the tender flesh between her thighs warm and moist and ready. Swearing only half under his breath at the intensity of her response, Alejandro thrust her back from him and started up the car.

'You shouldn't begin anything you can't finish,' she whispered helplessly, her body stabbing her with jagged regret over the loss of that so necessary physical contact with him.

Without warning Alejandro laughed and shot her a wicked long-lashed glance, his wide sensual mouth curling with amusement. 'I have every intention of finishing what I began, *tesora mia*.'

'It will take us well over an hour just to get home,' Jemima reminded him.

But only a few minutes later, Alejandro turned his Ferrari off the road and drew up outside a country hotel. She turned startled eyes on him. 'You can't be serious?'

'Only an acrobat could have good sex in this car,' Alejandro fielded, vaulting out and striding round the bonnet to open the passenger seat door and extract her.

'But we've got no luggage!' she protested in a panicked undertone, colouring hotly with self-consciousness when he strode over to the reception desk, his dark head held high, and asked for a room without the smallest hint of discomfiture.

'Your face is too well known. People will get to know about this,' she muttered ruefully when the door closed behind the porter and left them alone in a well-appointed room. Yet even as she sounded that note of caution she was excited by his audacity and his single-minded pursuit of satisfaction.

An unholy grin lit Alejandro's lean, darkly handsome features as he reached for her again. 'After imbibing a little too freely of the wine we had with lunch I was falling asleep at the wheel and rather than risk continuing our journey I did the sensible thing and took a break,' he mocked.

'The famous Spanish siesta, much written about but more rarely found in practice these days,' she teased.

'I promise that you will enjoy every moment of our siesta, *querida*,' Alejandro swore with a husky growl of anticipation edging his deep dark drawl.

And then he kissed her, and the heat and the craving

gripped her again with even greater power. He stripped off her clothes between passionate breathless kisses and she fought with his shirt buttons and his belt, already wildly, feverishly aware of the rigid fullness of his erection. She sank down on her knees and used her mouth on him until his hands closed tightly into her hair to restrain her and he was trembling against her.

He hauled her back up to him and tumbled her down on the crisp white linen sheets that awaited them. There was no need of further foreplay for either of them. He sank into her long and slow and deep and she quivered on a sexual high of intense response and so it continued until she hit a soul-shattering climax and her body convulsed in sweet spasms of delight around him.

'You can go to sleep now if you like,' Jemima whispered generously with a voluptuous stretch in the aftermath.

Laughing, Alejandro cradled her close and claimed another kiss. 'I have a much better idea.'

Jemima smiled, loving that physical closeness and relaxation and the charismatic smile tugging at the corners of his mouth as he gazed down at her. And suddenly new awareness of her emotions struck like an electric shock pulsing through her brain. Her eyes veiled when she registered that she could no longer imagine returning to England to live and work, could not picture herself ever leaving him again, indeed could not face the prospect of such a separation. Yet hadn't they both agreed to a three-month trial, which would very soon be up?

Although she had only been back in Spain with Alejandro for a brief period it had taken him a remarkably short time to break through her defensive barriers. She had started looking for him whenever he wasn't there, counting the hours when he was away from her until he was back again and within reach. She was falling for him all over again, she reflected worriedly, falling back in love with a guy who could only be programmed to hurt her for as long as he still believed that she had slept with his kid brother.

'What's up?' Alejandro queried, feeling her tension and lifting his tousled dark head to look down into her face with a frown.

'Nothing,' she swore, pushing close again, turning her lips up to his again and offering sex as a means of distraction.

And because Alejandro was and always had been a very passionate man, it worked a treat. There were no more awkward questions and there was an astounding amount of lovemaking until eventually they both drifted off to sleep exhausted. After dining at the hotel, they arrived back at the castle at quite a late hour. Maria, the housekeeper, greeted Jemima with the news that an Englishman had rung twice asking for her but had not left his name for her to call back.

Jemima had no idea who could have been calling her, for virtually all her connections back in England were female. 'Are you sure it was a man?' And at Maria's nod of confirmation, she shrugged and remarked, 'If it's important he'll ring back again.'

While she talked to the older woman, Beatriz had emerged from the salon and was speaking to her brother. Her sister-in-law's usual ready smile was absent and before Jemima's eyes Alejandro's stance transformed from relaxed to tense.

'Did something happen while we were out?' Jemima enquired when Beatriz hurried away again.

Alejandro settled his forbidding dark gaze on her, his lean bronzed face all Renaissance Man angles and hollows in the shadows cast by the wall lights, his jaw line as set as though it were carved from stone. 'Marco's come home for a visit. He's staying with his mother.'

And having dropped that bombshell, Alejandro said something flat about having work to do and, before she could part her lips, he was gone and she was standing alone in the echoing stone hall...

CHAPTER EIGHT

MARCO was back! It seemed a surprising coincidence that Alejandro's brother should choose to make his first visit home in years so soon after her own return to Spain. Jemima tossed and turned in her bed, unable to sleep while her thoughts ran on at a mad frantic pitch and refused to give her peace. She wondered too where Alejandro was and if he was really working.

Alejandro was less than pleased by news of his brother's arrival. Guilt squirmed through Jemima as she could remember when Alejandro was very fond of his younger brother and, whether she liked it or not, she had played an unwitting part in their estrangement. With hindsight, however, she recognised that Marco's feelings for his elder brother had always been less clear-cut. Idolised and spoiled by both parents as the baby of the family, Marco had nonetheless competed all his life within Alejandro's shadow and had never equalled or surpassed his sibling's achievements. Athletically gifted and academically brilliant, Alejandro had outshone Marco without effort and had set a bar that Marco could not reach. Even in business, Alejandro had triumphed while Marco had failed as an independent businessman and had eventually settled for a tailor-made position running one of the art galleries in his brother's empire.

But, those facts notwithstanding, Jemima had got on like a house on fire with Marco from the moment she had met him. Not that back then Marco had had much competition, since although Alejandro had been a brand-new husband at the time he had also been a workaholic and Jemima had been lonely, bored and unhappy. In the stiflingly formal household that Doña Hortencia had insisted on then, Marco had seemed like a breath of fresh air and Jemima had quickly warmed to her brother-in-law's light-hearted charm. In those days she had been blind to the reality that Marco might have a darker side to his nature than he had ever shown her.

How else could Marco have sacrificed a friendship with Jemima that he had once sworn meant a great deal to him? How else could he have allowed Alejandro to go on believing that his wife had slept with his brother? Why on earth had Marco done that? How could he have been so cruel and callous towards his brother and his former friend? She still didn't understand and *needed* to know the answer to those questions. What she did know was that Marco had gone to New York and embarked on a new life there, seemingly indifferent to the chaos and unhappiness he had left in his wake.

But while Jemima lay there ruminating on the past anger began to smoulder deep down inside her. Why was she feeling guilty about someone else's lies and another person's refusal to believe in her word? Marco was the one who had lied, at the very least by omission, and as a result Alejandro was convinced that his wife had been unfaithful. Alejandro had disbelieved and rejected Jemima's pleas of innocence. So why did she still feel as though she had done something she shouldn't have done? Why was she shouldering the blame when she was the victim of Marco's lies and her husband's distrust?

In a sudden movement, Jemima scrambled out of bed and at the speed of light she pulled on her long silky aquamarine wrap before heading downstairs in search of Alejandro. Acting like the guilty party would win her no prizes and, recalling Alejandro's coldness earlier in the day just saying his brother's name, she knew that forgiveness wasn't even on the cards.

Alejandro wasn't at work in his study. He was outside on the terrace, his classic profile hard as iron as he leant up against a stone pillar and stared out at a midnight-blue night sky studded with twinkling stars. Jemima came to an uncertain halt in the doorway, the electric light framing her curling mane of silvery pale hair to give it rosy highlights while darkening the violet hue of her eyes and accentuating the soft vulnerable pink of her mouth.

'I thought you would be asleep by now,' Alejandro confessed, awarding her a single studied glance that was cool and unreadable.

'I'm not quite that thick-skinned,' she fenced back. 'I don't like being made to feel bad when I haven't done anything wrong.'

'Let's not go digging, *mi dulzura.*'

'Marco's pulled quite some number on you,' she condemned, her slight shoulders rigid with resentment, her spine ramrod straight. 'In choosing to believe your brother rather than your wife you've given him the power to torment you—'

Alejandro spun round in a fast fluid motion that took her by surprise. His lean, strong face was taut with suppressed emotion but his eyes were as golden, dazzling and aggressive in their fiery heat as the sun. '*Porque Demonios!* Nobody torments me,' he declared, his lean, powerful body poised like a panther's, about to leap on its prey.

'All right—*I'm* being tormented by this!' Jemima proclaimed, willing to bend the point and take the hit if it persuaded him to listen to her. She took a hurried step out into the warm night air. 'It's like a big chasm is opening up between us again.'

A sardonic ebony brow quirked. 'And you're *surprised*?'

Her cheeks flamed with embarrassment. She felt angry and bitter, hurt and fearful, all at one and the same time. It was not a good recipe for tact. Her temper on a razor edge, she resisted a needling, worrying urge to move closer to him because for the first time since she had returned to Spain she was afraid of rejection. 'Don't do this to us,' she muttered in urgent appeal.

His attention lingered on her, sliding from the full pout of her lips down to her slender, elegant throat and the dim white sloping valley of her breasts interrupted by the ribboned edge of her nightgown. 'Go back to bed before we say things that we won't be able to forget,' Alejandro urged with curt emphasis.

Jemima recognised the reserve that restrained him from matching her candour and feared the damage such diffidence might do. In her opinion, bottling things up only made problems fester. 'I'm not scared. I'm not running away. I *want* to be with you.'

'But possibly I don't want to be with you right now,' Alejandro murmured smooth as silk.

That admission hit Jemima like a brick and momentarily she felt stunned and reeled dizzily from that rebuff. He had once told her that when she was cornered she reacted like an alley cat, eager to scratch and bite. 'Only because you won't let yourself want me,' she challenged, padding nearer him on bare feet cooled by the worn granite tiling.

'You can be such a baby sometimes.' His beautiful obsidian gaze had a lethal gleam in the moonlight, the anger and rawness tamped down out of her sight, patently too private for her viewing. 'If I could put it all behind me and no longer think about it, I would have done so by now.'

In comparison, a cascade of happy images gleaned from recent weeks was flooding Jemima's thoughts. Everything she valued, not just happiness, was at risk and it terrified her. She cursed Marco and wished she had never befriended him and she hovered within reach of Alejandro, wanting to be needed, needing to be wanted if that was all she could have.

'Come to bed,' she whispered soft and low, despising herself for sinking low enough to play that card.

'I'm not up for that either tonight,' Alejandro asserted with chilling bite.

Talking to him in such a mood was like death by a thousand tiny cuts, Jemima reflected wildly. He was too controlled to shout at her. He wouldn't tell her what he was thinking, but then he didn't really need to, did he? Not when his derision could seep through the cracks to show on the surface and burn her like acid sprinkled on tender skin.

'Why did you ask me to give our marriage another chance if you were planning to behave like this?' Jemima slung at him accusingly.

'I never pretended I could give you a clean slate but I believe I've done reasonably well in the circumstances—'

'Well, I disagree!' Jemima shot at him furiously, temper clawing up through her with such speed and ferocity that the strength of her anger almost took *her* by surprise. 'In fact I think you are screwing our relationship up this time just the way you did last time.'

Alejandro viewed her with cold dark eyes that reflected the silvery moonlight. If she was an alley cat in a fight, he was the equivalent of a deadly rapier blade flashing without warning. '*I* screwed it up?' he traded very drily.

'When you are finally forced to accept that I *never* had an affair with your brother, who are you going to blame then?' Jemima demanded between gritted teeth. 'But at the rate you're going now, we won't last that long. You might not be forgiving, Alejandro, but neither am I and I'm beginning to think that I've wasted enough of my youth on a dead relationship—'

His stunning bone structure was now visible below his bronzed skin, his potent tension patent in his set jaw line and the stillness of his tall muscular body. 'It's not dead—'

'Right at this minute it feels like it's as dead as a dodo,' Jemima pronounced, spelling out that comparison in defiant disagreement. 'I shouldn't be wasting time here on you. I should be getting a divorce and looking for a man who *really* wants me...not some guy tearing us both apart over an affair that never happened!'

'I *really* want you,' Alejandro bit out in raw dissent. 'I won't agree to a divorce.'

'Can't live with me, can't live without me,' Jemima parried shakily, fighting to get a grip on her flailing emotions. 'But I *can* get by without you. I've proved it. I had a good life in Charlbury St Helen's...'

His well-shaped mouth curled into a sardonic smile. 'But not so good that you weren't prepared to walk away from all of it to come back to a life of luxury with me!'

Turning pale with rage at that taunt, Jemima trembled. 'I only came back here to try again for Alfie's benefit. Don't you dare try to make out that I'm some sort of gold-digger!'

Silence fell like a blanket and it seemed to use up all the available oxygen as Jemima waited impatiently for him to take back that final taunt. He stared steadily back at her as if she had got what she deserved in that exchange and, in a way, she supposed she had. Her refusal to embrace the role of the disgraced wife caught out in adultery lay between them, an obstacle neither of them could overcome. Alejandro was very proud, but he might have managed to come to terms with what he believed she had done had she enabled him to believe that she was truly sorry. In the absence of that development there was no natural way forward and both of them were stuck in their respective opposite corners.

Her small face stiff, Jemima threw him a look of angry reproach. 'I never wanted you for your money,' she told him heatedly. 'I may have got in a bit of a mess and spent more money than I should have done when we were first married, but it wasn't done out of greed and there was never any plan to rip you off.'

His brilliant gaze was intent but wary and locked to her every changing expression. 'I can believe that,' he said, surprising her with that declaration of faith.

'I am really sorry about the money—I was stupid,' Jemima admitted, warming to a topic that she could be honest about on at least one level. She had indeed been stupid: she had thrown away thousands and thousands of pounds and yet she still could not bring herself to tell him what she had done with it.

Alejandro took a jerky step forward. 'It was a case of bad timing. My business enterprises were over-extended. The winds of recession were howling around us and I was struggling to just hold onto what I had. It was the worst possible moment for you to go mad with money… but then I shouldn't have left you access to so much of it.'

Jemima was breathing rapidly and by the time he had finished speaking her lower lip had dropped fully away from the upper while she gaped at him in unconcealed astonishment. 'Are you saying that you had financial problems a couple of years ago when we were still living together?' she gasped in disbelief. 'But why didn't you tell me?'

Alejandro's handsome mouth compressed into a wry line. 'I didn't want to worry you…'

Her wide eyes prickled with a sudden hot rush of spontaneous tears. 'But I thought you were *so* rich,' she framed before she could think better of using that immature phraseology.

'I know. I knew you hadn't a clue there was anything to worry about,' Alejandro murmured ruefully. 'But the truth is that my father left so much money to my stepmother and Marco when he died that up until quite recently it was a struggle for me just to keep the estate afloat.'

Jemima was shaking her head slowly back and forth in a negative motion. She could not hide how shocked she was by what he had confessed. 'I had no idea. You really should have told me, Alejandro. In fact, not only did you not tell me there was a problem, you seemed to go out of your way to throw loads of money and expensive gifts at me,' she reminded him tautly. 'Why the heck did you do that?'

'You wanted the whole fairy tale along with the castle and I very much wanted you to have it as well,' Alejandro admitted with a wry twist of his mouth. 'How could I tell you that I was in danger of losing it all?'

'All the hours you were working, turning night into day…you were never at home,' she muttered unsteadily, fighting to hold the tears back with all her might. 'You were trying to keep your businesses afloat?'

'Yes, and the extra work did pay off in one regard. I secured new contracts and in the end the financial tide turned, but by then it was too late: I had lost my wife,' Alejandro intoned bleakly.

Her generous mouth wobbled at that reminder. She wanted to hug him, but at the same time she wanted to slap him really hard for keeping secrets from her. He had treated her like a fragile little girl who couldn't cope with the grown up stuff when, in actuality, she had never been that naïve even as a child. She was appalled to appreciate that he had undertaken such a struggle and worked such long thankless hours while she went out on endless shopping trips and went out at night clubbing with Marco.

'Alejandro…if you had told me the truth, shared the bad stuff with me instead of leaving me in ignorance, things would have been so very different,' Jemima breathed unevenly, tears rolling down her cheeks unchecked until she dashed a hand across her face in an embarrassed gesture and sniffed furiously. 'I would've understood. I would have made allowances.'

Alejandro braced a hand to her slender spine and pressed her back indoors where he handed her a tissue. 'I'm not sure anything would have been different. You were very young and naïve and you were already pregnant and unhappy and at the time I don't think you could have coped with any more stress.'

He was wrong, but she didn't argue with him because she was too choked up to do so. She knew that as much as anything else his fierce pride would have prevented him from telling her that he had financial problems. He was an old-fashioned guy and he had always seen it as solely his role to provide for her needs. He had loved to spoil her with unexpected gifts and treats, to give her the frills he knew she had never had before she met him. She could have cried her heart out in that instant for all she had truly wanted from him two years earlier were his precious time and attention, not his wealth or what it could buy her.

'I didn't expect you to be my superhero all the time,' Jemima told him awkwardly, her voice hoarse as she dabbed at her damp cheeks. 'If you'd confided in me, I would never have spent so much time with your brother. I felt neglected. I thought you regretted marrying me and you were bored and that that's why you never came home.'

'It never would have occurred to me that telling you I was on the brink of losing everything, including our home, might save my marriage,' Alejandro confided, his cynical doubt in that likelihood unconcealed.

'Well, that just goes to show how very little you know about me. I'm very loyal and I would have stuck by you through thick and thin!' Jemima claimed proudly.

'But in those days I think you had much more in

common with my fun-loving brother,' Alejandro murmured with a derisive edge to his dark deep drawl.

'I wasn't that shallow.' Although she was back in control of her emotions and composed again, Jemima's fingers still bit into the damp tissue clutched between her fingers. She had really, really loved him two years earlier and she wished he could at least accept that the love had been genuine and real, even if it hadn't proved strong enough to withstand the misfortunes that had engulfed them both. 'But you didn't give me the chance to be anything else.'

Casting a last lingering look at his breathtakingly handsome features from below damp feathery lashes, Jemima walked back up to bed without another word. Her mobile phone was flashing on the dressing table and she lifted it. She had missed one phone call and there were two text messages. One was from Beatriz, saying that she hoped that Jemima didn't mind her having given her brother her phone number. The second text and the missed call were from Marco and she jerked in shock when she realised that he had actually dared to get in touch with her again.

Must see you to talk. Urgent, ran his message.

Jemima deleted the text with stabbing fingers and tossed the phone down again. Marco had to be joking. In the current climate she was not prepared to take the risk of seeing him again even if she did have questions of her own to ask. My goodness, wouldn't Alejandro just love that? The last thing her marriage needed was more fuel for the same fire.

The door opened, startling her. She froze when she saw Alejandro and then she slid out of bed like an eel and sped over to him, wrapping her arms round his neck and letting her head fall back as he meshed one strong hand into the depths of her pale hair and kissed her breathless.

'I thought you wouldn't come,' she confided, heart thrumming like a plucked string on a violin, the full effect pulsing through her entire body along with her intense relief that he had not stayed away from her.

'*Dios mio!* Living apart won't help us. Been there, done that, *querida*,' he reminded her darkly. 'We might as well have been living in different houses while you were pregnant with Alfie. It made everything worse.'

Her generous mouth swollen from the onslaught of his, Jemima got back into bed. His arrival had already made her feel two hundred per cent happier. 'Well, that was your choice, not mine,' she traded cheekily.

His ebony brows pleated as he shed his suit. 'It wasn't anyone's choice, it was a necessity.'

'How was it a necessity?' she questioned once he had emerged from the bathroom and joined her in bed.

'Right from the start, Dr Santos was afraid you would miscarry. He was quite frank with me. You are very small and slightly built and it was obvious early on that what we thought was one baby was going to be big. I didn't stay happy that you were pregnant for very long,' Alejandro admitted heavily, his arm tightening round her to pull her closer. 'I felt hugely guilty for putting you at risk.'

'I wasn't at risk.'

'I felt that you were and with my own mother having died from complications in childbirth it was not a matter I could ever take lightly.'

Jemima mulled that over, registering that her obstetrician had been more honest with her husband than he had been with her. Or had he been? Her Spanish had been less fluent in those days and it was perfectly possible that she had misunderstood some of what he told her, picking up only the gist rather than the full meaning of his advice. That he had shared his apprehension with Alejandro, however, was news to her and that Alejandro had been seriously worried about her was also a surprise. Suddenly she frowned as she made another deduction.

'Are you saying that you stopped making love to me because Dr Santos warned you off?'

'Why else would I have stopped?' Alejandro growled soft and low in her ear, tugging her back into the heat of his long, hard body. Her nostrils flared on the husky scent of his skin and she quivered with awareness. 'I used another bedroom, not only because I was keeping late hours and didn't want to waken you but also because I didn't trust myself in the same bed with you any more.'

'You should've explained—I had no idea.'

'I was present when the doctor warned you that you would have to be very careful indeed if you wanted the pregnancy to go to term. You had already had some bleeding,' he reminded her grimly. 'I know I didn't discuss it with you but what was there to say? We didn't have a choice.'

She pressed her mouth in silent apology against a bare bronzed shoulder. Consternation had a strong grip on her. She was shaken by how badly she had misjudged his past behaviour. She had viewed everything through the distorting prism of her unhappiness and insecurity and two and two had seemed to make four but she had added up the facts incorrectly. Alejandro had not been bored with her. He had not deliberately neglected her either.

At a difficult time he had simply done the best that he could for the two of them, while her behaviour had only added to their problems. That acknowledgement shamed her and made her appreciate just how much she had grown up since then.

'Let's make an agreement,' Alejandro breathed in a measured undertone above her head. 'You stay away from Marco. You don't speak to him, you don't see him. That will keep the peace.'

Jemima had stiffened, taken aback by that proposition coming at her out of the blue. She drew in a quivering breath. 'All right...if that's what you want.'

'That's how it *has* to be,' Alejandro countered in a tone of finality.

'I'm not arguing. I couldn't care less. It's not a problem,' she muttered in a small voice.

The tension in his big powerful frame eased and he smoothed a soothing hand over her hair. 'Go to sleep,' he intoned huskily. 'If you don't, you'll be too tired to join me for breakfast in the morning. I'm leaving early for a board meeting in Seville.'

That he was already planning breakfast in her company made her smile. She was remembering the hot sexual passion of the afternoon in the hotel room, but lying in his arms there in their own bed felt so much more intimate and significant. Even after news that neither one of them had wanted to hear, they were still together. The agreement Alejandro had demanded warned her that she would be walking a knife edge if she defied him, but she had no such intention. Marco might be home, but she was not prepared to allow him to damage her marriage a second time.

The following morning, Alejandro left her enjoying

her coffee on the roof and Alfie went downstairs with Placida so that their son could watch his father's helicopter take off from the front lawn. Jemima was still sitting outside, lightly clad in a cotton sundress, when Beatriz came up to join her. Her sister-in-law looked strained.

'Was I wrong to give Marco your cell-phone number last night?' the brunette prompted anxiously. 'He was so eager for the chance to speak to you that when he pressed me, I didn't know what to do for best.'

'I'm afraid I don't want to speak to him,' Jemima admitted quietly.

'But if you and Marco talked and then you talked to Alejandro, maybe all this bad feeling could be put away,' Beatriz suggested with unconcealed hope. 'The way things are now is very awkward for all of us and it's only going to get more difficult once word gets out that Marco is home again. Our relatives and neighbours will soon start including him in their invitations. Nobody outside these walls is aware that my brothers are at odds with each other—'

'How can that be? I assumed your stepmother would have told tales about me everywhere after I left Spain to go home,' Jemima admitted with an expressive shudder.

'Not when she believed her son might have been involved with you. Doña Hortencia is very proud of the family name and her goal was to protect Marco's reputation, rather than yours,' Beatriz told her ruefully. 'She's hoping that now he's home he'll find a girl to marry.'

Jemima stiffened at that comment. 'Your stepmother might have quite a long wait.'

Was that an answering glint of amusement in her

sister-in-law's dark eyes? It was there and then it was gone and Jemima wondered if she had imagined it. Not for the first time Jemima wondered just how much Beatriz might know about her younger brother's life. The habit of silence, however, kept her quiet for she could not credit that Beatriz might know what Alejandro did not even appear to suspect. It was never easy to tell with Beatriz, though, because the brunette was always very discreet and cautious even with her own family. Beatriz liked to mind her own business and steer clear of trouble, but lately it had come to light that she could also stand up for herself when she had to. She had helped her stepmother move into her very comfortable house on the estate and had withstood the storm of being accused of ingratitude and selfishness when she'd revealed that she was planning to stay on below her brother's roof. Jemima valued the other woman's friendship and wished that she could have confided in her. She missed Flora's company and chatter, she acknowledged ruefully, and wondered if her friend would be able to come out to Spain for a visit any time soon.

The following week, Jemima spent some time reor-ganising rooms with the housekeeper, Maria. She was keeping busy because Alejandro had spent several days working in Seville. A room was being set up for use as a smaller, cosier dining room in place of the huge banquet-ing space and even vaster pieces of antique furniture, which Doña Hortencia had considered necessary to her dignity. Jemima wondered if she should have discussed the change with Alejandro first, and then wrinkled her nose and decided to follow her own preferences. When she mentioned anything to do with the interior workings of the household Alejandro generally looked blank and hastened to disclaim either interest or authority. When Maria spoke to someone behind her, she was fixing some flowers for the table in an effort to give the room a touch of the feudal magnificence that the Vasquez family pretty much took for granted in their daily life.

'Jemima…'

Violet eyes wide, Jemima flipped round and focused on the tall broad-shouldered male in the doorway. She paled. With his coal black curls he was a very good-looking, younger version of his big brother, although he was not so tall nor so powerfully built. He was also so well dressed that he closely resembled a model who had stepped out of a glossy magazine.

'Marco?' she whispered in dismay. 'I didn't want to see you.'

'That's not very friendly, is it?' Marco said in re-proach. 'We are family, after all.'

CHAPTER NINE

JEMIMA reached a sudden decision and told Maria that she would finish the room on her own. As the house-keeper departed Jemima closed the door behind her, leant back against it and focused on Marco.

'I can't believe you've got the nerve to come any-where near me,' she admitted, her bright eyes sparkling with angry hostility.

Marco frowned. 'I don't understand why you are so angry with me.'

Registering that Alejandro's brother had decided to act as if he were ignorant of what he had done, Jemima tensed up like a racehorse at the start line. 'You're not stupid. You know very well why I'm angry. How *could* you allow Alejandro to believe that we had had an affair?'

'You had already left the country. Your marriage was over. What difference did it make to you what he thought?' he questioned, treating her to a level look that implied that he still had no real grasp of what the problem was.

'Doesn't it make a difference to you? It *should* do. Don't you have any affection for your brother that you could let him believe such a thing of us both?' Jemima slung back at him furiously.

Marco breathed in deep. 'All right, I'll try to be honest with you. I didn't really care what anyone thought if it gave me a good reason to leave home and move to New York. Dario and I needed the privacy to lead our own lives. As I honestly believed that you and Alejandro were all washed up as a couple, I didn't think it mattered.'

'You're not that innocent,' Jemima countered between compressed lips, any patience she had left fast shredding in the face of Marco's brazen refusal to express an ounce of regret, particularly when he was tossing his own relationship in her teeth and pointing out that he had wanted and needed it to prosper. 'You could have gone to New York with Dario and without hurting and humiliating your brother with that filthy lie!'

His smooth brow furrowed. 'I didn't actually tell any lies,' he retorted with an infuriating air of condescension. 'I didn't have to. Alejandro was convinced that you and I had had an affair and I didn't deny it. As far as I was concerned, if he wanted to believe something so ridiculous, that was his business and nothing to do with me—'

'It had everything to do with you!' Jemima yelled back at him. 'You didn't care who got hurt. You used our supposed relationship as an excuse—'

'Your marriage was over,' Marco reminded her afresh. 'I didn't know you were still pregnant—'

'I didn't know either at the time I left Spain,' Jemima conceded unwillingly.

'Naturally if I had known there was going to be a child it would have made a difference to what I allowed my brother to believe,' Marco argued. 'But I had no idea.'

'Well, you know now and I'm back with Alejandro

and we're trying to make a go of our marriage again,' Jemima pointed out. 'Only that's not very easy when he still thinks that I slept with you...'

'My brother has always had an easy ride through life. Everything always fell perfectly into place for him, at school, in business, with women,' Marco enumerated with a bitter resentment that he could not hide. 'A little bit of suffering over you and his marriage probably did wonders for his character.'

At that unfeeling crack, Jemima had to struggle to hang onto her temper because she had already decided that telling Marco exactly what she thought of him would be a counterproductive rather than positive act when she needed him to redress the wrong that he had done. Now she marvelled that she had not previously appreciated just how much Marco envied his brother's success in every field. Had she known what was really in Marco's heart she would never have made him her confidant or trusted him as much as she had. Just how much had his unrelenting negativity about her marriage influenced her when it came to making the decision to leave her husband? She did not want to think about that.

'You *have* to tell Alejandro the truth.'

Marco shook his handsome head, his eyes guarded. 'No can do.'

'Well, that's your decision,' Jemima said tightly in the tense silence, her teeth gritting on an urge to be a good deal more aggressive. 'But you can't expect me to stay quiet. If you won't tell Alejandro the truth, I *will*.'

Apprehension now tightening his boyish features, Marco strode forward. 'But you promised to keep my secret.'

Jemima lifted her chin, the anger in her clear gaze an open challenge. 'I didn't know then how much damage keeping your secret was likely to do to my marriage. Surely you can be honest now with your family?' she said forcefully. 'It may not be what they want for you, or expect, but families have got over worse revelations.'

'As far as my mother is concerned, there could be no *worse* revelation than the news that the love of my life is a boy and not a girl,' Marco declared in scornful disagreement. 'Have you ever heard her talking about gay people?'

Jemima grimaced and nodded confirmation. 'She is prejudiced but that could well change if you talked to her and gave her the chance to understand who you really are.'

'You've got to be joking!' Marco snapped back at her, angry colour edging his cheekbones. 'She'd throw me out of the house and cut off my allowance!'

Jemima's brows knitted and she studied him with narrowed eyes. 'I wasn't aware that you received an allowance from your mother.'

Marco released his breath in a weary groan. 'Do you really think that I could afford to live as comfortably as I do on an employee's salary?'

Stepping away from the door, Jemima stiffened. 'Your financial arrangements are none of my business, Marco. Whether you tell your mother or not is nothing to do with me either. But Alejandro is my business and I *do* expect you to tell him that you're gay so that he, at least, can appreciate that we did not have an affair.'

Marco sent her a furious look of umbrage. 'I'm certainly not telling Alejandro. He sacked the only gay man on his staff—did he tell you that?'

'Yes, but I believe the guy in question was also a bully and had had several warnings about the way he'd treated other staff before he was fired. I have never seen or heard Alejandro do or say anything which would lead me to believe that he has homophobic views. He doesn't share your mother's religious outlook on the issue either,' Jemima reasoned levelly. 'I'm not asking you to do this, Marco, I'm telling you that if you don't tell your brother, I will do it for you. I don't have to keep your secret when it's threatening to wreck my happiness and my child's.'

'You're blackmailing me,' Marco accused her angrily.

'I don't owe you any explanations or apologies after what you did to Alejandro,' Jemima contended, lifting her chin in challenge. 'I don't owe you anything.'

Registering that she was serious and not about to back down, Marco lost his temper. Throwing her a furious look of hostility, he swore at her. Then he yanked open the door with an impatient hand, stalked past the astonished housekeeper in the hall and straight back out of the castle. Jemima breathed in deep and slow and returned to the flower arrangement she had been doing. Beatriz joined her and admired the room, remarking that its more comfortable proportions would be a great deal warmer and more pleasant during the cooler months of the year when the fires were lit. For just a few minutes in the other woman's soothing company, it seemed to Jemima that the raw, distressing little scene with Marco had only taken place within her own imagination.

She couldn't help but think back to their former friendship. She had also just learned something from Marco that shed a rather different light on the past. Marco was financially dependent on his mother's continuing goodwill and, if Doña Hortencia's past pronouncements were anything to go by, it was very possible that Marco's admission that he was gay would lead to the kind of ructions that might well hit him hard in the pocket. Was that why Marco had always gone to such lengths to conceal his sexuality? Had money always been the primary reason for his silence on that issue? It occurred to Jemima that she had once been incredibly naïve and trusting when it came to Marco.

Retaining her brother-in-law's friendship, she acknowledged sadly, had come at a high cost, for she had been forced to conceal more and more from her husband. Marco had used her as an alibi and a front when he went places where he preferred not to be seen without female company. His Italian boyfriend, Dario, had often accompanied them on those nights out. What had happened to the open and honest nature that she had once prided herself on having? Almost from the start of her marriage she had begun to keep secrets from Alejandro.

That thought made her heart sink and her mind return to a place she didn't want to revisit. The past was best left untouched, she reckoned uneasily. There would be no advantage to digging everything up. Alejandro would be grateful for all of five minutes when she told him the truth of what she had done with the large sums of money that she had taken from their joint account over two years earlier. But five minutes after that he would wish she had kept quiet and he would see her in yet another unflattering light. Once again she would be shown up as his less than perfect match. She didn't think their marriage could withstand a second blow of that type.

'Marco can be very volatile,' his sister, Beatriz,

remarked gingerly, her attention locked to Jemima's troubled and expressive face.

'Yes,' Jemima agreed.

'But if you ignore his moods, I've found that he soon gets over them,' Beatriz added comfortably. 'Doña Hortencia indulged him too much when he was a child.'

The housekeeper came to the door to pass on a message from Alejandro. He had phoned to say that he would be spending the night at the family apartment in Seville. Jemima's slim shoulders sagged. Only when she learned that he wasn't coming back did she realise how much she had been looking forward to seeing him that evening. In addition she was a little hurt that he had not thought to speak to her personally about his change of plan.

'Jemima…go to Seville and be with my brother,' Beatriz urged, causing Jemima's violet eyes to fly to her in shock. 'You want to be with Alejandro and why shouldn't you be? I'll ensure that Alfie has his bath and his bedtime story. In fact if you wouldn't mind I'm planning to visit my friend, Serafina, this afternoon and I'd like to take Alfie with me. Serafina has a toddler as well.'

All concerns laid to rest by Beatriz's willingness to entertain her nephew, Jemima went upstairs to change. She was delighted by the idea of surprising Alejandro, for she had never done anything like that before, indeed had always shrunk from putting her feelings for him on the line, but the connection they had formed since her return to Spain really did feel much deeper and stronger. There was nothing wrong with being confident and optimistic, she told herself urgently. Once Marco did what he had to do the dark shadow that her brother-in-law had cast over her marriage would soon disappear.

She was in her bedroom when the phone call came. Engaged in checking her reflection in a raspberry-coloured dress with a draped neckline that clung to the curve of her breasts, outlined her tiny waist and bared a good deal of her legs, she snatched up the receiver by the bed to answer it.

'Jem…is that you?' a rough-edged male voice demanded. 'The woman said she'd put me straight through to you.'

Jemima froze, the animated colour in her face fading fast to leave her white as milk. Her heart sank to the soles of her feet and she almost tottered back against the bed for support on legs that felt too woolly to keep her standing upright. She had hoped never, ever to hear that voice again but fate, it seemed, was too cruel to grant her that escape from the memory of past connections and mistakes. Too late did she remember the phone calls from the unnamed male that Maria had mentioned that she had missed.

'How did you know where to find me?' she asked tautly.

'Your cousin, Ellie, saw a picture of you in a magazine and showed it to me. My little Jem in an evening dress mixing with all the toffs like she's one of them!' the older man jeered. 'So you went back to live with that high and mighty Spanish count of yours and you never even got in touch to tell me.'

'Why would I have?' Jemima asked her father sickly.

'The magazine mentioned that you have a kiddy as well now—my grandson and I've not even seen him,'

Stephen Grey complained. 'Maybe I should pay you a visit. If I was to come out of the woodwork now and embarrass you, you'd have a lot to lose, Jem.'

'I haven't got any money...I'm not giving you anything,' Jemima protested feverishly. 'You can't threaten me any more. Just leave me alone!'

Without waiting for a response, Jemima cut off the call and stood there clutching the receiver so hard in her hand that it hurt her fingers. She wouldn't let it start up again. She wouldn't be a pushover this time around. She would stand up for herself and refuse to be alarmed and intimidated by his threats. But in the back of her mind she was already wondering how much of the money in her bank account it would take to keep her father quiet.

He was an evil, frightening man, who had abused both his wife and his daughter with his nasty tongue and his brutal fists, finally throwing Jemima out onto the street as a teenager and washing his hands of responsibility for her. She had made her own way in life no thanks to Stephen Grey. He had no right to demand money from her, no right to terrorize her. He would phone back, she *knew* he would phone back, or worse... come and pay her a visit as he had once before. She had paid him to keep his distance and keep his mouth shut two years ago and his hopes would be riding high that she would crumble and make the same mistake again.

And she was in this position all because early on in her relationship with Alejandro she had told a little white lie that had seemed harmless, she thought in anguish. In fact at the time it had felt like simple common sense to conceal the ugly truth. Conscious that Alejandro came from a much more privileged and respectable

background than she did, she had seen no reason to
trail out all the dirty washing that accompanied her
own more humble beginnings. Indeed she had cringed
from the prospect of telling Alejandro that her father
had been imprisoned repeatedly, never mind broaching
the reality that he'd also regularly beaten up her mother.
She had lived a sad, grubby life as a child with a mother
who drank herself into a stupor daily to escape the world
and the husband she couldn't cope with.

In Seville, Jemima parked below the large office
building that housed Alejandro's headquarters. When
she arrived on the top floor she learned that he was in a
meeting and thought that perhaps it had been a bad idea
to spring a surprise on him when he was clearly so busy.
She was just getting comfortable in Reception when two
of Alejandro's executives passed by and, recognising
her, stopped to chat.

A very profitable contract renegotiated and agreed,
Alejandro saw his business colleagues and their lawyers
off the premises before he discovered his wife surrounded by a little ring of admiring men in Reception. She
was like a small but very powerful magnet, he conceded
bleakly, watching her violet eyes sparkle with natural
enticement as she laughed. Her jacket was hanging open,
her slender but curvy little body on display. His handsome mouth compressed into a hard, ruthless line.

Jemima's gaze fell on Alejandro and she scrambled
upright with a sunny smile to greet him. He looked
outrageously handsome although even at a glance she
recognised his leashed tension and assumed he was tired
after a stressful day. 'Are you too busy for me?' she
asked.

'I doubt if there is a man in the building who would

be too busy for you, *querida*,' he murmured, nodding as his executives acknowledged him and went on about their business. 'You look irresistible in that dress.'

But Jemima noticed that his brilliant answering smile didn't reach the cool darkness of his eyes and an odd little stab of alarm ran through her. As he guided her towards the lift with a firm hand at her spine that made her nerve-endings tingle she shot a glance at his hard bronzed profile. The dense screen of his black lashes cloaked his gaze even as an electrifying surge of awareness shimmied through her slender length. Within a heartbeat she was recalling the way his lean, powerful body had shuddered over hers in release around dawn and the all-consuming love that had overwhelmed her in his arms. She had never been a morning person but Alejandro had changed that. There was something intensely sexy about waking up next to his hot, hungry body. The merest touch made her ready for him and the reflection plunged her into a cascade of erotic imagery. By the time she emerged from that colourful daydream she was trembling and conscious that he had yet to break the heavy silence.

'Were you finished for the day?' she asked anxiously then. 'I mean, I didn't intend to just show up and force your hand.'

The lift doors whirred back to reveal the basement car park. 'I was ready to leave. Are you parked here?'

'Yes.'

'What brought you to Seville?' Alejandro enquired as his driver pulled in to pick them up a few yards from the lift.

Jemima went pink. 'You...I wanted to see you.'

Alejandro lifted a sardonic dark brow.

'Yes, I *did*!' Jemima proclaimed in the face of that disbelief.

'*Dios mio*—is it possible that you have something to tell me?' Alejandro enquired silkily.

Aware of the undertones of tension pulling at her, Jemima shifted uneasily and wondered why he was asking her that. 'No—what would I have to tell you?'

'Only you can answer that question,' Alejandro breathed icily.

Jemima shot him an enervated look and decided that while he always went for subtle she was more at home with being blunt. 'I'm no good at trick questions. Just tell me what's wrong.'

His lean dark features were taut, his eyes shielded. He said nothing. In the humming quiet, she stared out of the window at the crowded streets and waited in vain for his response.

'Well, this will certainly teach me a lesson. Don't go surprising you at the office...you're keeping such a distance from me I feel like Typhoid Mary!' she declared in flippant continuance, struggling to hide her hurt and mortification at the chilly welcome she had so far received from him.

'Exactly what did you expect from me?' Alejandro shot at her with dark eyes that flashed as golden as the heart of a fire.

As her bewilderment increased the limo came to a halt. They would walk the remaining distance through the pedestrian zone in the oldest part of Seville. The Vasquez apartment was in a gracious old building that had considerable character.

The anger that Alejandro could no longer hide was like a blast of heat on her unprotected skin. His driver opened the car door and they climbed out to walk down narrow streets past tall eighteenth-century houses and finally through a familiar flower-filled courtyard. By then her heart was beating as fast and loud as a jungle drum and a sheen of nervous perspiration had dampened her skin. They walked through tall gates and across the cobblestones towards an elegant building. She felt sick with apprehension.

'Why are you angry with me?' she prompted finally.

'Because you're a liar and I can't stay married to a woman I can't trust out of my sight!'

That thunderous aside punched through Jemima's defences like a hard physical blow. As she stepped into the old-fashioned lift fashioned of ornate wrought-iron folding gates she was in shock. She was a liar and he couldn't trust her? All of a sudden he was threatening to end their marriage? She could think of only one possible explanation for his behaviour.

Entering the cool, spacious apartment that spanned the equivalent of two buildings, Jemima stole an enervated glance at her tall, well-built husband and said abruptly, 'You know I've seen Marco, don't you? How?'

'When I phoned to speak to you, Maria mentioned that you were with him.'

Alejandro strode on into the airy drawing room where the shadows cast by the palm tree in the front courtyard were dancing in flickering spears of ghostly foliage across the pale walls. Once again the décor was new to her, the old darker, richer colours banished and replaced by shades that were light and new. The silence dragged horribly.

'Marco just came up to the castle to speak to me,'

Jemima told him jerkily, giving way first to the dreadful
tension. 'Probably because he texted me and called last
night and I didn't respond in any way.'

Alejandro rested unimpressed eyes on her, his wide
sensual mouth taking on a contemptuous twist. 'And
you didn't mention that fact to me, either.'

'Be fair,' Jemima urged in desperation. 'I didn't want
a stupid text message and a missed call from Marco to
cause more trouble between us.'

Alejandro turned blistering dark golden eyes on her.
His fabulous bone structure was set in hard lines of restraint. 'Without trust I can't live with you,' he breathed
with a suppressed savagery that raised gooseflesh on her
exposed skin. 'How could it be otherwise? I believed
that we were getting somewhere and then today I learned
that you were with Marco, in *spite* of your promise to
me.'

Jemima was trembling, nausea stirring in the pit of
her stomach. She had never felt as alone or scared since
childhood as she did at that moment. She could feel his
strength, his force of will and his immovable resolve.
If he decided that walking away from her was the right
thing to do, he would do it, no matter what the cost.
Unhappily for her she had promised not to see Marco
and she had broken her promise. How could she defend
herself from that charge?

It was not the moment, she sensed, to tell him that he
was being unreasonable, and that, for as long as Marco
was a family member with automatic access to their
home, avoiding the younger man would be a challenge.
Alejandro was not in a cool, rational state of mind, she
conceded inwardly. Indeed he was containing so many
powerful emotions that he radiated glowing energy. But

she could feel the distance in him, the wall he was already erecting between them. She had wounded him and he had taken a mental step back from her and their marriage. She was so appalled by the awareness that he was talking about a divorce that she could barely think straight. She could not bear to have got Alejandro back, to have tasted that happiness and then lose it and him again; it would be too cruel to bear.

Too late she saw where she had gone wrong. She had seriously underestimated the damage being done by Alejandro's conviction that she had been unfaithful. And she had made that cardinal error because she had known that she was innocent and had loftily dismissed the likely fallout from his destructive belief that she was not to be trusted. But she could also be a fast learner. When she feared losing Alejandro, no other loyalty had the power to hold her and she broke the silence in haste.

'There's never been anything between your brother and me and he will be speaking to you about that by the end of the week,' Jemima told Alejandro in a feverish rush, too worked up to stop and plan what she had to say before she spoke.

Alejandro was frowning at her. 'What are you talking about?'

'Marco informed me that he never actually told you that we had had an affair—he just didn't deny your accusation. But, by the start of the weekend, you'll know the truth because either he or I will tell you why there was never any possibility of an affair...'

'*Porque demonios!*' Alejandro exclaimed in frustration at that tangled explanation. 'Stop talking to me in riddles!'

'I gave my word to Marco that I would let him talk to you before I did.'

Outrage flared in Alejandro's brooding scrutiny. 'If there is something that I should know, I demand that you tell me now!'

The silence closed round them, thick and heavy as treacle.

'Marco is gay.' Jemima almost whispered the words, conscious of the pledge she had given and even while she refused to be bound by it she felt the bite of guilt and regret all the same. 'So there was never any question of anything intimate between us.'

Alejandro studied her in irate consternation. 'Are you trying to come up with a good cover story now? That's a despicable lie to tell me about my brother.'

'I appreciate that what I've just told you may come as a shock to you, but I'm not lying or trying to come up with a story,' Jemima protested fiercely.

'My brother has been dating...very extensively...since he was sixteen years old. I think we would know by now if he were gay,' Alejandro proclaimed very drily, his lean, strong face hard with denial.

'Marco has done everything possible to hide his true nature and he was at university before he reached the conclusion that he was gay. The girlfriends were just part of the pretence he put up. Didn't you ever wonder why he never hung onto any of them for longer than a couple of weeks?'

'Not many young men in his age group want a serious relationship.'

An uncertain laugh fell from Jemima's lips. 'I'm not getting anywhere with you, am I? You just don't believe me but I am telling you the truth. Marco didn't want anyone to know, not you and particularly not his mother. I know Doña Hortencia's outlook and Marco was afraid she would cut off the allowance she gives him.'

'As there is no question of my brother being gay, we will not discuss the matter further,' Alejandro pronounced with derision, his sensual mouth curling with disdain. 'But I would not have believed that even you would sink as low as to tell such lies.'

Having paled, Jemima took another tack in the hope of convincing him. 'From what I can understand Marco is still with Dario Ortini,' she remarked gingerly.

'What has that to do with anything? They were students together. They're old friends.'

'*No*, they are much more than that to each other.' Jemima shook her head slowly, her pale cloud of hair shifting round her strained face as she voiced that confident assurance. 'They're a couple, Alejandro. And pretty much inseparable. Didn't you think it strange that Dario went to New York as well?'

Alejandro parted his lips as if he was going to speak again to argue with her, and then suddenly he frowned and slowly closed his mouth again. She could literally see him thinking over what she had told him, making the connections, and while the uneasy silence stretched she watched him travel gradually from a state of incomprehension and angry disbelief to one of troubled and stunned acceptance.

'I can hardly believe it,' Alejandro muttered. 'Dario, now, he is less of a surprise. But their continuing friendship does stretch credulity too far.'

Jemima studied Alejandro fixedly, recognising that he was still fighting his astonishment.

'Evidently my brother has been leading a double life

for years,' he intoned between compressed lips. '*Dios mio*. Why couldn't he just tell me? Did he believe I would think less of him? It doesn't matter a damn to me—he is still my brother. But why the hell did Marco allow me to go on believing that you and he had had an affair?'

Jemima brushed her hair off her damp brow with an impatient hand. 'He's jealous of you, well, *very* jealous of everything you've achieved in life,' she divulged reluctantly.

'It is true that he has always been very competitive with me,' Alejandro acknowledged.

'I don't know how he could let you go on believing there had been an affair, but that's something you need to discuss with him rather than me.'

'Right now, what I need is a strong drink,' Alejandro admitted in a raw undertone, striding over to the drinks cabinet and asking her what she would like.

She closed a damp palm round the moisture-beaded tumbler he handed to her and pressed the glass against the overheated skin below her collarbone, all the while watching Alejandro, noticing how pale he was beneath his bronzed complexion and how prominent his hard bone structure seemed. His hands weren't quite steady either: he was really uptight.

'Are you all right?' she whispered worriedly.

'No,' he admitted flatly. 'I'm shattered, absolutely bloody shattered. My brother is gay and I never even suspected the fact.'

'That was how Marco wanted it. He didn't want his family to know.'

'My stepmother will throw a fit.' Alejandro scored long brown fingers through his luxuriant black hair, tousling it into disorder and turning his handsome head to study Jemima again with intense dark eyes. 'But, right at this moment, it is more important that I concentrate on what I've done to you and our marriage. I condemned you, misjudged you, refused to accept your word.'

Jemima gave an awkward shrug. 'I'm just grateful that you finally know and accept the truth. I can understand that when Marco didn't deny the affair you found it hard to believe that nothing had ever happened between us.'

'He used you to get at me. I should have had more faith in you.' Alejandro drained his glass and set it down in a hasty movement. 'Let's go out to eat.'

The abrupt change of mood and focus took her aback but it was very much Alejandro's way to reclaim his space and self-discipline. She had broken through his reserve with her revelation and he wanted the breathing space to put all those messy emotions back again where she couldn't see them. He continually frustrated her with his refusal to share what he thought and felt, she thought ruefully. She wanted to throw herself in his arms and tell him that she loved him enough to forgive him, but she sensed that that would not be a comfort. Alejandro was very proud. He had such high standards and, unhappily for him, he had just failed those standards. He had to come to terms with that and deal with it in his own way.

They dined only a few streets away in a tiny restaurant where the food melted in her mouth to be washed down by the finest wine. Alejandro had reinstated his iron self-control, for not a single reference to his brother passed his lips. In the candlelight she reached for his hand once and he gripped her fingers so tightly he almost crushed them.

'Don't say anything,' he urged in a roughened growl that was as much a plea as a command. 'I would rather have your anger than your pity, *tesora mia*.'

Sensing that a change of subject would be timely Jemima asked him when he had had the apartment redecorated.

'Soon after you left Spain, I still imagined you were waiting for me every time I walked through the door. I didn't like it,' he confessed, his dark, deep accented drawl as clipped as if he were talking business.

'And when you went into our bedroom at the castle?'

'The same.' He shrugged a broad shoulder in dismissal, subject closed.

He was more sensitive than she had ever appreciated, she conceded, and it was a discovery that troubled her more than it pleased her, for it made her think about the trauma he must have suffered when he'd believed she had betrayed him in his brother's arms. He hadn't needed to love her to be hurt. Marco had struck at the very roots of his sibling's pride and possessiveness, and his strong and protective family instincts, and it had been a devastating blow on all fronts.

Later, she slid naked and alone between the white linen sheets of the king-sized bed in the master bedroom. Alejandro had said he had work to catch up on before morning when they were to fly back home. Work, or a preference for his own company? She tossed and turned, wanting to be with him, refusing out of pride to make that move. He wasn't weak; why should she be? Giving into love was a weakness when it was for a man who did not love her back and who would despise any attempt to offer him reassurance. Eventually she fell into an uneasy doze, waking again with a jerk. She put on the light to check her watch and the empty bed. It was three in the morning and her resistance to natural promptings was at its lowest ebb. She thrust back the sheet and padded off in search of her missing husband.

And when she did, she discovered that Alejandro still had the power to surprise her...

CHAPTER TEN

JEMIMA knew drunk when she saw it. An awareness of
the signs was etched deep in her psyche after a childhood in which a man's stumbling steps or a mother's
shrill slurred complaints could make her turn cold with
fear or insecurity. And with them went an out-of-control
sensation that Jemima herself did not like, which was
why she never, ever drank and why she had been happy
to marry a man of abstemious habits.

But undeniably and disturbingly, Alejandro was
the worse for wear because of alcohol. He was in the
lounge, bathed only in moonlight as the curtains were
still open wide. He was barefoot, his jeans unbuttoned
at his narrow waist and his white shirt hung open on
his bronzed muscular chest. But as he lurched upright
to acknowledge her entrance he swayed and almost lost
his footing. He steadied himself with a timely hand on a
carved lamp table. His ebony hair was dishevelled, his
stubborn jaw line rough with stubble and his midnight-
dark eyes had a wild glitter unfamiliar to her.

'Alejandro?' Her violet eyes were full of concern; it
was a question as much as a greeting.

She watched him struggle to focus and regroup. 'I
can't talk to you right now—'

'You're going to talk to me whether you want to or not. Anything is better than you sitting drinking alone!' Jemima pronounced, a small hand pouncing on the bottle of spirits on the coffee table before he could reach for it again.

For a split second, outrage flashed over his lean dark features because he had been prevented from doing what he wanted to do. Then he froze as if he was registering that he had been caught in a less than presentable state and wasn't quite sure how to handle that exposure.

'You've been drinking and I want to know why,' Jemima spelt out.

With a visible effort, Alejandro squared his broad shoulders, muscles rippling across his flat, hard stomach as he sucked in a shuddering breath. 'Not now...'

Her violet eyes softened. 'I *need* to understand why,' she rephrased gently.

'Isn't that obvious? I got everything in our marriage wrong!' he launched at her with an explosive wrath that had finally escaped his containment. *'Everything!'*

Jemima sighed. 'It happens. You just have to live with it.'

'No sympathy?' A black brow lifted.

'You put me through hell. You don't deserve it,' she told him bluntly.

'You have the power to drive me mad with jealousy— you always did,' he confided harshly, his lean bronzed profile bleak. 'I saw you with another man once and I never forgot the way it made me feel.'

Jemima's brow had pleated. 'When?' she cut in.

'Long before we were married. That time you decided that if I was seeing other women you would see another man,' he specified.

Undaunted by the reminder, Jemima tilted her chin. 'That was fair enough,' she commented.

'You were in the street, smiling at him the same way you smiled at me and he was holding your hand,' Alejandro recalled, his dark eyes brooding with remembered hostility and recoil. 'I couldn't stand it. There is nothing I wouldn't have done to get him out of your life! But that predilection for jealousy stayed with me. It's in my nature.'

She remembered how fast their relationship had become exclusive once Alejandro had realised that the agreement had to cut both ways. But it was news to her that his demon jealousy had continued to dog him.

In the simmering silence, Alejandro clenched his hands into powerful fists. He sent her a burning look of condemnation from below the fringe of his lush black lashes. 'If you want honesty, I'll give it to you. I hated you spending so much time with my brother three years ago. I tried very hard to be reasonable about it. I knew I was working too many hours. I knew you were bored and unhappy, but you and Marco got on too well. You seemed so close. Of course it bothered me at a time when our marriage was under strain. I thought I was losing you. Naturally I began to believe that you had more than a platonic friendship going with my brother.'

'Even though I was pregnant with Alfie and was as sick as a dog for weeks on end?' Jemima pressed, keen to bring him to an awareness of how far-fetched his fears had been in the circumstances.

'Your friendship with Marco started months before that. He was always seeking you out, phoning you, sharing secret jokes with you...'

'I suppose we were too close for comfort. He told

me his big secret that he was gay and it made me feel privileged,' she muttered ruefully. 'I just didn't realise that you could be jealous of me because you never let me see it.'

'I was too proud to show you my Achilles' heel. But the jealousy tortured me and twisted the way I saw everything,' he revealed in a roughened admission. 'I thought you were taunting me with your preference for Marco's company.'

Jemima swallowed and then spoke up even though she didn't want to speak up on that angle. 'There was an element of that in my attitude. I so wanted your attention. I thought that if you saw how much Marco liked being with me it might make you want to spend more time with me,' she confessed unhappily. 'I didn't know that you were working so hard because you were trying to keep your businesses afloat. I thought you were bored with me.'

'I felt many things when we were first married but boredom never featured for even five minutes,' Alejandro revealed with a look of sardonic amusement marking his lean, darkly handsome features.

In the moonlight, which silvered his bronzed skin and accentuated the angles and hollows of his sculptured face, his sheer masculine beauty took her breath away. It crossed her mind that she now loved him much more deeply than she had when she first married him. She saw the man and his flaws. He wasn't perfect but it didn't matter because neither was she. But all that truly mattered to her just then was that he had never stopped wanting her before or after their marriage. Jealousy, assuming he could keep it within bounds, well, she could live with it by understanding that all that deep dark emotion of his had to occasionally find the wrong outlet.

'Why were you drinking?' she asked him worriedly.

Alejandro released a bleak laugh that was like a cold hand trailing down her spine. He settled haunted dark eyes on her, his tension unrelieved by their discussion. 'I let you down. I let you down in every way that mattered. You were my wife and, instead of supporting you and caring for you, I accused you of sleeping with my brother. Then I drove you away.'

'But now you know the truth.'

'And like many truths, it's not one I will enjoy living with.' Lean, powerful face grim, he yanked off his shirt in a physical move that startled her and strode past her, his steps even, his head high as though the very act of having had to talk to her had sobered him up. 'I need a shower.'

And Jemima went back to bed and lay awake waiting for him, but wherever he went to wash it wasn't in the en suite bathroom that adjoined the master bedroom. And wherever he slept it was not with her.

The next morning, however, it was business as usual for Alejandro. There was not a hint of the night's excesses visible in his crackling vitality and immaculately dressed appearance or, indeed, in his light and courteous conversation over breakfast. He'd made arrangements for the car she had driven to Seville to be returned to the estate and they left for the airfield and the short flight home. Alfie came running out into the garden to greet his parents and Alejandro snatched his son off his feet and hugged him close with an unashamed affection that touched Jemima's heart while making her crave the same treatment. Why were pride and perfection so important to Alejandro? Why could she accept his faults and live with them so much more easily than he could hers? She hadn't expected a perfect man and she hadn't got one. A more enlightened husband willing to accept that there was a learning curve in their marriage was the very best she could reasonably hope for. The difference between them was that she was already happy with the balance they had achieved now that he knew the truth about her supposed 'affair'.

It was the very next day that she received her second phone call from her father. She was with Alejandro when the call arrived and she excused herself to take it.

'It's normal for a man to expect his daughter to help him out,' Stephen Grey told her in a self-pitying whine. 'I'm not long out of prison, times are tough…'

'Have you tried to find work?' Jemima enquired flatly.

'It's not that easy.'

'You've never worked, never tried to keep yourself honestly. I'm not giving you any money this time.'

'How can you be so selfish? You're married to a very rich man. I've done my homework on him. You can afford to be generous—'

'I don't intend to spend the rest of my life being blackmailed by you. I've said no. You're out of luck. I'm not giving you a single euro of my husband's hard-earned cash. For a start, it's not mine to give,' Jemima asserted with cold clarity, and she replaced the phone receiver the instant she heard the warning rumble of her father's abusive response beginning.

She felt hot with shame when she recalled how she had first given way to her father's threats almost three years earlier, recklessly and fearfully handing over cash that she now knew Alejandro had not been able to afford just to keep the older man silent. Now she was calling Stephen Grey's bluff while dreading the prospect that he might go to the newspapers to reveal their relationship. The sleazy tale of her father's criminality and her unsavoury background and upbringing could only embarrass Alejandro and his family.

'Who was that on the phone?' Alejandro asked when she joined him and her son in the swimming pool, her slender body fetchingly clad in a ruffled apricot bikini.

'Oh, just someone from home.' Jemima struggled to telegraph casualness and lifted and dropped a thin shoulder while feeling the stiff discomfiture of virtually lying to him handicapping her pretence. 'Nobody important.'

It seemed to her that Alejandro's dark golden eyes rested on her a little longer than they need have done but, mercifully, he said nothing and went back to the task of teaching Alfie to swim. Very much a water baby, her son paddled over to her and giggled as he splashed her. The movement of the water was like cool silk lapping against Jemima's overheated skin. She rested back against the side and took in the sweeping view of the lush valley encircled by the snow-capped peaks. Her marriage had a horizon and a future again. She was not about to let go of that without a fight.

In the week that followed, Alejandro went out of his way to spend time with her and Alfie but, even though he returned to the marital bed, he didn't make love to her again. They dined out twice and on the second occasion he gave her a fabulous diamond ring just before they went out.

'What is this for?' she asked helplessly over dinner, watching the light flash blindingly on the glittering jewel and knowing that such magnificence must have cost at least two arms and a leg.

His ebony brows drew together, his dark golden eyes level. 'You're my wife. It's natural for me to want to give you gifts.'

'As long as it's not your guilty conscience talking,' Jemima cut in uncomfortably. 'You don't need to buy me, Alejandro. You already have me.'

'Do I? That's not something I would like to take for granted. You like pretty things,' he drawled softly. 'And I like giving them to you. I always did.'

Jemima turned a guilty pink. 'I had a fairly dismal childhood and I suppose I'm still making up for what I didn't get then.'

'You never talk about your childhood.'

Jemima tensed and shrugged, fixing a bright smile to her full mouth that felt hopelessly false. 'There's not much to talk about. We were always short of money and my parents didn't get on very well. It certainly wasn't a marriage made in heaven.'

'I seem to recall you telling me that your mother died in a car crash.'

'Yes. It was a sad time,' she said quickly, striving to steer him away from further discussion in that line because she did not want to be forced to tell him any more untruths. Somehow lies told in the past when they had seemed to have no relevance bothered her less than the prospect of having to tell more in the present.

After a stressful week, her nerves were still on a cliff edge of doubt, fear and uncertainty with regard to the future. Her father had phoned twice more, one call arriving when she was out and the second proving to be more or less a repeat of the first one she had received, in which he bemoaned his financial state, urged her to be generous and threatened to come and visit her in Spain. The last time Stephen Grey had insisted on being paid in untraceable cash, and although Jemima had sworn she would not pay blackmail money again, she knew to the last pound sterling how much money she had in her bank account, and also had a very good idea of how much of a breathing space it would buy her from her father's persistent demands.

'I've decided to meet up with Marco this weekend,' Alejandro told her. 'I don't think he's going to speak to me of his own free will, but I did want to give him the opportunity to make the first approach.'

'Give him some more time,' Jemima suggested.

'I can't, *tesora mia*,' Alejandro countered, his lean, strong face shadowing. 'I have to deal with him. This feud has gone on long enough, though I can see that it suited Marco to keep us all at a distance. By the way, Beatriz knows.'

'I suspected that she might,' Jemima confided.

'She knew for a fact that Dario was gay and worked it out from there. But, being Beatriz, she said nothing to anyone for fear of causing offence,' Alejandro remarked wryly. 'I could wish she had been less scrupulous. Is it the prospect of my confronting Marco which is making you so jumpy?'

Jemima tensed, violet eyes veiling. 'Jumpy?'

'This past week I've often had the feeling that you're worrying about something. I assure you that I have no plans to have a huge messy row with my brother. It's a little late for that.'

Taken aback that he had noticed that she was living on her nerves, Jemima nodded and tried to look unconcerned.

'For the sake of the family I'll keep it under control, but I don't think I could ever forgive him for what he allowed me to believe,' he admitted squarely.

'Let it go with Marco. It's all in the past and over and done with,' Jemima pointed out just before she climbed out of the car outside the castle.

Alejandro closed a possessive arm round her on the stairs. The tangy scent of his citrus-based aftershave flared her nostrils and sent a flood of helpless awareness travelling to the more sensitive parts of her body. Unfortunately that was as close as he came to instigating a more intimate connection. Later she lay in bed about a foot away from him and wondered why he was still keeping his distance. Of course she could have bridged the gap, but why risk rocking the boat when she was already so stressed and feeling far from daring? Even during the night hours she was always somehow waiting for another phone call to destroy her peace of mind.

On the surface, though, most things were now fine in their marriage and she was determined to accept that without looking for pitfalls and pressures that might not exist. After all, her one and only real problem was Stephen Grey and what he might do. She told herself that if she continued to stand up to her father, he would eventually give up and leave her alone.

So, Alejandro had never said that he loved her and he probably never would, she reflected ruefully. Well, that was life. You couldn't have everything and what you did get was rarely perfect. He was making a real effort to make her happy and he was also proving to be a terrific father. It didn't get much better than that, she bargained with herself, determined not to succumb to taking for granted what she did have in favour of craving the one thing she couldn't have. She had always loved him, had learned to get by without him when their marriage failed, but now she was older and wiser and she knew that no other man could make her feel as good about herself or as happy as Alejandro did without even trying very hard.

In the week that followed it seemed to Jemima that Alejandro was angling at winning some 'perfect husband' award. Even though he disliked nightclubs, he took her out in Seville and they stayed over in the apartment there. They had a picnic down by the castle lake in the shelter of the trees with Alfie on what felt like the hottest day of the year and she paddled at the water's edge with her son chuckling in her arms. In the cool of the evening they dined out on the terrace, a practice that Doña Hortencia had once dismissed as too common and undignified to even be considered.

At a family party held at Alejandro's uncle's home on the occasion of his seventieth birthday, Marco and Dario put in an appearance as a couple and Doña Hortencia claimed that she was ill and left early, while everyone else pretended not to have noticed anything in the least bit unusual. Jemima was asked if she would do the flowers for a cousin's wedding and Marco let it be known that he and his partner were heading back to New York that weekend. Doña Hortencia was popularly held to be prostrate with relief at the news that the closet door could be closed again. Marco, on the other hand, informed Jemima that his mother had taken the news without comment; she was certainly annoyed with him but was still giving him his allowance. He also confessed that he was surprised by his older brother's continuing coolness towards him, an admission that made Dario Ortini, who was more sensitive, glance at Jemima in some embarrassment.

The next morning, Jemima was making some notes of her ideas for the flowers for the family wedding when Maria announced a visitor in an unusually anxious and apologetic tone.

Even while she was frowning in surprise at the sound of the housekeeper's strained voice, Jemima was truly appalled to scramble upright and see her father walking into the huge salon as bold as brass. While not tall, he was a broadly built man. With his shaven head and diamond ear studs, not to mention a purple and pink striped sports shirt, Stephen Grey was quite a sight to his daughter's dismayed eyes.

'This place is in the back of beyond. I had to pay a taxi a fortune to get up here!' he complained, sweeping the beautifully furnished room with assessing eyes that were striving to tot up the price of everything he could see. 'I hope you're planning to make coming out to Spain worth my while!'

Mastering her consternation at the older man's appearance, Jemima sucked in a deep steadying breath. She was grateful that Alejandro was out on the estate and unlikely to return before evening. 'What are you doing here? I asked you to leave me alone.'

His bloodshot blue eyes hardened. 'You've got no business talking to me like that, Jem!' he retorted furiously, his voice rising steeply. 'I brought you into the world and raised you and I expect you to treat me with proper respect.'

Jemima was very pale but she didn't back off, even though he was too close and too loud for comfort. 'After the way you treated me and my mother, I don't owe you the time of day,' she argued with an anger she couldn't hide. 'You washed your hands of me when I was only a teenager. My son and I have a good life here and I'm not about to let you ruin it for me.'

'Aw…will your fancy-pants Spanish Count be too much of a snob to keep you, once he knows what stock you're from?' Stephen Grey sneered, strolling over to the fireplace to lift a miniature portrait off the wall beside it and give the delicate gold and pearl-studded frame an intent scrutiny.

Alarm ran through Jemima as she watched. 'Please put that back. It's very old…'

The older man sent her a knowing look. 'It must be worth a packet on the antique market, then. If you can't help me with some cash like the last time, you can at least close your eyes while I help myself to a few little items that I can sell.'

'*No!*' Jemima shot back at him, crossing the pastel embroidered rug to stand in front of him. 'You can't have it. Give it back to me!'

The older man slid the portrait into his pocket and studied her with scorn. 'Mind your own business, why don't you? Either I take some stuff now or I come back some night with a few mates and we help ourselves to a good deal more.'

'If there's ever a burglary here, I will tell Alejandro about you.'

Stephen Grey loosed a derisive laugh. 'You won't! You'll do anything to keep that husband of yours in ignorance. You're the one who set a price on keeping the truth from him.'

'Yes, and I was very wrong. I understand that now,' Jemima conceded painfully. 'Now give me that miniature back before I call the police—'

'You wouldn't dare call the police!' he bit out with smug assurance.

In a complete panic because she was afraid that he might be right on that score and its potential for extreme embarrassment, Jemima tried to slide a hand into his pocket to retrieve the miniature portrait from him. He struck her shoulder with a big clenched fist to push her out of his way and she went flying off her feet and fell backwards across the coffee table. A startled yelp escaped her as she struck her head against a wooden chair leg and she lay in a heap, momentarily in a daze, one hand flying up to the bump at the back of her head.

There was a loud noise as the door burst open and then an outburst of strident Spanish. An instant later, Alejandro was lifting Jemima bodily up off the floor, settling her down with care on a sofa and demanding to know how she had got hurt.

'He's my father and he's threatening me,' Jemima whispered dizzily, way beyond trying to cover up the sordid scene and present it other than how it was. 'He has one of the portrait miniatures in his pocket and he hit me when I tried to get it back off him.'

'Now you listen 'ere,' her parent began loudly.

'The portrait first,' Alejandro murmured flatly, extending an authoritative hand.

Scowling, the older man dug the item out and passed it over. Blinking, her head pounding less from the blow she had sustained than from the thud of the unbearable tension, Jemima watched her husband return it to the wall. She saw her father lean close and say something to Alejandro and a split second later, and to her intense shock, Alejandro swung round and punched her father hard. The older man reeled back with a gasp of pain while Alejandro flung open the door and told him to get out before he brought the police in. Two vineyard workers were waiting outside and, at a word from Alejandro, they marched in and propelled Stephen Grey, struggling and vociferously complaining, out of the room.

'How on earth did you know what was happening in here?' Jemima demanded shakily.

'He frightened Maria by forcing his way in to see you. She didn't like the look of him or the way he spoke to her. I was at the vineyard and she phoned me immediately to warn me that there might be trouble.'

'I suppose you'll never forgive me now for not telling you the truth,' Jemima mumbled shakily as Alejandro sank down beside her to turn her head and gently examine the slight swelling at the back of her head. 'But when we first met I no longer had any contact with my father and I pretended he was dead rather than tell you about his history.'

Alejandro released his breath on a slow hiss. 'I think I can understand why.'

'He has a criminal record as long as your arm,' Jemima confided. And then she stopped trying to pick her words and the whole sorry story of her childhood came tumbling out: her father's violence and long stays in prison, her mother's alcoholism and the toxic atmosphere in their home.

'That you had found a decent job for yourself and were fully independent when we first met says much more about your character than the accident of birth that gave you your parents,' Alejandro told her with quiet confidence. 'I'm not stupid. I always knew that there were things you were choosing not to talk about and I wish I had dug deeper but it never seemed important enough to me. I wanted you as my wife whoever you were and regardless of what background you came from...'

Jemima looked at him through tear-filled eyes, her emotions swelling and overflowing in the aftermath of that nasty, distressing confrontation with her father. 'Honestly?'

'Walking away was never an option for me. I met you and that was that—it was a done deal. Do you remember the weekends we spent together at the house I rented near the hotel where you worked?' Alejandro queried, dark eyes intent on her troubled face as she nodded uncertainly. 'Those weekends were some of the happiest of my life and I could never have let you go after that.'

'But when we were first seeing each other you kept on breaking dates or not phoning when you said you would.'

Alejandro groaned. 'I regret the way I behaved but, right from the start, I was fighting what I felt for you. It was unnerving to want you so much. I wasn't ready to settle down. After what I'd suffered through my father's obsession with his second wife, I was determined not to fall in love either.'

'The differences between us bothered you.'

'Until I began to see that those differences meant that we complemented each other. After that month when we were broken up, when we were first dating, I knew just how necessary you were to my peace of mind,'

Alejandro admitted tautly, his lean, strong face grave. 'You were like no other woman I had ever met and I was fascinated.'

'I thought...' Jemima breathed in deep and went ahead and said it anyway. 'I thought that for you it was just sex.'

'Just sex would have been easier to deal with,' Alejandro quipped. 'I didn't know at the time that you were my soul mate, I only knew that I wanted you in my life every day and not just on the weekends I could travel to England. When I was away from you I missed you so much that the only option left was to make you my wife.'

'It didn't seem like that then. You never mentioned needing me that much.'

'Of course, I didn't, *preciosa mia*. I was trying to play it cool and I never will be into sharing my every waking thought,' he pointed out wryly. 'But the point is that I stopped seeing other women so that I could have you all to myself, and the more I saw of you, the more I wanted you to be mine. It's my fault that you didn't feel you could tell me about your background—obviously I didn't make you feel secure enough.'

'Even before I met you I was telling people when they asked that both my parents were dead—it was easier than telling the truth,' she admitted. 'That's where some of the money I ran through went two years ago. Dad was threatening to go to the newspapers and tell all to embarrass you.'

'It won't embarrass me. Let him do his worst if he must,' Alejandro responded with immense assurance. 'And don't be upset if he carries out his threats. Most people will only have a passing interest in the fact that your father is a jailbird. So, you allowed him to black-mail you when we were first married?'

'Yes. I thought you'd be ashamed of me if you found out the truth of the kind of home I was from. You'd have to go back a generation to find any respectable relatives.'

Alejandro closed two hands over hers and held her fast. 'I just wish that you'd told me that you were being threatened and that you'd given me the chance to sort him out for you. Your father is like most bullies—once he saw that I wasn't afraid of him or what he might do, he was weak.'

'You must hate me, though, for giving all that money to him and wasting it,' Jemima reasoned, pale with shame and discomfiture.

'You were foolish. You could have trusted me even then.' Alejandro gazed down at her with dark eyes filled with regret. 'But I do appreciate that I wasn't a good enough husband in those days to inspire you with that trust. Without it, you were lost and your father got a stranglehold on you instead.'

'He's the other reason why I walked out then,' Jemima confided abruptly. 'It wasn't just your suspicions about my relationship with Marco, it was the fact that I also couldn't see an end to my father's demands for money. I just felt our marriage was cursed and that the best thing I could do was walk away from it.'

'The best thing you could have done was confide in me. I wouldn't let anyone harm you ever again,' Alejandro swore with conviction. 'But I made too much of a habit of feeling and thinking things that I didn't then share with you and that's one very good reason why our marriage broke down.'

Jemima looked up into his somber, darkly handsome face and stretched up to kiss him. For an instant he stiffened and then he kissed her back with such passionate fervour that she gasped beneath the onslaught. Her heart thumping like a piston, she pressed her hot face against his shoulder and struggled to catch her breath again. 'I was starting to think that you were never going to kiss me again.'

'I was playing safe by making no demands.'

Jemima looked blank. 'What on earth are you talking about?'

'Our agreement that we give our marriage a three-month trial,' Alejandro reminded her grimly. 'The three months were up this week and there you were acting strangely. Naturally, I thought that you were on edge because you were thinking of leaving me again and were worrying about how to go about it and retain custody of Alfie.'

Jemima was frowning. 'My word, I totally forgot about the three-month thing!'

'You *forgot*?' Alejandro exclaimed with incredulous emphasis. 'How could you forget an agreement like that? It's been haunting me ever since I was stupid enough to say yes to it.'

'Oh, so that's why you took me dancing,' Jemima guessed with a sudden giggle of appreciation.

'I got so much wrong in my relationship with you I had to make an effort to get some things right,' Alejandro pointed out darkly, his dignity clearly under threat from her growing amusement. 'I was scared that you had decided to return to England.'

Jemima rested a hand on his shirtfront, spreading her fingers to feel the solid pound of his heart and the heat of his muscular torso through the fine cotton. 'I want you for ever,' she told him without hesitation.

His hand covered hers. 'For ever?' he questioned with a frown.

'Like the castle in the fairy tale. For ever and ever... I'm greedy, I want it *all*.'

'All I want is you,' Alejandro confided in a roughened undertone. 'All I've ever wanted is you. I love you very much.'

Her heart leapt but so did her eyebrows. 'Since when?' she asked, initially suspicious of the claim.

'Since very soon after I met you, only I didn't want to admit it even to myself because it made me feel so powerless, *querida*,' he confided heavily.

'But you never told me that you loved me then.'

'I was stingy with the words,' Alejandro admitted ruefully. 'But why do you think I married you? We were dynamite in bed together, but I wouldn't have married you if I hadn't felt a great deal more for you. I was crushed when you walked out on our marriage.'

'Maybe it was for the best.' Jemima sighed, her violet eyes pools of deep reflective emotion. 'I needed to grow up a lot. I was too immature for you.'

'I knew you were too young to get married, but I couldn't face waiting any longer for you. I wouldn't even wait long enough for my stepmother to organise a wedding for us,' he pointed out.

'I didn't even know that that was ever an option.'

'It wasn't once I realised how long the arrangements would take. I was counting the days until I could bring you back to Spain. That's why I opted for a quick ceremony in England.'

For the first time she began believing in what he was

telling her and a wondering smile lit up her face. 'We rushed into getting married...'

'But with the very best of intentions,' he traded. 'Don't ever walk out on me again.'

'I won't.' Jemima hesitated as a long-suppressed thought occurred to her and then spoke up. 'After I left were there other women...affairs?'

'No. I told myself I would wait until I was divorced,' Alejandro extended. 'But I didn't want anyone else. I still wanted you.'

'There wasn't anyone else for me either,' Jemima volunteered.

He framed her cheekbones with long brown fingers and regarded her intently. 'Don't ever leave me again.'

'I'm not going anywhere,' she declared, and then she blushed. 'Apart from, well, if you should feel like it, our bedroom.'

It took a moment for Alejandro to grasp that invitation and then he wasted no time in vaulting upright and grasping her hand. 'Shouldn't I take you to a doctor to get that bruise on your head checked?'

'It's a bump and I saw stars for an instant, that's all. What I *really* want...'

'I'm more than ready to give you, *preciosa mia*,' Alejandro intoned with raging enthusiasm, pausing only to bundle her into his arms and mount the stairs with her clasped to his chest like a valued gift.

But Jessica had yet to forgive him for those nights she had lain awake wondering. 'I was worried that, maybe, as far as you were concerned, the passion had gone off the boil...'

'I'm on the boil round the clock!' Alejandro contradicted with a feeling groan, shouldering open the bedroom door and tumbling her down on the bed with an impressive amount of energy. 'I always want you.'

And he discarded her clothes and his in an untidy heap while he stole hot, hungry kisses from her willing mouth. His hands found her swollen breasts, the tender peaks and the moist heat between her legs. Seconds later he plunged into her and the intensity of her response hit fever pitch. Her orgasm roared up through her like an unstoppable fountain of burning sparks. She came apart in his arms, crying out her wild hot pleasure.

'Is this the optimum moment to tell you that I forgot to use a condom, *mi corazón*?' Alejandro drawled, his chest rising and falling rapidly as he struggled to catch his breath in the aftermath.

Jemima froze, thought about the possible consequences and then gave him a great big sunny smile because he had called her, 'my heart'. 'I suppose it must be because I forgot as well.'

'I would love to have another baby with you,' Alejandro husked, his dark golden eyes full of tenderness as he kissed her and held her close with possessive arms. 'I would like it very much indeed.'

'We could always try.'

Alejandro lifted his dark head and looked down at her with a heart stopping grin that made her feel all warm and squashy inside. 'I would like trying to get you pregnant very much as well, *preciosa mia*.'

'And if at first you don't succeed, try, try again,' Jemima reminded him with dancing eyes of amusement.

'That strikes me as the perfect blueprint for a second honeymoon. We'll go to the coast—Alfie will love the beach,' Alejandro forecast with satisfaction.

'I love you, Alejandro Navarro Vasquez,' Jemima told him, hugging him tightly to her.

'But not as much as I love you, *mi vide*,' Alejandro countered. 'You and Alfie are my whole world. Without you I would have nothing.'

Afloat on a wonderful cloud of happy contentment with all her worries and fears laid to rest, Jemima kissed him with tender loving appreciation.

A year later, Jemima gave birth to her daughter, Candice, a blue-eyed, black-haired little darling, who charmed both her parents and her big brother long before she gave them her first smile.

Jemima had sold her florist's shop in the village of Charlbury St Helens and had decided against opening a similar business in Spain because to make it a viable full-time enterprise she would have had to base it in Seville. Besides, decorating houses with flowers was less of a tradition in her adopted country. She did act as a floral consultant for several smart weddings and events in the extended family circle and once she learned that she was carrying her second child she was no longer concerned about how she would fill her time. Her fear that her pregnancy would be as difficult as the first proved unfounded and she suffered very little sickness and, when the time came, enjoyed a straightforward delivery. Raising her children, acting as Alejandro's hostess when they entertained at the castle, and continuing to take a strong interest in the charity that supported the women's shelter and enshrined the cause of battered women kept Jemima more than sufficiently busy.

Flora flew out every three months or so for a visit. Beatriz met an architect at a family christening and was married to him within six months. Currently expecting her first child, Beatriz was a good deal more confident than she had once been and remained Jemima's closest friend in Spain. Of all of them, Doña Hortencia had changed the least. Although Marco still visited his mother, relations were often strained between them because it remained a challenge for her to accept him as he was. On the other hand, her strong desire to retain her ties with the castle had ensured that the older woman had become much more polite to Jemima.

Alejandro and Marco had repaired their brotherly bond to some extent but past history ensured that Alejandro remained wary. Marco, however, was flourishing at the art gallery in New York and, having found his true métier, was steadily climbing the career ladder. In the field of business, the brothers shared a very strong bond indeed.

Alfie was thriving and had recently started preschool, which was improving his grasp of Spanish by leaps and bounds. Stephen Grey had sold a story about his wealthy daughter and son-in-law to a downmarket British tabloid but the article hadn't amounted to much and had attracted little attention. Since then Jemima had heard nothing from her father, although Alejandro had established that the older man had recently lost his freedom, having been returned to jail for committing an offence.

Jemima remained exuberantly happy with her life and never allowed herself to forget how close she had come to losing Alejandro and the marriage that had become the centre of her world. She told him just about everything and hid almost nothing from him and, in turn, he tried to talk more to her and share his deeper concerns. If he was working very long hours, Jemima stayed in Seville so that they saw more of each other. With a little compromise and mutual respect on both sides, they had ensured that they were closer than ever by the time that they celebrated the first anniversary of their reconciliation with a holiday in England.

Three months on from that, Jemima was in the Seville apartment, awaiting the sound of Alejandro's key in the lock on the front door. When she heard it, she flew out of bed and raced out to the hall, a slight figure in a black silk nightdress.

Alejandro leant back against the door to shut it, all the while studying her with appreciative dark golden eyes and a charismatic smile that made her tummy flip. 'You make coming home such an event, *esposa mia*,' he told her huskily.

'You've already eaten, haven't you?' she checked, moving forward to trail his jacket off his shoulders and lock flirtatious fingers round his tie to ease it slowly out from below his collar.

'I ordered in food once I knew that the talks would run late.' Keen to be of help, Alejandro jerked his shirt out of the waistband of his trousers and kicked off his shoes. He knew their housekeeper would find a trail of clothes leading down to the bedroom in the morning but he didn't care. He was delighted when his wife pounced on him. His shirt drifted down to the floor.

Jemima settled big violet eyes on his superb bronzed torso and uttered an appreciative sigh, which made him feel ten feet tall. On the threshold of the bedroom, he stepped out of his trousers and a step later paused to shed his socks.

'I really love being married to you,' Alejandro confessed raggedly as he came down on the bed.

Surveying Alejandro in his boxer shorts, Jemima had no complaints to make either. Indeed she was dizzily conscious of the sheer happiness bubbling through her. 'I love you too—more every day...'

He leant forward and kissed her and she quivered with pleasure and anticipation, revelling in the reality that it was a Friday and they had the whole night to enjoy each other. Much as they loved Alfie, it would be relaxing not to have a lively toddler sneaking into their bed at first light and ensuring that any fun had to be clean fun. The pressure of her handsome husband's mouth on hers was unbearably sexy.

'I love you...more than I have words to describe,' Alejandro told her thickly.

'I've got plenty of words,' she broke free to tell him.

'Shush,' he urged, kissing her again until she forgot what she had been talking about and settled up against his lean powerful body like an extra layer of skin. The silence that ensued was broken only by revealing little gasps, moans and sighs while Alfie and Candice's parents got thoroughly acquainted again after a day spent apart...

MILLS & BOON®

DECEMBER 2010 HARDBACK TITLES

ROMANCE

Naive Bride, Defiant Wife	Lynne Graham
Nicolo: The Powerful Sicilian	Sandra Marton
Stranded, Seduced...Pregnant	Kim Lawrence
Shock: One-Night Heir	Melanie Milburne
Innocent Virgin, Wild Surrender	Anne Mather
Her Last Night of Innocence	India Grey
Captured and Crowned	Janette Kenny
Buttoned-Up Secretary, British Boss	Susanne James
Surf, Sea and a Sexy Stranger	Heidi Rice
Wild Nights with her Wicked Boss	Nicola Marsh
Mistletoe and the Lost Stiletto	Liz Fielding
Rescued by his Christmas Angel	Cara Colter
Angel of Smoky Hollow	Barbara McMahon
Christmas at Candlebark Farm	Michelle Douglas
The Cinderella Bride	Barbara Wallace
Single Father, Surprise Prince!	Raye Morgan
A Christmas Knight	Kate Hardy
The Nurse Who Saved Christmas	Janice Lynn

HISTORICAL

Lady Arabella's Scandalous Marriage	Carole Mortimer
Dangerous Lord, Seductive Miss	Mary Brendan
Bound to the Barbarian	Carol Townend
Bought: The Penniless Lady	Deborah Hale

MEDICAL™

St Piran's: The Wedding of The Year	Caroline Anderson
St Piran's: Rescuing Pregnant Cinderella	Carol Marinelli
The Midwife's Christmas Miracle	Jennifer Taylor
The Doctor's Society Sweetheart	Lucy Clark

1110 Gen Std LP

DECEMBER 2010 LARGE PRINT TITLES

ROMANCE

The Pregnancy Shock — Lynne Graham
Falco: The Dark Guardian — Sandra Marton
One Night...Nine-Month Scandal — Sarah Morgan
The Last Kolovsky Playboy — Carol Marinelli
Doorstep Twins — Rebecca Winters
The Cowboy's Adopted Daughter — Patricia Thayer
SOS: Convenient Husband Required — Liz Fielding
Winning a Groom in 10 Dates — Cara Colter

HISTORICAL

Rake Beyond Redemption — Anne O'Brien
A Thoroughly Compromised Lady — Bronwyn Scott
In the Master's Bed — Blythe Gifford
Bought: The Penniless Lady — Deborah Hale

MEDICAL™

The Midwife and the Millionaire — Fiona McArthur
From Single Mum to Lady — Judy Campbell
Knight on the Children's Ward — Carol Marinelli
Children's Doctor, Shy Nurse — Molly Evans
Hawaiian Sunset, Dream Proposal — Joanna Neil
Rescued: Mother and Baby — Anne Fraser

MILLS & BOON®

JANUARY 2011 HARDBACK TITLES

ROMANCE

Hidden Mistress, Public Wife	Emma Darcy
Jordan St Claire: Dark and Dangerous	Carole Mortimer
The Forbidden Innocent	Sharon Kendrick
Bound to the Greek	Kate Hewitt
The Secretary's Scandalous Secret	Cathy Williams
Ruthless Boss, Dream Baby	Susan Stephens
Prince Voronov's Virgin	Lynn Raye Harris
Mistress, Mother...Wife?	Maggie Cox
With This Fling...	Kelly Hunter
Girls' Guide to Flirting with Danger	Kimberly Lang
Wealthy Australian, Secret Son	Margaret Way
A Winter Proposal	Lucy Gordon
His Diamond Bride	Lucy Gordon
Surprise: Outback Proposal	Jennie Adams
Juggling Briefcase & Baby	Jessica Hart
Deserted Island, Dreamy Ex!	Nicola Marsh
Rescued by the Dreamy Doc	Amy Andrews
Navy Officer to Family Man	Emily Forbes

HISTORICAL

Lady Folbroke's Delicious Deception	Christine Merrill
Breaking the Governess's Rules	Michelle Styles
Her Dark and Dangerous Lord	Anne Herries
How To Marry a Rake	Deb Marlowe

MEDICAL™

Sheikh, Children's Doctor...Husband	Meredith Webber
Six-Week Marriage Miracle	Jessica Matthews
St Piran's: Italian Surgeon, Forbidden Bride	Margaret McDonagh
The Baby Who Stole the Doctor's Heart	Dianne Drake

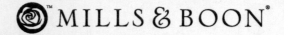

JANUARY 2011 LARGE PRINT TITLES

ROMANCE

HISTORICAL

MEDICAL™